TALES OF MYSTERY & THE

General Editor: David Stuart Davies

THE COMPLETE
FOUR JUST MEN

THE COMPLETE
FOUR JUST MEN

Edgar Wallace

with an Introduction by
David Stuart Davies

WORDSWORTH EDITIONS

For my husband
Anthony John Ranson

with love from your wife, the publisher

Eternally grateful for your unconditional
love, not just for me but for our children
Simon, Andrew and Nichola Trayler

Customers interested in other titles from
Wordsworth Editions are invited to visit our
website at www.wordsworth-editions.com

For our latest list and a full mail order service contact
Bibliophile Books, Unit 5 Datapoint,
South Crescent, London E16 4TL
Tel: +44 020 74 74 24 74
Fax: +44 020 74 74 85 89
orders@bibliophilebooks.com

This edition published 2012 by Wordsworth Editions Limited
8B East Street, Ware, Hertfordshire SG12 9HJ

ISBN 978 1 84022 684 3

This edition © Wordsworth Editions Limited 2012

Wordsworth® is a registered trademark of
Wordsworth Editions Limited, the company
founded by Michael Trayler in 1987

All rights reserved. This publication may not be reproduced,
stored in a retrieval system or transmitted, in any form or by
any means, electronic, mechanical, photocopying, recording
or otherwise, without the prior permission of the publishers.

Typeset in Great Britain by Roperford Editorial
Printed and bound by Clays Ltd, St Ives plc

CONTENTS

INTRODUCTION

The most lawless of us would hesitate to defend them, but the greater humanitarian could scarcely condemn them.

Edgar Wallace

The Four Just Men was one of Edgar Wallace's most famous novels and even today the title of this dramatic tale featuring the exploits of his four unconventional vigilantes is well known; but I doubt if many modern readers are aware that there were five other books featuring these cunning and reckless heroes. Most of the titles have been out of print from mainstream publishers for years and as far as I know they have not been collected in one bumper volume previously. Now Wordsworth have stepped into this particular breach and present you with *The Complete Four Just Men* – and what a thrilling rollercoaster collection it is, capturing as it does the air of intrigue, international tensions and conflicts, casual and brutal crime redolent of the early part of the twentieth century.

Edgar Richard Horatio Wallace (1875–1932) was the most prolific of authors. During his lifetime he wrote at a prodigious pace, producing one hundred and seventy three books and seventeen plays. His area of excellence was mainly crime, thrillers and adventure yarns, including such works as *Sanders of the River*, *The Terror*, the Mr J. G. Reeder series and *The Dark Eyes of London*. It is no wonder that by the time of his death he bore the sobriquet 'The King of Thrillers'.

His early life was turbulent and perhaps the bizarre events surrounding his birth and upbringing stimulated the imagination which created the dramatic scenarios of his fiction. He was born in Greenwich, the illegitimate son of penurious actors Marie (Polly) Richards and Richard Horatio Edgar Marriott, who kept him for a mere nine days after his birth. He was adopted by George Freeman, a fish porter, who brought him up with his other ten children. Wallace only learned the truth of his true parentage when he was eleven years old. This discovery came about because he needed a birth certificate in order to get a job. Like most things in his life, he took the shocking news in his stride.

Wallace had very little formal schooling but he was a quick learner and after a short spell in the army, he served as a correspondent during the Boer War for Reuters and South African and London newspapers. His journalistic work gave him a taste for creative writing. He loved language and the ability to describe scenes and create tension and suspense but he realised that factual reporting restricted his prose. He had a strong desire to formulate his own plots and characters, to let his imagination fly and dabble in the fantastic. In 1906 his fanciful newspaper work got him into trouble. When working on an article about Lever Brothers' threatened rise in soap prices he had grossly inflated the figures by quoting an 'unnamed washerwoman'. This was a lady conjured up from his own imagination. The article prompted Lever Brothers to take the newspaper to court.

With this flair for invention it was only natural that Wallace should try his hand at writing a novel. He knew that it had to be special and promoted in a unique fashion to catch the attention of the public. And so he concocted his first mystery novel featuring four respectable but ruthless vigilantes who find pleasure in administering justice when the law is incapable or unwilling to do so. Like most things in his life, the process of creating Wallace's first great writing success, *The Four Just Men*, was remarkably complicated.

On completing what he believed was a sure-fire bestseller, Wallace was dismayed to discover that publishers were not interested in his novel and so, undaunted by their indifference, he founded the Tallis Press and published the novel himself in 1905. The author intended to advertise *The Four Just Men* on an unprecedented scale. He ran a vast and successful campaign to promote the novel, which involved a huge publicity gimmick: a £500 reward was offered to any reader who could guess how the murder of the British Foreign Secretary was committed in the novel. At the time, Wallace was working for the *Daily Mail* newspaper, which was run by Alfred Harmsworth (later Lord Northcliffe), and it was in this paper that the story was first serialised along with the competition.

The author had advertisements placed on buses, hoardings, flyers, and so forth, running up an incredible bill of £2,000. Although he knew he needed the book to sell sufficient copies to make £2,500 before he saw any profit, Wallace rather foolishly believed that this was possible within three months of the book going on sale. This was not to be the case.

The gimmick generated tremendous sales, but Wallace had over-estimated his own cleverness in creating an unsolvable murder mystery plot for there were several correct responses and they all had to be paid. Only after the competition had closed and the correct solution printed as part of the final chapter dénouement did Edgar learn that he was legally obliged to pay every person who answered correctly the full prize amount.

Additionally, though his advertising campaign had worked, making *The Four Just Men* a runaway bestseller, Wallace discovered that instead of his woefully over-optimistic three months, the novel would have to continue selling consistently with no margin of error for two full years in order for him to recoup the £2,500 he needed to break even. Things were made worse when the number of entrants correctly guessing the right answer continued to rise.

As 1906 began and continued without any list of prize winners being printed, more and more suspicions were being voiced about the honesty of the competition. Friction already existed between the autocratic Harmsworth and his errant journalist and now the publisher was placed in the position of having to lend Wallace over £5,000 to protect the newspaper's reputation. Harmsworth's irritation simmered as, instead of receiving appropriate gratitude and contrition, Wallace recovered his ebullience and confidence, and appeared not to be in any hurry to repay the loan.

And so while the publication of *The Four Just Men* was financially disastrous, the novel made Edgar Wallace's name as a popular author.

Although the mystery surrounding the method of murder in the novel is clever and intricate, the plot itself is fairly straightforward. The Four Just Men, Leon Gonsalez, George Manfred, Raymond Poiccart, and Thery, are vigilantes, avengers who operate outside the law for the public good. Their name derives from the Jewish tradition that to each generation forty just gentiles are born who treat the Jewish people fairly and with justice. In this instance the Just Men announce that if Cabinet Minister Sir Philip Ramon doesn't withdraw his upcoming bill that will send many honest revolutionaries to certain death at the hands of their homeland's dictator, they will be forced to kill him. It is possible that Wallace was influenced by earlier works of fiction which used a similar vigilante concept as the cornerstone of their plot – books such as Eugène Sue's *The Mysteries of Paris* - which deal with heroes who set up their own underworld court systems to hand down justice to those whom the law could not touch.

In Wallace's novel, a brief summary of the career of the Just Men is compiled by the police:

> ' . . . The 'Four Just Men', as they sign themselves, are known collectively in almost every country under the sun. Who they are individually we should all very much like to know. Rightly or wrongly, they consider that justice as meted out here on earth is inadequate, and have set themselves about correcting the law. They were the people who assassinated General Trelovitch, the leader of the Servian Regicides: they hanged the French Army Contractor, Conrad, in the Place de la Concorde — with a hundred policemen within call. They shot Hermon le Blois, the poet-philosopher, in his study for corrupting the youth of the world with his reasoning.'

The morals and attitudes embedded in the book are typical of the time in which it was written when anarchists, nihilists, and the Fenians were very active, and it was still possible to romanticise figures seeking social justice such as the Just Men. Today we would judge them as terrorists. Like so much adventure fiction written in the early part of the Twentieth Century, the Bulldog Drummond stories for example, one must quell one's modern sensibilities and view these tales from a historical perspective and they emerge as exciting and engaging fun. As William Vivian Butler observes in his splendid book *The Durable Desperados* (1973), 'It is not the cleverness of the solution . . . that makes *The Four Just Men* such a fascinating subject for the student of thriller heroes . . . It is the staggering fact that so many thousands of readers eagerly, and never with the slightest scruple, accepted Wallace's invitation to align themselves with his quartet of high-handed political murderers.'

At the end of the book, the Just Men were down to three, but this did not deter Wallace from returning to the characters a few years later in 1908 with the second in the series, *The Council of Justice*. The remaining three Just Men are joined in the early part of the novel by their new partner 'a young man who calls himself Courlander', but who is really of noble birth. It is hinted by Wallace that he is a member of the Hapsburg dynasty. This time the vigilantes pit themselves against The Red Hundred, an organisation dedicated to international anarchy led by the charismatic and beautiful assassin, Maria, the Woman of Gratz, who forms a romantic attachment to George Manfred. The second outing for the Four Just Men is more extravagant in scope than the tightly focused first novel. The hand at the typewriter is more assured and indeed more expansive. This time we have international intrigue, prison breakouts, Zeppelin attacks, purpose built execution sheds in the mountains of Spain and a race across precipitous terrain as the Four Just Men attempt to defeat the villains. Admittedly the plot has many holes in it – where, for example do the Just Men obtain their information and how do they manage to track down people that even Scotland Yard cannot? However, the story moves at a thrilling pace, presenting the reader with so many exciting set pieces of drama and action that these questions do not seem to matter.

This novel sees the beginning of the Just Men's gradual rehabilitation with the establishment or, as Wallace himself put it, they gain 'a sort of unofficial approval'. While they were seen as enemies by the forces of law and order in the first book, in this exploit they receive reluctant cooperation from Scotland Yard. It was a deliberate move on the author's part to make the Just Men into international crime fighters rather than political vigilantes. Wallace hinted that these stories were easier to write and in shifting the focus of their operations, 'the public . . . can more readily appreciate the full significance of the Council's work.'

One of the criticisms of these novels and *The Council of Justice* in particular, is that the four heroes are fairly indistinguishable from each other. They are presented as mere ciphers and do not convince as living breathing characters. This is a fair observation. In many ways they are like chess pieces to be moved across the plot board to enliven the game. These are adventures stories of thrill and fantasy where the action is the most important element and certainly in this department they score highly.

Readers had to wait ten years for the third book in the series, *The Just Men of Cordova* (1918) and again there were more changes to the nature of the Just Men's work. What begins as an exotic thriller, in the style of the previous novel, soon settles down to be more of a detective story. It opens in Spain but very quickly the action moves to and stays in London. The plot includes a wide range of extra characters, including a young resourceful policeman, who often takes centre stage, thus side-lining the Just Men, who function mainly on the periphery of events. The central villain, the crooked financier Colonel Black, is a splendid creation, a creepy Bond-type mastermind who eliminates anyone who stands in his way, usually by means of an esoteric occult poison that kills the victim instantly.

So dangerous is this poison that Wallace adds a footnote to say that it would be inappropriate and dangerous to publish the real name of this fatal drug. It's a case of the old sensationalist at work again. The Just Men, maintaining their strange – and unexplained – omnipotence triumph in the end and get their man, but Scotland Yard are not far behind them.

The change in the Four Just Men stories was greatest in the next book, *The Law of the Four Just Men*, which contained a series of short stories in which only two of the avengers were operative, Leon Gonsalez and George Manfred, since one of the others has retired and the one who was killed has not been replaced in this book. Because the focus is only on two of the Four, there is much more scope for showing their individual characters. They operate mainly in London and can now be considered as 'alternative detectives'.

Wallace is perhaps at his best in the short-story format and in these well-constructed and often whimsical stories he presents the two heroes taking on a wide range of corrupt individuals such as cruel blackmailers, conscienceless money-lenders, owners of gambling houses and opium-dens, a mad scientist who has an irrational hatred of earthworms and common-or-garden murderers who kill for gain. Typical of the approach Wallace now takes is demonstrated in the first story in the collection, 'The Man Who Lived at Clapham', in which the Just Men set out to prove the innocence of a wrongly imprisoned man and bring the real culprit to justice. This is much more the territory of Sherlock Holmes, Lord Peter Wimsey or, indeed, another of Wallace's heroes Mr J. G. Reeder, than the old Just Men of the first book.

While the plot construction in these stories is sound and the suspense and excitement are well executed, the old weakness still pertains: Edgar Wallace conveniently fails to explain the modus operandi of the Just Men in achieving their ends and how they overcome formidable difficulties, content with just showing them at work and getting away with outrageous acts of vigilantism unscathed and with impunity.

The detective element is strengthened even further in the next and penultimate volume, *The Three Just Men* (1924). In this novel Manfred is running a detective agency in Curzon Street, with Gonsalez assuming the role of his chauffeur and Poiccart (inexplicably returned from retirement) that of his butler. This strange division of labour is never explained but it does not seem to interfere with their activities in tackling the nefarious activities of the villain of the piece,

Doktor Oberzohn. As suggested, Wallace had moved the Just Men into the territory of the detective thriller, but there is also a dash of the Bulldog Drummonds in a plot that includes poisonous snakes, an elixir of life, a secret boathouse, a kidnapped beauty and a climactic police siege. For sheer excitement and bravado, this is one of the best entries in the Just Men canon.

Wallace reverted to the short story format for his heroes' final volume, *Again the Three* (1928). In the first story, 'The Rebus', Wallace explained by means of a newspaper cutting from the *Megaphone*, how far the Just Men had moved from being desperate and dangerous criminal vigilantes to respectable crimefighters:

> Even the Four Just Men have become a respectable institution. Not more than fifteen years ago we spoke of them as 'a criminal organization'; rewards were offered for their arrest . . . today you may turn into Curzon Street and find a single triangle affixed to the sedate door which marks their professional headquarters . . . The hunted and reviled have become a most exclusive detective agency . . . We can only hope that their somewhat drastic methods of other times have been considerably modified.

Certainly these stories are more conventional in their scope. A client calls for help and they supply it, solving the mystery and handing out justice. The tales are entertaining and even amusing at times rather than thrilling.

No doubt there would have been more stories, more problems for the Just Men to tackle if Wallace had not died of diabetes in 1932. Nevertheless six books is quite a legacy for the Just Men, who have been unfairly neglected over the years. Here are all their yarns, scrapes, plots and thrilling exploits collected together for your entertainment. Of course we would regard some of the attitudes and characterisations as presented in the stories as politically incorrect these days, but they do accurately reflect the times in which they were written.

There have been two film versions, in 1921 and 1939, both loosely based on the first novel; and a TV series in 1959 which used the title and the basic idea of vigilante crimefighters but little else from Wallace's work. But for the real McCoy, you must read the stories – and here they all are ready and waiting to thrill you.

DAVID STUART DAVIES

THE FOUR JUST MEN

Prologue
Thery's trade

If you leave the Plaza del Mina, go down the narrow street, where, from ten till four, the big flag of the United States Consulate hangs lazily; through the square on which the Hôtel de la France fronts, round by the Church of Our Lady, and along the clean, narrow thoroughfare that is the High Street of Cadiz, you will come to the Café of the Nations.

At five o'clock there will be few people in the broad, pillared saloon, and usually the little round tables that obstruct the sidewalk before its doors are untenanted.

In the late summer (in the year of the famine) four men sat about one table and talked business.

Leon Gonsalez was one, Poiccart was another, George Manfred was a notable third, and one, Thery, or Saimont, was the fourth. Of this quartet, only Thery requires no introduction to the student of contemporary history. In the Bureau of Public Affairs you will find his record. As Thery, alias Saimont, he is registered.

You may, if you are inquisitive, and have the necessary permission, inspect his photograph taken in eighteen positions – with his hands across his broad chest, full faced, with a three-days' growth of beard, profile, with – but why enumerate the whole eighteen?

There are also photographs of his ears – and very ugly, bat-shaped ears they are – and a long and comprehensive story of his life.

Signor Paolo Mantegazza, Director of the National Museum of Anthropology, Florence, has done Thery the honour of including him in his admirable work (see chapter on 'Intellectual Value of a Face'); hence I say that to all students of criminology and physiognomy, Thery must need no introduction.

He sat at a little table, this man, obviously ill at ease, pinching his fat cheeks, smoothing his shaggy eyebrows, fingering the white scar on his unshaven chin, doing all the things that the lower classes do when they suddenly find themselves placed on terms of equality with their betters.

For although Gonsalez, with the light blue eyes and the restless hands, and Poiccart, heavy, saturnine, and suspicious, and George Manfred, with his grey-shot beard and single eyeglass, were less famous in the criminal world, each was a great man, as you shall learn.

Manfred laid down the *Heraldo di Madrid*, removed his eyeglass, rubbed it with a spotless handkerchief, and laughed quietly.

'These Russians are droll,' he commented.

Poiccart frowned and reached for the newspaper. 'Who is it – this time?'

'A governor of one of the Southern Provinces.'

'Killed?'

Manfred's moustache curled in scornful derision.

'Bah! Who ever killed a man with a bomb! Yes, yes; I know it has been done – but so clumsy, so primitive, so very much like undermining a city wall that it may fall and slay – amongst others – your enemy.'

Poiccart was reading the telegram deliberately and without haste, after his fashion.

'The Prince was severely injured and the would-be assassin lost an arm,' he read, and pursed his lips disapprovingly. The hands of Gonsalez, never still, opened and shut nervously, which was Leon's sign of perturbation.

'Our friend here – ' Manfred jerked his head in the direction of Gonsalez and laughed – 'our friend has a conscience and – '

'Only once,' interrupted Leon quickly, 'and not by my wish you remember, Manfred; you remember, Poiccart – ' he did not address Thery – 'I advised against it. You remember?' He seemed anxious to exculpate himself from the unspoken charge. 'It was a miserable little thing, and I was in Madrid,' he went on breathlessly, 'and they came to me, some men from a factory at Barcelona. They said what they were going to do, and I was horror-stricken at their ignorance of the elements of the laws of chemistry. I wrote down the ingredients and the proportions, and begged them, yes, almost on my knees, to use some other method. "My children," I said, "you are playing with something that even chemists are afraid to handle. If the owner of the factory is a bad man, by all means exterminate him, shoot him, wait on him after he has dined and is slow and dull, and present a petition with the right hand and – with the left hand – so!" ' Leon twisted his knuckles down and struck forward and upward at an imaginary oppressor. 'But they would listen to nothing I had to say.'

Manfred stirred the glass of creamy liquid that stood at his elbow and nodded his head with an amused twinkle in his grey eyes.

'I remember – several people died, and the principal witness at the trial of the expert in explosives was the man for whom the bomb was intended.'

Thery cleared his throat as if to speak, and the three looked at him curiously. There was some resentment in Thery's voice.

'I do not profess to be a great man like you, señors. Half the time I don't understand what you are talking about – you speak of governments and kings and constitutions and causes. If a man does me an injury I smash his head – ' he hesitated – 'I do not know how to say it . . . but I mean . . . well, you kill people without hating them, men who have not hurt you. Now, that is not my way . . . ' He hesitated again, tried to collect his thoughts, looked intently at the middle of the roadway, shook his head, and relapsed into silence.

The others looked at him, then at one another, and each man smiled. Manfred took a bulky case from his pocket, extracted an untidy cigarette, re-rolled it deftly and struck a government match on the sole of his boot.

'Your-way-my-dear-Thery – ' he puffed – 'is a fool's way. You kill for benefit; we kill for justice, which lifts us out of the ruck of professional slayers. When we see an unjust man oppressing his fellows; when we see an evil thing done against the good God – ' Thery crossed himself – 'and against man – and know that by the laws of man this evildoer may escape punishment – we punish.'

'Listen,' interrupted the taciturn Poiccart: 'once there was a girl, young and beautiful, up there – ' he waved his hand northward with unerring instinct – 'and a priest – a priest, you understand – and the parents winked at it because it is often done . . . but the girl was filled with loathing and shame, and would not go a second time, so he trapped her and kept her in a house, and then when the bloom was off turned her out, and I found her. She was nothing to me, but I said, 'Here is a wrong that the law cannot adequately right.' So one night I called on the priest with my hat over my eyes and said that I wanted him to come to a dying traveller. He would not have come then, but I told him that the dying man was rich and was a great person. He mounted the horse I had brought, and we rode to a little house on the mountain . . . I locked the door and he turned round – so! Trapped, and he knew it. 'What are you going to do?' he said with a gasping noise. 'I am going to kill you, señor,' I said, and he believed me. I told him the story of the girl . . . He screamed when I moved towards him, but he might as well have saved his breath. 'Let me see a priest,' he begged; and I handed him – a mirror.'

Poiccart stopped to sip his coffee.

'They found him on the road next day without a mark to show how he died,' he said simply.

'How?' They bent forward eagerly, but Poiccart permitted himself to smile grimly, and made no response.

They bent his brows and looked suspiciously from one to the other.

'If you can kill as you say you can, why have you sent for me? I was happy in Jerez working at the wine factory . . . there is a girl there . . . they call her Juan Samarez.' He mopped his forehead and looked quickly from one to the other. 'When I received your message I thought I should like to kill you – whoever you were – you understand I am happy . . . and there is the girl – and the old life I have forgotten – '

Manfred arrested the incoherent protests.

'Listen,' said he imperiously; 'it is not for you to inquire the wherefore and the why; we know who you are and what you are; we know more of you even than the police know; for we could send you to the garotte."

Poiccart nodded his head in affirmation and Gonsalez looked at Thery curiously, like the student of human nature that he was.

'We want a fourth man,' went on Manfred, 'for something we wish to do; we would have wished to have had one animated by no other desire than to see justice done. Failing that, we must have a criminal, a murderer if you like.'

Thery opened and shut his mouth as if about to speak.

'One whom we can at a word send to his death if he fails us; you are the man; you run no risk; you will be well rewarded; you may not be asked to slay. Listen,' went on Manfred, seeing that Thery had opened his mouth to speak. 'Do you know England? I see that you do not. You know Gibraltar? Well, this is the same people. It is a country up there – ' Manfred's expressive hands waved north – 'a curious, dull country, with curious, dull people. There is a man, a member of the Government, and there are men whom the Government have never heard of. You remember one Garcia, Manuel Garcia, leader in the Carlist movement; he is in England; it is the only country where he is safe; from England he directs the movement here, the great movement. You know of what I speak?'

Thery nodded.

'This year as well as last there has been a famine, men have been dying about the church doors, starving in the public squares; they have watched corrupt Government succeed corrupt Government; they have seen millions flow from the public treasury into the pockets of politicians. This year something will happen; the old regime must go. The Government know this; they know where the danger lies, they know their salvation can only come if Garcia is delivered into their hands before the organisation for revolt is complete. But Garcia is safe for the present and would be safe for all time were it not for a member of the English Government, who is about to introduce and pass into law a Bill. When that is passed, Garcia is as good as dead. You must help us to prevent that from ever becoming law; that is why we have sent for you.'

Thery looked bewildered. 'But how?' he stammered.

Manfred drew a paper from his pocket and handed it to Thery. 'This, I think,' he said, speaking deliberately, 'is an exact copy of the police description of yourself.' Thery nodded. Manfred leant over and, pointing to a word that occurred half way down the sheet, 'Is that your trade?' he asked.

Thery looked puzzled. 'Yes,' he replied.

'Do you really know anything about that trade?' asked Manfred earnestly; and the other two men leant forward to catch the reply.

'I know,' said Thery slowly, 'everything there is to be known: had it not been for a – mistake I might have earned great money.'

Manfred heaved a sigh of relief and nodded to his two companions.

'Then,' said he briskly, 'the English Minister is a dead man.'

Chapter 1
A newspaper story

On the fourteenth day of August, 19—, a tiny paragraph appeared at the foot of an unimportant page in London's most sober journal to the effect that the Secretary of State for Foreign Affairs had been much annoyed by the receipt of a number of threatening letters, and was prepared to pay a reward of fifty pounds to any person who would give such information as would lead to the apprehension and conviction of the person or persons, etc. The few people who read London's most sober journal thought, in their ponderous Athenaeum Club way, that it was a remarkable thing that a Minister of State should be annoyed at anything; more remarkable that he should advertise his annoyance, and most remarkable of all that he could imagine for one minute that the offer of a reward would put a stop to the annoyance.

News editors of less sober but larger circulated newspapers, wearily scanning the dull columns of Old Sobriety, read the paragraph with a newly acquired interest.

'Hullo, what's this?' asked Smiles of the *Comet*, and cut out the paragraph with huge shears, pasted it upon a sheet of copy-paper and headed it –

Who is Sir Philip's Correspondent?

As an afterthought – the *Comet* being in Opposition – he prefixed an introductory paragraph, humorously suggesting that the letters were from an intelligent electorate grown tired of the shilly-shallying methods of the Government.

The news editor of the *Evening World* – a white-haired gentleman of deliberate movement – read the paragraph twice, cut it out carefully, read it again and, placing it under a paperweight, very soon forgot all about it.

The news editor of the *Megaphone*, which is a very bright newspaper indeed, cut the paragraph as he read it, rang a bell, called a reporter, all in a breath, so to speak, and issued a few terse instructions.

'Go down to Portland Place, try to see Sir Philip Ramon, secure the story of that paragraph – why he is threatened, what he is threatened with; get a copy of one of the letters if you can. If you cannot see Ramon, get hold of a secretary.'

And the obedient reporter went forth.

He returned in an hour in that state of mysterious agitation peculiar to the reporter who has got a 'beat'. The news editor duly reported to the Editor-in-Chief, and that great man said, 'That's very good, that's very good indeed – ' which was praise of the highest order.

What was 'very good indeed' about the reporter's story may be gathered from the half-column that appeared in the *Megaphone* on the following day.

CABINET MINISTER IN DANGER

Threats to murder the Foreign Secretary
'The Four Just men' plot to arrest the
passage of the Aliens Extradition Bill –
Extraordinary revelations

Considerable comment was excited by the appearance in the news columns of yesterday's *National Journal* of the following paragraph –

The Secretary of State for Foreign Affairs (Sir Philip Ramon) has during the past few weeks been the recipient of threatening letters, all apparently emanating from one source and written by one person. These letters are of such a character that they cannot be ignored by His Majesty's Secretary of State for Foreign Affairs, who hereby offers a reward of Fifty pounds (L50) to any person or persons, other than the actual writer, who will lay such information as will lead to the apprehension and conviction of the author of these anonymous letters.

So unusual was such an announcement, remembering that anonymous and threatening letters are usually to be found daily in the letter-bags of every statesman and diplomat, that the *Daily Megaphone* immediately instituted inquiries as to the cause for this unusual departure.

A representative of this newspaper called at the residence of Sir Philip Ramon, who very courteously consented to be seen.

'It is quite an unusual step to take,' said the great Foreign Secretary, in answer to our representative's question, 'but it has been taken with the full concurrence of my colleagues of the

Cabinet. We have reasons to believe there is something behind the threats, and I might say that the matter has been in the hands of the police for some weeks past.

'Here is one of the letters,' and Sir Philip produced a sheet of foreign notepaper from a portfolio, and was good enough to allow our representative to make a copy.

It was undated, and beyond the fact that the handwriting was of the flourishing effeminate variety that is characteristic of the Latin races, it was written in good English.

It ran.

Your Excellency –

The Bill that you are about to pass into law is an unjust one . . . It is calculated to hand over to a corrupt and vengeful Government men who now in England find an asylum from the persecutions of despots and tyrants. We know that in England opinion is divided upon the merits of your Bill, and that upon your strength, and your strength alone, depends the passing into law of the Aliens Political Offences Bill.

Therefore it grieves us to warn you that unless your Government withdraws this Bill, it will be necessary to remove you, and not alone you, but any other person who undertakes to carry into law this unjust measure.

(Signed) Four Just Men

'The Bill referred to,' Sir Philip resumed, 'is of course the Aliens Extradition (Political Offences) Bill, which, had it not been for the tactics of the Opposition, might have passed quietly into law last session.'

Sir Philip went on to explain that the Bill was called into being by the insecurity of the succession in Spain.

'It is imperative that neither England nor any other country should harbour propagandists who, from the security of these, or other shores, should set Europe ablaze. Coincident with the passage of this measure similar Acts or proclamations have been made in every country in Europe. In fact, they are all in existence, having been arranged to come into law simultaneously with ours, last session.'

'Why do you attach importance to these letters?' asked the Daily *Megaphone* representative.

'Because we are assured, both by our own police and the continental police, that the writers are men who are in deadly earnest. The 'Four Just Men', as they sign themselves, are known collectively in almost every country under the sun. Who they are individually we should all very much like to know. Rightly or wrongly, they consider that justice as meted out here on earth is inadequate, and have set themselves about correcting the law. They were the people who assassinated General Trelovitch, the leader of the Servian Regicides: they hanged the French Army Contractor, Conrad, in the Place de la Concorde – with a hundred policemen within call. They shot Hermon le Blois, the poet-philosopher, in his study for corrupting the youth of the world with his reasoning.'

The Foreign Secretary then handed to our representative a list of the crimes committed by this extraordinary quartet.

Our readers will recollect the circumstance of each murder, and it will be remembered that until today – so closely have the police of the various nationalities kept the secret of the Four Men – no one crime has been connected with the other; and certainly none of the circumstances which, had they been published, would have assuredly revealed the existence of this band, have been given to the public before today.

The *Daily Megaphone* is able to publish a full list of sixteen murders committed by the four men.

'Two years ago, after the shooting of le Blois, by some hitch in their almost perfect arrangements, one of the four was recognised by a detective as having been seen leaving le Blois's house on the Avenue Kleber, and he was shadowed for three days, in the hope that the four might be captured together. In the end he discovered he was being watched, and made a bolt for liberty. He was driven to bay in a café in Bordeaux – they had followed him from Paris: and before he was killed he shot a sergeant de ville and two other policemen. He was photographed, and the print was circulated throughout Europe, but who he was or what he was, even what nationality he was, is a mystery to this day.'

'But the four are still in existence?'

Sir Philip shrugged his shoulders. 'They have either recruited another, or they are working shorthanded,' he said.

In conclusion the Foreign Secretary said –

'I am making this public through the Press, in order that the danger which threatens, not necessarily myself, but any public man who runs counter to the wishes of this sinister force, should be recognised. My second reason is that the public may in its knowledge assist those responsible for the maintenance of law and order in the execution of their office, and by their vigilance prevent the committal of further unlawful acts.'

Inquiries subsequently made at Scotland Yard elicited no further information on the subject beyond the fact that the Criminal Investigation Department was in communication with the chiefs of the continental police.

The following is a complete list of the murders committed by the Four Just Men, together with such particulars as the police have been able to secure regarding the cause for the crimes. We are indebted to the Foreign Office for permission to reproduce the list.

London, October 7, 1899. – Thomas Cutler, master tailor, found dead under suspicious circumstances. Coroner's jury returned a verdict of 'Wilful murder against some person or persons unknown'.

(Cause of murder ascertained by police: Cutler, who was a man of some substance, and whose real name was Bentvitch, was a sweater of a particularly offensive type. Three convictions under the Factory Act. Believed by the police there was a further and more intimate cause for the murder not unconnected with Cutler's treatment of women employees.)

Liège, February 28,1900. – Jacques Ellerman, prefect: shot dead returning from the Opera House. Ellerman was a notorious evil liver, and upon investigating his affairs after his death it was found that he had embezzled nearly a quarter of a million francs of the public funds.

Seattle (Kentucky), October, 1900. – Judge Anderson. Found dead in his room, strangled. Anderson had thrice been tried for his life on charges of murder. He was the leader of the Anderson faction in the Anderson-Hara feud. Had killed in all seven of the Hara clan, was three times indicted and three times released on a verdict of Not Guilty. It will be remembered that on the last occasion, when charged with the treacherous murder of the Editor of the *Seattle Star*, he shook hands with the packed jury and congratulated them.

New York, October 30, 1900. – Patrick Welch, a notorious grafter and stealer of public moneys. Sometime City Treasurer; moving spirit in the infamous Street Paving Syndicate; exposed by the *New York Journal*. Welch was found hanging in a little wood on Long Island. Believed at the time to have been suicide.

Paris, March 4, 1901. – Madame Despard. Asphyxiated. This also was regarded as suicide till certain information came to hands of French police. Of Madame Despard nothing good can be said. She was a notorious 'dealer in souls'.

Paris, March 4, 1902 (exactly a year later). – Monsieur Gabriel Lanfin, Minister of Communication. Found shot in his brougham in the Bois de Boulogne. His coachman was arrested but eventually discharged. The man swore he heard no shot or cry from his master. It was raining at the time, and there were few pedestrians in the Bois.

(Here followed ten other cases, all on a par with those quoted above, including the cases of Trelovitch and le Blois.)

*   *   *

It was undoubtedly a great story.

The Editor-in-Chief, seated in his office, read it over again and said, 'Very good indeed.'

The reporter – whose name was Smith – read it over and grew pleasantly warm at the consequences of his achievement.

The Foreign Secretary read it in bed as he sipped his morning tea, and frowningly wondered if he had said too much.

The chief of the French police read it – translated and telegraphed – in *Le Temps*, and furiously cursed the talkative Englishman who was upsetting his plans.

In Madrid, at the Café de la Paix, in the Place of the Sun, Manfred, cynical, smiling, and sarcastic, read extracts to three men – two pleasantly amused, the other heavy-jowled and pasty of face, with the fear of death in his eyes.

Chapter 2
The faithful Commons

Somebody – was it Mr Gladstone? – placed it on record that there is nothing quite so dangerous, quite so ferocious, quite so terrifying as a mad sheep. Similarly, as we know, there is no person quite so indiscreet, quite so foolishly talkative, quite so amazingly gauche, as the diplomat who for some reason or other has run off the rails.

There comes a moment to the man who has trained himself to guard his tongue in the Councils of Nations, who has been schooled to walk warily amongst pitfalls digged cunningly by friendly Powers, when the practice and precept of many years are forgotten, and he behaves humanly. Why this should be has never been discovered by ordinary people, although the psychological minority who can generally explain the mental processes of their fellows, have doubt-less very adequate and convincing reasons for these acts of dis-balancement.

Sir Philip Ramon was a man of peculiar temperament.

I doubt whether anything in the wide world would have arrested his purpose once his mind had been made up. He was a man of strong character, a firm, square-jawed, big-mouthed man, with that shade of blue in his eyes that one looks for in peculiarly heartless criminals, and particularly famous generals. And yet Sir Philip Ramon feared, as few men imagined he feared, the consequence of the task he had set himself.

There are thousands of men who are physically heroes and morally poltroons, men who would laugh at death – and live in terror of personal embarrassments. Coroner's courts listen daily to the tale of such men's lives – and deaths.

The Foreign Secretary reversed these qualities. Good animal men would unhesitatingly describe the Minister as a coward, for he feared pain and he feared death.

'If this thing is worrying you so much,' the Premier said kindly – it was at the Cabinet Council two days following the publication of the *Megaphone*'s story – 'why don't you drop the Bill? After all, there are matters of greater importance to occupy the time of the House, and we are getting near the end of the session.'

An approving murmur went round the table.

'We have every excuse for dropping it. There must be a horrible slaughtering of the innocents – Braithewaite's Unemployed Bill must go; and what the country will say to that, Heaven only knows.'

'No, no!' The Foreign Secretary brought his fist down on the table with a crash. 'It shall go through; of that I am determined. We are breaking faith with the Cortes, we are breaking faith with France, we are breaking faith with every country in the Union. I have promised the passage of this measure – and we must go through with it, even though there are a thousand "Just Men", and a thousand threats.'

The Premier shrugged his shoulders.

'Forgive me for saying so, Ramon,' said Bolton, the Solicitor, 'but I can't help feeling you were rather indiscreet to give particulars to the Press as you did. Yes, I know we were agreed that you should have a free hand to deal with the matter as you wished, but somehow I did not think you would have been quite so – what shall I say? – candid.'

'My discretion in the matter, Sir George, is not a subject that I care to discuss,' replied Ramon stiffly.

Later, as he walked across Palace Yard with the youthful-looking Chancellor, Mr Solicitor-General, smarting under the rebuff, said, a propos of nothing, 'Silly old ass.' And the youthful guardian of Britain's finances smiled.

'If the truth be told,' he said, 'Ramon is in a most awful funk. The story of the Four Just Men is in all the clubs, and a man I met at the Carlton at lunch has rather convinced me that there is really something to be feared. He was quite serious about it – he's just returned from South America and has seen some of the work done by these men.'

'What was that?'

'A president or something of one of these rotten little republics . . . about eight months ago – you'll see it in the list . . . They hanged him . . . most extraordinary thing in the world. They took him out of bed in the middle of the night, gagged him, blindfolded him, carried him to the public jail, gained admission, and hanged him on the public gallows – and escaped!'

Mr Solicitor saw the difficulties of such proceedings, and was about to ask for further information when an under-secretary button-holed the Chancellor and bore him off. 'Absurd,' muttered Mr Solicitor crossly.

There were cheers for the Secretary for Foreign Affairs as his brougham swept through the crowd that lined the approaches to the House. He was in no wise exalted, for popularity was not a possession he craved. He knew instinctively that the cheers were called forth by the public's appreciation of his peril; and the knowledge chilled and irritated him. He would have liked to think that the people scoffed at the existence of this mysterious four – it would have given him some peace of mind had he been able to think 'the people have rejected the idea.'

For although popularity or unpopularity was outside his scheme of essentials, yet he had an unswerving faith in the brute instincts of the mob. He was surrounded in the lobby of the House with a crowd of eager men of his party, some quizzical, some anxious, all clamouring for the latest information – all slightly in fear of the acid-tongued Minister.

'Look here, Sir Philip – ' it was the stout, tactless member for West Brondesbury – 'what is all this we hear about threatenin' letters? Surely you're not goin' to take notice of things of that sort – why, I get two or three every day of my life.'

The Minister strode impatiently away from the group, but Tester – the member – caught his arm.

'Look here – ' he began.

'Go to the devil,' said the Foreign Secretary plainly, and walked quickly to his room.

'Beastly temper that man's got, to be sure,' said the honourable member despairingly. 'Fact is, old Ramon's in a blue funk. The idea of making a song about threatenin' letters! Why, I get – '

A group of men in the members' smokeroom discussed the question of the Just Four in a perfectly unoriginal way.

'It's too ridiculous for words,' said one oracularly. 'Here are four men, a mythical four, arrayed against all the forces and established agencies of the most civilised nation on earth.'

'Except Germany,' interrupted Scott, MP, wisely.

'Oh, leave Germany out of it for goodness' sake,' begged the first speaker tartly. 'I do wish, Scott, we could discuss a subject in which the superiority of German institutions could not be introduced.'

'Impossible,' said the cheerful Scott, flinging loose the reins of his hobby horse: 'remember that in steel and iron alone the production per head of the employee has increased 43 per cent., that her shipping – '

'Do you think Ramon will withdraw the bill?' asked the senior member for Aldgate East, disentangling his attention from the babble of statistics.

'Ramon? Not he – he'd sooner die.'

'It's a most unusual circumstance,' said Aldgate East; and three boroughs, a London suburb, and a midland town nodded and 'thought it was'.

'In the old days, when old Bascoe was a young member – ' Aldgate East indicated an aged senator bent and white of beard and hair, who was walking painfully toward a seat – 'in the old days – '

'Thought old Bascoe had paired,' remarked an irrelevant listener.

'In the old days,' continued the member for the East End, 'before the Fenian trouble – '

' – talk of civilisation,' went on the enthusiastic Scott. 'Rheinbaken said last month in the Lower House, "Germany had reached that point where – " '

'If I were Ramon,' resumed Aldgate East profoundly, 'I know exactly what I should do. I should go to the police and say "Look here – " '

A bell rang furiously and continuously, and the members went scampering along the corridor. 'Division – 'vision.'

Clause Nine of the Medway Improvement Bill having been satisfactorily settled and the words 'Or as may hereafter be determined' added by a triumphant majority of twenty-four, the faithful Commons returned to the interrupted discussion.

'What I say, and what I've always said about a man in the Cabinet,' maintained an important individual, 'is that he must, if he is a true statesman, drop all consideration for his own personal feelings.'

'Hear!' applauded somebody.

'His own personal feelings,' repeated the orator. 'He must put his duty to the state before all other – er – considerations. You remember what I said to Barrington the other night when we were talking out the Estimates? I said, "The right honourable gentleman has not, cannot have, allowed for the strong and almost unanimous desires of the great body of the electorate. The action of a Minister of the Crown must primarily be governed by the intelligent judgment of the great body of the electorate, whose fine feelings" – no – "whose higher instincts" – no – that wasn't it – at any rate I made it very clear what the duty of a Minister was,' concluded the oracle lamely.

'Now I – ' commenced Aldgate East, when an attendant approached with a tray on which lay a greenish-grey envelope.

'Has any gentleman dropped this?' he inquired, and, picking up the letter, the member fumbled for his eyeglasses.

'To the Members of the House of Commons,' he read, and looked over his pince-nez at the circle of men about him.

'Company prospectus,' said the stout member for West Brondesbury, who had joined the party; 'I get hundreds. Only the other day – '

'Too thin for a prospectus,' said Aldgate East, weighing the letter in his hand.

'Patent medicine, then,' persisted the light of Brondesbury. 'I get one every morning – "Don't burn the candle at both ends", and all that sort of rot. Last week a feller sent me – '

'Open it,' someone suggested, and the member obeyed. He read a few lines and turned red.

'Well, I'm damned!' he gasped, and read aloud.

Citizens,

The Government is about to pass into law a measure which will place in the hands of the most evil Government of modern times men who are patriots and who are destined to be the saviours of their countries. We have informed the Minister in charge of this measure, the title of which appears in the margin, that unless he withdraws this Bill we will surely slay him.

We are loath to take this extreme step, knowing that otherwise he is an honest and brave gentleman, and it is with a desire to avoid fulfilling our promise that we ask the members of the Mother of Parliaments to use their every influence to force the withdrawal of this Bill.

Were we common murderers or clumsy anarchists we could with ease wreak a blind and indiscriminate vengeance on the members of this assembly, and in proof thereof, and as an earnest that our threat is no idle one, we beg you to search beneath the table near the recess in this room. There you will find a machine sufficiently charged to destroy the greater portion of this building.

(Signed) Four Just Men

Postscript. – We have not placed either detonator or fuse in the machine, which may therefore be handled with impunity.

As the reading of the letter proceeded the faces of the listeners grew pallid.

There was something very convincing about the tone of the letter, and instinctively all eyes sought the table near the recess.

Yes, there was something, a square black something, and the crowd of legislators shrank back. For a moment they stood spellbound – and then there was a mad rush for the door.

* * *

'Was it a hoax?' asked the Prime Minister anxiously, but the hastily summoned expert from Scotland Yard shook his head.

'Just as the letter described it,' he said gravely, 'even to the absence of fuses.'

'Was it really – '

'Enough to wreck the House, sir,' was the reply.

The Premier, with a troubled face, paced the floor of his private room.

He stopped once to look moodily through the window that gave a view of a crowded terrace and a mass of excited politicians gesticulating and evidently all speaking at once.

'Very, very serious – very, very serious,' he muttered. Then aloud, 'We said so much we might as well continue. Give the newspapers as full an account of this afternoon's happenings as they think necessary – give them the text of the letter.' He pushed a button and his secretary entered noiselessly.

'Write to the Commissioner telling him to offer a reward of a thousand pounds for the arrest of the man who left this thing and a free pardon and the reward to any accomplice.'

The Secretary withdrew and the Scotland Yard expert waited.

'Have your people found how the machine was introduced?'

'No, sir; the police have all been relieved and been subjected to separate interrogation. They remember seeing no stranger either entering or leaving the House.'

The Premier pursed his lips in thought.

'Thank you,' he said simply, and the expert withdrew.

On the terrace Aldgate East and the oratorical member divided honours.

'I must have been standing quite close to it,' said the latter impressively; ''pon my word it makes me go cold all over to think about it. You remember, Mellin? I was saying about the duty of the Ministry – '

'I asked the waiter,' said the member for Aldgate to an interested circle, 'when he brought the letter: "Where did you find it?"

' "On the floor, sir!" he said. "I thought it was a medicine advertisement; I wasn't going to open it, only somebody – " '

'It was me,' claimed the stout gentleman from Brondesbury proudly; 'you remember I was saying – '

'I knew it was somebody,' continued Aldgate East graciously. 'I opened it and read the first few lines. "Bless my soul," I said – '

'You said, "Well, I'm damned," ' corrected Brondesbury.

'Well, I know it was something very much to the point,' admitted Aldgate East. 'I read it – and, you'll quite understand, I couldn't grasp its significance, so to speak. Well – '

*   *   *

The three stalls reserved at the Star Music Hall in Oxford Street were occupied one by one. At half past seven prompt came Manfred, dressed quietly; at eight came Poiccart, a fairly prosperous middle-aged gentleman; at half past eight came Gonsalez, asking in perfect English for a programme. He seated himself between the two others.

When pit and gallery were roaring themselves hoarse over a patriotic song, Manfred smilingly turned to Leon, and said : 'I saw it in the evening papers.'

Leon nodded quickly.

'There was nearly trouble,' he said quietly. 'As I went in somebody said, "I thought Bascoe had paired," and one of them almost came up to me and spoke.'

Chapter 3
One thousand pounds reward

To say that England was stirred to its depths – to quote more than one leading article on the subject – by the extraordinary occurrence in the House of Commons, would be stating the matter exactly.

The first intimation of the existence of the Four Just Men had been received with pardonable derision, particularly by those newspapers that were behindhand with the first news. Only the *Daily Megaphone* had truly and earnestly recognised how real was the danger which threatened the Minister in charge of the obnoxious Act. Now, however, even the most scornful could not ignore the significance of the communication that had so mysteriously found its way into the very heart of Britain's most jealously guarded institution. The story of the Bomb Outrage filled the pages of every newspaper throughout the country, and the latest daring venture of the Four was placarded the length and breadth of the Isles.

Stories, mostly apocryphal, of the men who were responsible for the newest sensation made their appearance from day to day, and there was no other topic in the mouths of men wherever they met but the strange quartet who seemed to hold the lives of the mighty in the hollows of their hands.

Never since the days of the Fenian outrages had the mind of the public been so filled with apprehension as it was during the two days following the appearance in the Commons of the 'blank bomb', as one journal felicitously described it.

Perhaps in exactly the same kind of apprehension, since there was a general belief, which grew out of the trend of the letters, that the Four menaced none other than one man.

The first intimation of their intentions had excited widespread interest. But the fact that the threat had been launched from a small French town, and that in consequence the danger was very remote, had somehow robbed the threat of some of its force. Such was the vague reasoning of an ungeographical people that did not realise that Dax is no farther from London than Aberdeen.

But here was the Hidden Terror in the Metropolis itself. Why, argued London, with suspicious sidelong glances, every man we rub elbows with may be one of the Four, and we none the wiser.

Heavy, black-looking posters stared down from blank walls, and filled the breadth of every police noticeboard.

£1000 REWARD

Whereas, on August 18, at about 4.30 o'clock in the afternoon, an infernal machine was deposited in the Members' Smoke-Room by some person or persons unknown.

And whereas there is reason to believe that the person or persons implicated in the disposal of the aforesaid machine are members of an organised body of criminals known as The Four Just Men, against whom warrants have been issued on charges of wilful murder in London, Paris, New York, New Orleans, Seattle (USA), Barcelona, Tomsk, Belgrade, Christiania, Cape-town and Caracas.

Now, therefore, the above reward will be paid by His Majesty's Government to any person or persons who shall lay such information as shall lead to the apprehension of any of or the whole of the persons styling themselves The Four Just Men and identical with the band before mentioned.

And, furthermore, a free pardon and the reward will be paid to any member of the band for such information, providing the person laying such information has neither committed nor has been an accessory before or after the act of any of the following murders.

(Signed) Ryday Montgomery
His Majesty's Secretary of State for Home Affairs
J. B. Calfort
Commissioner of Police

[here followed a list of the sixteen crimes alleged against the four men]

GOD SAVE THE KING

All day long little knots of people gathered before the broadsheets, digesting the magnificent offer.

It was an unusual hue and cry, differing from those with which Londoners were best acquainted. For there was no appended description of the men wanted; no portraits by which they might be identified, no stereotyped 'when last seen was wearing a dark blue serge suit, cloth cap, check tie', on which the searcher might base his scrutiny of the passer-by.

It was a search for four men whom no person had ever consciously seen, a hunt for a will-o'-the-wisp, a groping in the dark after indefinite shadows.

Detective Superintendent Falmouth, who was a very plain-spoken man (he once brusquely explained to a Royal Personage that he hadn't got eyes in the back of his head), told the Assistant Commissioner exactly what he thought about it.

'You can't catch men when you haven't got the slightest idea who or what you're looking for. For the sake of argument, they might be women for all we know – they might be chinamen or niggers; they might be tall or short; they might – why, we don't even know their nationality! They've committed crimes in almost every country in the world. They're not French because they killed a man in Paris, or Yankee because they strangled Judge Anderson.'

'The writing,' said the Commissioner, referring to a bunch of letters he held in his hand.

'Latin; but that may be a fake. And suppose it isn't? There's no difference between the handwriting of a Frenchman, Spaniard, Portuguese, Italian, South American, or Creole – and, as I say, it might be a fake, and probably is.'

'What have you done?' asked the Commissioner.

'We've pulled in all the suspicious characters we know. We've cleaned out Little Italy, combed Bloomsbury, been through Soho, and searched all the colonies. We raided a place at Nunhead last night – a lot of Armenians live down there, but – '

The detective's face bore a hopeless look.

'As likely as not,' he went on, 'we should find them at one of the swagger hôtels – that's if they were fools enough to bunch together; but you may be sure they're living apart, and meeting at some unlikely spot once or twice a day.'

He paused, and tapped his fingers absently on the big desk at which he and his superior sat.

'We've had de Courville over,' he resumed. 'He saw the Soho crowd, and what is more important, saw his own man who lives amongst them – and it's none of them, I'll swear – or at least he swears, and I'm prepared to accept his word.'

The Commissioner shook his head pathetically.

'They're in an awful stew in Downing Street,' he said. 'They do not know exactly what is going to happen next.'

Mr Falmouth rose to his feet with a sigh and fingered the brim of his hat.

'Nice time ahead of us – I don't think,' he remarked paradoxically.

'What are the people thinking about it?' asked the Commissioner. 'You've seen the papers?'

Mr Commissioner's shrug was uncomplimentary to British journalism.

'The papers! Who in Heaven's name is going to take the slightest notice of what is in the papers!' he said petulantly.

'I am, for one,' replied the calm detective; 'newspapers are more often than not led by the public; and it seems to me the idea of running a newspaper in a nutshell is to write so that the public will say, "That's smart – it's what I've said all along." '

'But the public themselves – have you had an opportunity of gathering their idea?'

Superintendent Falmouth nodded.

'I was talking in the Park to a man only this evening – a masterman by the look of him, and presumably intelligent. "What's your idea of this Four Just Men business?" I asked. "It's very queer," he said: "do you think there's anything in it?" – and that,' concluded the disgusted police officer, 'is all the public thinks about it.'

But if there was sorrow at Scotland Yard, Fleet Street itself was all a-twitter with pleasurable excitement. Here was great news indeed: news that might be heralded across double columns, blared forth in headlines, shouted by placards, illustrated, diagrammised, and illuminated by statistics.

'Is it the Mafia?' asked the *Comet* noisily, and went on to prove that it was.

The *Evening World*, with its editorial mind lingering lovingly in the 'sixties, mildly suggested a vendetta, and instanced 'The Corsican Brothers'.

The *Megaphone* stuck to the story of the Four Just Men, and printed pages of details concerning their nefarious acts. It disinterred from dusty files, continental and American, the full circumstances of each murder; it gave the portraits and careers of the men who were slain, and, whilst in no way palliating the offence of the Four, yet set forth justly and dispassionately the lives of the victims, showing the sort of men they were.

It accepted warily the reams of contributions that flowed into the office; for a newspaper that has received the stigma 'yellow' exercises more caution than its more sober competitors. In newspaper-land a dull lie is seldom detected, but an interesting exaggeration drives an unimaginative rival to hysterical denunciations.

And reams of Four Men anecdotes did flow in. For suddenly, as if by magic, every outside contributor, every literary gentleman who made a speciality of personal notes, every kind of man who wrote, discovered that he had known the Four intimately all his life.

'When I was in Italy . . . ' wrote the author of *Come Again* (Hackworth Press, 6s.: 'slightly soiled', Farringdon Book Mart, 2d.) 'I remember I heard a curious story about these Men of Blood . . . '

Or –

'No spot in London is more likely to prove the hiding-place of the Four Villains than Tidal Basin,' wrote another gentleman, who stuck Collins in the north-east corner of his manuscript. 'Tidal Basin in the reign of Charles II was known as . . . '

'Who's Collins?' asked the super-chief of the *Megaphone* of his hard-worked editor.

'A liner,' described the editor wearily, thereby revealing that even the newer journalism had not driven the promiscuous contributor from his hard-fought field; 'he does police-courts, fires, inquests, and things. Lately he's taken to literature and writes Picturesque-Bits-of-Old London and Famous Tombstones-of-Hornsey epics . . . '

Throughout the offices of the newspapers the same thing was happening. Every cable that arrived, ever; piece of information that reached the sub-editor's basket was coloured with the impending tragedy uppermost in men's minds. Even the police-court reports contained some allusion to the Four. It was the overnight drunk and disorderly's justification for his indiscretion.

'The lad has always been honest,' said the peccant errand-boy's tearful mother; 'it's reading these horrible stories about the Four Foreigners that's made him turn out like this;' and the magistrate took a lenient view of the offence.

To all outward showing, Sir Philip Ramon, the man mostly interested in the development of the plot, was the least concerned.

He refused to be interviewed any further; he declined to discuss the possibilities of assassination, even with the Premier, and his answer to letters of appreciation that came to him from all parts of the country was an announcement in the *Morning Post* asking his correspondents to be good enough to refrain from persecuting him with picture postcards, which found no other repository than his wastepaper basket.

He had thought of adding an announcement of his intention of carrying the Bill through Parliament at whatever cost, and was only deterred by the fear of theatricality.

To Falmouth, upon whom had naturally devolved the duty of protecting the Foreign Secretary from harm, Sir Philip was unusually gracious, and incidentally permitted that astute officer to get a glimpse of the terror in which a threatened man lives.

'Do you think there's any danger, Superintendent?' he asked, not once but a score of times; and the officer, stout defender of an infallible police force, was very reassuring.

'For,' as he argued to himself, 'what is the use of frightening a man who is half scared to death already? If nothing happens, he will see I have spoken the truth, and if – if – well, he won't be able to call me a liar.'

Sir Philip was a constant source of interest to the detective, who must have shown his thoughts once or twice. For the Foreign Secretary, who was a remarkably shrewd man, intercepting a curious glance of the police officer, said sharply, 'You wonder why I still go on with the Bill knowing the danger? Well, it will surprise you to learn that I do not know the danger, nor can I imagine it! I have never been conscious of physical pain in my life, and in spite of the fact that I have a weak heart, I have never had so much as a single ache. What death will be, what pangs or peace it may bring, I have no conception. I argue with Epictetus that the fear of death is by way of being an impertinent assumption of a knowledge of the hereafter, and that we have no reason to believe it is any worse condition than our present. I am not afraid to die – but I am afraid of dying.'

'Quite so, sir,' murmured the sympathetic but wholly uncomprehending detective, who had no mind for nice distinctions.

'But,' resumed the Minister – he was sitting in his study in Portland Place – 'if I cannot imagine the exact process of dissolution, I can imagine and have experienced the result of breaking faith with the chancellories, and I have certainly no intention of laying up a store of future embarrassments for fear of something that may after all be comparatively trifling.'

Which piece of reasoning will be sufficient to indicate what the Opposition of the hour was pleased to term 'the tortuous mind of the right honourable gentleman'.

And Superintendent Falmouth, listening with every indication of attention, yawned inwardly and wondered who Epictetus was.

'I have taken all possible precautions, sir,' said the detective in the pause that followed the recital of this creed. 'I hope you won't mind for a week or two being followed about by some of my men. I want you to allow two or three officers to remain in the house whilst you are here, and of course there will be quite a number on duty at the Foreign Office.'

Sir Philip expressed his approval, and later, when he and the detective drove down to the House in a closed brougham, he understood why cyclists rode before and on either side of the carriage, and why two cabs followed the brougham into Palace Yard.

At Notice Time, with a House sparsely filled, Sir Philip rose in his place and gave notice that he would move the second reading of the Aliens Extradition (Political Offences) Bill, on Tuesday week, or, to be exact, in ten days.

* * *

That evening Manfred met Gonsalez in North Tower Gardens and remarked on the fairy-like splendour of the Crystal Palace grounds by night.

A Guards' band was playing the overture to *Tannhäuser*, and the men talked music.

Then –

'What of Thery?' asked Manfred.

'Poiccart has him today; he is showing him the sights.' They both laughed.

'And you?' asked Gonsalez.

'I have had an interesting day; I met that delightfully naive detective in Green Park, who asked me what I thought of ourselves!'

Gonsalez commented on the movement in G minor, and Manfred nodded his head, keeping time with the music.

'Are we prepared?' asked Leon quietly.

Manfred still nodded and softly whistled the number. He stopped with the final crash of the band, and joined in the applause that greeted the musicians.

'I have taken a place,' he said, clapping his hands. 'We had better come together.'

'Is everything there?'

Manfred looked at his companion with a twinkle in his eye.

'Almost everything.'

The band broke into the National Anthem, and the two men rose and uncovered.

The throng about the bandstand melted away in the gloom, and Manfred and his companion turned to go.

Thousands of fairy lamps gleamed in the grounds, and there was a strong smell of gas in the air.

'Not that way this time?' questioned, rather than asserted, Gonsalez.

'Most certainly not that way,' replied Manfred decidedly.

Chapter 4
Preparations

When an advertisement appeared in the *Newspaper Proprietor* announcing that there was –

> '*For sale*: An old-established zinco-engraver's business with a splendid new plant and a stock of chemicals'

everybody in the printing world said 'That's Etherington's.' To the uninitiated a photo-engraver's is a place of buzzing saws, and lead shavings, and noisy lathes, and big bright arc lamps.

To the initiated a photo-engraver's is a place where works of art are reproduced by photography on zinc plates, and consequently used for printing purposes.

To the very knowing people of the printing world, Etherington's was the worst of its kind, producing the least presentable of pictures at a price slightly above the average.

Etherington's had been in the market (by order of the trustees) for three months, but partly owing to its remoteness from Fleet Street (it was in Carnaby Street), and partly to the dilapidated condition of the machinery (which shows that even an official receiver has no moral sense when he starts advertising), there had been no bids.

Manfred, who interviewed the trustee in Carey Street, learnt that the business could be either leased or purchased; that immediate possession in either circumstances was to be had; that there were premises at the top of the house which had served as a dwelling-place to generations of caretakers, and that a banker's reference was all that was necessary in the way of guarantee.

'Rather a crank,' said the trustee at a meeting of creditors, 'thinks that he is going to make a fortune turning out photogravures of Murillo at a price within reach of the inartistic. He tells me that he is forming a small company to carry on the business, and that so soon as it is formed he will buy the plant outright.'

And sure enough that very day Thomas Brown, merchant; Arthur W. Knight, gentleman; James Selkirk, artist; Andrew Cohen, financial agent; and James Leech, artist, wrote to the Registrar of Joint Stock Companies, asking to be formed into a company, limited by shares, with the object of carrying on business as photo-engravers, with which object they had severally subscribed for the shares set against their names.

(In parenthesis, Manfred was a great artist.)

And five days before the second reading of the Aliens Extradition Act, the company had entered into occupation of their new premises in preparation to starting business.

'Years ago, when I first came to London,' said Manfred, 'I learned the easiest way to conceal one's identity was to disguise oneself as a public enemy. There's a wealth of respectability behind the word "limited", and the pomp and circumstance of a company directorship diverts suspicion, even as it attracts attention.'

Gonsalez printed a neat notice to the effect that the Fine Arts Reproduction Syndicate would commence business on October 1, and a further neat label that "no hands were wanted", and a further terse announcement that travellers and others could only be seen by appointment, and that all letters must be addressed to the Manager.

It was a plain-fronted shop, with a deep basement crowded with the dilapidated plant left by the liquidated engraver. The ground floor had been used as offices, and neglected furniture and grimy files predominated.

There were pigeonholes filled with old plates, pigeonholes filled with dusty invoices, pigeonholes in which all the debris that is accumulated in an office by a clerk with salary in arrear was deposited.

The first floor had been a workshop, the second had been a store, and the third and most interesting floor of all was that on which were the huge cameras and the powerful arc lamps that were so necessary an adjunct to the business.

In the rear of the house on this floor were the three small rooms that had served the purpose of the bygone caretaker.

In one of these, two days after the occupation, sat the four men of Cadiz.

Autumn had come early in the year, a cold driving rain was falling outside, and the fire that burnt in the Georgian grate gave the chamber an air of comfort.

This room alone had been cleared of litter, the best furniture of the establishment had been introduced, and on the ink-stained writing-table that filled the centre of the apartment stood the remains of a fairly luxurious lunch.

Gonsalez was reading a small red book, and it may be remarked that he wore gold-rimmed spectacles; Poiccart was sketching at a corner of the table, and Manfred was smoking a long thin cigar and studying a manufacturing chemist's price list. They (or as some prefer to call him Saimont) alone did nothing, sitting a brooding heap before the fire, twiddling his fingers, and staring absently at the leaping little flames in the grate.

Conversation was carried on spasmodically, as between men whose minds were occupied by different thoughts. They concentrated the attentions of the three by speaking to the point. Turning from his study of the fire with a sudden impulse he asked: 'How much longer am I to be kept here?'

Poiccart looked up from his drawing and remarked: 'That is the third time he has asked today.'

'Speak Spanish!' cried Thery passionately. 'I am tired of this new language. I cannot understand it, any more than I can understand you.'

'You will wait till it is finished,' said Manfred, in the staccato patois of Andalusia; 'we have told you that.'

Thery growled and turned his face to the grate.

'I am tired of this life,' he said sullenly. 'I want to walk about without a guard – I want to go back to Jerez, where I was a free man. I am sorry I came away.'

'So am I,' said Manfred quietly; 'not very sorry though – I hope for your sake I shall not be.'

'Who are you?' burst forth Thery, after a momentary silence. 'What are you? Why do you wish to kill? Are you anarchists? What money do you make out of this? I want to know.'

Neither Poiccart nor Gonsalez nor Manfred showed any resentment at the peremptory demand of their recruit. Gonsalez's clean-shaven, sharp-pointed face twitched with pleasurable excitement, and his cold blue eyes narrowed.

'Perfect! perfect!' he murmured, watching the other man's face: 'pointed nose, small forehead and – *articulorum se ipsos torquentium sonus; gemitus, mugitusque parum explanatis –* '

The physiognomist might have continued Seneca's picture of the Angry Man, but Thery sprang to his feet and glowered at the three.

'Who are you?' he asked slowly. 'How do I know that you are not to get money for this? I want to know why you keep me a prisoner, why you will not let me see the newspapers, why you never allow me to walk alone in the street, or speak to somebody who knows my language? You are not from Spain, nor you, nor you – your Spanish is – yes, but you are not of the country I know. You want me to kill – but you will not say how – '

Manfred rose and laid his hand on the other's shoulder.

'Señor,' he said – and there was nothing but kindness in his eyes – 'restrain your impatience, I beg of you. I again assure you that we do not kill for gain. These two gentlemen whom you see have each fortunes exceeding six million pesetas, and I am even richer; we kill and we will kill because we are each sufferers through acts of injustice, for which the law gave us no remedy. If – if – ' he hesitated, still keeping his grey eyes fixed unflinchingly on the Spaniard. Then he resumed gently: 'If we kill you it will be the first act of the kind.'

They was on his feet, white and snarling, with his back to the wall; a wolf at bay, looking from one to the other with fierce suspicion.

'Me – me!' he breathed, 'kill me?'

Neither of the three men moved save Manfred, who dropped his outstretched hand to his side.

'Yes, you.' He nodded as he spoke. 'It would be new work for us, for we have never slain except for justice – and to kill you would be an unjust thing.'

Poiccart looked at Thery pityingly.

'That is why we chose you,' said Poiccart, 'because there was always a fear of betrayal, and we thought – it had better be you.'

'Understand,' resumed Manfred calmly, 'that not a hair of your head will be harmed if you are faithful – that you will receive a reward that will enable you to live – remember the girl at Jerez.'

Thery sat down again with a shrug of indifference but his hands were trembling as he struck a match to light his cigarette.

'We will give you more freedom – you shall go out every day. In a few days we shall all return to Spain. They called you the silent man in the prison at Granada – we shall believe that you will remain so.'

After this the conversation became Greek to the Spaniard, for the men spoke in English.

'He gives very little trouble,' said Gonsalez. 'Now that we have dressed him like an Englishman, he does not attract attention. He doesn't like shaving every day; but it is necessary, and luckily he is fair. I do not allow him to speak in the street, and this tries his temper somewhat.'

Manfred turned the talk into a more serious channel.

'I shall send two more warnings, and one of those must be delivered in his very stronghold. He is a brave man.'

'What of Garcia?' asked Poiccart.

Manfred laughed.

'I saw him on Sunday night – a fine old man, fiery, and oratorical. I sat at the back of a little hall whilst he pleaded eloquently in French for the rights of man. He was a Jean-Jacques Rousseau, a Mirabeau, a broad-viewed Bright, and the audience was mostly composed of Cockney youths, who had come that they might boast they had stood in the temple of Anarchism.'

Poiccart tapped the table impatiently.

'Why is it, George, that an element of bathos comes into all these things?'

Manfred laughed.

'You remember Anderson? When we had gagged him and bound him to the chair, and had told him why he had to die – when there were only the pleading eyes of the condemned, and the half-dark room with a flickering lamp, and you and Leon and poor Clarice masked and silent, and I had just sentenced him to death – you remember how there crept into the room the scent of frying onions from the kitchen below.'

'I, too, remember,' said Leon, 'the case of the regicide.'

Poiccart made a motion of agreement.

'You mean the corsets,' he said, and the two nodded and laughed.

'There will always be bathos,' said Manfred; 'poor Garcia with a nation's destinies in his hand, an amusement for shop-girls – tragedy and the scent of onions – a rapier thrust and the whalebone of corsets – it is inseparable.'

And all the time Thery smoked cigarettes, looking into the fire with his head on his hands.

'Going back to this matter we have on our hands,' said Gonsalez. 'I suppose that there is nothing more to be done till – the day?'

'Nothing.'

'And after?'

'There are our fine art reproductions.'

'And after,' persisted Poiccart.

'There is a case in Holland, Hermannus van der Byl, to wit; but it will be simple, and there will be no necessity to warn.'

Poiccart's face was grave.

'I am glad you have suggested van der Byl, he should have been dealt with before – Hook of Holland or Flushing?'

'If we have time, the Hook by all means.'

'And Thery?'

'I will see to him,' said Gonsalez easily; 'we will go overland to Jerez – where the girl is,' he added laughingly.

The object of their discussion finished his tenth cigarette and sat up in his chair with a grunt.

'I forgot to tell you,' Leon went on, 'that today, when we were taking our exercise walk, Thery was considerably interested in the posters he saw everywhere, and was particularly curious to know why so many people were reading them. I had to find a lie on the spur of the minute, and I hate lying – ' Gonsalez was perfectly sincere. 'I invented a story about racing or lotteries or something of the sort, and he was satisfied.'

Thery had caught his name in spite of its anglicised pronunciation, and looked inquiry.

'We will leave you to amuse our friend,' said Manfred, rising. 'Poiccart and I have a few experiments to make.'

The two left the room, traversed the narrow passage, and paused before a small door at the end. A larger door on the right, padlocked and barred, led to the studio. Drawing a small key from his pocket, Manfred opened the door, and, stepping into the room, switched on a light that shone dimly through a dust-covered bulb. There had been some attempt at restoring order from the chaos. Two shelves had been cleared of rubbish, and on these stood rows of bright little phials, each bearing a number. A rough table had been pushed against the wall beneath the shelves, and on the green baize with which the table was covered was a litter of graduated measures, test tubes, condensers, delicate scales, and two queer-shaped glass machines, not unlike gas generators.

Poiccart pulled a chair to the table, and gingerly lifted a metal cup that stood in a dish of water. Manfred, looking over his shoulder, remarked on the consistency of the liquid that half filled the vessel, and Poiccart bent his head, acknowledging the remark as though it were a compliment.

'Yes,' he said, satisfied, 'it is a complete success, the formula is quite right. Some day we may want to use this.'

He replaced the cup in its bath, and reaching beneath the table, produced from a pail a handful of ice-dust, with which he carefully surrounded the receptacle.

'I regard that as the *multum in parvo* of explosives,' he said, and took down a small phial from the shelf, lifted the stopper with the crook of his little finger, and poured a few drops of a whitish liquid into the metal cup.

'That neutralises the elements,' said Poiccart, and gave a sigh of relief. 'I am not a nervous man, but the present is the first comfortable moment I have had for two days.'

'It makes an abominable smell,' said Manfred, with his handkerchief to his nose.

A thin smoke was rising from the cup.

'I never notice those things,' Poiccart replied, dipping a thin glass rod into the mess. He lifted the rod, and watched reddish drops dripping from the end.

'That's all right,' he said.

'And it is an explosive no more?' asked Manfred.

'It is as harmless as a cup of chocolate.'

Poiccart wiped the rod on a rag, replaced the phial, and turned to his companion.

'And now?' he asked.

Manfred made no answer, but unlocked an old-fashioned safe that stood in the corner of the room. From this he removed a box of polished wood. He opened the box and disclosed the contents.

'If Thery is the good workman he says he is, here is the bait that shall lure Sir Philip Ramon to his death,' he said.

Poiccart looked. 'Very ingenious,' was his only comment. Then – ' Does Thery know, quite know, the stir it has created?'

Manfred closed the lid and replaced the box before he replied.

'Does Thery know that he is the fourth Just Man?' he asked; then slowly, 'I think not – and it is as well as he does not know; a thousand pounds is roughly thirty-three thousand pesetas, and there is the free pardon – and the girl at Jerez,' he added thoughtfully.

*   *   *

A brilliant idea came to Smith, the reporter, and he carried it to the chief.

'Not bad,' said the editor, which meant that the idea was really very good – 'not bad at all.'

'It occurred to me,' said the gratified reporter, 'that one or two of the four might be foreigners who don't understand a word of English.'

'Quite so,' said the chief; 'thank you for the suggestion. I'll have it done tonight.'

Which dialogue accounts for the fact that the next morning the *Megaphone* appeared with the police notice in French, Italian, German – and Spanish.

Chapter 5
The outrage at the Megaphone

The editor of the *Megaphone*, returning from dinner, met the super-chief on the stairs. The super-chief, boyish of face, withdrew his mind from the mental contemplation of a new project (Megaphone House is the home of new projects) and inquired after the Four Just Men.

'The excitement is keeping up,' replied the editor. 'People are talking of nothing else but the coming debate on the Extradition Bill, and the Government is taking every precaution against an attack upon Ramon.'

'What is the feeling?'

The editor shrugged his shoulders.

'Nobody really believes that anything will happen in spite of the bomb.'

The super-chief thought for a moment, and then quickly: 'What do you think?'

The editor laughed.

'I think the threat will never be fulfilled; for once the Four have struck against a snag. If they hadn't warned Ramon they might have done something, but forewarned – '

'We shall see,' said the super-chief, and went home.

The editor wondered, as he climbed the stairs, how much longer the Four would fill the contents bill of his newspaper, and rather hoped that they would make their attempt, even though they met with a failure, which he regarded as inevitable.

His room was locked and in darkness, and he fumbled in his pocket for the key, found it, turned the lock, opened the door and entered.

'I wonder,' he mused, reaching out of his hand and pressing down the switch of the light . . .

There was a blinding flash, a quick splutter of flame, and the room was in darkness again.

Startled, he retreated to the corridor and called for a light.

'Send for the electrician,' he roared; 'one of these damned fuses has gone!'

A lamp revealed the room to be filled with a pungent smoke; the electrician discovered that every globe had been carefully removed from its socket and placed on the table.

From one of the brackets suspended a curly length of thin wire which ended in a small black box, and it was from this that thick fumes were issuing.

'Open the windows,' directed the editor; and a bucket of water having been brought, the little box was dropped carefully into it.

Then it was that the editor discovered the letter – the greenish-grey letter that lay upon his desk. He took it up, turned it over, opened it, and noticed that the gum on the flap was still wet.

Honoured Sir [ran the note], when you turned on your light this evening you probably imagined for an instant that you were a victim of one of those 'outrages' to which you are fond of referring. We owe you an apology for any annoyance we may have caused you. The removal of your lamp and the substitution of a 'plug' connecting a small charge of magnesium powder is the cause of your discomfiture. We ask you to believe that it would have been as simple to have connected a charge of nitroglycerine, and thus have made you your own executioner. We have arranged this as evidence of our inflexible intention to carry out our promise in respect of the Aliens Extradition Act. There is no power on earth that can save Sir Philip Ramon from destruction, and we ask you, as the directing force of a great medium, to throw your weight into the scale in the cause of justice, to call upon your Government to withdraw an unjust measure, and save not only the lives of many inoffensive persons who have found an asylum in your country, but also the life of a Minister of the Crown whose only fault in our eyes is his zealousness in an unrighteous cause.

(Signed) The Four Just Men

'Whew!' whistled the editor, wiping his forehead and eyeing the sodden box floating serenely at the top of the bucket.

'Anything wrong, sir?' asked the electrician daringly.

'Nothing,' was the sharp reply. 'Finish your work, refix these globes, and go.'

The electrician, ill-satisfied and curious, looked at the floating box and the broken length of wire.

'Curious-looking thing, sir,' he said. 'If you ask me – '

'I don't ask you anything; finish your work,' the great journalist interrupted.

'Beg pardon, I'm sure,' said the apologetic artisan.

Half an hour later the editor of the *Megaphone* sat discussing the situation with Welby.

Welby, who is the greatest foreign editor in London, grinned amiably and drawled his astonishment.

'I have always believed that these chaps meant business,' he said cheerfully, 'and what is more, I feel pretty certain that they will keep their promise. When I was in Genoa – ' Welby got much of his information first-hand – 'when I was in Genoa – or was it Sofia? – I met a man who told me about the Trelovitch affair. He was one of the men who assassinated the King of Servia, you remember. Well, one night he left his quarters to visit a theatre – the same night he was found dead in the public square with a sword thrust through his heart. There were two extraordinary things about it.' The foreign editor ticked them on off his fingers. 'First, the General was a noted swordsman, and there was every evidence that he had not been killed in cold blood, but had been killed in a duel; the second was that he wore corsets, as many of these Germanised officers do, and one of his assailants had discovered this fact, probably by a sword thrust, and had made him discard them; at any rate when he was found this frippery was discovered close by his body.'

'Was it known at the time that it was the work of the Four?' asked the editor.

Welby shook his head.

'Even I had never heard of them before,' he said resentfully. Then asked, 'What have you done about your little scare?'

'I've seen the hall porters and the messengers, and every man on duty at the time, but the coming and the going of our mysterious friend – I don't suppose there was more than one – is unexplained. It really is a remarkable thing. Do you know, Welby, it gives me quite an uncanny feeling; the gum on the envelope was still wet; the letter must have been written on the premises and sealed down within a few seconds of my entering the room.'

'Were the windows open?'

'No; all three were shut and fastened, and it would have been impossible to enter the room that way.'

The detective who came to receive a report of the circumstances endorsed this opinion.

'The man who wrote this letter must have left your room not longer than a minute before you arrived,' he concluded, and took charge of the letter.

Being a young and enthusiastic detective, before finishing his investigations he made a most minute search of the room, turning up carpets, tapping walls, inspecting cupboards, and taking laborious and unnecessary measurements with a foot-rule.

'There are a lot of our chaps who sneer at detective stories,' he explained to the amused editor, 'but I have read almost everything that has been written by Gaboriau and Conan Doyle, and I believe in taking notice of little things. There wasn't any cigar ash or anything of that sort left behind, was there?' he asked wistfully.

'I'm afraid not,' said the editor gravely.

'Pity,' said the detective, and wrapping up the 'infernal machine' and its appurtenances, he took his departure.

Afterwards the editor informed Welby that the disciple of Holmes had spent half an hour with a magnifying glass examining the floor.

'He found half a sovereign that I lost weeks ago, so it's really an ill wind – '

All that evening nobody but Welby and the chief knew what had happened in the editor's room. There was some rumour in the sub-editor's department that a small accident had occurred in the sanctum.

'Chief busted a fuse in his room and got a devil of a fright,' said the man who attended to the Shipping List.

'Dear me,' said the weather expert, looking up from his chart, 'do you know something like that happened to me: the other night – '

The chief had directed a few firm words to the detective before his departure.

'Only you and myself know anything about this occurrence,' said the editor, 'so if it gets out I shall know it comes from Scotland Yard.'

'You may be sure nothing will come from us,' was the detective's reply: 'we've got into too much hot water already.'

'That's good,' said the editor, and 'that's good' sounded like a threat.

So that Welby and the chief kept the matter a secret till half an hour before the paper went to press.

This may seem to the layman an extraordinary circumstance, but experience has shown most men who control newspapers that news has an unlucky knack of leaking out before it appears in type.

Wicked compositors – and even compositors can be wicked – have been known to screw up copies of important and exclusive news, and throw them out of a convenient window so that they have fallen close to a patient man standing in the street below and have been immediately hurried off to the office of a rival newspaper and sold for more than their weight in gold. Such cases have been known.

But at half past eleven the buzzing hive of Megaphone House began to hum, for then it was that the sub-editors learnt for the first time of the 'outrage'.

It was a great story – yet another *Megaphone* scoop, headlined half down the page with the 'Just Four' again – outrage at the office of the *Megaphone* – devilish ingenuity – Another Threatening Letter – The Four Will Keep Their Promise – Remarkable Document – Will the Police save Sir Philip Ramon?

'A very good story,' said the chief complacently, reading the proofs.

He was preparing to leave, and was speaking to Welby by the door.

'Not bad,' said the discriminating Welby. 'What I think – hullo!'

The last was addressed to a messenger who appeared with a stranger.

'Gentleman wants to speak to somebody, sir – bit excited, so I brought him up; he's a foreigner, and I can't understand him, so I brought him to you . . . ' – this to Welby.

'What do you want?' asked the chief in French.

The man shook his head, and said a few words in a strange tongue.

'Ah!' said Welby, 'Spanish – what do you wish?' he said in that language.

'Is this the office of that paper?' The man produced a grimy copy of the *Megaphone*.

'Yes.'

'Can I speak to the editor?'

The chief looked suspicious.

'I am the editor,' he said.

The man looked over his shoulder, then leant forward.

'I am one of The Four Just Men,' he said hesitatingly. Welby took a step towards him and scrutinised him closely.

'What is your name?' he asked quickly.

'Miguel Thery of Jerez,' replied the man.

* * *

It was half past ten when, returning from a concert, the cab that bore Poiccart and Manfred westward passed through Hanover Square and turned off to Oxford Street.

'You ask to see the editor,' Manfred was explaining; 'they take you up to the offices; you explain your business to somebody; they are very sorry, but they cannot help you; they are very polite, but not to the extent of seeing you off the premises, so, wandering about seeking your way out, you come to the editor's room and, knowing that he is out, slip in, make your arrangements, walk out, locking the door after you if nobody is about, addressing a few farewell words to an imaginary occupant, if you are seen, and *voilà*!'

Poiccart bit the end of his cigar.

'Use for your envelope a gum that will not dry under an hour and you heighten the mystery,' he said quietly, and Manfred was amused.

'The envelope-just-fastened is an irresistible attraction to an English detective.'

The cab speeding along Oxford Street turned into Edgware Road, when Manfred put up his hand and pushed open the trap in the roof.

'We'll get down here,' he called, and the driver pulled up to the sidewalk.

'I thought you said Pembridge Gardens?' he remarked as Manfred paid him.

'So I did,' said Manfred; 'goodnight.'

They waited chatting on the edge of the pavement until the cab had disappeared from view, then turned back to the Marble Arch, crossed to Park Lane, walked down that plutocratic thoroughfare and round into Piccadilly. Near the Circus they found a restaurant with a long bar and many small alcoves, where men sat around marble tables, drinking, smoking, and talking. In one of these, alone, sat Gonsalez, smoking a long cigarette and wearing on his clean-shaven mobile face a look of meditative content.

Neither of the men evinced the slightest sign of surprise at meeting him – yet Manfred's heart missed a beat, and into the pallid cheeks of Poiccart crept two bright red spots.

They seated themselves, a waiter came and they gave their orders, and when he had gone Manfred asked in a low tone, 'Where is Thery?'

Leon gave the slightest shrug.

'Thery has made his escape,' he answered calmly.

For a minute neither man spoke, and Leon continued: 'This morning, before you left, you gave him a bundle of newspapers?'

Manfred nodded.

'They were English newspapers,' he said. 'Thery does not know a word of English. There were pictures in them – I gave them to amuse him.'

'You gave him, amongst others, the *Megaphone*?'

'Yes – ha!' Manfred remembered.

'The offer of a reward was in it – and the free pardon – printed in Spanish.'

Manfred was gazing into vacancy.

'I remember,' he said slowly. 'I read it afterwards.'

'It was very ingenious,' remarked Poiccart commendingly.

'I noticed he was rather excited, but I accounted for this by the fact that we had told him last night of the method we intended adopting for the removal of Ramon and the part he was to play.'

Leon changed the topic to allow the waiter to serve the refreshments that had been ordered.

'It is preposterous,' he went on without changing his key, 'that a horse on which so much money has been placed should not have been sent to England at least a month in advance.'

'The idea of a bad Channel-crossing leading to the scratching of the favourite of a big race is unheard of,' added Manfred severely.

The waiter left them.

'We went for a walk this afternoon,' resumed Leon, 'and were passing along Regent Street, he stopping every few seconds to look in the shops, when suddenly – we had been staring at the window of a photographer's – I missed him. There were hundreds of people in the street – but no Thery . . . I have been seeking him ever since.'

Leon sipped his drink and looked at his watch.

The other two men did nothing, said nothing.

A careful observer might have noticed that both Manfred's and Poiccart's hands strayed to the top button of their coats.

'Perhaps not so bad as that,' smiled Gonsalez.

Manfred broke the silence of the two.

'I take all blame,' he commenced, but Poiccart stopped him with a gesture.

'If there is any blame, I alone am blameless,' he said with a short laugh. 'No, George, it is too late to talk of blame. We underrated the cunning of m'sieur, the enterprise of the English newspapers and – and – '

'The girl at Jerez,' concluded Leon.

Five minutes passed in silence, each man thinking rapidly.

'I have a car not far from here,' said Leon at length. 'You had told me you would be at this place by eleven o'clock; we have the naphtha launch at Burnham-on-Crouch – we could be in France by daybreak.'

Manfred looked at him. 'What do you think yourself?' he asked.

'I say stay and finish the work,' said Leon.

'And I,' said Poiccart quietly but decisively.

Manfred called the waiter.

'Have you the last editions of the evening papers?'

The waiter thought he could get them, and returned with two.

Manfred scanned the pages carefully, then threw them aside.

'Nothing in these,' he said. 'If They has gone to the police we must hide and use some other method to that agreed upon, or we could strike now. After all, They has told us all we want to know, but – '

'That would be unfair to Ramon.' Poiccart finished the sentence in such a tone as summarily ended that possibility. 'He has still two days, and must receive yet another, and last, warning.'

'Then we must find Thery.'

It was Manfred who spoke, and he rose, followed by Poiccart and Gonsalez.

'If Thery has not gone to the police – where would he go?'

The tone of Leon's question suggested the answer.

'To the office of the newspaper that published the Spanish advertisement,' was Manfred's reply, and instinctively the three men knew that this was the correct solution.

'Your motor-car will be useful,' said Manfred, and all three left the bar.

* * *

In the editor's room Thery faced the two journalists.

'Thery?' repeated Welby; 'I do not know that name. Where do you come from? What is your address?'

'I come from Jerez in Andalusia, from the wine farm of Sienor.'

'Not that,' interrupted Welby; 'where do you come from now – what part of London?'

Thery raised his hands despairingly.

'How should I know? There are houses and streets and people – and it is in London, and I was to kill a man, a Minister, because he had made a wicked law – they did not tell me – '

'They – who?' asked the editor eagerly.

'The other three.'

'But their names?'

Thery shot a suspicious glance at his questioner.

'There is a reward,' he said sullenly, 'and a pardon. I want these before I tell – '

The editor stepped to his desk.

'If you are one of the Four you shall have your reward – you shall have some of it now.' He pressed a button and a messenger came to the door.

'Go to the composing room and tell the printer not to allow his men to leave until I give orders.'

Below, in the basement, the machines were thundering as they flung out the first numbers of the morning news.

'Now – ' the editor turned to Thery, who had stood, uneasily shifting from foot to foot whilst the order was being given – 'now, tell me all you know.'

Thery did not answer; his eyes were fixed on the floor.

'There is a reward and a pardon,' he muttered doggedly.

'Hasten!' cried Welby. 'You will receive your reward and the pardon also. Tell us, who are the Four Just Men? Who are the other three? Where are they to be found?'

'Here,' said a clear voice behind him; and he turned as a stranger, closing the door as he entered, stood facing the three men – a stranger in evening dress, masked from brow to chin.

There was a revolver in the hand that hung at his side.

'I am one,' repeated the stranger calmly; 'there are two others waiting outside the building.'

'How did you get here – what do you want?' demanded the editor, and stretched his hand to an open drawer in his desk.

'Take your hand away – ' and the thin barrel of the revolver rose with a jerk. 'How I came here your doorkeeper will explain, when he recovers consciousness. Why I am here is because I wish to save my life – not an unreasonable wish. If Thery speaks I may be a dead man – I am about to prevent him speaking. I have no quarrel with either of you gentlemen, but if you hinder me I shall kill you,' he said simply. He spoke all the while in English, and Thery, with wide-stretched eyes and distended nostrils, shrank back against the wall, breathing quickly.

'You,' said the masked man, turning to the terror-stricken informer and speaking in Spanish, 'would have betrayed your comrades – you would have thwarted a great purpose, therefore it is just that you should die.'

He raised the revolver to the level of Thery's breast, and Thery fell on his knees, mouthing the prayer he could not articulate.

'By God – no!' cried the editor, and sprang forward.

The revolver turned on him.

'Sir,' said the unknown – and his voice sank almost to a whisper – 'for God's sake do not force me to kill you.'

'You shall not commit a cold-blooded murder,' cried the editor in a white heat of anger, and moved forward, but Welby held him back. 'What is the use?' said Welby in an undertone; 'he means it – we can do nothing.'

'You can do something,' said the stranger, and his revolver dropped to his side.

Before the editor could answer there was a knock at the door.

'Say you are busy'; and the revolver covered Thery, who was a whimpering, huddled heap by the wall.

'Go away,' shouted the editor, 'I am busy.'

'The printers are waiting,' said the voice of the messenger.

'Now,' asked the chief, as the footsteps of the boy died away; 'what can we do?'

'You can save this man's life.'

'How?'

'Give me your word of honour that you will allow us both to depart, and will neither raise an alarm nor leave this room for a quarter of an hour.'

The editor hesitated.

'How do I know that the murder you contemplate will not be committed as soon as you get clear?'

The other laughed under his mask.

'How do I know that as soon as I have left the room you will not raise an alarm?'

'I should have given my word, sir,' said the editor stiffly.

'And I mine,' was the quiet response; 'and my word has never been broken.'

In the editor's mind a struggle was going on; here in his hand was the greatest story of the century; another minute and he would have extracted from Thery the secret of the Four.

Even now a bold dash might save everything – and the printers were waiting . . . but the hand that held the revolver was the hand of a resolute man, and the chief yielded.

'I agree, but under protest,' he said. 'I warn you that your arrest and punishment is inevitable.'

'I regret,' said the masked man with a slight bow, 'that I cannot agree with you – nothing is inevitable save death. Come, Thery,' he said, speaking in Spanish. 'On my word as a Caballero I will not harm you.'

Thery hesitated, then slunk forward with his head bowed and his eyes fixed on the floor.

The masked man opened the door an inch, listened, and in the moment came the inspiration of the editor's life.

'Look here,' he said quickly, the man giving place to the journalist, 'when you get home will you write us an article about yourselves? You needn't give us any embarrassing particulars, you know – something about your aspirations, your *raison d'être*.'

'Sir,' said the masked man – and there was a note of admiration in his voice – 'I recognise in you an artist. The article will be delivered tomorrow'; and opening the door the two men stepped into the darkened corridor.

Chapter 6
The clues

Blood-red placards, hoarse newsboys, overwhelming headlines, and column after column of leaded type told the world next day how near the Four had been to capture. Men in the train leant forward, their newspapers on their knees, and explained what they would have done had they been in the editor of the *Megaphone*'s position. People stopped talking about wars and famines and droughts and street accidents and parliaments and ordinary everyday murders and the German Emperor, in order to concentrate their minds upon the topic of the hour. Would the Four Just Men carry out their promise and slay the Secretary for Foreign Affairs on the morrow?

Nothing else was spoken about. Here was a murder threatened a month ago, and, unless something unforeseen happened, to be committed tomorrow.

No wonder that the London Press devoted the greater part of its space to discussing the coming of Thery and his recapture.

' . . . It is not so easy to understand,' said the *Telegram*, 'why, having the miscreants in their hands, certain journalists connected with a sensational and halfpenny contemporary allowed them to go free to work their evil designs upon a great statesman whose unparalleled . . . We say if, for unfortunately in these days of cheap journalism every story emanating from the *sanctum sanctorum* of sensation-loving sheets is not to be accepted on its pretensions; so if, as it stated, these desperadoes really did visit the office of a contemporary last night . . . '

At noonday Scotland Yard circulated broadcast a hastily printed sheet.

£1000 REWARD

Wanted, on suspicion of being connected with a criminal organisation known as the Four Just Men, Miguel Thery, alias Saimont, alias le Chico, late of Jerez, Spain, a Spaniard speaking no English. Height 5 feet 8 inches. Eyes brown, hair black, slight black moustache, face broad. Scars: white scar on cheek, old knife wound on body. Figure, thick-set.

The above reward will be paid to any person or persons who shall give such information as shall lead to the identification of the said Thery with the band known as the Four Just Men and his apprehension.

From which may be gathered that, acting on the information furnished by the editor and his assistant at two o'clock in the morning, the Direct Spanish Cable had been kept busy; important personages had been roused from their beds in Madrid, and the history of Thery as recorded in the Bureau had been reconstructed from pigeon-hole records for the enlightenment of an energetic Commissioner of Police.

Sir Philip Ramon, sitting writing in his study at Portland Place, found a difficulty in keeping his mind upon the letter that lay before him.

It was a letter addressed to his agent at Branfell, the huge estate over which he, in the years he was out of office, played squire.

Neither wife nor chick nor child had Sir Philip. ' . . . If by any chance these men succeed in carrying out their purpose I have made ample provision not only for yourself but for all who have rendered me faithful service,' he wrote – from which may be gathered the tenor of his letter.

During these past few weeks, Sir Philip's feelings towards the possible outcome of his action had undergone a change.

The irritation of a constant espionage, friendly on the one hand, menacing on the other, had engendered so bitter a feeling of resentment, that in this newer emotion all personal fear had been swallowed up. His mind was filled with one unswerving determination, to carry through the measure he had in hand, to thwart the Four Just Men, and to vindicate the integrity of a Minister of the Crown. 'It would be absurd,' he wrote in the course of an article entitled 'Individuality in its Relation to the Public Service', and which was published some months later in the *Quarterly Review* – 'it would be monstrous to suppose that incidental criticism from a wholly unauthoritative source should affect or in any way influence a member of the Government in his conception of the legislation necessary for the millions of people entrusted to his care. He is the instrument, duly appointed, to put into tangible form the wishes and desires of those who naturally look to him not only to furnish means and methods for the betterment of their conditions, or the amelioration of irksome restrictions upon international commercial relations, but to find them protection from risks extraneous of purely commercial liabilities . . . in such a case a Minister of the Crown with a due appreciation of his responsibilities ceases to exist as a man and becomes merely an unhuman automaton.'

Sir Philip Ramon was a man with very few friends. He had none of the qualities that go to the making of a popular man. He was an honest man, a conscientious man, a strong man. He was the cold-blooded, cynical creature that a life devoid of love had left him. He had no enthusiasm – and inspired none. Satisfied that a certain procedure was less wrong than any other, he adopted it. Satisfied that a measure was for the immediate or ultimate good of his fellows, he carried that measure through to the bitter end. It may be said of him that he had no ambitions – only aims. He was the most dangerous man in the Cabinet, which he dominated in his masterful way, for he knew not the meaning of the blessed word 'compromise'.

If he held views on any subject under the sun, those views were to be the views of his colleagues.

Four times in the short history of the administration had 'Rumoured Resignation of a Cabinet Minister' filled the placards of the news-papers, and each time the Minister whose resignation was ultimately recorded was the man whose views had clashed with the Foreign Secretary. In small things, as in great, he had his way.

His official residence he absolutely refused to occupy, and No. 44 Downing Street was converted into half office, half palace. Portland Place was his home, and from there he drove every morning, passing the Horse Guards clock as it finished the last stroke of ten.

A private telephone wire connected his study in Portland Place with the official residence, and but for this Sir Philip had cut himself adrift from the house in Downing Street, to occupy which had been the ambition of the great men of his party.

Now, however, with the approach of the day on which every effort would be taxed, the police insisted upon his taking up his quarters in Downing Street.

Here, they said, the task of protecting the Minister would be simplified. No 44 Downing Street they knew. The approaches could be better guarded, and, moreover, the drive – that dangerous drive! – between Portland Place and the Foreign Office would be obviated.

It took a considerable amount of pressure and pleading to induce Sir Philip to take even this step, and it was only when it was pointed out that the surveillance to which he was being subjected would not be so apparent to himself that he yielded.

'You don't like to find my men outside your door with your shaving water,' said Superintendent Falmouth bluntly. 'You objected to one of my men being in your bathroom when you went in the other morning, and you complained about a plain-clothes officer driving on your box – well, Sir Philip, in Downing Street I promise that you shan't even see them.'

This clinched the argument.

It was just before leaving Portland Place to take up his new quarters that he sat writing to his agent whilst the detective waited outside the door.

The telephone at Sir Philip's elbow buzzed – he hated bells – and the voice of his private secretary asked with some anxiety how long he would be.

'We have got sixty men on duty at 44,' said the secretary, zealous and young, 'and today and tomorrow we shall – ' And Sir Philip listened with growing impatience to the recital.

'I wonder you have not got an iron safe to lock me in,' he said petulantly, and closed the conversation.

There was a knock at the door and Falmouth put his head inside.

'I don't want to hurry you, sir,' he said, 'but – '

So the Foreign Secretary drove off to Downing Street in something remarkably like a temper.

For he was not used to being hurried, or taken charge of, or ordered hither and thither. It irritated him further to see the now familiar cyclists on either side of the carriage, to recognise at every few yards an obvious policeman in mufti admiring the view from the sidewalk, and when he came to Downing Street and found it barred to all carriages but his own, and an enormous crowd of morbid sightseers gathered to cheer his ingress, he felt as he had never felt before in his life – humiliated.

He found his secretary waiting in his private office with the rough draft of the speech that was to introduce the second reading of the Extradition Bill.

'We are pretty sure to meet with a great deal of opposition,' informed the secretary, 'but Mainland has sent out three-line whips, and expects to get a majority of thirty-six – at the very least.'

Ramon read over the notes and found them refreshing.

They brought back the old feeling of security and importance. After all, he was a great Minister of State. Of course the threats were too absurd – the police were to blame for making so much fuss; and of course the Press – yes, that was it – a newspaper sensation.

There was something buoyant, something almost genial in his air, when he turned with a half-smile to his secretary.

'Well, what about my unknown friends – what do the blackguards call themselves? – the Four Just Men?'

Even as he spoke he was acting a part; he had not forgotten their title, it was with him day and night.

The secretary hesitated; between his chief and himself the Four Just Men had been a tabooed subject.

'They – oh, we've heard nothing more than you have read,' he said lamely; 'we know now who Thery is, but we can't place his three companions.'

The Minister pursed his lips.

'They give me till tomorrow night to recant,' he said.

'You have heard from them again?'

'The briefest of notes,' said Sir Philip lightly.

'And otherwise?'

Sir Philip frowned. 'They will keep their promise,' he said shortly, for the 'otherwise' of his secretary had sent a coldness into his heart that he could not quite understand.

* * *

In the top room in the workshop at Carnaby Street, Thery, subdued, sullen, fearful, sat facing the three. 'I want you to quite understand,' said Manfred, 'that we bear you no ill-will for what you have done. I think, and Señor Poiccart thinks, that Señor Gonsalez did right to spare your life and bring you back to us.'

Thery dropped his eyes before the half-quizzical smile of the speaker.

'Tomorrow night you will do as you agreed to do – if the necessity still exists. Then you will go – ' he paused.

'Where?' demanded Thery in sudden rage. 'Where in the name of Heaven? I have told them my name, they will know who I am – they will find that by writing to the police. Where am I to go?'

He sprang to his feet, glowering on the three men, his hands trembling with rage, his great frame shaking with the intensity of his anger.

'You betrayed yourself,' said Manfred quietly; 'that is your punishment. But we will find a place for you, a new Spain under other skies – and the girl at Jerez shall be there waiting for you.'

Thery looked from one to the other suspiciously. Were they laughing at him?

There was no smile on their faces; Gonsalez alone looked at him with keen, inquisitive eyes, as though he saw some hidden meaning in the speech.

'Will you swear that?' asked Thery hoarsely, 'will you swear that by the – '

'I promise that – if you wish it I will swear it,' said Manfred. 'And now,' he went on, his voice changing, 'you know what is expected of you tomorrow night – what you have to do?'

Thery nodded.

'There must be no hitch – no bungling; you and I and Poiccart and Gonsalez will kill this unjust man in a way that the world will never guess – such an execution as shall appal mankind. A swift death, a sure death, a death that will creep through cracks, that will pass by the guards unnoticed. Why, there never has been such a thing done – such – ' he stopped dead with flushed cheeks and kindling eyes, and met the gaze of his two companions. Poiccart impassive, sphinxlike, Leon interested and analytic. Manfred's face went a duller red.

'I am sorry,' he said almost humbly; 'for the moment I had forgotten the cause, and the end, in the strangeness of the means.'

He raised his hand deprecatingly.

'It is understandable,' said Poiccart gravely, and Leon pressed Manfred's arm.

The three stood in embarrassed silence for a moment, then Manfred laughed.

'To work!' he said, and led the way to the improvised laboratory.

Inside Thery took off his coat. Here was his province, and from being the cowed dependant he took charge of the party, directing them, instructing, commanding, until he had the men of whom, a few minutes before, he had stood in terror running from studio to laboratory, from floor to floor.

There was much to be done, much testing, much calculating, many little sums to be worked out on paper, for in the killing of Sir Philip Ramon all the resources of modern science were to be pressed into the service of the Four.

'I am going to survey the land,' said Manfred suddenly, and disappearing into the studio returned with a pair of step-ladders. These he straddled in the dark passage, and mounting quickly pushed up a trapdoor that led to the flat roof of the building.

He pulled himself up carefully, crawled along the leaden surface, and raising himself cautiously looked over the low parapet.

He was in the centre of a half mile circle of uneven roofs. Beyond the circumference of his horizon London loomed murkily through smoke and mist. Below was a busy street. He took a hasty survey of the roof with its chimney stacks, its unornamental telegraph pole, its leaden floor and rusty guttering; then, through a pair of field-glasses, made a long, careful survey southward. He crawled slowly back to the trapdoor, raised it, and let himself down very gingerly till his feet touched the top of the ladder. Then he descended rapidly, closing the door after him.

'Well?' asked Thery with something of triumph in his voice.

'I see you have labelled it,' said Manfred.

'It is better so – since we shall work in the dark,' said Thery.

'Did you see then – ?' began Poiccart.

Manfred nodded.

'Very indistinctly – one could just see the Houses of Parliament dimly, and Downing Street is a jumble of roofs.'

Thery had turned to the work that was engaging his attention. Whatever was his trade he was a deft workman. Somehow he felt that he must do his best for these men. He had been made forcibly aware of their superiority in the last days, he had now an ambition to assert his own skill, his individuality, and to earn commendation from these men who had made him feel his littleness.

Manfred and the others stood aside and watched him in silence. Leon, with a perplexed frown, kept his eyes fixed on the workman's face. For Leon Gonsalez, scientist, physiognomist (his translation of the Theologi Physiognomia Humana of Lequetius is regarded today as the finest), was endeavouring to reconcile the criminal with the artisan.

After a while Thery finished. 'All is now ready,' he said with a grin of satisfaction: 'let me find your Minister of State, give me a minute's speech with him, and the next minute he dies.'

His face, repulsive in repose, was now demoniacal. He was like some great bull from his own country made more terrible with the snuffle of blood in his nostrils.

In strange contrast were the faces of his employers. Not a muscle of either face stirred. There was neither exultation nor remorse in their expressions – only a curious something that creeps into the set face of the judge as he pronounces the dread sentence of the law. Thery saw that something, and it froze him to his very marrow.

He threw up his hands as if to ward them off.

'Stop! stop!' he shouted; 'don't look like that, in the name of God – don't, don't!' He covered his face with shaking hands.

'Like what, Thery?' asked Leon softly.

Thery shook his head.

'I cannot say – like the judge at Granada when he says – when he says, "Let the thing be done!" '

'If we look so,' said Manfred harshly, 'it is because we are judges – and not alone judges but executioners of our judgment.'

'I thought you would have been pleased,' whimpered Thery.

'You have done well,' said Manfred gravely.

'*Bueno, bueno*!' echoed the others.

'Pray God that we are successful,' added Manfred solemnly, and Thery stared at this strange man in amazement.

* * *

Superintendent Falmouth reported to the Commissioner that after-noon that all arrangements were now complete for the protection of the threatened Minister.

'I've filled up 44 Downing Street,' he said; 'there's practically a man in every room. I've got four of our best men on the roof, men in the basement, men in the kitchens.'

'What about the servants?' asked the Commissioner.

'Sir Philip has brought up his own people from the country, and now there isn't a person in the house from the private secretary to the doorkeeper whose name and history I do not know from A to Z.'

The Commissioner breathed an anxious sigh.

'I shall be very glad when tomorrow is over,' he said. 'What are the final arrangements?'

'There has been no change, sir, since we fixed things up the morn-ing Sir Philip came over. He remains at 44 all day tomorrow until half past eight, goes over to the House at nine to move the reading of the Bill, returns at eleven.'

'I have given orders for the traffic to be diverted along the Em-bankment between a quarter to nine and a quarter after, and the same at eleven,' said the Commissioner. 'Four closed carriages will drive from Downing Street to the House, Sir Philip will drive down in a car immediately afterwards.'

There was a rap at the door – the conversation took place in the Commissioner's office – and a police officer entered. He bore a card in his hand, which he laid upon the table.

'Señor Jose di Silva,' read the Commissioner. 'The Spanish Chief of Police,' he explained to the Superintendent. 'Show him in, please.'

Señor di Silva, a lithe little man, with a pronounced nose and a beard, greeted the Englishmen with the exaggerated politeness that is peculiar to Spanish official circles.

'I am sorry to bring you over,' said the Commissioner, after he had shaken hands with the visitor and had introduced him to Falmouth; 'we thought you might be able to help us in our search for Thery.'

'Luckily I was in Paris,' said the Spaniard; 'yes, I know Thery, and I am astounded to find him in such distinguished company. Do I know the Four? – ' his shoulders went up to his ears – 'who does? I know of them – there was a case at Malaga, you know? . . . Thery is not a good criminal. I was astonished to learn that he had joined the band.'

'By the way,' said the chief, picking up a copy of the police notice that lay on his desk, and running his eye over it, 'your people omitted to say – although it really isn't of very great importance – what is Thery's trade?'

The Spanish policeman knitted his brow.

'Thery's trade! Let me remember.' He thought for a moment. 'Thery's trade? I don't think I know; yet I have an idea that it is something to do with rubber. His first crime was stealing rubber; but if you want to know for certain – '

The Commissioner laughed.

'It really isn't at all important,' he said lightly.

Chapter 7
The messenger of the Four

There was yet another missive to be handed to the doomed Minister. In the last he had received there had occurred the sentence: 'One more warning you shall receive, and so that we may be assured it shall not go astray, our next and last message shall be delivered into your hands by one of us in person.'

This passage afforded the police more comfort than had any episode since the beginning of the scare. They placed a curious faith in the honesty of the Four Men; they recognised that these were not ordinary criminals and that their pledge was inviolable. Indeed, had they thought otherwise the elaborate precautions that they were taking to ensure the safety of Sir Philip would not have been made. The honesty of the Four was their most terrible characteristic.

In this instance it served to raise a faint hope that the men who were setting at defiance the establishment of the law would overreach themselves. The letter conveying this message was the one to which Sir Philip had referred so airily in his conversation with his secretary. It had come by post, bearing the date mark, Balham, 12.15.

'The question is, shall we keep you absolutely surrounded, so that these men cannot by any possible chance carry out their threat?' asked Superintendent Falmouth in some perplexity, 'or shall we apparently relax our vigilance in order to lure one of the Four to his destruction?'

The question was directed to Sir Philip Ramon as he sat huddled up in the capacious depths of his office chair.

'You want to use me as a bait?' he asked sharply.

The detective expostulated.

'Not exactly that, sir; we want to give these men a chance – '

'I understand perfectly,' said the Minister, with some show of irritation.

The detective resumed.

'We know now how the infernal machine was smuggled into the House; on the day on which the outrage was committed an old member, Mr Bascoe, the member for North Torrington, was seen to enter the House.'

'Well?' asked Sir Philip in surprise.

'Mr Bascoe was never within a hundred miles of the House of Commons on that date,' said the detective quietly. 'We might never have found it out, for his name did not appear in the division list. We've been working quietly on that House of Commons affair ever since, and it was only a couple of days ago that we made the discovery.'

Sir Philip sprang from his chair and nervously paced the floor of his room.

'Then they are evidently well acquainted with the conditions of life in England,' he asserted rather than asked.

'Evidently; they've got the lay of the land, and that is one of the dangers of the situation.'

'But,' frowned the other, 'you have told me there were no dangers, no real dangers.'

'There is this danger, sir,' replied the detective, eyeing the Minister steadily, and dropping his voice as he spoke. 'Men who are capable of making such disguise are really outside the ordinary run of criminals. I don't know what their game is, but whatever it is, they are playing it thoroughly. One of them is evidently an artist at that sort of thing, and he's the man I'm afraid of – today.'

Sir Philip's head tossed impatiently.

'I am tired of all this, tired of it – ' and he thrashed the edge of his desk with an open palm – 'detectives and disguises and masked murderers until the atmosphere is, for all the world, like that of a melodrama.'

'You must have patience for a day or two,' said the plain-spoken officer.

The Four Just Men were on the nerves of more people than the Foreign Minister.

'And we have not decided what is to be our plan for this evening,' he added.

'Do as you like,' said Sir Philip shortly, and then: 'Am I to be allowed to go to the House tonight?'

'No; that is not part of the programme,' replied the detective.

Sir Philip stood for a moment in thought.

'These arrangements; they are kept secret, I suppose?'

'Absolutely.'

'Who knows of them?'

'Yourself, the Commissioner, your secretary, and myself.'

'And no one else?'

'No one; there is no danger likely to arise from that source. If upon the secrecy of your movements your safety depended it would be plain sailing.'

'Have these arrangements been committed to writing?' asked Sir Philip.

'No, sir; nothing has been written; our plans have been settled upon and communicated verbally; even the Prime Minister does not know.'

Sir Philip breathed a sigh of relief.

'That is all to the good,' he said, as the detective rose to go.

'I must see the Commissioner. I shall be away for less than half an hour; in the meantime I suggest that you do not leave your room,' he said.

Sir Philip followed him out to the ante-room, in which sat Hamilton, the secretary.

'I have had an uncomfortable feeling,' said Falmouth, as one of his men approached with a long coat, which he proceeded to help the detective into, 'a sort of instinctive feeling this last day or two, that I have been watched and followed, so that I am using a car to convey me from place to place: they can't follow that, without attracting some notice.' He dipped his hand into the pocket and brought out a pair of motoring goggles. He laughed somewhat shamefacedly as he adjusted them. 'This is the only disguise I ever adopt, and I might say, Sir Philip,' he added with some regret, 'that this is the first time during my twenty-five years of service that I have ever played the fool like a stage detective.'

After Falmouth's departure the Foreign Minister returned to his desk.

He hated being alone: it frightened him. That there were two score detectives within call did not dispel the feeling of loneliness. The terror of the Four was ever with him, and this had so worked upon his nerves that the slightest noise irritated him. He played with the penholder that lay on the desk. He scribbled inconsequently on the blotting-pad before him, and was annoyed to find that the scribbling had taken the form of numbers of figure 4.

Was the Bill worth it? Was the sacrifice called for? Was the measure of such importance as to justify the risk? These things he asked himself again and again, and then immediately, What sacrifice? What risk?

'I am taking the consequence too much for granted,' he muttered, throwing aside the pen, and half turning from the writing-table. 'There is no certainty that they will keep their words; bah! it is impossible that they should – '

There was a knock at the door.

'Hullo, Superintendent,' said the Foreign Minister as the knocker entered. 'Back again already!'

The detective, vigorously brushing the dust from his moustache with a handkerchief, drew an official-looking blue envelope from his pocket.

'I thought I had better leave this in your care,' he said, dropping his voice; 'it occurred to me just after I had left; accidents happen, you know.'

The Minister took the document.

'What is it? 'he asked.

'It is something which would mean absolute disaster for me if by chance it was found in my possession,' said the detective, turning to go.

'What am I to do with it?'

'You would greatly oblige me by putting it in your desk until I return'; and the detective stepped into the anteroom, closed the door behind him and, acknowledging the salute of the plain-clothes officer who guarded the outer door, passed to the motor-car that awaited him.

Sir Philip looked at the envelope with a puzzled frown.

It bore the superscription, 'Confidential' and the address, 'Department A, CID, Scotland Yard'.

'Some confidential report,' thought Sir Philip, and an angry doubt as to the possibility of it containing particulars of the police arrangements for his safety filled his mind. He had hit by accident upon the truth had he but known. The envelope contained those particulars.

He placed the letter in a drawer of his desk and drew some papers towards him.

They were copies of the Bill for the passage of which he was daring so much.

It was not a long document. The clauses were few in number, the objects, briefly described in the preamble, were tersely defined. There was no fear of this Bill failing to pass on the morrow. The Government's majority was assured. Men had been brought back to town, stragglers had been whipped in, prayers and threats alike had assisted in concentrating the rapidly dwindling strength of the administration on this one effort of legislation; and what the frantic entreaties of the Whips had failed to secure, curiosity had accomplished, for members of both parties were hurrying to town to be present at a scene which might perhaps be history, and, as many feared, tragedy.

As Sir Philip conned the paper he mechanically formed in his mind the line of attack – for, tragedy or no, the Bill struck at too many interests in the House to allow of its passage without a stormy debate. He was a master of dialectics, a brilliant casuist, a coiner of phrases that stuck and stung. There was nothing for him to fear in the debate. If only – It hurt him to think of the Four Just Men. Not so much because they threatened his life – he had gone past that – but the mere thought that there had come a new factor into his calculations, a new and terrifying force, that could not be argued down or brushed aside with an acid jest, nor intrigued against, nor adjusted by any parliamentary method. He did not think of compromise. The possibility of making terms with his enemy never once entered his head.

'I'll go through with it!' he cried, not once but a score of times; 'I'll go through with it!' and now, as the moment grew nearer to hand, his determination to try conclusions with this new world-force grew stronger than ever.

The telephone at his elbow purred – he was sitting at his desk with his head on his hands – and he took the receiver. The voice of his house steward reminded him that he had arranged to give instructions for the closing of the house in Portland Place.

For two or three days, or until this terror had subsided, he intended his house should be empty. He would not risk the lives of his servants. If the Four intended to carry out their plan they would run no risks of failure, and if the method they employed were a bomb, then, to make assurance doubly sure, an explosion at Downing Street might well synchronize with an outrage at Portland Place.

He had finished his talk, and was replacing the receiver when a knock at the door heralded the entry of the detective.

He looked anxiously at the Minister.

'Nobody been, sir?' he asked.

Sir Philip smiled.

'If by that you mean have the Four delivered their ultimatum in person, I can comfort your mind – they have not.'

The detective's face was evidence of his relief.

'Thank Heaven!' he said fervently. 'I had an awful dread that whilst I was away something would happen. But I have news for you, sir.'

'Indeed!'

'Yes, sir, the Commissioner has received a long cable from America. Since the two murders in that country one of Pinkerton's men has been engaged in collecting data. For years he has been piecing together the scrappy evidence he has been able to secure, and this is his cable-gram.' The detective drew a paper from his pocket and, spreading it on the desk, read.

Pinkerton, Chicago, to Commissioner of Police,
Scotland Yard, London.
Warn Ramon that the Four do not go outside their promise. If they have threatened to kill in a certain manner at a certain time they will be punctual. We have proof of this characteristic. After Anderson's death small memorandum book was discovered outside window of room evidently dropped. Book was empty save for three pages, which were filled with neatly written memoranda headed 'Six methods of execution'. It was initialled 'C.' (third letter in alphabet). Warn Ramon against following: drinking coffee in any form, opening letters or parcels, using soap that has not been manufactured under eye of trustworthy agent, sitting in any room other than that occupied day and night by police officer. Examine his bedroom; see if there is any method by which heavy gases can be introduced. We are sending two men by *Lucania* to watch.

The detective finished reading. 'Watch' was not the last word in the original message, as he knew. There had been an ominous postscript, 'Afraid they will arrive too late.'

'Then you think – ?' asked the statesman.

'That your danger lies in doing one of the things that Pinkerton warns us against,' replied the detective. 'There is no fear that the American police are talking idly. They have based their warning on some sure knowledge, and that is why I regard their cable as important.'

There was a sharp rap on the panel of the door, and without waiting for invitation the private secretary walked into the room, excitedly waving a newspaper.

'Look at this!' he cried, 'read this! The Four have admitted their failure.'

'What!' shouted the detective, reaching for the journal.

'What does this mean?' asked Sir Philip sharply.

'Only this, sir: these beggars, it appears, have actually written an article on their "mission".'

'In what newspaper?'

'The *Megaphone*. It seems when they recaptured Thery the editor asked the masked man to write him an article about himself, and they've done it; and it's here, and they've admitted defeat, and – and – '

The detective had seized the paper and broke in upon the incoherent secretary's speech.

'The Creed of the Four Just Men,' he read. 'Where is their confession of failure?'

'Half way down the column – I have marked the passage – here'; and the young man pointed with a trembling finger to a paragraph.

' "We leave nothing to chance," ' read the detective, ' "if the slightest hitch occurs, if the least detail of our plan miscarries, we acknowledge defeat. So assured are we that our presence on earth is necessary for the carrying out of a great plan, so certain are we that we are the indispensable instruments of a divine providence, that we dare not, for the sake of our very cause, accept unnecessary risks. It is essential therefore that the various preliminaries to every execution should be carried out to the full. As an example, it will be necessary for us to deliver our final warning to Sir Philip Ramon; and to add point to this warning, it is, by our code, essential that that should be handed to the Minister by one of us in person. All arrangements have been made to carry this portion of our programme into effect. But such are the extraordinary exigencies of our system that unless this warning can be handed to Sir Philip in accordance with our promise, and before eight o'clock this evening, our arrangements fall to the ground, and the execution we have planned must be forgone." '

The detective stopped reading, with disappointment visible on every line of his face.

'I thought, sir, by the way you were carrying on that you had discovered something new. I've read all this, a copy of the article was sent to the Yard as soon as it was received.'

The secretary thumped the desk impatiently.

'But don't you see!' he cried, 'don't you understand that there is no longer any need to guard Sir Philip, that there is no reason to use him as a bait, or, in fact, to do anything if we are to believe these men – look at the time – '

The detective's hand flew to his pocket; he drew out his watch, looked at the dial, and whistled.

'Half past eight, by God!' he muttered in astonishment, and the three stood in surprised silence.

Sir Philip broke the silence.

'Is it a ruse to take us off our guard?' he said hoarsely.

'I don't think so,' replied the detective slowly, 'I feel sure that it is not; nor shall I relax my watch – but I am a believer in the honesty of these men – I don't know why I should say this, for I have been dealing with criminals for the past twenty-five years, and never once have I put an ounce of faith in the word of the best of 'em, but somehow I can't disbelieve these men. If they have failed to deliver their message they will not trouble us again.'

Ramon paced his room with quick, nervous steps.

'I wish I could believe that,' he muttered; 'I wish I had your faith.'

A tap on the door panel.

'An urgent telegram for Sir Philip,' said a grey-haired attendant.

The Minister stretched out his hand, but the detective was before him.

'Remember Pinkerton's wire, sir,' he said, and ripped open the brown envelope.

Just received a telegram handed in at Charing Cross 7.52. Begins: We have delivered our last message to the Foreign Secretary, signed Four. Ends. Is this true? Editor, Megaphone.

'What does this mean?' asked Falmouth in bewilderment when he had finished reading.

'It means, my dear Mr Falmouth,' replied Sir Philip testily, 'that your noble Four are liars and braggarts as well as murderers; and it means at the same time, I hope, an end to your ridiculous faith in their honesty.'

The detective made no answer, but his face was clouded and he bit his lips in perplexity.

'Nobody came after I left?' he asked.

'Nobody.'

'You have seen no person besides your secretary and myself?'

'Absolutely nobody has spoken to me, or approached within a dozen yards of me,' Ramon answered shortly.

Falmouth shook his head despairingly.

'Well – I – where are we?' he asked, speaking more to himself than to anybody in the room, and moved towards the door.

Then it was that Sir Philip remembered the package left in his charge.

'You had better take your precious documents,' he said, opening his drawer and throwing the package left in his charge on to the table.

The detective looked puzzled.

'What is this?' he asked, picking up the envelope.

'I'm afraid the shock of finding yourself deceived in your estimate of my persecutors has dazed you,' said Sir Philip, and added pointedly, 'I must ask the Commissioner to send an officer who has a better appreciation of the criminal mind, and a less childlike faith in the honour of murderers.'

'As to that, sir,' said Falmouth, unmoved by the outburst, 'you must do as you think best. I have discharged my duty to my own satisfaction; and I have no more critical taskmaster than myself. But what I am more anxious to hear is exactly what you mean by saying that I handed any papers into your care.'

The Foreign Secretary glared across the table at the imperturbable police officer.

'I am referring, sir,' he said harshly, 'to the packet which you returned to leave in my charge.'

The detective stared.

'I – did – not – return,' he said in a strained voice. 'I have left no papers in your hands.' He picked up the package from the table, tore it open, and disclosed yet another envelope. As he caught sight of the grey-green cover he gave a sharp cry.

'This is the message of the Four,' said Falmouth.

The Foreign Secretary staggered back a pace, white to the lips.

'And the man who delivered it?' he gasped.

'Was one of the Four Just Men,' said the detective grimly. 'They have kept their promise.'

He took a quick step to the door, passed through into the ante-room and beckoned the plain-clothes officer who stood on guard at the outer door.

'Do you remember my going out?' he asked.

'Yes, sir – both times.'

'Both times, eh!' said Falmouth bitterly, 'and how did I look the second time?'

His subordinate was bewildered at the form the question took.

'As usual, sir,' he stammered.

'How was I dressed?'

The constable considered. 'In your long dust-coat.'

'I wore my goggles, I suppose?'

'Yes, sir.'

'I thought so,' muttered Falmouth savagely, and raced down the broad marble stairs that led to the entrance-hall. There were four men on duty who saluted him as he approached.

'Do you remember my going out?' he asked of the sergeant in charge.

'Yes, sir – both times,' the officer replied.

'Damn your "both times"!' snapped Falmouth; 'how long had I been gone the first time before I returned?'

'Five minutes, sir,' was the astonished officer's reply.

'They just gave themselves time to do it,' muttered Falmouth, and then aloud, 'Did I return in my car?'

'Yes, sir.'

'Ah! – ' hope sprang into the detective's breast – 'did you notice the number?' he asked, almost fearful to hear the reply.

'Yes!'

The detective could have hugged the stolid officer.

'Good – what was it?'

'A 17164.'

The detective made a rapid note of the number.

'Jackson,' he called, and one of the men in mufti stepped forward and saluted.

'Go to the Yard; find out the registered owner of this car. When you have found this go to the owner; ask him to explain his movements; if necessary, take him into custody.'

Falmouth retraced his steps to Sir Philip's study. He found the statesman still agitatedly walking up and down the room, the secretary nervously drumming his fingers on the table, and the letter still unopened.

'As I thought,' explained Falmouth, 'the man you saw was one of the Four impersonating me. He chose his time admirably: my own men were deceived. They managed to get a car exactly similar in build and colour to mine, and, watching their opportunity, they drove to Downing Street a few minutes after I had left. There is one last chance of our catching him – luckily the sergeant on duty noticed the number of the car, and we might be able to trace him through that – hullo.' An attendant stood at the door.

Would the Superintendent see Detective Jackson?

Falmouth found him waiting in the hall below.

'I beg your pardon, sir,' said Jackson, saluting, 'but is there not some mistake in this number?'

'Why?' asked the detective sharply.

'Because,' said the man, 'A 17164 is the number of your own car.'

Chapter 8
The pocket-book

The final warning was brief and to the point.

We allow you until tomorrow evening to reconsider your position in the matter of the Aliens Extradition Bill. If by six o'clock no announcement is made in the afternoon newspapers of your withdrawing this measure we shall have no other course to pursue but to fulfil our promise. You will die at eight in the evening. We append for your enlightenment a concise table of the secret police arrangements made for your safety tomorrow. Farewell.

(Signed) Four Just Men

Sir Philip read this over without a tremor. He read too the slip of paper on which was written, in the strange foreign hand, the details that the police had not dared to put into writing.

'There is a leakage somewhere,' he said, and the two anxious watchers saw that the face of their charge was grey and drawn.

'These details were known only to four,' said the detective quietly, 'and I'll stake my life that it was neither the Commissioner nor myself.'

'Nor I!' said the private secretary emphatically.

Sir Philip shrugged his shoulders with a weary laugh.

'What does it matter? – they know,' he exclaimed; 'by what uncanny method they learnt the secret I neither know nor care. The question is, can I be adequately protected tomorrow night at eight o'clock?'

Falmouth shut his teeth.

'Either you'll come out of it alive or, by the Lord, they'll kill two,' he said, and there was a gleam in his eye that spoke for his determination.

* * *

The news that yet another letter had reached the great statesman was on the streets at ten o'clock that night. It circulated through the clubs and theatres, and between the acts grave-faced men stood in the vestibules discussing Ramon's danger. The House of Commons was seething with excitement. In the hope that the Minister would come down, a strong House had gathered, but the members were disappointed, for it was evident soon after the dinner recess that Sir Philip had no intention of showing himself that night.

'Might I ask the right honourable the Prime Minister whether it is the intention of His Majesty's Government to proceed with the Aliens Extradition (Political Offences) Bill,' asked the Radical Member for West Deptford, 'and whether he has not considered, in view of the extraordinary conditions that this Bill has called into life, the advisability of postponing the introduction of this measure?'

The question was greeted with a chorus of "hear-hears", and the Prime Minister rose slowly and turned an amused glance in the direction of the questioner.

'I know of no circumstance that is likely to prevent my right honourable friend, who is unfortunately not in his place tonight, from moving the second reading of the Bill tomorrow,' he said, and sat down.

'What the devil was he grinning at?' grumbled West Deptford to a neighbour.

'He's deuced uncomfortable, is JK,' said the other wisely, 'deuced uncomfortable; a man in the Cabinet was telling me today that old JK has been feeling deuced uncomfortable. "You mark my words," he said, "this Four Just Men business is making the Premier deuced uncomfortable," ' and the Hon. Member subsided to allow West Deptford to digest his neighbour's profundities.

'I've done my best to persuade Ramon to drop the Bill,' the Premier was saying, 'but he is adamant, and the pitiable thing is that he believes in his heart of hearts that these fellows intend keeping faith.'

'It is monstrous,' said the Colonial Secretary hotly; 'it is inconceivable that such a state of affairs can last. Why, it strikes at the root of everything, it unbalances every adjustment of civilisation.'

'It is a poetical idea,' said the phlegmatic Premier, 'and the standpoint of the Four is quite a logical one. Think of the enormous power for good or evil often vested in one man: a capitalist controlling the markets of the world, a speculator cornering cotton or wheat whilst mills stand idle and people starve, tyrants and despots with the destinies of nations between their thumb and finger – and then think of the four men, known to none; vague, shadowy figures stalking tragically through the world, condemning and executing the capitalist, the corner maker, the tyrant – evil forces all, and all beyond reach of the law. We have said of these people, such of us as are touched with mysticism, that God would judge them. Here are men arrogating to themselves the divine right of superior judgment. If we catch them they will end their lives unpicturesquely, in a matter-of-fact, commonplace manner in a little shed in Pentonville Gaol, and the world will never realise how great are the artists who perish.'

'But Ramon?'

The Premier smiled.

'Here, I think, these men have just overreached themselves. Had they been content to slay first and explain their mission afterwards I have little doubt that Ramon would have died. But they have warned and warned and exposed their hand a dozen times over. I know nothing of the arrangements that are being made by the police, but I should imagine that by tomorrow night it will be as difficult to get within a dozen yards of Ramon as it would be for a Siberian prisoner to dine with the Czar.'

'Is there no possibility of Ramon withdrawing the Bill?' asked the Colonies.

The Premier shook his head.

'Absolutely none,' he said.

The rising of a member of the Opposition front bench at that moment to move an amendment to a clause under discussion cut short the conversation.

The House rapidly emptied when it became generally known that Ramon did not intend appearing, and the members gathered in the smoking-room and lobby to speculate upon the matter which was uppermost in their minds.

In the vicinity of Palace Yard a great crowd had gathered, as in London crowds will gather, on the off-chance of catching a glimpse of the man whose name was in every mouth. Street vendors sold his portrait, frowsy men purveying the real life and adventures of the Four Just Men did a roaring trade, and itinerant street singers, introducing extemporised verses into their repertoire, declaimed the courage of that statesman bold, who dared for to resist the threats of coward alien and deadly anarchist.

There was praise in these poor lyrics for Sir Philip, who was trying to prevent the foreigner from taking the bread out of the mouths of honest working men.

The humour of which appealed greatly to Manfred, who, with Poiccart, had driven to the Westminster end of the Embankment; having dismissed their cab, they were walking to Whitehall.

'I think the verse about the "deadly foreign anarchist" taking the bread out of the mouth of the home-made variety is distinctly good,' chuckled Manfred.

Both men were in evening dress, and Poiccart wore in his button-hole the silken button of a Chevalier of the Légion d'Honneur.

Manfred continued: 'I doubt whether London has had such a sensation since – when?'

Poiccart's grim smile caught the other's eye and he smiled in sympathy.

'Well?'

'I asked the same question of the *maître d'hôtel*,' he said slowly, like a man loath to share a joke; '*he* compared the agitation to the atrocious East-End murders.'

Manfred stopped dead and looked with horror on his companion.

'Great heavens!' he exclaimed in distress, 'it never occurred to me that we should be compared with – him!'

They resumed their walk.

'It is part of the eternal bathos,' said Poiccart serenely; 'even De Quincey taught the English nothing. The God of Justice has but one interpreter here, and he lives in a public-house in Lancashire, and is an expert and dexterous disciple of the lamented Marwood, whose system he has improved upon.'

They were traversing that portion of Whitehall from which Scotland Yard runs.

A man, slouching along with bent head and his hands thrust deep into the pockets of his tattered coat, gave them a swift sidelong glance, stopped when they had passed, and looked after them. Then he turned and quickened his shuffle on their trail. A press of people and a seeming ceaseless string of traffic at the corner of Cockspur Street brought Manfred and Poiccart to a standstill, waiting for an opportunity to cross the road. They were subjected to a little jostling as the knot of waiting people thickened, but eventually they crossed and walked towards St Martin's Lane.

The comparison which Poiccart had quoted still rankled with Manfred.

'There will be people at His Majesty's tonight,' he said, 'applauding Brutus as he asks, "What villain touched his body and not for justice?" You will not find a serious student of history, or any commonplace man of intelligence, for the matter of that, who, if you asked, Would it not have been God's blessing for the world if Bonaparte had been assassinated on his return from Egypt? would not answer without hesitation, Yes. But we – we are murderers!'

'They would not have erected a statue of Napoleon's assassin,' said Poiccart easily, 'any more than they have enshrined Felton, who slew a profligate and debauched Minister of Charles I. Posterity may do us justice,' he spoke half mockingly; 'for myself I am satisfied with the approval of my conscience.'

He threw away the cigar he was smoking, and put his hand to the inside pocket of his coat to find another. He withdrew his hand without the cigar and whistled a passing cab.

Manfred looked at him in surprise.

'What is the matter? I thought you said you would walk?'

Nevertheless he entered the hansom and Poiccart followed, giving his direction through the trap, 'Baker Street Station.'

The cab was rattling through Shaftesbury Avenue before Poiccart gave an explanation.

'I have been robbed,' he said, sinking his voice, 'my watch has gone, but that does not matter; the pocketbook with the notes I made for the guidance of Thery has gone – and that matters a great deal.'

'It may have been a common thief,' said Manfred: 'he took the watch.'

Poiccart was feeling his pockets rapidly.

'Nothing else has gone,' he said; 'it may have been as you say, a pickpocket, who will be content with the watch and will drop the notebook down the nearest drain; but it may be a police agent.'

'Was there anything in it to identify you?' asked Manfred, in a troubled tone.

'Nothing,' was the prompt reply; 'but unless the police are blind they would understand the calculations and the plans. It may not come to their hands at all, but if it does and the thief can recognise us we are in a fix.'

The cab drew up at the down station at Baker Street, and the two men alighted.

'I shall go east,' said Poiccart, 'we will meet in the morning. By that time I shall have learnt whether the book has reached Scotland Yard. Goodnight.'

And with no other farewell than this the two men parted.

* * *

If Billy Marks had not had a drop of drink he would have been perfectly satisfied with his night's work. Filled, however, with that false liquid confidence that leads so many good men astray, Billy thought it would be a sin to neglect the opportunities that the gods had shown him. The excitement engendered by the threats of the Four Just Men had brought all suburban London to Westminster, and on the Surrey side of the bridge Billy found hundreds of patient suburbanites waiting for conveyance to Streatham, Camberwell, Clapham, and Greenwich.

So, the night being comparatively young, Billy decided to work the trams.

He touched a purse from a stout old lady in black, a Waterbury watch from a gentleman in a top hat, a small hand mirror from a dainty bag, and decided to conclude his operations with the exploration of a superior young lady's pocket.

Billy's search was successful. A purse and a lace handkerchief rewarded him, and he made arrangements for a modest retirement. Then it was that a gentle voice breathed into his ear. 'Hullo, Billy!'

He knew the voice, and felt momentarily unwell.

'Hullo, Mister Howard,' he exclaimed with feigned joy; ' 'ow are you, sir? Fancy meetin' you!'

'Where are you going, Billy?' asked the welcome Mr Howard, taking Billy's arm affectionately.

' 'Ome,' said the virtuous Billy.

'Home it is,' said Mr Howard, leading the unwilling Billy from the crowd; 'home, sweet home, it is, Billy.' He called another young man, with whom he seemed to be acquainted: 'Go on that car, Porter, and see who has lost anything. If you can find anyone bring them along'; and the other young man obeyed.

'And now,' said Mr Howard, still holding Billy's arm affectionately, 'tell me how the world has been using you.'

'Look 'ere, Mr Howard,' said Billy earnestly, 'what's the game? where are you takin' me?'

'The game is the old game,' said Mr Howard sadly – 'the same old game, Bill, and I'm taking you to the same old sweet spot.'

'You've made a mistake this time, guv'nor,' cried Bill fiercely, and there was a slight clink.

'Permit me, Billy,' said Mr Howard, stooping quickly and picking up the purse Billy had dropped.

At the police station the sergeant behind the charge desk pretended to be greatly overjoyed at Billy's arrival, and the gaoler, who put Billy into a steel-barred dock, and passed his hands through cunning pockets, greeted him as a friend.

'Gold watch, half a chain, gold, three purses, two handkerchiefs, and a red moroccer pocketbook,' reported the gaoler.

The sergeant nodded approvingly.

'Quite a good day's work, William,' he said.

'What shall I get this time?' inquired the prisoner, and Mr Howard, a plain-clothes officer engaged in filling in particulars of the charge, opined nine moons.

'Go on!' exclaimed Mr Billy Marks in consternation.

'Fact,' said the sergeant; 'you're a rogue and a vagabond, Billy, you're a petty larcenist, and you're for the sessions this time – Number Eight.'

This latter was addressed to the gaoler, who bore Billy off to the cells protesting vigorously against a police force that could only tumble to poor blokes, and couldn't get a touch on sanguinary murderers like the Four Just Men.

'What do we pay rates and taxes for?' indignantly demanded Billy through the grating of his cell.

'Fat lot you'll ever pay, Billy,' said the gaoler, putting the double lock on the door.

In the charge office Mr Howard and the sergeant were examining the stolen property, and three owners, discovered by PC Porter, were laying claim to their own.

'That disposes of all the articles except the gold watch and the pocketbook,' said the sergeant after the claimants had gone, 'gold watch, Elgin half-hunter No5029020, pocketbook containing no papers, no card, no address, and only three pages of writing. What this means I don't know.' The sergeant handed the book to Howard. The page that puzzled the policeman contained simply a list of streets. Against each street was scrawled a cabalistic character.

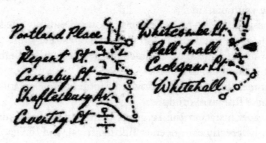

'Looks like the diary of a paperchase,' said Mr Howard. 'What is on the other pages?' They turned the leaf. This was filled with figures.

'H'm,' said the disappointed sergeant, and again turned overleaf. The contents of this page was understandable and readable although evidently written in a hurry as though it had been taken down at dictation.

'The chap who wrote this must have had a train to catch,' said the facetious Mr Howard, pointing to the abbreviations.

Will not leave D.S., except for Hs. Will drive to Hs in M.C. (4 dummy brghms first), 8.30. At 2 600 p arve traf divtd Embank, 80 spls. inside D.S. One each rm, three each cor, six basmt, six rf. All drs wide opn allow each off see another, all spls will carry revr. Nobody except F and H to approach R. In Hse strange gal filled with spl, all press vouched for. 200 spl. in cor. If nec battalion guards at disposal.

The policeman read this over slowly.

'Now what the devil does that mean?' asked the sergeant helplessly.

It was at that precise moment that Constable Howard earned his promotion.

'Let me have that book for ten minutes,' he said excitedly.

The sergeant handed the book over with wondering stare.

'I think I can find an owner for this,' said Howard, his hand trembling as he took the book, and ramming his hat on his head he ran out into the street.

He did not stop running until he reached the main road, and finding a cab he sprang in with a hurried order to the driver.

'Whitehall, and drive like blazes,' he called, and in a few minutes he was explaining his errand to the inspector in charge of the cordon that guarded the entrance of Downing Street.

'Constable Howard, 946 L reserve,' he introduced himself. 'I've a very important message for Superintendent Falmouth.'

That officer, looking tired and beaten, listened to the policeman's story.

'It looks to me,' went on Howard breathlessly, 'as though this has something to do with your case, sir. D.S. is Downing Street, and – '
He produced the book and Falmouth snatched at it.

He read a few words and then gave a triumphant cry.

'Our secret instructions,' he cried, and catching the constable by the arm he drew him to the entrance hall.

'Is my car outside?' he asked, and in response to a whistle a car drew up. 'Jump in, Howard,' said the detective, and the car slipped into Whitehall.

'Who is the thief?' asked the senior.

'Billy Marks, sir,' replied Howard; 'you may not know him, but down at Lambeth he is a well-known character.'

'Oh, yes,' Falmouth hastened to correct, 'I know Billy very well indeed – we'll see what he has to say.'

The car drew up at the police station and the two men jumped out.

The sergeant rose to his feet as he recognised the famous Falmouth, and saluted.

'I want to see the prisoner Marks,' said Falmouth shortly, and Billy, roused from his sleep, came blinking into the charge office.

'Now, Billy,' said the detective, 'I've got a few words to say to you.'

'Why, it's Mr Falmouth,' said the astonished Billy, and something like fear shaded his face. 'I wasn't in that 'Oxton affair, s'help me.'

'Make your mind easy, Billy; I don't want you for anything, and if you'll answer my questions truthfully, you may get off the present charge and get a reward into the bargain.'

Billy was suspicious. 'I'm not going to give anybody away if that's what you mean,' he said sullenly.

'Nor that either,' said the detective impatiently. 'I want to know where you found this pocketbook,' and he held it up.

Billy grinned. 'Found it lyin' on the pavement,' he lied.

'I want the truth,' thundered Falmouth.

'Well,' said Billy sulkily, 'I pinched it.'

'From whom?'

'I didn't stop to ask him his name,' was the impudent reply.

The detective breathed deeply. 'Now, look here,' he said, lowering his voice, 'you've heard about the Four Just Men?'

Billy nodded, opening his eyes in amazement at the question.

'Well,' exclaimed Falmouth impressively, 'the man to whom this pocketbook belongs is one of them.'

'What!' cried Billy.

'For his capture there is a reward of a thousand pounds offered. If your description leads to his arrest that thousand is yours.'

Marks stood paralysed at the thought.

'A thousand – a thousand?' he muttered in a dazed fashion, 'and I might just as easily have caught him.'

'Come, come!' cried the detective sharply, 'you may catch him yet – tell us what he looked like.'

Billy knitted his brows in thought.

'He looked like a gentleman,' he said, trying to recall from the chaos of his mind a picture of his victim; 'he had a white weskit, a white shirt, nice patent shoes – '

'But his face – his face!' demanded the detective.

'His face?' cried Billy indignantly, 'how do I know what it looked like? I don't look a chap in the face when I'm pinching his watch, do I?'

Chapter 9
The cupidity of Marks

'You cursed dolt, you infernal fool!' stormed the detective, catching Billy by the collar and shaking him like a rat. 'Do you mean to tell me that you had one of the Four Just Men in your hand, and did not even take the trouble to look at him?'

Billy wrenched himself free.

'You leave me alone!' he said defiantly. 'How was I to know it was one of the Four Just Men, and how do you know it was?' he added with a cunning twist of his face. Billy's mind was beginning to work rapidly. He saw in this staggering statement of the detective a chance of making capital out of the position which to within a few minutes he had regarded as singularly unfortunate.

'I did get a bit of a glance at 'em,' he said, 'they – '

'Them – they?' said the detective quickly. 'How many were there?'

'Never mind,' said Billy sulkily. He felt the strength of his position.

'Billy,' said the detective earnestly, 'I mean business; if you know anything you've got to tell us!'

'Ho!' cried the prisoner in defiance. 'Got to, 'ave I? Well, I know the lor as well as you – you can't make a chap speak if he don't want. You can't – '

The detective signalled the other police officers to retire, and when they were out of earshot he dropped his voice and said: 'Harry Moss came out last week.'

Billy flushed and lowered his eyes.

'I don't know no Harry Moss,' he muttered doggedly.

'Harry Moss came out last week,' continued the detective shortly, 'after doing three years for robbery with violence – three years and ten lashes.'

'I don't know anything about it,' said Marks in the same tone.

'He got clean away and the police had no clues,' the detective went on remorselessly, 'and they might not have caught him to this day, only – only "from information received" they took him one night out of his bed in Leman Street.'

Billy licked his dry lips, but did not speak.

'Harry Moss would like to know who he owes his three stretch to – and the ten. Men who've had the cat have a long memory, Billy.'

'That's not playing the game, Mr Falmouth,' cried Billy thickly. 'I – I was a bit hard up, an' Harry Moss wasn't a pal of mine – and the p'lice wanted to find out – '

'And the police want to find out now,' said Falmouth.

Billy Marks made no reply for a moment.

'I'll tell you all there is to be told,' he said at last, and cleared his throat. The detective stopped him.

'Not here,' he said. Then turning to the officer in charge: 'Sergeant, you may release this man on bail – I will stand sponsor.' The humorous side of this appealed to Billy at least, for he grinned sheepishly and recovered his former spirits.

'First time I've been bailed out by the p'lice,' he remarked facetiously.

The motor-car bore the detective and his charge to Scotland Yard, and in Superintendent Falmouth's office Billy prepared to unburden himself.

'Before you begin,' said the officer, 'I want to warn you that you must be as brief as possible. Every minute is precious.'

So Billy told his story. In spite of the warning there were embellishments, to which the detective was forced to listen impatiently.

At last the pickpocket reached the point.

'There was two of 'em, one a tall chap and one not so tall. I heard one say "My dear George" – the little one said that, the one I took the ticker from and the pocketbook. Was there anything in the notebook?' Billy asked suddenly.

'Go on,' said the detective.

'Well,' resumed Billy, 'I follered 'em up to the end of the street, and they was waitin' to cross towards Charing Cross Road when I lifted the clock, you understand?'

'What time was this?'

' 'Arf past ten – or it might've been eleven.'

'And you did not see their faces?'

The thief shook his head emphatically.

'If I never get up from where I'm sittin' I didn't, Mr Falmouth,' he said earnestly.

The detective rose with a sigh.

'I'm afraid you're not much use to me, Billy,' he said ruefully. 'Did you notice whether they wore beards, or were they clean-shaven, or – '

Billy shook his head mournfully.

'I could easily tell you a lie, Mr Falmouth,' he said frankly, 'and I could easily pitch a tale that would take you in, but I'm playin' it square with you.'

The detective recognised the sincerity of the man and nodded.

'You've done your best, Billy,' he said, and then: 'I'll tell you what I'm going to do. You are the only man in the world who has ever seen one of the Four Just Men – and lived to tell the story. Now, although you cannot remember his face, perhaps if you met him again in the street you would know him – there may be some little trick of walking, some habit of holding the hands that you cannot recall now, but if you saw again you would recognise. I shall therefore take upon myself the responsibility of releasing you from custody until the day after tomorrow. I want you to find this man you robbed. Here is a sovereign; go home, get a little sleep, turn out as early as you can and go west.' The detective went to his desk, and wrote a dozen words on a card. 'Take this: if you see the man or his companion, follow them, show this card to the first policeman you meet, point out the man, and you'll go to bed a thousand pounds richer than when you woke.'

Billy took the card.

'If you want me at any time you will find somebody here who will know where I am. Goodnight,' and Billy passed into the street, his brain in a whirl, and a warrant written on a visiting card in his waistcoat pocket.

The morning that was to witness great events broke bright and clear over London. Manfred, who, contrary to his usual custom, had spent the night at the workshop in Carnaby Street, watched the dawn from the flat roof of the building.

He lay face downwards, a rug spread beneath him, his head resting on his hands. Dawn with its white, pitiless light, showed his strong face, seamed and haggard. The white streaks in his trim beard were accentuated in the light of morning. He looked tired and disheartened, so unlike his usual self that Gonsalez, who crept up through the trap just before the sun rose, was as near alarmed as it was possible for that phlegmatic man to be. He touched him on the arm and Manfred started.

'What is the matter?' asked Leon softly.

Manfred's smile and shake of head did not reassure the questioner.

'Is it Poiccart and the thief?'

'Yes,' nodded Manfred. Then speaking aloud, he asked: 'Have you ever felt over any of our cases as you feel in this?'

They spoke in such low tones as almost to approach whispering. Gonsalez stared ahead thoughtfully.

'Yes,' he admitted, 'once – the woman at Warsaw. You remember how easy it all seemed, and how circumstance after circumstance thwarted us . . . till I began to feel, as I feel now, that we should fail.'

'No, no, no!' said Manfred fiercely. 'There must be no talk of failure, Leon, no thought of it.'

He crawled to the trapdoor and lowered himself into the corridor, and Gonsalez followed.

'Thery?' he asked.

'Asleep.'

They were entering the studio, and Manfred had his hand on the door handle when a footstep sounded on the bottom floor.

'Who's there?' cried Manfred, and a soft whistle from below sent him flying downstairs.

'Poiccart!' he cried.

Poiccart it was, unshaven, dusty, weary.

'Well?' Manfred's ejaculation was almost brutal in its bluntness.

'Let us go upstairs,' said Poiccart shortly. The three men ascended the dusty stairway, not a word being spoken until they had reached the small living-room.

Then Poiccart spoke.

'The very stars in their courses are fighting against us,' he said, throwing himself into the only comfortable chair in the room, and flinging his hat into a corner. 'The man who stole my pocketbook has been arrested by the police. He is a well-known criminal of a sneak-thief order, and unfortunately he had been under observation during the evening. The pocketbook was found in his possession, and all might have been well, but an unusually smart police officer associated the contents with us.

'After I had left you I went home and changed, then made my way to Downing Street. I was one of the curious crowd that stood watching the guarded entrance. I knew that Falmouth was there, and I knew, too, if there was any discovery made it would be communicated immediately to Downing Street. Somehow I felt sure the man was an ordinary thief, and that if we had anything to fear it was from a chance arrest. Whilst I was waiting a cab dashed up, and out an excited man jumped. He was obviously a policeman, and I had just time to engage a hansom when Falmouth and the new arrival came flying out. I followed them in the cab as fast as possible without exciting the suspicion of the driver. Of course, they outdistanced us, but their destination was evident. I dismissed the cab at the corner of the street in which the police station is situated, and walked down and found, as I had expected, the car drawn up at the door.

'I managed to get a fleeting glance at the charge room – I was afraid that any interrogation there might be would have been conducted in the cell, but by the greatest of good luck they had chosen the charge room. I saw Falmouth, and the policeman, and the prisoner. The latter, a mean-faced, long-jawed man with shifty eyes – no, no, Leon, don't question me about the physiognomy of the man – my view was for photographic purposes – I wanted to remember him.

'In that second I could see the detective's anger, the thief's defiance, and I knew that the man was saying that he could not recognise us.'

'Ha!' It was Manfred's sigh of relief that put a period to Poiccart's speech.

'But I wanted to make sure,' resumed the latter. 'I walked back the way I had come. Suddenly I heard the hum of the car behind me, and it passed me with another passenger. I guessed that they were taking the man back to Scotland Yard.

'I was content to walk back; I was curious to know what the police intended doing with their new recruit. Taking up a station that gave me a view of the entrance of the street, I waited. After a while the man came out alone. His step was light and buoyant. A glimpse I got of his face showed me a strange blending of bewilderment and gratification. He turned on to the Embankment, and I followed close behind.'

'There was a danger that he was being shadowed by the police, too,' said Gonsalez.

'Of that I was well satisfied,' Poiccart rejoined. 'I took a very careful survey before I acted. Apparently the police were content to let him roam free. When he was abreast of the Temple steps he stopped and looked undecidedly left and right, as though he were not quite certain as to what he should do next. At that moment I came abreast of him, passed him, and then turned back, fumbling in my pockets.

' "Can you oblige me with a match?" I asked.

'He was most affable; produced a box of matches and invited me to help myself.

'I took a match, struck it, and lit my cigar, holding the match so that he could see my face.'

'That was wise,' said Manfred gravely.

'It showed his face too, and out of the corner of my eye I watched him searching every feature. But there was no sign of recognition and I began a conversation. We lingered where we had met for a while and then by mutual consent we walked in the direction of Blackfriars, crossed the bridge, chatting on inconsequent subjects, the poor, the weather, the newspapers. On the other side of the bridge is a coffee-stall. I determined to make my next move. I invited him to take a cup of coffee, and when the cups were placed before us, I put down a sovereign. The stall-keeper shook his head, said he could not change it. "Hasn't your friend any small change?" he asked.

'It was here that the vanity of the little thief told me what I wanted to know. He drew from his pocket, with a nonchalant air – a sovereign. "This is all that I have got," he drawled. I found some coppers – I had to think quickly. He had told the police something, something worth paying for – what was it? It could not have been a description of ourselves, for if he had recognised us then, he would have known me when I struck the match and when I stood there, as I did, in the full glare of the light of the coffee-stall. And then a cold fear came to me. Perhaps he had recognised me, and with a thief's cunning was holding me in conversation until he could get assistance to take me.'

Poiccart paused for a moment, and drew a small phial from his pocket; this he placed carefully on the table.

'He was as near to death then as ever he has been in his life,' he said quietly, 'but somehow the suspicion wore away. In our walk we had passed three policemen – there was an opportunity if he had wanted it.

'He drank his coffee and said, "I must be going home."

' "Indeed!" I said. "I suppose I really ought to go home too – I have a lot of work to do tomorrow." He leered at me. "So have I," he said with a grin, "but whether I can do it or not I don't know."

'We had left the coffee-stall, and now stopped beneath a lamp that stood at the corner of the street.

'I knew that I had only a few seconds to secure the information I wanted – so I played bold and led directly to the subject. "What of these Four Just Men?" I asked, just as he was about to slouch away. He turned back instantly. "What about them?" he asked quickly. I led him on from that by gentle stages to the identity of the Four. He was eager to talk about them, anxious to know what I thought, but most concerned of all about the reward. He was engrossed in the subject, and then suddenly he leant forward, and, tapping me on the chest, with a grimy forefinger, he commenced to state a hypothetical case.'

Poiccart stopped to laugh – his laugh ended in a sleepy yawn.

'You know the sort of questions,' said he, 'and you know how very naive the illiterate are when they are seeking to disguise their identities by elaborate hypotheses. Well, that is the story. He – Marks is his name – thinks he may be able to recognise one of us by some extraordinary trick of memory. To enable him to do this, he has been granted freedom – tomorrow he would search London, he said.'

'A full day's work,' laughed Manfred.

'Indeed,' agreed Poiccart soberly, 'but hear the sequel. We parted, and I walked westward perfectly satisfied of our security. I made for Covent Garden Market, because this is one of the places in London where a man may be seen at four o'clock in the morning without exciting suspicion.

'I had strolled through the market, idly watching the busy scene, when, for some cause that I cannot explain, I turned suddenly on my heel and came face to face with Marks! He grinned sheepishly, and recognised me with a nod of his head.

'He did not wait for me to ask him his business, but started in to explain his presence.

'I accepted his explanation easily, and for the second time that night invited him to coffee. He hesitated at first, then accepted. When the coffee was brought, he pulled it to him as far from my reach as possible, and then I knew that Mr Marks had placed me at fault, that I had underrated his intelligence, that all the time he had been unburdening himself he had recognised me. He had put me off my guard.'

'But why – ?' began Manfred.

'That is what I thought,' the other answered. 'Why did he not have me arrested?' He turned to Leon, who had been a silent listener. 'Tell us, Leon, why?'

'The explanation is simple,' said Gonsalez quietly: 'why did not Thery betray us? – cupidity, the second most potent force of civilisation. He has some doubt of the reward. He may fear the honesty of the police – most criminals do so; he may want witnesses.' Leon walked to the wall, where his coat hung. He buttoned it thoughtfully, ran his hand over his smooth chin, then pocketed the little phial that stood on the table.

'You have slipped him, I suppose?' he asked.

Poiccart nodded.

'He lives – ?'

'At 700 Red Cross Street, in the Borough – it is a common lodging-house.'

Leon took a pencil from the table and rapidly sketched a head upon the edge of a newspaper.

'Like this? 'he asked.

Poiccart examined the portrait.

'Yes,' he said in surprise; 'have you seen him?'

'No,' said Leon carelessly, 'but such a man would have such a head.'

He paused on the threshold.

'I think it is necessary.' There was a question in his assertion. It was addressed rather to Manfred, who stood with his folded arms and knit brow staring at the floor.

For answer Manfred extended his clenched fist.

Leon saw the down-turned thumb, and left the room.

*   *   *

Billy Marks was in a quandary. By the most innocent device in the world his prey had managed to slip through his fingers. When Poiccart, stopping at the polished doors of the best hôtel in London, whither they had strolled, casually remarked that he would not be a moment and disappeared into the hôtel, Billy was nonplussed. This was a contingency for which he was not prepared. He had followed the suspect from Blackfriars; he was almost sure that this was the man he had robbed. He might, had he wished, have called upon the first constable he met to take the man into custody; but the suspicion of the thief, the fear that he might be asked to share the reward with the man who assisted him restrained him. And besides, it might not be the man at all, argued Billy, and yet –

Poiccart was a chemist, a man who found joy in unhealthy precipitates, who mixed evil-smelling drugs and distilled, filtered, carbonated, oxydized, and did all manner of things in glass tubes, to the vegetable, animal, and mineral products of the earth.

Billy had left Scotland Yard to look for a man with a discoloured hand. Here again, he might, had he been less fearful of treachery, have placed in the hands of the police a very valuable mark of identification.

It seems a very lame excuse to urge on Billy's behalf that this cupidity alone stayed his hand when he came face to face with the man he was searching for. And yet it was so. Then again there was a sum in simple proportion to be worked out. If one Just Man was worth a thousand pounds, what was the commercial value of four? Billy was a thief with a business head. There were no waste products in his day's labour. He was not a conservative scoundrel who stuck to one branch of his profession. He would pinch a watch, or snatch a till, or pass snide florins with equal readiness. He was a butterfly of crime, flitting from one illicit flower to another, and nor above figuring as the X of "information received".

So that when Poiccart disappeared within the magnificent portals of the Royal Hôtel in Northumberland Avenue, Billy was hipped. He realised in a flash that his captive had gone whither he could not follow without exposing his hand; that the chances were he had gone for ever. He looked up and down the street; there was no policeman in sight. In the vestibule, a porter in shirt sleeves was polishing brasses. It was still very early; the streets were deserted, and Billy, after a few moment's hesitation, took a course that he would not have dared at a more conventional hour.

He pushed open the swing doors and passed into the vestibule. The porter turned on him as he entered and favoured him with a suspicious frown.

'What do you want?' asked he, eyeing the tattered coat of the visitor in some disfavour.

'Look 'ere, old feller,' began Billy, in his most conciliatory tone.

Just then the porter's strong right arm caught him by the coat collar, and Billy found himself stumbling into the street.

'Outside – you,' said the porter firmly.

It needed this rebuff to engender in Marks the necessary self-assurance to carry him through.

Straightening his ruffled clothing, he pulled Falmouth's card from his pocket and returned to the charge with dignity.

'I am a p'lice officer,' he said, adopting the opening that he knew so well, 'and if you interfere with me, look out, young feller!'

The porter took the card and scrutinised it.

'What do you want?' he asked in more civil tones. He would have added "sir", but somehow it stuck in his throat. If the man is a detective, he argued to himself, he is very well disguised.

'I want that gentleman that came in before me,' said Billy.

The porter scratched his head.

'What is the number of his room?' he asked.

'Never mind about the number of his room,' said Billy rapidly. 'Is there any back way to this hôtel – any way a man can get out of it? I mean, besides through the front entrance?'

'Half a dozen,' replied the porter.

Billy groaned.

'Take me round to one of them, will you?' he asked. And the porter led the way.

One of the tradesmen's entrances was from a small back street; and here it was that a street scavenger gave the information that Marks had feared. Five minutes before a man answering to the description had walked out, turned towards the Strand and, picking up a cab in the sight of the street cleaner, had driven off.

Baffled, and with the added bitterness that had he played boldly he might have secured at any rate a share of a thousand pounds, Billy walked slowly to the Embankment, cursing the folly that had induced him to throw away the fortune that was in his hands. With hands thrust deep into his pockets, he tramped the weary length of the Embankment, going over again and again the incidents of the night and each time muttering a lurid condemnation of his error. It must have been an hour after he had lost Poiccart that it occurred to him all was not lost. He had the man's description, he had looked at his face, he knew him feature by feature. That was something, at any rate. Nay, it occurred to him that if the man was arrested through his description he would still be entitled to the reward – or a part of it. He dared not see Falmouth and tell him that he had been in company with the man all night without effecting his arrest. Falmouth would never believe him, and, indeed, it was curious that he should have met him.

This fact struck Billy for the first time. By what strange chance had he met this man? Was it possible – the idea frightened Marks – that the man he had robbed had recognised him, and that he had deliberately sought him out with murderous intent?

A cold perspiration broke upon the narrow forehead of the thief. These men were murderers, cruel, relentless murderers: suppose – ?

He turned from the contemplation of the unpleasant possibilities to meet a man who was crossing the road towards him. He eyed the stranger doubtingly. The newcomer was a young-looking man, clean-shaven, with sharp features and restless blue eyes. As he came closer, Marks noted that first appearance had been deceptive; the man was not so young as he looked. He might have been forty, thought Marks. He approached, looked hard at Billy, then beckoned him to stop, for Billy was walking away.

'Is your name Marks?' asked the stranger authoritatively.

'Yes, sir,' replied the thief.

'Have you seen Mr Falmouth?'

'Not since last night,' replied Marks in surprise.

'Then you are to come at once to him.'

'Where is he?'

'At Kensington Police Station – there has been an arrest, and he wants you to identify the man.'

Billy's heart sank.

'Do I get any of the reward?' he demanded, 'that is if I recognise 'im?'

The other nodded and Billy's hopes rose.

'You must follow me,' said the newcomer, 'Mr Falmouth does not wish us to be seen together. Take a first-class ticket to Kensington and get into the next carriage to mine – come.'

He turned and crossed the road toward Charing Cross, and Billy followed at a distance.

He found the stranger pacing the platform and gave no sign of recognition. A train pulled into the station and Marks followed his conductor through a crowd of workmen the train had discharged. He entered an empty first-class carriage, and Marks, obeying instructions, took possession of the adjoining compartment, and found himself the solitary occupant.

Between Charing Cross and Westminster Marks had time to review his position. Between the last station and St James's Park, he invented his excuses to the detective; between the Park and Victoria he had completed his justification for a share of the reward. Then as the train moved into the tunnel for its five minutes' run to Sloane Square, Billy noticed a draught, and turned his head to see the stranger standing on the footboard of the swaying carriage, holding the half-opened door.

Marks was startled.

'Pull up the window on your side,' ordered the man, and Billy, hypnotised by the authoritative voice, obeyed. At that moment he heard the tinkle of broken glass.

He turned with an angry snarl.

'What's the game?' he demanded.

For answer the stranger swung himself clear of the door and, closing it softly, disappeared.

'What's his game?' repeated Marks drowsily. Looking down he saw a broken phial at his feet, by the phial lay a shining sovereign. He stared stupidly at it for a moment, then, just before the train ran into Victoria Station, he stooped to pick it up . . .

Chapter 10
Three who died

A passenger leisurely selecting his compartment during the wait at Kensington opened a carriage door and staggered back coughing. A solicitous porter and an alarmed station official ran forward and pulled open the door, and the sickly odour of almonds pervaded the station.

A little knot of passengers gathered and peered over one another's shoulders, whilst the station inspector investigated. By and by came a doctor, and a stretcher, and a policeman from the street without.

Together they lifted the huddled form of a dead man from the carriage and laid it on the platform.

'Did you find anything?' asked the policeman.

'A sovereign and a broken bottle,' was the reply.

The policeman fumbled in the dead man's pockets.

'I don't suppose he'll have any papers to show who he is,' he said with knowledge. 'Here's a first-class ticket – it must be a case of suicide. Here's a card – '

He turned it over and read it, and his face underwent a change.

He gave a few hurried instructions, then made his way to the nearest telegraph office.

Superintendent Falmouth, who had snatched a few hours' sleep at the Downing Street house, rose with a troubled mind and an uneasy feeling that in spite of all his precautions the day would end disastrously. He was hardly dressed before the arrival of the Assistant Commissioner was announced.

'I have your report, Falmouth,' was the official's greeting; 'you did perfectly right to release Marks – have you had news of him this morning?'

'No.'

'H'm,' said the Commissioner thoughtfully. 'I wonder whether – ' He did not finish his sentence. 'Has it occurred to you that the Four may have realised their danger?'

The detective's face showed surprise.

'Why, of course, sir.'

'Have you considered what their probable line of action will be?'

'N – no – unless it takes the form of an attempt to get out of the country.'

'Has it struck you that whilst this man Marks is looking for them, they are probably seeking him?'

'Bill is smart,' said the detective uneasily.

'So are they,' said the Commissioner with an emphatic nod. 'My advice is, get in touch with Marks and put two of your best men to watch him.'

'That shall be done at once,' replied Falmouth; 'I am afraid that it is a precaution that should have been taken before.'

'I am going to see Sir Philip,' the Commissioner went on, and he added with a dubious smile, 'I shall be obliged to frighten him a little.'

'What is the idea?'

'We wish him to drop this Bill. Have you seen the morning papers?'

'No, sir.'

'They are unanimous that the Bill should be abandoned – they say because it is not sufficiently important to warrant the risk, that the country itself is divided on its merit; but as a matter of fact they are afraid of the consequence; and upon my soul I'm a little afraid too.'

He mounted the stairs, and was challenged at the landing by one of his subordinates.

This was a system introduced after the episode of the disguised 'detective'. The Foreign Minister was now in a state of siege. Nobody had to be trusted, a password had been initiated, and every precaution taken to ensure against a repetition of the previous mistake.

His hand was raised to knock upon the panel of the study, when he felt his arm gripped. He turned to see Falmouth with white face and startled eyes.

'They've finished Billy,' said the detective breathlessly. 'He has just been found in a railway carriage at Kensington.'

The Commissioner whistled.

'How was it done?' he asked.

Falmouth was the picture of haggard despair.

'Prussic acid gas,' he said bitterly; 'they are scientific. Look you, sir, persuade this man to drop his damned Bill.'

He pointed to the door of Sir Philip's room. 'We shall never save him. I have got the feeling in my bones that he is a doomed man.'

'Nonsense!' the Commissioner answered sharply.

'You are growing nervous – you haven't had enough sleep, Falmouth. That isn't spoken like your real self – we must save him.'

He turned from the study and beckoned one of the officers who guarded the landing.

'Sergeant, tell Inspector Collins to send an emergency call throughout the area for reserves to gather immediately. I will put such a cordon round Ramon today,' he went on addressing Falmouth, 'that no man shall reach him without the fear of being crushed to death.'

And within an hour there was witnessed in London a scene that has no parallel in the history of the Metropolis. From every district there came a small army of policemen. They arrived by train, by tramway car, by motorbus, by every vehicle and method of traction that could be requisitioned or seized. They streamed from the stations, they poured through the thoroughfares, till London stood aghast at the realisation of the strength of her civic defences.

Whitehall was soon packed from end to end; St James's Park was black with them. Automatically Whitehall, Charles Street, Birdcage Walk, and the eastern end of the Mall were barred to all traffic by solid phalanxes of mounted constables. St George's Street was in the hands of the force, the roof of every house was occupied by a uniformed man. Not a house or room that overlooked in the slightest degree the Foreign Secretary's residence but was subjected to a rigorous search. It was as though martial law had been proclaimed, and indeed two regiments of Guards were under arms the whole of the day ready for any emergency. In Sir Philip's room the Commissioner, backed by Falmouth, made his last appeal to the stubborn man whose life was threatened.

'I tell you, sir,' said the Commissioner earnestly, 'we can do no more than we have done, and I am still afraid. These men affect me as would something supernatural. I have a horrible dread that for all our precautions we have left something out of our reckoning; that we are leaving unguarded some avenue which by their devilish ingenuity they may utilise. The death of this man Marks has unnerved me – the Four are ubiquitous as well as omnipotent. I beg of you, sir, for God's sake, think well before you finally reject their terms. Is the passage of this Bill so absolutely necessary?' – he paused – 'is it worth your life?' he asked with blunt directness; and the crudity of the question made Sir Philip wince.

He waited some time before he replied, and when he spoke his voice was low and firm.

'I shall not withdraw,' he said slowly, with a dull, dogged evenness of tone. 'I shall not withdraw in any circumstance.

'I have gone too far,' he went on, raising his hand to check Falmouth's appeal. 'I have got beyond fear, I have even got beyond resentment; it is now to me a question of justice. Am I right in introducing a law that will remove from this country colonies of dangerously intelligent criminals, who, whilst enjoying immunity from arrest, urge ignorant men forward to commit acts of violence and treason? If I am right, the Four Just Men are wrong. Or are they right: is this measure an unjust thing, an act of tyranny, a piece of barbarism dropped into the very centre of twentieth-century thought, an anachronism? If these men are right, then I am wrong. So it has come to this, that I have to satisfy my mind as to the standard of right and wrong that I must accept – and I accept my own.'

He met the wondering gaze of the officers with a calm, unflinching countenance.

'You were wise to take the precautions you have,' he resumed quietly. 'I have been foolish to chafe under your protective care.'

'We must take even further precautions,' the Commissioner interrupted; 'between six and half past eight o'clock tonight we wish you to remain in your study, and under no circumstance to open the door to a single person – even to myself or Mr Falmouth. During that time you must keep your door locked.' He hesitated. 'If you would rather have one of us with you – '

'No, no,' was the Minister's quick reply; 'after the impersonation of yesterday I would rather be alone.'

The Commissioner nodded. 'This room is anarchist-proof,' he said, waving his hand round the apartment. 'During the night we have made a thorough inspection, examined the floors, the wall, the ceiling, and fixed steel shields to the shutters.'

He looked round the chamber with the scrutiny of a man to whom every visible object was familiar.

Then he noticed something new had been introduced. On the table stood a blue china bowl full of roses.

'This is new,' he said, bending his head to catch the fragrance of the beautiful flowers.

'Yes,' was Ramon's careless reply, 'they were sent from my house in Hereford this morning.'

The Commissioner plucked a leaf from one of the blooms and rolled it between his fingers. 'They look so real,' he said paradoxically, 'that they might even be artificial.'

As he spoke he was conscious that he associated the roses in some way with – what?

He passed slowly down the noble marble stairway – a policeman stood on every other step – and gave his views to Falmouth.

'You cannot blame the old man for his decision; in fact, I admire him today more than I have ever done before. But – ' there was a sudden solemnity in his voice – 'I am afraid – I am afraid.'

Falmouth said nothing.

'The notebook tells nothing,' the Commissioner continued, 'save the route that Sir Philip might have taken had he been anxious to arrive at 44 Downing Street by back streets. The futility of the plan is almost alarming, for there is so much evidence of a strong subtle mind behind the seeming innocence of this list of streets that I am confident that we have not got hold of the true inwardness of its meaning.'

He passed into the streets and threaded his way between crowds of policemen. The extraordinary character of the precautions taken by the police had the natural result of keeping the general public ignorant of all that was happening in Downing Street. Reporters were prohibited within the magic circle, and newspapers, and particularly the evening newspapers, had to depend upon such information as was grudgingly offered by Scotland Yard. This was scanty, while their clues and theories, which were many, were various and wonderful.

The *Megaphone*, the newspaper that regarded itself as being the most directly interested in the doings of the Four Just Men, strained every nerve to obtain news of the latest developments. With the coming of the fatal day, excitement had reached an extraordinary pitch; every fresh edition of the evening newspapers was absorbed as soon as it reached the streets. There was little material to satisfy the appetite of a sensation-loving public, but such as there was, was given. Pictures of 44 Downing Street, portraits of the Minister, plans of the vicinity of the Foreign Office, with diagrams illustrating existing police precautions, stood out from columns of letterpress dealing, not for the first but for the dozenth time, with the careers of the Four as revealed by their crimes.

And with curiosity at its height, and all London, all England, the whole of the civilised world, talking of one thing and one thing only there came like a bombshell the news of Marks's death.

Variously described as one of the detectives engaged in the case, as a foreign police officer, as Falmouth himself, the death of Marks grew from 'Suicide in a Railway Carriage' to its real importance.

Within an hour the story of tragedy, inaccurate in detail, true in substance, filled the columns of the Press. Mystery on mystery! Who was this ill-dressed man, what part was he playing in the great game, how came he by his death? asked the world instantly; and little by little, pieced together by ubiquitous newsmen, the story was made known. On top of this news came the great police march on Whitehall. Here was evidence of the serious view the authorities were taking.

'From my vantage place,' wrote Smith in the *Megaphone*, 'I could see the length of Whitehall. It was the most wonderful spectacle that London has ever witnessed. I saw nothing but a great sea of black helmets reaching from one end of the broad thoroughfare to the other. Police! the whole vicinity was black with police; they thronged side streets, they crowded into the Park, they formed not a cordon, but a mass through which it was impossible to penetrate.'

For the Commissioners of Police were leaving nothing to chance. If they were satisfied that cunning could be matched by cunning, craft by craft, stealth by counter-stealth, they would have been content to defend their charge on conventional lines. But they were outmanoeuvred. The stake was too high to depend upon strategy – this was a case that demanded brute force. It is difficult, writing so long after the event, to realise how the terror of the Four had so firmly fastened upon the finest police organisation in the world, to appreciate the panic that had come upon a body renowned for its clearheadedness.

The crowd that blocked the approaches to Whitehall soon began to grow as the news of Billy's death circulated, and soon after two o'clock that afternoon, by order of the Commissioner, Westminster Bridge was closed to all traffic, vehicular or passenger. The section of the Embankment that runs between Westminster and Hungerford Bridge was next swept by the police and cleared of curious pedestrians; Northumberland Avenue was barred, and before three o'clock there was no space within five hundred yards of the official residence of Sir Philip Ramon that was not held by a representative of the law. Members of Parliament on their way to the House were escorted by mounted men, and, taking on a reflected glory, were cheered by the crowd. All that afternoon a hundred thousand people waited patiently, seeing nothing, save, towering above the heads of a host of constabulary, the spires and towers of the Mother of Parliaments, or the blank faces of the buildings – in Trafalgar Square, along the Mall as far as the police would allow them, at the lower end of Victoria Street, eight deep along the Albert Embankment, growing in volume every hour. London waited, waited in patience, orderly, content to stare steadfastly at nothing, deriving no satisfaction for their weariness but the sense of being as near as it was humanly possible to be to the scene of a tragedy. A stranger arriving in London, bewildered by this gathering, asked for the cause. A man standing on the outskirts of the Embankment throng pointed across the river with the stem of his pipe.

'We're waiting for a man to be murdered,' he said simply, as one who describes a familiar function.

About the edge of these throngs newspaper boys drove a steady trade. From hand to hand the pink sheets were passed over the heads of the crowd. Every half hour brought a new edition, a new theory, a new description of the scene in which they themselves were playing an ineffectual if picturesque part. The clearing of the Thames Embankment produced an edition; the closing of Westminster Bridge brought another; the arrest of a foolish Socialist who sought to harangue the crowd in Trafalgar Square was worthy of another. Every incident of the day was faithfully recorded and industriously devoured.

All that afternoon they waited, telling and retelling the story of the Four, theorising, speculating, judging. And they spoke of the culmination as one speaks of a promised spectacle, watching the slow-moving hands of Big Ben ticking off the laggard minutes. 'Only two more hours to wait,' they said at six o'clock, and that sentence, or rather the tone of pleasurable anticipation in which it was said, indicated the spirit of the mob. For a mob is a cruel thing, heartless and unpitying.

Seven o'clock boomed forth, and the angry hum of talk ceased. London watched in silence, and with a quicker beating heart, the last hour crawl round the great clock's dial.

There had been a slight alteration in the arrangements at Downing Street, and it was after seven o'clock before Sir Philip, opening the door of his study, in which he had sat alone, beckoned the Commissioner and Falmouth to approach. They walked towards him, stopping a few feet from where he stood.

The Minister was pale, and there were lines on his face that had not been there before. But the hand that held the printed paper was steady and his face was sphinxlike.

'I am about to lock my door,' he said calmly. 'I presume that the arrangements we have agreed upon will be carried out?'

'Yes, sir,' answered the Commissioner quietly.

Sir Philip was about to speak, but he checked himself.

After a moment he spoke again.

'I have been a just man according to my lights,' he said half to himself. 'Whatever happens I am satisfied that I am doing the right thing – What is that?'

Through the corridor there came a faint roar.

'The people – they are cheering you,' said Falmouth, who just before had made a tour of inspection.

The Minister's lip curled in disdain and the familiar acid crept into his voice.

'They will be terribly disappointed if nothing happens,' he said bitterly. 'The people! God save me from the people, their sympathy, their applause, their insufferable pity.'

He turned and pushed open the door of his study, slowly closed the heavy portal, and the two men heard the snick of the lock as he turned the key.

Falmouth looked at his watch.

* * *

'Forty minutes,' was his laconic comment.

In the dark stood the Four Men.

'It is nearly time,' said the voice of Manfred, and Thery shuffled forward and groped on the floor for something.

'Let me strike a match,' he grumbled in Spanish.

'No!'

It was Poiccart's sharp voice that arrested him; it was Gonsalez who stooped quickly and passed sensitive fingers over the floor.

He found one wire and placed it in Thery's hand, then he reached up and found the other, and Thery deftly tied them together.

'Is it not time?' asked Thery, short of breath from his exertions.

'Wait.'

Manfred was examining the illuminated dial of his watch. In silence they waited.

'It is time,' said Manfred solemnly, and Thery stretched out his hand.

Stretched out his hand – and groaned and collapsed.

The three heard the groan, felt rather than saw the swaying figure of the man, and heard the thud of him as he struck the floor.

'What has happened?' whispered a tremorless voice; it was Gonsalez.

Manfred was at Thery's side fumbling at his shirt.

'They has bungled and paid the consequence,' he said in a hushed voice.

'But Ramon – '

'We shall see, we shall see,' said Manfred, still with his fingers over the heart of the fallen man.

* * *

That forty minutes was the longest that Falmouth ever remembered spending. He had tried to pass it pleasantly by recounting some of the famous criminal cases in which he had played a leading role. But he found his tongue wandering after his mind. He grew incoherent, almost hysterical. The word had been passed round that there was to be no talking in tones above a whisper, and absolute silence reigned, save an occasional sibilant murmur as a necessary question was asked or answered.

Policemen were established in every room, on the roof, in the basement, in every corridor, and each man was armed. Falmouth looked round. He sat in the secretary's office, having arranged for Hamilton to be at the House. Every door stood wide open, wedged back, so that no group of policemen should be out of sight of another.

'I cannot think what can happen,' he whispered for the twentieth time to his superior. 'It is impossible for those fellows to keep their promise – absolutely impossible.'

'The question, to my mind, is whether they will keep their other promise,' was the Commissioner's reply, 'whether having found that they have failed they will give up their attempt. One thing is certain,' he proceeded, 'if Ramon comes out of this alive, his rotten Bill will pass without opposition.'

He looked at his watch. To be exact, he had held his watch in his hand since Sir Philip had entered his room.

'It wants five minutes.' He sighed anxiously.

He walked softly to the door of Sir Philip's room and listened.

'I can hear nothing,' he said.

The next five minutes passed more slowly than any of the preceding.

'It is just on the hour,' said Falmouth in a strained voice. 'We have – '

The distant chime of Big Ben boomed once.

'The hour!' he whispered, and both men listened.

'Two,' muttered Falmouth, counting the strokes.

'Three.'

'Four.'

'Five – what's that?' he muttered quickly.

'I heard nothing – yes, I heard something.' He sprang to the door and bent his head to the level of the keyhole. 'What is that? What – '

Then from the room came a quick, sharp cry of pain, a crash – and silence.

'Quick – this way, men!' shouted Falmouth, and threw his weight against the door.

It did not yield a fraction of an inch.

'Together!'

Three burly constables flung themselves against the panels, and the door smashed open.

Falmouth and the Commissioner ran into the room.

'My God!' cried Falmouth in horror.

Sprawled across the table at which he had been sitting was the figure of the Foreign Secretary.

The paraphernalia that littered his table had been thrown to the floor as in a struggle.

The Commissioner stepped to the fallen man and raised him. One look at the face was sufficient.

'Dead!' he whispered hoarsely. He looked around – save for the police and the dead man the room was empty.

Chapter 11
A newspaper cutting

The court was again crowded today in anticipation of the evidence of the Assistant Commissioner of Police and Sir Francis Katling, the famous surgeon.

Before the proceedings recommenced the Coroner remarked that he had received a great number of letters from all kinds of people containing theories, some of them peculiarly fantastic, as to the cause of Sir Philip Ramon's death.

'The police inform me that they are eager to receive suggestions,' said the Coroner, 'and will welcome any view however bizarre.'

The Assistant Commissioner of Police was the first witness called, and gave in detail the story of the events that had led up to the finding of the late Secretary's dead body. He then went on to describe the appearance of the room. Heavy bookcases filled two sides of the room, the third or south-west was pierced with three windows, the fourth was occupied by a case containing maps arranged on the roller principle.

Were the windows fastened? – Yes.

And adequately protected? – Yes; by wooden folding shutters sheathed with steel.

Was there any indication that these had been tampered with? – None whatever.

Did you institute a search of the room? – Yes; a minute search.

By the Foreman of the Jury: Immediately? – Yes: after the body was removed every article of furniture was taken out of the room, the carpets were taken up, and the walls and ceilings stripped.

And nothing was found? – Nothing.

Is there a fireplace in the room? – Yes.

Was there any possibility of any person effecting an entrance by that method? – Absolutely none.

You have seen the newspapers? – Yes; some of them.

You have seen the suggestion put forward that the deceased was slain by the introduction of a deadly gas? – Yes.

Was that possible? – I hardly think so.

By the Foreman: Did you find any means by which such a gas could be introduced? – [*The witness hesitated*] None, except an old disused gaspipe that had an opening above the desk. [*Sensation*]

Was there any indication of the presence of such a gas? – Absolutely none.

No smell? – None whatever.

But there are gases which are at once deadly and scentless – carbon dioxide, for example? – Yes; there are.

By the Foreman: Did you test the atmosphere for the presence of such a gas? – No; but I entered the room before it would have had time to dissipate; I should have noticed it.

Was the room disarranged in any way? – Except for the table there was no disarrangement.

Did you find the contents of the table disturbed? – Yes.

Will you describe exactly the appearance of the table? – One or two heavy articles of table furniture, such as the silver candlesticks, etc., alone remained in their positions. On the floor were a number of papers, the inkstand, a pen, and [*here the witness drew a notecase from his pocket and extracted a small black shrivelled object*] a smashed flower bowl and a number of roses.

Did you find anything in the dead man's hand? – Yes, I found this.

The detective held up a withered rosebud, and a thrill of horror ran through the court.

That is a rose? – Yes.

The Coroner consulted the Commissioner's written report.

Did you notice anything peculiar about the hand? – Yes, where the flower had been there was a round black stain. [*Sensation*]

Can you account for that? – No.

By the Foreman: What steps did you take when you discovered this? – I had the flowers carefully collected and as much of the water as was possible absorbed by clean blotting-paper: these were sent to the Home Office for analysis.

Do you know the result of that analysis? – So far as I know, it has revealed nothing.

Did the analysis include leaves from the rose you have in your possession? – Yes.

The Assistant Commissioner then went on to give details of the police arrangements for the day. It was impossible, he emphatically stated, for any person to have entered or left 44 Downing Street without being observed. Immediately after the murder the police on duty were ordered to stand fast. Most of the men, said the witness, were on duty for twenty-six hours at a stretch.

At this stage there was revealed the most sensational feature of the inquiry. It came with dramatic suddenness, and was the result of a question put by the Coroner, who constantly referred to the Commissioner's signed statement that lay before him.

You know of a man called Thery? – Yes.

He was one of a band calling themselves "The Four Just Men"? – I believe so.

A reward was offered for his apprehension? – Yes.

He was suspected of complicity in the plot to murder Sir Philip Ramon? – Yes.

Has he been found? – Yes.

This monosyllabic reply drew a spontaneous cry of surprise from the crowded court.

When was he found? – This morning.

Where? – On Romney Marshes.

Was he dead? – Yes. [*Sensation*]

Was there anything peculiar about the body? [*The whole court waited for the answer with bated breath*] – Yes; on his right palm was a stain similar to that found on the hand of Sir Philip Ramon!

A shiver ran through the crowd of listeners.

Was a rose found in his hand also? – No.

By the Foreman: Was there any indication how Thery came to where he was found? – None.

The witness added that no papers or documents of any kind were found upon the man.

Sir Francis Katling was the next witness.

He was sworn and was accorded permission to give his evidence from the solicitor's table, on which he had spread the voluminous notes of his observations. For half an hour he devoted himself to a purely technical record of his examinations. There were three possible causes of death. It might have been natural: the man's weak heart was sufficient to cause such; it might have been by asphyxiation; it might have been the result of a blow that by some extraordinary means left no contusion.

There were no traces of poison? – None.

You have heard the evidence of the last witness? – Yes.

And that portion of the evidence that dealt with a black stain? – Yes.

Did you examine that stain? – Yes.

Have you formed any theories regarding it? – Yes; it seems to me as if it were formed by an acid.

Carbolic acid, for instance? – Yes; but there was no indication of any of the acids of commerce.

You saw the man Thery's hand? – Yes.

Was the stain of a similar character? – Yes, but larger and more irregular.

Were there any signs of acid? – None.

By the Foreman: You have seen many of the fantastic theories put forward by the Press and public? – Yes; I have paid careful attention to them.

And you see nothing in them that would lead you to believe that the deceased met his end by the method suggested? – No.

Gas? – Impossible; it must have been immediately detected.

The introduction into the room of some subtle poison that would asphyxiate and leave no trace? – Such a drug is unknown to medical science.

You have seen the rose found in Sir Philip's hand? – Yes.

How do you account for that? – I cannot account for it.

Nor for the stain? – No.

By the Foreman: You have formed no definite opinion regarding the cause of death? – No; I merely submit one of the three suggestions I have offered.

Are you a believer in hypnotism? – Yes, to a certain extent.

In hypnotic suggestion? – Again, to a certain extent.

Is it possible that the suggestion of death coming at a certain hour so persistently threatened might have led to death? – I do not quite understand you.

Is it possible that the deceased is a victim to hypnotic suggestion? – I do not believe it possible.

By the Foreman: You speak of a blow leaving no contusion. In your experience have you ever seen such a case? – Yes; twice.

But a blow sufficient to cause death? – Yes.

Without leaving a bruise or any mark whatever? – Yes; I saw a case in Japan where a man by exerting a peculiar pressure on the throat produced instant death.

Is that ordinary? – No; it is very unordinary; sufficiently so to create a considerable stir in medical circles. The case was recorded in the *British Medical Journal* in 1896.

And there was no contusion or bruise? – Absolutely none whatever.

The famous surgeon then read a long extract from the *British Medical Journal* bearing out this statement.

Would you say that the deceased died in this way? – It is possible.

By the Foreman: Do you advance that as a serious possibility? – Yes.

With a few more questions of a technical character the examination closed.

As the great surgeon left the box there was a hum of conversation, and keen disappointment was felt on all sides. It had been hoped that the evidence of the medical expert would have thrown light into dark places, but it left the mystery of Sir Philip Ramon's death as far from explanation as ever.

Superintendent Falmouth was the next witness called.

The detective, who gave his evidence in clear tones, was evidently speaking under stress of very great emotion. He seemed to appreciate very keenly the failure of the police to safeguard the life of the dead Minister. It is an open secret that immediately after the tragedy both the officer and the Assistant Commissioner tendered their resignations, which, at the express instruction of the Prime Minister, were not accepted.

Mr Falmouth repeated a great deal of the evidence already given by the Commissioner, and told the story of how he had stood on duty outside the Foreign Secretary's door at the moment of the tragedy. As he detailed the events of that evening a deathly silence came upon the court.

You say you heard a noise proceeding from the study? – Yes.

What sort of a noise? – Well, it is hard to describe what I heard; it was one of those indefinite noises that sounded like a chair being pulled across a soft surface.

Would it be a noise like the sliding of a door or panel? – Yes. [*Sensation*]

That is the noise as you described it in your report? – Yes.

Was any panel discovered? – No.

Or any sliding door? – No.

Would it have been possible for a person to have secreted himself in any of the bureaux or bookcases? – No; these were examined.

What happened next? – I heard a click and a cry from Sir Philip, and endeavoured to burst open the door.

By the Foreman: It was locked? – Yes.

And Sir Philip was alone? – Yes; it was by his wish: a wish expressed earlier in the day.

After the tragedy did you make a systematic search both inside and outside the house? – Yes.

Did you make any discovery? – None, except that I made a discovery curious in itself, but having no possible bearing on the case now.

What was this? – Well, it was the presence on the window-sill of the room of two dead sparrows.

Were these examined? – Yes; but the surgeon who dissected them gave the opinion that they died from exposure and had fallen from the parapet above.

Was there any trace of poison in these birds? – None that could be discovered.

At this point Sir Francis Katling was recalled. He had seen the birds. He could find no trace of poison.

Granted the possibility of such a gas as we have already spoken of – a deadly gas with the property of rapid dissipation – might not the escape of a minute quantity of such a fume bring about the death of these birds? – Yes, if they were resting on the window-sill.

By the Foreman: Do you connect these birds with the tragedy? – I do not, replied the witness emphatically.

Superintendent Falmouth resumed his evidence.

Were there any other curious features that struck you? – None.

The Coroner proceeded to question the witness concerning the relations of Marks with the police.

Was the stain found on Sir Philip's hand, and on the hand of the man Thery, found also on Marks? – No.

* * *

It was as the court was dispersing, and little groups of men stood discussing the most extraordinary verdict ever given by a coroner's jury, "Death from some unknown cause, and wilful murder against some person or persons unknown", that the Coroner himself met on the threshold of the court a familiar face.

'Hullo, Carson!' he said in surprise, 'you here too; I should have thought that your bankrupts kept you busy – even on a day like this – extraordinary case.'

'Extraordinary,' agreed the other.

'Were you there all the time?'

'Yes,' replied the spectator.

'Did you notice what a bright foreman we had?'

'Yes; I think he would make a smarter lawyer than a company promoter.'

'You know him, then?'

'Yes,' yawned the Official Receiver; 'poor devil, he thought he was going to set the Thames on fire, floated a company to reproduce photogravures and things – took Etherington's off our hands, but it's back again.'

'Has he failed?' asked the Coroner in surprise.

'Not exactly failed. He's just given it up, says the climate doesn't suit him – what is his name again?'

'Manfred,' said the Coroner.

Chapter 12
Conclusion

Falmouth sat on the opposite side of the Chief Commissioner's desk, his hands clasped before him. On the blotting-pad lay a thin sheet of grey notepaper. The Commissioner picked it up again and re-read it.

When you receive this [it ran] we who for want of a better title call ourselves 'The Four Just Men' will be scattered throughout Europe, and there is little likelihood of your ever tracing us. In no spirit of boastfulness we say: We have accomplished that which we set ourselves to accomplish. In no sense of hypocrisy we repeat our regret that such a step as we took was necessary.

Sir Philip Ramon's death would appear to have been an accident. This much we confess. Thery bungled – and paid the penalty. We depended too much upon his technical knowledge. Perhaps by diligent search you will solve the mystery of Sir Philip Ramon's death – when such a search is rewarded you will realise the truth of this statement. Farewell.

'It tells us nothing,' said the Commissioner. Falmouth shook his head despairingly. 'Search!' he said bitterly; 'we have searched the house in Downing Street from end to end – where else can we search?'

'Is there no paper amongst Sir Philip's documents that might conceivably put you on the track?'

'None that we have seen.'

The chief bit the end of his pen thoughtfully.

'Has his country house been examined?'

Falmouth frowned.

'I didn't think that necessary.'

'Nor Portland Place?'

'No: it was locked up at the time of the murder.'

The Commissioner rose.

'Try Portland Place,' he advised. 'At present it is in the hands of Sir Philip's executors.'

The detective hailed a hansom, and in a quarter of an hour found himself knocking upon the gloomy portals of the late Foreign Secretary's town house. A grave manservant opened the door; it was Sir Philip's butler, a man known to Falmouth, who greeted him with a nod.

'I want to make a search of the house, Perks,' he said. 'Has anything been touched?'

The man shook his head.

'No, Mr Falmouth,' he replied, 'everything is just as Sir Philip left it. The lawyer gentlemen have not even made an inventory.'

Falmouth walked through the chilly hall to the comfortable little room set apart for the butler.

'I should like to start with the study,' he said.

'I'm afraid there will be a difficulty, then, sir,' said Perks respectfully.

'Why?' demanded Falmouth sharply.

'It is the only room in the house for which we have no key. Sir Philip had a special lock for his study and carried the key with him. You see, being a Cabinet Minister, and a very careful man, he was very particular about people entering his study.'

Falmouth thought.

A number of Sir Philip's private keys were deposited at Scotland Yard.

He scribbled a brief note to his chief and sent a footman by cab to the Yard.

Whilst he was waiting he sounded the butler.

'Where were you when the murder was committed, Perks?' he asked.

'In the country: Sir Philip sent away all the servants, you will remember.'

'And the house?'

'Was empty – absolutely empty.'

'Was there any evidence on your return that any person had effected an entrance?'

'None, sir; it would be next to impossible to burgle this house. There are alarm wires fixed communicating with the police station, and the windows are automatically locked.'

'There were no marks on the doors or windows that would lead you to believe that an entrance had been attempted?'

The butler shook his head emphatically. 'None; in the course of my daily duty I make a very careful inspection of the paintwork, and I should have noticed any marks of the kind.'

In half an hour the footman, accompanied by a detective, returned, and Falmouth took from the plain-clothed officer a small bunch of keys.

The butler led the way to the first floor.

He indicated the study, a massive oaken door, fitted with a microscopic lock.

Very carefully Falmouth made his selection of keys. Twice he tried unsuccessfully, but at the third attempt the lock turned with a click, and the door opened noiselessly.

He stood for a moment at the entrance, for the room was in darkness.

'I forgot,' said Perks, 'the shutters are closed – shall I open them?'

'If you please,' said the detective.

In a few minutes the room was flooded with light.

It was a plainly furnished apartment, rather similar in appearance to that in which the Foreign Secretary met his end. It smelt mustily of old leather, and the walls of the room were covered with bookshelves. In the centre stood a big mahogany writing-table, with bundles of papers neatly arranged.

Falmouth took a rapid and careful survey of this desk. It was thick with accumulated dust. At one end, within reach of the vacant chair stood an ordinary table telephone.

'No bells,' said Falmouth.

'No,' replied the butler. 'Sir Philip disliked bells – there is a "buzzer".'

Falmouth remembered.

'Of course,' he said quickly. 'I remember – hullo!'

He bent forward eagerly.

'Why, what has happened to the telephone?'

He might well ask, for its steel was warped and twisted. Beneath where the vulcanite receiver stood was a tiny heap of black ash, and of the flexible cord that connected it with the outside world nothing remained but a twisted piece of discoloured wire.

The table on which it stood was blistered as with some great heat.

The detective drew a long breath.

He turned to his subordinate.

'Run across to Miller's in Regent Street – the electrician – and ask Mr Miller to come here at once.'

He was still standing gazing at the telephone when the electrician arrived.

'Mr Miller,' said Falmouth slowly, 'what has happened to this telephone?'

The electrician adjusted his pince-nez and inspected the ruin.

'H'm,' he said, 'it rather looks as though some linesman had been criminally careless.'

'Linesman? What do you mean?' demanded Falmouth.

'I mean the workmen engaged to fix telephone wires.' He made another inspection.

'Cannot you see?'

He pointed to the battered instrument.

'I see that the machine is entirely ruined – but why?'

The electrician stooped and picked up the scorched wire from the ground.

'What I mean is this,' he said. 'Somebody has attached a wire carrying a high voltage – probably an electric-lighting wire – to this telephone line: and if anybody had happened to have been at – ' He stopped suddenly, and his face went white.

'Good God!' he whispered, 'Sir Philip Ramon was electrocuted!'

For a while not one of the party spoke. Then Falmouth's hand darted into his pocket and he drew out the little notebook which Billy Marks had stolen.

'That is the solution,' he cried; 'here is the direction the wires took – but how is it that the telephone at Downing Street was not destroyed in a similar manner?'

The electrician, white and shaking, shook his head impatiently.

'I have given up trying to account for the vagaries of electricity,' he said; 'besides, the current, the full force of the current, might have been diverted – a short circuit might have been effected – anything might have happened.'

'Wait!' said Falmouth eagerly. 'Suppose the man making the connection had bungled – had taken the full force of the current himself – would that have brought about this result?'

'It might – '

' "Thery bungled – and paid the penalty," ' quoted Falmouth slowly. 'Ramon got a slight shock – sufficient to frighten him – he had a weak heart – the burn on his hand, the dead sparrows! By Heaven! it's as clear as daylight!'

Later, a strong force of police raided the house in Carnaby Street, but they found nothing – except a half-smoked cigarette bearing the name of a London tobacconist, and the counterfoil of a passage ticket to New York.

It was marked per RMS *Lucania*, and was for three first-class passengers.

When the *Lucania* arrived at New York she was searched from stem to stern, but the Four Just Men were not discovered.

It was Gonsalez who had placed the 'clue' for the police to find.

THE END

THE COUNCIL OF JUSTICE

Chapter 1
The Red Hundred

It is not for you or me to judge Manfred and his works. I say
'Manfred', though I might as well have said 'Gonsalez', or for the
matter of that 'Poiccart', since they are equally guilty or great
according to the light in which you view their acts. The most lawless
of us would hesitate to defend them, but the greater humanitarian
could scarcely condemn them.

From the standpoint of us, who live within the law, going about
our business in conformity with the code, and unquestioningly keeping to the left or to the right as the police direct, their methods were
terrible, indefensible, revolting.

It does not greatly affect the issue that, for want of a better word,
we call them criminals. Such would be mankind's unanimous designation, but I think – indeed, I know – that they were indifferent to
the opinions of the human race. I doubt very much whether they
expected posterity to honour them.

Their action towards the cabinet minister was murder, pure and
simple. Yet, in view of the large humanitarian problems involved,
who would describe it as pernicious?

Frankly I say of the three men who killed Sir Philip Ramon, and
who slew ruthlessly in the name of Justice, that my sympathies are
with them. There are crimes for which there is no adequate punishment, and offences that the machinery of the written law cannot
efface. Therein lies the justification for the Four Just Men –
the Council of Justice as they presently came to call themselves, a
council of great intellects, passionless.

And not long after the death of Sir Philip and while England
still rang with that exploit, they performed an act or a series of acts
that won not alone from the Government of Great Britain, but
from the Governments of Europe, a sort of unofficial approval and
Falmouth had his wish. For here they waged war against great
world-criminals – they pitted their strength, their cunning, and
their wonderful intellects against the most powerful organization

of the underworld – against past masters of villainous arts, and brains equally agile.

*   *   *

It was the day of days for the Red Hundred. The wonderful international congress was meeting in London, the first great congress of recognized Anarchism. This was no hole-and-corner gathering of hurried men speaking furtively, but one open and unafraid, with three policemen specially retained for duty outside the hall, a commissionaire to take tickets at the outer lobby, and a shorthand writer with a knowledge of French and Yiddish to make notes of remarkable utterances.

The wonderful congress was a fact. When it had been broached there were people who laughed at the idea; Niloff of Vitebsk was one because he did not think such openness possible. But little Peter (his preposterous name was Konoplanikova, and he was a reporter on the staff of the foolish *Russkoye Znamza*), this little Peter who had thought out the whole thing; whose idea it was to gather a conference of the Red Hundred in London; who hired the hall and issued the bills (bearing in the top left-hand corner the inverted triangle of the Hundred) asking those Russians in London interested in the building of a Russian Sailors' Home to apply for tickets; who, too, secured a hall where interruption was impossible; was happy – yea, little brothers, it was a great day for Peter.

'You can always deceive the police,' said little Peter enthusiastically; 'call a meeting with a philanthropic object and – *voilà*!'

Wrote Inspector Falmouth to the assistant commissioner of police –

Your respected communication to hand. The meeting to be held tonight at the Phoenix Hall, Middlesex Street, E., with the object of raising funds for a Russian Sailors' Home is, of course, the first international congress of the Red Hundred. Shall not be able to get a man inside, but do not think that matters much, as meeting will be engaged throwing flowers at one another and serious business will not commence till the meeting of the inner committee.

I enclose a list of men already arrived in London, and have the honour to request that you will send me portraits of undermentioned men.

There were three delegates from Baden, Herr Smidt from Freiburg, Herr Bleaumeau from Karlsruhe, and Herr Von Dunop from

Mannheim. They were not considerable persons, even in the eyes of the world of Anarchism; they called for no particular notice, and therefore the strange thing that happened to them on the night of the congress is all the more remarkable.

Herr Smidt had left his pension in Bloomsbury and was hurrying eastward. It was a late autumn evening and a chilly rain fell, and Herr Smidt was debating in his mind whether he should go direct to the rendezvous where he had promised to meet his two compatriots, or whether he should call a taxi and drive direct to the hall, when a hand grasped his arm.

He turned quickly and reached for his hip pocket. Two men stood behind him and but for themselves the square through which he was passing was deserted.

Before he could grasp the Browning pistol, his other arm was seized and the taller of the two men spoke.

'You are Augustus Smidt?' he asked.

'That is my name.'

'You are an anarchist?'

'That is my affair.'

'You are at present on your way to a meeting of the Red Hundred?'

Herr Smidt opened his eyes in genuine astonishment.

'How did you know that?' he asked.

'I am Detective Simpson from Scotland Yard, and I shall take you into custody,' was the quiet reply.

'On what charge?' demanded the German.

'As to that I shall tell you later.'

The man from Baden shrugged his shoulders.

'I have yet to learn that it is an offence in England to hold opinions.'

A closed motor-car entered the square, and the shorter of the two whistled and the chauffeur drew up near the group.

The anarchist turned to the man who had arrested him.

'I warn you that you shall answer for this,' he said wrathfully. 'I have an important engagement that you have made me miss through your foolery and – '

'Get in!' interrupted the tall man tersely.

Smidt stepped into the car and the door snapped behind him.

He was alone and in darkness. The car moved on and then Smidt discovered that there were no windows to the vehicle. A wild idea came to him that he might escape. He tried the door of the car; it was immovable. He cautiously tapped it. It was lined with thin sheets of steel.

'A prison on wheels,' he muttered with a curse, and sank back into the corner of the car.

He did not know London; he had not the slightest idea where he was going. For ten minutes the car moved along. He was puzzled. These policemen had taken nothing from him, he still retained his pistol. They had not even attempted to search him for compromising documents. Not that he had any except the pass for the conference and – the Inner Code!

Heavens! He must destroy that. He thrust his hand into the inner pocket of his coat. It was empty. The thin leather case was gone! His face went grey, for the Red Hundred is no fanciful secret society but a bloody-minded organization with less mercy for bungling brethren than for its sworn enemies. In the thick darkness of the car his nervous fingers groped through all his pockets. There was no doubt at all – the papers had gone.

In the midst of his search the car stopped. He slipped the flat pistol from his pocket. His position was desperate and he was not the kind of man to shirk a risk.

Once there was a brother of the Red Hundred who sold a password to the Secret Police. And the brother escaped from Russia. There was a woman in it, and the story is a mean little story that is hardly worth the telling. Only, the man and the woman escaped, and went to Baden, and Smidt recognized them from the portraits he had received from headquarters, and one night . . . You understand that there was nothing clever or neat about it. English newspapers would have described it as a 'revolting murder', because the details of the crime were rather shocking. The thing that stood to Smidt's credit in the books of the Society was that the murderer was undiscovered.

The memory of this episode came back to the anarchist as the car stopped – perhaps this was the thing the police had discovered? Out of the dark corners of his mind came the scene again, and the voice of the man . . . 'Don't! don't! O Christ! don't!' and Smidt sweated . . .

The door of the car opened and he slipped back the cover of his pistol.

'Don't shoot,' said a quiet voice in the gloom outside, 'here are some friends of yours.'

He lowered his pistol, for his quick ears detected a wheezing cough.

'Von Dunop!' he cried in astonishment.

'And Herr Bleaumeau,' said the same voice. 'Get in, you two.'

Two men stumbled into the car, one dumbfounded and silent –
save for the wheezing cough – the other blasphemous and voluble.

'Wait, my friend!' raved the bulk of Bleaumeau; 'wait! I will make
you sorry.'

The door shut and the car moved on.

The two men outside watched the vehicle with its unhappy passengers disappear round a corner and then walked slowly away.

'Extraordinary men,' said the taller.

'Most,' replied the other, and then, 'Von Dunop – isn't he – ?'

'The man who threw the bomb at the Swiss President – yes.'

The shorter man smiled in the darkness.

'Given a conscience, he is enduring his hour,' he said.

The pair walked on in silence and turned into Oxford Street as the
clock of a church struck eight.

The tall man lifted his walking-stick and a sauntering taxi pulled
up at the curb.

'Aldgate,' he said, and the two men took their seats.

Not until the taxi was spinning along Newgate Street did either of
the men speak, and then the shorter asked: 'You are thinking about
the woman?'

The other nodded and his companion relapsed into silence; then
he spoke again.

'She is a problem and a difficulty, in a way – yet she is the most
dangerous of the lot. And the curious thing about it is that if she were
not beautiful and young she would not be a problem at all. We're
very human, George. God made us illogical that the minor businesses of life should not interfere with the great scheme. And the
great scheme is that animal men should select animal women for the
mothers of their children.'

'*Venenum in auro bibitur*,' the other quoted, which shows that
he was an extraordinary detective, 'and so far as I am concerned it
matters little to me whether an irresponsible homicide is a beautiful
woman or a misshapen negro.'

They dismissed the taxi at Aldgate Station and turned into Middlesex Street.

The meeting-place of the great congress was a hall which was
originally erected by an enthusiastic Christian gentleman with a
weakness for the conversion of Jews to the New Presbyterian Church,
With this laudable object it had been opened with great pomp and the
singing of anthems and the enthusiastic proselytizer had spoken on
that occasion two hours and forty minutes by the clock.

After twelve months' labour the Christian gentleman discovered that the advantages of Christianity only appeal to very rich Jews indeed, to the Cohens who become Cowans, to the Isaacs who become Grahames, and to the curious low-down Jews who stand in the same relation to their brethren as White Kaffirs to a European community.

So the hall passed from hand to hand, and, failing to obtain a music and dancing licence, went back to the mission-hall stage.

Successive generations of small boys had destroyed its windows and beplastered its walls. Successive fly-posters had touched its blank face with colour. Tonight there was nothing to suggest that there was any business of extraordinary importance being transacted within its walls. A Russian or a Yiddish or any kind of reunion does not greatly excite Middlesex Street, and had little Peter boldly announced that the congress of the Red Hundred were to meet in full session there would have been no local excitement and – if the truth be told – he might still have secured the services of his three policemen and commissionaire.

To this worthy, a neat, cleanly gentleman in uniform, wearing on his breast the medals for the relief of Chitral and the Soudan Campaigns, the two men delivered the perforated halves of their tickets and passed through the outer lobby into a small room. By a door at the other end stood a thin man with a straggling beard. His eyes were red-rimmed and weak, he wore long narrow buttoned boots, and he had a trick of pecking his head forwards and sideways like an inquisitive hen.

'You have the word, brothers?' he asked, speaking German like one unaccustomed to the language.

The taller of the two strangers shot a swift glance at the sentinel that absorbed the questioner from his cracked patent leather boots to his flamboyant watch-chain. Then he answered in Italian.

'Nothing!'

The face of the guardian flushed with pleasure at the familiar tongue.

'Pass, brother; it is very good to hear that language.'

The air of the crowded hall struck the two men in the face like the blast from a destructor. It was unclean; unhealthy – the scent of an early-morning doss-house.

The hall was packed, the windows were closed and curtained, and as a precautionary measure, little Peter had placed thick blankets before the ventilators.

At one end of the hall was a platform on which stood a semicircle of chairs and in the centre was a table draped with red. On the wall behind the chairs – every one of which was occupied – was a huge red flag bearing in the centre a great white 'C'. It had been tacked to the wall, but one corner had broken away revealing a part of the painted scroll of the mission workers.

' . . . are the meek, for they shall inherit the earth.'

The two intruders pushed their way through a group that were gathered at the door. Three aisles ran the length of the building, and they made their way along the central gangway and found seats near the platform.

A brother was speaking. He was a good and zealous worker but a bad orator. He spoke in German and enunciated commonplaces with hoarse emphasis. He said all the things that other men had said and forgotten. 'This is the time to strike' was his most notable sentence, and notable only because it evoked a faint buzz of applause.

The audience stirred impatiently. The good Bentvitch had spoken beyond his allotted time; and there were other people to speak – and prosy at that. And it would be ten o'clock before the Woman of Gratz would rise.

The babble was greatest in the corner of the hall, where little Peter, all eyes and startled eyebrows, was talking to an audience of his own.

'It is impossible, it is absurd, it is most foolish!' his thin voice rose almost to a scream. 'I should laugh at it – we should all laugh, but the Woman of Gratz has taken the matter seriously, and she is afraid!'

'Afraid!'

'Nonsense!'

'Oh, Peter, the fool!'

There were other things said because everybody in the vicinity expressed an opinion. Peter was distressed, but not by the epithets. He was crushed, humiliated, beaten by his tremendous tidings. He was nearly crying at the horrible thought. The Woman of Gratz was afraid! The Woman of Gratz who . . . It was unthinkable.

He turned his eyes toward the platform, but she was not there.

'Tell us about it, Peter,' pleaded a dozen voices; but the little man with the tears twinkling on his fair eyelashes waved them off.

So far from his incoherent outburst they had learnt only this – that the Woman of Gratz was afraid.

And that was bad enough.

For this woman – she was a girl really, a slip of a child who should have been finishing her education somewhere in Germany – this same woman had once risen and electrified the world.

There had been a meeting in a small Hungarian town to discuss ways and means. And when the men had finished their denunciation of Austria, she rose and talked. A short-skirted little girl with two long flaxen braids of hair, thin-legged, flat-chested, angular, hipless – that is what the men of Gratz noticed as they smiled behind their hands and wondered why her father had brought her to the meeting.

But her speech . . . two hours she spoke and no man stirred. A little flat-chested girl full of sonorous phrases – mostly she had collected them from the talk in Old Joseph's kitchen. But with some power of her own, she had spun them together, these inconsiderable truisms, and had endowed them with a wondrous vitality.

They were old, old platitudes, if the truth be told, but at some time in the history of revolution, some long-dead genius had coined them, and newly fashioned in the furnace of his soul they had shaped men's minds and directed their great and dreadful deeds.

So the Woman of Gratz arrived, and they talked about her and circulated her speeches in every language. And she grew. The hollow face of this lank girl filled, and the flat bosom rounded and there came softer lines and curves to her angular figure, and, almost before they realized the fact, she was beautiful.

So her fame had grown until her father died and she went to Russia. Then came a series of outrages which may be categorically and briefly set forth –

1: General Maloff shot dead by an unknown woman in his private room at the Police Bureau, Moscow.

2: Prince Hazallarkoff shot dead by an unknown woman in the streets of Petrograd.

3: Colonel Kaverdavskov killed by a bomb thrown by a woman who made her escape.

And the Woman of Gratz leapt to a greater fame. She had been arrested half a dozen times, and whipped twice, but they could prove nothing against her and elicit nothing from her – and she was very beautiful.

Now to the thundering applause of the waiting delegates, she stepped upon the platform and took the last speaker's place by the side of the red-covered table.

She raised her hand and absolute and complete silence fell on the hall, so much so that her first words sounded strident and shrill, for she had attuned her voice to the din. She recovered her pitch and dropped her voice to a conversational tone.

She stood easily with her hands clasped behind her and made no gesture. The emotion that was within her she conveyed through her wonderful voice. Indeed, the power of the speech lay rather in its delivery than in its substance, for only now and then did she depart from the unwritten text of Anarchism: the right of the oppressed to overthrow the oppressor; the divinity of violence; the sacredness of sacrifice and martyrdom in the cause of enlightenment. One phrase alone stood apart from the commonplace of her oratory. She was speaking of the Theorists who counsel reform and condemn violence, 'These Christs who deputize their Calvaries', she called them with fine scorn, and the hall roared its approval of the imagery.

It was the fury of the applause that disconcerted her; the taller of the two men who sat watching her realized that much. For when the shouting had died down and she strove to resume, she faltered and stammered and then was silent. Then abruptly and with surprising vehemence she began again. But she had changed the direction of her oratory, and it was upon another subject that she now spoke. A subject nearer to her at that moment than any other, for her pale cheeks flushed and a feverish light came to her eyes as she spoke.

' . . . and now, with all our perfect organization, with the world almost within our grasp – there comes somebody who says "Stop!" – and we who by our acts have terrorized kings and dominated the councils of empires, are ourselves threatened!'

The audience grew deadly silent. They were silent before, but now the silence was painful.

The two men who watched her stirred a little uneasily, as though something in her speech had jarred. Indeed, the suggestion of braggadocio in her assertion of the Red Hundred's power had struck a discordant note.

The girl continued speaking rapidly.

'We have heard – you have heard – we know of these men who have written to us. They say – ' her voice rose – 'that we shall not do what we do. They threaten us – they threaten me – that we must change our methods, or they will punish as – as we – punish; kill as we kill – '

There was a murmuring in the audience and men looked at one another in amazement. For terror unmistakable and undisguised was written on her pale face and shone from those wondrous eyes of hers.

'But we will defy – '

Loud voices and the sound of scuffling in the little anteroom interrupted her, and a warning word shouted brought the audience to its feet.

'The police!'

A hundred stealthy hands reached for cunning pockets, but somebody leapt upon a bench, near the entrance, and held up an authoritative hand.

'Gentlemen, there is no occasion for alarm – I am Detective-Superintendent Falmouth from Scotland Yard, and I have no quarrel with the Red Hundred.'

Little Peter, transfixed for the moment, pushed his way towards the detective.

'Who do you want – what do you want?' he asked.

The detective stood with his back to the door and answered.

'I want two men who were seen to enter this hall: two members of an organization that is outside the Red Hundred. They – '

'Ha!' The woman who still stood upon the platform leant forward with blazing eyes.

'I know – I know!' she cried breathlessly; 'the men who threatened us – who threatened me – The Four Just Men!'

Chapter 2
The fourth man

The tall man's hand was in his pocket when the detective spoke.

When he had entered the hall he had thrown a swift glance round the place and taken in every detail. He had seen the beaded strip of unpainted wood which guarded the electric light cables, and had improved the opportunity whilst the prosy brother was speaking to make a further reconnaissance. There was a white porcelain switchboard with half a dozen switches at the left-hand side of the platform. He judged the distance and threw up the hand that held the pistol.

Bang! Bang!

A crash of broken glass, a quick flash of blue flame from the shattered fuses – and the hall was in darkness. It happened before the detective could spring from his form into the yelling, screaming crowd – before the police officer could get a glance at the man who fired the shots.

In an instant the place was a pandemonium.

'Silence!' Falmouth roared above the din; 'silence! Keep quiet, you miserable cowards – show a light here, Brown, Curtis – Inspector, where are your men's lanterns?'

The rays of a dozen bull's-eye lamps waved over the struggling throng.

'Open your lanterns – ' and to the scething mob, 'Silence!' Then a bright young officer remembered that he had seen gas-brackets in the room, and struggled through the howling mob till he came to the wall and found the gas-fitting with his lantern. He struck a match and lit the gas, and the panic subsided as suddenly as it had begun.

Falmouth, choked with rage, threw his eye round the hall. 'Guard the door,' he said briefly; 'the hall is surrounded and they cannot possibly escape.' He strode swiftly along the central aisle, followed by two of his men, and with an agile leap, sprang on to the platform and faced the audience. The Woman of Gratz, with a white set face, stood motionless, one hand resting on the little table, the other at her throat. Falmouth raised his hand to enjoin silence and the law-breakers obeyed.

'I have no quarrel with the Red Hundred,' he said. 'By the law of this country it is permissible to hold opinions and propagate doctrines, however objectionable they be – I am here to arrest two men who have broken the laws of this country. Two persons who are part of the organization known as the Four Just Men.'

All the time he was speaking his eyes searched the faces before him. He knew that one-half of the audience could not understand him and that the hum of talk that arose as he finished was his speech in course of translation.

The faces he sought he could not discern. To be exact, he hoped that his scrutiny would induce two men, of whose identity he was ignorant, to betray themselves.

There are little events, unimportant in themselves, which occasionally lead to tremendous issues. A skidding motor-bus that crashed into a private car in Piccadilly had led to the discovery that there were three vociferous foreign gentlemen imprisoned in the overturned vehicle. It led to the further discovery that the chauffeur had disappeared in the confusion of the collision. In the darkness, comparing notes, the three prisoners had arrived at a conclusion – to wit, that their abduction was a sequel to a mysterious letter each had received, which bore the signature 'The Four Just Men'.

So in the panic occasioned by the accident, they were sufficiently indiscreet to curse the Four Just Men by name, and, the Four Just Men being a sore topic with the police, they were questioned further, and the end of it was that Superintendent Falmouth motored eastward in great haste and was met in Middlesex Street by a reserve of police specially summoned.

He was at the same disadvantage he had always been – the Four Just Men were to him names only, symbols of a swift remorseless force that struck surely and to the minute – and nothing more.

Two or three of the leaders of the Red Hundred had singled themselves out and drew closer to the platform.

'We are not aware,' said François, the Frenchman, speaking for his companions in faultless English, 'we are not aware of the identity of the men you seek, but on the understanding that they are not brethren of our Society, and moreover – ' he was at a loss for words to put the fantastic situation – 'and moreover since they have threatened us – threatened us,' he repeated in bewilderment, 'we will afford you every assistance.'

The detective jumped at the opportunity.

'Good!' he said and formed a rapid plan.

The two men could not have escaped from the hall. There was a little door near the platform, he had seen that – as the two men he sought had seen it. Escape seemed possible through there; they had thought so, too. But Falmouth knew that the outer door leading from the little vestibule was guarded by two policemen. This was the sum of the discovery made also by the two men he sought. He spoke rapidly to François.

'I want every person in the hall to be vouched for,' he said quickly. 'Somebody must identify every man, and the identifier must himself be identified.'

The arrangements were made with lightning-like rapidity. From the platform in French, German and Yiddish, the leaders of the Red Hundred explained the plan. Then the police formed a line, and one by one the people came forward, and shyly, suspiciously or self-consciously, according to their several natures, they passed the police line.

'That is Simon Czech of Buda-Pest.'

'Who identifies him?'

'I' – a dozen voices.

'Pass.'

'This is Michael Ranekov of Odessa.'

'Who identifies him?'

'I,' said a burly man, speaking in German.

'And you?'

There was a little titter, for Michael is the best-known man in the Order. Some there were who, having passed the line, waited to identify their kinsfolk and fellow-countrymen.

'It seems much simpler than I could have imagined.'

It was the tall man with the trim beard, who spoke in a guttural tone which was neither German nor Yiddish. He was watching with amused interest the examination.

'Separating the lambs from the goats with a vengeance,' he said with a faint smile, and his taciturn companion nodded. Then he asked –

'Do you think any of these people will recognize you as the man who fired?'

The tall man shook his head decisively.

'Their eyes were on the police – and besides I am too quick a shot. Nobody saw me unless – '

'The Woman of Gratz?' asked the other, without showing the slightest concern.

'The Woman of Gratz,' said George Manfred.

They formed part of a struggling line that moved slowly toward the police barrier.

'I fear,' said Manfred, 'that we shall be forced to make our escape in a perfectly obvious way – the bull-at-the-gate method is one that I object to on principle, and it is one that I have never been obliged to employ.'

They were speaking all the time in the language of the harsh gutturals, and those who were in their vicinity looked at them in some perplexity, for it is a tongue unlike any that is heard in the Revolutionary Belt.

Closer and closer they grew to the inflexible inquisitor at the end of the police line. Ahead of them was a young man who turned from time to time as if seeking a friend behind. His was a face that fascinated the shorter of the two men, ever a student of faces. It was a face of deadly pallor, that the dark close-cropped hair and the thick black eyebrows accentuated. Aesthetic in outline, refined in contour, it was the face of a visionary, and in the restless, troubled eyes there lay a hint of the fanatic. He reached the barrier and a dozen eager men stepped forward for the honour of sponsorship. Then he passed and Manfred stepped calmly forward.

'Heinrich Rossenburg of Raz,' he mentioned the name of an obscure Transylvanian village.

'Who identifies this man?' asked Falmouth monotonously. Manfred held his breath and stood ready to spring.

'I do.'

It was the *spirituel* who had gone before him; the dreamer with the face of a priest.

'Pass.'

Manfred, calm and smiling, sauntered through the police with a familiar nod to his saviour. Then he heard the challenge that met his companion.

'Rolf Woolfund,' he heard Poiccart's clear, untroubled voice.

'Who identifies this man?'

Again he waited tensely.

'I do,' said the young man's voice again.

Then Poiccart joined him, and they waited a little.

Out of the corner of his eye Manfred saw the man who had vouched for him saunter toward them. He came abreast, then: 'If you would care to meet me at Reggiori's at King's Cross I shall be there in an hour,' he said, and Manfred noticed without emotion that this young man also spoke in Arabic.

They passed through the crowd that had gathered about the hall – for the news of the police raid had spread like wildfire through the East End – and gained Aldgate Station before they spoke.

'This is a curious beginning to our enterprise,' said Manfred. He seemed neither pleased nor sorry. 'I have always thought that Arabic was the safest language in the world in which to talk secrets – one learns wisdom with the years,' he added philosophically.

Poiccart examined his well-manicured finger-nails as though the problem centred there. 'There is no precedent,' he said, speaking to himself.

'And he may be an embarrassment,' added George; then, 'let us wait and see what the hour brings.'

The hour brought the man who had befriended them so strangely. It brought also a little in advance of him a fourth man who limped slightly but greeted the two with a rueful smile. 'Hurt?' asked Manfred.

'Nothing worth speaking about,' said the other carelessly, 'and now what is the meaning of your mysterious telephone message?'

Briefly Manfred sketched the events of the night, and the other listened gravely.

'It's a curious situation,' he began, when a warning glance from Poiccart arrested him. The subject of their conversation had arrived.

He sat down at the table, and dismissed the fluttering waiter that hung about him.

The four sat in silence for a while and the newcomer was the first to speak.

'I call myself Bernard Courtlander,' he said simply, 'and you are the organization known as the Four Just Men.'

They did not reply.

'I saw you shoot,' he went on evenly, 'because I had been watching you from the moment when you entered the hall, and when the police adopted the method of identification, I resolved to risk my life and speak for you.'

'Meaning,' interposed Poiccart calmly, 'you resolved to risk – our killing you?'

'Exactly,' said the young man, nodding, 'a purely outside view would be that such a course would be a fiendish act of ingratitude, but I have a closer perception of principles, and I recognize that such a sequel to my interference is perfectly logical.' He singled out

Manfred leaning back on the red plush cushions. 'You have so often shown that human life is the least considerable factor in your plan, and have given such evidence of your singleness of purpose, that I am fully satisfied that if my life – or the life of any one of you – stood before the fulfilment of your objects, that life would go – so!' He snapped his fingers. 'Well?' said Manfred. 'I know of your exploits,' the strange young man went on, 'as who does not?'

He took from his pocket a leather case, and from that he extracted a newspaper cutting. Neither of the three men evinced the slightest interest in the paper he unfolded on the white cloth. Their eyes were on his face.

'Here is a list of people slain – for justice's sake,' Courtlander said, smoothing the creases from a cutting from the *Megaphone*, 'men whom the law of the land passed by, sweaters and debauchers, robbers of public funds, corrupters of youth – men who bought "justice" as you and I buy bread.' He folded the paper again. 'I have prayed God that I might one day meet you.'

'Well?' It was Manfred's voice again.

'I want to be with you, to be one of you, to share your campaign and, and – ' he hesitated, then added soberly, 'if need be, the death that awaits you.'

Manfred nodded slowly, then looked toward the man with the limp.

'What do you say, Gonsalez?' he asked.

This Leon Gonsalez was a famous reader of faces – that much the young man knew – and he turned for the test and met the other's appraising eyes.

'Enthusiast, dreamer, and intellectual, of course,' said Gonsalez slowly; 'there is reliability which is good, and balance which is better – but – '

'But – ?' asked Courtlander steadily.

'There is passion, which is bad,' was the verdict.

'It is a matter of training,' answered the other quietly. 'My lot has been thrown with people who think in a frenzy and act in madness; it is the fault of all the organizations that seek to right wrong by indiscriminate crime, whose sense are senses, who have debased sentiment to sentimentality, and who muddle kings with kingship.'

'You are of the Red Hundred?' asked Manfred.

'Yes,' said the other, 'because the Red Hundred carries me a little way along the road I wish to travel.'

'In the direction?'

'Who knows?' replied the other. 'There are no straight roads, and you cannot judge where lies your destination by the direction the first line of path takes.'

'I do not tell you how great a risk you take upon yourself,' said Manfred, 'nor do I labour the extent of the responsibility you ask to undertake. You are a wealthy man?'

'Yes,' said Courtlander, 'as wealth goes; I have large estates in Hungary.'

'I do not ask that question aimlessly, yet it would make no difference if you were poor,' said Manfred. 'Are you prepared to sell your estates – Buda-Gratz I believe they are called – Highness?'

For the first time the young man smiled.

'I did not doubt but that you knew me,' he said; 'as to my estates, I will sell them without hesitation.'

'And place the money at my disposal?'

'Yes,' he replied, instantly.

'Without reservation?'

'Without reservation.'

'And,' said Manfred, slowly, 'if we felt disposed to employ this money for what might seem our own personal benefit, would you take exception?'

'None,' said the young man, calmly.

'And as a proof?' demanded Poiccart, leaning a little forward.

'The word of a Hap – '

'Enough,' said Manfred; 'we do not want your money – yet money is the supreme test.' He pondered awhile before he spoke again.

'There is the Woman of Gratz,' he said abruptly; 'at the worst she must be killed.'

'It is a pity,' said Courtlander, a little sadly.

He had answered the final test did he but know it.

A too willing compliance, an over-eagerness to agree with the supreme sentence of the 'Four', any one thing that might have betrayed the lack of that exact balance of mind, which their word demanded, would have irretrievably condemned him.

'Let us drink an arrogant toast,' said Manfred, beckoning a waiter. The wine was opened and the glasses filled, and Manfred muttered the toast.

'The Four who were three, to the Fourth who died and the Fourth who is born.'

Once upon a time there was a fourth who fell riddled with bullets in a Bordeaux café, and him they pledged.

* * *

In Middlesex Street, in the almost emptied hall, Falmouth stood at bay before an army of reporters.

'Were they the Four Just Men, Mr Falmouth?'

'Did you see them?'

'Have you any clue?'

Every second brought a fresh batch of newspaper men, taxi after taxi came into the dingy street, and the string of vehicles lined up outside the hall was suggestive of a fashionable gathering. The Telephone Tragedy was still fresh in the public mind, and it needed no more than the utterance of the magical words 'Four Just Men' to fan the spark of interest to flame again. The delegates of the Red Hundred formed a privileged throng in the little wilderness of a forecourt, and through these the journalists circulated industriously.

Smith of the *Megaphone* and his youthful assistant, Maynard, slipped through the crowd and found their taxi.

Smith shouted a direction to the driver and sank back in the seat with a whistle of weariness.

'Did you hear those chaps talking about police protection?' he asked; 'all the blessed anarchists from all over the world – and talking like a mothers' meeting! To hear 'em you would think they were the most respectable members of society that the world had ever seen. Our civilization is a wonderful thing,' he added, cryptically.

'One man,' said Maynard, 'asked me in very bad French if the conduct of the Four Just Men was actionable!'

At that moment, another question was being put to Falmouth by a leader of the Red Hundred, and Falmouth, a little ruffled in his temper, replied with all the urbanity that he could summon.

'You may have your meetings,' he said with some asperity, 'so long as you do not utter anything calculated to bring about a breach of the peace, you may talk sedition and anarchy till you're blue in the face. Your English friends will tell you how far you can go – and I might say you can go pretty far – you can advocate the assassination of kings, so long as you don't specify which king; you can plot against governments and denounce armies and grand dukes; in fact, you can do as you please – because that's the law.'

'What is – a breach of the peace?' asked his interrogator, repeating the words with difficulty.

Another detective explained.

François and one Rudulph Starque escorted the Woman of Gratz to her Bloomsbury lodgings that night, and they discussed the detective's answer.

This Starque was a big man, strongly built, with a fleshy face and little pouches under his eyes. He was reputed to be well off, and to have a way with women.

'So it would appear,' he said, 'that we may say "Let the kings be slain", but not "Let the king be slain"; also that we may preach the downfall of governments, but if we say "Let us go into this café" – how do you call it? – "public-house, and be rude to the *proprietaire*" we commit a – er – breach of the peace – *ne c'est pas?*

'It is so,' said François, 'that is the English way.'

'It is a mad way,' said the other.

They reached the door of the girl's pension. She had been very quiet during the walk, answering questions that were put to her in monosyllables. She had ample food for thought in the events of the night.

François bade her a curt good night and walked a little distance. It had come to be regarded as Starque's privilege to stand nearest the girl. Now he took her slim hands in his and looked down at her. Someone has said the East begins at Bukarest, but there is a touch of the Eastern in every Hungarian, and there is a crudeness in their whole attitude to womankind that shocks the more tender susceptibilities of the Western.

'Good night, little Maria,' he said in a low voice. 'Some day you will be kinder, and you will not leave me at the door.'

She looked at him steadfastly.

'That will never be,' she replied, without a tremor.

Chapter 3
Jessen, alias Long

The front page of every big London daily was again black with the story of the Four Just Men.

'What I should like,' said the editor of the *Megaphone*, wistfully, 'is a sort of official propaganda from the Four – a sort of inspired manifesto that we could spread into six columns.'

Charles Garrett, the *Megaphone*'s 'star' reporter, with his hat on the back of his head, and an apparently inattentive eye fixed on the electrolier, sniffed.

The editor looked at him reflectively.

'A smart man might get into touch with them.'

Charles said, 'Yes', but without enthusiasm.

'If it wasn't that I knew you,' mused the editor, 'I should say you were afraid.'

'I am,' said Charles shamelessly.

'I don't want to put a younger reporter on this job,' said the editor sadly, 'it would look bad for you; but I'm afraid I must.'

'Do,' said Charles with animation, 'do, and put me down ten shillings toward the wreath.'

He left the office a few minutes later with the ghost of a smile at the corners of his mouth, and one fixed determination in the deepest and most secret recesses of his heart. It was rather like Charles that, having by an uncompromising firmness established his right to refuse work of a dangerous character, he should of his own will undertake the task against which he had officially set his face. Perhaps his chief knew him as well as he knew himself, for as Charles, with a last defiant snort, stalked from the office, the smile that came to his lips was reflected on the editor's face.

Walking through the echoing corridors of Megaphone House, Charles whistled that popular and satirical song, the chorus of which runs –

> By kind permission of the *Megaphone*,
> By kind permission of the *Megaphone*.
> Summer comes when Spring has gone,
> And the world goes spinning on,
> By permission of the *Daily Megaphone*.

Presently, he found himself in Fleet Street, and, standing at the edge of the curb, he answered a taxi-driver's expectant look with a nod.

'Where to, sir?' asked the driver.

'37 Presley Street, Walworth – round by the "Blue Bob" and the second turning to the left.'

Crossing Waterloo Bridge it occurred to him that the taxi might attract attention, so half-way down the Waterloo Road he gave another order, and, dismissing the vehicle, he walked the remainder of the way.

Charles knocked at 37 Presley Street, and after a little wait a firm step echoed in the passage, and the door was half opened. The passage was dark, but he could see dimly the thick-set figure of the man who stood waiting silently.

'Is that Mr Long?' he asked.

'Yes,' said the man curtly.

Charles laughed, and the man seemed to recognize the voice and opened the door a little wider.

'Not Mr Garrett?' he asked in surprise.

'That's me,' said Charles, and walked into the house.

His host stopped to fasten the door, and Charles heard the snap of the well-oiled lock and the scraping of a chain. Then with an apology the man pushed past him and, opening the door, ushered him into a well-lighted room, motioned Charles to a deep-seated chair, seated himself near a small table, turned down the page of the book from which he had evidently been reading, and looked inquiringly at his visitor.

'I've come to consult you,' said Charles.

A lesser man than Mr Long might have been grossly flippant, but this young man – he was thirty-five, but looked older – did not descend to such a level.

'I wanted to consult you,' he said in reply.

His language was the language of a man who addresses an equal, but there was something in his manner which suggested deference.

'You spoke to me about Milton,' he went on, 'but I find I can't read him. I think it is because he is not sufficiently material.' He paused a little. 'The only poetry I can read is the poetry of the Bible, and that is because materialism and mysticism are so ingeniously blended – '

He may have seen the shadow on the journalist's face, but he stopped abruptly.

'I can talk about books another time,' he said. Charles did not make the conventional disclaimer, but accepted the other's interpretation of the urgency of his business.

'You know everybody,' said Charles, 'all the queer fish in the basket, and a proportion of them get to know you – in time.' The other nodded gravely.

'When other sources of information fail,' continued the journalist, 'I have never hesitated to come to you – Jessen.'

It may be observed that 'Mr Long' at the threshold of the house became 'Mr Jessen' in the intimacy of the inner room.

'I owe more to you than ever you can owe to me,' he said earnestly; 'you put me on the track,' he waved his hand round the room as though the refinement of the room was the symbol of that track of which he spoke. 'You remember that morning? – if you have forgotten, I haven't – when I told you that to forget – I must drink? And you said – '

'I haven't forgotten, Jessen,' said the correspondent quietly; 'and the fact that you have accomplished all that you have is a proof that there's good stuff in you.'

The other accepted the praise without comment.

'Now,' Charles went on, 'I want to tell you what I started out to tell: I'm following a big story. It's the Four Just Men story; you know all about it? I see that you do; well, I've got to get into touch with them somehow. I do not for one moment imagine that you can help me, nor do I expect that these chaps have any accomplices amongst the people you know.'

'They have not,' said Jessen; 'I haven't thought it worth while inquiring. Would you like to go to the Guild?'

Charles pursed his lips in thought.

'Yes,' he said slowly, 'that's an idea; yes, when?'

'Tonight – if you wish.'

'Tonight let it be,' said Charles.

His host rose and left the room.

He reappeared presently, wearing a dark overcoat and about his throat a black silk muffler that emphasized the pallor of his strong square face.

'Wait a moment,' he said, and unlocked a drawer, from which he took a revolver.

He turned the magazine carefully, and Charles smiled.

'Will that be necessary?' he asked.

Jessen shook his head.

'No,' he said with a little embarrassment, 'but – I have given up all my follies and fancies, but this one sticks.'

'The fear of discovery?'

Jessen nodded.

'It's the only folly left – this fear. It's the fly in the ointment.'

He led the way through the narrow passage, first having extinguished the lamp.

They stood together in the dark street, whilst Jessen made sure the fastening of the house.

'Now,' he said, and in a few minutes they found themselves amidst the raucous confusion of a Walworth Road market-night.

They walked on in silence, then turning into East Street, they threaded a way between loitering shoppers, dodged between stalls overhung by flaring naphtha lamps, and turned sharply into a narrow street.

Both men seemed sure of their ground, for they walked quickly and unhesitatingly, and striking off through a tiny court that connected one malodorous thoroughfare with the other, they stopped simultaneously before the door of what appeared to be a disused factory.

A peaky-faced youth who sat by the door and acted as doorkeeper thrust his hand forward as they entered, but recognizing them drew back without a word.

They ascended the flight of ill-lighted stairs that confronted them, and pushing open a door at the head of the stairs, Jessen ushered his friend into a large hall.

It was a curious scene that met the journalist's eye. Well acquainted with 'The Guild' as he was, and with its extraordinary composition, he had never yet put his foot inside its portals. Basing his conception upon his knowledge of working-men's clubs and philanthropic institutions for the regeneration of degraded youth, he missed the inevitable billiard-table; he missed, too, the table strewn with month-old literature, but most of all he missed the smell of free coffee.

The floor was covered with sawdust, and about the fire that crackled and blazed at one end of the room there was a semicircle of chairs occupied by men of varying ages. Old-looking young men and young-looking old men, men in rags, men well dressed, men flashily attired in loud clothing and resplendent with shoddy jewellery. And they were drinking.

Two youths at one end of the crescent shared a quart pewter pot; the flashy man whose voice dominated the conversation held a glass of whisky in one beringed hand, and the white-haired man with the scarred face who sat with bowed head listening had a spirit glass half filled with some colourless fluid.

Nobody rose to greet the newcomers.

The flashy man nodded genially, and one of the circle pushed his chair back to give place to Jessen.

'I was just a-saying – ' said the flashy man, then looked at Charles.

'All right,' signalled Jessen.

'I was just a-sayin' to these lads,' continued the flashy one, 'that takin' one thing with the other, there's worse places than "stir".'

Jessen made no reply to this piece of dogmatism, and he of the rings went on.

'An' what's the good of a man tryin' to go straight. The police will pull you all the same: not reportin' change of address, loitering with intent; it don't matter what you do if you've been in trouble once, you're sure to get in again.'

There was a murmur of assent.

'Look at me,' said the speaker with pride. 'I've never tried to go straight – been in twice an' it took six policemen to take me last time, and they had to use the "stick".'

Jessen looked at him with mild curiosity.

'What does that prove, except that the policemen were pretty soft?'

'Not a bit!' The man stood up.

Under the veneer of tawdry foppery, Charles detected the animal strength of the criminal.

'Why, when I'm fit, as I am now,' the man went on, 'there ain't two policemen, nor four neither, that could handle me.'

Jessen's hand shot out and caught him by the forearm.

'Get away,' he suggested, and the man swung round like lightning, but Jessen had his other arm in a grip of iron.

'Get away,' he said again; but the man was helpless, and knew it, and after a pause Jessen released his hold.

'How was that?' he asked.

The amused smiles of the men did not embarrass the prisoner.

'The guv'nor's different,' he explained easily; 'he's got a knack of his own that the police haven't got.'

Jessen drew up a chair, and whatever there was in the action that had significance, it was sufficient to procure an immediate silence.

He looked round the attentive faces that were turned toward him. Charles, an interested spectator, saw the eager faces that bent in his friend's direction, and marvelled not a little at the reproductive qualities of the seed he had sown.

Jessen began to speak slowly, and Charles saw that what he said was in the nature of an address. That these addresses of Jessen were nothing unusual, and that they were welcome, was evident from the attention with which they were received.

'What Falk has been telling you,' said Jessen, indicating the man with the rings, 'is true – so far as it goes. There are worse places than "stir", and it's true that the police don't give an old lag a chance, but that's because a lag won't change his job. And a lag won't change his job, because he doesn't know any other trade where he gets money so quickly. Wally – ' he jerked his head toward a weedy-looking youth – 'Wally there got a stretch for what? For stuff that fetched thirty pounds from a fence. Twelve months' hard work for thirty pounds! It works out at about 10s. 6d. a week. And his lawyer and the mouthpiece cost him a fiver out of that. Old man Garth – ' he pointed to the white-headed man with the gin – 'did a five stretch for less than that, and he's out on brief. His wage works out at about a shilling a week.'

He checked the impatient motion that Falk made.

'I know that Falk would say,' he went on smoothly, 'that what I'm saying is outside the bargain; when I fixed up the Guild, I gave my 'Davy that there wouldn't be any parson talk or Come-All-ye-Faithful singing. Everybody knows that being on the crook's a mug's game, and I don't want to rub it in. What I've always said and done is in the direction of making you fellows earn bigger money at your own trade.

'There's a man who writes about the army who's been trying to induce soldiers to learn trades, and he started right by making the Tommies dissatisfied with their own trade; and that is what I am trying to do. What did I do with young Isaacs? I didn't preach at him, and I didn't pray over him. Ike was one of the finest snide merchants in London. He used to turn out half-crowns made from pewter pots that defied detection. They rang true and they didn't bend. Ike got three years, and when he came out I found him a job. Did I try to make him a wood-chopper, or a Salvation Army plough-boy? No. He'd have been back on the crook in a week if I had. I got a firm of medal makers in Birmingham to take him, and when Ike found himself amongst plaster moulds and electric baths, and discovered he could work at his own trade honestly, he stuck to it.'

'We ain't snide merchants,' growled Falk discontentedly.

'It's the same with all branches,' Jessen went on, 'only you chaps don't know it. Take tale-pitching – '

It would not be fair to follow Jessen through the elaborate disquisition by which he proved to the satisfaction of his audience that the 'confidence' man was a born commercial traveller. Many of his arguments were as unsound as they could well be; he ignored first principles, and glossed over what seemed to such a clear-headed hearer as Charles to be insuperable obstacles in the scheme of regeneration. But his audience was convinced. The fringe of men round the fire was reinforced as he continued. Men came into the room singly, and in twos and threes, and added themselves to the group at the fire. The news had spread that Jessen was talking – they called him 'Mr Long', by the way – and some of the newcomers arrived breathlessly, as though they had run in order that no part of the address should be missed.

That the advocate of discontent had succeeded in installing into the minds of his hearers that unrest and dissatisfaction which he held to be the basis of a new moral code, was certain. For every face bore the stamp of introspective doubt.

Interesting as it all was, Charles Garrett had not lost sight of the object of his visit, and he fidgeted a little as the speaker proceeded.

Immediately on entering the room he had grasped the exact relationship in which Jessen stood to his pupils. Jessen he knew could put no direct question as to their knowledge of the Four Just Men without raising a feeling of suspicion which would have been fatal to the success of the mission, and indeed would have imperilled the very existence of the 'Guild'.

It was when Jessen had finished speaking, and had answered a dozen questions fired simultaneously from a dozen quarters, and had answered the questions that had arisen out of these queries, that an opening came from an unexpected quarter.

For, with the serious business of the meeting disposed of, the questions took the inevitable facetious turn.

'What trade would you give the Four Just Men?' asked Falk flippantly, and there was a little rumble of laughter.

The journalist's eyes met the reformer's for one second, and through the minds of both men flashed the answer. Jessen's mouth twitched a little, and his restless hands were even more agitated as he replied slowly: 'If anybody can tell me exactly what the Four Just Men – what their particular line of business is, I could reply to that.'

It was the old man sipping his gin in silence who spoke for the first time.

'D'ye remember Billy Marks?' he asked.

His voice was harsh, as is that of a man who uses his voice at rare intervals.

'Billy Marks is dead,' he continued, 'deader than a door-nail. He knew the Four Just Men; pinched the watch an' the notebook of one an' nearly pinched them.'

There was a man who sat next to Falk who had been regarding Charles with furtive attention.

Now he turned to Jessen and spoke to the point. 'Don't get any idea in your head that the likes of us will ever have anything to do with the Four,' he said. 'Why, Mr Long,' he went on, 'the Four Just Men are as likely to come to you as to us; bein' as you are a government official, it's very likely indeed.'

Again Jessen and Charles exchanged a swift glance, and in the eyes of the journalist was a strange light.

Suppose they came to Jessen! It was not unlikely. Once before, in pursuing their vengeance in a South American State, they had come to such a man as Jessen. It was a thought, and one worth following.

Turning the possibilities over in his mind Charles stood deep in thought as Jessen, still speaking, was helped into his overcoat by one of the men.

Then as they left the hall together, passing the custodian of the place at the foot of the stairs, the journalist turned to his companion.

'Should they come to you – ?'

Jessen shook his head.

'That is unlikely,' he said; 'they hardly require outside help.'

They walked the rest of the way in silence.

Charles shook hands at the door of Jessen's house.

'If by any chance they should come – ' he said.

Jessen laughed.

'I will let you know,' he said a little ironically.

Then he entered his house, and Charles heard again the snap of the lock as the strange man closed the door behind him.

Within twenty-four hours the newspapers recorded the mysterious disappearance of a Mr J. Long, of Presley Street. Such a disappearance would have been without interest, but for a note that was found on his table. It ran.

Mr Long being necessary for our purpose, we have taken him.
The Four Just Men

That the affair had connection with the Four was sufficient to give it an extraordinary news value. That the press was confounded goes without saying. For Mr Long was a fairly unimportant man with some self-education and a craze for reforming the criminal classes. But the Home Office, which knew Mr Long as 'Mr Jessen', was greatly perturbed, and the genius of Scotland Yard was employed to discover his whereabouts.

Chapter 4

The Red Bean

The Inner Council sent out an urgent call to the men who administer the affairs of the Red Hundred.

Starque came, François, the Frenchman, came, Hollom, the Italian, Paul Mirtisky, George Grabe, the American, and Lauder Bartholomew, the ex-captain of Irregular Cavalry, came also. Bartholomew was the best dressed of the men who gathered about the green table in Greek Street, for he had held the King's commission, which is of itself a sartorial education. People who met him vaguely remembered his name and frowned. They had a dim idea that there was 'something against him', but were not quite sure what it was. It had to do with the South African War and a surrender – not an ordinary surrender, but an arrangement with the enemy on a cash basis, and the transference of stores. There was a court martial, and a cashiering, and afterwards Bartholomew came to England and bombarded first the War Office and then the press with a sheaf of type-written grievances. Afterwards he went into the theatrical line of business and appeared in music-hall sketches as 'Captain Lauder Bartholomew – the Hero of Dopfontein'.

There were other chapters which made good reading, for he figured in a divorce case, ran a society newspaper, owned a few selling platers, and achieved the distinction of appearing in the Racing Calendar in a paragraph which solemnly and officially forbade his presence on Newmarket Heath.

That he should figure on the Inner Council of the Red Hundred is remarkable only in so far as it demonstrates how much out of touch with British sentiments and conditions is the average continental politician. For Bartholomew's secret application to be enrolled a member of the Red Hundred had been received with acclamation and his promotion to the Inner Council had been rapid. Was he not an English officer – an aristocrat? A member of the most exclusive circle of English society? Thus argued the Red Hundred, to whom a subaltern in a scallywag corps did not differ perceptibly from a Commander of the Household Cavalry.

Bartholomew lied his way to the circle, because he found, as he had all along suspected, that there was a strong business end to terrorism. There were grants for secret service work, and with his fertile imagination it was not difficult to find excuses and reasons for approaching the financial executive of the Red Hundred at frequent intervals. He claimed intimacy with royal personages. He not only stated as a fact that he was in their confidence, but he suggested family ties which reflected little credit upon his progenitors.

The Red Hundred was a paying speculation; membership of the Inner Council was handsomely profitable. He had drawn a bow at a venture when under distress – literally it was a distress warrant issued at the instance of an importunate landlord – he had indited a letter to a revolutionary offering to act as London agent for an organization which was then known as The Friends of the People, but which has since been absorbed into the body corporate of the Red Hundred. It is necessary to deal fully with the antecedents of this man because he played a part in the events that are chronicled in the Council of Justice that had effects further reaching than Bartholomew, the mercenary of anarchism, could in his wildest moments have imagined.

He was one of the seven that gathered in the dingy drawing-room of a Greek Street boarding-house, and it was worthy of note that five of his fellows greeted him with a deference amounting to humility. The exception was Starque, who, arriving late, found an admiring circle hanging upon the words of this young man with the shifty eyes, and he frowned his displeasure.

Bartholomew looked up as Starque entered and nodded carelessly.

Starque took his place at the head of the table, and motioned impatiently to the others to be seated. One, whose duty it was, rose from his chair and locked the door. The windows were shuttered, but he inspected the fastenings; then, taking from his pocket two packs of cards, he scattered them in a confused heap upon the table. Every man produced a handful of money and placed it before him.

Starque was an ingenious man and had learnt many things in Russia. Men who gather round a green baize-covered table with locked doors are apt to be dealt with summarily if no adequate excuse for their presence is evident, and it is more satisfactory to be fined a hundred roubles for gambling than to be dragged off at a moment's notice to an indefinite period of labour in the mines on suspicion of being concerned in a revolutionary plot.

Starque now initiated the business of the evening. If the truth be told, there was little in the earlier proceedings that differed from the procedure of the typical committee.

There were monies to be voted. Bartholomew needed supplies for a trip to Paris, where, as the guest of an Illustrious Personage, he hoped to secure information of vital importance to the Hundred.

'This is the fourth vote in two months, comrade,' said Starque testily, 'last time it was for information from your Foreign Office, which proved to be inaccurate.'

Bartholomew shrugged his shoulders with an assumption of carelessness.

'If you doubt the wisdom of voting the money, let it pass,' he said; 'my men fly high – I am not bribing policemen or sous-officiers of diplomacy.'

'It is not a question of money,' said Starque sullenly, 'it is a question of results. Money we have in plenty, but the success of our glorious demonstration depends upon the reliability of our information.'

The vote was passed, and with its passing came a grim element into the council.

Starque leant forward and lowered his voice.

There are matters that need your immediate attention,' he said. He took a paper from his pocket, and smoothed it open in front of him. 'We have been so long inactive that the tyrants to whom the name of Red Hundred is full of terror, have come to regard themselves as immune from danger. Yet,' his voice sank lower, 'yet we are on the eve of the greatest of our achievements, when the oppressors of the people shall be moved at one blow! And we will strike a blow at kingship as shall be remembered in the history of the world, aye, when the victories of Caesar and Alexander are forgotten and when the scenes of our acts are overlaid with the dust and debris of a thousand years. But that great day is not yet – first we must remove the lesser men that the blow may fall surer; first the servant, then the master.' He stabbed the list before him with a thick forefinger.

'Fritz von Hedlitz,' he read, 'Chancellor to the Duchy of Hamburg-Altoona.'

He looked round the board and smiled.

'A man of some initiative, comrades – he foiled our attempt on his master with some cunning – do I interpret your desire when I say – death?'

'Death!'

It was a low murmured chorus.

Bartholomew, renegade and adventurer, said it mechanically. It was nothing to him a brave gentleman should die for no other reason than that he had served his master faithfully.

'Marquis de Santo-Strato, private secretary to the Prince of the Escorial,' read Starque.

'Death!' Again the murmured sentence.

One by one, Starque read the names, stopping now and again to emphasize some enormity of the man under review.

'Here is Hendrik Houssmann,' he said, tapping the paper, 'of the Berlin Secret Police: an interfering man and a dangerous one. He has already secured the arrest and punishment of one of our comrades.'

'Death,' murmured the council mechanically.

The list took half an hour to dispose of.

'There is another matter,' said Starque.

The council moved uneasily, for that other matter was uppermost in every mind.

'By some means we have been betrayed,' the chairman went on, and his voice lacked that confidence which characterized his earlier speech; 'there is an organization – an organization of reaction – which has set itself to thwart us. That organization has discovered our identity.' He paused a little.

'This morning I received a letter which named me president of the Inner Council and threatened me.' Again he hesitated.

'It was signed "The Four Just Men".'

His statement was received in dead silence – a silence that perplexed him, for his compensation for the shock he had received had been the anticipation of the sensation his announcement would make.

He was soon enlightened as to the cause of the silence.

'I also have received a letter,' said François quietly.

'And I.'

'And I.'

'And I.'

Only Bartholomew did not speak, and he felt the unspoken accusation of the others.

'I have received no letter,' he said with an easy laugh – 'only these.' He fumbled in his waistcoat pocket and produced two beans. There was nothing peculiar in these save one was a natural black and the other had been dyed red.

'What do they mean?' demanded Starque suspiciously.

'I have not the slightest idea,' said Bartholomew with a contemptuous smile; 'they came in a little box, such as jewellery is sent in, and were unaccompanied either by letter or anything of the kind. These mysterious messages do not greatly alarm me.'

'But what does it mean?' persisted Starque, and every neck was craned toward the seeds; 'they must have some significance – think.'

Bartholomew yawned.

'So far as I know, they are beyond explanation,' he said carelessly; 'neither red nor black beans have played any conspicuous part in my life, so far as I – '

He stopped short and they saw a wave of colour rush to his face, then die away, leaving it deadly pale.

'Well?' demanded Starque; there was a menace in the question.

'Let me see,' faltered Bartholomew, and he took up the red bean with a hand that shook.

He turned it over and over in his hand, calling up his reserve of strength.

He could not explain, that much he realized.

The explanation might have been possible had he realized earlier the purport of the message he had received, but now with six pairs of suspicious eyes turned upon him, and with his confusion duly noted his hesitation would tell against him.

He had to invent a story that would pass muster.

'Years ago,' he began, holding his voice steady, 'I was a member of such an organization as this: and – and there was a traitor.' The story was plain to him now, and he recovered his balance. 'The traitor was discovered and we balloted for his life. There was an equal number for death and immunity, and I as president had to give the casting vote. A red bean was for life and a black for death – and I cast my vote for the man's death.'

He saw the impression his invention had created and elaborated the story. Starque, holding the red bean in his hand, examined it carefully.

'I have reason to think that by my action I made many enemies, one of whom probably sent this reminder.' He breathed an inward sigh of relief as he saw the clouds of doubt lifting from the faces about him. Then –

'And the £1,000?' asked Starque quietly.

Nobody saw Bartholomew bite his lip, because his hand was caressing his soft black moustache. What they all observed was the well-simulated surprise expressed in the lift of his eyebrows.

'The thousand pounds?' he said puzzled, then he laughed. 'Oh, I see you, too, have heard the story – we found the traitor had accepted that sum to betray us – and this we confiscated for the benefit of the Society – and rightly so,' he added, indignantly.

The murmur of approbation relieved him of any fear as to the result of his explanation. Even Starque smiled.

'I did not know the story,' he said, 'but I did see the "£1,000" which had been scratched on the side of the red bean; but this brings us no nearer to the solution of the mystery. Who has betrayed us to the Four Just Men?'

There came, as he spoke, a gentle tapping on the door of the room. François, who sat at the president's right hand, rose stealthily and tiptoed to the door.

'Who is there?' he asked in a low voice.

Somebody spoke in German, and the voice carried so that every man knew the speaker.

'The Woman of Gratz,' said Bartholomew, and in his eagerness he rose to his feet.

If one sought for the cause of friction between Starque and the ex-captain of Irregular Cavalry, here was the end of the search. The flame that came to the eyes of these two men as she entered the room told the story.

Starque, heavily made, animal man to his fingertips, rose to greet her, his face aglow.

'Madonna,' he murmured, and kissed her hand.

She was dressed well enough, with a rich sable coat that fitted tightly to her sinuous figure, and a fur toque upon her beautiful head.

She held a gloved hand toward Bartholomew and smiled.

Bartholomew, like his rival, had a way with women; but it was a gentle way, overladen with Western conventions and hedged about with set proprieties. That he was a contemptible villain according to our conceptions is true, but he had received a rudimentary training in the world of gentlemen. He had moved amongst men who took their hats off to their womenkind, and who controlled their actions by a nebulous code. Yet he behaved with greater extravagance than did Starque, for he held her hand in his, looking into her eyes, whilst Starque fidgeted impatiently.

'Comrade,' at last he said testily, 'we will postpone our talk with our little Maria. It would be bad for her to think that she is holding us from our work – and there are the Four – '

He saw her shiver.

'The Four?' she repeated. 'Then they have written to you, also?'

Starque brought his fist with a crash down on the table.

'You – you! They have dared threaten you? By Heaven – '

'Yes,' she went on, and it seemed that her rich sweet voice grew a little husky; 'they have threatened – me.'

She loosened the furs at her throat as though the room had suddenly become hot and the atmosphere unbreathable.

The torrent of words that came tumbling to the lips of Starque was arrested by the look in her face.

'It isn't death that I fear,' she went on slowly; 'indeed, I scarcely know what I fear.'

Bartholomew, superficial and untouched by the tragic mystery of her voice, broke in upon their silence. For silenced they were by the girl's distress.

'With such men as we about, why need you notice the theatrical play of these Four Just Men?' he asked, with a laugh; then he remembered the two little beans and became suddenly silent with the rest.

So complete and inexplicable was the chill that had come to them with the pronouncement of the name of their enemy, and so absolutely did the spectacle of the Woman of Gratz on the verge of tears move them, that they heard then what none had heard before – the ticking of the clock.

It was the habit of many years that carried Bartholomew's hand to his pocket, mechanically he drew out his watch, and automatically he cast his eyes about the room for the clock wherewith to check the time.

It was one of those incongruous pieces of commonplace that intrude upon tragedy, but it loosened the tongues of the council, and they all spoke together.

It was Starque who gathered the girl's trembling hands between his plump palms.

'Maria, Maria,' he chided softly, 'this is folly. What! the Woman of Gratz who defied all Russia – who stood before Mirtowsky and bade him defiance – what is it?'

The last words were sharp and angry and were directed to Bartholomew.

For the second time that night the Englishman's face was white, and he stood clutching the edge of the table with staring eyes and with his lower jaw drooping.

'God, man!' cried Starque, seizing him by the arm, 'what is it – speak – you are frightening her!'

'The clock!' gasped Bartholomew in a hollow voice, 'where – where is the clock?'

His staring eyes wandered helplessly from side to side. 'Listen,' he whispered, and they held their breath. Very plainly indeed did they hear the 'tick – tick – tick.'

'It is under the table,' muttered François.

Starque seized the cloth and lifted it. Underneath, in the shadow, he saw the black box and heard the ominous whir of clockwork. 'Out!' he roared and sprang to the door. It was locked and from the outside.

Again and again he flung his huge bulk against the door, but the men who pressed round him, whimpering and slobbering in their pitiable fright, crowded about him and gave him no room.

With his strong arms he threw them aside left and right; then leapt at the door, bringing all his weight and strength to bear, and the door crashed open.

Alone of the party the Woman of Gratz preserved her calm. She stood by the table, her foot almost touching the accursed machine, and she felt the faint vibrations of its working. Then Starque caught her up in his arms and through the narrow passage he half led, half carried her, till they reached the street in safety.

The passing pedestrians saw the dishevelled group, and, scenting trouble, gathered about them.

'What was it? What was it?' whispered François, but Starque pushed him aside with a snarl.

A taxi was passing and he called it, and lifting the girl inside, he shouted directions and sprang in after her.

As the taxi whirled away, the bewildered Council looked from one to the other.

They had left the door of the house wide open and in the hall a flickering gas-jet gyrated wildly.

'Get away from here,' said Bartholomew beneath his breath.

'But the papers – the records,' said the other wringing his hands.

Bartholomew thought quickly.

The records were such as could not be left lying about with impunity. For all he knew these madmen had implicated him in their infernal writings. He was not without courage, but it needed all he possessed to re-enter the room where a little machine in a black box ticked mysteriously.

'Where are they?' he demanded.

'On the table,' almost whispered the other. '*Mon Dieu*! what disaster!' The Englishman made up his mind.

He sprang up the three steps into the hall. Two paces brought him to the door, another stride to the table. He heard the 'tick' of the machine, he gave one glance to the table and another to the floor, and was out again in the street before he had taken two long breaths.

François stood waiting, the rest of the men had disappeared.

'The papers! the papers!' cried the Frenchman.

'Gone!' replied Bartholomew between his teeth.

* * *

Less than a hundred yards away another conference was being held.

'Manfred,' said Poiccart suddenly – there had been a lull in the talk – 'shall we need our friend?'

Manfred smiled. 'Meaning the admirable Mr Jessen?'

Poiccart nodded.

'I think so,' said Manfred quietly; 'I am not so sure that the cheap alarm-clock we put in the biscuit box will be a sufficient warning to the Inner Council – here is Leon.'

Gonsalez walked into the room and removed his overcoat deliberately.

Then they saw that the sleeve of his dress coat was torn, and Manfred remarked the stained handkerchief that was lightly bound round one hand.

'Glass,' explained Gonsalez laconically. 'I had to scale a wall.'

'Well?' asked Manfred.

'Very well,' replied the other; 'they bolted like sheep, and I had nothing to do but to walk in and carry away the extremely interesting record of sentences they have passed.'

'What of Bartholomew?'

Gonsalez was mildly amused.

'He was less panicky than the rest – he came back to look for the papers.'

'Will he – ?'

'I think so,' said Leon. 'I noticed he left the black bean behind him in his flight – so I presume we shall see the red.'

'It will simplify matters,' said Manfred gravely.

Chapter 5
The Council of Justice

Lauder Bartholomew knew a man who was farming in Uganda. It was not remarkable that he should suddenly remember his friend's existence and call to mind a three years' old invitation to spend a winter in that part of Africa. Bartholomew had a club. It was euphemistically styled in all the best directories as 'Social, Literary and Dramatic', but knowing men about town called it by a shorter title. To them it was a 'night club'. Poorly as were the literary members catered for, there were certain weeklies, *The Times*, and a collection of complimentary timetables to be obtained for the asking, and Bartholomew sought and found particulars of sailings. He might leave London on the next morning and overtake (via Brindisi and Suez) the German boat that would land him in Uganda in a couple of weeks.

On the whole he thought this course would be wise.

To tell the truth, the Red Hundred was becoming too much of a serious business; he had a feeling that he was suspect, and was more certain that the end of his unlimited financing was in sight. That much he had long since recognized, and had made his plans accordingly. As to the Four Just Men, they would come in with Menshikoff; it would mean only a duplication of treachery. Turning the pages of a Bradshaw, he mentally reviewed his position. He had in hand some seven hundred pounds, and his liabilities were of no account because the necessity for discharging them never occurred to him. Seven hundred pounds – and the red bean, and Menshikoff.

'If they mean business,' he said to himself, 'I can count on three thousand.'

The obvious difficulty was to get into touch with the Four. Time was everything and one could not put an advertisement in the paper: 'If the Four Just Men will communicate with L— B— they will hear of something to their advantage.'

Nor was it expedient to make in the agony columns of the London press even the most guarded reference to Red Beans after what had occurred at the Council Meeting. The matter of the Embassy was simple. Under his breath he cursed the Four Just Men for their unbusinesslike communication. If only they had mentioned or hinted at some rendezvous the thing might have been arranged.

A man in evening dress asked him if he had finished with the Bradshaw. He resigned it ungraciously, and calling a club waiter, ordered a whisky and soda and flung himself into a chair to think out a solution.

The man returned the Bradshaw with a polite apology.

'So sorry to have interrupted, but I've been called abroad at a moment's notice,' he said.

Bartholomew looked up resentfully. This young man's face seemed familiar.

'Haven't I met you somewhere?' he asked.

The stranger shrugged his shoulders.

'One is always meeting and forgetting,' he smiled. 'I thought I knew you, but I cannot quite place you.'

Not only the face but the voice was strangely familiar.

'Not English,' was Bartholomew's mental analysis, 'possibly French, more likely Slav – who the dickens can it be?'

In a way he was glad of the diversion, and found himself engaged in a pleasant discussion on fly fishing.

As the hands of the clock pointed to midnight, the stranger yawned and got up from his chair.

'Going west?' he asked pleasantly.

Bartholomew had no definite plans for spending the next hour, so he assented and the two men left the club together. They strolled across Piccadilly Circus and into Piccadilly, chatting pleasantly.

Through Half Moon Street into Berkeley Square, deserted and silent, the two men sauntered, then the stranger stopped. 'I'm afraid I've taken you out of your way,' he said. 'Not a bit,' replied Bartholomew, and was conventionally amiable. Then they parted, and the ex-captain walked back by the way he had come, picking up again the threads of the problem that had filled his mind in the earlier part of the evening.

Halfway down Half Moon Street was a motor-car, and as he came abreast, a man who stood by the curb – and whom he had mistaken for a waiting chauffeur – barred his further progress.

'Captain Bartholomew?' he asked respectfully.

'That is my name,' said the other in surprise.

'My master wishes to know whether you have decided.'

'What – ?'

'If,' went on his imperturbable examiner, 'if you have decided on the red – here is the car, if you will be pleased to enter.'

'And if I have decided on the black?' he asked with a little hesitation.

'Under the circumstances,' said the man without emotion, 'my master is of opinion that for his greater safety, he must take steps to ensure your neutrality.'

There was no menace in the tone, but an icy matter-of-fact confidence that shocked this hardened adventurer.

In the dim light he saw something in the man's hand – a thin bright something that glittered.

'It shall be red!' he said hoarsely.

The man bowed and opened the door of the car.

* * *

Bartholomew had regained a little of his self-assurance by the time he stood before the men.

He was not unused to masked tribunals. There had been one such since his elevation to the Inner Council.

But these four men were in evening dress, and the stagey setting that had characterized the Red Hundred's Court of Justice was absent. There was no weird adjustment of lights, or rollings of bells, or partings of sombre draperies. None of the cheap trickery of the Inner Council.

The room was evidently a drawing-room, very much like a hundred other drawing-rooms he had seen.

The four men who sat at equal distance before him were sufficiently ordinary in appearance save for their masks. He thought one of them wore a beard, but he was not sure. This man did most of the speaking.

'I understand,' he said smoothly, 'you have chosen the red.'

'You seem to know a great deal about my private affairs,' replied Bartholomew.

'You have chosen the red – again?' said the man.

'Why – again?' demanded the prisoner.

The masked man's eyes shone steadily through the holes in the mask.

'Years ago,' he said quietly, 'there was an officer who betrayed his country and his comrades.'

'That is an old lie.'

'He was in charge of a post at which was stored a great supply of foodstuffs and ammunition,' the mask went on. 'There was a commandant of the enemy who wanted those stores, but had not sufficient men to rush the garrison.'

'An old lie,' repeated Bartholomew sullenly.

'So the commandant hit upon the ingenious plan of offering a bribe. It was a risky thing, and in nine hundred and ninety-nine cases out of a thousand, it would have been a futile business. Indeed, I am sure that I am understating the proportion – but the wily old commandant knew his man.'

There is no necessity to continue,' said Bartholomew.

'No correspondence passed,' Manfred went on; 'our officer was too cunning for that, but it was arranged that the officer's answer should be conveyed thus.'

He opened his hand and Bartholomew saw two beans, one red and the other black, reposing in the palm.

'The black was to be a refusal, the red an acceptance, the terms were to be scratched on the side of the red bean with a needle – and the sum agreed was £1,000.' Bartholomew made no answer.

'Exactly that sum we offer you to place us from time to time in possession of such information as we require concerning the movements of the Red Hundred.'

'If I refuse?'

'You will not refuse,' replied the mask calmly; 'you need the money, and you have even now under consideration a plan for cutting yourself adrift from your friends.'

'You know so much – ' began the other with a shrug.

'I know a great deal. For instance, I know that you contemplate immediate flight – by the way, are you aware that the *Lucus Woerhmann* is in dock at Naples with a leaking boiler?'

Bartholomew started, as well he might, for nobody but himself knew that the *Lucus Woerhmann* was the ship he had hoped to overtake at Suez.

Manfred saw his bewilderment and smiled. 'I do not ask credit for supernatural powers,' he said; 'frankly, it was the merest guesswork, but you must abandon your trip. It is necessary for our greater success that you should remain.'

Bartholomew bit his lips. This scheme did not completely fall in with his plans. He affected a sudden geniality.

'Well, if I must, I must,' he said heartily, 'and since I agree, may I ask whom I have the honour of addressing, and further, since I am now your confidential agent, that I may see the faces of my employers?'

He recognized the contempt in Manfred's laugh.

'You need no introduction to us,' said Manfred coldly, 'and you will understand we do not intend taking you into our confidence. Our agreement is that we share your confidence, not that you shall share ours.'

'I must know something,' said Bartholomew doggedly. 'What am I to do? Where am I to report! How shall I be paid?'

'You will be paid when your work is completed.' Manfred reached out his hand toward a little table that stood within his reach.

Instantly the room was plunged into darkness.

The traitor sprang back, fearing he knew not what.

'Come – do not be afraid,' said a voice.

'What does this mean?' cried Bartholomew, and stepped forward.

He felt the floor beneath him yield and tried to spring backwards, but already he had lost his balance, and with a scream of terror he felt himself falling, falling . . .

* * *

'Here, wake up!'

Somebody was shaking his arm and he was conscious of an icy coldness and a gusty raw wind that buffeted his face.

He shivered and opened his eyes.

First of all he saw an iron camel with a load on its back; then he realized dimly that it was the ornamental support of a garden seat; then he saw a dull grey parapet of grimy stone. He was sitting on a seat on the Thames Embankment, and a policeman was shaking him, not ungently, to wakefulness.

'Come along, sir – this won't do, ye know.'

He staggered to his feet unsteadily. He was wearing a fur coat that was not his. 'How did I come here?' he asked in a dull voice.

The policeman laughed good humouredly.

'Ah, that's more than I can tell you – you weren't here ten minutes ago, that I'll swear.'

Bartholomew put his hand in his pocket and found some money.

'Call me a taxi,' he said shakily and one was found.

He left the policeman perfectly satisfied with the result of his morning's work and drove home to his lodgings. By what extraordinary means had he reached the Embankment? He remembered the Four, he remembered the suddenly darkened room, he remembered falling –

Perhaps he lost consciousness, yet he could not have been injured by his fall. He had a faint recollection of somebody telling him to breathe and of inhaling a sweet sickly vapour – and that was all.

The coat was not his. He thrust his hands into both pockets and found a letter. Did he but know, it was of the peculiar texture that had made the greenish-grey paper of the Four Just Men famous throughout Europe.

The letter was brief and to the point.

For faithful service, you will be rewarded; for treachery, there will be no net to break your fall.

He shivered again. Then his impotence, his helplessness, enraged him, and he swore softly and weakly.

He was ignorant of the locality in which the interview had taken place. On his way thither he had tried in vain to follow the direction the shuttered motor-car had taken.

By what method the Four would convey their instructions he had no idea. He was quite satisfied that they would find a way.

He reached his flat with his head swimming from the effects of the drug they had given him, and flung himself, dressed as he was, upon his bed and slept. He slept well into the afternoon, then rose stiff and irritable. A bath and a change refreshed him, and he walked out to keep an appointment he had made.

On his way he remembered impatiently that there was a call to the Council at five o'clock. It reminded him of his old rehearsal days. Then he recollected that no place had been fixed for the council meeting. He would find the quiet François in Leicester Square, so he turned his steps in that direction.

François, patient, smiling, and as deferential as ever, awaited him. 'The council was held at two o'clock,' he said, 'and I am to tell you that we have decided on two projects.' He looked left and right, with elaborated caution.

'There is at Gravesend – ' he pronounced it 'Gwayvse-end – ' 'a battleship that has put in for stores. It is the *Grondovitch*. It will be fresh in your mind that the captain is the nobleman Svardo – we have no reason to love him.'

'And the second?' asked Bartholomew.

Again François went through the pantomime that had so annoyed his companion before.

'It is no less than the Bank,' he said triumphantly.

Bartholomew was aghast.

'The Bank – the Bank of England! Why, you're mad – you have taken leave of your senses!'

François shrugged his shoulders tolerantly.

'It is the order,' he said; then, abruptly, '*Au revoir*,' he said, and, with his extravagant little bow, was gone.

If Bartholomew's need for cutting himself adrift from the Red Hundred existed before, the necessity was multiplied now a thousand times. Any lingering doubt he might have had, any remote twinge of conscience at the part he was playing, these vanished.

He glanced at his watch, and hurried to his destination.

It was the Red Room of the Hôtel Larboune that he sought.

He found a table and ordered a drink.

The waiter was unusually talkative.

He stood by the solitary table at which Bartholomew sat, and chatted pleasantly and respectfully. This much the other patrons of the establishment noticed idly, and wondered whether it was racing or house property that the two had in common.

The waiter was talking.

' . . . I am inclined to disbelieve the story of the *Grondovitch*, but the Embassy and the commander shall know – when do you leave?'

'Just as soon as I can,' said Bartholomew.

The waiter nodded and flicked some cigarette ash from the table with his napkin.

'And the Woman of Gratz?' he asked.

Bartholomew made a gesture of doubt.

'Why not,' said the waiter, looking thoughtfully out of the window, 'why not take her with you?'

There had been the germ of such a thought in Bartholomew's mind, but he had never given form to it – even to himself.

'She is very beautiful, and, it occurred to me, not altogether indifferent to your attractions – that kind of woman has a penchant for your type, and frankly we would gladly see her out of the way – or dead.'

M. Menshikoff was by no means vindictive, but there was obvious sincerity in his voice when he pronounced the last two words. M. Menshikoff had been right-hand man of the Grand Master of the Secret Police for too many years to feel any qualms at the project of removing an enemy to the system.

'I thought we had her once,' he said meditatively; 'they would have flogged her in the fortress of St Peter and Paul, but I stopped them. She was grateful I think, and almost human . . . but it passed off.'

Bartholomew paid for his drink, and ostentatiously tipped the obsequious man before him. He remembered as he did so that Menshikoff was reputedly a millionaire.

'Your change, m'sieur,' said Menshikoff gravely, and he handed back a few jingling coppers and two tightly folded banknotes for a hundred pounds. He was a believer in the principle of 'pay as you go'. Bartholomew pocketed the money carelessly.

'Good day,' he said loudly.

'*Au revoir, m'sieur, et bon voyage,*' said the waiter.

Chapter 6
Princess Revolutionary

The Woman of Gratz was very human. But to Bartholomew she seemed a thing of ice, passionless, just a beautiful woman who sat stiffly in a straight-backed chair, regarding him with calm, questioning eyes. They were in her flat in Bloomsbury on the evening of the day following his interview with Menshikoff. Her coolness chilled him, and strangled the very passion of his speech, and what he said came haltingly, and sounded lame and unconvincing.

'But why?' that was all she asked. Thrice he had paused appealingly, hoping for encouragement, but her answer had been the same.

He spoke incoherently, wildly. The fear of the Four on the one hand and the dread of the Reds on the other, were getting on his nerves.

He saw a chance of escape from both, freedom from the four-walled control of these organizations, and before him the wide expanse of a trackless wilderness, where the vengeance of neither could follow.

Eden in sight – he pleaded for an Eve.

The very thought of the freedom ahead overcame the depression her coldness laid upon him.

'Maria – don't you see? You are wasting your life doing this man's work – this assassin's work. You were made for love and for me!' He caught her hand and she did not withdraw it, but the palm he pressed was unresponsive and the curious searching eyes did not leave his face.

'But why?' she asked again. 'And how? I do not love you, I shall never love any man – and there is the work for you and the work for me. There is the cause and your oath. Your comrades – '

He started up and flung away her hand. For a moment he stood over her, glowering down at her upturned face.

'Work! – Comrades!' he grated with a laugh. 'D'ye think I'm going to risk my precious neck any further?'

He did not hear the door open softly, nor the footfall of the two men who entered.

'Are you blind as well as mad?' he went on brutally. 'Don't you see that the thing is finished? The Four Just Men have us all in the hollow of their hands! They've got us like that!' He snapped his fingers contemptuously. 'They know everything – even to the attempt that is to be made on the Prince of the Escorials! Ha! that startles you – yet it is true, every word I say – they know.'

'If it is true,' she said slowly, 'there has been a traitor.'

He waved his hand carelessly, admitting and dismissing the possibility.

'There are traitors always – when the pay for treachery is good,' he said easily; 'but traitor or no traitor, London is too hot for you and me.'

'For you,' corrected the girl.

'And for you,' he said savagely; he snatched up her hand again. 'You've got to come – do you hear – you beautiful snow woman – you've got to come with me!'

He drew her to him, but a hand grasped his arm, and he turned to meet the face of Starque, livid and puckered, and creased with silent anger.

Starque was prepared for the knife or for the pistol, but not for the blow that caught him full in the face and sent him staggering back to the wall.

He recovered himself quickly, and motioned to François, who turned and locked the door.

'Stand away from that door!'

'Wait!'

Starque, breathing quickly, wiped the blood from his face with the back of his hand.

'Wait,' he said in his guttural tone; 'before you go there is a matter to be settled.'

'At any time, in any place,' said the Englishman.

'It is not the blow,' breathed Starque, 'that is nothing; it is the matter of the Inner Council – traitor!'

He thrust out his chin as he hissed the last word.

Bartholomew had very little time to decide upon his course of action. He was unarmed; but he knew instinctively that there would be no shooting. It was the knife he had to fear and he grasped the back of a chair. If he could keep them at a distance he might reach the door and get safely away. He cursed his folly that he had delayed making the coup that would have so effectively laid Starque by the heels.

'You have betrayed us to the Four Just Men – but that we might never have known, for the Four have no servants to talk. But you sold us to the Embassy – and that was your undoing.' He had recovered his calm.

'We sent you a message telling you of our intention to destroy the Bank of England. The Bank was warned – by the Four. We told you of the attempt to be made on the *Grondovitch* – the captain was warned by the Embassy – you are doubly convicted. No such attempts were ever contemplated. They were invented for your particular benefit, and you fell into the trap.'

Bartholomew took a fresh grip of the chair. He realized vaguely that he was face to face with death, and for one second he was seized with a wild panic.

'Last night,' Starque went on deliberately, 'the Council met secretly, and your name was read from the list.'

The Englishman's mouth went dry.

'And the Council said with one voice . . .' Starque paused to look at the Woman of Gratz. Imperturbable she stood with folded hands, neither approving nor dissenting. Momentarily Bartholomew's eyes too sought her face – but he saw neither pity nor condemnation. It was the face of Fate, inexorable, unreasoning, inevitable.

'Death was the sentence,' said Starque in so soft a voice that the man facing him could scarcely hear him. 'Death . . .'

With a lightning motion he raised his hand and threw the knife . . . 'Damn you . . .' whimpered the stricken man, and his helpless hands groped at his chest . . . then he slid to his knees and François struck precisely . . .

Again Starque looked at the woman.

'It is the law,' he stammered, but she made no reply.

Only her eyes sought the huddled figure on the floor and her lips twitched.

'We must get away from here,' whispered Starque.

He was shaking a little, for this was new work for him. The forces of jealousy and fear for his personal safety had caused him to take upon himself the office that on other occasions he left to lesser men.

'Who lives in the opposite flat?'

He had peeped through the door.

'A student – a chemist,' she replied in her calm, level tone.

Starque flushed, for her voice sounded almost strident coming after the whispered conference between his companion and himself.

'Softly, softly,' he urged.

He stepped gingerly back to where the body was lying, made a circuit about it, and pulled down the blind. He could not have explained the instinct that made him do this. Then he came back to the door and gently turned the handle, beckoning the others. It seemed to him that the handle turned itself, or that somebody on the other side was turning at the same time.

That this was so he discovered, for the door suddenly jerked open, sending him staggering backward, and a man stood on the threshold.

With the drawn blind, the room was in semi-darkness, and the intruder, standing motionless in the door-way, could see nothing but the shadowy figures of the inmates.

As he waited he was joined by three others, and he spoke rapidly in a language that Starque, himself no mean linguist, could not understand. One of his companions opened the door of the student's room and brought out something that he handed to the watcher on the threshold.

Then the man entered the room alone and closed the door behind him, not quite close, for he had trailed what looked like a thick cord behind him and this prevented the shutting of the door.

Starque found his voice.

'What do you want?' he asked, quietly.

'I want Bartholomew, who came into this room half an hour ago,' replied the intruder.

'He has left,' said Starque, and in the darkness he felt at his feet for the dead man – he needed the knife.

'That is a lie,' said the stranger coolly; 'neither he nor you, Rudolph Starque, nor the Woman of Gratz, nor the murderer François has left.'

'Monsieur knows too much,' said Starque evenly, and lurched forward, swinging his knife.

'Keep your distance,' warned the stranger, and at that moment Starque and the silent François sprang forward and struck . . .

The exquisite agony of the shock that met them paralysed them for the moment. The sprayed threads of the 'live' wire the man held before him like a shield jerked the knife from Starque's hands, and he heard François groan as he fell.

'You are foolish,' said the voice again, 'and you, madame, do not move, I beg – tell me what has become of Bartholomew.'

A silence, then: 'He is dead,' said the Woman of Gratz.

She heard the man move.

'He was a traitor – so we killed him,' she continued calmly enough. 'What will you do – you, who stand as a self-constituted judge?'

He made no reply, and she heard the soft rustle of his fingers on the wall.

'You are seeking the light – as we all seek it,' she said, unmoved, and she switched on the light.

He saw her standing near the body of the man she had lured to his death, scornful, defiant, and strangely aloof from the sordidness of the tragedy she had all but instigated.

She saw a tanned man of thirty-five, with deep, grave eyes, a broad forehead, and a trim, pointed beard. A man of inches, with strength in every line of his fine figure, and strength in every feature of his face.

She stared at him insolently, uncaring, but before the mastery of his eyes, she lowered her lids.

It seemed the other actors in the drama were so inconsiderable as to be unworthy of notice. The dead man in his grotesque posture, the unconscious murderer at his feet, and Starque, dazed and stunned, crouching by the wall.

'Here is the light you want,' she went on, 'not so easily do we of the Red Hundred illuminate the gloom of despair and oppression – '

'Spare me your speech-making,' said Manfred coldly, and the scorn in his voice struck her like the lash of a whip. For the first time the colour came to her face and her eyes lit with anger.

'You have bad counsellors,' Manfred went on, 'you, who talk of autocrats and corrupt kingship – what are you but a puppet living on flattery? It is your whim that you should be regarded as a conspirator – a Corday. And when you are acclaimed Princess Revolutionary, it is satisfactory to your vanity – more satisfactory than your title to be hailed Princess Beautiful.'

He chose his words nicely.

'Yet men – such men as these,' he indicated Starque, 'think only of the Princess Beautiful – not the lady of the Inspiring Platitudes; not the frail, heroic Patriot of the Flaming Words, but the warm flesh and blood woman, lovable and adorable.'

He spoke in German, and there were finer shades of meaning in his speech than can be exactly or literally translated. He spoke of a purpose, evenly and without emotion. He intended to wound, and wound deeply, and he knew he had succeeded.

He saw the rapid rise and fall of her bosom as she strove to regain control of herself, and he saw, too, the blood on her lips where her sharp white teeth bit.

'I shall know you again,' she said with an intensity of passion that made her voice tremble. 'I shall look for you and find you, and be it the Princess Revolutionary or the Princess Beautiful who brings about your punishment, be sure I shall strike hard.'

He bowed.

'That is as it may be,' he said calmly; 'for the moment you are powerless. If I willed it you would be powerless forever – for the moment it is my wish that you should go.'

He stepped aside and opened the door.

The magnetism in his eyes drew her forward.

'There is your road,' he said when she hesitated. She was helpless; the humiliation was maddening.

'My friends – ' she began, as she hesitated on the threshold.

'Your friends will meet the fate that one day awaits you,' he said calmly.

White with passion, she turned on him.

'You! – threaten me! a brave man indeed to threaten a woman!'

She could have bitten her tongue at the slip she made. She as a woman had appealed to him as a man! This was the greatest humiliation of all.

There is your road,' he said again, courteously but uncompromisingly.

She was scarcely a foot from him, and she turned and faced him, her lips parted and the black devil of hate in her eyes.

'One day – one day,' she gasped, 'I will repay you!' Then she turned quickly and disappeared through the door, and Manfred waited until her footsteps had died away before he stooped to the half-conscious Starque and jerked him to his feet.

Chapter 7
The Government and Mr Jessen

In recording the events that followed the reappearance of the Four Just Men, I have confined myself to those which I know to have been the direct outcome of the Red Hundred propaganda and the counter-activity of the Four Just Men.

Thus I make no reference to the explosion at Woolwich Arsenal, which was credited to the Red Hundred, knowing, as I do, that the calamity was due to the carelessness of a workman. Nor to the blowing up of the main in Oxford Street, which was a much more simple explanation than the fantastic theories of the *Megaphone* would have you imagine. This was not the first time that a fused wire and a leaking gas main brought about the upheaval of a public thoroughfare, and the elaborate plot with which organized anarchy was credited was without existence.

I think the most conscientiously accurate history of the Red Hundred movement is that set forth in the series of ten articles contributed to the *Morning Leader* by Harold Ashton under the title of 'Forty Days of Terrorism', and, whilst I think the author frequently fails from lack of sympathy for the Four Just Men to thoroughly appreciate the single-mindedness of this extraordinary band of men, yet I shall always regard 'Forty Days of Terrorism' as being the standard history of the movement, and its failure.

On one point in the history alone I find myself in opposition to Mr Ashton, and that is the exact connection between the discovery of the Carlby Mansion Tragedy, and the extraordinary return of Mr Jessen of 37 Presley Street.

It is perhaps indiscreet of me to refer at so early a stage to this return of Jessen's, because whilst taking exception to the theories put forward in 'Forty Days of Terrorism', I am not prepared to go into the evidence on which I base my theories.

The popular story is that one morning Mr Jessen walked out of his house and demanded from the astonished milkman why he had omitted to leave his morning supply. Remembering that the disappearance of 'Long' – perhaps it would be less confusing to call him the name by which he was known in Presley Street – had created an extraordinary sensation; that pictures of his house and the interior of his house had appeared in all the newspapers; that the newspaper crime experts had published columns upon columns of speculative theories, and that 37 Presley Street had for some weeks been the Mecca of the morbid-minded, who, standing outside, stared the unpretentious façade out of countenance for hours on end; you may imagine that the milkman legend had the exact journalistic touch that would appeal to a public whose minds had been trained by generations of magazine-story writers to just such *dénouement* as this.

The truth is that Mr Long, upon coming to life, went immediately to the Home Office and told his story to the Under Secretary. He did not drive up in a taxi, nor was he lifted out in a state of exhaustion as one newspaper had erroneously had it, but he arrived on the top of a motor omnibus which passed the door, and was ushered into the Presence almost at once. When Mr Long had told his story he was taken to the Home Secretary himself, and the chief commissioner was sent for, and came hurriedly from Scotland Yard, accompanied by Superintendent Falmouth. All this is made clear in Mr Ashton's book.

'For some extraordinary reason,' I quote the same authority, 'Long, or Jessen, seems by means of documents in his possession to have explained to the satisfaction of the Home Secretary and the Police Authorities his own position in the matter, and moreover to have inspired the right hon. gentleman with these mysterious documents, that Mr Ridgeway, so far from accepting the resignation that Jessen placed in his hands, reinstated him in his position.'

As to how two of these documents came to Jessen or to the Four Just Men, Mr Ashton is very wisely silent, not attempting to solve a mystery which puzzled both the Quai d'Orsay and Petrograd.

For these two official forms, signed in the one case by the French President and in the other with the sprawling signature of Czar Nicholas, were supposed to be incorporated with other official memoranda in well-guarded national archives.

It was subsequent to Mr Jessen's visit to the Home Office that the discovery of the Garlby Mansions Tragedy was made, and I cannot do better than quote *The Times*, since that journal, jealous of the appearance in its columns of any news of a sensational character, reduced the intelligence to its most constricted limits. Perhaps the

Megaphone account might make better reading, but the space at my disposal will not allow of the inclusion in this book of the thirty-three columns of reading matter, headlines, portraits, and diagrammatic illustrations with which that enterprising journal served up particulars of the grisly horror to its readers. Thus, *The Times* –

Shortly after one o'clock yesterday afternoon and in consequence of information received, Superintendent Falmouth, of the Criminal Investigation Department, accompanied by Detective-Sergeants Boyle and Lawley, effected an entrance into No. 69, Carlby Mansions, occupied by the Countess Slienvitch, a young Russian lady of independent means. Lying on the floor were the bodies of three men who have since been identified as –

Lauder Bartholomew, aged 33, late of the Koondorp Mounted Rifles;

Rudolph Starque, aged 40, believed to be an Austrian and a prominent revolutionary propagandist;

Henri Delaye François, aged 36, a Frenchman, also believed to have been engaged in propaganda work.

The cause of death in the case of Bartholomew seems to be evident, but with the other two men some doubt exists, and the police, who preserve an attitude of rigid reticence, will await the medical examination before making any statement.

One unusual feature of the case is understood to be contained in a letter found in the room accepting, on behalf of an organization known as the Four Just Men, full responsibility for the killing of the two foreigners, and another, writes a correspondent, is the extraordinary structural damage to the room itself. The tenant, the Countess Slienvitch, had not, up to a late hour last night, been traced.

Superintendent Falmouth, standing in the centre of the room, from which most traces of the tragedy had been removed, was mainly concerned with the 'structural damage' that *The Times* so lightly passed over.

At his feet yawned a great square hole, and beneath, in the empty flat below, was a heap of plaster and laths, and the debris of destruction.

'The curious thing is, and it shows how thorough these men are,' explained the superintendent to his companion, 'that the first thing we found when we got there was a twenty-pound note pinned to the wall with a brief note in pencil saying that this was to pay the owner of the property for the damage.'

It may be added that by the express desire of the young man at his side he dispensed with all ceremony of speech.

Once or twice in speaking, he found himself on the verge of saying, 'Your Highness', but the young man was so kindly, and so quickly put the detective at his ease, that he overcame the feeling of annoyance that the arrival of the distinguished visitor with the letter from the commissioner had caused him, and became amiable.

'Of course, I have an interest in all this,' said the young man quietly; 'these people, for some reason, have decided I am not fit to encumber the earth – '

'What have you done to the Red Hundred, sir?'

The young man laughed.

'Nothing. On the contrary,' he added with a whimsical smile, 'I have helped them.'

The detective remembered that this hereditary Prince of the Escorial bore a reputation for eccentricity.

With a suddenness which was confusing, the Prince turned with a smile on his lips.

'You are thinking of my dreadful reputation?'

'No, no!' disclaimed the embarrassed Mr Falmouth. 'I – '

'Oh, yes – I've done lots of things,' said the other with a little laugh; 'it's in the blood – my illustrious cousin – '

'I assure your Highness,' said Falmouth impressively, 'my reflections were not – er – reflections on yourself – there is a story that you have dabbled in socialism – but that, of course – '

'Is perfectly true,' concluded the Prince calmly. He turned his attention to the hole in the floor.

'Have you any theory?' he asked.

The detective nodded.

It's more than a theory – it's knowledge – you see we've seen Jessen, and the threads of the story are all in hand.'

'What will you do?'

'Nothing,' said the detective stolidly; 'hush up the inquest until we can lay the Four Just Men by the heels.'

'And the manner of killing?'

'That must be kept quiet,' replied Falmouth emphatically. This conversation may furnish a clue as to the unprecedented conduct of the police at the subsequent inquest.

In the little coroner's court there was accommodation for three pressmen and some fifty of the general public. Without desiring in any way to cast suspicion upon the cleanest police force in the world, I can only state that the jury were remarkably well disciplined, that the general public found the body of the court so densely packed with broad-shouldered men that they were unable to obtain admission. As to the press, the confidential circular had done its work, and the three shining lights of journalism that occupied the reporters' desk were careful to carry out instructions.

The proceedings lasted a very short time, a verdict, ' . . . some person or persons unknown', was recorded, and another London mystery was added (I quote from the *Evening News*) to the already alarming and formidable list of unpunished crimes.

Charles Garrett was one of the three journalists admitted to the inquest, and after it was all over he confronted Falmouth.

'Look here, Falmouth,' he said pugnaciously, 'what's the racket?'

Falmouth, having reason to know, and to an extent stand in awe of, the little man, waggled his head darkly.

'Oh, rot!' said Charles rudely, 'don't be so disgustingly mysterious – why aren't we allowed to say these chaps died – ?'

'Have you seen Jessen?' asked the detective.

'I have,' said Charles bitterly, 'and after what I've done for that man; after I've put his big feet on the rungs of culture – '

'Wouldn't he speak?' asked Falmouth innocently.

'He was as close,' said Charles sadly, 'as the inside washer of a vacuum pump.'

'H'm!' the detective was considering. Sooner or later the connection must occur to Charles, and he was the only man who would be likely to surprise Jessen's secret. Better that the journalist should know now.

'If I were you,' said Falmouth quietly, 'I shouldn't worry Jessen; you know what he is, and in what capacity he serves the Government. Come along with me.'

He did not speak a word in reply to the questions Charles put until they passed through the showy portals of Carlby Mansions and a lift had deposited them at the door of the flat.

Falmouth opened the door with a key, and Charles went into the flat at his heels.

He saw the hole in the floor.

'This wasn't mentioned at the inquest,' he said; 'but what's this to do with Jessen?'

He looked up at the detective in perplexity, then a light broke upon him and he whistled.

'Well, I'm – ' he said, then he added softly – 'But what does the Government say to this?'

'The Government,' said Falmouth in his best official manner, smoothing the nap of his hat the while – 'the Government regard the circumstances as unusual, but they have accepted the situation with great philosophy.'

* * *

That night Mr Long (or Jessen) reappeared at the Guild as though nothing whatever had happened, and addressed his audience for half an hour on the subject of 'Do burglars make good caretakers?'

Chapter 8
Two incidents in the fight

From what secret place in the metropolis the Woman of Gratz reorganized her forces we shall never know; whence came her strength of purpose and her unbounded energy we can guess. With Starque's death she became virtually and actually the leader of the Red Hundred, and from every corner of Europe came reinforcements of men and money to strengthen her hand and to re-establish the shaking prestige of the most powerful association that Anarchism had ever known.

Great Britain had ever been immune from the active operations of the anarchist. It had been the sanctuary of the revolutionary for centuries, and Anarchism had hesitated to jeopardize the security of refugees by carrying on its propaganda on British soil. That the extremists of the movement had chafed under the restriction is well known, and when the Woman of Gratz openly declared war on England, she was acclaimed enthusiastically.

Then followed perhaps the most extraordinary duels that the world had ever seen. Two powerful bodies, both outside the pale of the law, fought rapidly, mercilessly, asking no quarter and giving none. And the eerie thing about it all was, that no man saw the agents of either of the combatants. It was as though two spirit forces were engaged in some titanic combat. The police were almost helpless. The fight against the Red Hundred was carried on, almost single-handedly, by the Four Just Men, or, to give them the title with which they signed their famous proclamation, 'The Council of Justice'.

There were occasions when the Council delegated its work to the police, as for instance when Scotland Yard received intimation of the attempt that was to be made on the House of Commons. But mainly they fought without assistance.

Who can remember without a thrill of horror the blood-red posters, marked with the triangle of the Red Hundred, which appeared by magic one night on all the prominent hoardings of London, announcing the coming destruction of London.

'Tomorrow,' ran the poster, 'from two airships controlled by our brethren, we will lay in ashes this hive of plutocracy and corruption . . . '

There were other and more flowery phrases in the edict.

'I underestimated her power,' confessed Manfred, and the three men who were with him in the Lewisham house looked grave.

This house in Lewisham was charmingly suburban, and had the prosperous appearance that the home of a bank manager usually bears. Years ago Manfred had purchased the house, and the old lady who acted as caretaker in his prolonged absences and cook and maid-of-all-works during his visits, satisfied the neighbours, as she satisfied herself, with the hint that Manfred was a foreign 'gentleman' in the 'music line'.

Though the information is of no consequence so far as the story goes, it might be said that Manfred had houses in other parts of London, in Paris, Berlin, Petrograd, Madrid, Vienna, and at Oyster Bay; in addition to which, I have reason to believe that the lease of 'Laing Kloof', that charming residence at Claremont, in Cape Colony, is also held by him.

The young man who called himself Courlander broke the silence that Manfred's speech caused.

'This airship – what do you intend doing?'

The conversation took place the night before the bills had been posted. A poster, wet from the press, had come to Manfred through one of his mysterious agencies.

Manfred smiled. 'It wasn't the thought of the balloons that induced the comment,' he said. 'As to these, I could destroy them tonight, or rather Leon could.'

'We have a fancy for a theatrical display,' said Leon. The book he was reading rested on his knees, and he held his pince-nez poised between his fingers.

He spoke half seriously, half jestingly; his thin scholarly face was a trifle paler, and there was more grey at his temples than in the days when he and Manfred and Poiccart and the man Thery had executed the cabinet minister. But the old fire still flamed in his eyes – that look of eager analysis that swept the face of every man he met until it seemed that every virtue, every weakness, every passion, that went to the moulding of that face had been valued and weighed and catalogued for future reference.

'The balloons are nothing,' Manfred went on. 'London will get a little panicky when it sees them overhead, and if, by chance, one of the bombs explodes in the street there might be damage done; mainly I am concerned with the knowledge that the continental party is sending fresh supplies to England.'

'Money?'

'The Pausique bomb,' said Manfred, 'a deadly form of explosive. They could never have been prepared here in England; as to the balloons, you shall see our new destroyer!'

* * *

The verger rather thought the gallery would be closed for the day. The Commissioner of Police had issued orders that the streets were to be cleared, and citizens had been warned to remain indoors until the danger was passed.

The verger, too, eyed the big box that Manfred carried, dubiously. Then Gonsalez showed him the permit, signed by the dean, that gave the party permission to photograph, and the 'camera' was passed.

The verger was a nervous man with wife and children living in Balham.

'Will you gentlemen be long?' he asked anxiously.

'About two hours,' said Manfred.

The verger groaned in spirit.

'But you needn't come up with us; we shall find our way out,' he said.

They left the verger at the foot of the winding stairway, by no means satisfied in his mind as to the proper course of action. From the gallery of St Paul's Cathedral, on a clear day, one may view a panorama like which there is nothing in the world. It was such a day as this, and London took on a new glory in the bright spring sunlight. The streets below were strangely deserted; here and there were little red groups of soldiers.

'Marksmen,' said Poiccart; 'your English soldier shoots rather well, does he not?'

Manfred nodded, and Courlander, looking a little puzzled, asked: 'Why have they not taken position in – such a place as this, for instance?'

'Three hundred feet one way or the other makes little difference,' explained Gonsalez. 'I should imagine they have all kinds of cumbersome apparatus for getting the range which would be impracticable in this restricted position – ah!'

He pointed southward.

High in the air appeared two tiny objects. Through his glasses Manfred made out their character.

'Cylinder shaped, ot course,' he muttered, 'on the Zeppelin plan, with the usual foolish motor and propellers; the wind's with them.'

They stood watching in silence. Then Gonsalez, sweeping the horizon with his binoculars, pointed to the Monument, from the cage of which came a sudden flash and a flicker of light.

'The military people have seen it and are sending the warning round. Aren't they in telegraphic communication?'

The flashes ceased for a little while, then recommenced with greater vigour than before.

Gonsalez spelt out the words.

'Over Chislehurst, heading for London at the rate of twenty miles an hour,' he read, and Manfred slid back a panel of the polished wooden box and surveyed the contents approvingly.

'If I know the Red Hundred,' said Courlander, 'there will first be a parade – a little cat-and-mouse play.'

Gonsalez smiled grimly.

'They will be sorry,' he said simply. He saw Courlander's eyes wandering to the box with a look in which doubt and amusement were blended.

'That was George's idea,' said Gonsalez regretfully; 'I almost grudge him that. George has had them for years. He foresaw the possibility.'

'This?' Courlander's hand waved inquiringly to where the two airships, growing larger every minute, sailed serenely in the sky.

'Oh, no,' said Leon; 'wars and things,' he added vaguely. 'George has the makings of a patriot – sentiment is his one failing.'

Manfred's amusement was checked by the silent Poiccart.

'In what order?' he asked abruptly.

'First St Paul's – ' began Manfred.

'Here!' said Courlander.

'Here,' smiled Manfred – 'I won't insult you by asking you if you're afraid – then the Tower, then the Mint, after that the National Gallery, and *en route* any particular public building that takes their fancy.'

He watched the nearing airships. They were so close now that the men in the skeleton car could be seen and the thud of the engines plainly heard.

'They are dropping a little,' reported Poiccart.

'So much the better,' said Manfred, and slipped on to his right hand a leathern gauntlet.

'Look!'

From the car of one of the airships, a small round object – absurdly small it seemed – fell straight as a plummet into the tangle of roofs and gables below. A second's pause, then, with a crash like thunder, a warehouse on the south side of the river burst into flames, shivered and collapsed like a house of cards.

'They have stopped,' said Poiccart.

The propellers had ceased to revolve and the airships caught by the wind swung slowly round.

'Idle curiosity has destroyed many a wary conspirator,' moralized Manfred, and slipped his gloved hand into the box. Twice he did this and each time he drew forth a bird.

Such a bird as few men see in these days, but which, in other times, the chivalry of England regarded with the pride and admiration that a later generation reserves for its racehorses.

'Falconry,' said Manfred, as he deftly slipped the hoods from the great hawks' heads, 'is a decaying sport – these have been well trained – but not for the snaring of pigeons'or pheasants or fowl – you shall see.'

As he slipped the falcons, Poiccart spoke. 'They are coming.'

'Good,' said Manfred, and watching the whirling death he had loosened.

For a moment they circled aimlessly, then with one accord they soared upward with one clean sweep of wing.

Straight for the two airships they made.

'They are over the river, I trust,' said Manfred calmly. 'Did you notice the steel spurs . . . ?'

High over the balloons the two hawks poised, then, as though each had singled out its enemy, they dropped like stones . . .

At that distance one could not hear the sibilant swish of slashed silk or the whistle of escaping gas. Only suddenly one of the balloons swayed and listed, and there appeared in its rigid side a great dent; then it fell.

It fell and no noise but one faint cry attended its falling.

'One,' said Manfred grimly, 'and in the river!'

The collapse of the second was not so rapid. It too, sagged across its broad back and rolled so that the car swayed wildly.

They could see the men who formed its crew holding on to the cordage, but all the time the airship was beating toward them.

They saw one of the crew release ballast and the balloon rose higher, then the engine stopped and the wind took charge of the great gas bag, and it drifted slowly back riverward.

Manfred made no sign; if he sighed a sigh of relief, he did so inwardly.

Then, as the airship, all crumpled and rolling, drifted backward, there was a bang: which echoed and reverberated through the London streets. Something went whining through the air, and over the airship appeared suddenly a puffy ball of white smoke, for the fraction of a second nothing happened.

Then a white jagged splash of flame sprang from the balloon and an ear-splitting explosion rent the air . . .

'Field artillery,' said Manfred. 'I saw a battery on the Embankment. I hope they haven't killed my bird.'

*   *   *

It is difficult to single out for special description the events of the ceaseless campaign that raged through London during that forty days. The episode of the airships was certainly one of the most picturesque, but by no means as far-reaching in its effects as others. In this history I have tried to avoid any bald categorical account of the incidents of the fight.

Since the days of the Fenian scare, London had never lived under the terror that the Red Hundred inspired. Never a day passed but preparations for some outrage were discovered, the most appalling of which was the attempt on the Tube Railway. If I refer to them as 'attempts', and if the repetition of that wearies the reader, it is because, thanks to the extraordinary vigilance of the Council of Justice, they were no more. Once only did the Red Hundred succeed, and the story of that success sent a thrill of horror through the civilized world.

It was three days after the events chronicled above that the Home Secretary called a meeting of the heads of the police.

'This sort of thing cannot go on,' he said petulantly. 'Here we have admittedly the finest police force in the world, and we must needs be under obligation to men for whom warrants exist on a charge of murder! "

The chief commissioner was sufficiently harassed, and was inclined to resent the criticism in the minister's voice.

'We've done everything that can be done, sir,' he said shortly; 'if you think my resignation would help you out of the difficulty – '

'Now for heaven's sake, don't be a fool,' pleaded the Home Secretary, in his best unparliamentary manner. 'Cannot you see – '

'I can see that no harm has been done so far,' said the commissioner doggedly; then he burst forth: 'Look here, sir! our people have very often to employ characters a jolly sight worse than the Four Just Men – if we don't employ them we exploit them. Mean little sneak-thieves, "narks" they call 'em, old lags, burglars – and once or twice something worse. We are here to protect the public; so long as the public is being protected, nobody can kick – '

'But it is not you who are protecting the public – you get your information – '

'From the Council of Justice, that is so; but where it comes from doesn't matter. Now, listen to me, sir.'

He was very earnest and emphasized his remarks with little raps on the desk.

'Get the Prince of the Escorial out of the country,' he said seriously. 'I've got information that the Reds are after his blood. No, I haven't been warned by the Just Men, that's the queer part about it. I've got it straight from a man who's selling me information. I shall see him tonight if they haven't butchered him.'

'But the Prince is our guest.'

'He's been here too long,' said the practical and unsentimental commissioner; 'let him go back to Spain – he's to be married in a month; let him go home and buy his trousseau or whatever he buys.'

'Is that a confession that you cannot safeguard him? "

The commissioner looked vexed. 'I could safeguard a child of six or a staid gentleman of sixty, but I cannot be responsible for a young man who insists on seeing London without a guide, who takes solitary motorcar drives, and refuses to give us any information beforehand as to his plans for the day – or if he does, breaks them!'

The minister was pacing the apartment with his head bent in thought.

'As to the Prince of the Escorial,' he said presently, 'advice has already been conveyed to His Highness – from the highest quarter – to make his departure at an early date. Tonight, indeed, is his last night in London.'

The Commissioner of Police made an extravagant demonstration of relief.

'He's going to the Auditorium tonight,' he said, rising. He spoke a little pityingly, and, indeed, the Auditorium, although a very first-class music hall, had a slight reputation. 'I shall have a dozen men in the house and we'll have his motor-car at the stage door at the end of the show.'

*   *   *

That night His Highness arrived promptly at eight o'clock and stood chatting pleasantly with the bareheaded manager in the vestibule. Then he went alone to his box and sat down in the shadow of the red velvet curtain.

Punctually at eight there arrived two other gentlemen, also in evening dress. Antonio Selleni was one and Karl Ollmanns was the other. They were both young men, and before they left the motor-car they completed their arrangement.

'You will occupy the box on the opposite side, but I will endeavour to enter the box. If I succeed – it will be finished. The knife is best;' there was pride in the Italian's tone. 'If I cannot reach him the honour will be yours.' He had the stilted manner of the young Latin.

The other man grunted. He replied in halting French. 'Once I shot an egg from between fingers – so,' he said.

They made their entry separately.

In the manager's office, Superintendent Falmouth relieved the tedium of waiting by reading the advertisements in an evening newspaper.

To him came the manager with a message that under no circumstances was His Highness in Box A to be disturbed until the conclusion of the performance.

In the meantime Signor Selleni made a cautious way to Box A. He found the road clear, turned the handle softly, and stepped quickly into the dark interior of the box.

Twenty minutes later Falmouth stood at the back of the dress circle issuing instructions to a subordinate.

'Have a couple of men at the stage door – my God!'

Over the soft music, above the hum of voices, a shot rang out and a woman screamed. From the box opposite the Prince's a thin swirl of smoke floated.

Karl Ollmanns, tired of waiting, had fired at the motionless figure sitting in the shadow of the curtain. Then he walked calmly out of the box into the arms of two breathless detectives.

'A doctor!' shouted Falmouth as he ran. The door of the Box A was locked, but he broke it open.

A man lay on the floor of the box very still and strangely stiff.

'Why, what – !' began the detective, for the dead man was bound hand and foot.

There was already a crowd at the door of the box, and he heard an authoritative voice demand admittance.

He looked over his shoulder to meet the eye of the commissioner.

'They've killed him, sir,' he said bitterly.

'Whom?' asked the commissioner in perplexity.

'His Highness.'

'His Highness!' The commissioner's eyebrows rose in genuine astonishment. 'Why, the Prince left Charing Cross for the Continent half an hour ago!'

The detective gasped.

'Then who in the name of fate is this?'

It was M. Menshikoff, who had come in with the commissioner, who answered.

He looked at the face of the stricken man.

'Antonio Selleni, an anarchist of Milan,' he reported.

Chapter 9
Don Emanuel builds a house

Carlos Ferdinand Bourbon, Prince of the Escorial, Duke of Buda-Gratz, and heir to three thrones, was to be married, and his many august cousins scattered throughout Europe had a sense of heartfelt relief.

A Prince with admittedly advanced views, an idealist, with Utopian schemes for the regeneration of mankind, and, coming down to the mundane practical side of life, a reckless motorcar driver, an outrageously daring horseman, and possessed of the indifference to public opinion which is equally the equipment of your fool and your truly great man, his marriage was looked forward to throughout the courts of Europe in the light of an international achievement.

Said his Imperial Majesty of Central Europe to the grizzled chancellor: 'Te Deums – you understand, von Hedlitz? In every church.'

'It is a great relief,' said the chancellor, wagging his head thoughtfully.

'Relief!' the Emperor stretched himself as though the relief were physical, 'that young man owes me two years of life. You heard of the London essay?'

The chancellor had heard – indeed, he had heard three or four times – but he was a polite chancellor and listened attentively. His Majesty had the true story-telling faculty, and elaborated the introduction.

' . . . if I am to believe his Highness, he was sitting quietly in his box when the Italian entered. He saw the knife in his hand and half rose to grapple with the intruder. Suddenly, from nowhere in particular, sprang three men, who had the assassin on the floor bound and gagged. You would have thought our Carlos Ferdinand would have made an outcry! But not he! He sat stock still, dividing his attention between the stage and the prostrate man and the leader of this mysterious band of rescuers.'

'The Four Just Men!' put in the chancellor.

'Three, so far as I can gather,' corrected the imperial story-teller. 'Well, it would appear that this leader, in quite a logical calm, matter-of-fact way, suggested that the prince should leave quietly; that his motor-car was at the stage door, that a saloon had been reserved at Charing Cross, a cabin at Dover, and a special train at Calais.'

His Majesty had a trick of rubbing his knee when anything amused him, and this he did now.

'Carl obeyed like a child – which seems the remarkably strange point about the whole proceedings – the captured anarchist was trussed and bound and sat on the chair, and left to his own unpleasant thoughts.'

'And killed,' said the chancellor.

'No, not killed,' corrected the Emperor. 'Part of the story I tell you is his – he told it to the police at the hospital – no, no, not killed – his friend was not the marksman he thought.'

*   *   *

Madrid was *en fête* for the wedding of the Prince. His illustrious kinsman, the King of Catalonia and of Aragon, had decreed it, and the people of Spain had a warm corner in their hearts for Carlos of the Escorial.

Therefore armies of workmen emplanted gaily draped masts, and twined garlands of flowers, and built miles of rough unpainted tribunes from whence a friendly populace might view the procession.

It was three days before the royal wedding, and when from all parts of the world visitors were flocking into Madrid, that the Commissioner of Police at Scotland Yard received certain information from a source that had served him so well before.

He summoned Falmouth.

'Shut the door,' he said quietly, as the detective entered; then, 'There's to be a week's truce, and I think we can safely slacken down for that period.'

'What is the cause, sir?' asked Falmouth.

'The royal wedding,' replied the commissioner, twisting in his fingers a soiled slip of paper; 'the Reds are furious at the trick played on them at the Auditorium; they are going to kill that young man.'

The young Prince had made many friends during his stay in England, and not least this stern colonel of engineers turned policeman.

'We can do nothing, of course, sir,' he considered, 'if you would care to go to Madrid for – a holiday you might be able to pick up a few threads.'

'I'll go,' said Falmouth, after a second's thought.

'Good,' said the chief commissioner, brightening up, 'er – Falmouth,' he called as the superintendent was making his departure, 'you may – er – find your Four Just friends there, by the way.'

Falmouth looked suspiciously at his chief, but the commissioner did not raise his eyes from the paper he was so diligently studying.

* * *

Gonsalez sat at a window writing. Outside, in the narrow Calle de Recoletos, electric cars went jangling by, and, but for these, Madrid was a city of the dead, for it was the hour of the *siesta*, when labour slept in the shade of the limes, and capital dozed in cool dark chambers.

In the high-ceilinged room, Gonsalez sat alone, and on the table before him, was a litter of papers and books which he consulted from time to time. Old registers, yellow plans, and surveyor's maps.

He wrote rapidly in the curious small cramped hand that usually denotes a life spent in the study of mathematics, and when he paused to consult an authority, it was a momentary pause.

There came a knock at the door and he rose and noiselessly unlocked it. 'Would the señor see the illustrious Don Emanuel de Silva?' The señor gravely nodded his head. The fact that illustrious Emanuel was a prosperous builder, fat and important with the self-assurance of the moneyed peasant, did not appeal to Gonsalez as possessing a humorous side. Long ago he had philosophically crystallized his attitude to the world in the sentence, 'If I am to laugh at the absurdities of life, I must laugh always.'

Don Emanuel found the grave, young-looking man with the face of a priest regarding him respectfully, and that was the attitude that Don Emanuel liked best.

They exchanged the conventional courtesies, and Gonsalez bowed his visitor to a seat.

'I have to inform your excellency,' said Don Emanuel elaborately, 'that your gracious commission is accomplished.'

Gonsalez nodded.

'The difficulties,' Emanuel went on impressively, 'were stupendous, unparalleled, heart-breaking. Labour! with the wedding feasts a few days removed. Ah, you know our people! And then there was material, and the difficulty of carriage – you chose a lonely spot for your shooting house.'

Gonsalez nodded again. He did not resent the 'thou' of the other.

'But I myself, Don Emanuel de Silva – I have the order of Isabel the Catholic, did you know that?' he thumbed the lapel of his coat where the fat rosette of nobility flamed red and yellow – 'I, who have erected palaces, I myself superintended the erection! Ah! those labourers of Avila! Señor, I raved, I stormed, I prayed and wept, but they would go their own pace. But night and day – ' he shrugged his shoulders ecstatically, and ended abruptly, 'it is finished.'

Again Gonsalez nodded. He opened a drawer at his hand and drew forth a thin sheet of paper.

'As specified?' he asked, and tapped the document.

'Even better than as specified,' breathed the builder with that quality of awe in his voice that comes to the man recounting his own achievements.

Gonsalez unlocked another drawer and brought out a thick pad of notes. He slipped off the rubber band that bound them together and deftly counted a number. These he laid on the table and recounted.

'Fifteen thousand pesetas,' he said. 'I am grateful to you, Don Emanuel,' and pushed the notes toward the builder.

There were some nourishing phrases of mutual satisfaction, a flourishing signature written across the King of Catalonia's face, yet another flourish of genteel wishes, and the builder prepared to take his departure.

' . . . it has been a great happiness to serve your excellency, but . . . naturally my workmen asked why this strange hut was built . . . built into the side of the hill itself, and lined with thick logs of wood – I must warn you that it will be damp, for the rains are heavy and the soil is treacherous . . . ' He was aching to ask questions.

All this Gonsalez saw.

'You are discreet, señor?' he asked quietly.

'As death,' answered the builder eagerly, if ambiguously. 'No workman knows for whom this hut, cave, call it what you will, is built – I have thought a thousand reasons.'

'And you employed only workmen of Avila?'

'That is so – it was your instruction; it would have been cheaper to have taken my own men.'

'Then,' said Gonsalez slowly, 'it will be well to take you into my confidence, Señor Don Emanuel – I am using this building for the same purpose as you used the little hut on the Sierras – you have forgotten, perhaps? You know the road that leads across the mountains of Tarifa?'

So far he got, noting the effect of his words. Then the stout prosaic builder sprang backward with a strangled cry, his eyes aglare with terror and his flabby face grey.

'I – I – ' he stammered.

Gonsalez waved his hands as though dismissing the subject. 'I do not desire to remind you of the indiscretions of your youth – no man would recognize in Don Emanuel de Silva – why did you take the Jewish name? – the sometime – '

'Enough,' gasped the other. 'Give me the money and let me go.'

Gonsalez handed the packet of notes to the trembling man.

'I may rely upon your discretion?' he asked calmly.

'To the death,' whispered the other, and left the room.

Gonsalez turned to his desk again with a quiet smile on his lips. Later he took a locked notebook from the desk and entered –

Emanuel Mandurez, smuggler: murdered Civil Guard 1886 at Guella in the district of Malaga. Afterwards disappeared; believed to be dead, but known to have settled down in Estremadura, where he became a successful business man. Dark hair, little beard, nose aquiline, cheek-bones high and large, strong jaw, eyes cold; projecting frontal eminence.'

Gonsalez was adding to that interesting collection of criminal data which was afterwards to appear in the form of that widely discussed book *Crime Facets*.

This done he locked the book and methodically replaced it, then resumed his writing.

Some day I should like to devote time to the study of Leon Gonsalez, dilettante, scientist, and philosopher; that I am so constantly discovering him, in the process of making this book, engaged in work which is apart from the purpose of the story is disconcerting. Luckily his present occupation carries the story forward, but once when tracing the movements of the Four (it was in recording the story of the Silver God of M'Beta), I, arriving hot-foot at the heels of Leon, in a state of excitement natural to the biographer whose subject is in mortal danger, found myself chilled by the spectacle of a fugitive from death, pausing to gather material for his history of the Borgias.

Gonsalez wrote on steadily until a carriage clock before him pointed to the hour of two.

Then he cleared away the litter of papers, locked his manuscripts into a box, lit a cigarette, and sauntered forth into the white hot glare of day. He boarded a tram-car, and rode along the Alcala till he reached the Calle de Sevilla, then dropped off, and crossed the road to the Café Fornos.

He found Manfred and Poiccart sitting at one of the tables at the far end of the dining-room, and, sitting down, ordered his lunch.

'Courlander?' he asked.

'Courlander is – well,' said Manfred, smiling.

They carried on their conversation in English.

'And the others?'

Manfred stroked his pointed beard thoughtfully.

'The others are here,' he said slowly; 'but the work is to be done by local men – that is a difficulty.'

Leon frowned.

'That sounds dangerous – the local men are few, and so far as I know, on one pretext or another, they have been arrested as a precautionary measure – Marshel, and Sumarez, and – '

'You needn't enumerate them,' said Poiccart shortly; 'none of those are likely to be employed – the Red Hundred has gone to Catalonia for its tool.'

Leon made no reply, but his eyes wandered absently about the crowded room.

'Tell me who will be the man,' he said at length, with a shade of grimness in his voice, 'and I will show you the place.'

The others regarded him attentively.

'There is only one spot in the whole of Madrid where such an attempt could be made with any hope of success,' Gonsalez went on. 'I've spent the morning with official survey maps, measuring the width of streets. The Alcala is too broad. The Puerta del Sol too vast . . . ' he took street by street to show their disabilities. 'The Calle Mayor – is an ideal spot. Just beyond the Plaza del Mayor, where the street narrows, and high houses overhang the tiny thoroughfare and a man can drop a bomb on the Royal carriage as easily as I could toss a biscuit on the floor.'

He stirred the soup that had been placed before him.

'Early this morning I promenaded – went to seek a place of vantage for the procession. There is a building on the identical spot, let off in flats. The first floor is irreproachable as to character. A countess and a marquess, and an official of the English Embassy – the second floor, bourgeois, but beyond suspicion. The top floor sub-let to well-known and easily identified local people, except one room, occupied in normal times by Genius in the shape of an artist.'

They listened without comment.

'To him comes a beautiful lady who is staying at the Hôtel de la Paix. Imagine our artist, hat in hand to the glorious foreigner who desires accommodation for her brother, arriving tonight by the train from Barcelona. Accommodation for *Monsieur le frère* at the Hôtel de la Paix is unprocurable – could she rent his room for a week? She paid well, and the artist, with a fine contempt for the pageantry of royalty, surrenders his right to view the procession from his window for a consideration of a thousand francs.'

Manfred nodded.

'He arrives tonight – and the woman?'

' "Slender and dark, with adorable eyes",' quoted Leon; ' "beautiful as the shadow of a summer valley".'

Manfred smiled.

'The artist's description?' he paused and looked at Poiccart; then, 'The Woman of Gratz,' he said soberly.

'The Woman of Gratz,' repeated Poiccart, nodding slowly.

They sat in silence, each thinking out his solution after his own fashion. Leon, rolling a Spanish cigarette with deft fingers, looked vacantly out of the great window, but the passing procession of light-hearted people was not his object.

'Heigh-ho!' he sighed at last.

'You were thinking of the woman?' accused Manfred.

Gonsalez displayed genuine astonishment at the suggestion.

'I was thinking of something quite different – have you ever noticed, George, how frequently mentally unsound people have full heavy chins and fine hair? I think it was Lambroso who said – '

'If you are going to talk physiognomy, I'm going,' said Poiccart with his heavy smile; 'yesterday you refused me a hearing on the subject of protoxides – and you missed a good story.'

Leon's hand was on his arm.

'I can spare myself the protoxides, but not the story,' he laughed.

'It is a queer little story,' said Poiccart, resuming his seat, 'but chemistry comes into it, and all the queer formulae that Leon so dislikes. It is about a chemist – he was in the Argentine – who was shamefully betrayed by a woman.'

Poiccart was never a great speaker and only in moments of rare excitement was he ever lucid.

Now he told his story hesitatingly.

'A woman betrayed this man for a few pieces of gold . . . somehow his rage was not directed against the woman, for she was terrified and confessed and threw the money at his feet, and he gathered the pieces up. It was the man who had betrayed the friendship against whom his rage was directed . . . '

Here he came to the part of his story with which he was more at home. He spoke of 'terchlorides' and 'protoxides', of chemical treatments, of a mysterious AuO_3 which, combined with caustic ammonia, formed something else, and the two men grew bewildered at the rapidity with which he handled the technical side of the subject.

Then, as the story neared its conclusion, as if by one accord, the eyes of Manfred and Gonsalez met.

As Poiccart finished Leon bent forward and looked curiously at the teller of the story.

'Do we understand your story to be a parable?' he asked.

Poiccart nodded, and Manfred asked: 'Would it be practicable?'

'I think so,' said Poiccart gravely.

This conversation, and particularly this story, had an important bearing upon the event which, more than any other, subsequently destroyed for ever the power of the Red Hundred – this and the little house that Don Emanuel built on the Sierras.

Chapter 10
In the Calle Mayor

The irregular-shaped dining-room of the Hôtel de la Paix was thronged. It was the hour when the brilliant assembly of guests dined.

The greater portion of the hôtel had been reserved by the Government for its illustrious guests, and the babel of talk that drowned the music of the orchestra was made up of a dozen different tongues. At the little white tables where silver and glass sparkled in the light of the shaded lamps, ministers of every nation, soldiers and attachés, austere court officials and secretaries to a score of special embassies, sat laughing and talking. Every table accommodated more than its usual quota, and scarcely a moment passed but there arrived some belated and apologetic attaché, for whom, with a great pushing of chairs and to the accompaniment of laughter, place had to be found.

One table alone was set for a solitary occupant, and toward her every masculine eye in the room strayed and strayed again.

'My word! that's a pretty girl.' The Major of the Lancers put up his eyeglass and gazed furtively.

'Who is the woman?' asked Prince Dalgouriski, of the Russian Mission, and stared.

The waiter in attendance supplied the information covertly.

'Very rich, your excellency – the Baroness von Zinnitt-Durnstadt; yes, I think she is married. It is said that she has large estates in Russia, but spends most of her time in Paris.'

'Wise woman,' growled the Russian. 'Russia is a cursed country, a thrice accursedly dull hole.'

The waiter smiled and made a mental note.

I step aside from the set course of my story to offer the above dialogue as a very reasonable explanation for Dalgouriski's subsequent banishment from Court, for all was fish that came to Menshikoff's net. Menshikoff's enemies have said that he so frequently adopted the rôle of waiter in pursuing his investigations, because in that capacity he was in his element; that, in fact, he had risen from that humble position, but there is little doubt that such a disguise gave him greater opportunities than any other.

The presence of the Woman of Gratz in Madrid he had all along anticipated. When he found that she had established herself at the Hôtel de la Paix his excellent credentials enabled him, with little difficulty, to secure service under the same roof. To very few people in Russia was Menshikoff known personally. In the main he was a name – and not always the same name. His duty in Madrid was to protect the Grand Duke, to whose suite he was in a measure attached; the Grand Duke himself was not aware of the presence in his retinue of such a person as M. Menshikoff.

Not inclined to interfere in matters outside his immediate province, he was not greatly concerned for the safety of the Prince of the Escorial. So long as his own charge was secure, it mattered very little who else might suffer.

He obeyed a signal from the beautiful woman who sat alone.

She was exquisitely dressed in a dress of soft black chiffon, un-relieved by ornament save a collar of pearls she wore about the tightly-fitting lace collar at her neck.

'The Red Hundred has spent money less advantageously,' thought Menshikoff as he bent forward deferentially to hear her order.

'I am expecting a visitor,' she said in French; 'he is to be shown into my *salon*.'

'*Oui, madame*,' said the agent; 'I will transmit your order to the *maître*.'

She looked at him with sudden interest.

'Your voice sounds familiar,' she said. 'Have you waited on me before?'

'Not to my recollection,' he said with the apologetic smirk of his assumed profession.

He hastened to carry out her instructions, and came back to tell her that the order had been given.

'I will take coffee,' she said, and looked at him again.

He bore the scrutiny placidly, skilfully and noiselessly removing the covers before her.

She sat at her coffee for ten minutes, taking a complete survey of the room. Cold, impassive, unsmiling, she felt and showed no response to the frothy gaiety of the place. Perfectly harmonious as she appeared in the splendid setting of gay uniforms and glittering orders, she was apart and aloof from it all. Not that this peasant's daughter experienced discomfort or embarrassment from the magnificence of her surroundings. Uncrowned queen of a terrible empire she was by right of her rare intellect, no less than by that beauty of hers which fired men's hearts to dreadful deeds.

Conscious of her limitless power, she could well afford to regard this chattering throng as so much background against which the vision of her schemes passed in slow review.

Hat in hand came the obsequious hall porter to tell her that 'M'sieur waited her excellency in her *salon*.'

She dismissed the man with a curt nod.

Then she rose and walked from the room, the focusing point of a hundred eyes.

Her suite was on the next floor; she declined the diminutive lift-boy's invitation and mounted the broad stairs.

At the door of her room she stopped a moment to take a paper from her pocket, then she turned the handle and entered. There was only one dim light in the great cheerless reception-room, and the man who rose to meet her was between her and the single lamp.

She stopped irresolutely, for it was not Von Dunop, whom she expected, but a taller man. She could not see his face.

'I am afraid – ' she began.

'I wish you were,' said the other easily; then she recognized the voice and the blood came to her pale cheeks.

'You!' she said almost under her breath.

The man bowed.

He had walked forward to meet her and now he was between her and the door, so that the light fell on him and she saw his face, and the sad eyes that had lived with her since the day she had first felt their power, held her again speechless.

'I wish you were afraid,' he went on a little bitterly; 'or that you had some human weakness or some soft womanly spot in your heart that could be reached.'

Her voice was uneven as she spoke.

'What do you desire?' she asked.

'The happiness of my fellows, security for the weak, justice for the oppressed,' he said simply.

'Who is it that deals in canting platitudes now?' she asked scornfully.

'Not I,' he said, 'nor my friends. My life is forfeit to every state in the civilized world because I believe in these principles – and, believing, have acted.'

'And now?' she asked calmly. She had recovered from the shock of the meeting, and was keenly alive to its possibilities. There would be no mistake this time. Once he had surprised her into a display which was wholly feminine; she was on her guard.

'And now,' he repeated, 'I have come to call a truce.'

'Ah!' The note of triumph left him unmoved.

'I have no reason for asking this,' he went on, 'save a desire to avoid useless bloodshed – the taking of lives which God knows might be more usefully and profitably employed than in the dreadful destructive work your people have undertaken – the casualties have been one-sided.'

'We have a score to settle,' she blazed forth.

He nodded. 'And we,' he said.

There was a sinister emphasis in his words.

'A score, indeed, madame!' he lowered his voice when she had expected him to raise it. It was a little thing, but it disconcerted her. He was always doing the unexpected.

'How many lives does the Red Hundred owe to civilization? Von Dunop, for instance, you expected him, did you not?'

'Is he dead?' she gasped.

Manfred smiled. After all, she was a woman, and it was the woman who observed the sweetness of that smile, and the little lines that came to the corners of his eyes. The woman thought that this must be the man who smiled often.

'No, he is not dead – did I not say a "truce" – but Von Dunop, has he personally no life to offer to the state? If he were slain, would his death lie on the conscience of any man? And Fritz Meister of Altona, and Carronalli, and De Vitzy – I could name a host who have struck in the name of the Red Hundred – what score does humanity hold against them?'

Her mind was moving quickly. She had a thought that grew and shaped as he spoke. It was to her back that he addressed his last words, for with a shrug of her shoulder, she had turned from him and walked to an open bureau.

Over her shoulder she flung the contemptuous question: 'And you?'

'Once only have we killed a good man,' he said gravely, 'and that, for humanity's sake.'

She was silent, then she turned and walked carelessly back to where she had stood when he began.

'There can be no truce,' she said, 'we have set ourselves to remove the obstacles in the path of struggling mankind – the accidental obstructions that old dead systems have bequeathed us. The sons of fathers who were the sons of fathers who had some time ruled by might, and left the legacy of their dominion to their haphazard progeny.'

She wheeled round on him with a burst of anger.

'If in England you race a horse and it wins your Derby, must the stock of that horse be acclaimed winners of the race from birth? Must their sons be Derby winners, though they do not race for the prize? Are your doctors' sons born doctors, or your judges born in ermines?'

'Yes and no,' he replied calmly; 'for the son of the Derby horse will win the race – if he is fit and trained. And the doctor's son will be a doctor, if he follows the course, and the king's son, wise and strong, will rule his people and dominate his councillors – if he has the training.'

'And if not?' she said fiercely. 'If he be a weakling or a madman?'

'Then his councillors will rule him,' said Manfred, a little wearily.

'You talk to me as though I were a child,' she raged on; 'as if I were to be humoured and persuaded and cajoled, as if every ounce of blood in my body did not throb for freedom, and every instinct cry "Death to kingship".'

'Another king will come – or the councillors, which is worse – or the dictator, who is worse than all,' he said sadly. 'You are fighting inevitable laws which decree that one man shall always have power over his fellows and rule them for the common good.'

'We're fighting ambition with terror,' she said; 'we are imposing our natural law upon another – the fear of death upon the hunger for power. One by one they shall go, these rulers of yours – ' she came closer and spoke rapidly, and he saw how quickly she breathed.

'King and councillors and dictator, till the lower steps of the throne are so set about with dead men's bones that even a crown shall not be worth the risk. And the men who oppose us shall go with the ruck – little and great, chancellor and courtier – even such men as you!'

He saw the flash of poignard and sprang to one side.

The razor-like edge of the knife caught his shoulder in passing, and before she could raise her hand again he had her in his arms; only for a second she felt herself crushed against him and his breath on her hair, then his hands slid down her arm, and her wrists were held.

She looked at him wildly.

The wave of passion that had swept her along had receded and left her white and trembling.

'Now,' she whispered huskily, 'you may kill me.'

He shook his head, and she saw the pain in his eyes.

'No,' he said shortly, and released her.

He stooped and picked up the dagger, looked at it curiously, and replaced it on the bureau.

Then he turned to her again.

'There is to be no truce?' he asked.

She made no reply.

'So be it,' he said, and turned to go.

He took two steps and reeled a little, steadying himself with his hand on the wall.

She was at his side in a moment, this extraordinary Woman of Gratz.

'You are hurt,' she cried, in a frenzy of alarm, and held his arm. 'Let me – !'

Manfred looked down at her from his height, and over his face came a strange shadow.

'Is there a truce?' he asked again. She drew back sharply, the fire rekindled in her eyes.

'Never!' she cried and stamped her foot.

Manfred bowed and left the room, walking slowly.

*   *   *

'Not a very serious wound,' said Gonsalez critically. 'The Woman of Gratz, of course – what did you do?'

'I left her unrepentant,' said Manfred with a grim smile.

Which may or may not have been true – for who shall say what induced the tears that the Woman of Gratz shed that night?

*   *   *

Carlos of the Escorial had conducted his courtship in that hurricane manner that was peculiarly his. With every chancellory of Europe making agitated search for precedent, with the Vatican ominously antagonistic, with the Grand Duchess of Sofia moving heaven and earth in a disinterested endeavour to break off the engagement – her daughter, the Princess Marie Teresa, will be thirty in March – the path of true love was made anything but smooth. But the young Prince held on his way untroubled by the succession of autographed letters that came to hand by special envoys. Father Mathias, his confessor, unwisely overstepped the bounds of discretion in lending gratuitous counsel, and was promptly dismissed. He came back in triumph with the support of Supreme Authority and was refused admittance. Then came a mission from Rome headed by a Prince of the Church, and Carlos listened courteously, and replied in brief.

'If you worry me I will turn Protestant.'

Because he was quite capable of carrying out this outrageous plan, they left him in peace. Then unexpected support came for him, from Central Europe, and most powerful of all, from the King of the Northern Islands. Such a combination was too tremendous for the quibblers, and they subsided, the Grand Duchess of Sofia talking to the last.

Of the high-born lady upon whom his choice fell, there is no need to tell here. That she was, and is, very beautiful, with wondrous blue eyes and hair of spun gold, all the world knows. That the young prince was head over heels in love with her goes without saying; for the rest, her life, her ancestral homes and illustrious progenitors, scenes of her early childhood, her dresses and such-like, I refer you to the picture postcards that sold by the million on the day of her marriage.

At three o'clock in the morning hawkers were crying their wares – pictures and favours, and bannerettes of the Royal colours. The streets were thronged when the first white rays of the sun flooded the Puerta del Sol – thronged with officers of every service, resplendent in gala dress, with their ladies, and peasantry from the outlying districts, their coats slung over their shoulders and their flat round caps a-tilt. The cafés were crowded, and as the sun rose higher, with brazen bugles waking the echoes, regiment after regiment passed to its station.

Almost barbaric was the splendour of the scene; such a feast of colour as Spain alone of the nations can spread for the eye grown weary of northern greys and drabs. The nobility vied one with the other to do honour to the Prince. From every balcony full lengths of priceless tapestry, from every window hung festoons of flowers, and the palaces of the nobility were all but hidden by a prodigality of decorations. As the morning wore on the heat became almost oppressive.

The two men who occupied the artist's room in the Calle Mayor felt it the more since it was necessary for their work to keep door and windows closed.

An open bottle of wine and a little fruit on the table, with a big bunch of flowers, lent them the appearance of holiday-makers, but the two polished steel cylinders and the loaded Browning pistols that stood amidst the flowers and fruit and wine gave a more sinister interpretation to their presence.

Now they lay stretched in deck chairs waiting.

They had heard the blare of music that signified the passing of the Royal party on the way to the church, and half an hour had slipped past.

One of them roused himself to reach for a glass.

'The way out – you are sure it is clear?' he asked.

The other yawned.

'There are three ways,' he said lazily. 'I have told you a dozen times, Manuel – are you nervous?'

The man grinned. He felt the broad belt about his waist, where, piece by piece, the gold had been carefully stored.

'It will create a sensation,' he said complacently.

'The more excitement the greater chance of escape,' said the first speaker, and lit a cigarette.

Manuel opened the window and looked down into the narrow street, then he came back into the room.

'The balconies below are crowded,' he reported, 'and the people are packed like oranges in a box in the street below – look!'

The other rose grumbling, and the two men stepped on to the balcony; then they turned back to the apartment . . .

A change had been effected in their few minutes of absence. Manuel, looking carelessly at the table, missed the pistols, and he observed, too, that the steel cylinders had been moved to the farther end of the table. He had not time to notice anything else.

Somebody's arm went round his neck – the thing was done in a flash, he was garrotted and helpless. He was luckier than his companion, because the practical Poiccart used a life-preserver.

The pressure on Manuel's throat relaxed, but with returning consciousness he realized the discomfort of his position. His hands were strapped, there was a stick in his mouth, and his legs were bound tightly to the chair. There was a strange roaring in his ears as he recovered consciousness, and after a little while he identified the noise with the people in the street. The Royal procession was passing, and he was sitting there helpless. The money had been paid and the work had not been accomplished. He looked round.

His friend was groaning noisily in much the same plight as himself.

The three men who had captured him were in consultation. He could not understand what they said, for they were speaking English.

'We can get them out of here – now,' said Manfred. He had his arm in a sling and looked tired.

'Not like this?' said Poiccart, and he pointed to the bonds.

'Then Leon must make them sleep – we can reach the yard below and the carriage,' said Manfred. 'When the streets are cleared we can take them away – but out of this room at once. Listen!'

The cheers in the street below had reached a frenzy.

'The Prince,' said Manfred . . . 'now . . . '

In the meantime the Woman of Gratz sat at the window of her room in the Hôtel de la Paix tearing her lace handkerchief into little shreds and listening for the explosion that did not come.

Chapter 11

The judgment

It was a commonplace table at which the three men sat, and the room, so far as Manuel could see in the light the smoky lamp gave, was ordinary enough. Perhaps a disused schoolroom, for it looked as if maps had been taken from the wall, and recently.

He was fettered with an unfamiliar handcuff; it looked clumsy enough, he thought, but after a furtive attempt to take advantage of its imperfections, he came to hold it in respect. He had observed earlier that the leader of these men had been wounded, and that he carried his arm stiffly; this leader did most of the talking.

'What is your name?'

'I refuse to answer.'

'Is it not Manuel Zaragoza?'

'Perhaps.'

'Are you an anarchist?'

'I am what it pays me to be.'

'And you,' to the second man, 'is your name Lomondo?'

'I do not answer,' snarled the other and spat on the floor.

'You are from Barcelona, both of you, and you are notorious characters,' Manfred went on, then turned to Gonsalez.

'What is known of Zaragoza?'

All that Leon recited as to these men was bad enough. It was a sordid record of assassination and outrage, of terrorized judges, of petitions for reprieve, and so on, in a cycle.'

'We have taken from you both five thousand francs in gold – who paid you this?'

No reply.

'Was this your only interest in the assassination you contemplated?'

'What other?' sneered the second man. 'Do I look the sort of fool who would kill profitlessly? What have you done with that money?' he demanded suddenly. 'Restore it and hand us to the judges.'

'In good time,' said Manfred calmly, 'the money shall come back to you – and we are your judges.'

Then the door behind the table opened and a fourth man came in. He was masked and bis form was hidden by a long Spanish cloak. The three men made no sign as he took his seat at the table.

'Did the Woman of Gratz pay you?' asked Manfred again.

'That I will tell the judge,' said the dogged prisoner.

It was the masked man who asked the next question.

'What have you against the Prince of the Escorial that you should seek his life?' he asked quietly.

The man shrugged his shoulders.

'I have no quarrel with the pig I kill for dinner,' he said roughly; 'prince or priest or water-seller, it is all one to me.'

'Years ago,' said the mask in his clear tone, 'you were tried.'

'Many times,' said the man with cheerful insolence.

'But this also was for murder – a bomb thrown at a religious procession.'

The man seemed amused.

'That Prince whose life you sought today pardoned you; he was a child then, but had power of life and death in your province.'

'I gave evidence,' said the man resentfully.

'And I,' said the other.

'You betrayed your employers – yes. But that was not sufficient to save your neck from the iron collar. It was that boy's mistaken belief that you were men maddened by persecution – was not that your defence? – that gave you your life.'

The more taciturn of the two shuffled his fettered feet impatiently.

'Have done with this talk,' he growled; 'hand us to the judge, if you will – restore the money you took from us, señor, we shall have need of that.'

'In good time,' said Manfred again; then to him who called himself Emanuel he said, 'You have some experience with bombs?'

'A little,' smiled the man.

'With chemistry generally?'

'I have dabbled,' with a deprecating shrug.

'A man, too, of some education.' Gonsalez interjected this.

'Why do you ask?' said the prisoner coolly.

'My question,' said Manfred, picking his words carefully, 'had some significance. I have said you shall have your gold again. Since it has left your possession it has undergone a slight change. My friend here is a chemist also.' He lifted from the table very carefully a glass phial half filled with a green powder.

'You see this?' he asked, and the man nodded pleasantly, as though all this was being done for his express amusement.

'Have you ever seen gold in this form?' asked Manfred, and the prisoner's brows contracted thoughtfully.

'No,' he said slowly.

'Yet,' Manfred went on, 'if you obtain the protoxide, which is known by the symbol AuO_3, and treat that with – '

'Caustic ammonia,' anticipated the other, a little pale.

'Exactly,' said Manfred; 'in that form we propose returning to yourself and to your friend the gold you accepted to wilfully slay in cold blood two young people against whom you had no grievance.'

'I demand justice,' cried the man Lomondo, 'trial by judge, and judgment according to evidence.'

'Justice you shall have,' said the masked man coldly. 'What man will deny me the right to judge you, or question the evidence on which you stand convicted? How say you?' He turned abruptly to the three who sat at the board.

Manfred nodded.

'It would be better,' he said quietly.

The masked man rose and walked to where the two men sat.

'Because you are what you are,' he said, 'it is fitting that you should die. Therefore I declare you outside the law and the protection of the law. The death you planned for others shall be yours, the brutal strength of the weapon you employ shall be turned upon you. The death that came swift from your hand to the helpless and the innocent shall come as surely to you.'

The face of Manuel was grey and his lips quivered.

'Señor, for God's sake, for the Blessed Virgin's sake, not that way!' he whimpered. 'Give me a chance, let me appeal to His Highness; he will be merciful.'

His judge towered above him, and for a moment slipped the mask from his face.

The man looked; then his eyes opened wide in terror, glared back at the three men seated at the table, and he fell whimpering to the floor. As for the man Lomondo, he looked down contemptuously at the grovelling figure and spat again. But he was not so well educated as Emanuel Zaragoza, and his imaginative faculties were more restricted.

*   *   *

The party that rode out in the early morning of the next day, and passed beyond the city's bounds, taking the road to the mountains, had to regulate its pace according to the speed of the lumbering coach.

But they had some eight hours' start of the woman who followed alone on the big lathering bay; she came swiftly in their wake. A motor-car might have taken her best part of the road, and an hour's search would have secured her an escort strong enough to deal with all possible contingencies. But she could not spare that hour. A spy had brought to her room one who had much to say – yet with many reservations. You can picture her walking this dingy apartment of hers, baffled, aglow with smouldering rage, a prey to a thousand conflicting doubts, bewildered by her helplessness – she with such potentialities at her command.

Complete this picture with the coming of the stout man, half pompous, half fearful, terror of the consequences of his act, fear for the dignity slipping so quickly away, awe for the beautiful creature before him, and superimposed upon the fabric of these emotions, the furbishing up of a tarnished manner which in the year '72 had been so effective with the women of Andalusia.

'Yes, yes, yes,' she interrupted impatiently. 'You built a house in the hills; but what is this to me?'

'Excellency,' said the flowery Don Emanuel, employing his more ornate diction, 'life is given to us for – '

'If you have anything to tell me, señor, I beg you to proceed.'

'Often it happens,' said the little man with dignity, 'that in the summer of life we regret the indiscretions of spring. Sometimes an unworthy wretch, knowing of these follies, will remind us, taunt us, upbraid us – such a man was this Don Leon Gonsalez – a man with pitiless prying eyes.'

She saw that she must let him tell his story his own way; that he had, for his vanity's sake, to gloss over a few of his own sins before he came to the object of his visit. She did not imagine that he had much to say that would interest her, but in a way he was a distraction, and her agent would not have sent him if the story was entirely without personal interest to her.

'Understanding, excellent señorita, that, by my discretion, my wealth of experience, by the patronage of the noble and discriminating aristocracy – induced by my very apparent qualities – I have raised myself so that today I am accounted rich, a member of the Ayuntimiento, a cavalier of Isabel the Catholic, and the Cortes before me: understanding all this, judge my sorrow, my despair, when there comes this man, this Señor Don Leon – may the devil eat salt with him this night, Amen! – to remind me of – a wild youth.'

His despair exaggerated, energetic, was graphically illustrated.

' "Build me a house," says he, "that shall be a hole in the solid hill, with such a thickness of plank, and such a foundation. With a hook there and an iron-cased door here. Let it be built by workmen who will not recognise the spot again, who will not talk or lead neighbours to see and speculate upon the purpose of this building." '

He paused and mopped his brow.

'Later I came with the house in my hand! It was finished; to the time prompt; every instruction noted and heeded! That is my way. Thus have I established myself in the hearts of my fellow-citizens: because of such qualities as these I secured the building of the Credit España on a tender ten thousand pesetas higher than any other; thus I secured also – '

She arrested the digression with a gesture.

'The Señor Don Leon – if that is indeed his name – paid me. In the whole history of this devilish business that one fact alone stands to his credit. Then he asked: "Are you discreet?"

' "As death!" said I. "Then," said he, "I am building this house to kill a man," just that and no more!'

Emanuel paused dramatically. Since his interpretation of the interview left something to the imagination, he hastened to fill it in.

'Here I return to the indiscretions of spring!' he said mournfully. 'There would be no need but for the fact that he must needs remind me. You accuse me of remaining silent,' he went on magnificently. 'You ask me why I did not fly to the alcalde and denounce the monster. You cry shame upon me – but, excellency, remember who I am, what I am – Spain's greatest builder, a cavalier of Isabel the Catholic. I sank with shame at the thought of the exposure of my early childish error; it was a trifle,' he added airily, and he really believed it was at the moment.

'What is all this to me?' she asked petulantly.

Don Emanuel held up a warning hand.

'Wait!' he said impressively, 'I have yet to finish. This morning, riding, as is my practice, in the cool of the morning – an English thoroughbred, excellency, that cost two thousand pesetas, though I fear I was robbed in the transaction – I saw a cavalcade on the road that leads from the city. Something induced me to conceal my presence in a little wood, some instinct with which I am fortunately endowed. The cavalcade passed. A coach drawn by eight mules, a señor driving, two others riding on either side of the carriage. He who drove the coach was – Señor Don Leon!'

He stepped back to notice the effect of his words upon the woman.

It was singularly disappointing, for she displayed no other emotion than a pardonable weariness.

'Listen!' he exclaimed, 'within that coach were two men! The blinds were drawn, but the wind lifted them a little, and I, Don Emanuel de Silva, saw them – bound hand and foot!'

This time his recital was rewarded. She looked interested. Indeed, if he might judge from her narrowing eyes, and the long breaths she drew, his description had roused her to an extraordinary extent.

'They were going in the direction of the house in the hill – to kill, as Don Leon had said – though he told me nothing of two men, particularly specifying one only.'

'These men,' she said rapidly, 'how do they look?'

'Don Leon is a man without a heart,' he began in his oracular vein; 'he has the face like a priest – '

'The others?' she said. 'Come – tell me quickly.'

'He was on the other side of the coach I could not see, but I do not doubt but that he has the face of a villain. The man nearest me was bearded.'

'Yes, yes,' she said eagerly.

'Short and pointed, and he rode using only one hand, the other being thrust in his coat.'

'So! – wait!' she flung open the desk and produced pen and paper.

'You are used to the drawing of plans,' she said quickly; 'sketch me the position of this house in the hill, the road I must take, the villages I must pass, and where I may secure horses – I will return.'

She almost thrust him into a chair, then swept out of the room.

To do justice to the honest Don Emanuel, it may be said that, ignorant of the character of the Woman of Gratz, and crediting her as the secret agent of a government, he had approached her in the hope that a man, who alive must always be a source of danger, might be effectively and legally removed from all possibility of contact.

Astounded and flattered at the stir his narrative had made, he was none the less puzzled. But he resolved to ask no questions, an inquisitive mind had been his undoing. When she came back, dressed in a riding-habit, she found him still busy with the plan.

'But, señora,' he said in astonishment, 'you will not ride – it is fifty kilometres and the road is bad – and alone!'

'Come with me,' she said a little maliciously, and smiled as he turned pale at the very suggestion.

She studied the plan.

'You may get horses here ' – he pointed out the village of Granja de la Flores – 'but it is doubtful; but, señora, these hill people are bad – suppose you are attacked?'

Her hard laugh was a revelation.

She bent over her desk to scribble a note.

'If you would deliver this, you will serve me,' she said. Then, without a word of thanks, she was gone, and through the window he saw her, with Madrid looking on in astonishment, canter across the streaming asphalt of the Puerta del Sol and take the road that led to the hills.

* * *

The difficulties of the road were greater than she had expected. Sometimes it was little more than a track across a boulder-strewn hillside. What advantage she had in the chase lay in keeping to this track, for the carriage must go the longer way round, keeping to the road. She found food at wayside houses, food of the roughest and wine with a resinous bite to it, but it served. Every hour or so the short cuts brought her to the road again, and the marks of the coach wheels on the white dust of the road were recent.

The sun was going down when she reached Granja de la Flores. Its grandiloquent title served to designate a wretched little village in a fold of the hills, a collection of whitewashed hovels, cowering about a big dominating church. Before the dilapidated *fonda* she pulled up and called for the landlord. Two or three unshaven men, sitting in the shade of a tattered sunblind, rose and swept off their hats mechanically, regarding her with suspicion. The landlord came at his leisure, rolling a cigarette and pausing at the door to cry a string of instructions over his shoulder.

'Can you supply me with a horse?' she asked.

The man looked up at her with a familiar grin.

'Beautiful lady, there is nothing in the world I cannot supply you with at the *fonda* of Granja – but a horse, no.'

He devoted his attention to the cigarette in making.

She made as though to dismount.

'Permit me, excellency,' he said quickly, and helped her down.

Her horse needed rest and food – she must spare a precious hour.

'Find me a room,' she said imperiously, and the man grinned again. There were two rooms beside the public room, and all three were unsavoury enough, but she found a dubious-looking sofa, and passed the hour dozing. She had no need to ask how long since the carriage had passed. Evidently her arrival had interrupted a discussion between the idlers before the *fonda* as to the exact hour the coach had left the village. This argument was now resumed. By their talk she gathered that she was less than two hours behind them, and they must halt as well as she. Her horse did not show signs of distress, the rest and food would help him.

At the end of the hour she rose and called for the horse. At their leisure the servants of the house brought it and she chafed under the delay. Also the landlord was unnecessarily familiar. It is not usual for beautiful young ladies to ride unattended in Spain.

His imprudence reached its culmination when she asked for assistance to mount.

'Better remain here, *bello mio*,' he sighed heavily; 'the roads are unsafe for such pretty birds as you.'

Then when she would have mounted unassisted, he held her arm gently but firmly, and she took a grip of her steel-ribbed riding-whip, and lashed him twice across the face. He went back shrieking with his hands to his eyes, and she sprang into the saddle. Then, as she turned her horse to the mountain road, he recovered and came at her bellowing with a knife in his hand. Perhaps he did not intend using it; it may be he expected to frighten her. I advance this excuse for the innkeeper's indiscretion, as the merest speculation. The solution of this little problem does not lie with us.

The Woman of Gratz, galloping along the mountain path, came suddenly face to face with a brown-faced member of the Guardia Civile. He reined back his horse into the undergrowth to allow her to pass and greeted her respectfully.

She checked her horse to exchange the customary civilities.

'I thought, señora, I heard a shot,' he said.

'Yes,' she replied; 'a man has been shot in the village.'

'If you will permit me I will leave you,' he said, and she heard the loose stones flying under the hoofs of his galloping charger.

The villagers gathered about the man, who lay full length in the white dust of the road, explained the circumstances, and the philosophical policeman looked grave.

'A reputation for Granja de la Flores!' he said with heavy sarcasm; 'that a foreign lady cannot come to your village without undergoing insult. Is this swine dead?'

'No,' said an apologetic bystander.

'Then take him into the house whilst I write a report,' said the magnificent custodian of the peace.

He met the innkeeper's wife at the doorway, arms akimbo, and very voluble. She defamed the Woman of Gratz, beginning with the probability of her irregular morals and ending with forecasting the destination of her immortal soul.

'And,' she added to clinch the matter, 'she has not paid for her room or for the fodder of the horse!'

'That,' said the policeman wisely, 'is a matter for the civil courts.'

Chapter 12
The house in the hill

In the cool of the evening the five men came to the house in the hill. They had left the coach in a little wood that marked the Castilian road. Two breakdowns had delayed them, and they were later than they had thought to be. It was difficult to find the door of the house, for Don Emanuel had carried out his orders to the letter. But Leon, making a rough calculation, fumbled amidst the drooping vines that covered the face of a small bluff and found what he sought.

'Here,' he said, and wrenched open the heavy door.

Into the dark interior the prisoners were pushed, and the door closed upon them.

The man called Zaragoza sniffed the newly planed pinewood and felt with his fingers the thickness of the lining of his strange prison.

Outside his captors lit a fire, and, from a 'thermos' bottle, Manfred poured out boiling hot coffee. He looked at his watch; it was seven o'clock.

'In two hours,' he said; 'in the meantime, let us prepare for our visitors.'

Leon rose and went down the hill to the little wood. He came back shortly with what looked like a bundle of sticks. These he carefully deposited beyond the reach of the fire.

They sat talking in low tones until a few minutes before eight, then Poiccart, seeking a soft piece of ground, bored, with a thick steel rod, a hole two feet deep. Into this he inserted one of the sticks, twisting it to make sure that it had full play.

He stood waiting, whilst Manfred sat, watch in hand, by the fire; then he nodded, and Poiccart stooped and applied a light.

With a roar like the roar of a mill-race the rocket swept up into the night. Higher and higher it soared, then slowly it described a curve and burst into a great mass of white stars, so brilliant that the plain beneath was for a few seconds illuminated, as with the light of a bright moon.

The people of the little village of Anmincio, seven miles away, saw it and wondered, crossing themselves reverently at the celestial token. Other people saw it also.

Von Dunop, on his fat mule, sweating in the darkness; Elbrecht, the German anarchist, jolting over the rough road in his one-horsed cart; Saromides, the Greek, riding down from the north, and Menshikoff, riding with the Judge of the First Court of Madrid. The Woman of Gratz saw it also, for she was nearest the hill, and tightened her rein.

Manfred heard the clatter of hoofs coming up the path, and smiled. She came into the circle of lights, and Gonsalez went toward her.

'Will you dismount?' he asked, and it seemed to her that her coming had been expected. She declined his help with a gesture and sprang lightly to the ground. The pistol she had used with effect in the village of Granja de la Flores was in her gloved hand; but they gave no sign that they had seen it.

'Will you sit down?' asked Gonsalez politely.

'I prefer to stand,' she said. It seemed ridiculous that she could think of no opening for her attack. That her presence had been anticipated seemed monstrously unfair somehow. Manfred, who had not spoken, read her thoughts.

'We expected you,' he said, speaking across the fire, 'but not quite so soon – and there are others.'

'I would rather think that you have invented your expectation on the spur of the moment,' she replied, and let the pistol swing pendulum fashion from her finger.

'And there are others,' he repeated coolly, 'else why did we fire the rocket save to guide our guests?'

He stirred the fire with his foot, and sent a shower of sparks flying. He looked reflectively into the red heart of it, and steadfastly refused to see the weapon in her hand.

'It was Leon who caused a message to be sent to the builder Don Emanuel,' he went on. 'The story he told you was carefully prepared for him. The bait was effective, and you are here.'

'Later – ' she began fiercely.

'Later will come your friends,' he finished complacently; 'that also I know. They will find – er – obstacles.'

'So it was a trap?' she breathed.

'An open trap,' he corrected. 'I shall not prevent your going – when we have finished with your mercenaries.'

'You will release them also,' she said steadily, and gathered the black blunt pistol in her hand so that it covered him. If he saw the action, he made no sign, nor did either of the men who were with him.

'Wait awhile,' he continued, still looking into the fire as though there the centre of interest lay. 'In a few minutes Von Dunop will be here, and Elbrecht – we have brought him a long journey from Hamburg – and Saromides, the Greek. He represents the Red Hundred effectively in the City of the Hills, does he not?'

From the foot of the hill came a wheezing cough, and Manfred seemed pleased.

Then with groans and curses and the thud of a falling stick, Von Dunop rode fearfully to the fireside.

First he saw the Woman of Gratz standing idly with her back to a young sapling, and he gave a satisfied grunt.

'Ach, so it is all well,' he said, and his obvious terror evaporated rapidly. 'I had feared that it was a trap, but the telegram gave the password, and I could not disobey.'

He saw Manfred and saluted him.

'I do not know these comrades,' he said, ponderously affable, and looked inquiringly at the woman.

He was not prepared for the introduction.

'These are they who call themselves the Four Just Men,' she said, and Von Dunop reeled back like a man stricken with vertigo.

'Hey!' he said loudly and put his hand to his hip.

Manfred did not move, nor the other men.

'A trap!' bellowed Von Dunop, with a great display of firearms.

'Yes,' Manfred permitted himself with sarcasm, 'a splendid trap'; he looked at their weapons meaningly.

One by one, guided by the fire, came the others, the Greek and the German, and, coming, they stayed, weapon in hand, muttering threats, puzzled, the lives of the three in their hands, yet withal a terror that lay on them like a weight, crushing their initiative. They took council in whispers, but the Woman of Gratz said neither yea nor nay to the hurried proposals they put before her. Then came the sound of two men upon the path, and the three men bent their heads, listening, and each had his hand to his face. When they raised their hands, the Woman of Gratz saw that they were masked. She took a step forward.

'This comedy ends,' she said sternly. 'Have you brought my friends here, from distant parts of Europe, to see a play? Are you mad that you think we can be held with words?' She pointed at Manfred. A splendidly tragic figure she made in her sombre close-fitting habit. The hand that gathered her dress held the pistol, and her finger was curled about the trigger.

'You!' she said, raising her voice, 'you! to add the humiliation of this farce to the slight you have already put upon me! Did you think the Red Hundred was so impotent, its powers so shattered, that you could call its leaders together to laugh at their weakness?'

So far she got when the men who were treading the path came into the light.

One of these, like the men at the fire, was masked and cloaked; the other was a man advanced in years, plainly dressed, but authority written in every line of his face.

He strode forward, bowing slightly to the woman and to the masked men by the fire.

Then something attracted the attention of the Woman of Gratz, and she involuntarily clutched Von Dunop's arm.

On the hills around and above, in the distant valley below, little fires were twinkling at regular intervals and through the trees that fringed the path she caught the glint of steel. Manfred saw also.

'Since we have promised you freedom – when we have finished – and since you have nothing to gain by resistance, for the hills above and the road below are held by the Pavia Hussars, you will listen and wait,' he said, and the old man came forward to the light of the fire.

They were puzzled and alarmed, these shining lights of the Red Hundred. To their strained hearing came the far-away jingle of steel, and once a trumpet-call woke the echoes of the hills.

Except for the Woman of Gratz, I am willing to believe, that the men who condemned their fellows to cruel and merciless deaths, and that without compunction, had a wholesome regard for their own lives, upon which they placed a value out of all proportion to their real worth.

'I must see the prisoners,' said the old man quietly, and Leon led them, blinking and frowning, into the light. The face of him who saw the Woman of Gratz first lit with hope, but the other, staring straight ahead at the grey-haired figure by the fire, shivered and dropped his eyes.

Then the old man called their names and they answered respectfully. Then he took a scroll from the hand of his masked companion, and read, with a curious old-world dignity, a document that began with a recital of the reader's style.

'Don Alberto de Mandeges y Carrilla y Ramundo, officer of the Order of Charles the Third . . . ' – there were a string of subsidiary dignitaries to be read – ' . . . a judge of the High Court, learned in the law . . . by these presents and in the name of His Most Catholic Highness, the Prince of the Escorial, confirm the sentence passed upon . . . ' – he read the names and aliases of each prisoner – ' . . . therefore it is right and proper in the manner arranged that these men should die . . . '

He finished reading and rolled the paper – then remembered and stepped forward to the prisoners, showing them that portion of the document bearing the neat signature of the Prince.

Then he fell back again to the other side of the fire, and there moved up to his side from the darkness about him a solid phalanx of civil guardsmen in their dark cloaks and high collars.

The woman was stupefied; she tried to think, to place these happenings in logical sequence. The Four Just Men were the law – in Spain. Higher than the law, for they might condemn without trial and execute without hope of reprieve.

She stood motionless whilst Gonsalez and Poiccart led the men back to the cell in the hill. They were absent longer than she expected, and when they returned Manfred rose.

'We will go,' he said.

She did not question his right to give the order. She was for the moment wholly under his domination. She followed meekly enough the tramping soldiers as they slipped and stumbled down the steep slopes. Two of them had lighted torches, and the difficulties of the descent were greater than she had thought.

Not until the party had halted in a clearing that commanded a view of the bluff – or would have done in daylight – did she speak.

'Hush, hush!' Von Dunop implored in a whisper. He was shaking like a jelly and his companions were in little better case. 'They have promised us we shall go – say nothing.'

'Say nothing!'

She could have struck the poltroon. 'Say nothing! when men who took our salt are being left to die in the darkness!'

Manfred had learnt something of the Woman of Gratz; he knew to a second how long a weapon might with safety be left in her hand. Now, Leon, standing close at hand, caught her wrist, and wrenched the pistol from her grasp.

'Later you may have it,' he said calmly.

She could have screamed in her fury.

'Some day, some day!' she muttered brokenly.

'Silence!' commanded a voice, and then Manfred began to speak.

It was to her he spoke, and to the men associated with her in the work.

'I have called you together that you may see. And seeing, remember. We, who are together in this work, have set ourselves the task of breaking for ever the organized power of anarchism. That we can prevent the acts of individuals privately moved to assassination by grievances existing only in their poor disordered brains, we cannot hope. That we can destroy for ever the association which exploits and directs these madmen for their profit, I am certain.'

'The Red Hundred lives,' she interrupted, tremulous with passion; 'though I die and the men with me, the Red Hundred will live – and avenge.'

'But for the fact that the Red Hundred is still powerful, I would not have brought you here,' he said calmly; 'but for my knowledge that your plans are complete for the continuation of your scheme of destruction in London, and that even now shipload upon shipload of material and men for the fight are pouring into England, we might dispense with your presence at this – ceremony.' His voice rang out sternly.

'There is no known faith or creed by which one may appeal to you. No better side or soft spot that ingenuity may reach. No concession with which to influence you. Blindly, insanely, uncaring, you move about your work, having no goal to pass or end to reach, filled with the lust of blood, slaying the innocent and sparing the guilty. God never provided for such aimless creatures as you – you are apart from His scheme. The fiercest hurricane brings rain to some pasture or other. The gales of the poles are breezes for the tropics; the deadly enemies of man who live in the African forests suppress other enemies – but you! Your hand is against all, your vengeance scattered broadcast, unintelligently – your very strength is a weakness pitiable and contemptible!

'Yonder in the darkness,' he went on, 'are two men – tools of such people as you. Hired murderers, paid with gold to commit a crime so foul that the brain that planned it could only be that of an illogical unbalanced woman.

'Your money is with them – ' he turned to the Woman of Gratz – 'my friend has converted it by chemical processes to an element that scientists know as fulminate of gold.

'The terror they have inspired they now suffer, and I would not spare them a moment of their agony. The bomb they would have thrown now hangs suspended by a chain above them.'

He lifted the terminal of a thin coil of wire that lay at her feet and she saw that the other end twisted into the bush.

'Give me a truce – hold back your people,' he said earnestly – 'in God's name give me your word that this bloody campaign of the Red Hundred shall end – and I will give you the lives of your servants.'

She reached out her hand and took the tiny switchboard from him, and it lay in her palm.

He could see the disfiguring fury of her face, and waited expectantly.

'My answer,' she cried, 'is this!'

With her fingers she slid back the little switch.

And instantly the hillside a hundred yards away heaved up with a blinding flash and a roar like thunder, and the ground beneath their feet shook again.

'That is my answer!' she cried. 'Long live Anarchy!'

Chapter 13

The terror and the suburbs

'So far as I can gather,' wrote Superintendent Falmouth, that admirable officer, to the Chief Commissioner, 'the F. J. M. had prepared somewhere in the hills a sort of bombproof house. It will give you an idea of the extraordinary foresight of these men, that they took the trouble to prearrange every little detail – down so far as to the purchase of the coach and horses that were to take their prisoners to the hills. From the fact that all their subsequent actions bore the impression of being semi-officially sanctioned, I gather that they have a "pull" in Spain. Madrid is quiet. Nobody knows anything at all about either the attempt or the execution – I need hardly say my information came from the F. J. M. themselves; they sent me particulars through the post . . . I found young Billy-Boy-Billy here with a few of the "heads", and sent him packing to Paris; but there were no English "toughs" in Madrid so far as I could discover.'

London was full of interest for the detective when he returned, for as his subordinate informed him, 'it had begun again', and there was no need to ask what 'it' was.

The outbreak of mysterious crime taxed the police to their utmost capacity; the importance and extent of the outrages may be judged from the fact that in one day alone the walls of Wandsworth Prison, wherein was incarcerated Jaurez, the firebrand socialist, was dynamited, a bomb was exploded in the Tate Gallery, and a determined attempt made to destroy London Bridge was only frustrated by the courage and watchfulness of the Thames Police. The outrages commenced two days after the Royal wedding in Madrid, or, to be exact, on the morning after the Woman of Gratz had made her decision in so dreadful a manner.

What connexion was there between this resumption of activities and the *urgente* telegram dispatched by the woman from Valladolid may be surmised. The most terrifying feature of the new campaign was the destruction of private houses in the suburbs. Not the houses or homes of the great law-makers, not the palaces of the aristocracy, but the humble dwellings of the 'nearly poor', as somebody aptly described them. This new attempt was devilishly ingenious, for, from the Terrorist point of view, it possessed two advantages. It was unattended by the risk that lay waiting for the anarchist whose object was the public building, and it struck fear into the hearts of the people – those people lying down of nights in fear and trembling lest their house be chosen for demolition. There was the advantage, too, that few of these attempts were unattended by fatalities. That no more powerful enemies to anarchy died than women and little children and poor helpless nursemaids did not perturb the bloody-minded agents of the organization. Terror was their aim, and it mattered little how that terror came. For three days they raged unchecked, and London sank to an ignoble panic. You had the spectacle of depleted offices and closed stores in the city, for merchants and clerks were also husbands and fathers, and the staid broker sat at home in his drawing-room with a shotgun across his knees, whilst his business went neglected.

You may be sure that the police did all that was humanly possible to cope with the situation. For the first time for many years free speech in public and through the columns of the Press was rigorously denied. Hyde Park was raided when Jean Froy, standing on his red rostrum, declaimed in broken English man's right to Revolution.

Greek Street, the little dens in Soho and Clerkenwell, where known and suspected anarchists were in residence, were cleared, and the county gaols of England filled with men 'under remand', who could by any stretch of imagination be regarded as suspects. All this was done in the first two days, for Scotland Yard moved with amazing rapidity.

The morning of the third day witnesses the blowing up of the New River Water Main and the destruction of the railway bridges that span the Grand Surrey Canal, south of London Bridge, the New Kent Road, and the bridge that is just outside Battersea Road Station. Small matters, but sufficient to effectively disorganize the continental train service. At 11 o'clock in the morning, the fish-boat *Mausor* of Grimsby, was sunk at her berth and the river-front of Billingsgate Market demolished by an explosion of melinite on the wharf. At 11.30, a bomb, placed by the approach of the Tower Bridge, destroyed the machinery used to raise the huge drawbridge; at 12.17 the Hop Exchange was the scene of yet another melinite outrage.

'You can trace their progress,' said the Commissioner bitterly. He was surveying the ruin at Billingsgate, when the roar of the Tower

Bridge explosion deafened him, and it was from Tower Bridge that he heard the second explosion.

At 1.35 a telephone message came through from New Cross that a bomb had been discovered under the seat of a council tramcar that had been run into the electric station during the slack time of the day, and it was followed by a message from Lewisham that a bank had been dynamited, a junior clerk and a book-keeper being killed.

The Commissioner literally wrung his hands in despair.

That was the last outrage of the day.

At 5 o'clock that evening some workmen, returning home and taking a short cut through a field two miles from Catford, saw a man hanging from a tree.

They ran across and found a fashionably dressed gentleman of foreign appearance. One of the labourers cut the rope with his knife, but the man was dead when they cut him down. Beneath the tree was a black bag, to which somebody had affixed a label bearing the warning, 'Do not touch – this bag contains explosives: inform the police.' More remarkable still was the luggage label tied to the lapel of the dead man's coat. It ran: 'This is Franz Kitsinger, convicted at Prague in 1904, for throwing a bomb: escaped from prison March 17, 1905: was one of the three men responsible for the outrages today. Executed by order of The Council of Justice.'

The Four Just Men had returned to London.

'It's a humiliating confession,' said the Chief Commissioner when they brought the news to him, 'but the presence of these men takes a load off my mind.'

But the Red Hundred were grimly persistent.

That night a man, smoking a cigar, strolled aimlessly past the policeman on point duty at the corner of Kensington Park Gardens, and walked casually into Ladbroke Square. He strolled on, turned a corner and crossing a road, till he came to where one great garden served for a double row of middle-class houses. The backs of these houses opened on to the square. He looked round and, seeing the coast clear, he clambered over the iron railings and dropped into the big pleasure ground, holding very carefully an object that bulged in his pocket.

He took a leisurely view of the houses before he decided on the victim. The blinds of this particular house were up and the French windows of the dining-room were open, and he could see the laughing group of young people about the table. There was a birthday party or something of the sort in progress, for there was a great parade of Parthian caps and paper sun-bonnets.

The man was evidently satisfied with the possibilities for tragedy, and he took a pace nearer . . .

Two strong arms were about him, arms with muscles like cords of steel.

'Not that way, my friend,' whispered a voice in his ear . . .

The man showed his teeth in a dreadful grin.

* * *

The sergeant on duty at Notting Hill Gate Station received a note at the hands of a grimy urchin, who for days afterwards maintained a position of enviable notoriety.

'A gentleman told me to bring this,' he said hoarsely; little boys of his class invariably speak hoarsely.

The sergeant looked at the small boy sternly and asked him if he ever washed his face. Then he read the letter:

'The second man of the three concerned in the outrages at the Tower Bridge, the Borough and Lewisham, will be found in the garden of Maidham Crescent, under the laurel bushes, opposite No. 72.'

It was signed 'The Council of Justice'.

The Commissioner was sitting over his coffee at the Ritz, when they brought him the news. Falmouth was a deferential guest, and the chief passed him the note without comment.

'This is going to settle the Red Hundred,' said Falmouth. 'These people are fighting them with their own weapons – assassination with assassination, terror with terror. Where do we come in?'

'We come in at the end,' said the Commissioner, choosing his words with great niceness, 'to clean up the mess, and take any scraps of credit, that are going – ' he paused and shook his head. 'I hope – I should be sorry – ' he began.

'So should I,' said the detective sincerely, for he knew that his chief was concerned for the ultimate safety of the men whose arrest it was his duty to effect. The Commissioner's brows were wrinkled thoughtfully.

'The biggest job of all,' he said presently, 'is to prevent any more of this stuff arriving in the country. It is coming put up ready for use, that I'll swear.'

'You mean the explosives?'

'Yes; we've tried every questionable steamer that has entered the Thames this past week, and the river police have done splendidly. It is a ticklish business, particularly when the ship's under a foreign flag.' He looked at the note again.

'Two,' he said musingly; 'now, how on earth do the Four Just Men know the number in this – and how did they track them down – and who is the third? – heavens! one could go on asking questions the whole of the night!'

On one point the Commissioner might have been informed earlier in the evening – he was not told until three o'clock the next morning.

The third man was our friend Von Dunop, newly arrived from Spain, smarting under the contempt of the Woman of Gratz, anxious to rehabilitate himself in her favour, and in deadly fear of this woman's caprice.

Von Dunop, equipped for the night's work, supremely satisfied with the result of the morning – he had returned to London a day ahead of the Four Just Men – and ignorant of the fate of his fellow-terrorists, sallied forth to complete the day notably.

The crowd at a theatre door started a train of thought, but he rejected that outlet to ambition. It was too public, and the chance of escape was nil. These British audiences did not lose their heads so quickly; they refused to be confounded by noise and smoke, and a writhing figure here and there. Von Dunop was no exponent of the Glory of Death school. He greatly desired glory, but the smaller the risk, the greater the glory. This was his code.

He stood for a moment outside the Hôtel Ritz. A party of diners were leaving, and motor-cars were being steered up to carry these accursed plutocrats to the theatre. One soldierly-looking gentleman, with a grey moustache, and attended by a quiet, observant, clean-shaven man, interested the anarchist.

He and the soldier exchanged glances.

'Who the dickens was that?' asked the Commissioner as he stepped into the taxi. 'I seem to know his face.'

'I have seen him before,' said Falmouth. 'I won't go with you, sir – I've a little business to do in this part of the world.'

Thereafter Von Dunop was not permitted to enjoy his walk in solitude, for, unknown to him, a man 'picked him up' and followed him throughout the evening. And as the hour grew later, that one man became two, at eleven o'clock he became three, and at a quarter to twelve, when Von Dunop had finally fixed upon the scene and scope of his exploit, he turned from Park Lane into Brook Street to discover, to his annoyance, quite a number of people within call. Yet he suspected nothing. He did not suspect the night wanderer mooching along the kerb with downcast eyes, seeking the gutter for the stray cigar end; nor the two loudly talking men in suits of violet check who wrangled as they walked concerning the relative merits of the favourites for the Derby; nor the commissionaire trudging home with his bag in his hand and a pipe in his mouth, nor the clean-shaven man in evening dress.

The Home Secretary had a house in Berkeley Square. Von Dunop knew the number very well. He slackened pace to allow the man in evening dress to pass. The slow-moving taxi that was fifty yards away he must risk. This taxi had been his constant attendant during the last hour, but he did not know it.

He dipped his hand into his overcoat pocket and drew forth the machine. It was one of Culverui's masterpieces and, to an extent, experimental – that much the master had warned him in a letter that bore the date mark 'Riga'. He felt with his thumb for the tiny key that 'set' the machine and pushed it.

Then he slipped into the doorway of No. 196 and placed the bomb. It was done in a second, and so far as he could tell no man had seen him leave the pathway and he was back again on the sidewalk very quickly. But as he stepped back, he heard a shout and a man darted across the road, calling on him to surrender. From the left two men were running, and he saw the man in evening dress blowing a whistle.

He was caught; he knew it. There was a chance of escape – the other end of the street was clear – he turned and ran like the wind. He could hear his pursuers pattering along behind him. His ear, alert to every phase of the chase, heard one pair of feet check and spring up the steps of 196. He glanced round. They were gaining on him, and he turned suddenly and fired three times. Somebody fell; he saw that much. Then right ahead of him a tall policeman sprang from the shadows and clasped him round the waist.

'Hold that man!" shouted Falmouth, running up. Blowing hard, came the night wanderer, a ragged object but skilful, and he had Von Dunop handcuffed in a trice.

It was he who noticed the limpness of the prisoner.

'Hullo!' he said, then held out his hand. 'Show a light here.'

There were half a dozen policemen and the inevitable crowd on the spot by now, and the rays of the bull's-eye focused on the detective's hand. It was red with blood. Falmouth seized a lantern and flashed it on the man's face.

There was no need to look farther. He was dead. Dead with the inevitable label affixed to the handle of the knife that killed him.

Falmouth rapped out an oath.

'It is incredible; it is impossible! He was running till the constable caught him, and he has not been out of our hands! Where is the officer who held him?'

Nobody answered, certainly not the tall policeman, who was at that moment being driven eastward, making a rapid change into the conventional evening costume of an English gentleman.

Chapter 14
The Ibex Queen

'We have said "check" to the Terrorists; how effective that check will be depends very largely upon the good sense and patience of the citizens of this city,' wrote Manfred in the course of his remarkable letter to *The Times*. Perhaps the most interesting letter that the famous newspaper has ever published, coming as it did from a man against whom a warrant existed on the capital charge, and who had rendered unique and dreadful service to a nation that would assuredly hang him, if Fate delivered him into her hands.

It would seem that the fires of the Red Hundred had been beaten down and finally extinguished by the catastrophes that overtook its most trusty lieutenants on the very day it had scored its greatest triumph. But those who knew the organization were not deceived. Not for a single second did Scotland Yard relax its vigilance, and the Four Just Men, from their unknown watch-tower, waited, without illusions. For the second check came from Scotland Yard. An uncanny prescience as to the presence of cargo not entered on the ship's papers brought the Yard into ill repute amongst certain skippers on the Baltic, and the Red Hundred needed weapons for their war.

'Keep them inactive for a month and they'll melt away,' said an authority, and there was wisdom in the reasoning.

One night the Woman of Gratz received a letter that roused her from her brooding, and rekindled the fire in her sulky eyes. Such a letter it was, illiterate, written in curious Greek characters, that set the hive of anarchy throughout London humming; that brought delegates who, from reasons of prudence, had scattered themselves over England, back to the headquarters of the Red Hundred.

By that same post a letter was delivered at Hill Lodge, Lewisham, which begged to acknowledge receipt of favour of 18th, and in reply to state goods would be shipped, et cetera, et cetera.

The men in the watch-tower – it was only a figurative watch-tower – were interested more than a little by this communication.

* * *

With heavy seas breaking on her port quarter, the ramshackle tramp *Ibex Queen*, a most unqueenly craft, came shuddering and shaking through the North Sea, and her chief officer, pulling a dilapidated golf cap down over his ear, spat reflectively over the side of the bridge and expressed himself: 'It's a lucky thing for us the wind's astern, old man.' Old man, smoking contentedly in the lee of the crazy chart-room, grunted approvingly, for not only was he master, but he was owner of the *Ibex Queen*.

The cautious and offensive attitude of Lloyd's, who refused to insure his craft after the mysterious disappearance of two boats of his, had given him a new interest in the art of navigation. Luckily he had not been master either of the *Miko* or the *Pride of Dawmish*, when they sank, and his ticket, in consequence, remained unsullied. Not so the unfortunate skippers, one of whom, a notoriously careless man, had gone down with his ship and the other had been suspended for six months, during which period he drank heavily and frequently, and was in receipt of a handsome allowance from 'friends'.

Now he was chief officer of the *Ibex Queen*, speaking familiarly with its captain – a significant fact, but one upon which I wish to lay no undue emphasis.

Because of the driving sleet that fell, they picked up no light till the revolving flash of the Nore Lightship.

The little ship plunged on in silence, lifting, wallowing, shuddering, an uneven way till the light was abreast, and then something broke the silence, a strident voice that hailed from the blackness of the night-enshrouded sea.

' . . . *Ibex Queen* ahoy!'

Part of the cry was blown away by the wind.

The mate, holding on, leant over the side of the bridge, and reached his battered megaphone.

'Ahoy!' he bellowed.

From the dark waters came the answer:

'Is that . . . *Queen*?'

'Ay.'

'Stop . . . coming aboard.'

The mate jerked back the handle of the telegraph.

'It's them fellers they told us about at Riga,' he grumbled. 'but how in hell they expect to get aboard, I don't know.

In a few minutes the *Ibex Queen* lay rolling in the trough of the sea.

It was indeed ticklish work getting aboard, for with the stopping of the vessel, the full force of the following gale struck her.

But out of the gloom overside a voice called for a rope, and an imperious demand came for steam in the donkey engine, and with some delay there arrived a sleepy donkey man who passed a steel hawser overboard.

Then in a comparative calm that followed a seventh wave, a voice ordered sharply: 'Hoist her in!'

Roaring and rattling, the drum of the engine spun round and overside came a drenched little motor-launch with two passengers in shining oilskins.

Whilst the half-dozen men who composed the crew of the *Ibex Queen* lashed the launch fast on deck, the taller of the two passengers made his way to the bridge. He saluted the mate with a nod.

'Well!'

'We've had rather a rough time,' said the tall passenger coolly. 'I didn't think we could live out the seas that were breaking.'

The shadowy figure of the old man shuffled forward.

'I'm the master of this boat,' he said, and added, 'and owner – if you've got business, come below.'

The first mate set the telegraph to full speed ahead.

'Am I in this?' he demanded.

The old man stopped with one foot on the companion.

'You are, and you ain't,' he said cautiously. 'I'll send the second to relieve you in a bit.'

'Send him quick,' growled the man suspiciously.

In the dingy saloon where an oil lamp swung leisurely to the extent of its tethering chain, the skipper viewed his visitors.

'Ain't I seen you before?' he asked.

Manfred laughed.

'Perhaps.'

'Bilbao or Vigo, or one of them Spanish ports maybe,' suggested the skipper.

'Very likely,' said Manfred carelessly; 'at any rate, I know you – I was once a passenger by the *Pride of Dawmish* when you were skipper.'

The old man coughed with some embarrassment.

'Very unfortunate business that,' he recited. 'If I'd had charge of her, nothing would have happened . . . valuable cargo . . . never got a penny from them swines of insurance people.'

Manfred's keen eyes were fixed on the old man.

'I thought the reverse,' he said dryly. 'Somebody told me – '

'Lies, all lies,' said the skipper doggedly. He was, in the light, an uncleanly old man, with dirty white tufts of whisker placed at irregular intervals over his face. He shifted uneasily under Manfred's scrutiny.

'What about this cargo?' he said abruptly, then checked himself. 'What d'yer want?' he modified his demand.

Manfred produced a pocket-book and from this extracted a printed sheet. The old man fumbled for his pince-nez and looked through the sheet.

'That's regular,' he said. 'Hundred and twenty bales of skins to the order of Mereowski, Leather Brokers, St. Ann's Wharf – well?'

'An insignificant cargo,' said Manfred quietly, 'for so high a freight.' It was a shot at random, but it went home.

The old man grinned.

'A freight without inquiries,' he said smugly, 'me not meetin' the charter parties and asking no questions.'

'I see,' said Manfred.

'And you're the consign–ee?' asked the skipper.

Manfred made a motion of assent.

'In fact – if not in intention,' was his cryptic reply, and then he went on.

'I want you to take a voyage, Captain Stansell – a pleasure trip.'

Again the old man grinned. 'It'll be a pleasure to me – if the money's all right.'

'Say to Gravesend,' Manfred continued, 'a straight trip to Gravesend, carrying passengers – shipwrecked passengers – tell the tale to the Trinity Masters.'

The old man was looking at Manfred from under his shaggy eyebrows.

'What – ' he began, when the door was flung open and the chief mate strode in.

'There's a tug standing out to us making signal,' he said, and the old man looked perplexed.

'Ah!' he said thoughtfully, 'the signal – come to think of it, mister, you showed no light?'

'That is so,' said the visitor carelessly; 'you see, we underestimated the bucketing we should get in our little boat, and the flare wouldn't burn – we shipped water in every locker.'

The two ship's officers were regarding Manfred and his companion with growing suspicion.

'How do I know you're the parties the stuff's intended for?' asked the skipper; 'them skins, I mean,' he added hastily, 'what I took aboard at Riga, me and the mate being ashore at the time, and not seeing 'em stowed.'

'*Qui s'excuse, s'accuse*,' quoted Manfred with a smile. 'I can make your mind easy on that point, because – ' he arrested his speech purposely – 'we're not!'

'Eh!'

'We are not the people to whom your bombs and melinite are consigned,' Manfred went on coolly, 'but we are prepared to take charge of the cargo, none the less – don't move,' he warned.

The mate scowled and backed to the door.

'Don't run either,' said Manfred, having in his hand sufficient argument to enforce his command, and the mate wisely stood his ground.

'This is piracy,' stammered the old man, his face pinched and his jaw chattering. 'This is a hangin' business, mister – me – friend.'

'You surprise me,' said the other ironically, and motioned the officers to the far end of the saloon.

'We must leave you for a little while, but we shall be within call,' he said, and they went out, locking the door.

The *Ibex Queen* rolled and dipped before the following seas, and Manfred, swinging himself up the narrow gangway ladder, reached the bridge. A shivering young man in the canvas shelter at the end of the bridge looked round.

'Where's the old man?' he asked.

'Temporarily confined to his cabin,' said Gonsalez flippantly.

'What's the game?' asked the youngster.

'Where's the tug?' asked Manfred.

'There she is – half a mile away,' grumbled the boy, then again: 'What's the racket?' he asked.

'Nothing much,' replied Manfred, 'only this old tub is running contraband, bombs and high explosives for the Port of London.'

'Good Lord!' said the astonished youth aghast, 'is the old man in it?'

'Up to his eyes – show the tug a flare.'

The young mate had jumped to the conclusion that these two men were police officers, and obeyed, and in a few seconds the sea was illuminated with the flare's ghostly light.

'When she comes alongside,' ordered Manfred, 'the crew can go ashore.'

'What about the ship?'

'I'll look after this beautiful craft,' was the quiet reply.

Twenty minutes later Poiccart summoned the two officers from the cabin, and they went on deck to find the scratch crew paraded with their bags – stokers, engineers, seamen and boys.

'What's the meaning of this?' roared the skipper in a flurry of alarm.

A voice from the darkness of the bridge informed him 'Stand by to abandon ship!' it said mockingly; 'there's a tug alongside with a few of your friends. If you stay, you'll be shot – move!'

A revolver bullet struck the deck at the old man's feet and he jumped for the companion ladder. The sea had fallen a little, but the tiny mast of the tug alongside gyrated dizzily.

Telling the story of the end of the *Ilex Queen* it may be said in truth, that the captain was the first to leave the ship, but that the chief officer was a close second.

Manfred watched the departure and shouted his farewells.

'*Bon voyage!*' he cried, then to the skipper of the tug: 'Let go – whilst you are safe!'

He heard the fussy little engines of the smaller craft panting, and watched her starboard light dipping and rising in the seas as she circled round for the shore trip.

Poiccart, slipping off his oilskins, clattered down the grimy ladder that led to the engine-room, and as the *Ibex Queen* gathered way again, Manfred swung her head to sea.

Through the speaking tube Poiccart gave him some information.

'Steam enough to get us into deep water,' he reported.

When the Admiralty chart showed seventy fathoms Manfred rung the telegraph to 'stop'.

'Luckily,' he said later, 'the sea has gone down considerably. This place will do remarkably well, and, besides, we want a little steam in hand for the donkey engine.'

Whilst Poiccart was busy in the hold, Manfred gave a last look round the horizon for signs of approaching steamers. The North Sea is never deserted, and away to the north-east a little light twinkled. The two men showed considerable seamanship in getting their boat overside.

'Goodbye, *Ibex Queen*,' said Manfred grimly, and started the purring engines of the launch.

He had left the lights burning on the doomed ship, and the men watched her unsteady roll.

'Not desiring publicity,' said Poiccart, 'I have arranged for a fairly unspectacular sinking.'

'Noiseless?'

'As far as possible,' said the other. A dull 'boom!' floated over the water.

'That was unavoidable,' said Poiccart apologetically, as the bow of the ship rose up. Then she went down by the stern, quickly, silently, mysteriously. Thus passed the *Ibex Queen*, and Lloyd's list knew her name no more.

* * *

The sometime captain of the *Ibex Queen* had outgrown his awe of beautiful women. If he shed senile tears in the presence of the Woman of Gratz, they were inspired by the pecuniary loss he had suffered in the loss of one of the finest twin-screw steamers that ever left the Clyde yard. This description is his. To exaggerate virtues of the departed is characteristically human, and the *Ibex Queen* was an ocean liner, sumptuously fitted, extravagantly manned, and the envy and admiration of the seaborne world.

'And now – !' he snivelled a little, wiping away the tears with a greasy cap – and now she lay in seventy fathoms of water, this Sea's Pride!

'And all through a bit of dirty business that I wouldn't have took on, but for the slack times!' he said slowly and added a practical request: what was she going to do about it?

'You were paid for the risk,' she said impatiently. She spoke through an interpreter, for her knowledge of English was limited.

'Paid!' The old man glared furiously. 'Paid a miserable thousand for a ship worth its weight in gold.'

But she had sources of information at hand that he had not expected.

'Your ship was worth its weight – in old iron,' she said coldly; 'it was such a wretched thing that no insurance company would risk a policy.'

He stormed, threatened, thrusting his seamed, mottled face into hers. He would have the law; the police should know, and a great deal more of the same kind of talk.

She eyed him curiously.

'Captain,' she said slowly, 'we, the brotherhood, the association, sympathize with you in your loss, we will even go so far as to compensate you – reasonably, but if you talk foolishly, we have the way and the will to make you silent.'

The old skipper tried to suppress a shudder, but without success. Wilfully blind to the character of the work he had undertaken, it came as a shock to see the veil of pretence torn from the 'business' and the grim reality of his enterprise shown, naked and ugly.

Seeking for an object for the display of rage which was necessary to cloak his fear, he happily hit upon the man who had brought about his misfortune, and his denunciations of Manfred and his works found instant response.

'You have lost a ship!' she said; 'seek the man who destroyed it and I will buy you a new one. Yes, I – I will buy you such a ship as you have never yet commanded. Give him into my hands, dead or alive. I ask for no greater service than that!'

She struck a bell and a man came into the room. She pointed to the captain.

'You will give this sailor a thousand pounds,' she said; 'you will also see that he is kept under observation. If he communicates with the police or endeavours in any way to betray us, you will kill him.'

The captain, trading as he did in the Baltic, had picked up a little Russian – sufficient, at any rate, to understand what she said.

Therefore he left the house in Maida Vale – where Madame Deloraine gave lessons in French to a never-ceasing stream of queer-looking pupils from 9 a.m. to 6 p.m. – with a dry mouth and – under the circumstances – a very natural unsteadiness of gait.

Chapter 15
The trial

To fathom the mind of the Woman of Gratz is no easy task, and one not to be lightly undertaken. Remembering her obscure beginning, the bare-legged child drinking in revolutionary talk in the Transylvanian kitchen, and the development of her intellect along unconventional lines – remembering, also, that early in life she made acquaintance with the extreme problems of life and death in their least attractive forms, and that the proportion of things had been grossly distorted by her teachers, you may arrive at a point where your vacillating judgement hesitates between blame and pity.

I would believe that the power of introspection had no real place in her mental equipment, else how can we explain her attitude towards the man whom she had once defied and reconcile those outbursts of hers wherein she called for his death, for his terrible punishment, wherein, too, she allowed herself the rare luxury of unrestrained speech, how can we reconcile these tantrums with the fact that this man's voice filled her thoughts day and night, the recollection of this man's eyes through his mask followed her every movement, till the image of him became an obsession?

It may be that I have no knowledge of women and their ways (there is no subtle smugness in the doubt I express) and that her inconsistency was general to her sex. But Manfred himself was never quite sure of her, and to Leon Gonsalez she had no material existence. To him she was a perverted intellect, and as such worthy of study. Poiccart crystallized her virtues and her weaknesses when he called her a 'dangerous fool'; beyond that this unemotional man was not prepared to go.

But Manfred, with all his genius, was only a man, and liable to a man's mistakes. As to Gonsalez, he was seemingly beyond the reach of passion, and judged cold-bloodedly. Poiccart was more human, but lacked romance. As for the fourth man, Courlander, who has flitted at intervals through the pages of this story, his judgment is for the moment under suspicion, for the sentiment with which

Gonzalez once charged him is very apparent in all his reasonings – for the moment.

With the knowledge of a market overstocked with stories, dealing intimately and with minute thoroughness, with the working of the human soul – with the example of the unparalleled case of the brother-author, who devoted a whole chapter to the psychology of a woman's smile, I feel how lame and incompetent is the bald statement that the Woman of Gratz hated George Manfred with an immeasurable hatred, and yet hungered for the sight of him. All the more remarkable was it, from the fact that for his companions she had neither hate nor thought. Yet she saw clearly enough that the other two were equal in wisdom and coolness and courage. To one of them at least she might well have owed a special debt of vengeance, for that night on the hills he had wrenched a pistol from her hand with unceremonious violence. As to the fourth, she had seen him twice. Once, masked by the fire on the Sierras, and once – it was a fleeting vision but clearly photographed in her mind – in the corridor on the day she first met Manfred.

It is curious that she should be thinking idly of the fourth man when they brought news of him to her. It must not be imagined that she had spared either trouble or money to secure the extermination of her enemies, and the enemies of the Red Hundred. She had described them after their first meeting, and portraits, sketched under her instruction, had been circulated by the officers of the Reds. Once or twice she had asked herself why, with the coming of the judge that night – she always went back in thought to the little house in the hill – the three had been masked. With the death of Von Dunop, the answer was clear enough. No man saw their faces and lived. Would they kill her? Would Manfred strike the blow, crushing her against him in his strong arms once more? That would be a death robbed of half its terrors . . . Thus she mused, sitting near the window of her house, lulled by the ceaseless hum of traffic in the street below, and half dozing.

The turning of the door-handle woke her from her dreams.

It was Smidt, the unspeakable Smidt, all perspiration and excitement. His round coarse face glowed with it, and he could scarcely bring his voice to tell the news.

'We have him! we have him!' he cried in glee, and snapped his fingers. 'Oh, the good news! – I am the first! Nobody has been, Little Friend? I have run and have taken taxis – '

'You have – whom?' she asked steadily. The colour left her face and her hand strayed to her breast. As she waited she could feel the dull throbbing of her heart.

'Speak, fool!' she blazed. The suspense sickened her. If it should be –

'The man – one of the men,' he said, 'who killed Starque and Francois, and – '

'Which – which man?' she said harshly.

He fumbled in his pocket and pulled out the discoloured sketch.

'Oh!' she said; it was not Manfred.

Was she relieved or disappointed? Disappointed indeed.

'Why, why?' she asked stormily, 'why only this man? Why not the others – why not the leader? – have they caught him and lost him?'

Chagrin and astonishment sat on Smidt's round face. His disappointment was almost comic.

'But, Little Mother!' he said, crestfallen and bewildered, 'this is one – we did not hope even for one and – '

The storm passed over.

'Yes, yes,' she said wearily, 'one – even one is good. They shall learn that the Red Hundred can still strike – this leader shall know – This man shall have a death,' she said, looking at Smidt, 'worthy of his importance. Tell me how he was captured.'

'It was the picture,' said the eager Smidt, 'the picture you had drawn. One of our comrades thought he recognized him and followed him to his house. To make sure he sent for me. I went and recognized him – '

'Why was I not told?' she asked sternly.

'There was no time – indeed there was no time,' he pleaded.

'But we might have taken them all.'

'No, no, no!' he said quickly; 'he lived alone, this man; that made it easier. Last night he went out – he walked quiet streets – soh!'

His gestures filled the blank spaces of the story.

'He shall be tried – tonight,' and she spent the day anticipating her triumph.

Conspirators do not always choose dark arches for their plottings. The Red Hundred especially were notorious for the likeliness of their rendezvous. They went to nature for a precedent, and as she endows the tiger with stripes that are undistinguishable from the jungle grass, so the Red Hundred would choose for their meetings such a place where meetings were usually held.

It was in the Lodge Room of the Pride of Millwall, A.O.S.A. – which may be amplified as the Associated Order of the Sons of Abstinence – that the trial took place. The financial position of the Pride of Millwall was not strong. An unusual epidemic of temperate seafaring men had called the Lodge into being, the influx of capital from eccentric bequests had built the tiny hall, and since the fiasco attending the first meeting of the League of London, much of its public business had been skilfully conducted in these riverside premises. It had been raided by the police during the days of terror, but nothing of an incriminating character had been discovered. Because of the success with which the open policy had been pursued the Woman of Gratz preferred to take the risk of an open trial in a hall liable to police raid.

The man must be so guarded that escape was impossible. Messengers sped in every direction to carry out her instruction. There was a rapid summoning of leaders of the movement, the choice of the place of trial, the preparation for a ceremony which was governed by well-established precedent, and the arrangement of the properties which played so effective a part in the trials of the Hundred.

In the black-draped chamber of trial the Woman of Gratz found a full company. Maliscrivona, Tchezki, Vellantini, De Romans, to name a few who were there sitting together side by side on the low forms, and they buzzed a welcome as she walked into the room and took her seat at the higher place. She glanced round the faces, bestowing a nod here and a glance of recognition there. She remembered the last time she had made an appearance before the rank and file of the movement. She missed many faces that had turned to her in those days: Starque, François, Kitsinger – dead at the hands of the Four Just Men. It fitted her mood to remember that tonight she would judge one who had at least helped in the slaying of Starque.

Abruptly she rose. Lately she had had few opportunities for the display of that oratory which was once her sole title to consideration in the councils of the Red Hundred. Her powers of organization had come to be respected later. She felt the want of practice as she began speaking. She found herself hesitating for words, and once she felt her illustrations were crude. But she gathered confidence as she proceeded and she felt the responsive thrill of a fascinated audience.

It was the story of the campaign that she told. Much of it we know; the story from the point of view of the Reds may be guessed. She finished her speech by recounting the capture of the enemy.

'Tonight we aim a blow at these enemies of progress; if they have been merciless, let us show them that the Red Hundred is not to be outdone in ferocity. As they struck, so let us strike – and, in striking, read a lesson to the men who killed our comrades, that they, nor the world, will ever forget.'

There was no cheering as she finished – that had been the order – but a hum of words as they flung their tributes of words at her feet – a ruck of incoherent phrases of praise and adoration.

Then two men led in the prisoner.

He was calm and interested, throwing out his square chin resolutely when the first words of the charge were called and twiddling the fingers of his bound hands absently.

He met the scowling faces turned to him serenely, but as they proceeded with the indictment, he grew attentive, bending his head to catch the words.

Once he interrupted. 'I cannot quite understand that,' he said in fluent Russian, 'my knowledge of German is limited.'

'What is your nationality?' demanded the woman.

'English,' he replied.

'Do you speak French?' she asked.

'I am learning,' he said naively, and smiled.

'You speak Russian,' she said. Her conversation was carried on in that tongue.

'Yes,' he said simply; 'I was there for many years.'

After this, the sum of his transgressions were pronounced in a language he understood. Once or twice as the reader proceeded – it was Ivan Oranvitch who read – the man smiled.

The Woman of Gratz recognized him instantly as the fourth of the party that gathered about her door the day Bartholomew was murdered. Formally she asked him what he had to say before he was condemned.

He smiled again.

'I am not one of the Four Just Men,' he said; 'whoever says I am – lies.'

'And is that all you have to say?' she asked scornfully.

'That is all,' was his calm reply.

'Do you deny that you helped slay our comrade Starque?'

'I do not deny it,' he said easily, 'I did not help – I killed him.'

'Ah!' the exclamation came simultaneously from every throat.

'Do you deny that you have killed many of the Red Hundred?'

He paused before he answered.

'As to the Red Hundred – I do not know; but I have killed many people.' He spoke with the grave air of a man filled with a sense of responsibility, and again the exclamatory hum ran through the hall. Yet, the Woman of Gratz had a growing sense of unrest in spite of the success of the examination.

'You have said you were in Russia – did men fall to your hand there?'

He nodded.

'And in England?'

'Also in England,' he said.

'What is your name?' she asked. By an oversight it was a question she had not put before.

The man shrugged his shoulders.

'Does it matter?' he asked.

A thought struck her. In the hall she had seen Magnus the Jew. He had lived for many years in England, and she beckoned him.

'Of what class is this man?' she asked in a whisper.

'Of the lower orders,' he replied; 'it is astounding – did you not notice when – no, you did not see his capture. But he spoke like a man of the streets, dropping his aspirates.'

He saw she looked puzzled and explained.

'It is a trick of the order – just as the Moujik says . . . ' he treated her to a specimen of colloquial Russian.

'What is your name?' she asked again.

He looked at her slyly.

'In Russia they called me Father Kopab . . . ' *

The majority of those who were present were Russian, and at the word they sprang to their feet, shrinking back with ashen faces, as though they feared contact with the man who stood bound and helpless in the middle of the room.

The Woman of Gratz had risen with the rest. Her lips quivered and her wide open eyes spoke her momentary terror.

'I killed Starque,' he went on, 'by authority. François also. Some day – ' he looked leisurely about the room – 'I shall also – '

'Stop!' she cried, and then: 'Release him,' she said, and, wonderingly, Smidt cut the bonds that bound him.

He stretched himself. 'When you took me,' he said, 'I had a book; you will understand that here in England I find – forgetfulness in books – and I, who have seen so much suffering and want caused through departure from the law, am striving as hard for the regeneration of mankind as you – but differently.'

---

* *Kopab*: literally, 'head-off'

Somebody handed him a book.

He looked at it, nodded, and slipped it into his pocket.

'Farewell,' he said as he turned to the open door.

'In God's name!' said the Woman of Gratz, trembling, 'go in peace, Little Father.'

And the man Jessen, sometime headsman to the Supreme Council, and latterly public executioner of England, walked out, no man barring his exit.

* * *

The power of the Red Hundred was broken. This much Falmouth knew. He kept an ever-vigilant band of men on duty at the great termini of London, and to these were attached the members of a dozen secret police forces of Europe. Day by day, there was the same report to make. Such and such a man, whose very presence in London had been unsuspected, had left via Harwich. So-and-so, surprisingly sprung from nowhere, had gone by the eleven o'clock train from Victoria; by the Hull and Stockholm route twenty had gone in one day, and there were others who made Liverpool, Glasgow, and Newcastle their port of embarkation.

I think that it was only then that Scotland Yard realized the strength of the force that had lain inert in the metropolis, or appreciated the possibilities for destruction that had been to hand in the days of the Terror.

Certainly every batch of names that appeared on the commissioner's desk made him more thoughtful than ever.

'Arrest them!' he said in horror when the suggestion was made. 'Arrest them! Look here, have you ever seen driver ants attack a house in Africa? Marching in, in endless battalions at midnight and clearing out everything living from chickens to beetles? Have you ever seen them re-form in the morning and go marching home again? You wouldn't think of arresting 'em, would you? No, you'd just sit down quietly out of their reach and be happy when the last little red leg has disappeared round the corner!'

Those who knew the Red Hundred best were heartily in accord with his philosophy.

'They caught Jessen,' reported Falmouth.

'Oh!' said the commissioner.

'When he disclosed his identity, they got rid of him quick.'

'I've often wondered why the Four Just Men didn't do the business of Starque themselves,' mused the Commissioner.

'It was rather rum,' admitted Falmouth, 'but Starque was a man under sentence, as also was François. By some means they got hold of the original warrants, and it was on these that Jessen – did what he did.'

The commissioner nodded. 'And now,' he asked, 'what about them?' Falmouth had expected this question sooner or later. 'Do you suggest that we should catch them, sir?' he asked with thinly veiled sarcasm; 'because if you do, sir, I have only to remind you that we've been trying to do that for some years.'

The chief commissioner frowned.

'It's a remarkable thing,' he said, 'that as soon as we get a situation such as – the Red Hundred scare and the Four Just Men scare, for instance, we're completely at sea, and that's what the papers will say. It doesn't sound creditable, but it's so.'

I place the superintendent's defence of Scotland Yard on record *in extenso*.

'What the papers say,' said Falmouth, 'never keeps me awake at night. Nobody's quite got the hang of the police force in this country – certainly the writing people haven't.

'There are two ways of writing about the police, sir. One way is to deal with them in the newspaper fashion with the headline "Another Police Blunder" or "The Police and The Public", and the other way is to deal with them in the magazine style, which is to show them as softies on the wrong scent, whilst an ornamental civilian is showing them their business, or as mysterious people with false beards who pop up at the psychological moment, and say in a loud voice, "In the name of the Law, I arrest you!"

'Well, I don't mind admitting that I know neither kind. I've been a police officer for twenty-three years, and the only assistance I've had from a civilian was from a man named Blackie, who helped me to find the body of a woman that had disappeared. I was rather prejudiced against him, but I don't mind admitting that he was pretty smart and followed his clues with remarkable ingenuity.

'The day we found the body I said to him: "Mr Blackie, you have given me a great deal of information about this woman's movements – in fact, you know a great deal more than you ought to know – so I shall take you into custody on the suspicion of having caused her death."

'Before he died he made a full confession, and ever since then I have always been pleased to take as much advice and help from outside as I could get.

'When people sometimes ask me about the cleverness of Scotland Yard, I can't tell 'em tales such as you read about. I've had murderers, anarchists, burglars, and average low-down people to deal with, but they have mostly done their work in a commonplace way and bolted. And as soon as they have bolted, we've employed fairly commonplace methods and brought 'em back.

'If you ask me whether I've been in dreadful danger, when arresting desperate murderers and criminals, I say "No".

'When your average criminal finds himself cornered, he says, "All right, Mr Falmouth; it's a cop," and goes quietly.

'Crime and criminals run in grooves. They're hardy annuals with perennial methods. Extraordinary circumstances baffle the police as they baffle other folks. You can't run a business on business lines and be absolutely prepared for anything that turns up. Whiteley's will supply you with a flea or an elephant, but if a woman asked a shopgirl to hold her baby whilst she went into the tinned meat department, the girl and the manager and the whole system would be floored, because there is no provision for holding babies. And if a Manchester goods merchant, unrolling his stuff, came upon a snake lying all snug in the bale, he'd be floored too, because natural history isn't part of their business training, and they wouldn't be quite sure whether it was a big worm or a boa constrictor.'

The Commissioner was amused.

'You've an altogether unexpected sense of humour,' he said, 'and the moral is – '

'That the unexpected always floors you, whether it's humour or crime,' said Falmouth, and went away fairly pleased with himself.

In his room he found a waiting messenger.

'A lady to see you, sir.'

'Who is it?' he asked in surprise.

The messenger handed him a slip of paper and when he read it he whistled.

'The unexpected, by — ! Show her up.'

On the paper was written – 'The Woman of Gratz' . . .

Chapter 16
Manfred

Manfred sat alone in his Lewisham house – he was known to the old lady who was his caretaker as 'a foreign gentleman in the music line – ' and in the subdued light of the shaded lamp, he looked tired. A book lay on the table near at hand, and a silver coffee-service and an empty coffee-cup stood on the stool by his side. Reaction he felt. This strange man had set himself to a task that was never-ending. The destruction of the forces of the Red Hundred was the end of a fight that cleared the ground for the commencement of another – but physically he was weary.

Gonsalez had left that morning for Paris, Poiccart went by the afternoon train, and he was to join them tomorrow.

The strain of the fight had told on them, all three. Financially, the cost of the war had been heavy, but that strain they could stand better than any other, for had they not the fortune of – Courtlander; in case of need they knew their man.

All the world had been searched before they – the first Four – had come together – Manfred, Gonsalez, Poiccart, and the man who slept eternally in the flower-grown grave at Bordeaux. As men taking the oaths of priesthood they lived down the passions and frets of life. Each man was an open book to the other, speaking his most secret thought in the faith of sympathy, one dominating thought controlling them all.

They had made the name of the Four Just Men famous or infamous (according to your point of reckoning) throughout the civilized world. They came as a new force into public and private life. There were men, free of the law, who worked misery on their fellows; dreadful human ghouls fattening on the bodies and souls of the innocent and helpless; great magnates calling the law to their aid, or pushing it aside as circumstances demanded. All these became amenable to a new law, a new tribunal. There had grown into being systems which defied correction; corporations beyond chastisement; individuals protected by cunningly drawn legislation, and others who knew to an inch the scope of toleration. In the name of justice, these men struck swiftly, dispassionately, mercilessly. The great swindler, the procureur, the suborner of witnesses, the briber of juries – they died.

There was no gradation of punishment: a warning, a second warning – then death.

Thus their name became a symbol, at which the evildoer went tremblingly about his work, dreading the warning and ready in most cases to heed it. Life became a sweeter, a more wholesome thing for many men who found the thin greenish-grey envelope on their breakfast-table in the morning; but others persisted on their way, loudly invoking the law, which in spirit, if not in letter, they had outraged. The end was very sure, and I do not know of one man who escaped the consequence.

Speculating on their identity, the police of the world decided unanimously upon two points. The first was that these men were enormously rich – as indeed they were, and the second that one or two of them were no mean scientists – that also was true. Of the fourth man who had joined them recently, speculation took a wider turn. Manfred smiled as he thought of this fourth member, of his honesty, his splendid qualities of heart and brain, his enthusiasm, and his proneness to 'lapse from the balance' – Gonsalez coined the phrase. It was an affectionate smile. The fourth man was no longer of the brotherhood; he had gone, the work being completed, and there were other reasons.

So Manfred was musing, till the little clock on the mantelpiece chimed ten, then he lit the spirit-kettle and brewed another cup of coffee. Thus engaged, he heard the far-away tinkle of a bell and the opening of a door. Then a murmur of voices and two steps on the stairs. He did not expect visitors, but he was always prepared for them at any hour.

'Come in,' he said, in answer to the knock; he recognized the apologetic rap of his housekeeper.

'A lady – a foreign lady to see you.'

'Show her in, please,' he said courteously.

He was busy with the kettle when she came in. He did not look up, nor did he ask who it was. His housekeeper stood a moment uncertain on the threshold, then went out, leaving them together.

'You will excuse me a moment,' he said. 'Please sit down.'

He poured out the coffee with a steady hand, walked to his desk, sorted a number of letters, tossed them into the grate, and stood for a moment watching them burn, then looked at her.

Taking no notice of his invitation, the girl stood waiting at ease, one hand on her hip, the other hanging loosely.

'Won't you sit down?' he asked again.

'I prefer to stand,' she said shortly.

'Then you are not so tired as I am,' he said, and sank back into the depths of his chair.

She did not reply, and for a few seconds neither spoke.

'Has the Woman of Gratz forgotten that she is an orator?' he said banteringly. It seemed to him that there was in those eyes of hers a great yearning, and he changed his tone.

'Sit down, Maria,' he said gently. He saw the flush that rose to her cheek, and mistook its significance.

'No, no!' he hastened to rectify an impression. 'I am serious now, I am not gibing – why have you not gone with the others?'

'I have work to do,' she said.

He stretched out his hands in a gesture of weariness.

'Work, work, work!' he said with a bitter smile, 'isn't the work finished? Isn't there an end to this work of yours?'

'The end is at hand,' she said, and looked at him strangely.

'Sit down,' he commanded, and she took the nearest chair and watched him.

Then she broke the silence.

'What are you?' she asked, with a note of irritation. 'Who gave you authority?'

He laughed.

'What am I – just a man, Maria. Authority? As you understand it – none.'

She was thoughtful for a moment.

'You have not asked me why I have come,' she said.

'I have not asked myself – yet it seems natural that you and I should meet again – to part.'

'What do they call you – your friends?' she asked suddenly. 'Do they say "the man with the beard", or "the tall man" – did any woman ever nurse you and call you by name?'

A shadow passed over his face for a second.

'Yes,' he said quietly; 'I have told you I am human; neither devil nor demi-god, no product of sea-foam or witches' cauldron,' he smiled, 'but a son of earthly parents – and men call me George Manfred.'

'George,' she repeated as though learning a lesson. 'George Manfred.' She looked at him long and earnestly, and frowned.

'What is it you see that displeases you?' he asked.

'Nothing,' she said quickly, 'only I am – I cannot understand – you are different – '

'From what you expected.'

She bent her head.

'You expected me to air a triumph. To place myself in defence?'

She nodded again.

'No, no,' he went on, 'that is finished. I do not pursue a victory – I am satisfied that the power of your friends is shattered. I dissociate you from the humiliation of their defeat.'

'I am no better nor worse than they,' she said defiantly.

'You will be better when the madness passes,' he said gravely, 'when you realize that your young life was not meant for the dreadful sacrifice of anarchy.'

He leant over and took her listless hand and held it between his palms.

'Child, you must leave this work,' he said softly, 'forget the nightmare of your past – put it out of your mind, so that you will come to believe that the Red Hundred never existed.'

She did not draw away her hand, nor did she attempt to check the tears that came to her eyes. Something had entered her soul – an influence that was beyond all description or definition. A wonderful element that had dissolved the thing of granite and steel, that she had fondly thought was her heart, and left her weak and shaking in the process.

'Maria, if you ever knew a mother's love – ' how soft his voice was – 'think of that: have you ever realized what your tiny life was to her – how she planned and thought and suffered for you – and to what end? That the hands she kissed should be set against men's lives! Did she pray to God that He might keep you strong in health and pure in soul – only that His gifts should prove a curse to His beautiful world?'

With the tenderness of a father he drew her to him, till she was on her knees before him and her weeping face was pressed closely against him.

His strong arms were about her, and his hand smoothed her hair.

'I am a wicked woman,' she sobbed, 'a wicked, wicked woman.'

'Hush,' he said sadly; 'do not let us take our conception of wickedness from our deeds, but from our intentions, however mistaken, however much they traverse the written law.'

But her sobbing grew wilder, and she clutched him as though in fear that he would leave her.

He talked to her as though she were a frightened child, chiding her, laughing at her in gentle raillery, and she grew calmer and presently lifted her stained face to his.

'Listen,' she said; 'I – I – oh, I cannot, I cannot say it.' And she buried her face on her breast.

Then with an effort she raised her head again.

'If I asked you – if I begged you to do something for me – would you?'

He looked into her eyes, smiling.

'You have done many things – you have killed – yes – yes, let me say it – I know I am hurting you, but let me finish.'

'Yes,' he said simply; 'I have killed.'

'Have you – pitied as you killed?'

He shook his head.

'Yet you would,' she went on, and her distress moved him, 'you would if you thought that you could kill a body and save a soul.'

He shook his head again.

'Yes, yes,' she whispered, and tried to speak. Twice she attempted to frame the words, and twice she failed. Then she pushed herself slowly backwards with her hands at his chest, and crouched before him with parted lips and heaving bosom.

'Kill me,' she breathed, 'for I have betrayed you to the police.'

Still he made no sign, sitting there all huddled in the big chair, as though every muscle of his body had relaxed.

'Do you hear?' she cried fiercely. 'I have betrayed you because – I think – I love you – but I – I did not know it – I did not know it! I hated you so that I pitied you – and always I thought of you!'

She knew by the look of pain in his eyes what her words had cost him.

Somehow she divined that the betrayal hurt least.

'I have never said it to myself,' she whispered; 'I have never thought it in my most secret thoughts – yet it was there, there all the time, waiting for expression – and I am happier, though you die, and though every hour of my life be a lifetime of pain, I am happier that I have said it, happier than I thought I could ever be.

'I have wondered why I remembered you, and why I thought of you, and why you came into my every dream. I thought it was because I hated you, because I wanted to kill you, and to hold you at my mercy – but I know now, I know now.'

She rocked from side to side, clasping her hands in the intensity of her passion.

'You do not speak?' she cried. 'Do you not understand, beloved? I have handed you over to the police, because – O God! because I love you! It must be that I do!'

He leant forward and held out his hands and she came to him half swooning.

'Marie, child,' he murmured, and she saw how pale he was, 'we are strangely placed, you and I, to talk of love. You must forget this, little girl; let this be the waking point of your bad dream; go forth into the new life – into a life where flowers are, and birds sing, and where rest and peace is.'

She had no thought now save for his danger.

'They are below,' she moaned. 'I brought them here – I guided them.'

He smiled into her face.

'I knew,' he said.

She looked at him incredulously.

'You knew,' she said, slowly.

'Yes – when you came – ' he pointed to the heap of burnt papers in the grate – 'I knew.'

He walked to the window and looked out. What he saw satisfied him.

He came back to where she still crouched on the floor and lifted her to her feet.

She stood unsteadily, but his arm supported her. He was listening, he heard the door open below.

'You must not think of me,' he said again.

She shook her head helplessly, and her lips quivered.

'God bless you and help you,' he said reverently, and kissed her.

Then he turned to meet Falmouth.

'George Manfred,' said the officer, and looked at the girl in perplexity.

'That is my name,' said Manfred quietly. 'You are Inspector Falmouth.'

'Superintendent,' corrected the other.

'I'm sorry,' said Manfred.

'I shall take you into custody,' said Falmouth, 'on suspicion of being a member of an organization known as the Four Just Men, and accordingly concerned in the following crimes – '

'I will excuse you the recital,' said Manfred pleasantly, and held out his hands. For the first time in his life he felt the cold contact of steel at his wrists.

The man who snapped the handcuffs on was nervous and bungled, and Manfred, after an interested glance at the gyves, lifted his hands.

'This is not quite fastened,' he said.

Then as they closed round him, he half turned toward the girl and smiled.

'Who knows how bright are the days in store for us both?' he said softly.

Then they took him away.

Charles Garrett, admirable journalist, had written the last line of a humorous description of a local concert at which a cabinet minister had sung pathetic ballads. Charles wrote with difficulty, for the situation had been of itself so funny, that extracting its hidden humours was a more than ordinarily heartbreaking thing. But he had finished and the thick batch of copy lay on the chief sub-editor's desk – Charles wrote on an average six words to a folio, and a half a column story from his pen bulked like a three-volume novel.

Charles stopped to threaten an office-boy who had misdirected a letter, strolled into various quiet offices to 'see who was there' and with his raincoat on his arm, and his stick in his hand, stopped at the end of his wanderings before the chattering tape machine. He looked through the glass box that shielded the mechanism, and was interested in a message from Teheran in the course of transmission.

' . . . at early date. Grand Vizier has informed Exchange Correspondent that the construction of line will be pushed forward . . . '

The tape stopped its stuttering and buzzed excitedly, then came a succession of quick jerks that cleared away the uncompleted message.

Then ' . . . the leader of the Four Just Men was arrested in London tonight,' said the tape, and Charles broke for the editor's room.

He flung open the door without ceremony, and repeated the story the little machine had told.

The grey chief received the news quietly, and the orders he gave in the next five minutes inconvenienced some twenty or thirty unoffending people.

The construction of the 'story' of the Four Just Men began at the lower rung of the intellectual ladder.

'You boy! get half a dozen taxicabs here quick . . . Poynter, 'phone the reporters in . . . get the Lambs Club on the 'phone and see if O'Mahony or any other of our bright youths are there . . . There are five columns about the Four Just Men standing in the gallery, get it pulled up, Mr Short . . . pictures – h'm . . . yet wire Massonni to get down to the police station and see if he can find a policeman who'll give him material for a sketch . . . Off you go, Charles, and get the story.'

There was no flurry, no rush; it was for all the world like the scene on a modern battleship when 'clear lower deck for action' had sounded. Two hours to get the story into the paper was ample, and there was no need for the whip.

Later, with the remorseless hands of the clock moving on, taxi after taxi flew up to the great newspaper office, discharging alert young men who literally leapt into the building. Later, with waiting operators sitting tensely before the keyboards of the linotypes, came Charles Garrett doing notable things with a stump of pencil and a ream of thin copy paper.

It was the *Megaphone* that shone splendidly amidst its journalistic fellows, with pages – I quote the envenomed opinion of the news editor of the *Mercury* – that 'shouted like the checks on a bookmaker's waistcoat'.

It was the *Megaphone* that fed the fires of public interest, and was mainly responsible for the huge crowds that gathered outside Greenwich Police Court, and overflowed in dense masses to the foot of Blackheath Hill, whilst Manfred underwent his preliminary inquiries.

'George Manfred, aged 39, of no occupation, residing at Hill Crest Lodge, St John's.' In this prosaic manner he was introduced to the world.

* * *

He made a striking figure in the steel-railed dock. A chair was placed for him, and he was guarded as few prisoners had been guarded. A special cell had been prepared for his reception, and departing from established custom, extra warders were detailed to watch him. Falmouth took no risks.

The charge that had been framed had to do with no well-known case. Many years before, one Samuel Lipski, a notorious East End sweater, had been found dead with the stereotyped announcement that he had fallen to the justice of the Four. Upon this the Treasury founded its case for the prosecution – a case which had been very thoroughly and convincingly prepared, and pigeon-holed against such time as arrest should overtake one or the other of the Four Just Men.

Reading over the thousands of newspaper cuttings dealing with the preliminary examination and trial of Manfred, I am struck with the absence of any startling feature, such as one might expect to find in a great state trial of this description. Summarizing the evidence that was given at the police court, one might arrange the 'parts' of the dozen or so commonplace witnesses so that they read –

A policeman: 'I found the body.'

An inspector: 'I read the label.'

A doctor: 'I pronounced him dead.'

An oily man with a slight squint and broken English: 'This man Lipski, I known him, he were a goot man and make the business wit the head, ker-vick.'

And the like.

Manfred refused to plead 'guilty' or 'not guilty'. He spoke only once during the police court proceedings, and then only when the formal question had been put to him.

'I am prepared to abide by the result of my trial,' he said clearly, 'and it cannot matter much one way or the other whether I plead "guilty" or "not guilty".'

'I will enter your plea as "not guilty",' said the magistrate.

Manfred bowed.

'That is at your worship's discretion,' he said.

On the seventh of June he was formally committed for trial. He had a short interview with Falmouth before he was removed from the police-court cells.

Falmouth would have found it difficult to analyse his feelings towards this man. He scarcely knew himself whether he was glad or sorry that fate had thrown the redoubtable leader into his hands.

His attitude to Manfred was that of a subordinate to a superior, and that attitude he would have found hardest to explain.

When the cell door was opened to admit the detective, Manfred was reading. He rose with a cheery smile to greet his visitor.

'Well, Mr Falmouth,' he said lightly, 'we enter upon the second and more serious act of the drama.'

'I don't know whether I'm glad or sorry,' said Falmouth bluntly.

'You ought to be glad,' said Manfred with his quizzical smile. 'For you've vindicated – '

'Yes, I know all about that,' said Falmouth dryly, 'but it's the other part I hate.'

'You mean – ?'

Manfred did not complete the question.

'I do – it's a hanging job, Mr Manfred, and that is the hateful business after the wonderful work you've done for the country.'

Manfred threw back his head, and laughed in unrestrained amusement.

'Oh, it's nothing to laugh about,' said the plain-spoken detective, 'you are against a bad proposition – the Home Secretary is a cousin of Ramon's, and he hates the very name of the Four Just Men.'

'Yet I may laugh,' said Manfred calmly, 'for I shall escape.'

There was no boastfulness in the speech, but a quiet assurance that had the effect of nettling the other.

'Oh, you will, will you?' he said grimly. 'Well, we shall see.'

There was no escape for Manfred in the dozen yards or so between his cell door and the prison van. He was manacled to two warders, and a double line of policemen formed an avenue through which he was marched. Not from the van itself that moved in a solid phalanx of mounted men with drawn swords. Nor from the gloomy portals of Wandsworth Gaol where silent, uniformed men closed round him and took him to the triple-locked cell.

Once in the night, as he slept, he was awakened by the sound of the changing guard, and this amused him.

If one had the space to write, one could compile a whole book concerning Manfred's life during the weeks he lay in gaol awaiting trial. He had his visitors. Unusual laxity was allowed in this respect. Falmouth hoped to find the other two men. He generously confessed his hope to Manfred.

'You may make your mind easy on that point,' said Manfred; 'they will not come.'

Falmouth believed him.

'If you were an ordinary criminal, Mr Manfred,' he said smilingly, 'I should hint the possibilities of King's evidence, but I won't insult you.'

Manfred's reply staggered him.

'Of course not,' he said with an air of innocence; 'if they were arrested, who on earth would arrange my escape?'

The Woman of Gratz did not come to see him, and he was glad.

He had his daily visits from the governor, and found him charmingly agreeable. They talked of countries known to both, of people whom each knew equally well, and tacitly avoided forbidden subjects. Only –

'I hear you are going to escape?' said the governor, as he concluded one of these visits. He was a largely built man, sometime Major of Marine Artillery, and he took life seriously. Therefore he did not share Falmouth's view of the projected escape as being an ill-timed jest.

'Yes,' replied Manfred.

'From here?'

Manfred shook his head solemnly.

'The details have not yet been arranged,' he said with admirable gravity. The governor frowned.

'I don't believe you're trying to pull my leg – it's too devilishly serious a matter to joke about – but it would be an awkward thing for me if you got away.' He was of the prisoner's own caste and he had supreme faith in the word of the man who discussed prison-breaking so lightheartedly.

'That I realize,' said Manfred with a little show of deference, 'and I shall accordingly arrange my plans, so that the blame shall be equally distributed.'

The governor, still frowning thoughtfully, left the cell. He came back in a few minutes.

'By the way, Manfred,' he said, 'I forgot to tell you that you'll get a visit from the chaplain. He's a very decent young fellow, and I know I needn't ask you to let him down lightly.'

With this subtle assumption of mutual paganism, he left finally.

'That is a worthy gentleman,' thought Manfred.

The chaplain was nervously anxious to secure an opening, and sought amidst the trivialities that led out of the conventional exchange of greetings a fissure for the insertion of a tactful inquiry.

Manfred, seeing his embarrassment, gave him the chance, and listened respectfully while the young man talked, earnestly, sincerely, manfully.

'N – no,' said the prisoner after a while, 'I don't think, Mr Summers, that you and I hold very different opinions, if they were all reduced to questions of faith and appreciation of God's goodness – but I have got to a stage where I shrink from labelling my inmost beliefs with this or that creed, or circumscribing the boundless limits of my faith with words. I know you will forgive me and believe that I do not say this from any desire to hurt you, but I have reached, too, a phase of conviction where I am adamant to outside influence. For good or ill, I must stand by the conceptions that I have built out of my own life and its teachings.

'There is another, and a more practical reason,' he added, 'why I should not do you or any other chaplain the disservice of taking up your time – I have no intention of dying.'

With this, the young minister was forced to be content. He met Manfred frequently, talking of books and people and of strange religions.

To the warders and those about him, Manfred was a source of constant wonder. He never wearied them with the recital of his coming attempt. Yet all that he said and did seemed founded on that one basic article of faith: I shall escape.

The governor took every precaution to guard against rescue. He applied for and secured reinforcements of warders, and Manfred, one morning at exercise seeing strange faces amongst his guards, bantered him with over-nervousness.

'Yes,' said the Major, 'I've doubled the staff. I'm taking you at your word, that is all – one must cling tight to the last lingering shreds of faith one has in mankind. You say that you're going to escape, and I believe you.' He thought a moment, 'I've studied you,' he added.

'Indeed?'

'Not here,' said the governor, comprehending the prison in a sweep of his hand, 'but outside – read about you and thought about you and a little dimly understood you – that makes me certain that you've got something at the back of your mind when you talk so easily of escape.'

Manfred nodded. He nodded many times thoughtfully, and felt a new interest in the bluff, brusque man.

'And whilst I'm doubling the guard and that sort of thing, I know in my heart that that "something" of yours isn't "something" with dynamite in it, or "something" with brute force behind it, but it's "something" that's devilishly deep – that's how I read it.'

He jerked his head in farewell, and the cell door closed behind him with a great jangling and snapping of keys.

He might have been tried at the sessions following his committal, but the Crown applied for a postponement, and being informed and asked whether he would care to raise any objection to that course, he replied that so far from objecting, he was grateful, because his arrangements were not yet completed, and when they asked him, knowing that he had refused solicitor and counsel, what arrangements he referred to, he smiled enigmatically and they knew he was thinking of this wonderful plan of escape. That such persistent assurances of delivery should eventually reach the public through the public press was only to be expected, and although 'Manfred says he will escape from Wandsworth' in the *Megaphone* headline, became 'A prisoner's strange statement' in *The Times*, the substance of the story was the same, and you may be sure that it lost nothing in the telling. A Sunday journal, with a waning circulation, rallied on the discovery that Manfred was mad, and published a column-long account of this 'poor lunatic gibbering of freedom'.

Being allowed to read the newspapers, Manfred saw this, and it kept him amused for a whole day.

The warders in personal attendance on him were changed daily, he never had the same custodian twice till the governor saw a flaw in the method that allowed a warder with whom he was only slightly acquainted, and of whose integrity he was ignorant, to come into close contact with his prisoner. Particularly did this danger threaten from the new officers who had been drafted to Wandsworth to reinforce the staff, and the governor went to the other extreme, and two trusted men, who had grown old in the service, were chosen for permanent watch-dogs.

'You won't be able to have any more newspapers,' said the governor one morning. 'I've had orders from headquarters – there have been some suspicious-looking "agonies" in the *Megaphone* this last day or so.'

'I did not insert them,' said Manfred, smiling.

'No – but you may have read them,' said the governor drily.

'So I might have,' said the thoughtful Manfred.

'Did you?'

Manfred made no reply.

'I suppose that isn't a fair question,' said the governor cheerfully; 'anyhow, no more papers. You can have books – any books you wish within limits.'

So Manfred was denied the pleasure of reading the little paragraphs that described the movements and doings of the fashionable world. Just then these interested him more than the rest of the newspaper put together. Such news as he secured was of a negative kind and through the governor. 'Am I still mad?' he asked.

'No.'

'Was I born in Brittany – the son of humble parents?'

'No – there's another theory now.'

'Is my real name still supposed to be Isadore something-or-other?'

'You are now a member of a noble family, disappointed at an early age by a reigning princess,' said the governor impressively.

'How romantic!' said Manfred in hushed tones. The gravity of his years, that was beyond his years, fell away from him in that time of waiting. He became almost boyish again. He had a never-ending fund of humour that turned even the tremendous issues of his trial into subject-matter of amusement.

Armed with the authority of the Home Secretary came Luigi Fressini, the youthful director of the Anthropological Institute of Rome.

Manfred agreed to see him and made him as welcome as the circumstances permitted. Fressini was a little impressed with his own importance, and had the professional manner strongly developed. He had a perky way of dropping his head on one side when he made observations, and reminded Manfred of a horse-dealer blessed with a little knowledge, but anxious to discover at all hazards the 'points' that fitted in with his preconceived theories. 'I would like to measure your head,' he said.

'I'm afraid I cannot oblige you,' said Manfred coolly; 'partly because I object to the annoyance of it, and partly because head-measuring in anthropology is as much out of date as bloodletting in surgery.'

The director was on his dignity.

'I'm afraid I cannot take lessons in the science – ' he began.

'Oh, yes, you can,' said Manfred, 'and you'd be a greater man if you did. As it is Antonio de Costa and Felix Hedeman are both beating you on your own ground – that monograph of yours on "Cerebral Dynamics" was awful nonsense.'

Whereupon Fressini went very red and spluttered and left the cell, afterwards in his indiscretion granting an interview to an evening newspaper, in the course of which he described Manfred as a typical homicide with those peculiarities of parietal development, that are invariably associated with cold-blooded murderers. For publishing what constituted a gross contempt of court, the newspaper was heavily fined, and at the instance of the British Government, Fressini was reprimanded, and eventually superseded by that very De Costa of whom Manfred spoke.

All these happenings formed the comedy of the long wait, and as to the tragedy, there was none.

A week before the trial Manfred, in the course of conversation, expressed a desire for a further supply of books.

'What do you want?' asked the governor, and prepared to take a note.

'Oh, anything,' said Manfred lazily – 'travel, biography, science, sport – anything new that's going.'

'I'll get you a list,' said the governor, who was not a booky man. 'The only travel books I know are those two new things, *Three Months in Morocco* and *Through the Ituri Forest*. One of them's by a new man, Theodore Max – do you know him?'

Manfred shook his head.

'But I'll try them,' he said.

'Isn't it about time you started to prepare your defence?' the governor asked gruffly.

'I have ho defence to offer,' said Manfred, 'therefore no defence to prepare.'

The governor seemed vexed.

'Isn't life sufficiently sweet to you – to urge you to make an effort to save it?' he asked roughly, 'or are you going to give it up without a struggle?'

'I shall escape,' said Manfred again; 'aren't you tired of hearing me tell you why I make no effort to save myself?'

'When the newspapers start the "mad" theory again,' said the exasperated prison official, 'I shall feel most inclined to break the regulations and write a letter in support of the speculation.'

'Do,' said Manfred cheerfully, 'and tell them that I run round my cell on all fours biting visitors' legs.'

The next day the books arrived. *The Mysteries of the Ituri Forest* remained mysteries, but *Three Months in Morocco* (big print, wide margins, 12s. 6d.) he read with avidity from cover to cover, notwithstanding the fact that the reviewers to a man condemned it as being the dullest book of the season. Which was an unkindly reflection upon the literary merits of its author, Leon Gonsalez, who had worked early and late to prepare the book for the press, writing far into the night, whilst Poiccart, sitting at the other side of the table, corrected the damp proofs as they came from the printer.

Chapter 18
The 'Rational Faithers'

In the handsomely furnished sitting-room of a West Kensington flat, Gonsalez and Poiccart sat over their post-prandial cigars, each busy with his own thoughts. Poiccart tossed his cigar into the fireplace and pulled out his polished briar and slowly charged it from a gigantic pouch. Leon watched him under half-closed lids, piecing together the scraps of information he had collected from his persistent observation.

'You are getting sentimental, my friend,' he said.

Poiccart looked up inquiringly.

'You were smoking one of George's cigars without realizing it. Halfway through the smoke you noticed the band had not been removed, so you go to tear it off. By the band you are informed that it is one of George's favourite cigars, and that starts a train of thought that makes the cigar distasteful to you, and you toss it away.'

Poiccart lit his pipe before replying.

'Spoken like a cheap little magazine detective,' he said frankly. 'If you would know I was aware that it was George's, and from excess of loyalty I was trying to smoke it; halfway through I reluctantly concluded that friendship had its limits; it is you who are sentimental.'

Gonsalez closed his eyes and smiled. 'There's another review of your book in the *Evening Mirror* tonight,' Poiccart went on maliciously; 'have you seen it?'

The recumbent figure shook its head.

'It says,' the merciless Poiccart continued, 'that an author who can make Morocco as dull as you have done, would make – '

'Spare me,' murmured Gonsalez half asleep.

They sat for ten minutes, the tick-tick of the little clock on the mantelpiece and the regular puffs from Poiccart's pipe breaking the silence.

'It would seem to me,' said Gonsalez, speaking with closed eyes, 'that George is in the position of a master who has set his two pupils a difficult problem to solve, quite confident that, difficult as it is, they will surmount all obstacles and supply the solution.'

'I thought you were asleep,' said Poiccart.

'I was never more awake,' said Gonsalez calmly. 'I am only marshalling details. Do you know Mr Peter Sweeney?'

'No,' said Poiccart.

'He's a member of the Borough Council of Chelmsford. A great and a good man.'

Poiccart made no response.

'He is also the head and front of the "Rational Faith" movement, of which you may have heard.'

'I haven't,' admitted Poiccart, stolid but interested.

'The "Rational Faithers",' Gonsalez explained sleepily, 'are an offshoot of the New Unitarians, and the New Unitarians are a hotchpotch people with grievances.'

Poiccart yawned.

'The "Rational Faithers",' Gonsalez went on, 'have a mission in life, they have also a brass band, and a collection of drivelling songs, composed, printed and gratuitously distributed by Mr Peter Sweeney, who is a man of substance.'

He was silent after this for quite a minute.

'A mission in life, and a nice loud brassy band – the members of which are paid monthly salaries – by Peter.'

Poiccart turned his head and regarded his friend curiously.

'What is all this about?' he asked.

'The "Rational Faithers",' the monotonous Gonsalez continued, 'are the sort of people who for all time have been in the eternal minority. They are against things, against public-houses, against music-halls, against meat eating, and vaccination – and capital punishment,' he repeated softly.

Poiccart waited.

Years ago they were regarded as a nuisance – rowdies broke up their meetings; the police prosecuted them for obstruction, and some of them were sent to prison and came out again, being presented with newly furbished haloes at meat breakfasts – Peter presiding.

'Now they have lived down their persecutions – martyrdom is not to be so cheaply bought – they are an institution like the mechanical spinning jenny and fashionable socialism – which proves that if you go on doing things often enough and persistently, saying with a loud voice, "*pro bono publico*", people will take you at your own valuation, and will tolerate you.'

Poiccart was listening intently now.

'These people demonstrate – Peter is really well off, with heaps of slum property, and he has lured other wealthy ladies and gentlemen into the movement. They demonstrate on all occasions. They have chants – Peter calls them "chants", and it is a nice distinction, stamping them as it does with the stamp of semi-secularity – for these festive moments, chants for the confusion of vaccinators, and eaters of beasts, and such. But of all their "Services of Protest" none is more thorough, more beautifully complete, than that which is specially arranged to express their horror and abhorrence of capital punishment.'

His pause was so long that Poiccart interjected an impatient – 'Well?'

'I was trying to think of the chant,' said Leon thoughtfully. 'If I remember right one verse goes –

> Come fight the gallant fight,
>   This horror to undo;
> Two blacks will never make a white,
>   Nor legal murder too.

'The last line,' said Gonsalez tolerantly, 'is a trifle vague, but it conveys with delicate suggestion the underlying moral of the poem. There is another verse which has for the moment eluded me, but perhaps I shall think of it later.'

He sat up suddenly and leant over, dropping his hand on Poiccart's arm.

'When we were talking of – our plan the other day you spoke of our greatest danger, the one thing we could not avoid. Does it not seem to you that the "Rational Faithers" offer a solution with their querulous campaigns, their demonstrations, their brassy brass band, and their preposterous chants?'

Poiccart pulled steadily at his pipe.

'You're a wonderful man, Leon,' he said.

Leon walked over to the cupboard, unlocked it, and drew out a big portfolio such as artists use to carry their drawings in. He untied the strings and turned over the loose pages. It was a collection that had cost the Four Just Men much time and a great deal of money.

'What are you going to do?' asked Poiccart, as the other, slipping off his coat and fixing his pince-nez, sat down before a big plan he had extracted from the portfolio. Leon took up a fine drawing-pen from the table, examined the nib with the eye of a skilled craftsman, and carefully uncorked a bottle of architect's ink.

'Have you ever felt a desire to draw imaginary islands?' he asked, 'naming your own bays, christening your capes, creating towns with a scratch of your pen, and raising up great mountains with herringbone strokes? Because I'm going to do something like that – I feel in that mood which in little boys is eloquently described as "trying", and I have the inclination to annoy Scotland Yard.'

* * *

It was the day before the trial that Falmouth made the discovery. To be exact it was made for him. The keeper of a Gower Street boarding house reported that two mysterious men had engaged rooms. They came late at night with one portmanteau bearing divers foreign labels; they studiously kept their faces in the shadow, and the beard of one was obviously false. In addition to which they paid for their lodgings in advance, and that was the most damning circumstance of all. Imagine mine host, showing them to their rooms, palpitating with his tremendous suspicion, calling to the full upon his powers of simulation, ostentatiously nonchalant, and impatient to convey the news to the police-station round the corner. For one called the other Leon, and they spoke despairingly in stage whispers of 'poor Manfred'.

They went out together, saying they would return soon after midnight, ordering a fire for their bedroom, for the night was wet and chilly.

Half an hour later the full story was being told to Falmouth over the telephone.

'It's too good to be true,' was his comment, but gave orders. The hôtel was well surrounded by midnight, but so skilfully that the casual passer-by would never have suspected it. At three in the morning, Falmouth decided that the men had been warned, and broke open their doors to search the rooms. The portmanteau was their sole find. A few articles of clothing, bearing the 'tab' of a Parisian tailor, was all they found till Falmouth, examining the bottom of the portmanteau, found that it was false.

'Hullo!' he said, and in the light of his discovery the exclamation was modest in its strength, for, neatly folded, and cunningly hidden, he came upon the plans. He gave them a rapid survey and whistled. Then he folded them up and put them carefully in his pocket.

'Keep the house under observation,' he ordered. 'I don't expect they'll return, but if they do, take 'em.'

Then he flew through the deserted streets as fast as a motor-car could carry him, and woke the chief commissioner from a sound sleep.

'What is it?' he asked as he led the detective to his study.

Falmouth showed him the plans.

The commissioner raised his eyebrows, and whistled.

'That's what I said,' confessed Falmouth.

The chief spread the plans upon the big table.

'Wandsworth, Pentonville and Reading,' said the commissioner, 'Plans, and remarkably good plans, of all three prisons.'

Falmouth indicated the writing in the cramped hand and the carefully ruled lines that had been drawn in red ink.

'Yes, I see them,' said the commissioner, and read ' "Wall 3 feet thick – dynamite here, warder on duty here – can be shot from wall, distance to entrance to prison hall 25 feet; condemned cell here, walls 3 feet, one window, barred 10 feet 3 inches from ground".'

'They've got the thing down very fine – what is this – Wandsworth?'

'It's the same with the others, sir,' said Falmouth. 'They've got distances, heights and posts worked out; they must have taken years to get this information.'

'One thing is evident,' said the commissioner; 'they'll do nothing until after the trial – all these plans have been drawn with the condemned cell as the point of objective.'

Next morning Manfred received a visit from Falmouth.

'I have to tell you, Mr Manfred,' he said, 'that we have in our possession full details of your contemplated rescue.'

Manfred looked puzzled.

'Last night your two friends escaped by the skin of their teeth, leaving behind them elaborate plans – '

'In writing?' asked Manfred, with his quick smile.

'In writing,' said Falmouth solemnly. 'I think it is my duty to tell you this, because it seems that you are building too much upon what is practically an impossibility, an escape from gaol.'

'Yes,' answered Manfred absently, 'perhaps so – in writing I think you said.'

'Yes, the whole thing was worked out – ' he thought he had said quite enough, and turned the subject. 'Don't you think you ought to change your mind and retain a lawyer?'

'I think you're right,' said Manfred slowly. 'Will you arrange for a member of some respectable firm of solicitors to see me?'

'Certainly,' said Falmouth, 'though you've left your defence – '

'Oh, it isn't my defence,' said Manfred cheerfully; 'only I think I ought to make a will.'

They were privileged people who gained admission to the Old Bailey, people with tickets from sheriffs, reporters, great actors, and very successful authors. The early editions of the evening newspapers announced the arrival of these latter spectators. The crowd outside the court contented themselves with discussing the past and the probable future of the prisoner.

The *Megaphone* had scored heavily again, for it published *in extenso* the particulars of the prisoner's will. It referred to this in its editorial columns variously as 'An Astounding Document' and 'An Extraordinary Fragment'. It was remarkable alike for the amount bequeathed, and for the generosity of its legacies.

Nearly half a million was the sum disposed of, and of this the astonishing sum of £60,000 was bequeathed to 'the sect known as the "Rational Faithers" for the furtherance of their campaign against capital punishment', a staggering legacy remembering that the Four Just Men knew only one punishment for the people who came under its ban.

'You want this kept quiet, of course,' said the lawyer when the will had been attested.

'Not a bit,' said Manfred; 'in fact I think you had better hand a copy to the *Megaphone*.'

'Are you serious?' asked the dumbfounded lawyer.

'Perfectly so,' said the other. 'Who knows,' he smiled, 'it might influence public opinion in – er – my favour.'

So the famous will became public property, and when Manfred, climbing the narrow wooden stairs that led to the dock of the Old Bailey, came before the crowded court, it was this latest freak of his that the humming court discussed.

'Silence!'

He looked round the big dock curiously, and when a warder pointed out the seat, he nodded, and sat down. He got up when the indictment was read.

'Are you guilty or not guilty?' he was asked, and replied briefly: 'I enter no plea.'

He was interested in the procedure. The scarlet-robed judge with his old, wise face and his quaint, detached air interested him mostly. The businesslike sheriffs in furs, the clergyman who sat with crossed legs, the triple row of wigged barristers, the slaving bench of reporters with their fierce whispers of instructions as they passed their copy to the waiting boys, and the strong force of police that held the court: they had all a special interest for him.

The leader for the Crown was a little man with a keen, strong face and a convincing dramatic delivery. He seemed to be possessed all the time with a desire to deal fairly with the issues, fairly to the Crown and fairly to the prisoner. He was not prepared, he said, to labour certain points which had been brought forward at the police-court inquiry, or to urge the jury that the accused man was wholly without redeeming qualities.

He would not even say that the man who had been killed, and with whose killing Manfred was charged, was a worthy or a desirable citizen of the country. Witnesses who had come forward to attest their knowledge of the deceased, were ominously silent on the point of his moral character. He was quite prepared to accept the statement he was a bad man, an evil influence on his associates, a corrupting influence on the young women whom he employed, a breaker of laws, a blackguard, a debauchee.

'But, gentlemen of the jury,' said the counsel impressively, 'a civilized community such as ours has accepted a system – intricate and imperfect though it may be – by which the wicked and the evil-minded are punished. Generation upon generation of wise law-givers have moulded and amended a scale of punishment to meet every known delinquency. It has established its system laboriously, making great national sacrifices for the principles that system involved. It has wrested with its life-blood the charters of a great liberty – the liberty of a law administered by its chosen officers and applied in the spirit of untainted equity.'

So he went on to speak of the Four Just Men who had founded a machinery for punishment, who had gone outside and had over-ridden the law; who had condemned and executed their judgment independent and in defiance of the established code.

'Again I say, that I will not commit myself to the statement that they punished unreasonably: that with the evidence against their victims, such as they possessed, the law officers of the Crown would have hesitated at initiating a prosecution. If it had pleased them to have taken an abstract view of this or that offence, and they had said this or that man is deserving of punishment, we, the representatives of the established law, could not have questioned for one moment the justice of their reasoning. But we have come into conflict on the question of the adequacy of punishment, and upon the more serious question of the right of the individual to inflict that punishment, which results in the appearance of this man in the dock on a charge of murder.'

Throughout the opening speech, Manfred leant forward, following the counsel's words.

Once or twice he nodded, as though he were in agreement with the speaker, and never once did he show sign of dissent.

The witnesses came in procession. The constable again, and the doctor, and the voluble man with the squint. As he finished with each, the counsel asked whether he had any question to put, but Manfred shook his head.

'Have you ever seen the accused before?' the judge asked the last witness.

'No, sar, I haf not,' said the witness emphatically, 'I haf not'ing to say against him.'

As he left the witness-box, he said audibly: 'There are anoder three yet – I haf no desire to die,' and amidst the laughter that followed this exhibition of caution, Manfred recalled him sharply.

'If you have no objection, my lord?' he said.

'None whatever,' replied the judge courteously.

'You have mentioned something about another three,' he said. 'Do you suggest that they have threatened you?'

'No, sar – no!' said the eager little man.

'I cannot examine counsel,' said Manfred, smiling; 'but I put it to him, that there has been no suggestion of intimidation of witnesses in this case.'

'None whatever,' counsel hastened to say; 'it is due to you to make that statement.'

'Against this man – ' the prisoner pointed to the witness-box – 'we have nothing that would justify our action. He is a saccharine smuggler, and a dealer in stolen property – but the law will take care of him.'

'It's a lie,' said the little man in the box, white and shaking; 'it is libellous!'

Manfred smiled again and dismissed him with a wave of his hand.

The judge might have reproved the prisoner for his irrelevant accusation, but allowed the incident to pass.

The case for the prosecution was drawing to a close when an official of the court came to the judge's side and, bending down, began a whispered conversation with him.

As the final witness withdrew, the judge announced an adjournment and the prosecuting counsel was summoned to his lordship's private room.

In the cells beneath the court, Manfred received a hint at what was coming and looked grave.

After the interval, the judge, on taking his seat, addressed the jury.

'In a case presenting the unusual features that characterize this,' he said, 'it is to be expected that there will occur incidents of an almost unprecedented nature. The circumstances under which evidence will be given now, are, however, not entirely without precedent.' He opened a thick law book before him at a place marked by a slip of paper. 'Here in the Queen against Forsythe, and earlier, the Queen against Berander, and earlier still and quoted in all these rulings, the King against Sir Thomas Mandory, we have parallel cases.' He closed the book.

'Although the accused has given no intimation of his desire to call witnesses on his behalf, a gentleman has volunteered his evidence. He desires that his name shall be withheld, and there are peculiar circumstances that compel me to grant his request. You may be assured, gentlemen of the jury, that I am satisfied both as to the identity of the witness, and that he is in every way worthy of credence.'

He nodded a signal to an officer, and through the judge's door to the witness box there walked a young man. He was dressed in a tightly fitting frock coat, and across the upper part of his face was a half mask.

He leant lightly over the rail, looking at Manfred with a little smile on his clean-cut mouth, and Manfred's eyes challenged him.

'You come to speak on behalf of the accused?' asked the judge.

'Yes, my lord.'

It was the next question that sent a gasp of surprise through the crowded court.

'You claim equal responsibility for his actions?'

'Yes, my lord!'

'You are, in fact, a member of the organization known as the Four Just Men?'

'I am.'

He spoke calmly, and the thrill that the confession produced, left him unmoved.

'You claim, too,' said the judge, consulting a paper before him, 'to have participated in their councils?'

'I claim that.'

There were long pauses between the questions, for the judge was checking the replies and counsel was writing busily.

'And you say you are in accord both with their objects and their methods?'

'Absolutely.'

'You have helped carry out their judgment?'

'I have.'

'And have given it the seal of your approval?'

'Yes.'

'And you state that their judgments were animated with a high sense of their duty and responsibility to mankind?'

'Those were my words.'

'And that the men they killed were worthy of death?'

'Of that I am satisfied.'

'You state this as a result of your personal knowledge and investigation?'

'I state this from personal knowledge in two instances, and from the investigations of myself and the independent testimony of high legal authority.'

'Which brings me to my next question,' said the judge. 'Did you ever appoint a commission to investigate all the circumstances of the known cases in which the Four Just Men have been implicated?'

'I did.'

'Was it composed of a Chief Justice of a certain European State, and four eminent criminal lawyers?'

'It was.'

'And what you have said is the substance of the finding of that Commission?'

'Yes.'

The Judge nodded gravely and the public prosecutor rose to cross-examination.

'Before I ask you any question,' he said, 'I can only express myself as being in complete agreement with his lordship on the policy of allowing your identity to remain hidden.' The young man bowed.

'Now,' said the counsel, 'let me ask you this. How long have you been in association with the Four Just Men?'

'Six months,' said the other.

'So that really you are not in a position to give evidence regarding the merits of this case – which is five years old, remember.'

'Save from the evidence of the Commission.'

'Let me ask you this – but I must tell you that you need not answer unless you wish – are you satisfied that the Four Just Men were responsible for that tragedy?'

'I do not doubt it,' said the young man instantly.

'Would anything make you doubt it?'

'Yes,' said the witness smiling, 'if Manfred denied it, I should not only doubt it, but be firmly assured of his innocence.'

'You say you approve both of their methods and their objects?'

'Yes.'

'Let us suppose you were the head of a great business firm controlling a thousand workmen, with rules and regulations for their guidance and a scale of fines and punishments for the preservation of discipline. And suppose you found one of those workmen had set himself up as an arbiter of conduct, and had superimposed upon your rules a code of his own.'

'Well?'

'Well, what would be your attitude toward that man?'

'If the rules he initiated were wise and needful I would incorporate them in my code.'

'Let me put another case. Suppose you governed a territory, administering the laws – '

'I know what you are going to say,' interrupted the witness, 'and my answer is that the laws of a country are as so many closely-set palings erected for the benefit of the community. Yet try as you will, the interstices exist, and some men will go and come at their pleasure, squeezing through this fissure, or walking boldly through that gap.'

'And you would welcome an unofficial form of justice that acted as a kind of moral stop-gap?'

'I would welcome clean justice.'

'If it were put to you as an abstract proposition, would you accept it?'

The young man paused before he replied.

'It is difficult to accommodate one's mind to the abstract, with such tangible evidence of the efficacy of the Four Just Men's system before one's eyes,' he said.

'Perhaps it is,' said the counsel, and signified that he had finished.

The witness hesitated before leaving the box, looking at the prisoner, but Manfred shook his head smilingly, and the straight slim figure of the young man passed out of court by the way he had come.

The unrestrained buzz of conversation that followed his departure was allowed to go unchecked as judge and counsel consulted earnestly across the bench.

Garrett, down amongst the journalists, put into words the vague thought that had been present in every mind in court.

'Do you notice, Jimmy,' he said to James Sinclair of the *Review*, 'how blessed unreal this trial is? Don't you miss the very essence of a murder trial, the mournfulness of it and the horror of it? Here's a feller been killed and not once has the prosecution talked about "this poor man struck down in the prime of life" or said anything that made you look at the prisoner to see how he takes it. It's a philosophical discussion with a hanging at the end of it.'

'Sure,' said Jimmy.

'Because,' said Garrett, 'if they find him guilty, he's got to die. There's no doubt about that; if they don't hang him, crack! goes the British Constitution, the Magna Charta, the Diet of Worms, and a few other things that Bill Seddon was gassing about.'

His irreverent reference was to the prosecutor's opening speech. Now Sir William Seddon was on his feet again, beginning his closing address to the jury. He applied himself to the evidence that had been given, to the prisoner's refusal to call that evidence into question, and conventionally traced step by step the points that told against the man in the dock. He touched on the appearance of the masked figure in the witness-box. For what it was worth it deserved their consideration, but it did not affect the issue before the court. The jury were there to formulate a verdict in accordance with the law as it existed, not as if it did not exist at all, to apply the law, not to create it – that was their duty. The prisoner would be offered an opportunity to speak in his own defence. Counsel for the Crown had waived his right to make the final address. They would, if he spoke, listen attentively to the prisoner, giving him the benefit of any doubt that might be present in their minds. But he could not see, he could not conceivably imagine, how the jury could return any but one verdict.

It seemed for a while that Manfred did not intend availing himself of the opportunity, for he made no sign, then he rose to his feet, and, resting his hands on the inkstand ledge before him, 'My lord,' he said, and turned apologetically to the jury, 'and gentlemen.'

The court was so still that he could hear the scratchings of the reporters' pens, and unexpected noises came from the street outside.

'I doubt either the wisdom or the value of speaking,' he said, 'not that I suggest that you have settled in your minds the question of my guilt without very excellent and convincing reasons.

'I am under an obligation to Counsel for the Treasury,' he bowed to the watchful prosecutor, 'because he spared me those banalities of speech which I feared would mar this trial. He did not attempt to whitewash the man we killed, or to exonerate him from his gross and sordid crimes. Rather, he made plain the exact position of the law in relation to myself, and with all he said I am in complete agreement. The inequalities of the law are notorious, and I recognize the impossibility, as society is constituted, of amending the law so that crimes such as we have dealt with shall be punished as they deserve. I do not rail against the fate that sent me here. When I undertook my mission, I undertook it with my eyes open, for I, too,' he smiled at the upturned faces at the counsels' bench, 'I too am learned in the law – and other things.'

'There are those who imagine that I am consumed with a burning desire to alter the laws of this country; that is not so. Set canons, inflexible in their construction, cannot be adapted according to the merits of a case, and particularly is this so when the very question of "merit" is a contentious point. The laws of England are good laws, wise and just and equitable. What other commendation is necessary than this one fact, that I recognize that my life is forfeit by those laws, and assent to the justice which condemns me'?

'None the less, when I am free again,' he went on easily, 'I shall continue to merit your judgment because there is that within me, which shows clearly which way my path lies, and how best I may serve humanity. If you say that to choose a victim here and a victim there for condemnation, touching only the veriest fringe of the world of rascaldom, I am myself unjust – since I leave the many and punish the few – I answer that for every man we slew, a hundred turned at the terror of our name and walked straightly; that the example of one death saved thousands. And if you should seriously ask: Have you helped reform mankind, I answer as seriously – Yes.'

He talked all this time to the judge.

'It would be madness to expect a civilized country to revert to the barbarism of an age in which death was the penalty for every other crime, and I will not insult your intelligence by denying that such a return to the bad days was ever suggested by me. But there has come into existence a spurious form of humanitarianism, the exponents of which have, it would appear, lost their sense of proportion, and have promoted the Fear of Pain to a religion; who have forgotten that the Age of Reason is not yet, and that men who are animal in all but human semblance share the animal's obedience to corrective discipline, share too his blind fear of death – and are amenable to methods that threaten his comfort or his life.'

He flung out his hand toward the judge.

'You, my lord,' he cried, 'can you order the flogging of a brute who has half killed one of his fellows, without incurring the bleating wrath of men and women, who put everything before physical pain – honour, patriotism, justice? Can you sentence a man to death for a cruel murder without a thousand shrieking products of our time rushing hither and thither like ants, striving to secure his release? Without a chorus of pity – that was unexcited by the mangled victim of his ferocity? "Killing, deliberate, wolfish killing by man", say they in effect, "is the act of God; but the legal punishment of death, is murder." That is why I expect no sympathy for the methods the Four Just Men adopted. We represented a law – we executed expeditiously. We murdered if you like. In the spirit and the letter of the laws of England, we did murder. I acknowledge the justice of my condemnation. I do not desire to extenuate the circumstances of my crime. Yet none the less the act I cannot justify to your satisfaction I justify to my own.'

He sat down.

A barrister, leaning over the public prosecutor's back, asked: 'What do you think of that?'

Sir William shook his head.

'Bewildering,' he said in despair.

The judge's summing up was one of the briefest on record.

The jury had to satisfy their minds that the prisoner committed the crime with which he was charged, and must not trouble themselves with any other aspect of the case but that part plainly before them. Was the man in the dock responsible for the killing of Lipski?

Without leaving the box, the jury returned its verdict.

'Guilty!'

Those used to such scenes noticed that the judge in passing sentence of death omitted the striking and sombre words that usually accompany the last sentence of the law, and that he spoke, too, without emotion.

'Either he's going to get a reprieve or else the judge is certain he'll escape,' said Garrett, 'and the last explanation seems ridiculous.'

'By the way,' said his companion as they passed slowly with the crowd into the roadway, 'who was that swell that came late and sat on the bench?'

'That was his Highness the Prince of the Escorial,' said Charles, 'he's in London just now on his honeymoon.'

'I know all about that,' said Jimmy, 'but I heard him speaking to the sheriff just before we came out, and it struck me that I'd heard his voice before.'

'It seemed so to me,' said the discreet Charles – so discreet indeed that he never even suggested to his editor that the mysterious mask who gave evidence on behalf of George Manfred was none other than his Royal Highness.

They took Manfred back to Wandsworth Gaol on the night of the trial. The governor, standing in the gloomy courtyard as the van drove in with its clanking escort, received him gravely.

'Is there anything you want?' he asked when he visited the cell that night.

'A cigar,' said Manfred, and the governor handed him the case. Manfred selected with care, the prison-master watching him wonderingly.

'You're an extraordinary man,' he said.

'And I need to be,' was the reply, 'for I have before me an ordeal which is only relieved of its gruesomeness by its uniqueness.'

'There will be a petition for reprieve, of course,' said the governor.

'Oh, I've killed that,' laughed Manfred, 'killed it with icy blast of satire – although I trust I haven't discouraged the "Rational Faithers" for whom I have made such handsome posthumous provision.'

'You are an extraordinary man,' mused the governor again. 'By the way, Manfred, what part does the lady play in your escape?'

'The lady?' Manfred was genuinely astonished.

'Yes, the woman who haunts the outside of this prison; a lady in black, and my chief warder tells me singularly beautiful.'

'Ah, the woman,' said Manfred, and his face clouded. 'I had hoped she had gone.'

He sat thinking.

'If she is a friend of yours, an interview would not be difficult to obtain,' said the governor.

'No, no, no,' said Manfred hastily, 'there must be no interview – at any rate here.'

The governor thought that the interview 'here' was very unlikely, for the Government had plans for the disposal of their prisoner, which he did not feel his duty to the State allowed him to communicate. He need not, had he known, have made a mystery of the scheme.

Manfred kicked off the clumsy shoes the prison authorities had provided him with – he had changed into convict dress on his return to the gaol – and laid himself down dressed as he was, pulling a blanket over him.

One of the watching warders suggested curtly that he should undress.

'It is hardly worth while,' he said, 'for so brief a time.'

They thought he was referring again to the escape, and marvelled a little at his madness. Three hours later when the governor came to the cell, they were dumbfounded at his knowledge.

'Sorry to disturb you,' said the Major, 'but you're to be transferred to another prison – why, you aren't undressed!'

'No,' said Manfred, lazily kicking off the cover, 'but I thought the transfer would be earlier.'

'How did you know?'

'About the transfer – oh, a little bird told me,' said the prisoner, stretching himself. 'Where is it to be – Pentonville?'

The governor looked at him a little strangely.

'No,' he said.

'Reading?'

'No,' said the governor shortly.

Manfred frowned.

'Wherever it is, I'm ready,' he said.

He nodded to the attendant warder as he left and took an informal but cheery farewell of the governor on the deserted railway station where a solitary engine with brake van attached stood waiting.

'A special, I perceive,' he said.

'Goodbye, Manfred,' said the governor and offered his hand.

Manfred did not take it – and the Major flushed in the dark.

'I cannot take your hand,' said Manfred, 'for two reasons. The first is that your excellent chief warder has handcuffed me, behind – '

'Never mind about the other reason,' said the governor with a little laugh, and then as he squeezed the prisoner's arm he added, 'I don't wish the other man any harm, but if by chance that wonderful escape of yours materializes, I know a respected officer in the Prison Service who will not be heartbroken.'

Manfred nodded, and as he stepped into the train he said: 'That lady – if you see her, tell her I am gone.'

'I will – but I'm afraid I may not tell her where.'

'That is at your discretion,' said Manfred as the train moved off. The warders drew down the blinds, and Manfred composed himself to sleep.

He woke with the chief warder's hand on his arm and stepped out on to the platform as the day was breaking. His quick eye searched the advertisement boards on the station. He would have done this ordinarily, because they would tell him where he was, supposing for some reason the authorities had wished to keep his destination a secret from him. But he had a particular interest in advertising just then. The station was smothered with the bills of a travelling cheap jack – an unusual class of advertisement for the austere notice boards of a railway station. Huge flaming posters that said 'Everything is Right', and in smaller type underneath 'Up to-date'. Little bills that said, 'Write to your cousin in London . . . and tell her that Gipsy Jack's bargain,' etc. 'Go by the book!' said another. Marching down the stairs he observed opposite the station yet further evidence of this extravagant cheap jack's caprice, for there were big illuminated signs in evidence, all to the same effect. In the shuttered darkness of the cab, Manfred smiled broadly. There was really no limit to the ingenuity of Leon Gonsalez. Next morning when the governor of Chelmsford Gaol visited him, Manfred expressed his intention of writing a letter to his cousin – in London.

* * *

'Did you see him?' asked Poiccart.

'Just a glimpse,' said Leon. He walked over to the window of the room and looked out. Right in front of him rose the grim façade of the gaol. He walked back to the table and poured himself out a cup of tea. It was not yet six o'clock, but he had been up the greater part of the night.

'The Home Secretary,' he said between gasps as he drank the scalding hot liquid, 'is indiscreet in his correspondence and is generally a most careless man.'

It was apropos of Manfred's coming.

'I have made two visits to the right honourable gentleman's house in this past fortnight, and I am bursting with startling intelligence. Do you know that Willington, the President of the Board of Trade, has had an "affair", and that a junior Lord of the Admiralty drinks like a sponge, and the Chancellor hates the War Secretary, who will talk all the time, and – '

'Keeps a diary?' asked Poiccart, and the other nodded.

'A diary full of thousands of pounds' worth of gossip, locked with a sixpenny-ha'penny lock. His house is fitted with the Magno-Sellie system of burglar alarms, and he keeps three servants.'

'You are almost encyclopedic,' said Poiccart.

'My dear Poiccart,' said Leon resentfully, 'you have got a trick of accepting the most wonderful information from me without paying me the due of adopting the following flattering attitudes: primary, incredulous surprise; secondary, ecstatic wonder; tertiary, admiration blended with awe.'

Poiccart laughed outright: an unusual circumstance.

'I have ceased to wonder at your cleverness, illustrious,' he said, speaking in Spanish, the language these two men invariably used when alone.

'All these things are beyond me,' Poiccart went on, 'yet no man can say for all my slow brain that I am a sluggard in action.'

Leon smiled.

The work of the last few weeks had fallen heavily on them both. It was no light task, the preparation of *Three Months in Morocco*. The first word of every seventh paragraph formed the message that he had to convey to Manfred – and it was a long message. There was the task of printing it, arranging the immediate publication, the placing of the book in the list, and generally thrusting it under the noses of an unappreciative public. As sailors store life-belts for possible contingencies, so, in every country had the Four Just Men stored the equipment of rescue against their need. Poiccart, paying many flying visits to the Midlands, brought back with him from time to time strange parts of machinery. The lighter he carried with his luggage, the heavier parts he smuggled into Chelmsford in a strongly-built motor-car.

The detached house facing the prison was fortunately for sale, and the agent who conducted the rapid negotiations that resulted in its transfer had let fall the information that the clients hoped to establish a garage on the Colchester Road that would secure a sensible proportion of the Essex motor traffic. The arrival of two rough-painted chassis supported this view of the new owners' business. They were enterprising people, these new arrivals, and it was an open secret 'on the road', that Gipsy Jack, whose caravan was under distress, and in the hands of the bailiff, had found financial support at their hands. Albeit Jack protested vigorously at the ridiculous suggestion that he should open in Chelmsford at an unpropitious season, and sniffed contemptuously at the extravagant billing of the town. Nor did he approve of the wording of the posters, which struck him as being milder than the hilarious character of his business-entertainment called for.

'Them Heckfords are going to make a failure,' said Mr Peter Sweeney in the bosom of his family. He occupied 'Faith Home', an ornate villa on the Colchester Road. Before his momentous conception of the 'Rational Faithers', it had borne the more imposing title of 'Palace Lodge', this by the way.

'They've got no business ability, and they're a bit gone on the sherbet.' For a high-priest of a new cult, Peter's language was neither pure nor refined. 'And they haven't got the common politeness of pigs,' he added ambiguously. 'I took the petition there today,' Peter went on indignantly, 'and the chap that come to the door! Oh, what a sight! Looked as if he'd been up all night, eyes red, face white, and all of a shake.'

'"Good mornin', Mr Heckford," says I, "I've come about the petition."

' "What petition?" says he.

' "The petition for the poor creature now lyin' in Chelmsford," says I, "under sentence of death – which is legal murder," I says.

' "Go to the devil" he says; they were his exact words, "Go to the devil." I was that upset that I walked straight away from the door – he didn't even ask me in – an' just as I got to the bottom of the front garden, he shouts, "What do you want him reprieved for – hasn't he left you a pot of money?"'

Mr Peter Sweeney was very much agitated as he repeated this callous piece of cynicism.

'That idea,' said Peter solemnly and impressively, 'Must Not be Allowed to Grow.'

It was to give the lie to the wicked suggestion that Peter arranged his daily demonstration, from twelve to two. There had been such functions before, 'Mass' meetings with brass bands at the very prison gates, but they were feeble mothers' meetings compared to these demonstrations on behalf of Manfred.

The memory of the daily 'service' is too fresh in the minds of the public, and particularly the Chelmsford public, to need any description here. Crowds of three thousand people were the rule, and Peter's band blared incessantly, whilst Peter himself grew hoarse from the effect of railing his denunciation of the barbarous methods of a medieval system.

Heckford Brothers, the new motor-car firm, protested against the injury these daily paraders were inflicting on their business. That same dissipated man, looking more dissipated than ever, who had been so rude to him, called upon Peter and threatened him with injunctions. This merely had the effect of stiffening Peter Sweeney's back, and next day the meeting lasted three hours.

In the prison, the pandemonium that went on outside penetrated even to the seclusion of Manfred's cell, and he was satisfied.

The local police were loath to interfere – and reopen the desperate quarrel that had centred around such demonstrations before.

So Peter triumphed, and the crowd of idlers that flocked to the midday gathering grew in proportion as the interest in the condemned man's fate arose.

And the augmented band blared and the big drum boomed the louder and Rational Faith gained many new converts.

A sightseer, attracted by curiosity, was standing on the fringe of the crowd one day. He could not see the band from where he stood but he made a remarkable observation; it was nothing less than a gross reflection upon a valued member of the orchestra.

'That chap,' said this unknown critic, 'is beating out of time – or else there's two drums going.'

The man to whom he addressed his remarks listened attentively, and agreed.

The crowd had swayed back to the railings before the premises of the motor manufacturers, and as it dispersed – Peter's party 'processed' magnificently to the town before breaking up – one of the new tenants came to the door and stood, watching the melting crowd. He overheard this remark concerning the big drummer's time, and it vexed him. When he came back to the sitting-room, where a pallid Poiccart lay supinely on a couch, he said: 'We must be careful,' and repeated the conversation.

Until six o'clock these men rested – as men must rest who have been working under a monstrous pressure of air – then they went to clear away the results of their working.

At midnight they ceased, and washed away the stains of their labours.

'Luckily,' said Poiccart, 'we have many rooms to fill yet; the drawing-room can hold little more, the dining-room we need, the morning-room is packed. We must start upstairs tomorrow.'

As the work proceeded, the need for caution became more and more apparent; but no accident marred their progress, and three days before the date fixed for the execution, the two men, coming to their barely furnished living-room, looked at each other across the uncovered table that separated them, and sighed thankfully, for the work was almost finished.

'Those fellows,' said Mr Peter Sweeney, 'are not so Bad as I thought they was. One of 'em come to me today and Apologized. He was lookin' better too, and offered to sign the petition.' Peter always gave you the impression in speaking that he was using words that began with capital letters.

'Pa,' said his son, who had a mind that dealt in material issues, 'what are you going to do with Manfred's money?'

His parent looked at him sternly.

'I shall Devote it to the Cause,' he said shortly.

'That's you, ain't it?' asserted the innocent child.

Peter disdained to answer.

'These young men,' he went on, 'might do worse than they have done. They are more business-like than I thought. Clarker, the town electrician, tells me that they had got a power current in their works, they have got a little gas-engine too, and from the way one of them was handling a big car today on the London road, it strikes me they know something about the business of motor-car running.'

Gonsalez, coming back from a trial trip on his noisy car, had to report a disquieting circumstance.

'She's here,' he said, as he was washing the grime from his hands.

Poiccart looked up from his work – he was heating something in a crucible over an electric stove.

'The Woman of Gratz?' he asked.

Leon nodded.

'That is natural,' Poiccart said, and went on with his experiment.

'She saw me,' said Leon calmly.

'Oh!' said the other, unconcerned. 'Manfred said – '

'That she would betray no more – I believe that, and George asked us to be good to her, that is a command.'

(There was a great deal more in Manfred's letter to 'his cousin in London' than met the governor's eye.)

'She is an unhappy woman,' said Gonsalez gravely; 'it was pitiable to see her at Wandsworth, where she stood day after day with those tragic eyes of hers on the ugly gate of the prison; here, with the result of her work in sight, she must be suffering the tortures of the damned.'

'Then tell her,' said Poiccart.

'That – '

'That George will escape.'

'I thought of that. I think George would wish it.'

'The Red Hundred has repudiated her,' Leon went on. 'We were advised of that yesterday; I am not sure that she is not under sentence. You remember Herr Smidt, he of the round face? It was he who denounced her.'

Poiccart nodded and looked up thoughtfully.

'Smidt – Smidt,' he puzzled. 'Oh yes – there is something against him, a cold-blooded murder, was it not?'

'Yes,' said Leon very quietly, and they did not speak again of Herr Smidt of Prague. Poiccart was dipping thin glass rods into the seething, bubbling contents of the crucible, and Leon watched idly.

'Did she speak?' Poiccart asked after a long interval of silence.

'Yes.'

Another silence, and then Leon resumed: 'She was not sure of me – but I made her the sign of the Red Hundred. I could not speak to her in the open street. Falmouth's people were in all probability watching her day and night. You know the old glove trick for giving the hour of assignation. Drawing on the glove slowly and stopping to admire the fit of one, two, or three fingers . . . so I signalled to her to meet me in three hours' time.'

'Where?'

'At Wivenhoe – that was fairly simple too . . . imagine me leaning over the side of the car to demand of the willing bystanders how long it would take me to reach Wivenhoe – the last word loudly – would it take me three hours? Whilst they volunteered their counsel, I saw her signal of assent.'

Poiccart hummed as he worked.

'Well – are you going?' he asked.

'I am,' said the other, and looked at his watch.

After midnight, Poiccart, dozing in his chair, heard the splutter and the Gatling-gun explosions of the car as it turned into the extemporized garage.

'Well?' he asked as Leon entered.

'She's gone,' said Gonsalez with a sigh of relief. 'It was a difficult business, and I had to lie to her – we cannot afford the risk of betrayal. Like the remainder of the Red Hundred, she clings to the idea that we have thousands of people in our organization; she accepted my story of storming the prison with sheer brute force. She wanted to stay, but I told her that she would spoil everything – she leaves for the continent tomorrow.'

'She has no money, of course,' said Poiccart with a yawn.

'None – the Red Hundred has stopped supplies – but I gave her – '

'Naturally,' said Poiccart.

'It was difficult to persuade her to take it; she was like a mad thing between her fear of George, her joy at the news I gave her – and remorse.

'I think,' he went on seriously, 'that she had an affection for George.'

Poiccart looked at him.

'You surprise me,' he said ironically, and went to bed.

Day found them working. There was machinery to be dismantled, a heavy open door to be fixed, new tires to be fitted to the big car. An hour before the midday demonstration came a knock at the outer door. Leon answered it and found a polite chauffeur. In the roadway stood a car with a solitary occupant.

The chauffeur wanted petrol; he had run himself dry. His master descended from the car and came forward to conduct the simple negotiation. He dismissed the mechanic with a word.

'There are one or two questions I would like to ask about my car,' ne said distinctly.

'Come inside, sir,' said Leon, and ushered the man into the sitting-room.

He closed the door and turned on the fur-clad visitor.

'Why did you come?' he asked quickly; 'it is terribly dangerous – for you.'

'I know,' said the other easily, 'but I thought there might be something I could do – what is the plan?'

In a few words Leon told him, and the young man shivered.

'A gruesome experience for George,' he said.

'It's the only way,' replied Leon, 'and George has nerves like ice.'

'And after – you're leaving that to chance?'

'You mean where shall we make for – the sea, of course. There is a good road between here and Clacton, and the boat lies snug between there and Walton.'

'I see,' said the young man, and he made a suggestion.

'Excellent – but you?' said Leon.

'I shall be all right?' said the cheerful visitor.

'By the way, have you a telegraph map of this part of the world?'

Leon unlocked a drawer and took out a folded paper.

'If you would arrange that,' he said, 'I should be grateful.'

The man who called himself Courtlander marked the plan with a pencil.

'I have men who may be trusted to the very end,' he said. 'The wires shall be cut at eight o'clock, and Chelmsford shall be isolated from the world.'

Then, with a tin of petrol in his hand, he walked back to his car.

Chapter 21
The Execution

If you pass through the little door that leads to the porter's lodge (the door will be locked and bolted behind you) your conductor will pass you through yet another door into a yard that is guarded by the ponderous doors of the prison at the one end and by a big steel gate at the other. Through this gate you reach another courtyard, and bearing to the right, you come to a flight of stone steps that bring you to the governor's tiny office. If you go straight along the narrow passage from which the office opens, descend a flight of stairs at the other end, through a well-guarded doorway, you come suddenly into the great hall of the prison. Here galleries run along both sides of the hall, and steel gangways and bridges span the width at intervals. Here, too, polished stairways criss-cross, and the white face of the two long walls of the hall are pitted with little black doors.

On the ground floor, the first cell on the right as you enter the hall from the governor's office is larger and more commodious than its fellows. There is, too, a suspicion of comfort in the strip of matting that covers the floor, in the naked gaslight which flares in its wire cage by day and night, in the table and chair, and the plain comfortable bed. This is the condemned cell. A dozen paces from its threshold is a door that leads to another part of the yard, and a dozen more paces along the flagged pathway brings you to a little unpretentious one-storeyed house without windows, and a doorway sufficiently wide to allow two men to pass abreast. There is a beam where a rope may be made fast, and a trapdoor, and a brick-lined pit, coloured with a salmon-pink distemper.

From his cell, Manfred was an interested listener, as day by day the uproar of the demonstration before the gates increased.

He found in the doctor who visited him daily a gentleman of some wit. In a sense, he replaced the governor of Wandsworth as an intellectual companion, for the master of Chelmsford was a reserved man, impregnated with the traditions of the system. To the doctor, Manfred confided his private opinion of the 'Rational Faithers'.

'But why on earth have you left them so much money?' asked the surprised medico.

'Because I dislike cranks and narrow, foolish people most intensely,' was the cryptic reply.

'This Sweeney – ' he went on.

'How did you hear of Sweeney?' asked the doctor.

'Oh, one hears,' said Manfred carelessly. 'Sweeney had an international reputation; besides,' he added, not moving a muscle of his face, 'I know about everybody.'

'Me, for instance?' challenged the man of medicine.

'You,' repeated Manfred wisely. 'From the day you left Clifton to the day you married the youngest Miss Arbuckle of Chertsey.'

'Good Lord!' gasped the doctor.

'It isn't surprising, is it,' explained Manfred, 'that for quite a long time I have taken an interest in the various staffs of the prisons within reach of London?'

'I suppose it isn't,' said the other. None the less he was impressed.

Manfred's life in Chelmsford differed in a very little degree from his life in Wandsworth.

The routine of prison life remained the same: the daily exercises, the punctilious visits of governor, doctor and chaplain.

On one point Manfred was firm. He would receive no spiritual ministrations, he would attend no service. He made his position clear to the scandalized chaplain.

'You do not know to what sect I am attached,' he said, 'because I have refused to give any information upon that point. I feel sure you have no desire to proselytize or convert me from my established beliefs.'

'What are your beliefs?' asked the chaplain.

'That,' said Manfred, 'is my own most secret knowledge, and which I do not intend sharing with any man.'

'But you cannot die like a heathen,' said the clergyman in horror.

'Point of view is everything,' was the calm rejoinder, 'and I am perfectly satisfied with the wholesomeness of my own; in addition to which,' he added, 'I am not going to die just yet, and being aware of this, I shrink from accepting from good men the sympathy and thought which I do not deserve.'

To the doctor he was a constant source of wonder, letting fall surprising items of news mysteriously acquired.

'Where he gets his information from, puzzles me, sir,' he confessed to the governor. 'The men who are guarding him – '

'Are above suspicion,' said the governor promptly.

'He gets no newspapers?'

'No, only the books he requires. He expressed a desire the other day for *Three Months in Morocco*, said he had half finished it when he was at Wandsworth, and wanted to read it again to "make sure" – so I got it.'

Three days before the date fixed for the execution, the governor had informed Manfred that, despite the presentation of a petition, the Home Secretary saw no reason for advising the remission of the sentence.

'I never expected a reprieve,' he replied without emotion.

He spent much of his time chatting with the two warders. Strict sense of duty forced them to reply in monosyllables, but he interested them keenly with his talk of the strange places of the world. As far as they could, they helped him pass the time, and he appreciated their restricted tightness.

'You are named Perkins,' he said one day.

'Yes,' said the warder.

'And you're Franklin,' he said to the other, and the man replied in the affirmative. Manfred nodded.

'When I am at liberty,' he said, 'I will make you some recompense for your exemplary patience.'

At exercise on the Monday – Tuesday was the fatal day fixed by the High Sheriff – he saw a civilian walking in the yard and recognized him, and on his return to his cell he requested to see the governor.

'I would like to meet Mr Jessen,' he said when the officer came, and the governor demurred.

'Will you be good enough to refer my request to the Home Secretary by telegraph?' asked Manfred, and the governor promised that he would.

To his surprise, an immediate reply gave the necessary permission.

Jessen stepped into the cell and nodded pleasantly to the man who sat on the edge of the couch.

'I wanted to speak to you, Jessen,' Manfred said, and motioned him to a seat. 'I wanted to put the business of Starque right, once and for all.'

Jessen smiled. 'That was all right – it was an order signed by the Czar and addressed personally to me – I could do no less than hang him,' he said.

'Yet you may think,' Manfred went on, 'that we took you for this work because – '

'I know why I was taken,' said the quiet Jessen. 'Starque and François were within the law, condemned by the law, and you strike only at those the law has missed.'

Then Manfred inquired after the Guild, and Jessen brightened.

'The Guild is flourishing,' he said cheerfully. 'I am now converting the luggage thieves – you know, the men who haunt railway stations.'

'Into – ?' asked the other.

'The real thing – the porters they sometimes impersonate,' said the enthusiast, and added dolefully, 'It's terribly uphill business though, getting characters for the men who want to go straight and have only a ticket of leave to identify them.'

As he rose to go, Manfred shook hands.

'Don't lose heart,' he said.

'I shall see you again,' said Jessen, and Manfred smiled.

Again, if you grow weary of that repetition 'Manfred smiled', remember that the two words best describe his attitude in those dreadful days in Chelmsford.

There was no trace of flippancy in his treatment of the oppressing situation. His demeanour on the occasions when he met the chaplain was one to which the most sensitive could take no exception, but the firmness was insuperable.

'It is impossible to do anything with him,' said the despairing minister. 'I am the veriest child in his hands. He makes me feel like a lay preacher interviewing Socrates.'

There was no precedent for the remarkable condition of affairs, and finally, at Manfred's request, it was decided to omit the ceremony of the religious service altogether.

In the afternoon, taking his exercise, he lifted his eyes skyward, and the warders, following his gaze, saw in the air a great yellow kite, bearing a banner that advertised some brand or other of motor tires.

'Yellow kite, all right,' he improvised, and hummed a tune as he marched round the stone circle.

That night, after he had retired to rest, they took away his prison clothes and returned the suit in which he had been arrested. He thought he heard the measured tramping of feet as he dozed, and wondered if the Government had increased the guard of the prison. Under his window the step of the sentry sounded brisker and heavier.

'Soldiers,' he guessed, and fell asleep.

He was accurate in his surmise. At the eleventh hour had arisen a fear of rescue, and half a battalion of guards had arrived by train in the night and held the prison.

The chaplain made his last effort, and received an unexpected rebuff, unexpected because of the startling warmth with which it was delivered.

'I refuse to see you,' stormed Manfred. It was the first exhibition of impatience he had shown.

'Have I not told you that I will not lend myself to the reduction of a sacred service to a farce? Can you not understand that I must have a very special reason for behaving as I do, or do you think I am a sullen boor rejecting your kindness out of pure perversity?'

'I did not know what to think,' said the chaplain sadly, and Manfred's voice softened as he replied: 'Reserve your judgement for a few hours – then you will know.'

The published accounts of that memorable morning are to the effect that Manfred ate very little, but the truth is that he partook of a hearty breakfast, saying, 'I have a long journey before me, and need my strength.'

At five minutes to eight a knot of journalists and warders assembled outside the cell door, a double line of warders formed across the yard, and the extended line of soldiers that circled the prison building stood to attention. At a minute to eight came Jessen with the straps of office in his hand. Then with the clock striking the hour, the governor, beckoning Jessen, entered the cell.

Simultaneously and in a dozen different parts of the country, the telegraph wires which connect Chelmsford with the rest of the world were cut.

It was a tragic procession, robbed a little of its horror by the absence of the priest, but sufficiently dreadful. Manfred, with strapped hands, followed the governor, a warder at each arm, and Jessen walking behind. They guided him to the little house without windows and stood him on a trap and drew back, leaving the rest to Jessen. Then, as Jessen put his hand to his pocket, Manfred spoke.

'Stand away for a moment,' he said; 'before the rope is on my neck I have something to say,' and Jessen stood back. 'It is,' said Manfred slowly, 'farewell!'

As he spoke he raised his voice, and Jessen stooped to pick up the coil of rope that dragged on the floor. Then without warning, before the rope was raised, or any man could touch him, the trap fell with a crash and Manfred shot out of sight.

Out of sight indeed, for from the pit poured up a dense volume of black smoke, that sent the men at the edge reeling and coughing backwards to the open air.

'What is it? What is it?' a frantic official struggled through the press at the door and shouted an order.

'Quick! the fire hose!'

The clanging of a bell sent the men to their stations. 'He is in the pit,' somebody cried, but a man came with a smoke helmet and went down the side. He was a long time gone, and when he returned he told his story incoherently.

'The bottom of the pit's been dug out – there's a passage below and a door – the smoke – I stopped that, it's a smoke cartridge!'

The chief warder whipped a revolver from his holster.

'This way,' he shouted, and went down the dangling rope hand over hand.

It was dark, but he felt his way; he slipped down the sharp declivity where the tunnel dipped beneath the prison wall and the men behind him sprawled after him. Then without warning he ran into an obstacle and went down bruised and shaken.

One of the last men down had brought a lamp, and the light of it came flickering along the uneven passage. The chief warder shouted for the man to hurry.

By the light he saw that what confronted him was a massive door made of unpainted deal and clamped with iron. A paper attracted his attention. It was fastened to the door, and he lifted the lantern to read it.

'The tunnel beyond this point is mined.'

That was all it said.

'Get back to the prison,' ordered the warder sharply. Mine or no mine, he would have gone on, but he saw that the door was well nigh impregnable.

He came back to the light stained with clay and sweating with his exertions.

'Gone!' he reported curtly; 'if we can get the men out on the roads and surround the town – '

'That has been done,' said the governor, 'but there's a crowd in front of the prison, and we've lost three minutes getting through.'

He had a grim sense of humour, this fierce silent old man, and he turned on the troubled chaplain.

'I should imagine that you know why he didn't want the service now?'

'I know,' said the minister simply, 'and knowing, I am grateful.'

* * *

Manfred felt himself caught in a net. Deft hands loosened the straps at his wrists and lifted him to his feet. The place was filled with the pungent fumes of smoke.

'This way.'

Poiccart, going ahead, flashed the rays of his electric lamp over the floor. They took the slope with one flying leap, and stumbled forward as they landed; reaching the open door, they paused whilst Leon crashed it closed and slipped the steel bolts into their places.

Poiccart's lamp showed the smoothly cut sides of the tunnel, and at the other end they had to climb the debris of dismantled machinery.

'Not bad,' said Manfred, viewing the work critically. 'The "Rational Faithers" were useful,' he added. Leon nodded.

'But for their band you could have heard the drills working in the prison,' he said breathlessly.

Up a ladder at the end they raced, into the earth strewn 'dining-room' through the passage, inches thick with trodden clay.

Leon held the thick coat for him and he slipped into it. Poiccart started the motor.

'Right!' They were on the move thumping and jolting through a back lane that joined the main road five hundred yards below the prison.

Leon, looking back, saw the specks of scarlet struggling through the black crowds at the gates. 'Soldiers to hold the roads,' he said; 'we're just in time – let her rip, Poiccart.'

It was not until they struck the open country that Poiccart obeyed, and then the great racer leapt forward, and the rush of wind buffeted the men's faces with great soft blows.

Once in the loneliest part of the road they came upon telegraph wires that trailed in the hedge.

Leon's eyes danced at the sight of it.

'If they've cut the others, the chase is over,' he said; 'they'll have cars out in half an hour and be following us; we are pretty sure to attract attention, and they'll be able to trace us.'

Attract attention they certainly did, for leaving Colchester behind, they ran into a police trap, and a gesticulating constable signalled them to stop.

They left him behind in a thick cloud of dust. Keeping to the Clacton road, they had a clear run till they reached a deserted strip where a farm wagon had broken down and blocked all progress.

A grinning wagoner saw their embarrassment.

'You cairn't pass here, mister,' he said gleefully, 'and there ain't another road for two miles back.'

'Where are your horses?' asked Leon quickly.

'Back to farm,' grinned the man.

'Good,' said Leon. He looked round, there was nobody in sight.

'Go back there with the car,' he said, and signalled Poiccart to reverse the engine.

'What for?'

Leon was out of the car, walking with quick steps to the lumbering wreck in the road.

He stooped down, made a swift examination, and thrust something beneath the huge bulk. He lit a match, steadied the flame, and ran backward, clutching the slow-moving yokel and dragging him with him.

'Ere, wot's this?' demanded the man, but before he could reply there was a deafening crash, like a clap of thunder, and the air was filled with wreckage.

Leon made a second examination and called the car forward.

As he sprang into his seat he turned to the dazed rustic.

'Tell your master that I have taken the liberty of dynamiting his cart,' he said; and then, as the man made a movement as if to clutch his arm, Leon gave him a push which sent him flying, and the car jolted over the remainder of the wagon.

The car turned now in the direction of Walton, and after a short run, turned sharply toward the sea.

*   *   *

Twenty minutes later two cars thundered along the same road, stopping here and there for the chief warder to ask the question of the chance-met pedestrian.

They too swung round to the sea and followed the cliff road.

'Look!' said a man.

Right ahead, drawn up by the side of the road, was a car. It was empty.

They sprang out as they reached it – half a dozen warders from each car. They raced across the green turf till they came to the sheer edge of the cliff.

There was no sign of the fugitive.

The serene blue of sea was unbroken, save where, three miles away, a beautiful white steam yacht was putting out to sea.

Attracted by the appearance of the warders, a little crowd came round them.

'Yes,' said a wondering fisherman, 'I seed 'em, three of 'em went out in one of they motor boats that go like lightenin' – they're out o' sight by now.'

'What ship is that?' asked the chief warder quickly and pointed to the departing yacht.

The fisherman removed his pipe and answered: 'That's the Royal Yacht.'

'What Royal Yacht?'

'The Prince of the Escorials,' said the fisherman impressively.

The chief warder groaned.

'Well, they can't be on her!' he said.

THE END

THE JUST MEN
OF CORDOVA

Chapter 1

Three men of Cordova

The man who sat at the marble-topped table of the Café of the Great Captain – if I translate the sign aright – was a man of leisure. A tall man, with a trim beard and grave grey eyes that searched the street absently as though not quite certain of his quest. He sipped a coffee *con leche* and drummed a little tune on the table with his slender white hands.

He was dressed in black, which is the conventional garb in Spain, and his black cloak was lined with velvet. His cravat was of black satin, and his well-fitting trousers were strapped under his pointed boots, in the manner affected by certain caballero.

These features of his attire were the most striking, though he was dressed conventionally enough – for Cordova. He might have been a Spaniard, for grey eyes are a legacy of the Army of Occupation, and many were the unions between Wellington's rollicking Irishmen and the susceptible ladies of the Estremadura.

His speech was flawless. He spoke with the lisp of Andalusia, clipping his words as do the folk of the South. Also, there was evidence of his Southern origin in his response to the whining beggar that shuffled painfully to him, holding out crooked fingers for largesse.

'In the name of the Virgin, and the Saints, and the God who is above all, I beseech you, Señor, to spare me ten centimes.'

The bearded man brought his far-seeing eyes to focus on the palm.

'God will provide,' he said, in the slurred Arabic of Spanish Morocco.

'Though I live a hundred years,' said the beggar monotonously, 'I will never cease to pray for your lordship's happiness.'

He of the velvet-lined cloak looked at the beggar.

The mendicant was a man of medium height, sharp-featured, unshaven, after the way of his kind, terribly bandaged across his head and one eye.

Moreover, he was lame. His feet were shapeless masses of swathed bandages, and his discoloured hands clutched a stick fiercely.

'Señor and Prince,' he whined, 'there is between me and the damnable pangs of hunger ten centimes, and your worship would not sleep this night in comfort thinking of me tossing in famine.'

'Go in peace,' said the other patiently.

'Exalted,' moaned the beggar, 'by the *chico* that lay on your mother's knee' – he crossed himself – 'by the gallery of the Saints and the blessed blood of martyrs, I beseech you not to leave me to die by the wayside, when ten centimes, which is as the paring of your nails, would lead me to a full stomach.'

The man at the table sipped his coffee unmoved.

'Go with God,' he said.

Still the man lingered.

He looked helplessly up and down the sunlit street. He peered into the cool dark recess of the café, where an apathetic waiter sat at a table reading the *Heraldo*.

Then he leant forward, stretching out a slow hand to pick a crumb of cake from the next table.

'Do you know Dr Essley?' he asked in perfect English.

The cavalier at the table looked thoughtful.

'I do not know him. Why?' he asked in the same language.

'You should know him,' said the beggar; 'he is interesting.'

He said no more, shuffling a painful progress along the street. The *caballero* watched him with some curiosity as he made his way slowly to the next café.

Then he clapped his hands sharply, and the apathetic waiter, now nodding significantly over his Heraldo, came suddenly to life, collected the bill, and a tip which was in proportion to the size of the bill. Though the sky was cloudless and the sun threw blue shadows in the street, those same shadows were immensely cold, for these were the chilly days before the first heat of spring.

The gentleman, standing up to his full height – he was well over the six-feet mark – shook his cloak and lightly threw one end across his shoulder; then he began to walk slowly in the direction taken by the beggar.

The way led him through narrow streets, so narrow that in the walls on either side ran deep recesses to allow the boxes of cartwheels to pass. He overtook the man in the Calle Paraiso, passed him, threading the narrow streets that led to San Fernando. Down this he went, walking very leisurely, then turned to the street of Carrera de Puente, and so came to the shadows of the mosque-cathedral which is dedicated to God and to Allah with delightful impartiality. He stood irresolutely before the gates that opened on to the courtyards, seemed half in doubt, then turned again, going downhill to the Bridge of Calahorra. Straight as a die the bridge runs, with its sixteen arches that the ancient Moors built. The man with the cloak reached the centre of the bridge and leant over, watching with idle interest the swollen yellow waters of the Guadalquivir.

Out of the corner of his eye he watched the beggar come slowly through the gate and walk in his direction. He had a long time to wait, for the man's progress was slow. At last he came sidling up to him, hat in hand, palm outstretched. The attitude was that of a beggar, but the voice was that of an educated Englishman.

'Manfred,' he said earnestly, 'you must see this man Essley. I have a special reason for asking.'

'What is he?'

The beggar smiled.

'I am dependent upon memory to a great extent,' he said, 'the library at my humble lodgings being somewhat limited, but I have a dim idea that he is a doctor in a suburb of London, rather a clever surgeon.'

'What is he doing here?'

The redoubtable Gonsalez smiled again.

'There is in Cordova a Dr Cajalos. From the exalted atmosphere of the Paseo de Gran Capitan, wherein I understand you have your luxurious suite, no echo of the underworld of Cordova comes to you. Here' – he pointed to the roofs and the untidy jumble of buildings at the farther end of the bridge – 'in the Campo of the Verdad, where men live happily on two pesetas a week, we know Dr Cajalos. He is a household word – a marvellous man, George, performing miracles undreamt of in your philosophy: making the blind to see, casting spells upon the guilty, and creating infallible love philtres for the innocent! He'll charm a wart or arrest the ravages of sleeping sickness.'

Manfred nodded. 'Even in the Paseo de la Gran Capitan he is not without honour,' he said with a twinkle in his eye. 'I have seen him and consulted him.'

The beggar was a little astonished. 'You're a wonderful man,' he said, with admiration in his voice. 'When did you do it?'

Manfred laughed softly.

'There was a certain night, not many weeks ago, when a beggar stood outside the worthy doctor's door, patiently waiting till a mysterious visitor, cloaked to his nose, had finished his business.'

'I remember,' said the other, nodding. 'He was a stranger from Ronda, and I was curious – did you see me following him?'

'I saw you,' said Manfred gravely. 'I saw you from the corner of my eye.'

'It was not you?' asked Gonsalez, astonished.

'It was I,' said the other. 'I went out of Cordova to come into Cordova.'

Gonsalez was silent for a moment.

'I accept the humiliation,' he said. 'Now, since you know the doctor, can you see any reason for the visit of a commonplace English doctor to Cordova? He has come all the way without a halt from England by the Algeciras Express. He leaves Cordova tomorrow morning at daybreak by the same urgent system, and he comes to consult Dr Cajalos.'

'Poiccart is here: he has an interest in this Essley – so great an interest that he comes blandly to our Cordova, Baedeker in hand, seeking information of the itinerant guide and submitting meekly to his inaccuracies.'

Manfred stroked his little beard, with the same grave thoughtful expression in his wise eyes as when he had watched Gonsalez shuffling from the Café de la Gran Capitan. 'Life would be dull without Poiccart,' he said.

'Dull, indeed – ah, Señor, my life shall be your praise, and it shall rise like the smoke of holy incense to the throne of Heaven.'

He dropped suddenly into his whine, for a policeman of the town guard was approaching, with a suspicious eye for the beggar who stood with expectant hand outstretched.

Manfred shook his head as the policeman strolled up.

'Go in peace,' he said.

'Dog,' said the policeman, his rough hand descending on the beggar's shoulder, 'thief of a thief, begone lest you offend the nostrils of this illustrious.'

With arms akimbo, he watched the man limp away, then he turned to Manfred.

'If I had seen this scum before, excellency,' he said fiercely, 'I should have relieved your presence of his company.'

'It is not important,' said Manfred conventionally.

'As for me,' the policeman went on, releasing one hand from his hip to curl an insignificant moustache, 'I have hard work in protecting rich and munificent *caballeros* from these swine. And God knows my pay is poor, and with three hungry mouths to fill, not counting my wife's mother, who comes regularly on feast days and must be taken to the bull-fight, life is hard. More especially, Señor, since she is one of those damned proud Andalusian women who must have a seat in the shade at two pesetas.* For myself, I have not tasted rioja since the feast of Santa Therese – '

Manfred slipped a peseta into the hand of the uniformed beggar. The man walked by his side to the end of the bridge, retailing his domestic difficulties with the freedom and intimacy which is possible nowhere else in the world. They stood chattering near the principal entrance to the Cathedral.

'Your excellency is not of Cordova?' asked the officer.

'I am of Malaga,' said Manfred without hesitation.

'I had a sister who married a fisherman of Malaga,' confided the policeman. 'Her husband was drowned, and she now lives with a señor whose name I forget. She is a pious woman, but very selfish. Has your excellency been to Gibraltar?'

Manfred nodded. He was interested in a party of tourists which was being shown the glories of the Puerta del Perdon.

One of the tourists detached himself from his party and came towards them. He was a man of middle height and strongly built. There was a strange reserve in his air and a saturnine imperturbability in his face.

'Can you direct me to the Paseo de la Gran Capitan?' he asked in bad Spanish.

'I am going that way,' said Manfred courteously; 'if the Señor would condescend to accompany me – '

'I shall be grateful,' said the other.

They chatted a little on divers subjects – the weather, the delightful character of the mosque-cathedral.

'You must come along and see Essley,' said the tourist suddenly. He spoke in perfect Spanish.

'Tell me about him.' said Manfred. 'Between you and Gonsalez, my dear Poiccart, you have piqued my curiosity.'

'This is an important matter,' said the other earnestly. 'Essley is a doctor in a suburb of London. I have had him under observation for some months. He has a small practice – quite a little one – and he attends a few cases. Apparently he does no serious work in his suburb, and his history is a strange one. He was a student at University College, London, and soon after getting his degree left with a youth named Henley for Australia. Henley had been a hopeless failure and

---

* At a bull-fight the seats in the sun are the cheaper, those in the shade being double the price.

had been badly ploughed in his exams, but the two were fast friends, which may account for their going away together to try their luck in a new country. Neither of them had a relation in the world, except Henley, who had a rich uncle settled somewhere in Canada, and whom he had never seen. Arrived in Melbourne, the two started off up country with some idea of making for the new gold diggings, which were in full swing at that time. I don't know where the diggings were; at any rate, it was three months before Essley arrived – alone, his companion having died on the road!'

'He does not seem to have started practising,' Poiccart went on, 'for three or four years. We can trace his wanderings from mining camp to mining camp, where he dug a little, gambled a lot, and was generally known as Dr S. – probably an abbreviation of Essley. Not until he reached Western Australia did he attempt to establish himself as a doctor. He had some sort of a practice, not a very high-class one, it is true, but certainly lucrative. He disappeared from Coolgardie in 1900; he did not reappear in England until 1908.'

They had reached the Paseo by now. The streets were better filled than they had been when Manfred had followed the beggar.

'I've some rooms here,' he said. 'Come in and we will have some tea.'

He occupied a flat over a jeweller's in the Calle Moreria. It was a well-furnished apartment, 'and especially blessed in the matter of light,' explained Manfred as he inserted the key. He put a silver kettle on the electric stove.

'The table is laid for two?' questioned Poiccart.

'I have visitors,' said Manfred with a little smile. 'Sometimes the begging profession becomes an intolerable burden to our Leon and he enters Cordova by rail, a most respectable member of society, full of a desire for the luxury of life – and stories. Go on with yours, Poiccart; I am interested.'

The 'tourist' seated himself in a deep armchair. 'Where was I?' he asked. 'Oh, yes. Dr Essley disappeared from Coolgardie, and after an obliteration of eight years reappeared in London.'

'In any exceptional circumstances?'

'No, very ordinarily. He seems to have been taken up by the newest kind of Napoleon.'

'A Colonel Black?' asked Manfred, raising his eyebrows.

Poiccart nodded.

'That same meteor,' he said. 'At any rate, Essley, thanks to what practice he could steal from other practitioners in his own suburb –

somewhere in the neighbourhood of Forest Hill – and what practice Napoleon's recommendation gives him, seems to be fairly well off. He first attracted my attention – '

There came a tap at the door, and Manfred raised his finger warningly. He crossed the room and opened the door. The concierge stood outside, cap in hand; behind him and a little way down the stairs was a stranger – obviously an Englishman.

'A señor to see your excellency,' said the concierge.

'My house is at your disposal,' said Manfred, addressing the stranger in Spanish.

'I am afraid I do not speak good Spanish,' said the man on the stairs.

'Will you come up?' asked Manfred, in English.

The other mounted the stairs slowly.

He was a man of fifty. His hair was grey and long. His eyebrows were shaggy, and his under-jaw stuck out and gave his face an appearance which was slightly repulsive. He wore a black coat and carried a big, soft wideawake in his gloved hand.

He peered round the room from one to the other.

'My name,' he said, 'is Essley.'

He pronounced the word, lingering upon the double 'ss' till it sounded like a long hiss.

'Essley,' he repeated as though he derived some satisfaction from the repetition – 'Dr Essley.'

Manfred motioned him to a chair, but he shook his head.

'I'll stand,' he said harshly. 'When I have business, I stand.' He looked suspiciously at Poiccart. 'I have private business,' he said pointedly.

'My friend has my complete confidence,' said Manfred.

He nodded grudgingly. 'I understand,' he said, 'that you are a scientist and a man of considerable knowledge of Spain.'

Manfred shrugged his shoulders. In his present role he enjoyed some reputation as a quasi-scientific *littérateur*, and under the name of 'de la Monte' had published a book on *Modern Crime*.

'Knowing this,' said the man, 'I came to Cordova, having other business also – but that will keep.'

He looked round for a chair and Manfred offered one, into which he sat, keeping his back to the window.

'Mr de la Monte,' said the doctor, leaning forward with his hands on his knees and speaking very deliberately, 'you have some knowledge of crime.'

'I have written a book on the subject,' said Manfred, 'which is not necessarily the same thing.'

'I had that fear,' said the other bluntly. 'I was also afraid that you might not speak English. Now I want to ask you a plain question and I want a plain answer.'

'So far as I can give you this, I shall be most willing,' said Manfred.

The doctor twisted his face nervously, then – 'Have you ever heard of the Four Just Men?' he asked.

There was a little silence.

'Yes,' said Manfred calmly, 'I have heard of them.'

'Are they in Spain?' The question was put sharply.

'I have no exact knowledge,' said Manfred. 'Why do you ask?'

'Because – ' The doctor hesitated. 'Oh, well – I am interested. It is said that they unearth villainy that the law does not punish; they – they kill – eh?' His voice was sharper, his eyelids narrowed till he peered from one to the other through slits.

'Such an organization is known to exist,' said Manfred, 'and one knows that they do happen upon unpunished crime – and punish.'

'Even to – to killing?'

'They even kill,' said Manfred gravely.

'And they go free!' – the doctor leapt to his feet with a snarl and flung out his hands in protest – 'they go free! All the laws of all nations cannot trap them! A self-appointed tribunal – who are they to judge and condemn? Who gave them the right to sit in judgment? There is a law, if a man cheats it – '

He checked himself suddenly, shook his shoulders and sank heavily into the chair again.

'So far as I can secure information upon the subject,' he said roughly, 'these men are no longer an active force – they are outlawed – there are warrants for them in every country.'

Manfred nodded.

'That is very true,' he said gently; 'but whether they are an active force, time must reveal.'

'There were three?' – the doctor looked up quickly – 'and they usually find a fourth – an influential fourth.'

Manfred nodded again. 'So I understand.'

Dr Essley twisted uncomfortably in his chair. It was evident that the information or assurance he expected to receive from this expert in crime was not entirely satisfactory to him.

'And they are in Spain?' he asked.

'So it is said.'

'They are not in France; they are not in Italy; they are not in Russia; nor in any of the German States,' said the doctor resentfully. 'They must be in Spain.'

He brooded awhile in silence.

'Pardon me,' said Poiccart, who had been a silent listener, 'but you seem very interested in these men. Would it be offensive to you if I asked you to satisfy my curiosity as to why you should be anxious to discover their whereabouts?'

'Curiosity also,' said the other quickly; 'in a sense I am a modest student of crime, as our friend de la Monte is.'

'An enthusiastic student,' said Manfred quietly.

'I hoped that you would be able to give me some help,' Essley went on, unmindful of the significant emphasis of the other's tones; 'beyond the fact that they may be in Spain, which, after all, is conjectural, I have learnt nothing.'

'They may not even be in Spain,' said Manfred, as he accompanied his visitor to the door; 'they may not even be in existence – your fears may be entirely groundless.'

The doctor whipped round, white to the lips. 'Fears?' he said, breathing quickly. 'Did you say fears?'

'I am sorry,' laughed Manfred easily; my English is perhaps not good.'

'Why should I fear them?' demanded the doctor aggressively. 'Why should I? Your words are chosen very unwisely, sir. I have nothing to fear from the Four Just Men – or from any other source.'

He stood panting in the doorway like a man who is suddenly deprived of breath. With an effort he collected himself, hesitated a moment, and then with a stiff little bow left the room.

He went down the stairs, out to the street, and turned into the Paseo. There was a beggar at the corner who raised a languid hand. '*Por deos* – ' he whined.

With an oath, Essley struck at the hand with his cane, only to miss it, for the beggar was singularly quick and, for all the discomforts he was prepared to face, Gonsalez had no desire to endure a hand seamed and wealed – those sensitive hands of his were assets to Gonsalez.

The doctor pursued a savage way to his hôtel. Reaching his room, he locked the door and threw himself into a chair to think. He cursed his own folly – it was madness to have lost his temper even before so insignificant a person as a Spanish dilettante in science. There was the first half of his mission finished – and it was a failure. He took from the pocket of his overcoat, hanging behind the door, a Spanish Baedeker. He turned the leaves till he came to a map of Cordova. Attached to this was a smaller plan, evidently made by somebody who knew the topography of the place better than he understood the rules of cartography.

He had heard of Dr Cajalos first from a Spanish anarchist he had met in some of his curious nocturnal prowlings in London. Under the influence of good wine this bold fellow had invested the wizard of Cordova with something approaching miraculous powers – he had also said things which had aroused the doctor's interest to an extraordinary degree. A correspondence had followed: the visit was the result.

Essley looked at his watch. It was nearly seven o'clock. He would dine, then go to his room and change. He made a hasty ablution in the growing darkness of the room – curiously enough he did not switch on the light; then he went to dinner. He had a table to himself and buried himself in an English magazine he had brought with him. Now and again as he read he would make notes in a little book which lay on the table by the side of his plate.

They had no reference to the article he read; they had little association with medical science. On the whole, they dealt with certain financial aspects of a certain problem which came into his mind.

He finished his dinner, taking his coffee at the table. Then he rose, put the little notebook in his pocket, the magazine under his arm, and made his way back to his room. He turned on the light, pulled down the blinds, and drew a light dressing-table beneath the lamp. He produced his note-book again and, with the aid of a number of closely-written sheets of paper taken from his valise, he compiled a little table. He was completely engrossed for a couple of hours. As if some invisible and unheard alarum clock warned him of his engagement, he closed the book, locked his memoranda in the valise, and struggled into his coat. With a soft felt hat pulled down over his eyes, he left the hôtel and without hesitation took the path which led down to the Calahorra Bridge. The streets through which he passed were deserted, but he had no hesitation, knowing well the lawful character of these unprepossessing little Spanish suburbs.

He plunged into a labyrinth of narrow streets – he had studied his plan to some purpose – and only hesitated when he reached a cul-de-sac which was more spacious than the street from which it opened. One oil lamp at the farther end added rather to the gloom. Tall, windowless houses rose on either side, and each was pierced by a door. On the left door the doctor, after a moment's hesitation, knocked twice.

Instantly it opened noiselessly. He hesitated.

'Enter,' said a voice in Spanish; 'the Señor need not fear.'

He stepped into the black void and the door closed behind him. 'Come this way,' said the voice. In the pitch darkness he could make out the indistinct figure of a little man.

The doctor stepped inside and surreptitiously wiped the sweat from his forehead. The old man lit a lamp, and Essley took stock of him. He was very little, scarcely more than four feet in height. He had a rough white beard and head as bald as an egg. His face and hands were alike grimy, and his whole appearance bore evidence of his aversion to water.

A pair of black twinkling eyes were set deeply in his head, and the puckering lines about them revealed him as a man who found humour in life. This was Dr Cajalos, a famous man in Spain, though he had no social standing.

'Sit down,' said Cajalos; 'we will talk quietly, for I have a señora of high quality to see me touching a matter of lost affection.'

Essley took the chair offered to him and the doctor seated himself on a high stool by the table. A curious figure he made, with his dangling little legs, his old, old face and his shining bald pate.

'I wrote to you on the subject of certain occult demonstrations,' began the doctor, but the old man stopped him with a quick jerk of the hand.

'You came to see me, Señor, because of a drug I have prepared,' he said, 'a preparation of — ' *

Essley sprang to his feet. 'I – I did not tell you so,' he stammered.

'The green devil told me,' said the other seriously. 'I have many talks with the foot-draggers, and they speak very truly.'

'I thought – '

'Look!' said the old man. He leapt down from his high perch with agility. In the dark corner of one of the rooms were some boxes, to which he went. Essley heard a scuffling, and by and by the old man came back, holding by the ears a wriggling rabbit. With his disengaged hand he unstoppered a little green bottle on the table. He picked a feather from the table, dipped the point gingerly into

---

* In the story, as it appeared in serial form, the name of the poison occurred. It has been represented to the author (and he agrees) that it is wholly undesirable that the name of this drug should appear in a work of fiction. It is one well known to oculists and its action is faithfully described in these pages.

the bottle. Then very carefully he lightly touched the nose of the rabbit with the end of the feather – so lightly, indeed, that the feather hardly brushed the muzzle of the animal.

Instantly, with no struggle, the rabbit went limp, as though the life essence had been withdrawn from the body. Cajalos replaced the stopper and thrust the feather into a little charcoal fire that burnt dully in the centre of the room.

'P—e,' he said briefly; 'but my preparation.' He laid the dead animal on the floor at the feet of the other. 'Señor,' he said proudly, 'you shall take that animal and examine it; you shall submit it to tests beyond patience; yet you shall not discover the alkaloid that killed it.'

'That is not so,' said Essley, 'for there will be a contraction of the pupil which is an invariable sign.'

'Search also for that,' said the old man triumphantly.

Essley made the superficial tests. There was not even this invariable symptom.

A dark figure, pressed close to the wall outside, listened. He was standing by the shuttered window. He held to his ear a little ebonite tube with a microphonic receiver, and the rubber which covered the bell-like end was pressed against the shutter.

For half an hour he stood thus, almost motionless, then he withdrew silently and disappeared into the shadows of the orange grove that grew in the centre of the long garden.

As he did so, the door of the house opened and, with lantern in hand, Cajalos showed his visitor into the street.

'The devils are greener than ever,' chuckled the old man. 'Hey! there will be happenings, my brother!'

Essley said nothing. He wanted to be in the street again. He stood quivering with nervous impatience as the old man unfastened the heavy door, and when it swung open he almost leapt into the street outside.

'Goodbye,' he said.

'Go with God,' said the old man, and the door closed noiselessly.

Chapter 2
Colonel Black, financier

The firm of Black and Gram had something of a reputation in City circles. Gram might have been a man beyond reproach – a veritable Bayard of finance, a churchgoer, and a generous subscriber to charities. Indeed, Black complained with good-humoured irritation – if the combination can be visualized – that Gram would ruin him one of these fine days by his quixotic munificence.

Gram allowed his heart to dictate to his head; he was too soft for business, too retiring. The City was very sceptical about Gram. It compared him with a certain Mrs Harris, but Black did not fly into a temper; he smiled mysteriously at all the suspicion which the City entertained or expressed, and went on deploring the criminal rustiness of a man who apparently sought, by Black's account, to made the firm reputable in spite of the rumours which centred about Colonel J. Black.

In this way did Black describe himself, though the Army list was innocent of his name, and even a search through the voluminous rolls of the American honorary ranks failed to reveal any association.

Black and Gram floated companies and dealt largely in stocks and shares. They recommended to their clients certain shares, and the clients bought or sold according to the advice given, and at the end of a certain period of time. Black and Gram wrote politely regretting that the cover deposited had been exhausted, and urgently requesting, with as little delay as possible, the discharge of those liabilities which in some extraordinary fashion the client had incurred. This, at any rate, was the humble beginnings of a firm which was destined to grow to important proportions. Gram went out of the business – was never in it, if the truth be told. One doubts if he ever breathed the breath of life – and Black grew in prosperity. His was a name to conjure with in certain circles. In others it was never mentioned. The financial lords of the City – the Farings, the Wertheiners, the Scott-Teasons – had no official knowledge of his existence. They went about their business calmly, loaning their millions at a ridiculously small percentage, issuing Government loans, discounting bills, buying bullion, and such-like operations which filled the hours between eleven o'clock, when their electric broughams set them down in Threadneedle Street, and four o'clock, when their electric broughams picked them up again.

They read of Colonel Black in their grave way, because there were days when he dominated the financial columns. They read of his mighty stock deals, of his Argentine electric deal, his rubber flotations and his Canadian copper mines. They read about him, neither approving nor disapproving. They regarded him with that dispassionate interest which a railway engine has for a motorcar.

When, on one never-to-be-forgotten occasion, he approached the financial lords with a promising proposition, they 'regretted they were unable to entertain Colonel Black's interesting suggestion'. A little baffled, a little annoyed, he approached the big American group, for it was necessary for the success of his scheme that there should be names on his prospectus. Shrewd fellows, these Americans, thought Colonel Black, and he set forth his proposals in terms which were at once immodest and alluring. In reply – 'Dear friend,' (it was one of those American businesses that turn down a million dollars with five cents' worth of friendship), 'we have carefully considered your proposition, and whilst we are satisfied that you will make money by its fruition, we are not so certain that we shall.'

Black came to the City of London one afternoon to attend a board of directors' meeting. He had been out of town for a few days, recruiting in advance, as he informed the board with a touch of facetiousness, for the struggle that awaited him.

He was a man of middle height, broad of shoulder. His face was thin and lank, his complexion sallow, with a curious uniform yellowness. If you saw Colonel Black once you would never forget him – not only because of that yellow face of his, that straight black bar of eyebrow and the thin-lipped mouth, but the very personality of the man impressed itself indelibly on the mind of the observer.

His manner was quick, almost abrupt; his replies brusque. A sense of finality marked his decisions. If the financial lords knew him not, there were thousands that did. His name was a household word in England. There was hardly a middle-class family that did not hold his stock. The little 'street punters' hung on his word, his issues were subscribed for twice over. And he had established himself in five years; almost unknown before, he had risen to the dizziest heights in that short space of time.

Punctual to the minute, he entered the board-room of the suite of offices he occupied in Moorgate Street.

The meeting had threatened to be a stormy one. Again an amalgamation was in the air, and again the head of one group of ironmasters – it was an iron combine he was forming – had stood against the threats and blandishments of Black and his emissaries.

'The others are weakening,' said Fanks, that big, hairless man; 'you promised us that you would put him straight.'

'I will keep my promise.' said Black shortly.

'Widdison stood out, but he died,' continued Fanks. 'We can't expect Providence to help us all the time.'

Black's eyebrows lowered.

'I do not like jests of that kind,' he said. 'Sandford is an obstinate man, a proud man; he needs delicate handling. Leave him to me.'

The meeting adjourned lamely enough, and Black was leaving the room when Fanks beckoned to him.

'I met a man yesterday who knew your friend, Dr Essley, in Australia,' he said.

'Indeed.' Colonel Black's face was expressionless.

'Yes – he knew him in his very early days – he was asking me where he could find him.'

The other shrugged his shoulders. 'Essley is abroad, I think – you don't like him?'

Augustus Fanks shook his head. 'I don't like doctors who come to see me in the middle of the night, who are never to be found when they are wanted, and are always jaunting off to the Continent.'

'He is a busy man,' excused Black. 'By the way, where is your friend staying?'

'He isn't a friend, he's a sort of prospector, name of Weld, who has come to London with a mining proposition. He is staying at Varlet's Temperance Hôtel in Bloomsbury.'

'I will tell Essley when he returns,' said Black, nodding his head.

He returned to his private office in a thoughtful mood. All was not well with Colonel Black. Reputedly a millionaire, he was in the position of many a financier who counted his wealth in paper. He had got so far climbing on the shadows. The substance was still beyond his reach. He had organized successful combinations, but the cost had been heavy. Millions had flowed through his hands, but precious little had stuck. He was that curious contradiction – a dishonest man with honest methods. His schemes were financially sound, yet it had needed almost superhuman efforts to get them through.

He was in the midst of an unpleasant reverie when a tap on the door aroused him. It opened to admit Fanks. He frowned at the intruder, but the other pulled up a chair and sat down. 'Look here, Black,' he said, 'I want to say something to you.'

'Say it quickly.'

Fanks took a cigar from his pocket and lit it. 'You've had a marvellous career,' he said. 'I remember when you started with a little bucket-shop – well, we won't call it a bucket-shop,' he said hastily as he saw the anger rising in the other's face, 'outside broker's. You had a mug – I mean an inexperienced partner who found the money.'

'Yes.'

'Not the mysterious Gram, I think?'

'His successor – there was nothing mysterious about Gram.'

'A successor named Flint?'

'Yes.'

'He died unexpectedly, didn't he?'

'I believe he did,' said Black abruptly.

'Providence again,' said Fanks slowly; 'then you got the whole of the business. You took over the flotation and a rubber company, and it panned out. Well, after that you floated a tin mine or something – there was a death there, wasn't there?'

'I believe there was – one of the directors; I forget his name.'

Fanks nodded. 'He could have stopped the flotation – he was threatening to resign and expose some methods of yours.'

'He was a very headstrong man.'

'And he died.'

'Yes,' – a pause – 'he died.'

Fanks looked at the man who sat opposite to him.

'Dr Essley attended him.'

'I believe he did.'

'And he died.'

Black leant over the desk. 'What do you mean?' he asked. 'What are you suggesting about my friend, Dr Essley?'

'Nothing, except that Providence has been of some assistance to you,' said Fanks. 'The record of your success is a record of death – you sent Essley to see me once.'

'You were ill.'

'I was,' said Fanks grimly, 'and I was also troubling you a little.' He flicked the ash from his cigar to the carpet. 'Black, I'm going to resign all my directorships on your companies.'

The other man laughed unpleasantly.

'You can laugh, but it isn't healthy, Black. I've no use for money that is bought at too heavy a price.'

'My dear man, you can resign,' said Colonel Black, 'but might I ask if your extraordinary suspicions are shared by anybody else?'

Fanks shook his head.

'Not at present,' he said.

They looked at one another for the space of half a minute, which was a very long time.

'I want to clear right out,' Fanks continued. 'I reckon my holdings are worth £150,000 – you can buy them.'

'You amaze me,' said Black harshly.

He opened a drawer of his desk and took out a little green bottle and a feather. 'Poor Essley,' he smiled, 'wandering about Spain seeking the secrets of Moorish perfumery – he would go off his head if he knew what you thought of him.'

'I'd sooner he went off his head than that I should go off the earth,' said Fanks stolidly. 'What have you got there?'

Black unstoppered the bottle and dipped in the feather. He withdrew it and held it close to his nose.

'What is it?' asked Fanks curiously. For answer, Black held up the feather for the man to smell.

'I can smell nothing,' said Fanks. Tilting the end quickly downwards. Black drew it across the lips of the other. 'Here . . . ' cried Fanks, and went limply to the ground.

*　　*　　*

'Constable Fellowe!'

Frank Fellowe was leaving the charge-room when he heard the snappy tones of the desk-sergeant calling him.

'Yes, sergeant?' he said, with a note of inquiry in his voice. He knew that there was something unpleasant coming. Sergeant Gurden seldom took any opportunity of speaking to him, except in admonishment. The sergeant was a wizen-faced man, with an ugly trick of showing his teeth when he was annoyed, and no greater contrast could be imagined than that which was afforded by the tall, straight-backed young man in the constable's uniform, standing before the desk, and the shrunken figure that sat on the stool behind.

Sergeant Gurden had a dead-white face, which a scrubby black moustache went to emphasize. In spite of the fact that he was a man of good physical development, his clothing hung upon him awkwardly, and indeed the station-sergeant was awkward in more ways than one. Now he looked at Fellowe, showing his teeth. 'I have had another complaint about you,' he said, 'and if this is repeated it will be a matter for the Commissioner.'

The constable nodded his head respectfully. 'I am very sorry, sergeant,' he said, 'but what is the complaint?'

'You know as well as I do,' snarled the other; 'you have been annoying Colonel Black again.'

A faint smile passed across Fellowe's lips. He knew something of the solicitude in which the sergeant held the colonel.

'What the devil are you smiling at?' snapped the sergeant. 'I warn you,' he went on, 'that you are getting very impertinent, and this may be a matter for the Commissioner.'

'I had no intention of being disrespectful, sergeant,' said the young man. 'I am as tired of these complaints as you are, but I have told you, as I will tell the Commissioner, that Colonel Black lives in a house in Serrington Gardens and is a source of some interest to me – that is my excuse.'

'He complains that you are always watching the house,' said the sergeant, and Constable Fellowe smiled.

'That is his conscience working,' he said. 'Seriously, sergeant, I happen to know that the colonel is not too friendly disposed – '

He stopped himself.

'Well?' demanded the sergeant.

'Well,' repeated Constable Fellowe, 'it might be as well perhaps if I kept my thoughts to myself.'

The sergeant nodded grimly.

'If you get into trouble you will only have yourself to blame,' he warned. 'Colonel Black is an influential man. He is a ratepayer. Don't forget that, constable. The ratepayers pay your salary, find the coat for your back, feed you – you owe everything to the ratepayers.'

'On the other hand,' said the young man, 'Colonel Black is a ratepayer who owes me something.'

Hitching his cape over his arm, he passed from the charge-room down the stone steps into the street without. The man on duty at the door bade him a cheery farewell.

* * *

Fellowe was an annoying young man, more annoying by reason of the important fact that his antecedents were quite unknown to his most intimate friends. He was a man of more than ordinary education, quiet, restrained, his voice gently modulated; he had all the manners and attributes of a gentleman.

He had a tiny little house in Somers Town where he lived alone, but no friend of his, calling casually, had ever the good fortune to find him at home when he was off duty. It was believed he had other interests.

What those interests were could be guessed when, with exasperating unexpectedness, he appeared in the amateur boxing championship and carried off the police prize, for Fellowe was a magnificent boxer – hard-hitting, quick, reliable, scientific.

The bad men of Somers Town were the first to discover this, and one, Grueler, who on one never-to-be-forgotten occasion had shown fight on the way to the station, testified before breathless audiences as to the skill and science of the young man.

His breezy independence had won for him many friends, but it had made him enemies too, and as he walked thoughtfully along the street leading from the station, he realized that in the sergeant he had an enemy of more than average malignity.

Why should this be? It puzzled him. After all, he was only doing his duty. That he was also exceeding his duty did not strike him as being sufficient justification for the resentment of his superior, for he had reached the enthusiastic age of life where only inaction was unpardonable. As to Black, Frank shrugged his shoulders. He could not understand it. He was not of a nature to suspect that the sergeant had any other motive than the perfectly natural desire which all blasé superiors have, to check their too impulsive subordinates.

Frank admitted to himself that he was indeed a most annoying person, and in many ways he understood the sergeant's antagonism to himself. Dismissing the matter from his mind, he made his way to his tiny house in Croome Street and let himself into his small dining-room.

The walls were distempered, and the few articles of furniture that were within were such as are not usually met with in houses of this quality. The old print above the mantelpiece must have been worth a working-man's annual income. The small gate-legged table in the centre of the felt-covered floor was indubitably Jacobean, and the chairs were Sheraton, as also was the sideboard. Though the periods may not have harmonized, there is harmony enough in great age. A bright fire was burning in the grate, for the night was bitterly cold. Fellowe stopped before the mantelpiece to examine two letters which stood awaiting him, replaced them from where he had taken them, and passed through the folding doors of the room into a tiny bedroom.

He had an accommodating landlord. Property owners in Somers Town, and especially the owners of small cottages standing on fairly valuable ground, do not as a rule make such renovations as Fellowe required. The average landlord, for instance, would not have built the spacious bathroom which the cottage boasted, but then Fellowe's landlord was no ordinary man.

The young man bathed, changed himself into civilian clothing, made himself a cup of tea, and, slipping into a long overcoat which reached to his heels, left the house half an hour after he had entered.

Frank Fellowe made his way West. He found a taxi-cab at King's Cross and gave an address in Piccadilly. Before he had reached that historic thoroughfare he tapped at the window-glass and ordered the cabman to drop him.

At eleven o'clock that night Sergeant Gurden, relieved from his duty, left the station-house. Though outwardly taciturn and calm, he was boiling internally with wrath.

His antipathy to Fellowe was a natural one, but it had become intensified during the past few weeks by the attitude which the young man had taken up towards the sergeant's protégé.

Gurden was as much of a mystery to the men in his division as Fellowe, and even more so, because the secrecy which surrounded Gurden's life had a more sinister import than the reservation of the younger man.

Gurden was cursed with an ambition. He had hoped at the outset of his career to have secured distinction in the force, but a lack of education, coupled with an address which was apt to be uncouth and brusque, had militated against his enthusiasm.

He had recognized the limitations placed upon his powers by the authorities over him. He had long since come to realize that hope of promotion, first to an inspectorship, and eventually to that bright star which lures every policeman onward, and which is equivalent to the baton popularly supposed to be in every soldier's knapsack, a superintendentship, was not for him.

Thwarted ambition had to find a new outlet, and he concentrated his attention upon acquiring money. It became a passion for him, an obsession. His parsimony, his meanness, and his insatiable greed were bywords throughout the Metropolitan police force.

It had become a mania with him, this collecting of money, and his bitterest enmity was reserved for those who placed the slightest obstacle between the officer and the gratification of his ambitions.

It must be said of Colonel Black that he had been most kind. Cupidity takes a lenient view of its benefactor's morals, and though Sergeant Gurden was not the kind of man willingly to help the lawless, no person could say that an outside broker, undetected of fraud, was anything but a desirable member of society.

Black had made an appointment with him. He was on his way now to keep it. The colonel lived in one of those one-time fashionable squares in Camden Town. He was obviously well off, ran a car of his own, and had furnished No. 60 Serrington Gardens, with something like lavish comfort.

The sergeant had no time to change. There was no necessity, he told himself, for his relations with Black were of such a character that there was no need to stand on ceremony.

The square was deserted at this time of night, and the sergeant made his way to the kitchen entrance in the basement and rang the bell. The door was opened almost instantly by a man-servant.

'Is that you, sergeant?' said a voice from the darkness, as Gurden made his way upstairs to the unlighted hall above. Colonel Black turned on the light. He held out a long muscular hand in welcome to the police officer. 'I am so glad you have come,' he said.

The sergeant took the hand and shook it warmly. 'I have come to apologize to you. Colonel Black,' he said. 'I have severely reprimanded Police-Constable Fellowe.'

Black waved his hand deprecatingly. 'I do not wish to get any member of your admirable force into trouble,' he said, 'but really this man's prying into my business is inexcusable and humiliating.'

The sergeant nodded. 'I can well understand your annoyance, sir,' he said, 'but you will understand that these young constables are always a little over-zealous, and when a man is that way he is inclined to overdo it a little.'

He spoke almost pleadingly in his desire to remove any bad impression that might exist in Black's mind as to his own part in Police-Constable Fellowe's investigations.

Black favoured him with a gracious bow.

'Please do not think of it, I beg of you,' he said. 'I am perfectly sure that the young constable did not intend willingly to hurt my amour-propre.' He led the way to a spacious dining-room situated at the back of the house. Whisky and cigars were on the table. 'Help yourself, sergeant,' said Colonel Black. He pushed a big comfortable chair forward.

With a murmured word of thanks, the sergeant sank into its luxurious depths. 'I am due back at the station in half an hour,' he said, 'if you will excuse me then.'

Black nodded. 'We shall be able to do our business in that time,' he said, 'but before we go any further, let me thank you for what you have already done.'

From the inside pocket of his coat he took a flat pocket-book, opened it and extracted two bank-notes. He laid them on the table at the sergeant's elbow. The sergeant protested feebly, but his eyes twinkled at the sight of the crinkling paper. 'I don't think I have done anything to deserve this,' he muttered.

Colonel Black smiled, and his big cigar tilted happily. 'I pay well for little services, sergeant,' he said. 'I have many enemies – men who will misrepresent my motives – and it is essential that I should be forewarned.'

He strode up and down the apartment thoughtfully, his hands thrust into his trousers pockets.

'It is a hard country, England,' he said, 'for men who have had the misfortune to dabble in finance.'

Sergeant Gurden murmured sympathetically.

'In our business, sergeant,' the aggrieved colonel went on, 'it frequently happens that disappointed people – people who have not made the profits which they anticipated – bring extraordinary accusations against those responsible for the conduct of those concerns in which their money is invested. I had a letter today – ' he shrugged his shoulders – 'accusing me – me! – of running a bucket-shop.'

The sergeant nodded; he could well understand that aspect of speculation.

'And one has friends,' Black went on, striding up and down the apartment, 'one has people one wants to protect against similar annoyances – take my friend Dr Essley – Essley, E double S L E Y,' he spelt the name carefully; 'you have heard of him?'

The sergeant had not heard of any such body, but was willing to admit that he had.

'There is a man,' said the colonel, 'a man absolutely at the head of his profession – I shouldn't be surprised to learn that even he is no safer from the voice of slander.'

The sergeant thought it very likely, and murmured to the effect.

'There is always a possibility that malignity will attach itself to the famous,' the colonel continued, 'and because I know that you would be one of the first to hear such slander, and that you would moreover afford me an opportunity – a private opportunity – of combating such slander, that I feel such security. God bless you, sergeant!' He patted the other's shoulder, and Gurden was genuinely affected.

'I can quite understand your position, sir,' he said, 'and you may be sure that when it is possible to render you any assistance I shall be most happy and proud to render it.'

Again Colonel Black favoured his visitor with a little pat.

'Or to Dr Essley,' he said; 'remember the name. Now, sergeant,' he went on, 'I sent for you tonight,' – he shrugged his shoulders – 'when I say sent for you, that, of course, is an exaggeration. How can a humble citizen like myself command the services of an officer of the police?'

Sergeant Gurden fingered his moustache self-consciously.

'It is rather,' the colonel went on, 'that I take advantage of your inestimable friendship to seek your advice.'

He stopped in his walk, drew a chair opposite to where the sergeant was sitting, and seated himself.

'Constable Fellowe, the man of whom I have complained, had the good fortune to render a service to the daughter of Mr Theodore Sandford – I see you know the gentleman.'

The sergeant nodded; he had heard of Mr Theodore Sandford, as who had not? For Theodore Sandford was a millionaire ironmaster who had built a veritable palace at Hampstead, had purchased the Dennington Velasquez, and had presented it to the nation.

'Your constable,' continued Colonel Black, 'sprang upon a motor-car Miss Sandford was driving down a steep hill, the brakes of which had gone wrong, and at some risk to himself guided the car through the traffic when, not to put too fine a point on it, Miss Sandford had lost her head.'

'Oh, it was him, was it?' said the sergeant disparagingly.

'It was him,' agreed the colonel out of sheer politeness. 'Now these young people have met unknown to the father of Miss Sandford, and – well, you understand.'

The sergeant did not understand, but said nothing.

'I do not suggest,' said the colonel, 'that there is anything wrong – but a policeman, sergeant, not even an officer like yourself – a policeman!'

Deplorable! said the sergeant's head, eyes and hands.

'For some extraordinary reason which I cannot fathom,' the colonel proceeded, 'Mr Sandford tolerates the visits of this young man; that, I fear, is a matter which we cannot go into, but I should like you – well, I should like you to use your influence with Fellowe.'

Sergeant Gurden rose to depart. He had no influence, but some power. He understood a little of what the other man was driving at, the more so when –

'If this young man gets into trouble, I should like to know,' said Colonel Black, holding out his firm hand; 'I should like to know very much indeed.'

'He is a rare pushful fellow, that Fellowe,' said the sergeant severely. 'He gets to know the upper classes in some way that I can't under-stand, and I dare say he has wormed himself into their confidence. I always say that the kitchen is the place for the policeman, and when I see a constable in the drawing-room I begin to suspect things. There is a great deal of corruption – ' He stopped, suddenly realizing that he himself was in a drawing-room, and that corruption was an ugly and an incongruous word.

Colonel Black accompanied him to the door.

'You understand, sergeant,' he said, 'that this man – Fellowe, did you call him? – may make a report over your head or behind your back. I want you to take great care that such a report, if it is made, shall come to me. I do not want to be taken by surprise. If there is any charge to answer I want to know all about it in advance. It will make the answering ever so much easier, as I am a busy man.'

He shook hands with the sergeant and saw him out of the house.

Sergeant Gurden went back to the station with a brisk step and a comforting knowledge that the evening had been well spent.

Chapter 3

An adventure in Pimlico

In the meantime our constable had reached a small tavern in the vicinity of Regent Street. He entered the bar and, ordering a drink, took a seat in the corner of the spacious saloon. There were two or three people about; there were two or three men drinking at the bar and talking – men in loud suits, who cast furtive glances at every newcomer. He knew them to be commonplace criminals of the first type. They did not engage his attention: he flew higher.

He sat in the corner, apparently absorbed in an evening paper, with his whisky and soda before him scarcely touched, waiting. It was not the first time he had been here, nor would it be the first time he had waited without any result. But he was patient and dogged in the pursuit of his object.

The clock pointed to a quarter after ten, when the swing-doors were pushed open and two men entered. For the greater part of half an hour the two were engaged in a low-voiced consultation. Over his paper Frank could see the face of Sparks. He was the jackal of the Black gang, the man-of-all-trades. To him were deputed the meanest of Black's commissions, and worthily did he serve his master. The other was known to Frank as Jakobs, a common thief and a pensioner of the benevolent colonel.

The conversation was punctuated either by glances at the clock above the bar or at Sparks' watch, and at a quarter to eleven the two men rose and went out. Frank followed, leaving his drink almost untouched.

The men turned into Regent Street, walked a little way up, and then hailed a taxi. Another cab was passing. Frank beckoned it. 'Follow that yellow cab,' he said to the driver, 'and keep a reasonable distance behind, and when it sets down, pass it and drop me farther along the street.'

The man touched his cap. The two cabs moved on. They went in the direction of Victoria, passed the great station on the left, turned down Grosvenor Road on the right, and were soon in the labyrinth of streets that constitute Pimlico. The first cab pulled up at a big gaunt house in a street which had once been fashionable, but which now hovered indescribably between slums and shabby gentility. Frank saw the two men get out, and descended himself a few hundred yards farther along on the opposite side of the street. He had marked the house. There was no difficulty in distinguishing it; a brass plate was attached to the door announcing it to be an employment agency – as, indeed, it was.

His quarry had entered before he strode across towards the house. He crossed the road and took a position from whence he could watch the door. The half-hour after twelve had chimed from a neighbouring church before anything happened. A policeman on his beat had passed Frank with a resentful sidelong glance, and the few pedestrians who were abroad at that hour viewed him with no less suspicion.

The chime of the neighbouring church had hardly died away when a private car came swiftly along the road and pulled up with a jerk in front of the house. A man descended. From where he stood Frank had no difficulty in recognizing Black. That he was expected was evident from the fact that the door was immediately opened to him.

Three minutes later another car came down the street and stopped a few doors short of the house, as though the driver was not quite certain as to which was his destination. The newcomer was a stranger to Frank. In the uncertain light cast by a street lamp he seemed to be fashionably dressed. As he turned to give instructions to his chauffeur, Fellowe caught a glimpse of a spotless white shirt-front beneath the long dark overcoat. He hesitated at the foot of the steps which led to the door, and ascended slowly and fumbled for a moment at the bell. Before he could touch it the door opened. There was a short parley as the new man entered.

Frank, waiting patiently on the other side of the road, saw a light appear suddenly on the first floor.

Did he but know, this gathering was in the nature of a board meeting, a board meeting of a company more heavily financed than some of the most respected houses in the City, having its branches in various parts of the world, its agents, its business system – its very books, if they could be found and the ciphered entries unravelled.

Black sat at one end of the long table and the last arrival at the other. He was a florid young man of twenty-six, with a weak chin and a slight yellow moustache. His face would be familiar to all racing men, for this was the sporting baronet, Sir Isaac Tramber. There was something about Sir Isaac which kept him on the outside fringe of good society, in spite of the fact that he came of a stock which was indelibly associated with England's story: the baronetcy had been created as far back as the seventeenth century. It was a proud name, and many of his ancestors had borne it proudly. None the less, his name was taboo, his invitations politely refused, and never reciprocated.

There had been some unfathomable scandal associated with his name. Society is very lenient to its children. There are crimes and sins which it readily, or if not readily, at any rate eventually, forgives and condones, but there are some which are unpardonable, unforgivable. Once let a man commit those crimes, or sin those sins, and the doors of Mayfair are closed for ever against him. Around his head was a cloud of minor scandal, but that which brought down the bar of good society was the fact that he had ridden his own horse at one of the Midland meetings. It had started a hot favourite – five to two on.

The circumstances of that race are inscribed in the annals of the Jockey Club. How an infuriated mob broke down the barriers and attempted to reach this amateur jockey was ably visualized by the sporting journalists who witnessed the extraordinary affair. Sir Isaac was brought before the local stewards and the case submitted to the stewards of the Jockey Club. The next issue of the Racing Calendar contained the ominous announcement that Sir Isaac Tramber had been 'warned off' Newmarket Heath.

Under this ban he sat for four years, till the withdrawal of the notice. He might again attend race-meetings and own horses, and he did both, but the ban of society, that unwritten 'warning off' notice, had not been withdrawn. The doors of every decent house were closed to him. Only one friend he had in the fashionable world, and there were people who said that the Earl of Verlond, that old and crabbed and envenomed man, merely championed his unpromising protégé out of sheer perversity, and there was ample justification for this contention of a man who was known to have the bitterest tongue in Europe.

The descent to hell is proverbially easy, and Sir Isaac Tramber's descent was facilitated by that streak of decadence which had made itself apparent even in his early youth. As he sat at one end of the board-table, both hands stuffed into his trousers pockets, his head on one side like a perky bird, he proved no mean man of business, as Black had discovered earlier in their acquaintanceship.

'We are all here now, I think,' said Black, looking humorously at his companion. They had left Sparks and his friend in a room below.

'I have asked you to come tonight,' he said, 'to hear a report of this business. I am happy to tell you that we have made a bigger profit this year than we have ever made in the course of our existence.'

He went on to give details of the work for which he had been responsible, and he did so with the air and in the manner of one who was addressing a crowded board-room.

'People would say,' said the colonel oracularly, 'that the business of outside broker is inconsistent with my acknowledged position in the world of finance; therefore I deem it expedient to dissociate myself from our little firm. But the outside broker is a useful person – especially the outside broker who has a hundred thousand clients. There are stocks of mine which he can recommend with every evidence of disinterestedness, and just now I am particularly desirous that these stocks should be recommended.'

'Do we lose anything by Fanks's death?' asked the baronet carelessly. 'Hard luck on him, wasn't it? But he was awfully fat.'

The colonel regarded the questioner with a calm stare. 'Do not let us refer to Fanks,' he said evenly. 'The death of Fanks has very much upset me – I do not wish to speak about it.'

The baronet nodded. 'I never trusted him, poor chap,' he said, 'any more than I trusted the other chap who made such an awful scene here a year ago – February, wasn't it?'

'Yes' said the colonel briefly.

'It's lucky for us he died too,' said the tactless aristocrat, 'because – '

'We'll get on with the business.' Colonel Black almost snarled the words. But the baronet had something to say. He was troubled about his own security. It was when Black showed some sign of ending the business that Sir Isaac leant forward impatiently.

'There is one thing we haven't discussed, Black,' he said.

Black knew what the thing was, and had carefully avoided mention of the subject. 'What is it?' he asked innocently.

'These fellows who are threatening us, or rather threatening you; they haven't any idea who it is who is running the show, have they?' he asked, with some apprehension.

Black shook his head smilingly. 'I think not,' he said. 'You are speaking, of course, of the Four Just Men.'

Sir Isaac gave a short nod. 'Yes,' Black went on, with an assumption of indifference, 'I have had an anonymous letter from these gentlemen. As a matter of fact, my dear Sir Isaac, I haven't the slightest doubt that the whole thing is a bluff.'

'What do you mean by a bluff?' demanded the other.

Black shrugged his shoulders. 'I mean that there is no such organization as the Four Just Men. They are a myth. They have no existence. It is too melodramatic for words. Imagine four people gathered together to correct the laws of England. It savours more of the sensational novel than of real life.' He laughed with apparent ease. 'These things,' he said, wagging his finger jocosely at the perturbed baronet, 'do not happen in Pimlico. No, I suspect that our constable, the man I spoke to you about, is at the bottom of it. He is probably the whole Four of these desperate conspirators.' He laughed again.

Sir Isaac fingered his moustache nervously. 'It's all rot to say they don't exist; we know what they did six years ago, and I don't like this other man a bit,' he grumbled.

'Don't like which other man?'

'This interfering policeman,' he replied irritably. 'Can't he be squared?'

'The constable?'

'Yes; you can square constables, I suppose, if you can square sergeants.' Sir Isaac Tramber had the gift of heavy sarcasm.

Black stroked his chin thoughtfully. 'Curiously enough,' he said, 'I have never thought of that. I think we can try.' He glanced at his watch. 'Now I'll ask you just to clear out,' he said. 'I have an appointment at half-past one.'

Sir Isaac smiled slowly. 'Rather a curious hour for an appointment,' he said.

'Ours is a curious business,' replied Colonel Black.

They rose, and Sir Isaac turned to Black. 'What is the appointment?' he asked.

Black smiled mysteriously. 'It is rather a peculiar case,' he began.

He stopped suddenly. There were hurried footsteps on the stairs without. A second later the door was flung open and Sparks burst into the room. 'Guv'nor,' he gasped, 'they're watching the house.'

'Who is watching?'

'There's a busy on the other side of the road,' said the man, speaking graphically. 'I spotted him, and the moment he saw I noticed him he moved off. He's back again now. Me and Willie have been watching him.'

The two followed the agitated Sparks downstairs, where from a lower window they might watch, unobserved, the man who dared spy on their actions.

'If this is the police,' fumed Black, 'that dog Gurden has failed me. He told me Scotland Yard were taking no action whatever.'

Frank, from his place of observation, was well aware that he had caused some consternation. He had seen Sparks turn back hurriedly with Jakobs and re-enter the house. He observed the light go out suddenly on the first floor, and now he had a pretty shrewd idea that they were watching him through the glass panel of the doorway.

There was no more he could learn. So far his business had been a failure. It was no secret to him that Sir Isaac Tramber was an associate of Black's, or that Jakobs and the estimable Sparks were also partners in this concern. He did not know what he hoped to find, or what he had hoped to accomplish.

He was turning away in the direction of Victoria when his attention was riveted on the figure of a young man which was coming slowly along on the opposite sidewalk, glancing from time to time at the numbers which were inscribed on the fanlights of the doors.

He watched him curiously, then in a flash he realized his objective as he stopped in front of No. 63.

In half a dozen steps he had crossed the road towards him. The boy – he was little more – turned round, a little frightened at the sudden appearance.

Frank Fellowe walked up to him and recognized him.

'You need not be scared,' he said, 'I am a police officer. Are you going into that house?'

The young man looked at him for a moment and made no reply. Then, in a voice that shook, he said 'Yes.'

'Are you going there to give Colonel Black certain information about your employer's business?'

The young man seemed hypnotized by fear. He nodded.

'Is your employer aware of the fact?'

Slowly he shook his head.

'Did *he* send you?' he asked suddenly, and Frank observed a note of terror in his voice.

'No,' he smiled, wondering internally who the 'he' was. 'I am here quite on my own, and my object is to warn you against trusting Colonel Black.'

He jerked up his head, and Frank saw the flush that came to his face. 'You are Constable Fellowe,' he said suddenly.

To say that Frank was a little staggered is to express the position mildly. 'Yes,' he repeated, 'I am Constable Fellowe.'

Whilst he was talking the door of the house had opened. From the position in which he stood Frank could not see this. Black emerged stealthily and came down the steps towards him.

The agent had no other desire than to discover the identity of the man who was shadowing him. He was near enough to hear what the young man said.

'Fellowe,' he boomed, and came down the rest of the steps at a run. 'So it's you, is it?' he snarled. 'It's you interfering with my business again.'

'Something like that,' said Frank coolly. He turned to the young man again.

'I tell you,' he said in a tone of authority, 'that if you go into this house, or have anything whatever to do with this man, you will regret it to the last day of your life.'

'You shall pay for this!' fumed Black. 'I'll have your coat from your back, constable. I'll give you in charge. I'll – I'll – '

'You have an excellent opportunity,' said Frank. His quick eye had detected the figure of a constable on the other side of the road, walking slowly towards them. 'There's a policeman over there; call him now and give me in charge. There is no reason why you shouldn't – no reason why you should want to avoid publicity of the act.'

'Oh, no, no!' It was the youth who spoke. 'Colonel Black, I must come another time.'

He turned furiously on Frank. 'As to you – ' he began, gaining courage from Black's presence.

'As to you,' retorted Frank, 'avoid bad company!'

He hesitated, then turned and walked quickly away, leaving the two men alone on the pavement.

The three watchers in the hall eyed the scene curiously, and two of them at least anticipated instructions from Black which would not be followed by pleasant results for Frank.

With an effort, however, Black controlled his temper. He, too, had seen the shadow on the other side of the road.

'Look here, Constable Fellowe,' he said, with forced geniality, 'I know you're wrong, and you think you're right. Just come inside and let's argue this matter out.'

He waited, his nimble mind evolving a plan for dealing with this dangerous enemy. He did not imagine that Frank would accept the invitation, and he was genuinely astounded when, without another word, the constable turned and slowly ascended the steps to the door.

Chapter 4

The men who sat in judgment

Frank heard a little scuffling in the hall, and knew that the men who had been watching him had gone to cover. He had little fear, though he carried no weapon. He was supremely confident in his own strength and science.

Black, following him in, shut the door behind him. Frank heard the snick of a bolt being shot into its socket in the dark. Black switched on the light.

'We're playing fair, Constable Fellowe.' he said, with an amiable smile. 'You see, we do not try any monkey tricks with you. Everything is straight and above-board.'

He led the way up the thickly-carpeted stairs, and Frank followed. The young man noticed the house was luxuriously furnished. Rich engravings hung on the walls, the curtains that veiled the big stairway window were of silk, cabinets of Chinese porcelain filled the recesses.

Black led the way to a room on the first floor. It was not the room in which the board meeting had been held, but a small one which led off from the board-room. Here the luxury was less apparent. Two desks formed the sole furniture of the room; the carpet under foot was of the commonplace type to be found in the average office. A great panel of tapestry – the one touch of luxury – covered one wall, and a cluster of lights in the ceiling afforded light to the room. A little fire was burning in the grate. On a small table near one of the desks supper had been laid for two. Frank noticed this, and Black, inwardly cursing his own stupidity, smiled.

'It looks as though I expected you,' he said easily, 'though, as a matter of fact, I have some friends here tonight, and one of them is staying to supper.'

Frank nodded. He knew the significance of that supper-table and the white paper pads ready for use.

'Sit down,' said Black, and himself sat at one of the desks. Frank seated himself slowly at some distance from the other, half turning to face the man whom he had set himself to ruin.

'Now, let us get to business,' said Black briskly. 'There is no reason in the world why you and I should not have an understanding. I'm a business man, you're a business man, and a smart young man too,' he said approvingly.

Frank made no reply. He knew what was coming.

'Now suppose,' Black continued reflectively, 'suppose we make an arrangement like this. You imagine that I am engaged in a most obnoxious type of business. Oh, I know!' he went on deprecatingly, 'I know! You're under the impression that I'm making huge profits, that I'm robbing people by bucket-shop methods. I needn't tell you, constable, that I am most grieved and indignant that you should have entertained so low an opinion of my character.'

His voice was neither grieved nor indignant. Indeed, the tone he employed was a cheerful admission of fault.

'Now, I am quite content you should investigate my affairs first hand. You know we receive a large number of accounts from all over the Continent and that we pay away enormous sums to clients who – well, shall we say – gamble on margins?'

'You can say what you like,' said Frank.

'Now,' said Black, 'suppose you go to Paris, constable, you can easily get leave, or go into the provinces, to any of the big towns in Great Britain where our clients reside, and interview them for yourself as to our honesty. Question them – I'll give you a list of them. I don't want you to do this at your own expense – ' his big hands were outstretched in protest. 'I don't suppose you have plenty of money to waste on that variety of excursion. Now, I will hand you tonight, if you like, a couple of hundred pounds, and you shall use this just as you like to further your investigations. How does that strike you?'

Frank smiled. 'It strikes me as devilish ingenious,' he said. 'I take the couple of hundred, and I can either use it for the purpose you mention or I can put it to my own account, and no questions will be asked. Do I understand aright?'

Colonel Black smiled and nodded. His strong, yellow face puckered in internal amusement. 'You are a singularly sharp young man,' he said.

Frank rose. 'There's nothing doing,' he said.

Colonel Black frowned. 'You mean you refuse?' he said.

Frank nodded. 'I refuse,' he said, 'absolutely. You can't bribe me with two hundred pounds, or with two thousand pounds, Black. I am not to be bought. I believe you are one of the most dangerous people society knows. I believe that both here and in the City you are running on crooked lines; I shall not rest until I have you in prison.'

Black rose slowly to his feet. 'So that's it, is it?' he said. There was menace and malignity in his tones. A look of implacable hatred met Fellowe's steady gaze. 'You will regret this,' he went on gratingly. 'I have given you a chance that most young men would jump at. I could make that three hundred – '

'If you were to make it thirty-three hundred, or thirty-three thousand,' said Frank impatiently, 'there would be no business done. I know you too well, Black. I know more about you than you think I know.'

He took up his hat and examined the interior thoughtfully.

'There is a man wanted in France – an ingenious man who initiated Get-rich-quick banks all over the country, particularly in Lyons and the South – his name is Olloroff,' he said carefully. 'There's quite a big reward offered for him. He had a partner who died suddenly – '

Black's face went white. The hand that rose to his lips shook a little. 'You know too much, I think,' he said. He turned swiftly and left the room. Frank sprang back to the door. He suspected treachery, but before he could reach it the door closed with a click. He turned the handle and pulled, but it was fast.

He looked round the room, and saw another door at the farther end. He was half-way towards this when all the lights in the room went out. He was in complete darkness. What he had thought to be a window at one end turned out to be a blank wall, so cunningly draped with curtains and ingeniously-shaped blinds as to delude the observer. The real window, which looked out on to the street below, was heavily shuttered.

The absence of light was no inconvenience to him. He had a small electric lamp in his pocket, which he flashed round the room. It had been a tactical error on his part to put Black on his guard, but the temptation to give the big man a fright had been too great. He realized that he was in a position of considerable danger. Save the young man he had seen in the street, and who in such an extraordinary manner had recognized him, nobody knew of his presence in that house.

He made a swift search of the room and listened intently at both doors, but he could hear nothing. On the landing outside the door through which he had entered there were a number of antique Eastern arms hung on the wall. He had a slight hope that this scheme of decoration might have been continued in the room, but before he began his search he knew his quest was hopeless. There would be no weapons here. He made a careful examination of the floor; he wanted to be on his guard against traps and pitfalls.

There was no danger from this. He sat down on the edge of a desk and waited. He waited half an hour before the enemy gave a sign. Then, close to his ear, it seemed, a voice asked 'Are you going to be sensible, constable?'

Frank flashed the rays of his lamp in the direction from which the voice came. He saw what appeared to him to be a hanging Eastern lantern. He had already observed that the stem from which it hung was unusually thick; now he realized that the bell-shaped lamp was the end of a speaking-tube. He guessed, and probably correctly, that the device had been hung rather to allow Black to overhear than for the purpose of communicating with the occupants of the room.

He made no reply. Again the question was repeated, and he raised his head and answered. 'Come and see,' he challenged.

All the time he had been waiting in the darkness his attention had been divided between the two doors. He was on the alert for the thin pencil of light which would show him the stealthy opening. In some extraordinary manner he omitted to take into consideration the possibility of the outside lights being extinguished.

He was walking up and down the carpeted centre of the room, which was free of any impediment, when a slight noise behind him arrested his attention. He had half turned when a noose was slipped over his body, a pair of desperate arms encircled his legs, and he was thrown violently to the floor. He struggled, but it was against uneven odds. The lasso which had pinioned him prevented the free use of his arms. He found himself lying face downwards upon the carpet. A handkerchief was thrust into his mouth, something cold and hard encircled his wrists and pulled them together. He heard a click, and knew that he was handcuffed behind.

'Pull him up,' said Black's voice.

At that moment the lights in the room went on. Frank staggered to his feet, assisted ungently by Jakobs. Black was there. Sparks was there, and a stranger Frank had seen enter the house was also there, but a silk handkerchief was fastened over the lower half of his face, and all that Frank could see was the upper half of a florid countenance and a pair of light blue eyes that twinkled shiftily.

'Put him on that sofa,' said Black. 'Now,' he said, when his prisoner had been placed according to instructions, 'I think you are going to listen to reason.'

It was impossible for Frank Fellowe to reply. The handkerchief in his mouth was an effective bar to any retort that might have risen in his mind, but his eyes, clear, unwavering, spoke in unmistakable language to the smiling man who faced him.

'My proposition is very simple,' said Black: 'you're to hold your tongue, mind your own business, accept a couple of hundred on account, and you will not be further molested. Refuse, and I'm going to put you where I can think about you.' He smiled crookedly. 'There are some five cellars in this house,' said Black; 'if you are a student of history, as I am, Mr Fellowe, you should read the History of the Rhine Barons. You would recognize then that I have an excellent substitute for the donjon keeps of old. You will be chained there by the legs, you will be fed according to the whims of a trusted custodian, who, I may tell you, is a very absent-minded man, and there you will remain until you are either mad or glad – glad to accept our terms – or mad enough to be incarcerated in some convenient asylum, where nobody will take your accusations very seriously.'

Black turned his head. 'Take that gag out,' he said; 'we will bring him into the other room. I do not think that his voice will be heard, however loudly he shouts, in there.'

Jakobs pulled the handkerchief roughly from Frank's mouth. He was half pushed, half led, to the door of the board-room, which was in darkness. Black went ahead and fumbled for the switch, the others standing in the doorway. He found the light at last, and then he stepped back with a cry of horror.

Well he might, for four strangers sat at the board – four masked men. The door leading into the board-room was a wide one. The three men with their prisoner stood grouped in the centre, petrified into immobility. The four who sat at the table uttered no sound.

Black was the first to recover his self-possession. He started forward, then stopped. His face worked, his mouth opened, but he could frame no words. 'What – what?' he gasped.

The masked man who sat at the head of the table turned his bright eyes upon the proprietor of the establishment. 'You did not expect me, Mr Olloroff?' he said bluntly.

'My name is Black,' said the other violently. 'What are you doing here?'

'That you shall discover,' said the masked man. 'There are seats.'

Then Black saw that seats had been arranged at the farther end of the table.

'First of all,' the masked man went on, 'I will relieve you of your prisoner. You take those handcuffs off, Sparks.'

The man fumbled in his pocket for the key, but not in his waistcoat pocket – his hand went farther down.

'Keep your hand up,' said the man at the table, sharply. He made a little gesture with his hand, and Black's servant saw the gleam of a pistol. 'You need have no fear,' he went on, 'our little business will have no tragic sequence tonight – tonight!' he repeated significantly. 'You have had three warnings from us, and we have come to deliver the last in person.'

Black was fast recovering his presence of mind. 'Why not report to the police?' he scoffed.

'That we shall do in good time,' was the polite reply, 'but I warn you personally, Black, that you have almost reached the end of your tether.'

In some ways Black was no coward. With an oath, he whipped out a revolver and sprang into the room. As he did so the room went dark, and Frank found himself seized by a pair of strong hands and wrenched from the loose grip of his captor.

He was pushed forward, a door slammed behind him. He found himself tumbling down the carpeted stairs into the hall below. Quick hands removed the handcuffs from his wrists, the street door was opened by somebody who evidently knew the ways of the house, and he found himself, a little bewildered, in the open street, with two men in evening dress by his side.

They still wore their masks. There was nothing to distinguish either of them from the ordinary man in the street.

'This is your way, Mr Fellowe,' said one, and he pointed up the street in the direction of Victoria.

Frank hesitated. He was keen to see the end of this adventure. Where were the other two of this vigilant four? Why had they been left behind? What were they doing?

His liberators must have guessed his thoughts, for one of them said, 'Our friends are safe, do not trouble about them. You will oblige us, constable, by going very quickly.'

With a word of thanks, Frank Fellowe turned and walked quickly up the street. He looked back once, but the two men had disappeared into the darkness.

Chapter 5
The Earl of Verlond

Colonel Black was amused. He was annoyed, too, and the two expressions resulted in a renewed irritation.

His present annoyance rose from another cause. A mysterious tribunal, which had examined his papers, had appeared from and disappeared to nowhere, had annoyed him – had frightened him, if the truth be told; but courage is largely a matter of light with certain temperaments, and strong in the security of the morning sunshine and with the satisfaction that there was nothing tangible for the four men to discover, he was bold enough.

He was sitting in his dressing-gown at breakfast, and his companion was Sir Isaac Tramber.

Colonel Black loved the good things of life, good food and the comforts of civilization. His breakfast was a very ample one.

Sir Isaac's diet was more simple: a brandy and water and an apple comprised the menu. 'What's up?' he growled. He had had a late night and was not in the best of tempers.

Black tossed a letter across to him.

'What do you think of that?' he asked. 'Here's a demand from Tangye's, the brokers, for ten thousand pounds, and a hint that failing its arrival I shall be posted as a defaulter.'

'Pay it,' suggested Sir Isaac languidly, and the other laughed.

'Don't talk rot,' he said, with offensive good humour. 'Where am I going to get ten thousand pounds? I'm nearly broke; you know that, Tramber; we're both in the same boat. I've got two millions on paper, but I don't think we could raise a couple of hundred ready between us if we tried.'

The baronet pushed back his plate. 'I say,' he said abruptly, 'you don't mean what you said?'

'About the money?'

'About the money – yes. You nearly gave me an attack of heart disease. My dear chap, we should be pretty awkwardly fixed if money dried up just now.'

Colonel Black smiled. 'That's just what has happened,' he said. 'Fix or no fix, we're in it. I'm overdrawn in the bank; I've got about a hundred pounds in the house, and I suppose you've got another hundred.'

'I haven't a hundred farthings,' said the other.

'Expenses are very heavy,' Black went on; 'you know how these things turn up. There are one or two in view, but beyond that we have nothing. If we could bring about the amalgamation of those Northern Foundries we might both sign cheques for a hundred thousand.'

'What about the City?'

The Colonel sliced off the top of his egg without replying. Tramber knew the position in the City as well as he did.

'H'm,' said Sir Isaac, 'we've got to get money from somewhere, Black.'

'What about your friend?' asked Colonel Black. He spoke carelessly, but the question was a well-considered one.

'Which friend?' asked Sir Isaac, with a hoarse laugh. 'Not that I have so many that you need particularize any. Do you mean Verlond?'

Black nodded.

'Verlond, my dear chap,' said the baronet, 'is the one man I must not go to in this world for money.'

'He is a very rich man,' mused Black.

'He is a very rich man,' said the other grimly, 'and he may have to leave his money to me.'

'Isn't there an heir?' asked the colonel, interested.

'There was,' said the baronet with a grin, 'a high-spirited nephew, who ran away from home, and is believed to have been killed on a cattle-ranch in Texas. At any rate, Lord Verlond intends applying to the court to presume his death.'

'That was a blow for the old man,' said Black.

This statement seemed to amuse Sir Isaac. He leant back in his chair and laughed loud and long.

'A blow!' he said. 'My dear fellow, he hated the boy worse than poison. You see, the Verlond stock – he's a member of the cadet branch of the family. The boy was a real Verlond. That's why the old man hated him. I believe he made his life a little hell. He used to have him up for week-ends to bully him, until at last the kid got desperate, collected all his pocket-money and ran away.

'Some friends of the family traced him; the old man didn't move a step to search for him. They found work for him for a few months in a printer's shop in London. Then he went abroad – sailed to America on an emigrant's ticket.

'Some interested people took the trouble to follow his movements. He went out to Texas and got on to a pretty bad ranch. Later, a man after his description was shot in a street fight; it was one of those little ranching towns that you see so graphically portrayed in cinema palaces.'

'Who is the heir?' asked Black.

'To the title, nobody. To the money, the boy's sister. She is quite a nice girl.'

Black was looking at him through half-closed eyes.

The baronet curled his moustache thoughtfully and repeated, as if to himself, 'Quite a nice girl.'

'Then you have – er – prospects?' asked Black slowly.

'What the devil do you mean, Black?' asked Sir Isaac, sitting up stiffly.

'Just what I say,' said the other. 'The man who marries the lady gets a pretty large share of the swag. That's the position, isn't it?'

'Something like that,' said Sir Isaac sullenly.

The colonel got up and folded his napkin carefully. Colonel Black needed ready money so badly that it mattered very little what the City said. If Sandford objected that would be another matter, but Sandford was a good sportsman, though somewhat difficult to manage.

He stood for a moment looking down on the baronet thoughtfully.

'Ikey,' he said, 'I have noticed in you of late a disposition to look upon our mutual interests as something of which a man might be ashamed – I have struck an unexpected streak of virtue in you, and I confess that I am a little distressed.'

His keen eyes were fixed on the other steadily.

'Oh, it's nothing,' said the baronet uneasily, 'but the fact is, I've got to keep my end up in society.'

'You owe me a little,' began Black.

'Four thousand,' said the other promptly, 'and it is secured by a £50,000 policy on my life.'

'The premiums of which I pay,' snarled the colonel grimly; 'but I wasn't thinking of money.'

His absorbed gaze took in the baronet from head to foot.

'Fifty thousand pounds!' he said facetiously. 'My dear Ikey, you're worth much more murdered than alive.'

The baronet shivered. 'Don't make those rotten jokes,' he said, and finished his brandy at a gulp.

The other nodded. 'I'll leave you to your letters.' he said.

Colonel Black was a remarkably methodical and neat personage. Wrapped in his elaborate dressing-gown, he made his way through the flat and, reaching his study alone, he closed the door behind him and let it click.

He was disturbed in his mind at this sudden assumption of virtue on the part of his confederate; it was more than disconcerting, it was alarming. Black had no illusions. He did not trust Sir Isaac Tramber any more than he did other men.

It was Black's money that had, to some extent, rehabilitated the baronet in society; it was Black's money that had purchased race-horses and paid training bills. Here again, the man was actuated by no altruistic desire to serve one against whom the doors of society were shut and the hands of decent men were turned.

An outcast, Sir Isaac Tramber was of no value to the colonel: he had even, on one occasion, summarized his relationship with the baronet in a memorable and epigrammatic sentence: 'He was the most dilapidated property I have ever handled; but I refurnished him, redecorated him, and today, even if he is not beautiful, he is very letable.'

And very serviceable Sir Isaac had proved – well worth the money spent on him, well worth the share he received from the proceeds of that business he professed to despise.

Sir Isaac Tramber feared Black. That was half the secret of the power which the stronger man wielded over him. When at times he sought to escape from the tyranny his partner had established, there were sleepless nights. During the past few weeks something had happened which made it imperative that he should dissociate himself from the confederacy; that 'something' had to do with the brightening of his prospects.

Lady Mary Cassilirs was more of a reality now than she had ever been. With Lady Mary went that which Black in his vulgar way described as 'swag'.

The old earl had given him to understand that his addresses would not be unwelcome. Lady Mary was his ward, and perhaps it was because she refused to be terrorized by the wayward old man and his fits of savage moroseness, and because she treated his terrible storms of anger as though they did not exist and never had existed, that in the grim old man's hard and apparently wicked heart there had kindled a flame of respect for her.

Sir Isaac went back to his own chambers in a thoughtful frame of mind. He would have to cut Black, and his conscience had advanced so few demands on his actions that he felt justified in making an exception in this case.

He felt almost virtuous as he emerged again, dressed for the park, and he was in his brightest mood when he met Lord Verlond and his beautiful ward.

There were rude people who never referred to the Earl of Verlond and his niece except as 'Beauty and the Beast'. She was a tall girl and typically English – straight of back, clear of skin, and bright of eye. A great mass of chestnut hair, two arched eyebrows, and a resolute little chin made up a face of special attractiveness. She stood almost head and shoulders above the old man at her side. Verlond had never been a beauty. Age had made his harsh lines still harsher; there was not a line in his face which did not seem as though it had been carved from solid granite, so fixed, so immovable and cold it was.

His lower jaw protruded, his eyes were deep set. He gave you the uncanny impression when you first met him that you had been longer acquainted with his jaw than with his eyes.

He snapped a greeting to Sir Isaac. 'Sit down, Ikey,' he smiled. The girl had given the baronet the slightest of nods, and immediately turned her attention to the passing throng.

'Not riding today?' asked Sir Isaac.

'Yes,' said the peer, 'I am at this moment mounted on a grey charger, leading a brigade of cavalry.'

His humour took this one form, and supplied answers to unnecessary questions. Then suddenly his face went sour, and after a glance round to see whether the girl's attention had been attracted elsewhere, he leant over towards Sir Isaac and, dropping his voice, said, 'Ikey, you're going to have some difficulty with her.'

'I am used to difficulties,' said Sir Isaac airily.

'Not difficulties like this,' said the earl. 'Don't be a fool, Ikey, don't pretend you're clever. I know – the difficulties – I have to live in the same house with her. She's an obstinate devil – there's no other word for it.'

Sir Isaac looked round cautiously. 'Is there anybody else?' he asked.

He saw the earl's brows tighten, his eyes were glaring past him, and, following their direction, Sir Isaac saw the figure of a young man coming towards them with a smile that illuminated the whole of his face.

That smile was directed neither to the earl nor to his companion; it was unmistakably intended for the girl, who, with parted lips and a new light in her eyes, beckoned the newcomer forward.

Sir Isaac scowled horribly. 'The accursed cheek of the fellow,' he muttered angrily.

'Good morning,' said Horace Gresham to the earl; 'taking the air?'

'No,' growled the old man, 'I am bathing, I am deep-sea fishing, I am aeroplaning. Can't you see what I am doing? I'm sitting here – at the mercy of every jackass that comes along to address his insane questions to me.'

Horace laughed. He was genuinely amused. There was just this touch of perverse humour in the old man which saved him from being absolutely repulsive. Without further ceremony he turned to the girl. 'I expected to find you here,' he said.

'How is that great horse of yours?' she asked.

He shot a smiling glance at Tramber.

'Oh, he'll be fit enough on the day of the race,' he said. 'We shall make Timbolino gallop.'

'Mine will beat yours, wherever they finish, for a thousand,' said Sir Isaac angrily.

'I should not like to take your money,' said the young man. 'I feel that it would be unfair to you, and unfair to – your friend.'

The last words were said carelessly, but Sir Isaac Tramber recognized the undertone of hostility, and read in the little pause which preceded them the suggestion that this cheery young man knew much more about his affairs than he was prepared for the moment to divulge.

'I am not concerned about my friend,' said the baronet angrily. 'I merely made a fair and square sporting offer. Of course, if you do not like to accept it – ' He shrugged his shoulders.

'Oh, I would accept it all right,' said the other. He turned deliberately to the girl.

'What's Gresham getting at?' asked Verlond, with a grin at his friend's discomfiture.

'I didn't know he was a friend of yours,' said Sir Isaac; 'where did you pick him up?'

Lord Verlond showed his yellow teeth in a grin. 'Where one picks up most of one's undesirable acquaintances,' he said, 'in the members' enclosure. But racing is getting so damned respectable, Ikey, that a real top-notch undesirable is hard to meet. The last race-meeting I went to, what do you think I found? The tea-room crammed, you couldn't get in at the doors; the bar empty. Racing is going to the dogs, Ikey.'

He was on his favourite hobby now, and Sir Isaac shifted uneasily, for the old man was difficult to divert when in the mood for reminiscent chatter.

'You can't bet nowadays like you used to bet,' the earl went on. 'I once backed a horse for five thousand pounds at 20-1, without altering the price. Where could you do that nowadays?'

'Let us walk about a little,' said the girl.

Lord Verlond was so engrossed in his grievance against racing society that he did not observe the two young people rise and stroll away.

Sir Isaac saw them, and would have interrupted the other's garrulity, but for the wholesome fear he had of the old man's savage temper.

'I can't understand,' said Horace, 'how your uncle can stick that bounder.'

The girl smiled. 'Oh, he can "stick" him all right,' she said dryly. 'Uncle's patience with unpleasant people is proverbial.'

'He's not very patient with me,' said Mr Horace Gresham.

She laughed. 'That is because you are not sufficiently unpleasant,' she said. 'You have to be hateful to everybody else in the world before uncle likes you.'

'And I'm not that, am I?' he asked eagerly.

She flushed a little. 'No, I wouldn't say you were that,' she said, glancing at him from under her eyelashes. 'I am sure you are a very nice and amiable young man. You must have lots of friends. Ikey, on the other hand, has such queer friends. We saw him at the Blitz the other day, lunching with a perfectly impossible man – do you know him?' she asked.

He shook his head. 'I don't know any perfectly impossible persons,' he said promptly.

'A Colonel Black?' she suggested.

He nodded. 'I know of him,' he replied.

'Who is this Black?' she asked.

'He is a colonel.'

'In the army?'

'Not in our army,' said Horace with a smile. 'He is what they call in America a "pipe colonel", and he's – well, he's a friend of Sir Isaac – ' he began, and hesitated.

'That doesn't tell me very much, except that he can't be very nice,' she said.

He looked at her eagerly. 'I'm so glad you said that,' he said. 'I was afraid – ' Again he stopped, and she threw a swift glance at him.

'You were afraid?' she repeated.

It was remarkable to see this self-possessed young man embarrassed, as he was now.

'Well,' he went on, a little incoherently, 'one hears things – rumours. I know what a scoundrel he is, and I know how sweet you are – the fact is, Mary, I love you better than anything in life.'

She went white and her hand trembled. She had never anticipated such a declaration in a crowd. The unexpectedness of it left her speechless. She looked at his face: he, too, was pale.

'You shouldn't,' she murmured, 'at this time in the morning.'

Chapter 6

The policeman and a lady

Frank Fellowe was agitating a punch-ball in one of the upper rooms of his little cottage, and with good reason.

He was 'taking out' of the ball all the grievances he had against the petty irritants of life.

Sergeant Gurden had bothered him with a dozen and one forms of petty annoyance. He had been given the least congenial of jobs; he had been put upon melancholy point work; and he seemed to be getting more than his share of extra duty. And, in addition, he had the extra worry of checking, at the same time, the work of Black's organization. He might, had he wished, put away all the restrictions which hampered his movements, but that was not his way. The frustration of Black's plans was one of Frank's absorbing passions. If he had other passions which threatened to be equally absorbing, he had the sense to check them – for a while –

The daughter of a millionaire, violently introduced, subsequently met with heart-flutterings on the one side and not a little perturbation on the other; her gratitude and admiration began on a wayward two-seater with defective brakes, and progressed by way of the Zoo, for which she sent him a Sunday ticket – for she was anxious to see just what he was like.

She went in some fear of disillusionment, because an heroic constable in uniform, whose face is neatly arranged by helmet-peak and chin-strap, may be less heroic in clothes of his own choosing, to say nothing of cravats and shoes.

But she braced herself for the humiliation of discovering that one who could save her life could also wear a ready-made tie. She was terribly self-conscious, kept to the unfrequented walks of the Zoo, and was found by a very good-looking gentleman who was dressed irreproachably in something that suggested neither the butcher's boy at a beanfeast nor a plumber at a funeral.

She showed him the inmates of exactly two cages, then he took her in hand and told her things about wild beasts that she had never known before. He showed her the subtle distinction between five varieties of lynx, and gave her little anecdotes of the jungle fellowship that left her breathless with admiration. Moreover, he took her to the most unlikely places – to rooms where the sick and lame of the animal kingdom were nursed to health. It would appear that there was no need to have sent him the ticket, because he was a Fellow of the Society There was too much to be seen on one day.

She went again and yet again; rode with him over Hampstead Heath in the early hours of the morning. She gathered that he jobbed his horse, yet it was not always the same animal he rode.

'How many horses have you in your stable?' she asked banteringly one morning.

'Six,' he said readily. 'You see,' he added hastily, 'I do a lot of hunting in the season – '

He stopped, realizing that he was further in the mire.

'But you are a constable – a policeman!' she stammered. 'I mean – forgive me if I'm rude.'

He turned in his saddle, and there was a twinkle in his eye.

'I have a little money of my own,' he said. 'You see, I have only been a constable for twelve months; previous to that I – I wasn't a constable!'

He was not very lucid: by this time he was apparently embarrassed, and she changed the subject, wondering and absurdly pleased.

It was inconsistent of her to realize after the ride that these meetings were wrong. They were wrong before, surely? Was it worse to ride with a man who had revealed himself to be a member of one's own class than with a policeman? Nevertheless, she knew it was wrong and met him – and that is where Constable Fellowe and Miss Sandford became 'May' and 'Frank' to one another. There had been nothing clandestine in their meetings.

Theodore Sandford, a hard-headed man, was immensely democratic. He joked about May's policeman, made ponderous references to stolen visits to his palatial kitchen in search of rabbit-pie, and then there arose from a jesting nothing the question of Frank's remaining in the force. He had admitted that he had independent means. Why remain a ridiculous policeman? From jest it had passed into a very serious discussion and the presentation of an ultimatum, furiously written, furiously posted, and as furiously regretted.

Theodore Sandford looked up from his writing-table with an amused smile.

'So you're really angry with your policeman, are you?' he asked.

But it was no joke to the girl. Her pretty face was set determinedly.

'Of course,' she shrugged her pretty shoulders, 'Mr Fellowe can do as he wishes – I have no authority over him – ' this was not true – 'but one is entitled to ask of one's friends – '

There were tears of mortification in her eyes, and Sandford dropped his banter. He looked at the girl searchingly, anxiously. Her mother had died when May was a child; he was ever on the look-out for some sign of the fell disease which carried off the woman who had been his all.

'Dearest!' he said tenderly 'you mustn't be worried or bothered by your policeman; I'm sure he'd do anything in the world for you, if he is only half a human man. You aren't looking well,' he said anxiously.

She smiled. 'I'm tired tonight, daddy,' she said, putting her arm about his neck.

'You're always tired nowadays,' he said. 'Black thought so the other day when he saw you. He recommended a very clever doctor – I've got his address somewhere.'

She shook her head with vigour. 'I don't want to see doctors,' she said decidedly.

'But – '

'Please – please!' she pleaded, laughing now. 'You mustn't!'

There was a knock at the door and a footman came in. 'Mr Fellowe, madam,' he announced.

The girl looked round quickly. 'Where is he?' she asked. Her father saw the pink in her cheeks and shook his head doubtingly.

'He is in the drawing-room,' said the man.

'I'll go down, daddy.' She turned to her father.

He nodded. 'I think you'll find he's fairly tractable – by the way, the man is a gentleman.'

'A gentleman, daddy!' she answered with lofty scorn, 'of course he's a gentleman!'

'I'm sorry I mentioned it,' said Mr Theodore Sandford humbly.

Frank was reading her letter – the letter which had brought him to her – when she came in. He took her hand and held it for a fraction of a second, then he came straight to the point. It was hard enough, for never had she so appealed to him as she did this night.

There are some women whose charms are so elusive, whose beauty is so unordinary in character, as to baffle adequate description. May Sandford was one of these. No one feature goes to the making of a woman, unless, indeed, it be her mouth. There is something in the poise of the head, in the method of arranging the hair, in the clearness and peach-like bloom of the complexion, in the carriage of the shoulders, the suppleness of the body, the springy tread – each characteristic furnished something to the beautiful whole.

May Sandford was a beautiful girl. She had been a beautiful child, and had undergone none of the transition from prettiness to plainness, from beauty to awkwardness. It was as though the years had each contributed their quota to the creation of the perfect woman.

'Surely,' he said, 'you do not mean this? That is not your view?' He held out her letter. She bent her head.

'I think it would be best,' she said in a low tone. 'I don't think we shall agree very well on – on things. You've been rather horrid lately, Mr Fellowe.'

His face was very pale. 'I don't remember that I have been particularly horrid,' he said quietly.

'It is impossible for you to remain a policeman,' she went on tremulously. She went up to him and laid her hands upon his shoulders. 'Don't you see – even papa jokes about it, and it's horrid. I'm sure the servants talk – and I'm not a snob really – '

Frank threw back his head and laughed.

'Can't you see, dearie, that I should not be a policeman if there was not excellent reason? I am doing this work because I have promised my superior that I would do it.'

'But – but,' she said, bewildered, 'if you left the force you would have no superior.'

'I cannot give up my work,' he said simply. He thought a moment, then shook his head slowly. 'You ask me to break my word,' he said. 'You ask me to do greater mischief than that which I am going to undo. You wouldn't, you couldn't, impose that demand upon me.'

She drew back a little, her head raised, pouting ever so slightly. 'I see,' she said, 'you would not.' She held out her hand. 'I shall never ask you to make another sacrifice.'

He took her hand, held it tightly a moment, then let it drop. Without another word the girl left the room. Frank waited a moment, hoping against hope that she would repent. The door remained closed.

He left the house with an overwhelming sense of depression.

Chapter 7

Dr Essley meets a man

Dr Essley was in his study, making a very careful microscopic examination. The room was in darkness save for the light which came from a powerful electric lamp directed to the reflector of the instrument. What he found on the slide was evidently satisfactory, for by and by he removed the strip of glass, threw it into the fire and turned on the lights.

He took up a newspaper cutting from the table and read it. It interested him, for it was an account of the sudden death of Mr Augustus Fanks.

'The deceased gentleman,' ran the account, 'was engaged with Colonel Black, the famous financier, discussing the details of the new iron amalgamation, when he suddenly collapsed and, before medical assistance could be procured, expired, it is believed, of heart failure.'

There had been no inquest, for Fanks had in truth a weak heart and had been under the care of a specialist, who, since his speciality was heart trouble, discovered symptoms of the disease on the slightest pretext.

So that was the end of Fanks. The doctor nodded slowly. Yes, that was the end of him. And now? He took a letter from his pocket. It was addressed to him in the round sprawling calligraphy of Theodore Sandford.

Essley had met him in the early days when Sandford was on friendly terms with Black. He had been recommended to the ironmaster by the financier, and had treated him for divers ills. 'My suburban doctor,' Sandford had called him.

'Though I am not seeing eye to eye with our friend Black,' he wrote, 'and we are for the moment at daggers drawn, I trust that this will not affect our relationships, the more so since I wish you to see my daughter.'

Essley remembered having seen her once: a tall girl, with eyes that danced with laughter and a complexion of milk and roses.

He put the letter in his pocket, went into his little surgery and locked the door. When he came out he wore his long overcoat and carried a little satchel. He had just time to catch a train for the City, and at eleven o'clock he found himself in Sandford's mansion.

'You are a weird man, doctor,' said the ironmaster with a smile, as he greeted his visitor. 'Do you visit most of your patients by night?'

'My aristocratic patients,' said the other coolly.

'A bad job about poor Fanks,' said the other. 'He and I were only dining together a few weeks ago. Did he tell you that he met a man who knew you in Australia?'

A shadow of annoyance passed over the other's face. 'Let us talk about your daughter,' he said brusquely. 'What is the matter with her?'

The ironmaster smiled sheepishly. 'Nothing, I fear; yet you know, Essley, she is my only child, and I sometimes imagine that she is looking ill. My doctor in Newcastle tells me that there is nothing wrong with her.'

'I see,' said Essley. 'Where is she?'

'She is at the theatre,' confessed the father. You must think I am an awful fool to bring you up to town to discuss the health of a girl who is at the theatre, but something upset her pretty badly last night, and I was today glad to see her take enough interest in life to visit a musical comedy.'

'Most fathers are fools,' said the other. 'I will wait till she comes in.' He strolled to the window and looked out. 'Why have you quarrelled with Black?' he asked suddenly.

The older man frowned. 'Business,' he said shortly. 'He is pushing me into a corner. I helped him four years ago – '

'He helped you, too.' interrupted the doctor.

'But not so much as I helped him,' said the other obstinately. 'I gave him his chance. He floated my company and I profited, but he profited more. The business has now grown to such vast proportions that it will not pay me to come in. Nothing will alter my determination.'

'I see.'

Essley whistled a little tune as he walked again to the window.

Such men as this must be broken, he thought. Broken! And there was only one way: that daughter of his. He could do nothing tonight, that was evident – nothing.

'I do not think I will wait for your daughter,' he said. 'Perhaps I will call in tomorrow evening.'

'I am so sorry – '

But the doctor silenced him. 'There is no need to be sorry,' he said with acerbity; 'you will find my visit charged in my bill.'

The ironmaster laughed as he saw him to the door. 'You are almost as good a financier as your friend,' he said.

'Almost,' said the doctor dryly.

His waiting taxi dropped him at Charing Cross, and he went straight to the nearest call-office and rang up a Temperance Hôtel at Bloomsbury. He had reasons for wishing to meet a Mr Weld who knew him in Australia.

He had no difficulty in getting the message through. Mr Weld was in the hôtel. He waited whilst the attendant found him. By and by a voice spoke:

'I am Weld – do you want me?'

'Yes; my name is Cole. I knew you in Australia. I have a message for you from a mutual friend. Can you see me tonight?'

'Yes; where?'

Dr Essley had decided the place of meeting. 'Outside the main entrance of the British Museum,' he said. 'There are few people about at this time of night, and I am less likely to miss you.'

There was a pause at the other end of the wire. 'Very good,' said the voice; in a quarter of an hour?'

'That will suit me admirably – goodbye.'

He hung up the receiver. Leaving his satchel at the cloak-room at Charing Cross Station, he set out to walk to Great Russell Street. He would take no cab. There should be no evidence of that description. Black would not like it. He smiled at the thought. Great Russell Street was deserted, save for a constant stream of taxi-cabs passing and repassing and an occasional pedestrian. He found his man waiting; rather tall and slight, with an intellectual, refined face.

'Dr Essley?' he asked, coming forward as the other halted.

'That is my – ' Essley stopped. 'My name is Cole,' he said harshly. 'What made you think I was Essley?'

'Your voice,' said the other calmly. 'After all, it does not matter what you call yourself; I want to see you.'

'And I you,' said Essley.

They walked along side by side until they came to a side street.

'What do you want of me?' asked the doctor.

The other laughed.

'I wanted to see you. You are not a bit like the Essley I knew. He was slighter and had not your colouring, and I was always under the impression that the Essley who went up into the bush died.'

'It is possible,' said Essley in an absent way. He wanted to gain time. The street was empty. A little way down there was a gateway in which a man might lie unobserved until a policeman came.

In his pocket he had an impregnated feather carefully wrapped up in lint and oiled silk. He drew it from his pocket furtively and with his hands behind him he stripped it of its covering.

' . . . in fact, Dr Essley,' the man was saying, 'I am under the impression that you are an impostor.'

Essley faced him. 'You think too much,' he said in a low voice, 'and after all, I do not recognize – turn your face to the light.'

The young man obeyed. It was a moment. Quick as thought the doctor raised the feather . . .

A hand of steel gripped his wrist. As if from the ground, two other men had appeared. Something soft was thrust into his face; a sickly aroma overpowered him. He struggled madly, but the odds were too many, and then a shrill police-whistle sounded and he dropped to the ground . . .

He awoke to find a policeman bending over him. Instinctively he put his hand to his head.

'Hurt, sir?' asked the man.

'No.' He struggled to his feet and stood unsteadily. 'Did you capture the men?'

'No, sir, they got away. We just spotted them as they downed you, but, bless your heart, they seemed to be swallowed up by the earth.'

He looked around for the feather: it had disappeared. With some reluctance he gave his name and address to the constable, who called a taxi-cab.

'You're sure you've lost nothing, sir?' asked the man.

'Nothing,' said Essley testily. 'Nothing – look here, constable, do not report this.' He slipped a pound into the man's hand. 'I do not wish this matter to get into the papers.'

The constable handed the money back. 'I'm sorry, sir,' he said, 'I couldn't take this even if I was willing.' He looked round quickly and lowered his voice. 'I've got a gentleman from the Yard with me,' he said, 'one of the assistant commissioners.'

Essley followed the direction of the policeman's eyes. In the shadow of the wall a man was standing.

'He was the chap who saw you first,' said the policeman, young and criminally loquacious.

Obeying some impulse he could not define, Essley walked towards the man in the shadow.

'I owe you a debt of gratitude,' he said. 'I can only hope that you will add to your kindness by letting the matter drop – I should hate to see the thing referred to in the newspapers.'

'I suppose you would,' said the unknown. He was in evening dress, and the red glow of his cigar rather concealed than defined his face. 'But this is a matter, Dr Essley, where you must allow us full discretion.'

'How do you know my name?' asked the doctor suspiciously. The other smiled in the darkness and turned away.

'One moment!' Essley took a stride forward and peered into the other's face. 'I seem to recognize your voice,' he said.

'That is possible,' said the other, and pushed him gently, but firmly, away. Essley gasped. He himself was no weakling, but this man had an arm like steel.

'I think you had better go, sir,' said the police-constable anxiously. He desired neither to offend an obviously influential member of the public nor his superior – that mysterious commissioner who appeared and disappeared in the various divisions and who left behind him innumerable casualties amongst the different members of the force.

'I'll go,' said the doctor, 'but I should like to know this gentleman's name.'

'That cannot possibly interest you,' said the stranger, and Essley shrugged his shoulders. With that he had to be content. He drove home to Forest Hill, thinking, thinking. Who were these three – what object had they? Who was the man who had stood in the shadows? Was it possible that his assailants were acting in collusion with the police?

He was no nearer the solution when he reached his home. He unlocked the door and let himself in. There was nobody in the house but himself and the old woman upstairs. His comings and goings were so erratic that he had organized a system which allowed him the most perfect freedom of movement.

There must be an end to Dr Essley, he decided. Essley must disappear from London. He need not warn Black – Black would know. He would settle the business of the iron-master and his daughter, and then – there would be a finish.

He unlocked his study, entered and switched on the lights. There was a letter on his writing-table, a letter enclosed in a thin grey envelope. He picked it up and examined it. It had been delivered by hand, and bore his name written in a firm hand. He looked at the writing-table and started back. The letter had been written in the room and blotted on the pad!

There was no doubt at all about it. The blotting-paper had been placed there fresh that day, and the reverse of the bold handwriting on the envelope was plain to see. He looked at the envelope again.

It could not have been a patient: he never admitted patients – he had none worth mentioning. The practice was a blind. Besides, the door had been locked, and he alone had the key. He tore the envelope open and took out the contents. It was a half-sheet of note-paper. The three lines of writing ran –

You escaped tonight, and have only seven days to prepare your-self for the fate which awaits you.

The Four Just Men

He sank into his chair, crushed by the knowledge. They were the Just Men – and he had escaped them. The Just Men! He buried his face in his hands and tried to think. Seven days they gave him. Much could be done in seven days. The terror of death was upon him, he who had without qualm or remorse sent so many on the long journey. But this was he – himself! He clutched at his throat and glared round the room. Essley the poisoner – the expert; a specialist in death – the man who had revived the lost art of the Medicis and had hoodwinked the law. Seven days! Well, he would settle the business of the ironmaster. That was necessary to Black.

He began to make feverish preparations for the future. There were no papers to destroy. He went into the surgery and emptied three bottles down the sink. The fourth he would want. The fourth had been useful to Black: a little green bottle with a glass stopper. He slipped it into his pocket.

He let the tap run to wash away all trace of the drug he had spilt. The bottles he smashed and threw into a waste-bin.

He went upstairs to his room, but he could not sleep. He locked his door and put a chair against it. With a revolver in his hand, he searched the cupboard and beneath the bed. He placed the revolver under his pillow and tried to sleep.

Next morning found him haggard and ill, but none the less he made his toilet with customary care. Punctually at noon he presented himself at Hampstead and was shown into the drawing-room. The girl was alone when he entered. He noted with approval that she was very beautiful.

That May Sandford did not like him he knew by instinct. He saw the cloud come to her pretty face as he came into her presence, and was amused in his cold way.

'My father is out.' she said.

'That is good,' said Essley, 'for now we can talk.' He seated himself without invitation.

'I think it is only right to tell you, Dr Essley, that my father's fears regarding me are quite groundless.'

At that moment the ironmaster came in and shook hands warmly with the doctor. 'Well, how do you think she looks?' he asked.

'Looks tell you nothing,' said the other. It was not the moment for the feather. He had other things to do, and the feather was not the way. He chatted for a while and then rose. 'I will send you some medicine,' he said.

She pulled a wry face.

'You need not worry to take it,' he said, with the touch of rancour that was one of his characteristics.

'Can you come to dinner on Tuesday?' asked Sandford.

Essley considered. This was Saturday – three days out of seven, and anything might turn up in the meantime. 'Yes,' he said, 'I will come.'

He took a cab to some chambers near the Thames Embankment. He had a most useful room there.

Chapter 8

Colonel Black has a shock

Mr Sandford had an appointment with Colonel Black. It was the final interview before the break.

The City was busy with rumours. A whisper had circulated; all was not well with the financier – the amalgamation on which so much depended had not gone through. Black sat at his desk that afternoon, idly twiddling a paper-knife. He was more sallow than usual; the hand that held the knife twitched nervously. He looked at his watch. It was time Sandford came. He pushed a bell by the side of his desk and a clerk appeared.

'Has Mr Sandford arrived?' he asked.

'He has just come, sir,' said the man.

'Show him in.'

The two men exchanged formal greetings, and Black pointed to a chair. 'Sit down, Sandford,' he said curtly. 'Now, exactly how do we stand?'

'Where we did,' said the other uncompromisingly.

'You will not come into my scheme?'

'I will not,' said the other.

Colonel Black tapped the desk with his knife, and Sandford looked at him. He seemed older than when he had last seen him. His yellow face was seamed and lined.

'It means ruin for me,' he said suddenly. 'I have more creditors than I can count. If the amalgamation went through I should be established. There are lots of people in with me too – Ikey Tramber – you know Sir Isaac? He's a friend of – er – the Earl of Verlond.'

But the elder man was not impressed. 'It is your fault if you're in a hole,' said he. 'You have taken on too big a job – more than that, you have taken too much for granted.'

The man at the desk looked up from under his straight brows. 'It is all very well for you to sit there and tell me what I should do,' he said, and the shakiness of his voice told the other something of the passion he concealed. 'I do not want advice or homily – I want money. Come into my scheme and amalgamate, or – '

'Or – ' repeated the ironmaster quietly.

'I do not threaten you,' said Black sullenly; 'I warn you. You are risking more than you know.'

'I'll take the risk,' said Sandford. He got up on to his feet. 'Have you anything more to say?'

'Nothing.'

'Then I'll bid you goodbye.'

The door closed with a slam behind him, and Black did not move. He sat there until it was dark, doing no more than scribble aimlessly upon his blotting-pad. It was nearly dark when he drove back to the flat he occupied in Victoria Street and let himself in.

'There is a gentleman waiting to see you, sir,' said the man who came hurrying to help him out of his coat.

'What sort of a man?'

'I don't know exactly, sir, but I have got a feeling that he is a detective.'

'A detective?' He found his hands trembling, and cursed his folly. He stood uncertainly in the centre of the hall. In a minute he had mastered his fears and turned the handle of the door.

A man rose to meet him. He had a feeling that he had met him before. It was one of those impressions that it is so difficult to explain.

'You wanted to see me?' he asked.

'Yes, sir,' said the man, a note of deference in his voice. 'I have called to make a few inquiries.'

It was on the tip of Black's tongue to ask him whether he was a police officer, but somehow he had not the courage to frame the words. The effort was unnecessary, as it proved, for the next words of the man explained his errand.

'I have been engaged,' he said, 'by a firm of solicitors to discover the whereabouts of Dr Essley.'

Black looked hard at him.

'There ought to be no difficulty,' he said, 'in that. The doctor's name is in the Directory.'

'That is so,' said the man, 'and yet I have had the greatest difficulty in running him to earth. As a matter of fact,' explained the man, 'I was wrong when I said I wanted to discover his whereabouts. It is his identity I wish to establish.'

'I do not follow you,' said the financier.

'Well,' said the man, 'I don't know exactly how to put it. If you know Dr Essley, you will recall the fact that he was for some years in Australia.'

'That is true,' said Black. 'He and I came back together.'

'And you were there some years, sir?'

'Yes, we were there for a number of years, though we were not together all the time.'

'I see,' said the man. 'You went out together, I believe?'

'No,' replied the other sharply, 'we went at different periods.'

'Have you seen him recently?'

'No, I have not seen him, although I have frequently written to him on various matters.' Black was trying hard not to lose his patience. It would not do for this man to see how much the questions were irritating him.

The man jotted down something in his notebook, closed it and put it in his pocket. 'Would you be surprised to learn,' he asked quietly, 'that the real Dr Essley who went out to Australia died there?'

Black's fingers caught the edge of the table and he steadied himself.

'I did not know that,' he said. 'Is that all you have to ask?' he said, as the man finished.

'I think that will do, sir,' said the detective.

'Can I ask you on whose behalf you are inquiring?' demanded the colonel.

'That I am not at liberty to tell.'

After he had gone, Black paced the apartment, deep in thought.

He took down from the shelf a continental Baedeker and worked out with a pencil and paper a line of retirement. The refusal of Sandford to negotiate with him was the crowning calamity.

He crossed the room to the safe which stood in the corner, and opened it. In the inside drawer were three flat packets of notes. He picked them out and laid them on the table. They were notes on the Bank of France, each for a thousand francs.

It would be well to take no risks. He put them in the inside pocket of his coat. If all things failed, they were the way to freedom. As for Essley – he smiled.He must go any way. He left his flat and drove eastwards to the City. Two men followed him, though this he did not know.

* * *

Black boasted that his corporation kept no books, maintained no record, and this fact was emphasized the night that the Four had visited him unbidden. Their systematic search for evidence, which they had intended to use against him at a recognized tribunal, had failed to disclose the slightest vestige of documentary evidence which might be employed. Yet, if the truth be told, Black kept a very complete set of books, only they were in a code of his own devising, the key of which he had never put on paper, and which he only could understand.

He was engaged on the evening of the detective's visit in placing even these ledgers beyond the reach of the Four. He had good reason for his uneasiness. The Four had been very active of late, and they had thought fit to issue another challenge to Colonel Black. He was busy from nine o'clock to eleven, tearing up apparently innocent letters and burning them. When that hour struck, he looked at his watch and confirmed the time. He had very important business that night.

He wrote a note to Sir Isaac Tramber, asking him to meet him that night. He had need of every friend, every pull, and every bit of help that could come to him.

Chapter 9

Lord Verlond gives a dinner

Lord Verlond was an afternoon visitor at the Sandford establishment. He had come for many reasons, not the least of which nobody expected. He was a large shareholder in the Sandford Foundries, and with rumours of amalgamation in the air there was excuse enough for his visit. Doubly so, it seemed, when the first person he met was a large, yellow-faced man, confoundedly genial (in the worst sense of the word) and too ready to fraternize for the old man's liking.

'I have heard of you, my lord,' said Colonel Black.

'For the love of Heaven, don't call me "my lord"!' snapped the earl. 'Man' alive, you are asking me to be rude to you!'

But no man of Verlond's standing could be rude to the colonel, with his mechanical smile and his beaming eye.

'I know a friend of yours, I think,' he said, in that soothing tone which in a certain type of mind passes for deference.

'You know Ikey Tramber, which is not the same thing,' said the earl.

Colonel Black made a noise indicating his amusement. 'He always – ' he began.

'He always speaks well of me and says what a fine fellow I am, and how the earth loses its savour if he passes a day without seeing me,' assisted Lord Verlond, his eyes alight with pleasant malice, 'and he tells you what a good sportsman I am, and what a true and kindly heart beats behind my somewhat unprepossessing exterior, and how if people only knew me they would love me – he says all this, doesn't he?'

Colonel Black bowed.

'I don't think!' said Lord Verlond vulgarly. He looked at the other for a while. 'You shall come to dinner with me tonight – you will meet a lot of people who will dislike you intensely.'

'I shall be delighted,' murmured the colonel.

He was hoping that in the conference which he guessed would be held between Sandford and his lordship he would be invited to participate. In this, however, he was disappointed. He might have taken his leave there and then, but he chose to stay and discuss art (which he imperfectly understood) with a young and distracted lady who was thinking about something else all the time.

She badly wanted to bring the conversation round to the Metropolitan police force, in the hope that a rising young constable might be mentioned. She would have asked after him, but her pride prevented her. Colonel Black himself did not broach the subject.

He was still discussing lost pictures when Lord Verlond emerged from the study with Sandford. 'Let your daughter come,' the earl was saying.

Sandford was undecided. 'I'm greatly obliged – I should not like her to go alone.'

Something leapt inside Colonel Black's bosom. A chance . . . !

'If you are talking of the dinner tonight,' he said with an assumption of carelessness, 'I shall be happy to call in my car for you.'

Still Sandford was not easy in his mind. It was May who should make the decision.

'I think I'd like to, daddy,' she said.

She did not greatly enjoy the prospect of going anywhere with the colonel, but it would only be a short journey.

'If I could stand *in loco parentis* to the young lady,' said Black, nearly jocular, 'I should esteem it an honour.'

He looked round and caught a curious glint in Lord Verlond's eyes. The earl was watching him closely, eagerly almost, and a sudden and unaccountable fear gripped the financier's heart.

'Excellent, excellent!' murmured the old man, still watching him through lowered lids. 'It isn't far to go, and I think you'll stand the journey well.'

The girl smiled, but the grim fixed look on the earl's face did not relax.

'As you are an invalid, young lady,' he went on, despite May's laughing protest – 'as you're an invalid, young lady, I will have Sir James Bower and Sir Thomas Bigland to meet you – you know those eminent physicians, colonel? Your Dr Essley will, at any rate – experts both on the action of vegetable alkaloids.'

Great beads of sweat stood on Black's face, but his features were under perfect control. Fear and rage glowed in his eyes, but he met the other's gaze defiantly. He smiled even – a slow, laboured smile. 'That puts an end to any objection,' he said almost gaily.

The old man took his leave and was grinning to himself all the way back to town.

The Earl of Verlond was a stickler for punctuality: a grim, bent old man, with a face that, so Society said, told eloquently the story of his life, his bitter tongue was sufficient to maintain for him the respect – or if not the respect, the fear that so ably substitutes respect – of his friends.

'Friends' is a word which you would never ordinarily apply to any of the earl's acquaintances. He had apparently no friends save Sir Isaac Tramber. 'I have people to dine with me,' he had said cynically when this question of friendship was once discussed by one who knew him sufficiently well to deal with so intimate a subject.

That night he was waiting in the big library of Carnarvon Place. The earl was one of those men who observed a rigid time-table every day of his life. He glanced at his watch; in two minutes he would be on his way to the drawing-room to receive his guests.

Horace Gresham was coming. A curious invitation, Sir Isaac Tramber had thought, and had ventured to remark as much, presuming his friendship.

'When I want your advice as to my invitation list, Ikey,' said the earl, 'I will send you a prepaid telegram.'

'I thought you hated him,' grumbled Sir Isaac.

'Hate him! Of course I hate him. I hate everybody. I should hate you, but you are such an insignificant devil,' said the earl. 'Have you made your peace with Mary?'

'I don't know what you mean by "making my peace",' said Sir Isaac complainingly. 'I tried to be amiable to her, and I only seemed to succeed in making a fool of myself.'

'Ah!' said the nobleman with a little chuckle, 'she would like you best natural.'

Sir Isaac shot a scowling glance at his patron. 'I suppose you know,' he said, 'that I want to marry Mary.'

'I know that you want some money without working for it,' said the earl. 'You have told me about it twice. I am not likely to forget it. It is the sort of thing I think about at nights.'

'I wish you wouldn't pull my leg,' growled the baronet. 'Are you waiting for any other guests?'

'No,' snarled the earl, 'I am sitting on the top of Mont Blanc eating rice pudding.' There was no retort to this. 'I've invited quite an old friend of yours,' said the earl suddenly, 'but it doesn't look as if he was turning up.'

Ikey frowned. 'Old friend?'

The other nodded. 'Military gent,' he said laconically. 'A colonel in the army, though nobody knows the army.'

Sir Isaac's jaw dropped. 'Not Black?'

Lord Verlond nodded. He nodded several times, like a gleeful child confessing a fault of which it was inordinately proud. 'Black it is,' he said, but made no mention of the girl.

He looked at his watch again and pulled a little face. 'Stay here,' he commanded. 'I'm going to telephone.'

'Can I – '

'You can't!' snapped the earl. He was gone some time, and when he returned to the library there was a smile on his face. 'Your pal's not coming,' he said, and offered no explanation either for the inexplicable behaviour of the colonel or for his amusement.

At dinner Horace Gresham found himself seated next to the most lovely woman in the world. She was also the kindest and the easiest to amuse. He was content to forget the world, and such of the world who were gathered about the earl, but Lord Verlond had other views.

'Met a friend of yours today,' he said abruptly and addressing Horace.

'Indeed, sir?' The young man was politely interested.

'Sandford – that terribly prosperous gentleman from Newcastle.'

Horace nodded cautiously.

'Friend of yours too, ain't he?' The old man turned swiftly to Sir Isaac. 'I asked his daughter to come to dinner – father couldn't come. She ain't here.'

He glared round the table for the absent girl.

'In a sense Sandford is a friend of mine,' said Sir Isaac no less cautiously, since he must make a statement in public without exactly knowing how the elder man felt on the subject of the absent guests; 'at least, he's a friend of a friend.'

'Black,' snarled Lord Verlond, 'bucket-shop swindler – are you in it?'

'I have practically severed my connection with him,' Sir Isaac hastened to say.

Verlond grinned. 'That means he's broke,' he said, and turned to Horace. 'Sandford's full of praise for a policeman who's mad keen on his girl – friend of yours?'

Horace nodded. 'He's a great friend of mine,' he said quietly.

'Who is he?'

'Oh, he's a policeman,' said Horace.

'And I suppose he's got two legs and a head and a pair of arms,' said the earl. 'You're too full of information – I know he's a policeman. Everybody seems to be talking about him. Now, what does he do, where does he come from – what the devil does it all mean?'

'I'm afraid I can't give you any information,' said Horace. 'The only thing that I am absolutely certain about in my own mind is that he is a gentleman.'

'A gentleman and a policeman?' asked the earl incredulously.

Horace nodded.

'A new profession for the younger son, eh?' remarked Lord Verlond sardonically. 'No more running away and joining the army; no more serving before the mast; no more cow-punching on the pampas – '

A look of pain came into Lady Mary's eyes. The old lord swung round on her.

'Sorry' he growled. 'I wasn't thinking of that young fool. No more dashing away to the ends of the earth for the younger son; no dying picturesquely in the Cape Mounted Rifles, or turning up at an appropriate hour with a bag of bullion under each arm to save the family from ruin. Join the police force, that's the game. You ought to write a novel about that: a man who can write letters to the sporting papers can write anything.'

'By the way,' he added, 'I am coming down to Lincoln on Tuesday to see that horse of yours lose.'

'You will make your journey in vain,' said Horace. 'I have arranged for him to win.'

He waited later for an opportunity to say a word in private to the old man. It did not come till the end of the dinner, when he found himself alone with the earl. 'By the way,' he said, with an assumption of carelessness, 'I want to see you on urgent private business.'

'Want money?' asked the earl, looking at him suspiciously from underneath his shaggy brows.

Horace smiled. 'No, I – don't think I am likely to borrow money,' he said.

'Want to marry my niece?' asked the old man with brutal directness.

'That's it,' said Horace coolly. He could adapt himself to the old man's mood.

'Well, you can't,' said the earl. 'You have arranged for your horse to win, I have arranged for her to marry Ikey. At least,' he corrected himself, 'Ikey has arranged with me.'

'Suppose she doesn't care for this plan?' asked Horace.

'I don't suppose she does,' said the old man with a grin. 'I can't imagine anybody liking Ikey, can you? I think he's a hateful devil. He doesn't pay his debts, he has no sense of honour, very little sense of decency; his associates, including myself, are the worst men in London.'

He shook his head suspiciously.

'He's being virtuous now,' he growled, 'told me so confidentially; informed me that he was turning over a new leaf. What a rotten confession for a man of his calibre to make! I mistrust him in his penitent mood.'

He looked up suddenly.

'You go and cut him out,' he said, the tiny flame of malice, which gave his face such an extraordinary character, shining in his eyes. 'Good idea, that! Go and cut him out; it struck me Mary was a little keen on you. Damn Ikey! Go along!'

He pushed the astonished youth from him.

Horace found the girl in the conservatory. He was bubbling over with joy. He had never expected to make so easy a conquest of the old man – so easy that he almost felt frightened. It was as if the Earl of Verlond, with that sardonic humour of his, was devising some method of humiliating him. Impulsively he told her all that had happened.

'I can't believe it,' he cried, 'he was so ready, so willing. He was brutal, of course, but that was natural.'

She looked at him with a little glint of amusement in her eyes. 'I don't think you know uncle,' she said quietly.

'But – but – ' he stammered.

'Yes, I know,' she went on, 'everybody thinks they do. They think he's the most horrid old man in the world. Sometimes,' she confessed, 'I have shared their opinion. I can never understand why he sent poor Con away.'

'That was your brother?' he asked.

She nodded. Her eyes grew moist.

'Poor boy,' she said softly, 'he didn't understand uncle. I didn't then. I sometimes think uncle doesn't understand himself very well,' she said with a sad little smile. 'Think of the horrid things he says about people – think of the way he makes enemies – '

'And yet, I am ready to believe he is a veritable Gabriel,' said Horace fervently. 'He is a benefactor of the human race, a king among men, the distributor of great gifts – '

'Don't be silly,' she said, and laying her hand on his arm, she led him to the farther end of the big palm court.

Whatever pleasure the old lord brought to Horace, it found no counterpart in his dealings with Sir Isaac.

He alternately patted and kicked him, until the baronet was writhing with rage. The old man seemed to take a malicious pleasure in ruffling the other. That the views he expressed at ten o'clock that night were in absolute contradiction to those that he had put into words at eight o'clock on the same night did not distress him; he would have changed them a dozen times during the course of twenty-four hours if he could have derived any pleasure from so doing.

Sir Isaac was in an evil frame of mind when a servant brought him a note. He looked round for a quiet place in which to read it. He half suspected its origin. But why had Black missed so splendid an opportunity of meeting Lord Verlond? The note would explain, perhaps.

He crossed the room and strolled towards the conservatory, reading the letter carefully. He read it twice, then he folded it up and put it into his pocket; he had occasion to go to that pocket again almost immediately, for he pulled out his watch to see the time.

When he had left the little retreat on his way to the hall, he left behind him a folded slip of paper on the floor.

This an exalted Horace, deliriously happy, discovered on his way back to the card-room. He handed it to Lord Verlond who, having no scruples, read it – and, reading it in the seclusion of his study, grinned.

Chapter 10
A policeman's business

There was living at Somers Town at that time a little man named Jakobs. He was a man of some character, albeit an unfortunate person with 'something behind him'. The something behind him, however, had come short of a lagging. 'Carpets' (three months' hard labour) almost innumerable had fallen to his share, but a lagging had never come his way.

A little wizened-faced man, with sharp black eyes, very alert in his manner, very neatly dressed, he conveyed the impression that he was enjoying a day off, but so far as honest work was concerned Jakobs's day was an everlasting one.

Mr Jakobs had been a pensioner of Colonel Black's for some years. During that period of time Willie Jakobs had lived the life of a gentleman. That is to say, he lived in the manner which he thought conformed more readily to the ideal than that which was generally accepted by the wealthier classes.

There were moments when he lived like a lord – again he had his own standard – but these periods occurred at rare intervals, because Willie was naturally abstemious. But he certainly lived like a gentleman, as all Somers Town agreed, for he went to bed at whatsoever hour he chose, arose with such larks as were abroad at the moment, or stayed in bed reading his favourite journal.

A fortunate man was he, never short of a copper for a half-pint of ale, thought no more of spending a shilling on a race than would you or I, was even suspected of taking his breakfast in bed, a veritable hall-mark of luxury and affluence by all standards.

To him every Saturday morning came postal orders to the value of two pounds sterling from a benefactor who asked no more than that the recipient should be happy and forget that he ever saw a respected dealer in stocks and shares in the act of rifling a dead man's pockets.

For this William Jakobs had seen.

Willie was a thief, born so, and not without pride in his skilful-fingered ancestry. He had joined the firm of Black and Company less with the object of qualifying for a pension twenty years hence than on the off chance of obtaining an immediate dividend.

He was guarded by the very principles which animated the head of his firm.

There was an obnoxious member of the board – obnoxious to the genial Colonel Black – who had died suddenly. A subsequent inquisition came to the conclusion that he died from syncope: even Willie knew no better. He had stolen quietly into the managing director's office one day in the ordinary course of business, for Master Jakobs stole quietly, but literally and figuratively. He was in search of unconsidered stamps and such loose coinage as might be found in the office of a man notoriously careless in the matter of small change. He had expected to find the room empty, and was momentarily paralysed to see the great Black himself bending over the recumbent figure of a man, busily searching the pockets of a dead man for a letter – for the silent man on the floor had come with his resignation in his pocket and had indiscreetly embodied in this letter his reasons for taking the step. Greatest indiscretion of all, he had revealed the existence of this very compromising document to Colonel Black.

Willie Jakobs knew nothing about the letter – had no subtle explanation for the disordered pocket-book. To his primitive mind Colonel Black was making a search for money: it was, in fact, a stamp-hunt on a large scale, and in his agitation he blurted this belief.

At the subsequent inquest Mr Jakobs did not give evidence. Officially he knew nothing concerning the matter. Instead he retired to his home in Somers Town, a life pensioner subject to a continuation of his reticence. Two years later, one Christmas morning, Mr Jakobs received a very beautiful box of chocolates by post, "with every good wish", from somebody who did not trouble to send his or her name. Mr Jakobs, being no lover of chocolate drops, wondered what it had cost and wished the kindly donor had sent beer.

'Hi, Spot, catch!' said Mr Jakobs, and tossed a specimen of the confectioner's art to his dog, who possessed a sweet tooth.

The dog ate it, wagging his tail, then he stopped wagging his tail and lay down with a shiver – dead.

It was some time before Willie Jakobs realized the connection between the stiff little dog and this bland and ornate Christmas gift.

He tried a chocolate on his landlord's dog, and it died. He experimented on a fellow-lodger's canary, and it died too – he might have destroyed the whole of Somers Town's domestic menagerie but for the timely intervention of his landlord, who gave him in charge for his initial murder. Then the truth came out. The chocolates were poisoned. Willie Jakobs found his photograph in the public Press as the hero of a poisoning mystery: an embarrassment for Willie, who was promptly recognized by a Canning Town tradesman he had once victimized, and was arrested for the second time in a week.

Willie came out of gaol (it was a 'carpet') expecting to find an accumulation of one-pound postal orders awaiting him. Instead he found one five-pound note and a typewritten letter, on perfectly plain uncompromising paper, to the effect that the sender regretted that further supplies need not be expected.

Willie wrote to Colonel Black, and received in reply a letter in which 'Colonel Black could not grasp the contents of yours of the 4th. He has never sent money, and fails to understand why the writer should have expected', etc., etc.

Willie, furious and hurt at the base ingratitude and duplicity of his patron, carried the letter and a story to a solicitor, and the solicitor said one word – 'Blackmail!' Here, then, was a disgruntled Willie Jakobs forced to work: to depend upon chance bookings and precarious liftings. Fortunately his right hand had not lost its cunning, nor, for the matter of that, had his left. He 'clicked' to good stuff, fenced it with the new man in Eveswell Road (he was lagged eventually because he was only an amateur and gave too much for the stuff), and did well – so well, indeed, that he was inclined to take a mild view of Black's offences.

On the evening of Lord Verlond's dinner party – though, to do him justice, it must be confessed that Jakobs knew nothing of his lordship's plans – he sallied forth on business intent.

He made his way through the tiny court and narrow streets which separated him from Stibbington Street, there turning southwards to the Euston Road, and taking matters leisurely, he made his way to Tottenham Court Road, *en route* to Oxford Street.

Tottenham Court Road, on that particular night, was filled with interested people.

They were interested in shop windows, interested in one another, interested in boarding and alighting from buses. It was an ideal crowd from Jakobs's point of view.

He liked people who concentrated, who fixed their minds on one thing and had no thought for any other. In a sense he was something of a psychologist, and he looked round to find some opulent person whose powers of concentration might be of service to himself.

Gathered round the steps of an omnibus, impatiently waiting for other passengers to disembark, was a little crowd of people, and Jakobs, with his quick, keen eye, spotted a likely client.

He was a stout man of middle age. His hat was placed at such an angle on his head that the Somers Towner diagnosed him as 'canned'. He may or may not have been right in his surmise. It is sufficient that he appeared comfortably off, and that not only was his coat of good material, but he had various indications of an ostentatious character testifying to his present affluence. Willie Jakobs had had no intention of taking a bus ride. I doubt very much whether he changed his plans even now, but certain it is that he began to elbow his way into the little throng which surrounded the bus, by this time surging forward to board it.

He elbowed his way with good effect, for suddenly ceasing his efforts, as though he had remembered some very important engagement, he began to back out. He reached the outskirts of the little knot, then turned to walk briskly away.

At that moment a firm hand dropped on his shoulder in quite a friendly way. He looked round quickly. A tall young man in civilian dress stood behind him.

'Hullo!' said the young man, kindly enough, 'aren't you going on?'

'No, Mr Fellowe,' he said. 'I was going down for a blow, but I remember I left the gas burning at home.'

'Let's go back and put it out,' said Constable Fellowe, who was on a very special duty that night.

'On second thoughts,' said Jakobs reflectively, 'I don't think it's worth while. After all, it's one of those penny-in-the-slot machines and it can only burn itself out.'

'Then come along and see if my gas is burning,' said Frank humorously.

He held the other's arm lightly, but when Jakobs attempted to disengage himself he found the pressure on his arm increased. 'What's the game?' he asked innocently.

'The same old game,' said Frank, with a little smile. 'Hullo. Willie, you've dropped something.'

He stooped quickly, without releasing his hold, and picked up a pocket-book.

The bus was on the point of moving off as Frank swung round and with a signal stopped the conductor.

'I think someone who has just boarded your bus has lost a pocket-book. I think it is that stoutish gentleman who has just gone inside.'

The stoutish gentleman hastily descended to make a public examination of his wardrobe. He discovered himself minus several articles which should, by all laws affecting the right of property, have been upon his person.

Thereafter the matter became a fairly commonplace incident.

'It's a cop,' said Willie philosophically. I didn't see you around, Mr Fellowe.'

'I don't suppose you did, yet I'm big enough.'

'And ugly enough,' added Willie impartially.

Frank smiled. 'You're not much of an authority on beauty, Willie, are you?' he asked jocosely, as they threaded their way through the streets which separated them from the nearest police-station.

'Oh, I don't know,' said Willie, ' 'andsome is as 'andsome does. Say, Mr Fellowe, why don't the police go after a man like Olloroff? What are they worrying about a little hook like me for – getting my living at great inconvenience, in a manner of speaking. He is a fellow who makes his thousands, and has ruined his hundreds. Can you get him a lagging?'

'In time I hope we shall,' said Frank.

'There's a feller!' said Willie. 'He baits the poor little clerk – gets him to put up a fiver to buy a million pounds' worth of gold mines. Clerk puts it – pinches the money from the till, not meanin' to be dishonest, in a manner of speakin', but expectin' one day to walk into his boss, covered with fame and diamonds, and say, "Look at your long-lost Horace!" See what I mean?'

Frank nodded.

' "Look at your prodigal cashier",' Jakobs continued, carried away by his imagination. ' "Put your lamps over my shiners, run your hooks over me Astrakhan collar. Master, it is I, thy servant!" '

It was not curious that they should speak of Black. There had been a case in court that day in which a too-credulous client of Black's, who had suffered as a result of that credulity, had sued the colonel for the return of his money, and the case had not been defended.

'I used to work for him,' said Mr Jakobs, reminiscently. 'Messenger at twenty-nine shillings a week – like bein' messenger at a mortuary.'

He looked up at Frank.

'Ever count up the number of Black's friends who've died suddenly?' he asked. 'Ever reckon that up? He's a regular jujube tree, he is.'

' "Upas" is the word you want, Willie,' said Frank gently.

'You wait till the Four get him,' warned Mr Jakobs cheerfully. 'They won't half put his light out.'

He said no more for a while, then he turned suddenly to Frank.

'Come to think of it, Fellowe,' he said, with the gross familiarity of the habitué in dealing with his captor, 'this is the third time you've pinched me.'

'Come to think of it,' admitted Frank cheerfully, 'it is.'

'Harf a mo'.' Mr Jakobs halted and surveyed the other with a puzzled air. 'He took me in the Tottenham Court Road, he took me in the Charin' Cross Road, an' he apperryhended me in Cheapside.'

'You've a wonderful memory,' smiled the young man.

'Never on his beat,' said Mr Jakobs to himself, 'always in plain clothes, an' generally watchin' me – now, why?'

Frank thought a moment. 'Come and have a cup of tea, Willie,' he said, 'and I will tell you a fairy story.'

'I think we shall be gettin' at facts very soon,' said Willie, in his best judicial manner.

'I am going to be perfectly frank with you, my friend,' said Fellowe, when they were seated in a neighbouring coffee-shop.

'If you don't mind,' begged Willie, 'I'd rather call you by your surname – I don't want it to get about that I'm a pal of yours.'

Frank smiled again. Willie had ever been a source of amusement.

'You have been taken by me three times,' he said, 'and this is the first time you have mentioned our friend Black. I think I can say that if you had mentioned him before it might have made a lot of difference to you, Willie.'

Mr Jakobs addressed the ceiling. 'Come to think of it,' he said, 'he 'inted at this once before.'

'I 'int at it once again,' said Frank. 'Will you tell me why Black pays you two pounds a week?'

'Because he don't,' said Willie promptly. 'Because he's a sneakin' hook an' because he's a twister, because he's a liar – '

'If there's any reason you haven't mentioned, give it a run,' said Constable Fellowe in the vernacular.

Willie hesitated. 'What's the good of my tellin' you?' he asked. 'Sure as death you'll tell me I'm only lyin'.'

'Try me,' said Frank, and for an hour they sat talking, policeman and thief.

At the end of that time they went different ways – Frank to the police-station, where he found an irate owner of property awaiting him, and Mr Jakobs, thankfully, yet apprehensively, to his Somers Town home.

His business completed at the station, and a station sergeant alternately annoyed and mystified by the erratic behaviour of a plain-clothes constable, who gave orders with the assurance of an Assistant-Commissioner, Frank found a taxi and drove first to the house of Black, and later (with instructions to the driver to break all the rules laid down for the regulation of traffic) to Hampstead.

May Sandford was expecting the colonel. She stood by the drawing-room fire, buttoning her glove and endeavouring to disguise her pleasure that her sometime friend had called.

'Where are you going?' was his first blunt greeting, and the girl stiffened.

'You have no right to ask in that tone,' she said quietly, 'but I will tell you. I am going to dinner.'

'With whom?'

The colour came to her face, for she was really annoyed. 'With Colonel Black,' she said an effort to restrain her rising anger.

He nodded. 'I'm afraid I cannot allow you to go,' he said coolly.

The girl stared. 'Once and for all, Mr Fellowe,' she said with quiet dignity, 'you will understand that I am my own mistress. I shall do as I please. You have no right to dictate to me – you have no right whatever – ' she stamped her foot angrily – 'to say what I may do and what I may not do. I shall go where and with whom I choose.'

'You will not go out tonight, at any rate,' said Frank grimly.

An angry flush came to her cheeks. 'If I chose to go tonight, I should go tonight,' she said.

'Indeed, you will do nothing of the sort.' He was quite cool now – master of himself – completely under control.

'I shall be outside this house,' he said, 'for the rest of the night. If you go out with this man I shall arrest you.'

She started and took a step back.

'I shall arrest you,' he went on determinedly. 'I don't care what happens to me afterwards. I will trump up any charge against you. I will take you to the station, through the streets, and put you in the iron dock as though you were a common thief. I'll do it because I love you,' he said passionately, 'because you are the biggest thing in the world to me – because I love you better than life, better than you can love yourself, better than any man could love you. And do you know why I will take you to the police-station?' he went on earnestly. 'Because you will be safe there, and the women who look after you will allow no dog like this fellow to have communication with you – because he dare not follow you there, whatever else he dare. As for him – '

He turned savagely about as a resplendent Black entered the room.

Black stopped at the sight of the other's face and dropped his hand to his pocket.

'You look out for me,' said Frank, and Black's face blanched.

The girl had recovered her speech.

'How dare you – how dare you!' she whispered. 'You tell me that you will arrest me. How dare you! And you say you love me!' she said scornfully.

He nodded slowly. 'Yes,' he said, quietly enough. 'I love you. I love you enough to make you hate me. Can I love you any more than that?'

His voice was bitter, and there was something of helplessness in it too, but the determination that underlay his words could not be mistaken.

He did not leave her until Black had taken his leave, and in his pardonable perturbation he forgot that he intended searching the colonel for a certain green bottle with a glass stopper.

* * *

Colonel Black returned to his flat that night to find unmistakable evidence that the apartment had been most systematically searched. There existed, however, no evidence as to how his visitors had gained admission. The doors had been opened, despite the fact that they were fastened by a key which had no duplicate, and with locks that were apparently unpickable. The windows were intact, and no attempt had been made to remove money and valuables from the desk which had been ransacked. The only proof of identity they had left behind was the seal which he found attached to the blotting-pad on his desk.

They had gone methodically to work, dropped a neat round splash of sealing-wax, and had as neatly pressed the seal of the organization upon it. There was no other communication, but in its very simplicity this plain 'IV' was a little terrifying. It seemed that the members of the Four defied all his efforts at security, laughed to scorn his patent locks, knew more about his movements than his most intimate friends, and chose their own time for their visitations.

This would have been disconcerting to a man of less character than Black; but Black was one who had lived through a score of years –

each year punctuated, at regular intervals, with threats of the most terrible character. He had ever lived in the shadow of reprisal, yet he had never suffered punishment.

It was his most fervent boast that he never lost his temper, that he never did anything in a flurry. Now, perhaps for the first time in his life, he was going to work actuated by a greater consideration than self-interest – a consideration of vengeance.

It made him less careful than he was wont to be. He did not look for shadowers that evening, yet shadowers there had been – not one but many.

To Lincoln races

Sir Isaac Tramber went to Lincoln in an evil frame of mind. He had reserved a compartment, and cursed his luck when he discovered that his reservation adjoined that of Horace Gresham.

He paced the long platform at King's Cross, waiting for his guests. The Earl of Verlond had promised to go down with him and to bring Lady Mary, and it was no joy to Sir Isaac to observe on the adjoining carriage the label, 'Reserved for Mr Horace Gresham and party'.

Horace came along about five minutes before the train started. He was as cheerful as the noonday sun, in striking contrast to Sir Isaac, whose night had not been too wisely spent. He nodded carelessly to Sir Isaac's almost imperceptible greeting.

The baronet glanced at his watch and inwardly swore at the old earl and his caprices. It wanted three minutes to the hour at which the train left. His tongue was framing a bitter indictment of the old man when he caught a glimpse of his tall, angular figure striding along the platform.

'Thought we weren't coming. I suppose?' asked the earl, as he made his way to the compartment. 'I say, you thought we weren't coming?' he repeated, as Lady Mary entered the compartment, assisted with awkward solicitude by Sir Isaac.

'Well, I didn't expect you to be late.'

'We are not late,' said the earl.

He settled himself comfortably in a corner seat – the seat which Sir Isaac had specially arranged for the girl. Friends of his and of the old man who passed nodded. An indiscreet few came up to speak.

'Going up to Lincoln, Lord Verlond?' asked one idle youth.

'No,' said the earl sweetly, 'I am going to bed with the mumps.' He snarled the last word, and the young seeker after information fled.

'You can sit by me, Ikey – leave Mary alone,' said the old man sharply. 'I want to know all about this horse. I have £150 on this thoroughbred of yours; it is far more important than those fatuous inquiries you intend making of my niece.'

'Inquiries?' grumbled Sir Isaac resentfully.

'Inquiries!' repeated the other. 'You want to know whether she slept last night; whether she finds it too warm in this carriage; whether she would like a corner seat or a middle seat, her back to the engine or her face to the engine. Leave her alone, leave her alone, Ikey. She'll decide all that. I know her better than you.'

He glared, with that amusing glint in his eyes, across at the girl.

'Young Gresham is in the next carriage. Go and tap at the window and bring him out. Go along!'

'He's got some friends there, I think, uncle,' said the girl.

'Never mind about his friends,' said Verlond irritably. 'What the devil does it matter about his friends? Aren't you a friend? Go and tap at the door and bring him out.'

Sir Isaac was fuming.

'I don't want him in here,' he said loudly. 'You seem to forget, Verlond, that if you want to talk about horses, this is the very chap who should know nothing about Timbolino.'

'Ach!' said the earl testily, 'don't you suppose he knows all there is to be known. What do you think sporting papers are for?'

'Sporting papers can't tell a man what the owner knows,' said Sir Isaac importantly.

'They tell me more than he knows,' he said. 'Your horse was favourite yesterday morning – it isn't favourite any more, Ikey.'

'I can't control the investments of silly asses,' grumbled Sir Isaac.

'Except one,' said the earl rudely. 'But these silly asses you refer to do not throw their money away – remember that, Ikey. When you have had as much racing as I have had, and won as much money as I have won, you'll take no notice of what owners think of their horses. You might as well ask a mother to give a candid opinion of her own daughter's charms as to ask an owner for unbiased information about his own horse.'

The train had slipped through the grimy purlieus of London and was now speeding through green fields to Hatfield. It was a glorious spring day, mellow with sunlight: such a day as a man at peace with the world might live with complete enjoyment.

Sir Isaac was not in this happy position, nor was he in a mood to discuss either the probity of racing men or the general question of the sport itself.

He observed with an inward curse the girl rise and walk, apparently carelessly, into the corridor. He could have sworn he heard a tap at the window of the next compartment, but in this, of course, he was wrong. She merely moved across the vision of the little coterie who sat laughing and talking, and in an instant Horace had come out.

'It is not my fault this, really,' she greeted him, with a little flush in her cheeks. 'It was uncle's idea.'

'Your uncle is an admirable old gentleman,' said Horace fervently. 'I retract anything I may have said to his discredit.'

'I will tell him,' she said, with mock gravity.

'No, no,' cried Horace, 'I don't want you to do that exactly.'

'I want to talk to you seriously,' said she suddenly. 'Come into our compartment. Uncle and Sir Isaac are so busy discussing the merits of Timbolino – is that the right name?' He nodded, his lips twitching with amusement. 'That they won't notice anything we have to say,' she concluded.

The old earl gave him a curt nod. Sir Isaac only vouchsafed a scowl. It was difficult to maintain anything like a confidential character in their conversation, but by manoeuvring so that they spoke only of the more important things when Sir Isaac and his truculent guest were at the most heated point of their argument, she was able to unburden the anxiety of her mind.

'I am worried about uncle,' she said in a low tone.

'Is he ill?' asked Horace.

She shook her head. 'No, it isn't his illness – yet it may be. But he is so contradictory; I am so afraid that it might react to our disadvantage. You know how willing he was that you should . . . ' She hesitated, and his hand sought hers under the cover of an open newspaper.

'It was marvellous,' he whispered, 'wasn't it? I never expected for one moment that the old dev – that your dear uncle,' he corrected himself, 'would have been so amenable.'

She nodded again. 'You see,' she said, taking advantage of another heated passage between the old man and the irritated baronet, 'what he does so impetuously he can undo just as easily. I am so afraid he will turn and rend you.'

'Let him try,' said Horace. 'I am not easily rent.'

Their conversation was cut short abruptly by the intervention of the man they were discussing.

'Look here, Gresham,' snapped the earl shortly, 'you're one of the cognoscenti, and I suppose you know everything. Who are the Four Just Men I hear people talking about?'

Horace was conscious of the fact that the eyes of Sir Isaac Tramber were fixed on him curiously. He was a man who made no disguise of his suspicion.

'I know no more than you,' said Horace. 'They seem to me to be an admirable body of people who go about correcting social evils.'

'Who are they to judge what is and what is not evil?' growled the earl, scowling from under his heavy eyebrows. 'Infernal cheek! What do we pay judges and jurymen and coroners and policemen and people of that sort for, eh? What do we pay taxes for, and rent for, and police rates, and gas rates, and water rates, and every kind of dam' rate that the devilish ingenuity of man can devise? Do we do it that these jackanapes can come along and interfere with the course of justice? It's absurd! It's ridiculous!' he stormed.

Horace threw out a protesting hand.

'Don't blame me,' he said.

'But you approve of them,' accused the earl. 'Ikey says you do, and Ikey knows everything – don't you, Ikey?'

Sir Isaac shifted uncomfortably in his seat. 'I didn't say Gresham knew anything about it,' he began lamely.

'Why do you lie, Ikey; why do you lie?' asked the old man testily. 'You just told me that you were perfectly sure that Gresham was one of the leading spirits of the gang.'

Sir Isaac, inured as he was to the brutal indiscretions of his friends, went a dull red. 'Oh, I didn't mean that exactly,' he said awkwardly and a little angrily. 'Dash it, Lord Verlond, don't embarrass a fellow by rendering him liable to heavy damages and all that sort of thing.'

Horace was unperturbed by the other's confusion. 'You needn't bother yourself,' he said coolly. 'I should never think of taking you to a court of justice.'

He turned again to the girl, and the earl claimed the baronet's attention. The old man had a trick of striking off at a tangent; from one subject to another he leapt like a will-o'-the-wisp. Before Horace had framed half a dozen words the old man was dragging his unwilling victim along a piscatorial road, and Sir Isaac was floundering out of his depths in a morass – if the metaphor be excused – of salmon-fishing, trout-poaching, pike-fishing – a sport on which Sir Isaac Tramber could by no means deem himself an authority.

It was soon after lunch that the train pulled into Lincoln. Horace usually rented a house outside the town, but this year he had arranged to go and return to London on the same night. At the station he parted with the girl.

'I shall see you on the course,' he said. 'What are your arrangements? Do you go back to town tonight?'

She nodded. 'Is this a very important race for you to win?' she asked, a little anxiously.

He shook his head.

'Nobody really bothers overmuch about the Lincolnshire Handicap,' he said. 'You see, it's too early in the season for even the gamblers to put their money down with any assurance. One doesn't know much, and it is almost impossible to tell what horses are in form. I verily believe that Nemesis will win but everything is against her.

'You see, the Lincoln,' continued Horace doubtfully, 'is a race which is not usually won by a filly, and then, too, she is a sprinter. I know sprinters have won the race before, and every year have been confidently expected to win it again; but the averages are all against a horse like Nemesis.'

'But I thought,' she said in wonder, 'that you were so confident about her.'

He laughed a little. 'Well, you know, one is awfully confident on Monday and full of doubts on Tuesday. That is part of the game; the form of horses is not half as inconsistent as the form of owners. I shall probably meet a man this morning who will tell me that some horse is an absolute certainty for the last race of the day. He will hold me by the buttonhole and he will drum into me the fact that this is the most extraordinarily easy method of picking up money that was ever invented since racing started. When I meet him after the last race he will coolly inform me that he did not back that horse, but had some tip at the last moment from an obscure individual who knew the owner's aunt's sister. You mustn't expect one to be consistent.

'I still think Nemesis will win,' he went on, 'but I am not so confident as I was. The most cocksure of students gets a little glum in the face of the examiner.'

The earl had joined them and was listening to the conversation with a certain amount of grim amusement. 'Ikey is certain Timbolino will win,' he said, 'even in the face of the examiner. Somebody has just told me that the examiner is rather soft under foot.'

'You mean the course?' asked Horace, a little anxiously.

The earl nodded. 'It won't suit yours, my friend,' he said. 'A sprinter essaying the Lincolnshire wants good going. I can see myself taking £1,500 back to London today.'

'Have you backed Timbolino?'

'Don't ask impertinent questions,' said the earl curtly. 'And unnecessary questions,' he went on. 'You know infernally well I've backed Timbolino. Don't you believe me? I've backed it and I'm afraid I'm not going to win.'

'Afraid?'

Whatever faults the old man had, Horace knew him for a good loser. The earl nodded.

He was not amused now. He had dropped like a cloak the assumption of that little unpleasant leering attitude. He was, Horace saw for the first time, a singularly good-looking old man. The firm lines of the mouth were straight, and the pale face, in repose, looked a little sad.

'Yes. I'm afraid.' he said. His voice was even and without the bitter quality of cynicism which was his everlasting pose.

'This race makes a lot of difference to some people. It doesn't affect me very much,' he said, and the corner of his mouth twitched a little. 'But there are people,' he went on seriously, 'to whom this race makes a difference between life and death.' There was a sudden return to his usual abrupt manner. 'Eh? How does that strike you for good melodrama, Mr Gresham?'

Horace shook his head in bewilderment. 'I'm afraid I don't follow you at all, Lord Verlond.'

'You may follow me in another way,' said the earl briskly. 'Here is my car. Good morning.'

Horace watched him out of sight and then made his way to the racecourse.

The old man had puzzled him not a little. He bore, as Horace knew, a reputation which, if not unsavoury, was at least unpleasant. He was credited with having the most malicious tongue in London. But when Horace came to think, as he did, walking along the banks of the river on his way to the course, there was little that the old man had ever said which would injure or hurt innocent people. His cynicism was in the main directed against his own class, his savageness most manifested against notorious sinners. Men like Sir Isaac Tramber felt the lash of his tongue.

His treatment of his heir was, of course, inexcusable. The earl himself never excused it; he persistently avoided the subject, and it would be a bold man who would dare to raise so unpleasant a topic against the earl's wishes.

He was known to be extraordinarily wealthy, and Horace Gresham had reason for congratulating himself that he had been specially blessed with this world's goods. Otherwise his prospects would not have been of the brightest. That he was himself enormously rich precluded any suggestion (and the suggestion would have been inevitable) that he hunted Lady Mary's fortune. It was a matter of supreme indifference to himself whether she inherited the Verlond millions or whether she came to him empty-handed.

There were other people in Lincoln that day who did not take so philosophical a view of the situation.

Sir Isaac had driven straight to the house on the hill leading to the Minster, which Black had engaged for two days. He was in a very bad temper when at last he reached his destination. Black was sitting at lunch.

Black looked up as the other entered. 'Hullo, Ikey,' he said, 'come and sit down.'

Sir Isaac looked at the menu with some disfavour.

'Thanks,' he said shortly, 'I've lunched on the train. I want to talk to you.'

'Talk away,' said Black, helping himself to another cutlet. He was a good trencherman – a man who found exquisite enjoyment in his meals.

'Look here. Black,' said Isaac, 'things are pretty desperate. Unless that infernal horse of mine wins today I shall not know what to do for money.'

'I know one thing you won't be able to do,' said Black coolly, 'and that is, come to me. I am in as great straits as you.' He pushed back his plate and took a cigar-case from his pocket. 'What do we stand to win on this Timbolino of yours?'

'About £25,000,' said Sir Isaac moodily. 'I don't know if the infernal thing will win. It would be just my luck if it doesn't. I am afraid of this horse of Gresham's.'

Black laughed softly. 'That's a new fear of yours,' he said. 'I don't remember having heard it before.'

'It's no laughing matter,' said the other. 'I had my trainer, Tubbs, down watching her work. She is immensely fast. The only thing is whether she can stay the distance.'

'Can't she be got at?' asked Black.

'Got at!' said the other impatiently. 'The race will be run in three hours' time! Where do you get your idea of racing from?' he asked irritably. 'You can't poison horses at three hours' notice. You can't even poison them at three days' notice, unless you've got the trainer in with you. And trainers of that kind only live in novels.'

Black was carefully cutting the end of his cigar. 'So if your horse loses we shall be in High Street, Hellboro'?' he reflected. 'I have backed it to save my life.' He said this in grim earnest.

He rang a bell. The servant came in.

'Tell them to bring round the carriage,' he said. He looked at his watch. 'I am not particularly keen on racing, but I think I shall enjoy this day in the open. It gives one a chance of thinking.'

Chapter 12

The race

The curious ring on the Carholme was crowded. Unusually interested in the Lincoln handicap was the sporting world, and this, together with the glorious weather, had drawn sportsmen from north and south to meet together on this great festival of English racing.

Train and steamer had brought the wanderers back to the fold. There were men with a tan of Egypt on their cheeks, men who had been to the south to avoid the vigorous and searching tests of an English winter; there were men who came from Monte Carlo, and lean, brown men who had spent the dark days of the year amongst the snows of the Alps.

There were regular followers of the game who had known no holiday, and had followed the jumping season with religious attention. There were rich men and comparatively poor men; little tradesmen who found this the most delightful of their holidays; members of Parliament who had snatched a day from the dreariness of the Parliamentary debates; sharpers on the look-out for possible victims; these latter quiet, unobtrusive men whose eyes were constantly on the move for a likely subject. There was a sprinkling of journalists, cheery and sceptical, young men and old men, farmers in their gaiters – all drawn together in one great brotherhood by a love of the sport of kings.

In the crowded paddock the horses engaged in the first race were walking round, led by diminutive stable-lads, the number of each horse strapped to the boy's arm.

'A rough lot of beggars,' said Gresham, looking them over. Most of them still had their winter coats; most of them were grossly fat and unfitted for racing. He was ticking the horses off on his card; some he immediately dismissed as of no account. He found Lady Mary wandering around the paddock by herself. She greeted him as a shipwrecked mariner greets a sail.

'I'm so glad you've come,' she said. 'I know nothing whatever about racing.' She looked round the paddock. 'Won't you tell me something. Are all these horses really fit?'

'You evidently know something about horses,' he smiled. 'No, they're not.'

'But surely they can't win if they're not fit,' she said in astonishment.

'They can't all win,' replied the young man, laughing. 'They're not all intended to win, either. You see, a trainer may not be satisfied his horse is top-hole. He sends him out to have a feeler, so to speak, at the opposition. The fittest horse will probably win this race. The trainer who is running against him with no hope of success will discover how near to fitness his own beast is!'

'I want to find Timbolino,' she said, looking at her card. 'That's Sir Isaac's, isn't it?'

He nodded.

'I was looking for him myself,' he said. 'Come along, and let's see if we can find him.'

In a corner of the paddock they discovered the horse – a tall, upstanding animal, well muscled, so far as Horace could judge, for the horse was still in his cloths.

'A nice type of horse for the Lincoln,' he said thoughtfully. 'I saw him at Ascot last year. I think this is the fellow we've got to beat.'

'Does Sir Isaac own many horses?' she asked.

'A few,' he said. 'He is a remarkable man.'

'Why do you say that?' she asked.

He shrugged his shoulders.

'Well, one knows . . . '

Then he realized that it wasn't playing cricket to speak disparagingly of a possible rival, and she rightly interpreted his silence.

'Where does Sir Isaac make his money?' she asked abruptly.

He looked at her. 'I don't know,' he said. 'He's got some property somewhere, hasn't he?'

She shook her head. 'No,' she said. 'I am not asking,' she went on quickly, 'because I have any possible interest in his wealth or his prospects. All my interest is centred – elsewhere.'

She favoured him with a dazzling little smile.

Although the paddock was crowded and the eyes of many people were upon him, the owner of the favourite had all his work to restrain himself from taking her hand.

She changed the subject abruptly. 'So now let's come and see your great horse,' she said gaily.

He led her over to one of the boxes where Nemesis was receiving the attention of an earnest groom.

There was not much of her. She was of small build, clean of limb, with a beautiful head and a fine neck not usually seen in so small a thoroughbred. She had run a good fourth in the Cambridgeshire of the previous year, and had made steady improvement from her three-year-old to her four-year-old days.

Horace looked her over critically. His practised eye could see no fault in her condition. She looked very cool, ideally fit for the task of the afternoon. He knew that her task was a difficult one; he knew, too, that he had in his heart really very little fear that she could fail to negotiate the easy mile of the Carholme. There were many horses in the race who were also sprinters, and they would make the pace a terrifically fast one. If stamina was a weak point, it would betray her.

The previous day, on the opening of the racing season, his stable had run a horse in a selling plate, and it was encouraging that this animal, though carrying top weight, beat his field easily. It was this fact that had brought Nemesis to the position of short-priced favourite.

Gresham himself had very little money upon her; he did not bet very heavily, though he was credited with making and losing fabulous sums each year. He gained nothing by contradicting these rumours. He was sufficiently indifferent to the opinions of his fellows not to suffer any inconvenience from their repetition.

But the shortening of price on Nemesis was a serious matter for the connection of Timbolino. They could not cover their investments by 'saving' on Nemesis without a considerable outlay.

Horace was at lunch when the second race was run. He had found Lord Verlond wonderfully gracious; to the young man's surprise his lordship had accepted his invitation with such matter-of-fact heartiness as to suggest he had expected it. 'I suppose,' he said, with a little twinkle in his eye, 'you haven't invited Ikey?'

Gresham shook his head smilingly.

'No, I do not think Sir Isaac quite approves of me.'

'I do not think he does,' agreed the other. 'Anyway, he's got a guest of his own, Colonel Black. I assure you it is through no act of mine. Ikey introduced him to me, somewhat unnecessarily, but Ikey is always doing unnecessary things.

'A very amiable person,' continued the earl, busy with his knife and fork; 'he "lordshipped" me and "my lorded" me as though he were the newest kind of barrister and I was the oldest and wiliest of assize judges. He treated me with that respect which is only accorded to those who are expected to pay eventually for the privilege. Ikey was most anxious that he should create a good impression.'

It may be said with truth that Black saw the net closing round him. He knew not what mysterious influences were at work, but day by day, in a hundred different ways, he found himself thwarted, new obstacles put in his way. He was out now for a final kill.

He was recalled to a realization of the present by the strident voices of the bookmakers about him; the ring was in a turmoil. He heard a voice shout, 'Seven to one, bar one! Seven to one Nemesis!' and he knew enough of racing to realize what had happened to the favourite.

He came to a bookmaker he knew slightly. 'What are you barring?' he asked.

'Timbolino,' was the reply.

He found Sir Isaac near the enclosure. The baronet was looking a muddy white, and was biting his finger-nails with an air of perturbation.

'What has made your horse so strong a favourite?'

'I backed it again,' said Sir Isaac.

'Backed it again?'

'I've got to do something,' said the other savagely. 'If I lose, well, I lose more than I can pay. I might as well add to my liabilities. I tell you I'm down and out if this thing doesn't win,' he said, 'unless you can do something for me. You can, can't you, Black, old sport?' he asked entreatingly. 'There's no reason why you and I should have any secrets from one another.'

Black looked at him steadily. If the horse lost he might be able to use this man to greater advantage.

Sir Isaac's next words suggested that in case of necessity help would be forthcoming.

'It's that beastly Verlond,' he said bitterly. 'He put the girl quite against me – she treats me as though I were dirt – and I thought I was all right there. I've been backing on the strength of the money coming to me.'

'What has happened recently?' asked Black.

'I got her by myself just now,' said the baronet, 'and put it to her plain; but it's no go. Black, she gave me the frozen face – turned me down proper. It's perfectly damnable,' he almost wailed.

Black nodded. At that moment there was a sudden stir in the ring. Over the heads of the crowd from where they stood they saw the bright-coloured caps of the jockeys cantering down to the post.

Unlike Sir Isaac, who had carefully avoided the paddock after a casual glance at his candidate, Horace was personally supervising the finishing touches to Nemesis. He saw the girths strapped and gave his last instructions to the jockey. Then, as the filly was led to the course, with one final backward and approving glance at her, he turned towards the ring.

'One moment, Gresham!' Lord Verlond was behind him. 'Do you think your horse,' said the old man, with a nod towards Nemesis, 'is going to win?'

Horace nodded. 'I do now,' he said; 'in fact, I am rather confident.'

'Do you think,' the other asked slowly, 'that if your horse doesn't, Timbolino will?'

Horace looked at him curiously. 'Yes, Lord Verlond, I do,' he said quietly.

Again there was a pause, the old man fingering his shaven chin absently. 'Suppose, Gresham,' he said, without raising his voice, 'suppose I asked you to pull your horse?'

The face of the young man went suddenly red.

'You're joking, Lord Verlond,' he answered stiffly.

'I'm not joking,' said the other. 'I'm speaking to you as a man of honour, and I am trusting to your respecting my confidence. Suppose I asked you to pull Nemesis, would you do it?'

'No, frankly, I would not,' said the other, 'but I can't – '

'Never mind what you can't understand,' said Lord Verlond, with a return of his usual sharpness. 'If I asked you and offered you as a reward what you desired most, would you do it?'

'I would not do it for anything in the world,' said Horace gravely.

A bitter little smile came to the old man's face. 'I see,' he said.

'I can't understand why you ask me,' said Horace, who was still bewildered. 'Surely you – you know – '

'I only know that you think I want you to pull your horse because I have backed the other,' said the old earl, with just a ghost of a smile on his thin lips. 'I would advise you not to be too puffed up with pride at your own rectitude,' he said unpleasantly, though the little smile still lingered, 'because you may be very sorry one of these days that you did not do as I asked.'

'If you would tell me,' began Horace, and paused. This sudden request from the earl, who was, with all his faults, a sportsman, left him almost speechless.

'I will tell you nothing,' said the earl, 'because I have nothing to tell you,' he added suavely.

Horace led the way up the stairs to the county stand. To say that he was troubled by the extraordinary request of the old man would be to put it mildly. He knew the earl as an eccentric man; he knew him by reputation as an evil man, though he had no evidence as to this. But he never in his wildest and most uncharitable moments had imagined that this old rascal – so he called him – would ask him to pull a horse. It was unthinkable. He remembered that Lord Verlond was steward of one or two big meetings, and that he was a member of one of the most august sporting clubs in the world.

He elbowed his way along the top of the stand to where the white osprey on Lady Mary's hat showed.

'You look troubled,' she said as he reached her side. 'Has uncle been bothering you?'

He shook his head. 'No,' he replied, with unusual curtness.

'Has your horse developed a headache?' she asked banteringly.

'I was worried about something I remembered,' he said incoherently.

The field was at the starting-post.

'Your horse is drawn in the middle,' she said.

He put up his glasses. He could see the chocolate and green plainly enough.

Sir Isaac's – grey vertical stripes on white, yellow cap – was also easy to see. He had drawn the inside right.

The field was giving the starter all the trouble that twenty-four high-spirited thoroughbreds could give to any man. For ten minutes they backed and sidled and jumped and kicked and circled before the two long tapes. With exemplary patience the starter waited, directing, imploring almost, commanding and, it must be confessed, swearing, for he was a North-country starter who had no respect for the cracks of the jockey world.

The wait gave Horace an opportunity for collecting his thoughts. He had been a little upset by the strange request of the man who was now speaking so calmly at his elbow.

For Sir Isaac the period of waiting had increased the tension. His hands were shaking, his glasses went up and down, jerkily; he was in an agony of apprehension, when suddenly the white tape swung up, the field bunched into three sections, then spread again and, like a cavalry regiment, came thundering down the slight declivity on its homeward journey.

'They're off!'

A roar of voices. Every glass was focused on the oncoming field. There was nothing in it for two furlongs; the start had been a splendid one. They came almost in a dead line. Then something on the rail shot out a little: it was Timbolino, going with splendid smoothness.

'That looks like the winner,' said Horace philosophically. 'Mine's shut in.'

In the middle of the course the jockey on Nemesis, seeking an opening, had dashed his mount to one which was impossible.

He found himself boxed between two horses, the riders of which showed no disposition to open out for him. The field was half-way on its journey when the boy pulled the filly out of the trap and 'came round his horses'.

Timbolino had a two-length clear lead of Colette, which was a length clear of a bunch of five; Nemesis, when half the journey was done, was lying eighth or ninth.

Horace, on the stand, had his stop-watch in his hand. He clicked it off as the field passed the four-furlong post and hastily examined the dial.

'It's a slow race,' he said, with a little thrill in his voice.

At the distance, Nemesis, with a quick free stride, had shot out of the ruck and was third, three lengths behind Timbolino.

The boy on Sir Isaac's horse was running a confident race. He had the rails and had not moved on his horse. He looked round to see where the danger lay, and his experienced eye saw it in Nemesis, who was going smoothly and evenly.

A hundred yards from the post the boy on Gresham's filly shook her up, and in half a dozen strides she had drawn abreast of the leader.

The rider of Timbolino saw the danger – he pushed his mount, working with hands and heels upon the willing animal under him.

They were running now wide of each other, dead level. The advantage, it seemed, lay with the horse on the rails, but Horace, watching with an expert eye from the top of the stand, knew that the real advantage lay with the horse in the middle of the track.

He had walked over the course that morning, and he knew that it was on the crown of the track that the going was best. Timbolino responded nobly to the efforts of his rider; once his head got in front, and the boy on Nemesis took up his whip, but he did not use it. He was watching the other. Then, with twenty yards to go, he drove Nemesis forward with all the power of his splendid hands.

Timbolino made one more effort, and as they flew past the judge's box there was none save the judge who might separate them.

Horace turned to the girl at his side with a critical smile.

'Oh, you've won,' she said. 'You did win, didn't you?'

Her eyes were blazing with excitement.

He shook his head smilingly.

'I'm afraid I can't answer that,' he said. 'It was a very close thing.'

He glanced at Sir Isaac. The baronet's face was livid, the hand that he raised to his lips trembled like an aspen leaf.

'There's one man,' thought Horace, 'who's more worried about the result than I am.'

Down below in the ring there was a Babel of excited talk. It rose up to them in a dull roar. They were betting fast and furiously on the result, for the numbers had not yet gone up.

Both horses had their partisans. Then there was a din amounting to a bellow. The judge had hoisted two noughts in the frame. It was a dead-heat!

'By Jove!' said Horace.

It was the only comment he made.

He crossed to the other side of the enclosure as quickly as he could, Sir Isaac following closely behind. As the baronet elbowed his way through the crowd somebody caught him by the arm. He looked round. It was Black.

'Run it off,' said Black, in a hoarse whisper. 'It was a fluke that horse got up. Your jockey was caught napping. Run it off.'

Sir Isaac hesitated. 'I shall get half the bets and half the stakes,' he said.

'Have the lot,' said Black. 'Go along, there is nothing to be afraid of. I know this game; run it off. There's nothing to prevent you winning.'

Sir Isaac hesitated, then walked slowly to the unsaddling enclosure. The steaming horses were being divested of their saddles.

Gresham was there, looking cool and cheerful. He caught the baronet's eye.

'Well, Sir Isaac,' he said pleasantly, 'what are you going to do?'

'What do you want to do?' asked Sir Isaac suspiciously.

It was part of his creed that all men were rogues. He thought it would be safest to do the opposite to what his rival desired. Like many another suspicious man, he made frequent errors in his diagnosis.

'I think it would be advisable to divide,' said Horace. 'The horses have had a very hard race, and I think mine was unlucky not to win.'

That decided Sir Isaac.

'We'll run it off,' he said.

'As you will,' said Horace coldly, 'but I think it is only right to warn you that my horse was boxed in half-way up the course and but for that would have won very easily. She had to make up half a dozen – '

'I know all about that,' interrupted the other rudely, 'but none the less, I'm going to run it off.'

Horace nodded. He turned to consult with his trainer. If the baronet decided to run the dead-heat off, there was nothing to prevent it, the laws of racing being that both owners must agree to divide.

Sir Isaac announced his intention to the stewards, and it was arranged that the run-off would take place after the last race of the day.

He was shaking with excitement when he rejoined Black. 'I'm not so sure that you're right,' he said dubiously. 'This chap Gresham says his horse was boxed in. I didn't see the beast in the race, so I can't tell. Ask somebody.'

'Don't worry,' said Black, patting him on the back, 'there is nothing to worry about; you'll win this race just as easily as I shall walk from this ring to the paddock.'

Sir Isaac was not satisfied. He waited till he saw a journalist whom he knew by sight returning from the telegraph office.

'I say,' he said, 'did you see the race?'

The journalist nodded. 'Yes, Sir Isaac,' he said with a smile. 'I suppose Gresham insisted on running it off?'

'No, he didn't,' said Sir Isaac, 'but I think I was unlucky to lose.'

The journalist made a little grimace. 'I'm sorry I can't agree with you,' he said. 'I thought that Mr Gresham's horse ought to have won easily, but that he was boxed in in the straight.'

Sir Isaac reported this conversation to Black.

'Take no notice of these racing journalists,' said Black contemptuously. 'What do they know? Haven't I got eyes as well as they?'

But this did not satisfy Sir Isaac. 'These chaps are jolly good judges,' he said. 'I wish to heaven I had divided.'

Black slapped him on the shoulder. 'You're losing your nerve, Ikey,' he said. 'Why, you'll be thanking me at dinner tonight for having saved you thousands of pounds. He didn't want to run it off?'

'Who?' asked Sir Isaac. 'Gresham?'

'Yes; did he?' asked Black.

'No, he wasn't very keen. He said it wasn't fair to the horses.'

Black laughed. 'Rubbish!' he said scornfully. 'Do you imagine a man like that cares whether his horse is hard raced or whether it isn't? No! He saw the race as well as I did. He saw that your fool of a jockey had it won and was caught napping. Of course he didn't want to risk a run-off. I tell you that Timbolino will win easily.'

Somewhat reassured by his companion's optimism, Sir Isaac awaited the conclusion of the run-off in better spirits. It added to his assurance that the ring took a similar view to that which Black held. They were asking for odds about Timbolino. You might have got two to one against Nemesis.

But only for a little while. Gresham had gone into the tea-room with the girl, and was standing at the narrow entrance of the county stand, when the cry, 'Two to one Nemesis!' caught his ear.

'They're not laying against my horse!' he exclaimed in astonishment. He beckoned a man who was passing. 'Are they laying against Nemesis?' he asked.

The man nodded. He was a commission agent, who did whatever work the young owner required. 'Go in and back her for me. Put in as much money as you possibly can get. Back it down to evens,' said Gresham decidedly.

He was not a gambling man. He was shrewd and business-like in all his transactions, and he could read a race. He knew exactly what had happened. His money created some sensation in a market which was not over-strong. Timbolino went out, and Nemesis was a shade odds on.

Then it was that money came in for Sir Isaac's horse.

Black did not bet to any extent, but he saw a chance of making easy money. The man honestly believed all he had said to Sir Isaac. He was confident in his mind that the jockey had ridden a 'jolly race'. He had sufficient credit amongst the best men in the ring to invest fairly heavily.

Again the market experienced an extraordinary change. Timbolino was favourite again. Nemesis went out – first six to four, then two to one, then five to two.

But now the money began to come in from the country. The results of the race and its description had been published in the stop-press editions in hundreds of evening papers up and down England, Ireland and Scotland. Quick to make their decisions, the little punters of Great Britain were re-investing – some to save their stakes, others to increase what they already regarded as their winnings.

And here the money was for Nemesis. The reporters, unprejudiced, had no other interest but to secure for the public accurate news and to describe things as they saw them. And the race as they saw it was the race which Sir Isaac would not believe and at which Black openly scoffed.

The last event was set for half-past four, and after the field had come past the post, and the winner was being led to the unsaddling enclosure, the two dead-heaters of the memorable Lincolnshire Handicap came prancing from the paddock on to the course.

The question of the draw was immaterial. There was nothing to choose between the jockeys, two experienced horsemen, and there was little delay at the post. It does not follow that a race of two runners means an equable start, though it seemed that nothing was likely to interfere with the tiny field getting off together. When the tapes went up, however, Nemesis half-turned and lost a couple of lengths.

'I'll back Timbolino,' yelled somebody from the ring, and a quick staccato voice cried, 'I'll take three to one.'

A chorus of acceptances met the offer.

Sir Isaac was watching the race from the public stand. Black was at his side.

'What did I tell you?' asked the latter exultantly. 'The money is in your pocket, Ikey, my boy. Look, three lengths in front. You'll win at a walk.'

The boy on Nemesis had her well balanced. He did not drive her out. He seemed content to wait those three lengths in the rear. Gresham, watching them through his glasses, nodded his approval.

'They're going no pace,' he said to the man at his side. 'She was farther behind at this point in the race itself.'

Both horses were running smoothly. At the five-furlong post the lad on Nemesis let the filly out just a little. Without any apparent effort she improved her position. The jockey knew now exactly what were his resources and he was content to wait behind. The rest of the race needs very little description. It was a procession until they had reached the distance. Then the boy on Timbolino looked round.

'He's beaten,' said Gresham, half to himself. He knew that some jockeys looked round when they felt their mount failing under them.

Two hundred yards from the post Nemesis, with scarcely an effort, drew level with the leader. Out came the other jockey's whip.

One, two, he landed his mount, and the horse went ahead till he was a neck in front. Then, coming up with one long run, Nemesis first drew up, then passed the fast-stopping Timbolino, and won with consummate ease by a length and a half.

Sir Isaac could not believe his eyes. He gasped, dropped his glasses, and stared at the horses in amazement.

It was obvious that he was beaten long before the winning-post was reached.

'He's pulling the horse,' he cried, beside himself with rage and chagrin. 'Look at him! I'll have him before the stewards. He is not riding the horse!'

Black's hand closed on his arm. 'Drop it, you fool,' he muttered. 'Are you going to give away the fact that you are broke to the world before all these people? You're beaten fairly enough. I've lost as much as you have. Get out of this.'

Sir Isaac Tramber went down the stairs of the grand-stand in the midst of a throng of people, all talking at once in different keys. He was dazed. He was more like a man in a dream. He could not realize what it meant to him. He was stunned, bewildered. All that he knew was that Timbolino had lost. He had a vague idea at the back of his mind that he was a ruined man, and only a faint ray of hope that Black would in some mysterious way get him out of his trouble.

'The horse was pulled,' he repeated dully. 'He couldn't have lost. Black, wasn't it pulled?'

'Shut up,' snarled the other. 'You're going to get yourself into pretty bad trouble unless you control that tongue of yours.' He got the shaking man away from the course and put a stiff glass of brandy and water in his hand. The baronet awoke to his tragic position.

'I can't pay, Black,' he wailed. 'I can't pay – what an awful business for me. What a fool I was to take your advice – what a fool! Curse you, you were standing in with Gresham. Why did you advise me? What did you make out of it?'

'Dry up,' said Black shortly. 'You're like a babe, Ikey. What are you worrying about? I've told you I've lost as much money as you. Now we've got to sit down and think out a plan for making money. What have you lost?'

Sir Isaac shook his head weakly. 'I don't know,' he said listlessly. 'Six or seven thousand pounds. I haven't got six or seven thousand pence,' he added plaintively. 'It's a pretty bad business for me, Black. A man in my position – I shall have to sell off my horses – '

'Your position!' Black laughed harshly. 'My dear good chap, I shouldn't let that worry you. Your reputation,' he went on. 'You're living in a fool's paradise, my man,' he said with savage banter. 'Why, you've no more reputation than I have. Who cares whether you pay your debts of honour or whether you don't? It would surprise people more if you paid than if you defaulted. Get all that nonsense out of your head and think sensibly. You will make all you've lost and much more. You've got to marry – and quick, and then she's got to inherit my lord's money, almost as quickly.'

Ikey looked at him in despairing amazement.

'Even if she married me,' he said pettishly, 'I should have to wait years for the money.'

Colonel Black smiled.

They were moving off the course when they were overtaken by a man, who touched the baronet on the arm.

'Excuse me, Sir Isaac,' he said, and handed him an envelope.

'For me?' asked Ikey wonderingly, and opened the envelope. There was no letter – only a slip of paper and four bank-notes for a thousand pounds each. Sir Isaac gasped and read: 'Pay your debts and live cleanly; avoid Black like the devil and work for your living.'

The writing was disguised, but the language was obviously Lord Verlond's.

Chapter 13

Who are the Four?

Lord Verlond sat at breakfast behind an open copy of *The Times*. Breakfast was ever an unsociable meal at Verlond House. Lady Mary, in her neat morning dress, was content to read her letters and her papers without expecting conversation from the old man.

He looked across at her. His face was thoughtful. In repose she had always thought it rather fine, and now his grave eyes were watching her with an expression she did not remember having seen before.

'Mary,' he asked abruptly, 'are you prepared for a shock?'

She smiled, though somewhat uneasily. These shocks were often literal facts. 'I think I can survive it,' she said.

There was a long pause, during which his eyes did not leave her face.

'Would you be startled to know that that young demon of a brother of yours is still alive?'

'Alive!' she exclaimed, starting to her feet.

There was no need for the old man to ask exactly how she viewed the news. Her face was flushed with pleasure – joy shone in her eyes.

'Oh, is it really true?' she cried.

'It's true enough,' said the old man moodily. 'Very curious how things turn out. I thought the young beggar was dead, didn't you?'

'Oh, don't talk like that, uncle, you don't mean it.'

'I mean it all right,' snapped the earl. 'Why shouldn't I? He was infernally rude to me. Do you know what he called me before he left?'

'But that was sixteen years ago,' said the girl.

'Sixteen grandmothers,' said the old man. 'It doesn't make any difference to me if it was sixteen hundred years – he still said it. He called me a tiresome old bore – what do you think of that?'

She laughed, and a responsive gleam came to the old man's face.

'It's all very well for you to laugh,' he said, 'but it's rather a serious business for a member of the House of Lords to be called a tiresome old bore by a youthful Etonian. Naturally, remembering his parting words and the fact that he had gone to America, added to the very important fact that I am a Churchman and a regular subscriber to Church institutions, I thought he was dead. After all, one expects some reward from an All-wise Providence.'

'Where is he?' she asked.

'I don't know,' said the earl. 'I traced him to Texas – apparently he was on a farm there until he was twenty-one. After that his movements seem to have been somewhat difficult to trace.'

'Why,' she said suddenly, pointing an accusing finger at him, 'you've been trying to trace him.'

For a fraction of a second the old man looked confused.

'I've done nothing of the sort,' he snarled. Do you think I'd spend my money to trace a rascal who – '

'Oh, you have,' she went on. 'I know you have. Why do you pretend to be such an awful old man?'

'Anyway, I think he's found out,' he complained. 'It takes away a great deal of the fortune which would have come to you. I don't suppose Gresham will want you now.'

She smiled. He rose from the table and went to the door.

'Tell that infernal villain – '

'Which one?'

'James,' he replied, 'that I'm not to be disturbed. I'm going to my study. I'm not to be disturbed by anyone for any reason; do you understand?'

If it was a busy morning for his lordship, it was no less so for Black and his friend, for it was Monday, and settling day, and in numerous clubs in London expectant bookmakers, in whose volumes the names of Black and Sir Isaac were freely inscribed, examined their watches with feelings that bordered upon apprehension.

But, to the surprise of everybody who knew the men, the settlements were made.

An accession of wealth had come to the 'firm'.

Sir Isaac Tramber spent that afternoon pleasantly. He was raised from the depths of despair to the heights of exaltation. His debts of honour were paid; he felt it was possible for him to look the world in the face. As a taxi drove him swiftly to Black's office, he was whistling gaily, and smiling at the politely veiled surprise of one of his suspicious bookmakers.

The big man was not at his office, and Sir Isaac, who had taken the precaution of instructing his driver to wait, re-directed him to the Chelsea flat.

Black was dressing for dinner when Sir Isaac arrived.

'Hullo!' he said, motioning him to a seat. 'You're the man I want. I've got a piece of information that will please you. You are the sort of chap who is scared by these Four Just Men. Well, you needn't be any more. I've found out all about them. It's cost me £200 to make the discovery, but it's worth every penny.'

He looked at a sheet of paper lying before him.

'Here is the list of their names. A curious collection, eh? You wouldn't suspect a Wesleyan of taking such steps as these chaps have taken. A bank manager in South London – Mr Charles Grimburd – you've heard of him: he's the art connoisseur, an unexpected person, eh? And Wilkinson Despard – he's the fellow I suspected most of all. I've been watching the papers very carefully. The *Post Herald*, the journal he writes for, has always been very well informed upon these outrages of the Four. They seem to know more about it than any other paper, and then, in addition, this man Despard has been writing pretty vigorously on social problems. He's got a place in Jermyn Street. I put a man on to straighten his servant, who had been betting. He had lost money. My man has been at him for a couple of weeks. There they are.' He tossed the sheet across. 'Less awe-inspiring than when they stick to their masks and their funny titles.'

Sir Isaac studied the list with interest.

'But there are only three here,' he said. 'Who is the fourth?'

'The fourth is the leader: can't you guess who it is? Gresham, of course.'

'Gresham?'

'I haven't any proof,' said Black; 'it's only surmise. But I would stake all I have in the world that I'm right. He is the very type of man to be in this – to organize it, to arrange the details.'

'Are you sure the fourth is Gresham?' asked Sir Isaac again.

'Pretty sure,' said Black. He had finished his dressing and was brushing his dress-coat carefully with a whisk brush.

'Where are you going?' asked Sir Isaac.

'I have a little business tonight,' replied the other. 'I don't think it would interest you very much.'

He stopped his brushing. For a moment he seemed deep in thought.

'On consideration,' he said slowly, 'perhaps it will interest you. Come along to the office with me. Have you dined?'

'No, not yet.'

'I'm sorry I can't dine you,' said Black. 'I have an important engagement after this which is taking all my attention at present. You're not dressed,' he continued. 'That's good. We're going to a place where people do not as a rule dress for dinner'

Over his own evening suit he drew a long overcoat, which he buttoned to the neck. He selected a soft felt hat from the wardrobe in the room and put it on before the looking-glass.

'Now, come along,' he said.

It was dusk, and the wind which howled through the deserted street justified the wrapping he had provided. He did not immediately call a cab, but walked until they came to Vauxhall Bridge Road. By this time Sir Isaac's patience and powers of pedestrianism were almost exhausted.

'Oh, Lord!' he said irritably, 'this is not the kind of job I like particularly.'

'Have a little patience,' said Black. 'You don't expect me to call cabs in Chelsea and give my directions for half a dozen people to hear. You don't seem to realize, Ikey, that you and I are being very closely watched.'

'Well, they could be watching us now,' said Sir Isaac with truth.

'They may be, but the chances are that nobody will be near enough when we give directions to the driver as to our exact destination.'

Even Sir Isaac did not catch it, so low was the voice of Black instructing the driver.

Through the little pane at the back of the cab Black scrutinized the vehicles following their route.

'I don't think there is anybody after us at present,' he said. 'It isn't a very important matter, but if the information came to the Four that their plans were being checkmated it might make it rather awkward for us.'

The cab passed down the winding road which leads from the Oval to Kennington Green. It threaded a way through the traffic and struck the Camberwell Road. Half-way down, Black put out his head, and the cab turned sharply to the left. Then he tapped at the window and it stopped.

He got out, followed by Sir Isaac.

'Just wait for me at the end of the street,' he said to the driver.

He handed the man some money as a guarantee of his *bona fides*, and the two moved off. The street was one of very poor artisan houses, and Black had recourse to an electric lamp which he carried in his pocket to discover the number he wanted. At last he came to a small house with a tiny patch of garden in front and knocked.

A little girl opened the door.

'Is Mr Farmer in?' said Black.

'Yes, sir,' said the little girl, 'will you go up?'

She led the way up the carpeted stairs and knocked at a small door on the left. A voice bade them come in. The two men entered. Seated by the table in a poorly-furnished room, lit only by the fire, was a man. He rose as they entered.

'I must explain,' said Black, 'that Mr Farmer has rented this room for a couple of weeks. He only comes here occasionally to meet his friends. This,' he went on, motioning to Sir Isaac, 'is a great friend of mine.'

He closed the door, and waited till the little girl's footsteps on the stairs had died away.

'The advantage of meeting in this kind of house,' said the man called Farmer, 'is that the slightest movement shakes the edifice from roof to basement.'

He spoke with what might be described as a 'mock-culture' voice. It was the voice of a common man who had been much in the company of gentlemen, and who endeavoured to imitate their intonation without attempting to acquire their vocabulary.

'You can speak freely, Mr Farmer,' said Black. 'This gentleman is in my confidence. We are both interested in this ridiculous organization. I understand you have now left Mr Wilkinson Despard's employment?'

The man nodded.

'Yes, sir,' he said, with a little embarrassed cough. 'I left him yesterday.'

'Now, have you found out who the fourth is?'

The man hesitated.

'I am not sure, sir. It is only fair to tell you that I am not absolutely certain. But I think you could gamble on the fact that the fourth gentleman is Mr Horace Gresham.'

'You didn't say that,' said Black, 'until I suggested the name myself.'

The man did not flinch at the suspicion involved in the comment. His voice was even as he replied: 'That I admit, sir. But the other three gentlemen I knew. I had nothing to do with the fourth. He used to come to Mr Despard's late at night, and I admitted him. I never saw his face and never heard his voice. He went straight to Mr Despard's study, and if you knew how the house was portioned out you would realize that it was next to impossible to hear anything!'

'How did you come to know that these men were the Four?' asked Black.

'Well, sir,' said the other, obviously ill at ease, 'by the way servants generally find things out – I listened.'

'And yet you never found out who the leader was?'

'No, sir.'

'Have you discovered anything else of which I am not aware?'

'Yes, sir,' said the man eagerly. I discovered before I left Mr Despard's employ that they've got you set. That's an old army term which means that they've marked you down for punishment.'

'Oh, they have, have they?' said Black.

'I overheard that last night. You see, the meeting generally consisted of four. The fourth very seldom turned up unless there was something to do. But he was always the leading spirit. It was he who found the money when money was necessary. It was he who directed the Four to their various occupations. And it was he who invariably chose the people who had to be punished. He has chosen you, I know, sir. They had a meeting, the night before last. They were discussing various people, and I heard your name.'

'How could you hear?'

'I was in the next room, sir. There's a dressing-room leading out of Mr Despard's room, where these conferences were held. I had a duplicate key.'

Black rose as if to go.

'It almost seems a pity you have left that Johnnie. Did they ever speak about me?' asked Sir Isaac, who had been an attentive listener.

'I don't know your name, sir,' said the servant deferentially.

'No, and you jolly well won't,' answered the baronet promptly.

'I hope, gentlemen,' said the man, 'that now I have lost my employment you'll do whatever you can to find me another place. If either of you gentlemen want a reliable man-servant – '

He looked inquiringly at Sir Isaac, as being the more likely of the two.

'Not me,' said the other brutally. 'I find all my work cut out to keep my own secrets, without having any dam' eavesdropping man on the premises to spy on me.'

The man against whom this was directed did not seem particularly hurt by the bluntness of the other. He merely bowed his head and made no reply.

Black took a flat case from his inside pocket, opened it and extracted two notes.

'Here are twenty pounds,' he said, 'which makes £220 you have had from me. Now, if you can find out anything else worth knowing I don't mind making it up to £300 – but it has got to be something good. Keep in with the servants. You know the rest of them. Is there any reason why you shouldn't go back to the flat?'

'No, sir,' said the man. 'I was merely discharged for carelessness.'

'Very good,' said Black. 'You know my address and where to find me. If anything turns up let me know.'

'Yes, sir.'

'By the way,' said Black, as he made a move to go, 'do the Four contemplate taking any action in the immediate future?'

'No, sir,' said the man eagerly. 'I am particularly sure of that. I heard them discussing the advisability of parting. One gentleman wanted to go to the Continent for a month, and another wanted to go to America to see about his mining property. By the way, they all agreed there was no necessity to meet for a month. I gathered that for the time being they were doing nothing.'

'Excellent!' said Black.

He shook hands with the servant and departed.

'Pretty beastly sort of man to have about the house,' said Sir Isaac as they walked back to the cab.

'Yes,' said Black, good-humouredly, 'but it isn't my house, and I feel no scruples in the matter. I do not,' he added virtuously, 'approve of tapping servants for information about their masters and mistresses, but there are occasions when this line of conduct is perfectly justified.'

Chapter 14
Willie Jakobs tells

Left alone, the man whom they had called Farmer waited a few minutes. Then he took down his coat, which hung behind the door, put on his hat and gloves deliberately and thoughtfully, and left the house. He walked in the direction which Black and Sir Isaac had taken, but their taxi-cab was flying northward long before he reached the spot where it had waited.

He pursued his way into the Camberwell Road and boarded a tram-car. The street lamps and the lights in the shop windows revealed him to be a good-looking man, a little above the average height, with a pale refined face. He was dressed quietly, but well.

He alighted near the Elephant and Castle and strode rapidly along the New Kent Road, turning into one of the poorer streets which lead to a labyrinth of smaller and more poverty-stricken thoroughfares in that district which is bounded on the west by East Street and on the east by the New Kent Road. A little way along, some of the old houses had been pulled down and new buildings in yellow brick had been erected. A big red lamp outside a broad entrance notified the neigh-bourhood that this was the free dispensary, though none who lived within a radius of five miles needed any information as to the existence of this institution.

In the hall-way was a board containing the names of three doctors, and against them a little sliding panel, which enabled them to inform their visitors whether they were in or out. He paused before the board.

The little indicator against the first name said 'Out.'

Farmer put up his hand and slid the panel along to show the word 'In'. Then he passed through the door, through the large waiting-room into a small room, which bore the name 'Dr Wilson Graille'.

He closed the door behind him and slipped a catch. He took off his hat and coat and hung them up. Then he touched a bell, and a servant appeared.

'Is Dr O'Hara in?' he asked.

'Yes, doctor,' replied the man.

'Ask him to come along to me, will you, please?'

In a few minutes a man of middle height, but powerfully built, came in and closed the door behind him.

'Well, how did you get on,' he inquired, and, uninvited, drew up a chair to the table.

'They jumped at the bait,' said Gonsalez with a little laugh. 'I think they have got something on. They were most anxious to know whether we were moving at all. You had better notify Manfred. We'll have a meeting tonight. What about Despard? Do you think he would object to having his name used?'

His voice lacked the mock culture which had so deceived Black.

'Not a bit. I chose him purposely because I knew he was going abroad tonight.'

'And the others?'

'With the exception of the art man, they are non-existent.'

'Suppose he investigates?'

'Not he. He will be satisfied to take the most prominent of the four – Despard, and the other chap whose name I have forgotten. Despard leaves tonight, and the other on Wednesday for America. You see, that fits in with what I told Black.'

He took from his pocket the two ten-pound notes and laid them on the table. 'Twenty pounds,' he said, and handed them to the other man. 'You ought to be able to do something with that.'

The other stuffed them into his waistcoat pocket.

'I shall send those two Brady children to the seaside,' he said. 'It probably won't save their lives, but it will give the little devils some conception of what joy life holds – for a month or so.'

The same thought seemed to occur to both, and they laughed.

'Black would not like to know to what base use his good money is being put,' said Graille, or Farmer, or Gonsalez – call him what you will – with a twinkle in his blue eyes.

'Were they anxious to know who was the fourth man?' asked Poiccart.

'Most keen on it,' he said. 'But I wondered if they would have believed me if I had confessed myself to be one of the four, and had I at the same time confessed that I was as much in the dark as to the identity of the fourth as they themselves.'

Poiccart rose and stood irresolutely, with his hands stuffed into his trousers pockets, looking into the fire.

'I often wonder,' he said, 'who it is. Don't you?'

'I've got over those sensations of curiosity,' said Gonsalez. 'Whoever he is, I am of course satisfied that he is a large-hearted man, working with a singleness of purpose.'

The other nodded in agreement.

'I am sure,' said Graille enthusiastically, 'that he has done great work, justifiable work, and honourable work.'

Poiccart nodded gravely.

'By the way,' said the other, 'I went to old Lord Verlond – you remember, No. 4 suggested our trying him. He's a pretty bitter sort of person with a sharp tongue.'

Poiccart smiled. 'What did he do? Tell you to go to the devil?'

'Something of the sort,' said Dr Gonsalez. 'I only got a grudging half-guinea from him, and he regaled me all the time with more than half a guinea's worth of amusement.'

'But it wasn't for this work,' said the other.

Gonsalez shook his head. 'No, for another department,' he said with a smile.

They had little more time for conversation. Patients began to come in, and within a quarter of an hour the two men were as busy as men could be attending to the injuries, the diseases and the complaints of the people of this overcrowded neighbourhood.

This great dispensary owed its erection and its continuance to the munificence of three doctors who appeared from nowhere. Who the man was who had contributed £5,000 to the upkeep, and who had afterwards appeared in person, masked and cloaked, and had propounded to three earnest workers for humanity his desire to be included in the organization, nobody knew, unless it was Manfred. It was Manfred the wise who accepted not only the offer, but the *bona fides* of the stranger – Manfred who accepted him as a co-partner.

Casual observers described the three earnest medicos not only as cranks, but fanatics. They were attached to no organization; they gave no sign to the world that they could be in any way associated with any of the religious organizations engaged in medical work. It is an indisputable fact that they possessed the qualifications to practise, and that one – Leon Gonsalez – was in addition a brilliant chemist.

No man ever remembered their going to church, or urging attendance at any place of worship. The religious bodies that laboured in the neighbourhood were themselves astonished.

One by one they had nibbled at the sectarian question. Some had asked directly to what religious organization these men were attached. No answer was offered satisfactory to the inquirers.

It was nearly eleven o'clock that night when the work of the two dispensers had finished. The last patient had been dismissed, the last fretful whimper of an ailing child had died away; the door had been locked, the sweepers were engaged in cleaning up the big waiting-room.

The two men sat in the office – tired, but cheerful. The room was well furnished; it was the common room of the three. A bright fire burnt in the fire-place, big roomy armchairs and settees were in evidence. The floor was carpeted thickly, and two or three rare prints hung on the distempered walls.

They were sitting discussing the events of the evening – comparing notes, retailing particulars of interest in cases which had come under their notice. Manfred had gone out earlier in the evening and had not returned.

Then a bell rang shrilly. Leon looked up at the indicator.

'That is the dispensary door,' he said in Spanish. I suppose we'd better see who it is.'

'It will be a small girl,' said Poiccart. ' "Please will you come to father; he's either dead or drunk." '

There was a little laugh at this reminiscence of an incident which had actually happened.

Poiccart opened the door. A man stood in the entrance.

'There's a bad accident just round the corner,' he said. 'Can I bring him in here, doctor?'

'What sort of an accident?' said Poiccart.

'A man has been knifed.'

'Bring him in,' said Poiccart.

He went quickly to the common room. 'It's a stabbing case,' he said. 'Will you have him in your surgery, Leon?'

The young man rose swiftly. 'Yes,' he said; 'I'll get the table ready.'

In a few minutes half a dozen men bore in the unconscious form of the victim. It was a face familiar to the two. They laid him tenderly upon the surgical table, and with deft hands ripped away the clothing from the wound, whilst the policeman who had accompanied the party pushed back the crowd from the surgery door.

The two men were alone with the unconscious man.

They exchanged glances.

'Unless I am mistaken' said Gonsalez carefully, 'this is the late Mr Willie Jakobs.'

*   *   *

That evening May Sandford sat alone in her room reading. Her father, when he had come in to say goodbye to May before going to a directors' dinner, had left her ostensibly studying an improving book, but the volume now lay unheeded at her side.

That afternoon she had received an urgent note from Black, asking her to meet him 'on a matter of the greatest importance'. It concerned her father, and it was very secret. She was alarmed, and not a little puzzled. The urgency and the secrecy of the note distressed her unaccountably.

For the twentieth time she began to read the improving plays of Monsieur Molière, when a knock at the door made her hastily conceal the paper.

'There is a man who wishes to see you,' said the girl who had entered in response to her 'Come in'.

'What sort of man?'

'A common-looking man,' said the maid.

She hesitated. The butler was in the house, otherwise she would not have seen the visitor.

'Show him into father's study,' she said. 'Tell Thomas this man is here and ask him to be handy in case I ring for him.'

She had never seen the man whom she found waiting. Instinctively she distrusted his face, though there was something about him which compelled her sympathy. He was white and haggard, black shadows encircled his eyes, and his hands, by no means clean, shook.

'I am sorry to bother you, miss,' he said, 'but this is important.'

'It is rather a late hour,' she said. 'What is it you want?'

He fumbled with his hat and looked at the waiting girl. At a nod from May she left the room.

'This is rather important to you, miss,' said the man again. 'Black treated me pretty badly.'

For a moment an unworthy suspicion flashed through her mind. Had Frank sent his man to her to shake her faith in Black? A feeling of resentment arose against her visitor and the man she thought was his employer.

'You may save your breath,' she said coolly, 'and you can go back to the gentleman who sent you and tell him – '

'Nobody sent me, miss,' he said eagerly. 'I come on my own. I tell you they've done me a bad turn. I've kept my mouth shut for Black for years, and now he's turned me down. I'm ill, miss, you can see that for yourself,' he said, throwing out his arms in despair. 'I've been almost starving and they haven't given me a bean. I went to Black's house today and he wouldn't see me.'

He almost whimpered in his helpless anger.

'He's done me a bad turn and I'm going to do him one,' he said fiercely. 'You know what his game is?'

'I do not want to know,' she said again, the old suspicion obscuring her vision. 'You will gain nothing by speaking against Colonel Black.'

'Don't be foolish, miss,' he pleaded, 'don't think I've come for money. I don't expect money – I don't want it. I dare say I can get help from Mr Fellowe.'

'Ah!' she said, 'so you know Mr Fellowe: it was he who sent you. I will not hear another word,' she went on hotly. 'I know now where you come from – I've heard all this before.'

She walked determinedly across the room and rang the bell. The butler came in.

'Show this man out,' said May.

The man looked at her sorrowfully. 'You've had your chance, miss,' he said ominously. 'Black's Essley, that's all!'

With this parting shot he shuffled through the hall, down the steps into the night.

Left alone, the girl shrank into her chair. She was shaking from head to foot with indignation and bewilderment. It must have been Frank who sent this man. How mean, how inexpressibly mean!

'How dare he? How dare he?' she asked.

It was the policeman in Frank which made him so horrid, she thought. He always believed horrid things of everybody. It was only natural. He had lived his life amongst criminals; he had thought of nothing but breaches of the law. She looked at the clock: it was a quarter to ten. He had wasted her evening, this visitor. She did not know exactly what to do. She could not read; it was too early to go to bed. She would have liked to have gone for a little walk, but there was nobody to take her. It was absurd asking the butler to walk behind her; she smiled at the thought.

Then she started. She had heard the distant ring of the front-door bell. Who could it be?

She had not long to wait in doubt. A few minutes afterwards the girl had announced Colonel Black. He was in evening dress and very cheerful.

'Forgive this visit,' he said, with that heartiness of voice which carried conviction of his sincerity. 'I happened to be passing and I thought I'd drop in.'

This was not exactly true. Black had carefully planned this call. He knew her father was out; knew also, so bitter had been a discussion of that afternoon, that he would not have sanctioned the visit.

May gave him her hand, and he grasped it warmly.

She came straight to the point. 'I'm so glad you've come,' she said. 'I've been awfully bothered.'

He nodded sympathetically, though a little at sea.

'And now this man has come.'

'This man – which man?' he asked sharply.

'I forget his name – he came this evening. In fact, he's only been gone a little time. And he looked awfully ill. You know him, I think?'

'Not Jakobs?' he breathed.

She nodded. 'I think that is the name,' she said.

'Jakobs?' he repeated, and his face went a little white. 'What did he say?' he asked quickly.

She repeated the conversation as nearly as she could remember it. When she had finished he rose.

'You're not going?' she said in astonishment.

'I'm afraid I must,' he said. 'I've a rather important engagement and – er – I only called in passing. Which way did this man go? Did he give you any idea as to his destination?'

She shook her head.

'No. All he said was that there were people who would be glad of the information he could give about you.'

'He did, did he?' said Black, with an heroic attempt at a smile. 'I never thought Jakobs was that kind of man. Of course, there is nothing that I should mind everybody knowing, but one has business secrets, you know. Miss Sandford. He is a discharged employee of mine who has stolen some contracts. You need not worry about the matter.'

He smiled confidently at her as he left the room.

He drove straight from the house to his city office. The place was in darkness, but he knew his way without the necessity of lighting up. He ran upstairs into the boardroom.

There was a little door in one corner of the room, concealed from view by a hanging curtain.

He closed the shutters and pulled down the blinds before he switched on the light. He pushed the curtain aside and examined the face of the door. There was no sign that it had been forced. Jakobs knew of the existence of this little retiring-room, and had, in his indiscretion, mentioned its existence in one of his letters of demand.

Black drew from his pocket a small bunch of keys attached to a silver chain. The door of the room opened easily. There was a smaller room disclosed – no larger than a big cupboard. A single incandescent electric burner slung from the ceiling supplied all the light necessary. There was a dressing-table, a chair, a big looking-glass, and a number of hooks from which were suspended a dozen articles of attire. Air was admitted through two ventilators let into the wall and communicating with the main ventilating shaft of the building.

He opened the door of the dressing-table and drew out a number of wigs. They were wigs such as only Fasieur can supply – perfectly modelled and all of one shade of hair, though differently arranged.

He tossed them on to the table impatiently, groping for something which he knew should be there, and was there unless a thief skilled in the use of skeleton keys, and having, moreover, some knowledge of the office, had taken it. He stopped his search suddenly and examined a pad of paper which lay on the table.

It was a pad which he kept handy for note-taking – to jot down memoranda. On the white face of the paper was a large brown thumb-mark, and though Colonel Black knew little of the science of anthropology, he was sufficiently well acquainted with the sign to know that it was the mark of a thumb which ought never to have been in this secret office of his.

Then it was Willie! Willie Jakobs, the befriended, the pensioned, and the scorned, who had removed a certain green bottle, the duplicate of which was in his pocket at that moment.

Black did not lose his nerve. He went to a drawer in the desk of his outer office and took out a Browning pistol. It was loaded. He balanced it in his right hand, looked at it reflectively, then put it back again. He hated firearms; they made a great deal of unnecessary noise, and they left behind them too sure an indication of the identity of their user. Men have been traced by bullets.

There were other ways. He lifted from the drawer a long thin knife. It was an Italian stiletto of the sixteenth century – the sort of toy a man might use in these prosaic days for opening his letters. And indeed this was the ostensible reason why Black kept the weapon at hand.

He drew it from its ornate leather sheath and tested its temper, felt its edge and gingerly fingered its point; then he put the stiletto in its case in his overcoat pocket, switched out the light and went out. This was not a case which demanded the employment of the little bottle. There was too little of the precious stuff left, and he had need of it for other purposes.

There were two or three places where he might find the man. A little public-house off Regent Street was one. He drove there, stopping the cab a few paces from the spot. He strode into the bar, where men of Jakobs's kind were to be found, but it was empty. The man he sought was not there.

He made a tour of other likely places with no better success. Willie would be at home. He had moved to lodgings on the south side of the Thames.

It was coming from a little public-house off the New Kent Road that Black found his man. Willie had been spending the evening brooding over his grievance, and was on his way home to prepare for his big adventure when Black clapped him on the shoulder.

'Hullo, Willie,' he said.

The man turned round with a start.

'Keep your hands off me,' he said hastily, stumbling against the wall.

'Now, don't be silly,' said Black. 'Let's talk this matter out reasonably. You're a reasonable man, aren't you? I've got a cab waiting round the corner.'

'You don't get me into no cabs,' said Jakobs. 'I've had enough of you, Black. You've turned round on me. You cast me out like a dog. Is that the way to treat a pal?'

'You've made a mistake, my friend,' said Black smoothly. 'We're all liable to make mistakes. I've made many, and I dare say you've made a few. Now, let's talk business.'

Willie said nothing. He was still suspicious. Once he thought he saw the other's hand steal to his breast-pocket. He guessed the motive of the action. This, then, was where the bottle was.

Black was an adept in the art of cajolery. He knew the weak places of all the men who had been associated with him. Very slowly he led the other aimlessly, so it seemed, from one street to another until they reached a little cul-de-sac. Stables occupied one side of the tiny street and artisan houses the other. One street-lamp half-way down showed a dim light.

Willie hesitated. 'There's no thoroughfare,' he said.

'Oh yes, there is,' said Black confidently. 'I know this neighbourhood rather well. Now, there's one thing I want to ask you, Willie. I'm sure you are feeling more friendly towards me now, aren't you?'

His hand rested almost affectionately on the other's shoulder.

'You didn't play the game,' persisted the other.

'Let bygones be bygones,' said Black. 'What I want to know is, Willie, why did you take the bottle?'

He asked the question in a matter-of-fact tone. He did not raise his voice or give the query unusual emphasis.

The other man was taken off his guard. 'Well, I felt sore,' he said.

'And I suppose,' said Black, with gentle reproach, 'you're waiting to hand that bottle to our friend Fellowe?'

'I haven't handed it to anybody yet,' said Willie, 'but to tell you the truth – '

He said no more. The big man's hand suddenly closed round his throat with a grip like steel. Willie struggled, but he was like a child in the grasp of the other.

'You dog,' breathed Black.

He shook the helpless man violently. Then with his disengaged hand he whipped the tell-tale phial from the other's pocket and pushed him against the wall.

'And I'll teach you that that's nothing to what you'll get if you ever come across me again.'

Jakobs dropped, white and ghastly, against the wall. 'You've got the bottle, Black,' he said, 'but I know everything that you've done with it.'

'You do, do you?'

'Yes, everything,' said the other desperately. 'You're not going to cast me off, do you hear? You've got to pension me, same as you've done other people. I know enough to send you for a lagging without – '

'I thought you did,' said Black.

Something glittered in the light of the lamp, and without a cry Jakobs went down in a huddled heap to the ground.

Black looked round. He wiped the blade of the stiletto carefully on the coat of the stricken man, carefully replaced the weapon in its leather case, and examined his own hands with considerable care for any signs of blood. But these Italian weapons make small wounds.

He turned and, pulling on his gloves, made his way back to where the cab was still waiting.

Chapter 15

Sir Isaac's fears

Under the bright light of a bronze lamp, all that was mortal of Jakobs lay extended upon the operating-table. About the body moved swiftly the shirt-sleeved figures of the doctors.

'I don't think there is much we can do for him,' said Gonsalez. 'He's had an arterial perforation. It seems to me that he's bleeding internally.'

They had made a superficial examination of the wound, and Poiccart had taken so serious a view of the man's condition that he had dispatched a messenger for a magistrate.

Willie was conscious during the examination, but he was too weak and too exhausted to give any account of what had happened.

'There's just a chance,' said Gonsalez, if we could get a J.P. up in time, that we could give him sufficient strychnine to enable him to tell us who had done this.'

'It's murder, I think,' said Gonsalez, 'the cut's a clean one. Look, there's hardly half an inch of wound. The man who did this used a stiletto, I should say, and used it pretty scientifically. It's a wonder he wasn't killed on the spot.'

The hastily-summoned justice of the peace appeared on the scene much sooner than they had anticipated. Gonsalez explained the condition of the man.

'He tried to tell me, after we had got him on the table, who had done it,' he said, 'but I couldn't catch the name.'

'Do you know him?' asked the J.P.

'I know him,' he said, 'and I've rather an idea as to who has done it, but I can't give any reasons for my suspicions.'

Jakobs was unconscious, and Gonsalez seized the first opportunity that presented itself of consulting with his colleague.

'I believe this is Black's work,' he said hurriedly. 'Why not send for him? We know Jakobs has been in his employ and was pensioned by him, and that's sufficient excuse. Possibly, if we can get him down before this poor chap dies, we shall learn something.'

'I'll get on the telephone,' said the other.

He drew from his pocket a memorandum book and consulted its pages. Black's movements and his resorts were fairly well tabulated, but the telephone failed to connect the man they wanted.

At a quarter to two in the morning Jakobs died, without having regained consciousness, and it looked as though yet another mystery had been added to a list which was already appallingly large.

The news came to May Sandford that afternoon. The tragedy had occurred too late that night to secure descriptions in the morning papers; but from the earlier editions of the afternoon journals she read with a shock of the man's terrible fate.

It was only by accident that she learnt of it from this source, for she was still reading of his death in the paper when Black, ostentatiously agitated, called upon her. 'Isn't it dreadful, Miss Sandford?' he said.

He was quite beside himself with grief, the girl thought.

'I shall give evidence, of course, but I shall take great care to keep your name out of it. I think the poor man had very bad associates indeed,' he said frankly. 'I had to discharge him for that reason. Nobody need know he ever came here,' he suggested. 'It wouldn't be pleasant for you to be dragged into a sordid case like this.'

'Oh, no, no,' she said. 'I don't want to be mixed up in it at all. I'm awfully sorry, but I can't see how my evidence would help.'

'Of course,' agreed Black. It had only occurred to him that morning how damning might be the evidence that this girl was in a position to give, and he had come to her in a panic lest she had already volunteered it.

She thought he looked ill and worried, as indeed he was, for Black had slept very little that night. He knew that he was safe from detection. None had seen him meet the man, and although he had visited the resorts which the man frequented, he had not inquired after him.

Yet Black was obsessed by the knowledge that a net was drawing round him. Who were the hunters he could not guess. There came to him at odd moments a strange feeling of terror.

Nothing was going exactly right with him. Sir Isaac had showed signs of revolt.

Before the day was out he found that he had quite enough to bother him without the terrors which the unknown held. The police had made most strenuous inquiries regarding his whereabouts on the night of the murder. They had even come to him and questioned him with such persistence that he suspected a directing force behind them. He had not bothered overmuch with the Four Just Men. He had accepted the word of his informant that the Four had separated for the time being, and the fact that Wilkinson Despard had left for America confirmed all that the man had told him.

He was getting short of money again. The settlement of his bets had left him short. Sandford must be 'persuaded'. Every day it was getting more and more of a necessity.

One morning Sir Isaac had telephoned him asking him to meet him in the park.

'Why not come here?' asked Black.

'No,' said the baronet's voice. 'I'd rather meet you in the park.'

He named the spot, and at the hour Black met him, a little annoyed that his day's programme should be interrupted by this eccentricity on the part of Sir Isaac Tramber.

The baronet himself did not at once come to the point. He talked around, hummed and hawed, and at last blurted out the truth.

'Look here, Black,' he said, 'you and I have been good pals – we've been together in some queer adventures, but now I am going to – I want – '

He stammered and spluttered.

'What do you want?' asked Black with a frown.

'Well, to tell the truth,' said Sir Isaac, with a pathetic attempt to be firm, 'I think it is about time that you and I dissolved partnership.'

'What do you mean?' asked Black.

'Well, you know, I'm getting talked about,' said the other disjointedly. 'People are spreading lies about me, and one or two chaps recently have asked me what business you and I are engaged in, and – it's worrying me, Black.' he said with the sudden exasperation of a weak man. 'I believe I have lost my chance with Verlond because of my association with you.'

'I see,' said Black. It was a favourite expression of his. It meant much; it meant more than usual now.

'I understand,' he said, 'that you think the ship is sinking, and, rat-like, you imagine it is time to swim to the shore.'

'Don't be silly, dear old fellow,' protested the other, 'and don't be unreasonable. You see how it is. When I joined you, you were goin' to do big things – big amalgamations, big trusts, stuffin' an' all that sort of thing. Of course,' he admitted apologetically, 'I knew all about the bucket-shop, but that was a side-line.'

Black smiled grimly. 'A pretty profitable side-line for you,' he said dryly.

'I know, I know,' said Ikey, patient to an offensive degree, 'but it wasn't a matter of millions an' all that, now was it?'

Black was thoughtful, biting his nails and looking down at the grass at his feet.

'People are talkin', dear old fellow,' Tramber went on, 'sayin' the most awful rotten things. You've been promisin' this combination with Sandford's foundries, you've practically issued shares in Amalgamated Foundries of Europe without havin' the goods.'

'Sandford won't come in,' said Black, without looking up, 'unless I pay him a quarter of a million cash – he'll take the rest in shares. I want him to take his price in shares.'

'He's no mug,' said the baronet coarsely. 'Old Sandford isn't a mug – and I'll bet he's got Verlond behind him. He's no mug either.'

There was a long and awkward silence – awkward for Sir Isaac, who had an unaccountable desire to bolt.

'So you want to sneak out of it, do you?' said Black, meeting his eyes with a cold smile.

'Now, my dear old chap,' said Sir Isaac hastily, 'don't take that uncharitable view.

Partnerships are always being dissolved, it's what they're for,' he said with an attempt at humour. 'And I must confess I don't like some of your schemes.'

'You don't like!' Black turned round on him with a savage oath. 'Do you like the money you've got for it? The money paid in advance for touting new clients? The money given to you to settle your debts at the club? You've got to go through with it, Ikey, and if you don't, I'll tell the whole truth to Verlond and to every pal you've got.'

'They wouldn't believe you,' said Sir Isaac calmly. 'You see, my dear chap, you've got such an awful reputation, and the worst of having a bad reputation is that no one believes you. If it came to a question of believing you or believing me, who do you think Society would believe – a man of some position, one in the baronetage of Great Britain, or a man – well, not to put too fine a point on it – like you?'

Black looked at him long and steadily.

'Whatever view you take,' he said slowly, 'you've got to stand your corner. If, as a result of any of the business we are now engaged in, I am arrested, I shall give information to the police concerning you. We are both in the same boat – we sink or swim together.'

He noticed the slow-spreading alarm on Sir Isaac's face.

'Look here,' he said, 'I'll arrange to pay you back that money I've got. I'll give you bills – '

Black laughed. 'You're an amusing devil,' he said. 'You and your bills! I can write bills myself, can't I? I'd as soon take a crossing-sweeper's bills as yours. Why, there's enough of your paper in London to feed Sandford's furnaces for a week.'

The words suggested a thought. 'Let's say no more about this matter till after the amalgamation. It's coming off next week. It may make all the difference in our fortune, Ikey,' he said in gentler tones. 'Just drop the idea of ratting.'

'I'm not ratting,' protested the other. 'I'm merely – '

'I know,' said Black. 'You're merely taking precautions – well, that's all the rats do. You're in this up to your neck – don't deceive yourself. You can't get out of it until I say "Go".'

'It will be awkward for me if the game is exposed,' said Sir Isaac, biting his nails. 'It will be jolly unpleasant if it is discovered I am standing in with you.'

'It will be more awkward for you,' answered Black ominously, 'if, at the psychological moment, you are *not* standing in with me.'

* * *

Theodore Sandford, a busy man, thrust his untidy grey head into the door of his daughter's sitting-room.

'May,' said he, 'don't forget that I am giving a dinner tonight in your honour – for unless my memory is at fault and the cheque you found on your breakfast-tray was missupplied, you are twenty-two today.'

She blew him a kiss.

'Who is coming?' she asked. 'I ought really to have invited everybody myself.'

'Can't stop to tell you,' said her father with a smile. 'I'm sorry you quarrelled with young Fellowe. I should like to have asked him.'

She smiled gaily. 'I shall have to get another policeman,' she said.

He looked at her for a long time. 'Fellowe isn't an ordinary policeman,' he said quietly. 'Do you know that I saw him dining with the Home Secretary the other day?'

Her eyebrows rose.

'In uniform?' she asked.

He laughed.

'No, you goose,' he chuckled, 'in his dressing-gown.'

She followed him down the corridor. 'You've learnt that from Lord Verlond,' she said reproachfully.

She waited till the car had carried her father from view, then walked back to her room, happy with the happiness which anticipates happiness.

The night before had been a miserable one till, acting on an impulse, she had humbled herself, and found strange joy in the humiliation.

The knowledge that this young man was still her ideal, all she would have him to be, had so absorbed her that for the time being she was oblivious of all else.

She recalled with a little start the occasion of their last meeting, and how they had parted.

The recollection made her supremely miserable again, and, jumping up from her stool, she had opened her little writing-bureau and scribbled a hurried, penitent, autocratic little note, ordering and imploring him to come to her the instant he received it.

Frank came promptly. The maid announced his arrival within ten minutes of Mr Sandford's departure.

May ran lightly downstairs and was seized with a sudden fit of shyness as she reached the library door. She would have paused, but the maid, who was following her, regarded her with so much sympathetic interest that she was obliged to assume a nonchalance that she was far from feeling and enter the room.

Frank was standing with his back to the door, but he turned quickly on hearing the light rustle of her gown.

May closed the door, but she made no effort to move away from it.

'How do you do?' she began.

The effort she was making to still the wild beating of her heart made her voice sound cold and formal.

'I am very well, thank you.' Frank's tone reflected her own.

'I – I wanted to see you,' she continued, with an effort to appear natural.

'So I gathered from your note,' he replied.

'It was good of you to come,' she went on conventionally. 'I hope it has not inconvenienced you at all.'

'Not at all.' Again Frank's voice was an expressive echo. 'I was just on the point of going out, so came at once.'

'Oh, I am sorry – won't you keep your other appointment first? Any time will suit me; it – it is nothing important.'

'Well, I hadn't an appointment exactly.' It was the young man's turn to hesitate. 'To tell the truth, I was coming here.'

'Oh, Frank! Were you really?'

'Yes, really and truly, little girl.' May did not answer, but something Frank saw in her face spoke more plainly than words could do.

Mr Sandford returned that afternoon to find two happy people sitting in the half-darkness of the drawing-room; and ten members of the Criminal Investigation Department waited at Scotland Yard, alternately swearing and wringing their hands.

Chapter 16

Colonel Black meets a just man

Dr Essley's house at Forest Hill stood untenanted. The red lamp before the door was unlit, and though the meagre furnishings had not been removed, the house, with its drawn blinds and grimy steps, had the desolate appearance of emptiness.

The whisper of a rumour had agitated the domestic circles of that respectable suburb – a startling rumour which, if it were true, might well cause Forest Hill to gasp in righteous indignation.

'Dr' Essley was an unauthorized practitioner, a fraud of the worst description, for he had taken the name and the style of a dead man.

'All I know,' explained Colonel Black, whom a reporter discovered at his office, 'is that I met Dr Essley in Australia, and that I was impressed by his skill. I might say,' he added in a burst of frankness, 'that I am in a sense responsible for his position in England, for I not only advanced him money to buy his practice, but I recommended him to all my friends, and naturally I am upset by the revelation.'

No, he had no idea as to the 'doctor's' present location. He had last seen him a month before, when the 'doctor' spoke of going to the Continent.

Colonel Black had as much to tell – and no more – to the detectives who came from Scotland Yard. They came with annoying persistence and never seemed tired of coming. They waited for him on the doorstep and in his office. They waited for him in the vestibules of the theatres, at the entrance doors of banks. They came as frequently as emissaries of houses to whom Colonel Black was under monetary obligation.

A week after the events chronicled in the last chapter. Colonel Black sat alone in his flat with a light heart. He had collected together a very considerable amount of money. That it was money to which he had no legal right did not disturb the smooth current of his thoughts. It was sufficient that it was money, and that a motor-car which might carry him swiftly to Folkestone was within telephone-call day and night. Moreover, he was alive.

The vengeance of an organization vowed against Dr Essley had passed over the head of Colonel Black – he might be excused if he thought that the matter of a grey wig and a pair of shaggy eyebrows, added to some knowledge of medicine, had deceived the astute men who had come to England to track him down.

This infernal man Fellowe, who appeared and disappeared as if by magic, puzzled him – almost alarmed him.

Fellowe was not one of the Four Just Men – instinct told him that much. Fellowe was an official.

A Sergeant Gurden who had been extremely useful to Black had been suddenly transferred to a remote division, and nobody knew why. With him had disappeared from his familiar beats a young police-constable who had been seen dining with Cabinet Ministers.

It was very evident that there was cause for perturbation – yet, singularly enough, Colonel Black was cheerful; but there was a malignant quality to his cheerfulness. He busied himself with the destruction of such of his papers – and they were few – which he had kept by him.

He turned out an old pocket-book and frowned when he saw its contents. It was a *wagon-lit* coupon for the journey from Paris to Madrid, and was made out in the name of Dr Essley – a mad slip which might have led to serious consequences, he told himself. He burnt the incriminating sheet and crumbled the ashes before he threw them into the fire-place.

It was dark before he had finished his preparations, but he made no attempt to light the room. His dress-suit was laid out in an adjoining room, his trunks stood packed.

He looked at his watch. In half an hour he would be on his way to the Sandfords. Here was another risk which none but a madman would take – so he told himself, but he contemplated the outcome of his visit with equanimity.

He went into his bedroom and began his preparations, then remembered that he had left a bundle of notes on his writing-table, and went back. He found the notes and was returning when there was a click, and the room was flooded with light.

He whipped round with an oath, dropping his hand to his hippocket.

'Don't move, please,' quietly.

'You!' gasped Black.

The tall man with the little pointed beard nodded.

'Keep your hand away from your pocket, colonel,' he said; 'there is no immediate danger.'

He was unarmed. The thin cigar between his white teeth testified his serenity.

'De la Monte!' stammered Black.

Again the bearded man nodded. 'The last time we met was in Cordova,' he said, 'but you have changed since then.'

Black forced a smile.

'You are confusing me with Dr Essley,' he said.

'I am confusing you with Dr Essley,' agreed the other. 'Yet I think I am justified in my confusion.'

He did not remove his cigar, seemed perfectly at ease, even going so far as to cast an eye upon a chair, inviting invitation.

'Essley or Black,' he said steadily, 'your day is already dusk, and the night is very near.'

A cold wave of terror swept over the colonel. He tried to speak, but his throat and his mouth were dry, and he could only make inarticulate noises. 'Tonight – now?' he croaked – his shaking hands went up to his mouth. Yet he was armed and the man before him bore no weapon. A quick movement of his hand and he would lay the spectre which had at one time terrorized Europe. He did not doubt that he was face to face with one of the dreaded Four, and he found himself endeavouring to memorize the face of the man before him for future use. Yet he did not touch the pistol which lay snug in his hip-pocket. He was hypnotized, paralysed by the cool confidence of the other. All that he knew was that he wanted the relief which could only come if this calm man were to go. He felt horribly trapped, saw no way of escape in the presence of this force.

The other divined what was going on in Black's mind.

'I have only one piece of advice to offer you,' he said, 'and that is this – keep away from the Sandfords' dinner.'

'Why – why?' stammered Black.

The other walked to the fire-place and flicked the ash of his cigar into the grate.

'Because,' he said, without turning round, 'at the Sandford dinner you come within the jurisdiction of the Four Just Men – who, as you may know, are a protecting force. Elsewhere – '

'Yes – elsewhere?'

'You come within the jurisdiction of the law, Colonel Black, for at this present moment an energetic young Assistant-Commissioner of Police is applying for a warrant for your arrest on the charge of murder.'

With a little nod, Manfred turned his back and walked leisurely towards the door.

'Stop!' The words were hissed. Black, revolver in hand, was livid with rage and fear.

Manfred laughed quietly. He did not check his walk, but looked backward over his shoulder.

'Let the cobbler stick to his last,' he quoted. 'Poison, my dear colonel, is your last – or the knife in the case of Jakobs. An explosion, even of a Webley revolver, would shatter your nerves.'

He opened the door and walked out, closing it carefully behind him.

Black sank into the nearest chair, his mouth working, the perspiration streaming down his face.

This was the end. He was a spent force. He crossed the room to the telephone and gave a number. After a little while he got an answer.

Yes, the car was in readiness; there had been no inquiries. He hung up the telephone and called up six depots where cars could be hired. To each he gave the same instructions. Two cars were to be waiting – he changed the locality with each order. Two fast cars, each able to cover the eighty miles to Dover without fear of a breakdown.

'I shall take one,' he said, 'the other must follow immediately behind – yes, empty. I am going to Dover to meet a party of people.'

He would take no risk of a breakdown. The second car must be close at hand in case he had an accident with the first.

He was something of an organizer. In the short space of time he was at the telephone, he arranged the cars so that whatever avenue of escape he was forced to take he would find the vehicles waiting. This done, he completed his dressing. The reaction from the fear had come. He was filled with black hate for the men who had put a period to his career of villainy. Most of all he hated Sandford, the man who could have saved him.

He would take the risk of the Four – take his chance with the police.

Curiously, he feared the police least of all. One final blow he would strike and break the man whose obstinacy had broken him.

He was mad with anger – he saw nothing but the fulfilment of his plan of revenge. He went into his room, unlocked a cupboard and took out the green bottle. There was no need for the feather, he would do the job thoroughly.

He finished his dressing, pocketed his bank-notes, and slipped the little green bottle into his waistcoat pocket. One last look round he gave, then, with a sense of the old exhilaration which had been his before the arrival of Manfred, he put on his hat, threw an overcoat over his arm and went out.

* * *

It was a gay little party that assembled at the Great South Central Hôtel. May Sandford had invited a girl friend, and Mr Sandford had brought back the junior partner of one of the City houses he did business with.

Black was late and did not arrive till a quarter of an hour after the time settled for dinner. Sandford had given orders for the meal to be served when the colonel came in.

'Sit down, Black,' said Sandford.

There was a chair between the ironmaster and his daughter, and into this he dropped. His hand shook as he took up the spoon to his soup.

He put the spoon down again and unfolded his serviette. A letter dropped out. He knew those grey envelopes now, and crushed the letter into his pocket without attempting to read it.

'Busy man, Black, eh?' smiled Sandford. He was a florid, hearty man with a wisp of white whisker on either side of his rubicund face, and in his pleasant moments he was a very lovable man. 'You ought to be grateful I did not agree to the amalgamations – you would have been worked to death.'

'Yes,' said the colonel shortly. He stuck out his jaw – a trick he had when he was perturbed.

'In a way,' bantered the elder man, 'you're an admirable chap. If you were a little more reasonable you would be more successful.'

'Wouldn't you call me successful?'

Sandford pouted thoughtfully.

'Yes and no,' he said. 'You are not altogether successful. You see, you have achieved what you would call success too easily.'

Colonel Black did not pursue the subject, nor did he encourage the other to go any further. He needed opportunity. For a time he had to sit patiently, joining in, with such scraps of speech as he could muster, the conversation that rippled about him.

At his left hand were the girl's wine-glasses. She refused the lighter wines and drew forth a laughing protest from her father.

'Dearie, on your birthday – you must sip some champagne!'

'Champagne, then!' she said gaily. She was happy for many reasons, but principally because – well, just because.

That was the opportunity.

Absent-mindedly he drew her glass nearer, then he found the bottle in his pocket. With one hand he removed the cork and spilt half the contents of the phial on to his serviette. He re-corked the bottle and slipped it into his pocket. He took the glass on to his lap. Twice he wiped the edge of it with the damp napkin. He replaced the glass unnoticed.

Now it was done he felt better. He leant back in his chair, his hands thrust deep into his trousers pockets. It was an inelegant attitude, but he derived a sense of comfort.

'Black, wake up, my dear fellow!' Sandford was talking to him, and he roused himself with a start. 'My friend here was rude enough to comment on your hair.'

'Eh?' Black put up his hand to his head.

'Oh, it's all right and it isn't disarranged – but how long has it been white?'

'White?'

He had heard of such things and was mildly interested.

'White? Oh – er – quite a time.'

He did not further the discussion. The waiters were filling the glasses. He looked across to Sandford. How happy, how self-sufficient he was. He intercepted the tender little looks that passed between father and daughter. There was perfect sympathy between the two. It was a pity that in a minute or so one should be dead and the other broken. She so full of life, so splendid of shape, so fresh and lovely. He turned his head and looked at her. Curious, very curious, how frail a thing is life, that a milligram of a colourless fluid should be sufficient to snap the cord that binds soul to body.

The waiter filled the glasses – first the girl's, then his.

He raised his own with unconcern and drank it off.

The girl did not touch hers. She was talking to the man on her left. Black could see only the rounded cheek and one white shoulder. He waited impatiently.

Sandford tried to bring him into the conversation, but he refused to be drawn. He was content to listen, he said. To listen, to watch and to wait. He saw the slim white fingers close round the stem of the glass, saw her half raise it, still looking towards her partner.

Black pushed his chair a little to one side as the glass reached her lips. She drank, not much, but enough.

The colonel held his breath. She replaced the glass, still talking with the man on her left.

Black counted the slow seconds. He counted sixty – a hundred, oblivious to the fact that Sandford was talking to him.

The drug had failed!

'Are you ill, colonel?'

Everybody was staring at him.

'Ill?' he repeated hoarsely. 'No, I am not ill – why should I be ill?'

'Open one of those windows, waiter.'

A blast of cold air struck him and he shivered.

He left the table hurriedly and went blundering blindly from the room. There was an end to it all.

In the corridor of the hôtel he came in his haste into collision with a man. It was the man who had called upon him some time before.

'Excuse me,' said the man, catching his arm. 'Colonel Black, I believe.'

'Stand out of my way.' Black spat out the words savagely.

'I am Detective-Sergeant Kay from Scotland Yard, and I shall take you into custody.'

At the first hint of danger the colonel drew back. Suddenly his fist shot out and caught the officer under the jaw. It was a terrific blow and the detective was unprepared. He went down like a log.

The corridor was empty. Leaving the man upon the floor, the fugitive sped into the lobby. He was hatless, but he shaded his face and passed through the throng in the vestibule into the open air. He signalled a taxi.

'Waterloo, and I will give you a pound if you catch my train.'

He was speeding down the Strand in less than a minute. He changed his instructions before the station was reached.

'I have lost the train – drop me at the corner of Eaton Square.'

At Eaton Square he paid the cabman and dismissed him. With little difficulty he found two closed cars that waited.

'I am Colonel Black,' he said, and the first chauffeur touched his cap. 'Take the straightest road to Southampton and let the second man follow behind.'

The car had not gone far before he changed his mind.

'Go first to the Junior Turf Club in Pall Mall,' he said.

Arrived at the club, he beckoned the porter. 'Tell Sir Isaac Tramber that he is wanted at once,' he directed.

Ikey was in the club – it was a chance shot of the colonel's, but it bagged his man.

'Get your coat and hat,' said Black hurriedly to the flustered baronet.

'But – '

'No buts,' snarled the other savagely. 'Get your coat and hat, unless you want to be hauled out of your club to the nearest police-station.'

Reluctantly Ikey went back to the club and returned in a few seconds struggling into his great-coat.

'Now what the devil is this all about?' he demanded peevishly; then, as the light of a street lamp caught the colonel's uncovered head, he gasped: 'Good Lord! Your hair has gone white! You look just like that fellow Essley!'

Chapter the last

Justice

'Where are we going?' asked Sir Isaac faintly.

'We are going to Southampton,' growled Black in his ear. 'We shall find some friends there.' He grinned in the darkness. Then, leaning forward, he gave instructions in a low tone to the chauffeur.

The car jerked forward and in a few minutes it had crossed Hammersmith Broadway and was speeding towards Barnes.

Scarcely had it cleared the traffic when a long grey racing car cut perilously across the crowded space, dodging with extraordinary agility a number of vehicles, and, unheeding the caustic comments of the drivers, it went on in the same direction as Black's car had taken.

He had cleared Kingston and was on the Sandown road when he heard the loud purring of a car behind. He turned and looked, expecting to find his second car, but a punctured tyre held Black's reserve on Putney Heath. Black was a little uneasy, though it was no unusual thing for cars to travel the main Portsmouth road at that hour of the night.

He knew, too, that he could not hope to keep ahead of his pursuer. He caught the unmistakable sound which accompanies the racing car in motion.

'We'll wait till the road gets a little broader,' he said, 'and then we'll let that chap pass us.'

He conveyed the gist of this intention to the chauffeur.

The car behind showed no disposition to go ahead until Sandown and Cobham had been left behind and the lights of Guildford were almost in sight.

Then, on a lonely stretch of road, two miles from the town, the car, without any perceptible effort, shot level with them and then drew ahead on the off side. Then it slowed, and the touring car had perforce to follow its example.

Black watched the manoeuvre with some misgiving. Slower and slower went the racing car till it stopped crossways in the road; it stopped, too, in a position which made it impossible for the touring car to pass.

Black's man drew up with a jerk.

They saw, by the light of their lamps, two men get out of the motor ahead and make what seemed to be a cursory examination of a wheel. Then one walked back, slowly and casually, till he came to where Black and his companion sat.

'Excuse me,' said the stranger. 'I think I know you.'

Of a sudden an electric lamp flashed in Black's face. More to the point, in the spreading rays of the light, clear to be seen was the nickel-plated barrel of a revolver, and it was pointed straight at Black.

'You will alight, Mr Black – you and your companion,' said the unknown calmly.

In the bright light that flooded him, Black could make no move. Without a word he stepped down on to the roadway, his companion following him.

'Go ahead,' said the man with the revolver.

The two obeyed. Another flood of light met them. The driver of the first car was standing up, electric torch in one hand, revolver in the other. He directed them curtly to enter the tonneau. The first of their captors turned to give directions to the chauffeur of the grey touring car, then he sprang into the body in which they sat and took a seat opposite them.

'Put your hands on your knees,' he commanded, as his little lamp played over them.

Black brought his gloved hands forward reluctantly. Sir Isaac, half dead with fright, followed his example.

The car moved forward. Their warder, concentrating his lamp upon their knees, kept watch while his companion drove the car forward at a racing pace.

They struck off from the main road and took a narrow country lane which was unfamiliar to Black, and for ten minutes they twisted and turned in what seemed the heart of the country. Then they stopped.

'Get down!' ordered the man with the lamp.

Neither Black nor his friend had spoken one word up till now.

'What is the game?' asked Black.

'Get down!' commanded the other. With a curse, the big man descended.

There were two other men waiting for them.

'I suppose this is the Four Just Men farce,' said Black with a sneer.

'That you shall learn,' said one of those who were waiting.

They were conducted by a long, rough path through a field, through a little copse, until ahead of them in the night loomed a small building.

It was in darkness. It gave Black the impression of being a chapel. He had little time to take any note of its construction. He heard Sir Isaac's quick breathing behind him and the snick of a lock. The hand that held his arm now relaxed.

'Stay where you are,' said a voice.

Black waited. There was growing in his heart a sickly fear of what all this signified.

'Step forward,' said a voice.

Black moved two steps forward and suddenly the big room in which he stood blazed with light. He raised his hand to veil his eyes from the dazzling glow.

The sight he saw was a remarkable one. He was in a chapel; he saw the stained-glass windows, but in place of the altar there was a low platform which ran along one end of the building.

It was draped with black and set with three desks. It reminded him of nothing so much as a judge's desk, save that the hangings were of purple, the desks of black oak, and the carpet that covered the dais of the same sombre hue.

Three men sat at the desks. They were masked, and a diamond pin in the cravat of one glittered in the light of the huge electrolier which hung from the vaulted roof. Gonsalez had a weakness for jewels.

The remaining member of the Four was to the right of the prisoners.

With the stained-glass windows, the raftered roof, and the solemn character of the architecture, the illusion of the chapel ended. There was no other furniture on the floor; it was tiled and bare of chair or pew.

Black took all this in quickly. He noted a door behind the three, through which they came and apparently made their exit. He could see no means of escape save by the way he had come.

The central figure of the three at the desk spoke in a voice which was harsh and stern and uncompromising.

'Morris Black,' he said solemnly, 'what of Fanks?'

Black shrugged his shoulders and looked round as though weary of a question which he found it impossible to answer.

'What of Jakobs, of Coleman, of a dozen men who have stood in your way and have died?' asked the voice.

Still Black was silent.

His eye took in the situation. Behind him were two doors, and he observed that the key was in the lock. He could see that he was in an old Norman chapel which private enterprise had restored for a purpose.

The door was modern and of the usual 'churchy' type.

'Isaac Tramber,' said Number One, 'what part have you played?'

'I don't know,' stammered Sir Isaac. 'I am as much in the dark as you are. I think the bucket-shop idea is perfectly beastly. Now look here, is there anything else I can tell you, because I am most anxious to get out of this affair with clean hands?'

He made a step forward and Black reached out a hand to restrain him, but was pulled back by the man at his side.

'Come here,' said Number One.

His knees shaking under him, Sir Isaac walked quickly up the aisle floor.

'I'll do anything I can,' he said eagerly, as he stood like a penitent boy before the master's figure. 'Any information I can give you I shall be most happy to give.'

'Stop!' roared Black. His face was livid with rage. 'Stop,' he said hoarsely, 'you don't know what you're doing, Ikey. Keep your mouth shut and stand by me and you'll not suffer.'

'There is only one thing I know,' Sir Isaac went on, 'and that is that Black had a bit of a row with Fanks – '

The words were scarcely out of his mouth when three shots rang out in rapid succession. The Four had not attempted to disarm Black. With lightning-like rapidity he had whipped out his Browning pistol and had fired at the traitor.

In a second he was at the door. An instant later the key was turned and he was through.

'Shoot – shoot, Manfred,' said a voice from the dais. But they were too late – Black had vanished into the darkness. As the two men sprang after him, they stood for a moment silhouetted against the light from the chapel within.

'Crack! crack!' A nickel bullet struck the stone supports of the doorway and covered them with fine dust and splinters of stone.

'Put the lights out and follow,' said Manfred quickly.

He was too late, for Black had a start, and the fear and hatred in him lent him unsuspected speed.

The brute instinct in him led him across the field unerringly. He reached the tiny road, turned to the left, and found the grey racing car waiting, unattended.

He sprang to the crank and turned it. He was in the driver's seat in an instant. He had to take risks – there might be ditches on either side of the road, but he turned the wheel over till it almost locked and brought his foot down over the pedal.

The car jumped forward, lurched to the side, recovered itself, and went bumping and crashing along the road.

'It's no good,' said Manfred. He saw the tail-lights of the car disappearing. 'Let's get back.'

He had slipped off his mask.

They raced back to the chapel. The lights were on again. Sir Isaac Tramber lay stone-dead on the floor. The bullet had struck him in the left shoulder and had passed through this heart.

But it was not to him they looked. Number One lay still and motionless on the floor in a pool of blood.

'Look to the injury,' he said, 'and unless it is fatal do not unmask me.'

Poiccart and Gonsalez made a brief examination of the wound.

'It's pretty serious.'

In this terse sentence they summarized their judgment.

'I thought it was,' said the wounded man quietly. 'You had better get on to Southampton. He'll probably pick up Fellowe – ' he smiled through his mask – 'I suppose I ought to call him Lord Francis Ledborough now. He's a nephew of mine and a sort of a police-commissioner himself. I wired him to follow me. You might pick up his car and go on together. Manfred can stay with me. Take this mask off.'

Gonsalez stooped down and gently removed the silk half-mask. Then he started back.

'Lord Verlond!' he exclaimed with surprise, and Manfred, who knew, nodded.

* * *

The road was clear of traffic at this hour of the night. It was dark and none too wide in places for a man who had not touched the steering-wheel of a car for some years, but Black, bareheaded, sat and drove the big machine ahead without fear of consequences. Once he went rocking through a little town at racing speed.

A policeman who attempted to hold him up narrowly escaped with his life. Black reached open road again with no injury save a shattered mud-guard that had caught a lamp-post on a sharp turn. He went through Winchester at top speed – again there was an attempt to stop him. Two big wagons had been drawn up in the main street, but he saw them in time and took a side turning, and cleared town again more by good luck than otherwise. He knew now that his flight was known to the police. He must change his plans. He admitted to himself that he had few plans to change: he had arranged to leave England by one of two ports, Dover or Southampton.

He had hoped to reach the Havre boat without attracting attention, but that was now out of the question. The boats would be watched, and he had no disguise which would help him.

Eight miles south of Winchester he overtook another car and passed it before he realized that this must be the second car he had hired. With the realization came two reports – the front tyres of his car had punctured.

His foot pressed on the brake and he slowed the car to a standstill. Here was luck! To come to grief at the very spot where his relief was at hand!

He jumped out of the car and stood revealed in the glare of the lamps of the oncoming car, his arms outstretched.

The car drew up within a few feet of him.

'Take me on to Southampton; I have broken down,' he said, and the chauffeur said something unintelligible.

Black opened the door of the car and stepped in. The door slammed behind him before he was aware that there were other occupants.

'Who – ?' he began.

Then two hands seized him, something cold and hard snapped on his wrists, and a familiar voice said: 'I am Lord Francis Ledborough, an assistant-commissioner of police, and I shall take you into custody on a charge of wilful murder.'

'Ledborough?' repeated Black dully.

'You know me best as Constable Fellowe,' said the voice.

* * *

Black was hanged at Pentonville gaol on the 27th of March, 19— , and Lord Francis Ledborough, sitting by the side of an invalid uncle's bed, read such meagre descriptions as were given to the press.

'Did you know him, sir?' he asked.

The old earl turned fretfully.

'Know him?' he snarled. 'Of course I knew him; he is the only friend of mine that has ever been hanged.'

'Where did you meet him?' persisted a sceptical A.C. of Police.

'I never met him,' said the old man grimly, 'he met me.'

And he made a little grimace, for the wound in his shoulder was still painful.

THE END

THE LAW OF THE
FOUR JUST MEN

The Man who lived at Clapham

'The jury cannot accept the unsupported suggestion – unsupported even by the prisoner's testimony since he has not gone into the box – that Mr Noah Stedland is a blackmailer and that he obtained a large sum of money from the prisoner by this practice. That is a defence which is rather suggested by the cross-examination than by the production of evidence. The defence does not even tell us the nature of the threat which Stedland employed . . . '

The remainder of the summing up was creditable to the best traditions of the Bar, and the jury, without retiring, returned a verdict of 'Guilty'.

There was a rustle of movement in the court and a thin babble of whispered talk as the Judge fixed his pince-nez and began to write.

The man in the big oaken pen looked down at the pale drawn face of a girl turned to him from the well of the court and smiled encouragingly. For his part, he did not blanch and his grave eyes went back to the figure on the Bench – the puce-gowned, white-headed figure that was writing so industriously. What did a Judge write on these occasions, he wondered? Surely not a précis of the crime. He was impatient now to have done with it all; this airy court, these blurred rows of pink faces in the gloom of the public gallery, the indifferent counsel and particularly with the two men who had sat near the lawyer's pews watching him intently.

He wondered who they were, what interest they had in the proceedings. Perhaps they were foreign authors, securing first-hand impressions. They had the appearance of foreigners. One was very tall (he had seen him rise to his feet once), the other was slight and gave an impression of boyishness, though his hair was grey. They were both clean-shaven and both were dressed in black and balanced on their knees broad-brimmed hats of soft black felt.

A cough from the Judge brought his attention back to the Bench.

'Jeffrey Storr,' said his lordship, 'I entirely agree with the verdict of the jury. Your defence that Stedland robbed you of your savings and that you broke into his house for the purpose of taking the law into your own hands and securing the money and a document, the character of which you do not specify but which you allege proved his guilt, could not be considered seriously by any Court of Justice. Your story sounds as though you had read of that famous, or infamous, association called the Four Just Men, which existed some years ago, but which is now happily dispersed. Those men set themselves to punish where the law failed. It is a monstrous assumption that the law ever fails! You have committed a very serious offence, and the fact that you were at the moment of your arrest and capture in possession of a loaded revolver, serves very gravely to aggravate your crime. You will be kept in penal servitude for seven years.'

Jeffrey Storr bowed and without so much as a glance at the girl in the court, turned and descended the steps leading to the cells.

The two foreign-looking men who had excited the prisoner's interest and resentment were the first to leave the court.

Once in the street the taller of the two stopped.

'I think we will wait for the girl,' he said.

'Is she the wife?' asked the slight man.

'Married the week he made his unfortunate investment,' replied the tall man, then, 'It was a curious coincidence, that reference of the Judge's to the Four Just Men.'

The other smiled.

'It was in that very court that you were sentenced to death, Manfred,' he said, and the man called Manfred nodded.

'I wondered whether the old usher would remember me,' he answered, 'he has a reputation for never forgetting a face. Apparently the loss of my beard has worked a miracle, for I actually spoke to him. Here she is.'

Fortunately the girl was alone. A beautiful face, thought Gonsalez, the younger of the two men. She held her chin high and there was no sign of tears. As she walked quickly toward Newgate Street they followed her. She crossed the road into Hatton Garden and then it was that Manfred spoke.

'Pardon me, Mrs Storr,' he said, and she turned and stared at the foreign-looking man suspiciously.

'If you are a reporter – ' she began.

'I'm not,' smiled Manfred, 'nor am I a friend of your husband's, though I thought of lying to you in that respect in order to find an excuse for talking to you.'

His frankness procured her interest.

'I do not wish to talk about poor Jeffrey's terrible trouble,' she said. 'I just want to be alone.'

Manfred nodded.

'I understand that,' he said sympathetically, 'but I wish to be a friend of your husband's and perhaps I can help him. The story he told in the box was true – you thought that too, Leon?'

Gonsalez nodded.

'Obviously true,' he said, 'I particularly noticed his eyelids. When a man lies he blinks at every repetition of the lie. Have you observed, my dear George, that men cannot tell lies when their hands are clenched and that when women lie they clasp their hands together?'

She looked at Gonsalez in bewilderment. She was in no mood for a lecture on the physiology of expression and even had she known that Leon Gonsalez was the author of three large books which ranked with the best that Lombroso or Mantegazza had given to the world, she would have been no more willing to listen.

'The truth is, Mrs Storr,' said Manfred, interpreting her new distress, 'we think that we can free your husband and prove his innocence. But we want as many facts about the case as we can get.'

She hesitated only a moment.

'I have some furnished lodgings in Gray's Inn Road,' she said, 'perhaps you will be good enough to come with me.

'My lawyer does not think there is any use in appealing against the sentence,' she went on as they fell in one on either side of her. Manfred shook his head.

'The Appeal Court would uphold the sentence,' he said quietly, 'with the evidence you have there is no possibility of your husband being released.'

She looked round at him in dismay and now he saw that she was very near to tears.

'I thought . . . you said . . . ?' she began a little shakily.

Manfred nodded.

'We know Stedland,' he said, 'and – '

'The curious thing about blackmailers, is that the occiput is hardly observable,' interrupted Gonsalez thoughtfully. 'I examined sixty-two heads in the Spanish prisons and in every case the occipital protuberance was little more than a bony ridge. Now in homicidal heads the occiput sticks out like a pigeon's egg.'

'My friend is rather an authority upon the structure of the head,' smiled Manfred. 'Yes, we know Stedland. His operations have been reported to us from time to time. You remember the Wellingford case, Leon?'

Gonsalez nodded.

'Then you are detectives?' asked the girl.

Manfred laughed softly.

'No, we are not detectives – we are interested in crime. I think we have the best and most thorough record of the unconvicted criminal class of any in the world.'

They walked on in silence for some time.

'Stedland is a bad man,' nodded Gonsalez as though the conviction had suddenly dawned upon him. 'Did you observe his ears? They are unusually long and the outer margins are pointed – the Darwinian tubercle, Manfred. And did you remark, my dear friend, that the root of the helix divides the concha into two distinct cavities and that the lobule was adherent? A truly criminal ear. The man has committed murder. It is impossible to possess such an ear and not to murder.'

The flat to which she admitted them was small and wretchedly furnished. Glancing round the tiny dining-room, Manfred noted the essential appointments which accompany a 'furnished' flat.

The girl, who had disappeared into her room to take off her coat, now returned, and sat by the table at which, at her invitation, they had seated themselves.

'I realise that I am being indiscreet,' she said with the faintest of smiles; 'but I feel that you really want to help me, and I have the curious sense that you can! The police have not been unkind or unfair to me and poor Jeff. On the contrary, they have been most helpful. I fancy that they suspected Mr Stedland of being a black-mailer, and they were hoping that we could supply some evidence. When that evidence failed, there was nothing for them to do but to press forward the charge. Now, what can I tell you?'

'The story which was not told in court,' replied Manfred.

She was silent for a time. 'I will tell you,' she said at last. 'Only my husband's lawyer knows, and I have an idea that he was sceptical as to the truth of what I am now telling you. And if he is sceptical,' she said in despair, 'how can I expect to convince you?'

The eager eyes of Gonsalez were fixed on hers, and it was he who answered.

'We are already convinced, Mrs Storr,' and Manfred nodded.

Again there was a pause. She was evidently reluctant to begin a narrative which, Manfred guessed, might not be creditable to her; and this proved to be the case.

'When I was a girl,' she began simply, 'I was at school in Sussex – a big girls' school; I think there were over two hundred pupils. I am not going to excuse anything I did,' she went on quickly. 'I fell in love with a boy – well, he was a butcher's boy! That sounds dreadful, doesn't it? But you understand I was a child, a very impressionable child – oh, it sounds horrible, I know; but I used to meet him in the garden leading out from the prep. room after prayers; he climbed over the wall to those meetings, and we talked and talked, sometimes for an hour. There was no more in it than a boy and girl love affair, and I can't explain just why I committed such a folly.'

'Mantegazza explains the matter very comfortably in his *Study of Attraction*,' murmured Leon Gonsalez. 'But forgive me, I interrupted you.'

'As I say, it was a boy and girl friendship, a kind of hero worship on my part, for I thought he was wonderful. He must have been the nicest of butcher boys,' she smiled again, 'because he never offended me by so much as a word. The friendship burnt itself out in a month or two, and there the matter might have ended, but for the fact that I had been foolish enough to write letters. They were very ordinary, stupid love-letters, and perfectly innocent – or at least they seemed so to me at the time. Today, when I read them in the light of a greater knowledge they take my breath away.'

'You have them, then?' said Manfred.

She shook her head.

'When I said "them" I meant one, and I only have a copy of that, supplied me by Mr Stedland. The one letter that was not destroyed fell into the hands of the boy's mother, who took it to the headmistress, and there was an awful row. She threatened to write to my parents who were in India, but on my solemn promise that the acquaintance should be dropped, the affair was allowed to blow over. How the letter came into Stedland's hands I do not know; in fact, I had never heard of the man until a week before my marriage with Jeff. Jeff had saved about two thousand pounds, and we were looking forward to our marriage day when this blow fell. A letter from a perfectly unknown man, asking me to see him at his office, gave me my first introduction to this villain. I had to take the letter with me, and I went in some curiosity, wondering why I had been sent for. I was not to wonder very long. He had a little office off Regent Street, and after he had very carefully taken away the letter he had sent me, he explained, fully and frankly, just what his summons had meant.'

Manfred nodded.

'He wanted to sell you the letter,' he said, 'for how much?'

'For two thousand pounds. That was the diabolical wickedness of it,' said the girl vehemently. 'He knew almost to a penny how much Jeff had saved.'

'Did he show you the letter?'

She shook her head.

'No, he showed me a photographic reproduction and as I read it and recalled what construction might be put upon this perfectly innocent note, my blood went cold. There was nothing to do but to tell Jeff, because the man had threatened to send facsimiles to all our friends and to Jeffrey's uncle, who had made Jeffrey his sole heir. I had already told Jeffrey about what happened at school, thank heaven, and so I had no need to fear his suspicion. Jeffrey called on Mr Stedland, and I believe there was a stormy scene; but Stedland is a big, powerful man in spite of his age, and in the struggle which ensued poor Jeffrey got a little the worst of it. The upshot of the matter was, Jeffrey agreed to buy the letter for two thousand pounds, on condition that Stedland signed a receipt, written on a blank page of the letter itself. It meant the losing of his life savings; it meant the possible postponement of our wedding; but Jeffrey would not take any other course. Mr Stedland lives in a big house near Clapham Common – '

'184 Park View West,' interrupted Manfred.

'You know?' she said in surprise. 'Well, it was at this house Jeffrey had to call to complete the bargain. Mr Stedland lives alone except for a manservant, and opening the door himself, he conducted Jeffrey up to the first floor, where he had his study. My husband, realising the futility of argument, paid over the money, as he had been directed by Stedland, in American bills – '

'Which are more difficult to trace, of course,' said Manfred.

'When he had paid him, Stedland produced the letter, wrote the receipt on the blank page, blotted it and placed it in an envelope, which he gave to my husband. When Jeffrey returned home and opened the envelope, he found it contained nothing more than a blank sheet of paper.'

'He had rung the changes,' said Manfred.

'That was the expression that Jeffrey used,' said the girl. 'Then it was that Jeffrey decided to commit this mad act. You have heard of the Four Just Men?'

'I have heard of them,' replied Manfred gravely.

'My husband is a great believer in their methods, and a great admirer of them too,' she said. 'I think he read everything that has ever been written about them. One night, two days after we were married – I had insisted upon marrying him at once when I discovered the situation – he came to me.

' "Grace," he said, "I am going to apply the methods of the Four to this devil Stedland."

'He outlined his plans. He had apparently been watching the house, and knew that except for the servant the man slept in the house alone, and he had formed a plan for getting in. Poor dear, he was an indifferent burglar; but you heard today how he succeeded in reaching Stedland's room. I think he hoped to frighten the man with his revolver.'

Manfred shook his head.

'Stedland graduated as a gun-fighter in South Africa,' he said quietly. 'He is the quickest man on the draw I know, and a deadly shot. Of course, he had your husband covered before he could as much as reach his pocket.'

She nodded.

'That is the story,' she said quietly. 'If you can help Jeff, I shall pray for you all my life.'

Manfred rose slowly.

'It was a mad attempt,' he said. 'In the first place Stedland would not keep a compromising document like that in his house, which he leaves for six hours a day. It might even have been destroyed, though that is unlikely. He would keep the letter for future use. Blackmailers are keen students of humanity, and he knows that money may still be made, from that letter of yours. But if it is in existence – '

'If it is in existence,' she repeated – and now the reaction had come and her lips were trembling –

'I will place it in your hands within a week,' said Manfred, and with this promise left her.

Mr Noah Stedland had left the Courts of Justice that afternoon with no particular sense of satisfaction save that he was leaving it by the public entrance. He was not a man who was easily scared, but he was sensitive to impressions; and it seemed to him that the Judge's carefully chosen words had implied, less in their substance than in their tone, a veiled rebuke to himself. Beyond registering this fact, his sensitiveness did not go. He was a man of comfortable fortune, and that fortune had been got together in scraps – sometimes the scraps were unusually large – by the exercise of qualities which were not handicapped by such imponderable factors as conscience or remorse. Life to this tall, broad-shouldered, grey-faced man was a game, and Jeffrey Storr, against whom he harboured no resentment, was a loser.

He could think dispassionately of Storr in his convict clothes, wearing out the years of agony in a convict prison, and at the mental picture could experience no other emotion than that of the successful gambler who can watch his rival's ruin with equanimity.

He let himself into his narrow-fronted house, closed and double-locked the door behind him, and went up the shabbily carpeted stairs to his study. The ghosts of the lives he had wrecked should have crowded the room; but Mr Stedland did not believe in ghosts. He rubbed his finger along a mahogany table and noted that it was dusty, and the ghost of a well-paid charlady took shape from that moment.

As he sprawled back in his chair, a big cigar between his gold-spotted teeth, he tried to analyse the queer sensation he had experienced in court. It was not the Judge, it was not the attitude of the defending counsel, it was not even the possibility that the world might censure him, which was responsible for his mental perturbation. It was certainly not the prisoner and his possible fate, or the white-faced wife. And yet there had been a something or a somebody which had set him glancing uneasily over his shoulder.

He sat smoking for half an hour, and then a bell clanged and he went down the stairs and opened the front door. The man who was waiting with an apologetic smile on his face, a jackal of his, was butler and tout and general errand-boy to the hard-faced man.

'Come in, Jope,' he said, closing the door behind the visitor. 'Go down to the cellar and get me a bottle of whisky?'

'How was my evidence, guv'nor?' asked the sycophant, smirking expectantly.

'Rotten,' growled Stedland. 'What did you mean by saying you heard me call for help?'

'Well, guv'nor, I thought I'd make it a little worse for him,' said Jope humbly.

'Help!' sneered Mr Stedland. 'Do you think I'd call on a guy like you for help? A damned lot of use you would be in a rough house! Get that whisky!'

When the man came up with a bottle and a syphon, Mr Stedland was gazing moodily out of the window which looked upon a short, untidy garden terminating in a high wall. Behind that was a space on which a building had been in course of erection when the armistice put an end to Government work. It was designed as a small factory for the making of fuses, and was an eyesore to Mr Stedland, since he owned the ground on which it was built.

'Jope,' he said, turning suddenly, 'was there anybody in court we know?'

'No, Mr Stedland,' said the man, pausing in surprise. 'Not that I know, except Inspector – '

'Never mind about the Inspector,' answered Mr Stedland impatiently. 'I know all the splits who were there. Was there anybody else – anybody who has a grudge against us?'

'No, Mr Stedland. What does it matter if there was?' asked the valorous Jope. 'I think we're a match for any of 'em.'

'How long have we been in partnership?' asked Stedland unpleasantly, as he poured himself out a tot of whisky.

The man's face twisted in an ingratiating smile.

'Well, we've been together some time now, Mr Stedland,' he said.

Stedland smacked his lips and looked out of the window again.

'Yes,' he said after a while, 'we've been together a long time now. In fact, you would almost have finished your sentence, if I had told the police what I knew about you seven years ago – '

The man winced, and changed the subject. He might have realised, had he thought, that the sentence of seven years had been commuted by Stedland to a sentence of life servitude, but Mr Jope was no thinker.

'Anything for the Bank today, sir?' he asked.

'Don't be a fool,' said Stedland. 'The Bank closed at three. Now, Jope,' he turned on the other, 'in future you sleep in the kitchen.'

'In the kitchen, sir?' said the astonished servant, and Stedland nodded.

'I'm taking no more risks of a night visitor,' he said. 'That fellow was on me before I knew where I was, and if I hadn't had a gun handy he would have beaten me. The kitchen is the only way you can break into this house from the outside, and I've got a feeling at the back of my mind that something might happen.'

'But he's gone to gaol.'

'I'm not talking about him,' snarled Stedland. 'Do you understand, take your bed to the kitchen.'

'It's a bit draughty – ' began Jope.

'Take your bed to the kitchen,' roared Stedland, glaring at the man.

'Certainly, sir,' said Jope with alacrity.

When his servant had gone, Stedland took off his coat and put on one of stained alpaca, unlocked the safe, and took out a book. It was a pass-book from his bank, and its study was very gratifying. Mr Stedland dreamed dreams of a South American ranch and a life of ease and quiet. Twelve years' strenuous work in London had made him a comparatively rich man. He had worked cautiously and patiently and had pursued the business of blackmail in a businesslike manner. His cash balance was with one of the best-known of the private bankers. Sir William Molbury & Co., Ltd. Molbury's Bank had a reputation in the City for the privacy and even mystery which enveloped the business of its clients – a circumstance which suited Mr Stedland admirably. It was, too, one of those old-fashioned banks which maintain a huge reserve of money in its vaults; and this was also a recommendation to Mr Stedland, who might wish to gather in his fluid assets in the shortest possible space of time.

The evening and the night passed without any untoward incident, except as was revealed when Mr Jope brought his master's tea in the morning, and told, somewhat hoarsely, of a cold and unpleasant night. 'Get more bedclothes,' said Stedland curtly. He went off to his city office after breakfast, and left Mr Jope to superintend the operations of the charwoman and to impress upon her a number of facts, including the high rate at which she was paid, the glut of good charwomen on the market and the consequences which would overtake her if she left Mr Stedland's study undusted.

At eleven o'clock that morning came a respectable and somewhat elderly looking gentleman in a silk hat, and him Mr Jope interviewed on the door-mat.

'I've come from the Safe Deposit,' said the visitor.

'What Safe Deposit?' asked the suspicious Mr Jope.

'The Fetter Lane Deposit,' replied the other. 'We want to know if you left your keys behind the last time you came?'

Jope shook his head. 'We haven't any Safe Deposit,' he said with assurance, 'and the governor's hardly likely to leave his keys behind.'

'Then evidently I've come to the wrong house,' smiled the gentleman. 'This is Mr Smithson's?'

'No, it ain't,' said the ungracious Jope, and shut the door in the caller's face.

The visitor walked down the steps into the street and joined another man who was standing at a corner.

'They know nothing of Safe Deposits, Manfred,' he said.

'I hardly thought it would be at a Safe Deposit,' said the taller of the two. 'In fact, I was pretty certain that he would keep all his papers at the bank. You saw the man Jope, I suppose?'

'Yes,' said Gonsalez dreamily. 'An interesting face. The chin weak, but the ears quite normal. The frontal bones slope irregularly backward, and the head, so far as I can see, is distinctly oxycephalic.'

'Poor Jope!' said Manfred without a smile. 'And now, Leon, you and I will devote our attention to the weather. There is an anticyclone coming up from the Bay of Biscay, and its beneficent effects are already felt in Eastbourne. If it extends northwards to London in the next three days we shall have good news for Mrs Storr.'

'I suppose,' said Gonsalez, as they were travelling back to their rooms in Jermyn Street, 'I suppose there is no possibility of rushing this fellow.'

Manfred shook his head.

'I do not wish to die,' he said, 'and die I certainly should, for Noah Stedland is unpleasantly quick to shoot.'

Manfred's prophecy was fulfilled two days later, when the influence of the anticyclone spread to London and a thin yellow mist descended on the city. It lifted in the afternoon, Manfred saw to his satisfaction, but gave no evidence of dispersing before nightfall.

Mr Stedland's office in Regent Street was small but comfortably furnished. On the glass door beneath his name was inscribed the magic word: 'Financier,' and it is true that Stedland was registered as a moneylender and found it a profitable business; for what Stedland the moneylender discovered, Stedland the blackmailer exploited, and it was not an unusual circumstance for Mr Stedland to lend at heavy interest money which was destined for his own pocket. In this way he could obtain a double grip upon his victim.

At half past two that afternoon his clerk announced a caller.

'Man or woman?'

'A man, sir,' said the clerk, 'I think he's from Molbury's Bank.'

'Do you know him?' asked Stedland.

'No, sir, but he came yesterday when you were out, and asked if you'd received the Bank's balance sheet.' Mr Stedland took a cigar from a box on the table and lit it.

'Show him in,' he said, anticipating nothing more exciting than a dishonoured cheque from one of his clients.

The man who came in was obviously in a state of agitation. He closed the door behind him and stood nervously fingering his hat.

'Sit down,' said Stedland. 'Have a cigar, Mr – '

'Curtis, sir,' said the other huskily. 'Thank you, sir, I don't smoke.'

'Well, what do you want?' asked Stedland.

'I want a few minutes' conversation with you, sir, of a private character.' He glanced apprehensively at the glass partition which separated Mr Stedland's office from the little den in which his clerks worked.

'Don't worry,' said Stedland humorously. 'I can guarantee that screen is sound-proof. What's your trouble?'

He scented a temporary embarrassment, and a bank clerk temporarily embarrassed might make a very useful tool for future use.

'I hardly know how to begin, Mr Stedland,' said the man, seating himself on the edge of a chair, his face twitching nervously. 'It's a terrible story, a terrible story.'

Stedland had heard about these terrible stories before, and sometimes they meant no more than that the visitor was threatened with bailiffs and was anxious to keep the news from the ears of his employers. Sometimes the confession was more serious – money lost in gambling, and a desperate eleventh-hour attempt to make good a financial deficiency.

'Go on,' he said. 'You won't shock me.' The boast was a little premature, however.

'It's not about myself, but about my brother, John Curtis, who's been cashier for twenty years, sir,' said the man nervously. 'I hadn't the slightest idea that he was in difficulties, but he was gambling on the Stock Exchange, and only today he has told me the news. I am in terrible distress about him, sir. I fear suicide. He is a nervous wreck.'

'What has he done?' asked Stedland impatiently.

'He has robbed the Bank, sir,' said the man in a hushed voice. 'It wouldn't matter if it had happened two years ago, but now, when things have been going so badly and we've had to stretch a point to make our balance sheet plausible, I shudder to think what the results will be.'

'Of how much has he robbed the Bank?' asked Stedland quickly.

'A hundred and fifty thousand pounds,' was the staggering reply, and Stedland jumped to his feet.

'A hundred and fifty thousand?' he said incredulously.

'Yes, sir. I was wondering whether you could speak for him; you are one of the most highly respected clients of the Bank!'

'Speak for him!' shouted Stedland, and then of a sudden he became cool. His quick brain went over the situation, reviewing every possibility. He looked up at the clock. It was a quarter to three.

'Does anybody in the Bank know?'

'Not yet, sir, but I feel it is my duty to the general manager to tell him the tragic story. After the Bank closes this afternoon I am asking him to see me privately and – '

'Are you going back to the Bank now?' asked Stedland.

'Yes, sir,' said the man in surprise.

'Listen to me, my friend.' Stedland's grey face was set and tense. He took a case from his pocket, opened it and extracted two notes. 'Here are two notes for fifty,' he said. 'Take those and go home.'

'But I've got to go to the Bank, sir. They will wonder – '

'Never mind what they wonder,' said Stedland. 'You'll have a very good explanation when the truth comes out. Will you do this?'

The man took up the money reluctantly.

'I don't quite know what you – '

'Never mind what I want to do,' snapped Stedland. 'That is to keep your mouth shut and go home. Do you understand plain English?'

'Yes, sir,' said the shaking Curtis.

Five minutes later Mr Stedland passed through the glass doors of Molbury's Bank and walked straight to the counter. An air of calm pervaded the establishment and the cashier, who knew Stedland, came forward with a smile.

> 'Unconscious of their awful doom,
>   The little victims play;'

quoted Stedland to himself. It was a favourite quotation of his, and he had used it on many appropriate occasions.

He passed a slip of paper across the counter, and the cashier looked at it and raised his eyebrows.

'Why, this is almost your balance, Mr Stedland,' he said.

Stedland nodded.

'Yes, I am going abroad in a hurry,' he said. 'I shall not be back for two years, but I am leaving just enough to keep the account running.'

It was a boast of Molbury's that they never argued on such occasions as these.

'Then you will want your box?' said the cashier politely.

'If you please,' said Mr Noah Stedland. If the Bank passed into the hands of the Receiver, he had no wish for prying strangers to be unlocking and examining the contents of the tin box he had deposited with the Bank, and to the contents of which he made additions from time to time.

Ten minutes later, with close on a hundred thousand pounds in his pockets, a tin box in one hand, the other resting on his hip pocket – for he took no chances – Mr Stedland went out again on the street and into the waiting taxicab. The fog was cleared, and the sun was shining at Clapham when he arrived.

He went straight up to his study, fastened the door and unlocked the little safe. Into this he pushed the small box and two thick bundles of notes, locking the safe door behind him. Then he rang for the faithful Jope, unfastening the door to admit him.

'Have we another camp bed in the house?' he asked.

'Yes, sir,' said Jope.

'Well, bring it up here. I am going to sleep in my study tonight.'

'Anything wrong, sir?'

'Don't ask jackass questions. Do as you're told!'

Tomorrow, he thought, he would seek out a safer repository for his treasures. He spent that evening in his study and lay down to rest, but not to sleep, with a revolver on a chair by the side of his camp bed. Mr Stedland was a cautious man. Despite his intention to dispense with sleep for one night, he was dozing when a sound in the street outside roused him.

It was a familiar sound – the clang of fire bells – and apparently fire engines were in the street, for he heard the whine of motors and the sound of voices. He sniffed; there was a strong smell of burning, and looking up he saw a flicker of light reflected on the ceiling. He sprang out of bed to discover the cause. It was immediately discernible, for the fuse factory was burning merrily, and he caught a glimpse of firemen at work and a momentary vision of a hose in action. Mr Stedland permitted himself to smile. That fire would be worth money to him, and there was no danger to himself.

And then he heard a sound in the hall below; a deep voice boomed an order, and he caught the chatter of Jope, and unlocked the door. The lights were burning in the hall and on the stairway. Looking over the banisters he saw the shivering Jope, with an overcoat over his pyjamas, expostulating with a helmeted fireman.

'I can't help it,' the latter was saying, 'I've got to get a hose through one of these houses, and it might as well be yours.'

Mr Stedland had no desire to have a hose through his house, and thought he knew an argument which might pass the inconvenience on to his neighbour.

'Just come up here a moment,' he said. 'I want to speak to one of those firemen.'

The fireman came clumping up the stairs in his heavy boots, a fine figure of a man in his glittering brass.

'Sorry,' he said, 'but I must get the hose – '

'Wait a moment, my friend,' said Mr Stedland with a smile. 'I think you will understand me after a while. There are plenty of houses in this road, and a tenner goes a long way, eh? Come in.'

He walked back into his room and the fireman followed and stood watching as he unlocked the safe. Then: 'I didn't think it would be so easy,' he said.

Stedland swung round.

'Put up your hands,' said the fireman, 'and don't make trouble, or you're going out, Noah. I'd just as soon kill you as talk to you.'

Then Noah Stedland saw that beneath the shade of the helmet the man's face was covered with a black mask.

'Who – who are you?' he asked hoarsely.

'I'm one of the Four Just Men – greatly reviled and prematurely mourned. Death is my favourite panacea for all ills . . . '

At nine o'clock in the morning Mr Noah Stedland still sat biting his nails, a cold uneaten breakfast spread on a table before him.

To him came Mr Jope wailing tidings of disaster, interrupted by Chief Inspector Holloway and a hefty subordinate who followed the servant into the room.

'Coming for a little walk with me, Stedland?' asked the cheery inspector, and Stedland rose heavily.

'What's the charge?' he asked heavily.

'Blackmail,' replied the officer. 'We've got evidence enough to hang you – delivered by special messenger. You fixed that case against Storr too – naughty, naughty!'

As Mr Stedland put on his coat the inspector asked: 'Who gave you away?'

Mr Stedland made no reply. Manfred's last words before he vanished into the foggy street had been emphatic.

'If he wanted to kill you, the man called Curtis would have killed you this afternoon when we played on your cunning; we could have killed you as easily as we set fire to the factory. And if you talk to the police of the Four Just Men, we will kill you, even though you be in Pentonville with a regiment of soldiers round you.'

And somehow Mr Stedland knew that his enemy spoke the truth. So he said nothing, neither there nor in the dock at the Old Bailey, and went to penal servitude without speaking.

The Man with the Canine Teeth

'Murder, my dear Manfred is the most accidental of crimes,' said Leon Gonsalez, removing his big shell-rimmed glasses and looking across the breakfast-table with that whimsical earnestness which was ever a delight to the handsome genius who directed the operations of the Four Just Men.

'Poiccart used to say that murder was a tangible expression of hysteria,' he smiled, 'but why this grisly breakfast-table topic?'

Gonsalez put on his glasses again and returned, apparently, to his study of the morning newspaper. He did not wilfully ignore the question, but his mind, as George Manfred knew, was so completely occupied by his reflections that he neither heard the query nor, for the matter of that, was he reading the newspaper. Presently he spoke again.

'Eighty per cent of the men who are charged with murder are making their appearance in a criminal court for the first time,' he said: 'therefore, murderers as a class are not criminals – I speak, of course, for the Anglo-Saxon murderer. Latin and Teutonic criminal classes supply sixty per cent of the murderers in France, Italy and the Germanic States. They are fascinating people, George, fascinating!'

His face lighted up with enthusiasm, and George Manfred surveyed him with amusement.

'I have never been able to take so detached a view of those gentlemen,' he said, 'To me they are completely horrible – for is not murder the apotheosis of injustice?' he asked.

'I suppose so,' said Gonsalez vacantly.

'What started this line of thought?' asked Manfred, rolling his serviette.

'I met a true murderer type last night,' answered the other calmly. 'He asked me for a match and smiled when I gave it to him. A perfect set of teeth, my dear George, perfect – except – '

'Except?'

'The canine teeth were unusually large and long, the eyes deep set and amazingly level, the face anamorphic – which latter fact is not necessarily criminal.'

'Sounds rather an ogre to me,' said Manfred.

'On the contrary,' Gonsalez hastened to correct the impression, 'he was quite good-looking. None but a student would have noticed the irregularity of the face. Oh no, he was most presentable.'

He explained the circumstances of the meeting. He had been to a concert the night before – not that he loved music, but because he wished to study the effect of music upon certain types of people. He had returned with hieroglyphics scribbled all over his programme, and had sat up half the night elaborating his notes.

'He is the son of Professor Tableman. He is not on good terms with his father, who apparently disapproves of his choice of fiancée, and he loathes his cousin,' added Gonsalez simply.

Manfred laughed aloud.

'You amusing person! And did he tell you all this of his own free will, or did you hypnotise him and extract the information? You haven't asked me what I did last night.'

Gonsalez was lighting a cigarette slowly and thoughtfully.

'He is nearly two metres – to be exact, six feet two inches – in height, powerfully built, with shoulders like that!' He held the cigarette in one hand and the burning match in the other to indicate the breadth of the young man. 'He has big, strong hands and plays football for the United Hospitals. I beg your pardon, Manfred; where *were* you last night?'

'At Scotland Yard,' said Manfred; but if he expected to produce a sensation he was to be disappointed. Probably knowing his Leon, he anticipated no such result.

'An interesting building,' said Gonsalez. 'The architect should have turned the western façade southward – though its furtive entrances are in keeping with its character. You had no difficulty in making friends?'

'None. My work in connection with the Spanish Criminal Code and my monograph on Dactyology secured me admission to the chief.'

Manfred was known in London as 'Señor Fuentes', an eminent writer on criminology, and in their roles of Spanish scientists both men bore the most compelling of credentials from the Spanish Minister of Justice. Manfred had made his home in Spain for many years. Gonsalez was a native of that country, and the third of the famous four – there had not been a fourth for twenty years – Poiccart, the stout and gentle, seldom left his big garden in Cordova.

To him Leon Gonsalez referred when he spoke.

'You must write and tell our dear friend Poiccart,' he said. 'He will be interested. I had a letter from him this morning. Two new litters of little pigs have come to bless his establishment, and his orange trees are in blossom.'

He chuckled to himself, and then suddenly became serious.

'They took you to their bosom, these policemen?'

Manfred nodded.

'They were very kind and charming. We are lunching with one of the Assistant Commissioners, Mr Reginald Fare, tomorrow. British police methods have improved tremendously since we were in London before, Leon. The finger-print department is a model of efficiency, and their new men are remarkably clever.'

'They will hang us yet,' said the cheerful Leon.

'I think not!' replied his companion.

The lunch at the Ritz-Carlton was, for Gonsalez especially, a most pleasant function. Mr Fare, the middle-aged Commissioner, was, in addition to being a charming gentleman, a very able scientist. The views and observations of Marro, Lombroso, Fere, Mantegazza and Ellis flew from one side of the table to the other.

'To the habitual criminal the world is an immense prison, alternating with an immense jag,' said Fare. 'That isn't my description but one a hundred years old. The habitual criminal is an easy man to deal with. It is when you come to the non-criminal classes, the murderers, the accidental embezzlers – '

'Exactly!' said Gonsalez. 'Now my contention is – '

He was not to express his view, for a footman had brought an envelope to the Commissioner, and he interrupted Gonsalez with an apology to open and read its contents.

'H'm!' he said. 'That is a curious coincidence . . . '

He looked at Manfred thoughtfully.

'You were saying the other night that you would like to watch Scotland Yard at work close at hand, and I promised you that I would give you the first opportunity which presented – your chance has come!'

He had beckoned the waiter and paid his bill before he spoke again.

'I shall not disdain to draw upon your ripe experience,' he said, 'for it is possible we may need all the assistance we can get in this case.'

'What is it?' asked Manfred. as the Commissioner's car threaded the traffic at Hyde Park Corner.

'A man has been found dead in extraordinary circumstances,' said the Commissioner. 'He holds rather a prominent position in the scientific world – a Professor Tableman – you probably know the name.'

'Tableman?' said Gonsalez, his eyes opening wide. 'Well, that is extraordinary! You were talking of coincidences, Mr Fare. Now I will tell you of another.'

He related his meeting with the son of the Professor on the previous night.

'Personally,' Gonsalez went on, 'I look upon all coincidences as part of normal intercourse. It is a coincidence that, if you receive a bill requiring payment, you receive two or more during the day, and that if you receive a cheque by the first post, be sure you will receive a cheque by your second or third post. Some day I shall devote my mind to the investigation of that phenomenon.'

'Professor Tableman lives in Chelsea. Some years ago he purchased his house from an artist, and had the roomy studio converted into a laboratory. He was a lecturer in physics and chemistry at the Bloomsbury University,' explained Fare, though he need not have done so, for Manfred recalled the name; 'and he was also a man of considerable means.'

'I knew the Professor and dined with him about a month ago,' said Fare. 'He had had some trouble with his son. Tableman was an arbitrary, unyielding old man, one of those types of Christians who worship the historical figures of the Old Testament but never seem to get to the second book.'

They arrived at the house, a handsome modern structure in one of the streets abutting upon King's Road, and apparently the news of the tragedy had not leaked out, for the usual crowd of morbid loungers had not gathered. A detective was waiting for them, and conducted the Commissioner along a covered passage-way running by the side of the house, and up a flight of steps directly into the studio. There was nothing unusual about the room save that it was very light, for one of the walls was a huge window and the sloping roof was also of glass. Broad benches ran the length of two walls, and a big table occupied the centre of the room, all these being covered with scientific apparatus, whilst two long shelves above the benches were filled with bottles and jars, apparently containing chemicals.

A sad-faced, good-looking young man rose from a chair as they entered.

'I am John Munsey,' he said, 'the Professor's nephew. You remember me, Mr Fare? I used to assist my uncle in his experiments.'

Fare nodded. His eyes were occupied with the figure that lay upon the ground, between table and bench.

'I have not moved the Professor,' said the young man in a low voice. 'The detectives who came moved him slightly to assist the doctor in making his examination, but he has been left practically where he fell.'

The body was that of an old man, tall and spare, and on the grey face was an unmistakable look of agony and terror.

'It looks like a case of strangling,' said Fare. 'Has any rope or cord been found?'

'No, sir,' replied the young man. 'That was the view which the detectives reached, and we made a very thorough search of the laboratory.'

Gonsalez was kneeling by the body, looking with dispassionate interest at the lean neck. About the throat was a band of blue about four inches deep, and he thought at first that it was a material bandage of some diaphanous stuff, but on close inspection he saw that it was merely the discoloration of the skin. Then his keen eye rose to the table, near where the Professor fell.

'What is that?' he asked. He pointed to a small green bottle by the side of which was an empty glass.

'It is a bottle of crême de menthe,' said the youth; 'my uncle took a glass usually before retiring.'

'May I?' asked Leon, and Fare nodded.

Gonsalez picked up the glass and smelt it, then held it to the light.

'This glass was not used for liqueur last night, so he was killed before he drank,' the Commissioner said. 'I'd like to hear the whole story from you, Mr Munsey. You sleep on the premises, I presume?'

After giving a few instructions to the detectives, the Commissioner followed the young man into a room which was evidently the late Professor's library.

'I have been my uncle's assistant and secretary for three years,' he said, 'and we have always been on the most affectionate terms. It was my uncle's practice to spend the morning in his library, the whole of the afternoon either in his laboratory or at his office at the University, and he invariably spent the hours between dinner and bedtime working at his experiments.'

'Did he dine at home?' asked Fare.

'Invariably,' replied Mr Munsey, 'unless he had an evening lecture or there was a meeting of one of the societies with which he was connected, and in that case he dined at the Royal Society's Club in St James's Street.

'My uncle, as you probably know, Mr Fare, has had a serious disagreement with his son, Stephen Tableman, and my cousin and very good friend. I have done my best to reconcile them, and when, twelve months ago, my uncle sent for me in this very room and told me that he had altered his will and left the whole of his property to me and had cut his son entirely from his inheritance, I was greatly distressed. I went immediately to Stephen and begged him to lose no time in reconciling himself with the old man. Stephen just laughed and said he didn't care about the Professor's money, and that, sooner than give up Miss Faber – it was about his engagement that the quarrel occurred – he would cheerfully live on the small sum of money which his mother left him. I came back and saw the Professor and begged him to restore Stephen to his will. I admit,' he half smiled, 'that I expected and would appreciate a small legacy. I am following the same scientific course as the Professor followed in his early days, and I have ambitions to carry on his work. But the Professor would have none of my suggestion. He raved and stormed at me, and I thought it would be discreet to drop the subject, which I did. Nevertheless, I lost no opportunity of putting in a word for Stephen, and last week, when the Professor was in an unusually amiable frame of mind, I raised the whole question again and he agreed to see Stephen. They met in the laboratory; I was not present, but I believe that there was a terrible row. When I came in, Stephen had gone, and Mr Tableman was livid with rage. Apparently, he had again insisted upon Stephen giving up his fiancée, and Stephen had refused point-blank.'

'How did Stephen arrive at the laboratory?' asked Gonsalez. 'May I ask that question, Mr Fare?'

The Commissioner nodded.

'He entered by the side passage. Very few people who come to the house on purely scientific business enter the house.'

'Then access to the laboratory is possible at all hours?'

'Until the very last thing at night, when the gate is locked,' said the young man. 'You see, Uncle used to take a little constitutional before going to bed, and he preferred using that entrance.'

'Was the gate locked last night?'

John Munsey shook his head.

'No.' he said quietly. 'That was one of the first things I investigated. The gate was unfastened and ajar. It is not so much of a gate as an iron grille, as you probably observed.'

'Go on,' nodded Mr Fare.

'Well, the Professor gradually cooled down, and for two or three days he was very thoughtful, and I thought a little sad. On Monday – what is today? Thursday? – yes, it was on Monday, he said to me: "John, let's have a little talk about Steve. Do you think I have treated him very badly?" – "I think you were rather unreasonable, Uncle," I said. "Perhaps I was," he replied. "She must be a very fine girl for Stephen to risk poverty for her sake." That was the opportunity I had been praying for, and I think I urged Stephen's case with an eloquence which he would have commended. The upshot of it was that the old man weakened and sent a wire to Stephen, asking him to see him last night. It must have been a struggle for the Professor to have got over his objection to Miss Faber; he was a fanatic on the question of heredity – '

'Heredity?' interrupted Manfred quickly. 'What was wrong with Miss Faber?'

'I don't know,' shrugged the other, 'but the Professor had heard rumours that her father had died in an inebriates' home. I believe those rumours were baseless.'

'What happened last night?' asked Fare.

'I understand that Stephen came,' said Munsey. 'I kept carefully out of the way; in fact, I spent my time in my room, writing off some arrears of correspondence. I came downstairs about half past eleven, but the Professor had not returned. Looking from this window you can see the wall of the laboratory, and as the lights were still on, I thought the Professor's conversation had been protracted, and, hoping that the best results might come from this interview, I went to bed. It was earlier than I go as a rule, but it was quite usual for me to go to bed even without saying good night to the Professor.

'I was awakened at eight in the morning by the housekeeper, who told me that the Professor was not in his room. Here again, this was not an unusual circumstance. Sometimes the Professor would work very late in the laboratory and then throw himself into an armchair and go off to sleep. It was a habit of which I had remonstrated as plainly as I dared; but he was not a man who bore criticism with equanimity.

'I got into my dressing-gown and my slippers, and went along to the laboratory, which is reached, as you know, by the way we came here. It was then that I discovered him on the floor, and he was quite dead.'

'Was the door of the laboratory open?' asked Gonsalez.

'It was ajar.'

'And the gate also was ajar?'

Munsey nodded.

'You heard no sound of quarrelling?'

'None.'

There was a knock, and Munsey walked to the door.

'It is Stephen,' he said, and a second later Stephen Tableman, escorted by two detectives, came into the room. His big face was pale, and when he greeted his cousin with a little smile, Manfred saw the extraordinary canines, big and cruel-looking. The other teeth were of normal size, but these pointed fangs were notably abnormal.

Stephen Tableman was a young giant, and, observing those great hands of his, Manfred bit his lip thoughtfully.

'You have heard the sad news, Mr Tableman?'

'Yes, sir,' said Stephen in a shaking voice. 'Can I see my father?'

'In a little time,' said Fare, and his voice was hard. 'I want you to tell me when you saw your father last.'

'I saw him alive last night,' said Stephen Tableman quickly. 'I came by appointment to the laboratory, and we had a long talk.'

'How long were you there with him?'

'About two hours, as near as I can guess.'

'Was the conversation of a friendly character?'

'Very,' said Stephen emphatically. 'For the first time since over a year ago' – he hesitated – 'we discussed a certain subject rationally.'

'The subject being your fiancée, Miss Faber?'

Stephen looked at the interrogator steadily.

'That was the subject, Mr Fare,' he replied quietly.

'Did you discuss any other matters?'

Stephen hesitated.

'We discussed money,' he said. 'My father cut off his allowance, and I have been rather short; in fact, I have been overdrawn at my bank, and he promised to make that right, and also spoke about – the future.'

'About his will?'

'Yes, sir, he spoke about altering his will.' He looked across at Munsey, and again he smiled. 'My cousin has been a most persistent advocate, and I can't thank him half enough for his loyalty to me in those dark times,' he said.

'When you left the laboratory, did you go out by the side entrance?'

Stephen nodded.

'And did you close the door behind you?'

'My father closed the door,' he said. 'I distinctly remember hearing the click of the lock as I was going up the alley.'

'Can the door be opened from outside?'

'Yes,' said Stephen, 'there is a lock which has only one key, and that is in my father's possession – I think I am right, John?'

John Munsey nodded.

'So that, if he closed the door behind you, it could only be opened again by somebody in the laboratory – himself, for example?'

Stephen looked puzzled.

'I don't quite understand the meaning of this enquiry,' he said. 'The detective told me that my father had been found dead. What was the cause?'

'I think he was strangled,' said Fare quietly, and the young man took a step back.

'Strangled!' he whispered. 'But he hadn't an enemy in the world.'

'That we shall discover.' Fare's voice was dry and businesslike. 'You can go now, Mr Tableman.'

After a moment's hesitation the big fellow swung across the room through a door in the direction of the laboratory. He came back after an absence of a quarter of an hour, and his face was deathly white.

'Horrible, horrible!' he muttered. 'My poor father!'

'You are on the way to being a doctor, Mr Tableman? I believe you are at the Middlesex Hospital,' said Fare. 'Do you agree with me that your father was strangled?'

The other nodded.

'It looks that way,' he said, speaking with difficulty. 'I couldn't conduct an examination as if he had been – somebody else, but it looks that way.'

The two men walked back to their lodgings. Manfred thought best when his muscles were most active. Their walk was in silence, each being busy with his own thoughts.

'You observed the canines?' asked Leon with quiet triumph after a while.

'I observed too his obvious distress,' said Manfred, and Leon chuckled.

'It is evident that you have not read friend Mantegazza's admirable monograph on the "Physiology of Pain",' he said smugly – Leon was delightfully smug at times – 'nor examined his most admirable tables on the "Synonyms of Expression", or otherwise you would be aware that the expression of sorrow is indistinguishable from the expression of remorse.'

Manfred looked down at his friend with that quiet smile of his.

'Anybody who did not know you, Leon, would say that you were convinced that Professor Tableman was strangled by his son.'

'After a heated quarrel,' said Gonsalez complacently.

'When young Tableman had gone, you inspected the laboratory. Did you discover anything?'

'Nothing more than I expected to find,' said Gonsalez. 'There were the usual air apparatus, the inevitable liquid-air still, the ever-to-be-expected electric crucibles. The inspection was superfluous, I admit, for I knew exactly how the murder was committed – for murder it was – the moment I came into the laboratory and saw the thermos flask and the pad of cotton wool.'

Suddenly he frowned and stopped dead.

'*Santa Miranda*!' he ejaculated. Gonsalez always swore by this non-existent saint. 'I had forgotten!'

He looked up and down the street.

'There is a place from whence we can telephone,' he said. 'Will you come with me, or shall I leave you here?'

'I am consumed with curiosity,' said Manfred.

They went into the shop and Gonsalez gave a number. Manfred did not ask him how he knew it, because he too had read the number which was written on the telephone disc that stood on the late Professor's table.

'Is that you, Mr Munsey?' asked Gonsalez. 'It is I. You remember I have just come from you? Yes, I thought you would recognise my voice. I want to ask you where are the Professor's spectacles.'

There was a moment's silence.

'The Professor's spectacles?' said Munsey's voice. 'Why, they're with him, aren't they?'

'They were not on the body or near it,' said Gonsalez. 'Will you see if they are in his room? I'll hold the line.'

He waited, humming a little aria from *El Perro Chico*, a light opera which had its day in Madrid fifteen years before; and presently he directed his attention again to the instrument.

'In his bedroom, were they? Thank you very much.'

He hung up the receiver. He did not explain the conversation to Manfred, nor did Manfred expect him to, for Leon Gonsalez dearly loved a mystery. All he permitted himself to say was, 'Canine teeth!'

And this seemed to amuse him very much.

When Gonsalez came to breakfast the next morning, the waiter informed him that Manfred had gone out early. George came in about ten minutes after the other had commenced breakfast, and Leon Gonsalez looked up.

'You puzzle me when your face is so mask-like, George,' he said. 'I don't know whether you're particularly amused or particularly depressed.'

'A little of the one and a little of the other,' said Manfred, sitting down to breakfast. 'I have been to Fleet Street to examine the files of the sporting press.'

'The sporting press?' repeated Gonsalez, staring at him, and Manfred nodded.

'Incidentally, I met Fare. No trace of poison has been found in the body, and no other sign of violence. They are arresting Stephen Tableman today.'

'I was afraid of that,' said Gonsalez gravely. 'But why the sporting press, George?'

Manfred did not answer the question, but went on: 'Fare is quite certain that the murder was committed by Stephen Tableman. His theory is that there was a quarrel and that the young man lost his temper and choked his father. Apparently, the examination of the body proved that extraordinary violence must have been used. Every blood-vessel in the neck is congested. Fare also told me that at first the doctor suspected poison, but there is no sign of any drug to be discovered, and the doctors say that the drug that would cause that death with such symptoms is unknown. It makes it worse for Stephen Tableman because for the past few months he has been concentrating his studies upon obscure poisons.'

Gonsalez stretched back in his chair, his hands in his pockets.

'Well, whether he committed that murder or not,' he said after a while, 'he is certain to commit a murder sooner or later. I remember once a doctor in Barcelona who had such teeth. He was a devout Christian, a popular man, a bachelor, and had plenty of money, and there seemed no reason in the world why he should murder anybody, and yet he did. He murdered another doctor who threatened to expose some error he made in an operation. I tell you, George, with teeth like that – ' He paused and frowned thoughtfully. 'My dear George,' he said, 'I am going to ask Fare if he will allow me the privilege of spending a few hours alone in Professor Tableman's laboratory.'

'Why on earth – ' began Manfred, and checked himself. 'Why, of course, you have a reason, Leon. As a rule I find no difficulty in solving such mysteries as these. But in this case I am puzzled, though

I have confidence that you have already unravelled what mystery there is. There are certain features about the business which are particularly baffling. Why should the old man be wearing thick gloves – '

Gonsalez sprang to his feet, his eyes blazing.

'What a fool! What a fool!' he almost shouted. 'I didn't see those. Are you sure, George?' he asked eagerly. 'He had thick gloves? Are you certain?'

Manfred nodded, smiling his surprise at the other's perturbation.

'That's it!' Gonsalez snapped his fingers. 'I knew there was some error in my calculations! Thick woollen gloves, weren't they?' He became suddenly thoughtful. 'Now, I wonder how the devil he induced the old man to put 'em on?' he said half to himself.

The request to Mr Fare was granted, and the two men went together to the laboratory. John Munsey was waiting for them.

'I discovered those spectacles by my uncle's bedside,' he said as soon as he saw them.

'Oh, the spectacles?' said Leon absently. 'May I see them?' He took them in his hand. 'Your uncle was very short-sighted. How did they come to leave his possession, I wonder?'

'I think he went up to his bedroom to change; he usually did after dinner,' explained Mr Munsey. 'And he must have left them there. He usually kept an emergency pair in the laboratory, but for some reason or other he doesn't seem to have put them on. Do you wish to be alone in the laboratory?' he asked.

'I would rather,' said Leon. 'Perhaps you would entertain my friend whilst I look round?'

Left alone, he locked the door that communicated between the laboratory and the house, and his first search was for the spectacles that the old man usually wore when he was working.

Characteristically enough, he went straight to the place where they were – a big galvanised ash-pan by the side of the steps leading up to the laboratory. He found them in fragments, the horn rims broken in two places, and he collected what he could and returned to the laboratory, and, laying them on the bench, he took up the telephone.

The laboratory had a direct connection with the exchange, and after five minutes waiting, Gonsalez found himself in communication with Stephen Tableman.

'Yes, sir,' was the surprised reply. 'My father wore his glasses throughout the interview.'

'Thank you, that is all,' said Gonsalez and hung up the 'phone.

Then he went to one of the apparatus in a corner of the laboratory and worked steadily for an hour and a half. At the end of that time he went to the telephone again. Another half hour passed, and then he pulled from his pocket a pair of thick woollen gloves, and unlocking the door leading to the house, called Manfred.

'Ask Mr Munsey to come,' he said.

'Your friend is interested in science,' said Mr Munsey as he accompanied Manfred along the passage.

'I think he is one of the cleverest in his own particular line,' said Manfred.

He came into the laboratory ahead of Munsey, and to his surprise, Gonsalez was standing near the table, holding in his hand a small liqueur glass filled with an almost colourless liquid. Almost colourless, but there was a blue tinge to it, and to Manfred's amazement a faint mist was rising from its surface.

Manfred stared at him, and then he saw that the hands of Leon Gonsalez were enclosed in thick woollen gloves.

'Have you finished?' smiled Mr Munsey as he came from behind Manfred; and then he saw Leon and smiled no more. His face went drawn and haggard, his eyes narrowed, and Manfred heard his laboured breathing.

'Have a drink, my friend?' said Leon pleasantly. 'A beautiful drink. You'd mistake it for crême de menthe or any old liqueur – especially if you were a short-sighted, absent-minded old man and somebody had purloined your spectacles.'

'What do you mean?' asked Munsey hoarsely. 'I – I don't understand you.'

'I promise you that this drink is innocuous, that it contains no poison whatever, that it is as pure as the air you breathe,' Gonsalez went on.

'Damn you!' yelled Munsey, but before he could leap at his tormentor, Manfred had caught him and slung him to the ground.

'I have telephoned for the excellent Mr Fare, and he will be here soon, and also Mr Stephen Tableman. Ah, here they are.'

There was a tap at the door.

'Will you open, please, my dear George? I do not think our young friend will move. If he does, I will throw the contents of this glass in his face.'

Fare came in, followed by Stephen, and with them an officer from Scotland Yard.

'There is your prisoner, Mr Fare,' said Gonsalez. 'And here is the means by which Mr John Munsey encompassed the death of his uncle – decided thereto, I guess, by the fact that his uncle had been reconciled with Stephen Tableman, and that the will which he had so carefully manoeuvred was to be altered in Stephen Tableman's favour.'

'That's a lie!' gasped John Munsey. 'I worked for you – you know I did, Stephen. I did my best for you – '

'All part of the general scheme of deception – again I am guessing,' said Gonsalez. 'If I am wrong, drink this. It is the liquid your uncle drank on the night of his death.'

'What is it?' demanded Fare quickly.

'Ask him,' smiled Gonsalez, nodding to the man.

John Munsey turned on his heels and walked to the door, and the police officer who had accompanied Fare followed him.

'And now I will tell you what it is,' said Gonsalez. 'It is liquid air!'

'Liquid air!' said the Commissioner. 'Why, what do you mean? How can a man be poisoned with liquid air?'

'Professor Tableman was not poisoned. Liquid air is a fluid obtained by reducing the temperature of air to two hundred and seventy degrees below zero. Scientists use the liquid for experiments, and it is usually kept in a thermos flask, the mouth of which is stopped with cotton wool, because, as you know, there would be danger of a blow up if the air was confined.'

'Good God?' gasped Tableman in horror. 'Then that blue mark about my father's throat – '

'He was frozen to death. At least his throat was frozen solid the second that liquid was taken. Your father was in the habit of drinking a liqueur before he went to bed, and there is no doubt that, after you had left, Munsey gave the Professor a glassful of liquid air and by some means induced him to put on gloves.'

'Why did he do that? Oh, of course, the cold,' said Manfred.

Gonsalez nodded.

'Without gloves he would have detected immediately the stuff he was handling. What artifice Munsey used we may never know. It is certain he himself must have been wearing gloves at the time. After your father's death he then began to prepare evidence to incriminate somebody else. The Professor had probably put away his glasses preparatory to going to bed, and the murderer, like myself, overlooked the fact that the body was still wearing gloves.'

'My own theory,' said Gonsalez later, 'is that Munsey has been working for years to oust his cousin from his father's affections. He probably invented the story of the dipsomaniac father of Miss Faber.'

Young Tableman had come to their lodgings, and now Gonsalez had a shock. Something he said had surprised a laugh from Stephen, and Gonsalez stared at him.

'Your – your teeth!' he stammered.

Stephen flushed.

'My teeth?' he repeated, puzzled.

'You had two enormous canines when I saw you last,' said Gonsalez. 'You remember, Manfred?' he said, and he was really agitated. 'I told you – '

He was interrupted by a burst of laughter from the young student.

'Oh, they were false,' he said awkwardly. 'They were knocked out at a rugger match, and Benson, who's a fellow in our dental department and is an awfully good chap, though a pretty poor dentist, undertook to make me two to fill the deficiency. They looked terrible, didn't they? I don't wonder your noticing them. I got two new ones put in by another dentist.'

'It happened on the thirteenth of September last year. I read about it in the sporting press,' said Manfred, and Gonsales fixed him with a reproachful glance.

'You see, my dear Leon – ' Manfred laid his hand on the other's shoulder – 'I knew they were false, just as you knew they were canines.'

When they were alone, Manfred said: 'Talking about canines – '

'Let us talk about something else,' snapped Leon.

The Man who hated Earthworms

'The death has occurred at Staines of Mr Falmouth, late Super-intendent of the Criminal Investigation Department. Mr Falmouth will best be remembered as the Officer who arrested George Man-fred, the leader of the Four Just Men gang. The sensational escape of this notorious man is perhaps the most remarkable chapter in criminal history. The "Four Just Men" was an organisation which set itself to right acts of injustice which the law left unpunished. It is believed that the members were exceedingly rich men who devoted their lives and fortunes to this quixotic but wholly unlawful purpose. The gang has not been heard of for many years.'

Manfred read the paragraph from the *Morning Telegram* and Leon Gonsalez frowned.

'I have an absurd objection to being called a "gang",' he said, and Manfred smiled quietly.

'Poor old Falmouth,' he reflected, 'well, he knows! He was a nice fellow.'

'I liked Falmouth,' agreed Gonsalez. 'He was a perfectly normal man except for a slight progenism – '

Manfred laughed.

'Forgive me if I appear dense, but I have never been able to keep up with you in this particular branch of science,' he said, 'what is a "progenism"?'

'The unscientific call it an "underhung jaw",' explained Leon, 'and it is mistaken for strength. It is only normal in Piedmont where the brachycephalic skull is so common. With such a skull, progenism is almost a natural condition.'

'Progenism or not, he was a good fellow,' insisted Manfred and Leon nodded. 'With well-developed wisdom teeth,' he added slyly, and Gonsalez went red, for teeth formed a delicate subject with him. Nevertheless he grinned.

'It will interest you to know, my dear George,' he said trium-phantly, 'that when the famous Dr Carrara examined the teeth of four hundred criminals and a like number of non-criminals – you will find his detailed narrative in the monograph "Sullo Sviluppo Del Terzo Dente Morale Net Criminali" – he found the wisdom tooth more frequently present in normal people.'

'I grant you the wisdom tooth,' said Manfred hastily. 'Look at the bay! Did you ever see anything more perfect?'

They were sitting on a little green lawn overlooking Babbacombe Beach. The sun was going down and a perfect day was drawing to its close. High above the blue sea towered the crimson cliffs and green fields of Devon.

Manfred looked at his watch.

'Are we dressing for dinner?' he asked, 'or has your professional friend Bohemian tastes?'

'He is of the new school,' said Leon, 'rather superior, rather immaculate, very Balliol. I am anxious that you should meet him, his hands are rather fascinating.'

Manfred in his wisdom did not ask why.

'I met him at golf,' Gonsalez went on, 'and certain things happened which interested me. For example, every time he saw an earthworm he stopped to kill it and displayed such an extraordinary fury in the assassination that I was astounded. Prejudice has no place in the scientific mind. He is exceptionally wealthy. People at the club told me that his uncle left him close on a million, and the estate of his aunt or cousin who died last year was valued at another million and he was the sole legatee. Naturally a good catch. Whether Miss Moleneux thinks the same I have had no opportunity of gauging,' he added after a pause.

'Good lord!' cried Manfred in consternation as he jumped up from his chair. 'She is coming to dinner too, isn't she?'

'And her mamma,' said Leon solemnly. 'Her mamma has learnt Spanish by correspondence lessons, and insists upon greeting me with "*habla usted Espanol?*" '

The two men had rented Cliff House for the spring. Manfred loved Devonshire in April when the slopes of the hills were yellow with primroses and daffodils made a golden path across the Devon lawns. 'Señor Fuentes' had taken the house after one inspection and found the calm and the peace which only nature's treasury of colour and fragrance could bring to his active mind.

Manfred had dressed and was sitting by the wood fire in the drawing-room when the purr of a motor-car coming cautiously down the cliff road brought him to his feet and through the open French window.

Leon Gonsalez had joined him before the big limousine had come to a halt before the porch.

The first to alight was a man and George observed him closely. He was tall and thin. He was not bad looking, though the face was lined and the eyes deep-set and level. He greeted Gonsalez with just a tiny hint of patronage in his tone.

'I hope we haven't kept you waiting, but my experiments detained me. Nothing went right in the laboratory today. You know Miss Moleneux and Mrs Moleneux?'

Manfred was introduced and found himself shaking hands with a grave-eyed girl of singular beauty.

Manfred was unusually sensitive to 'atmosphere' and there was something about this girl which momentarily chilled him. Her frequent smile, sweet as it was and undoubtedly sincere, was as undoubtedly mechanical. Leon, who judged people by reason rather than instinct, reached his conclusion more surely and gave shape and definite description to what in Manfred's mind was merely a distressful impression. The girl was afraid! Of what? wondered Leon. Not of that stout, complacent little woman whom she called mother, and surely not of this thin-faced academic gentleman in pince-nez.

Gonsalez had introduced Dr Viglow and whilst the ladies were taking off their cloaks in Manfred's room above, he had leisure to form a judgment. There was no need for him to entertain his guest. Dr Viglow spoke fluently, entertainingly and all the time.

'Our friend here plays a good game of golf,' he said, indicating Gonsalez, 'a good game of golf indeed for a foreigner. You two are Spanish?'

Manfred nodded. He was more thoroughly English than the doctor, did that gentleman but know, but it was as a Spaniard and armed, moreover, with a Spanish passport that he was a visitor to Britain.

'I understood you to say that your investigations have taken rather a sensational turn, Doctor,' said Leon and a light came into Dr Viglow's eyes.

'Yes,' he said complacently, and then quickly, 'who told you that?'

'You told me yourself at the club this morning.'

The doctor frowned.

'Did I?' he said and passed his hand across his forehead. 'I can't recollect that. When was this?'

'This morning,' said Leon, 'but your mind was probably occupied with much more important matters.'

The young professor bit his lip and frowned thoughtfully.

'I ought not to have forgotten what happened this morning,' he said in a troubled tone.

He gave the impression to Manfred that one half of him was struggling desperately to overcome a something in the other half. Suddenly he laughed.

'A sensational turn!' he said. 'Yes indeed, and I rather think that within a few months I shall not be without fame, even in my own country! It is, of course, terribly expensive. I was only reckoning up today that my typists' wages come to nearly £60 a week.'

Manfred opened his eyes at this.

'Your typists' wages?' he repeated slowly. 'Are you preparing a book?'

'Here are the ladies,' said Dr Felix.

His manner was abrupt to rudeness and later when they sat round the table in the little dining-room Manfred had further cause to wonder at the boorishness of this young scientist. He was seated next to Miss Moleneux and the meal was approaching its end when most unexpectedly he turned to the girl and in a loud voice said: 'You haven't kissed me today, Margaret.'

The girl went red and white and the fingers that fidgeted with the table-ware before her were trembling when she faltered: 'Haven't – haven't I, Felix?'

The bright eyes of Gonsalez never left the doctor. The man's face had gone purple with rage.

'By God! This is a nice thing!' he almost shouted. 'I'm engaged to you. I've left you everything in my will and I'm allowing your mother a thousand a year and you haven't kissed me today!'

'Doctor!' It was the mild but insistent voice of Gonsalez that broke the tension. 'I wonder whether you would tell me what chemical is represented by the formula Cl_2O_5.'

The doctor had turned his head slowly at the sound of Leon's voice and now was staring at him. Slowly the strange look passed from his face and it became normal.

'Cl_2O_5 is Oxide of Chlorine,' he said in an even voice, and from thenceforward the conversation passed by way of acid reactions into a scientific channel.

The only person at the table who had not been perturbed by Viglow's outburst had been the dumpy complacent lady on Manfred's right. She had tittered audibly at the reference to her allowance, and when the hum of conversation became general she lowered her voice and leant toward Manfred.

'Dear Felix is so eccentric,' she said, 'but he is quite the nicest, kindest soul. One must look after one's girls, don't you agree, Señor?'

She asked this latter question in very bad Spanish and Manfred nodded. He shot a glance at the girl. She was still deathly pale.

'And I am perfectly certain she will be happy, much happier than she would have been with that impossible person.'

She did not specify who the 'impossible person' was, but Manfred sensed a whole world of tragedy. He was not romantic, but one look at the girl had convinced him that there was something wrong in this engagement. Now it was that he came to a conclusion which Leon had reached an hour before, that the emotion which dominated the girl was fear. And he pretty well knew of whom she was afraid.

Half an hour later when the tail light of Dr Viglow's limousine had disappeared round a corner of the drive the two men went back to the drawing-room and Manfred threw a handful of kindling to bring the fire to a blaze.

'Well, what do you think?' said Gonsalez, rubbing his hands together with evidence of some enjoyment.

'I think it's rather horrible,' replied Manfred, settling himself in his chair. 'I thought the days when wicked mothers forced their daughters into unwholesome marriages were passed and done with. One hears so much about the modern girl.'

'Human nature isn't modern,' said Gonsalez briskly, 'and most mothers are fools where their daughters are concerned. I know you won't agree but I speak with authority. Mantegazza collected statistics of 843 families – '

Manfred chuckled.

'You and your Mantegazza!' he laughed. 'Did that infernal man know everything?'

'Almost everything,' said Leon. 'As to the girl,' he became suddenly grave, 'she will not marry him of course.'

'What is the matter with him?' asked Manfred. 'He seems to have an ungovernable temper.'

'He is mad,' replied Leon calmly and Manfred looked at him.

'Mad?' he repeated incredulously. 'Do you mean to say that he is a lunatic?'

'I never use the word in a spectacular or even in a vulgar sense,' said Gonsalez, lighting a cigarette carefully. 'The man is undoubtedly mad. I thought so a few days ago and I am certain of it now. The most ominous test is the test of memory. People who are on the verge of madness or entering its early stages do not remember what happened a short time before. Did you notice how worried he was when I told him of the conversation we had this morning?'

'That struck me as peculiar,' agreed Manfred.

'He was fighting,' said Leon, 'the sane half of his brain against the insane half. The doctor against the irresponsible animal. The doctor told him that if he had suddenly lost his memory for incidents which had occurred only a few hours before, he was on the high way to lunacy. The crazy half of the brain told him that he was such a wonderful fellow that the rules applying to ordinary human beings did not apply to him. We will call upon him tomorrow to see his laboratory and discover why he is paying £60 a week for typists,' he said. 'And now, my dear George, you can go to bed. I am going to read the excellent but often misguided Lombroso on the male delinquent.'

Dr Viglow's laboratory was a new red building on the edge of Dartmoor. To be exact, it consisted of two buildings, one of which was a large army hut which had been recently erected for the accommodation of the doctor's clerical staff.

'I haven't met a professor for two or three years,' said Manfred as they were driving across the moor, en route to pay their call, 'nor have I been in a laboratory for five. And yet within the space of a few weeks I have met two extraordinary professors, one of whom I admit was dead. Also I have visited two laboratories.'

Leon nodded.

'Some day I will make a very complete examination of the phenomena of coincidence,' he said.

When they reached the laboratory they found a post-office van, backed up against the main entrance, and three assistants in white overalls were carrying post bags and depositing them in the van.

'He must have a pretty large correspondence,' said Manfred in wonder.

The doctor, in a long white overall, was standing at the door as they alighted from their car, and greeted them warmly.

'Come into my office,' he said, and led the way to a large airy room which was singularly free from the paraphernalia which Gonsalez usually associated with such work-rooms.

'You have a heavy post,' said Leon and the doctor laughed quietly.

'They are merely going to the Torquay post office,' he said. 'I have arranged for them to be despatched when – ' he hesitated, 'when I am sure. You see,' he said, speaking with great earnestness, 'a scientist has to be so careful. Every minute after he has announced a discovery he is tortured with the fear that he has forgotten something, some essential, or has reached a too hasty conclusion. But I think I'm right,' he said, speaking half to himself. 'I'm sure I'm right, but I must be even more sure!'

He showed them round the large room, but there was little which Manfred had not seen in the laboratory of the late Professor Tableman. Viglow had greeted them genially, indeed expansively, and yet within five minutes of their arrival he was taciturn, almost silent, and did not volunteer information about any of the instruments in which Leon showed so much interest, unless he was asked.

They came back to his room and again his mood changed and he became almost gay.

'I'll tell you,' he said, 'by Jove, I'll tell you! And no living soul knows this except myself, or realises or understands the extraordinary work I have been doing.'

His face lit up, his eyes sparkled and it seemed to Manfred that he grew taller in this moment of exaltation. Pulling open a drawer of a table which stood against the wall he brought out a long porcelain plate and laid it down. From a wire-netted cupboard on the wall he took two tin boxes and with an expression of disgust which he could not disguise, turned the contents upon the slab. It was apparently a box full of common garden mould and then Leon saw to his amazement a wriggling little red shape twisting and twining in its acute discomfort. The little red fellow sought to hide himself and burrowed sinuously into the mould.

'Curse you! Curse you!' The doctor's voice rose until it was a howl. His face was twisted and puckered in his mad rage. 'How I hate you!'

If ever a man's eyes held hate and terror, they were the eyes of Dr Felix Viglow.

Manfred drew a long breath and stepped back a pace the better to observe him. Then the man calmed himself and peered down at Leon.

'When I was a child,' he said in a voice that shook, 'I hated them and we had a nurse named Martha, a beastly woman, a wicked woman, who dropped one down my neck. Imagine the horror of it!'

Leon said nothing. To him the earthworm was a genus of chaetopod in the section *oligochaeta* and bore the somewhat pretentious name of *lumbricus terrestris*. And in that way, Dr Viglow, eminent naturalist and scientist, should have regarded this beneficent little fellow.

'I have a theory,' said the doctor. He was calmer now and was wiping the sweat from his forehead with a handkerchief, 'that in cycles every type of living thing on the earth becomes in turn the dominant creature. In a million years' time man may dwindle to the size of an ant and the earthworm, by its super-intelligence, its cunning and its ferocity, may be pre-eminent in the world! I have always thought that,' he went on when neither Leon nor Manfred offered any comment. 'It is still my thought by day and my dream by night. I have devoted my life to the destruction of this menace.'

Now the earthworm is neither cunning nor intelligent and is moreover notoriously devoid of ambition.

The doctor again went to the cupboard and took out a wide-necked bottle filled with a greyish powder. He brought it back and held it within a few inches of Leon's face.

'This is the work of twelve years,' he said simply. 'There is no difficulty in finding a substance which will kill these pests, but this does more.'

He took a scalpel and tilting the bottle brought out a few grains of the powder on the edge of it. This he dissolved in a twenty-ounce measure which he filled with water. He stirred the colourless fluid with a glass rod, then lifting the rod he allowed three drops to fall upon the mould wherein the little creature was hidden. A few seconds passed, there was a heaving of the earth where the victim was concealed.

'He is dead,' said the doctor triumphantly and scraped away the earth to prove the truth of his words. 'And he is not only dead, but that handful of earth is death to any other earthworm that touches it.'

He rang a bell and one of his attendants came in.

'Clear away that,' he said with a shudder and walked gloomily to his desk.

Leon did not speak all the way back to the house. He sat curled up in the corner of the car, his arms lightly folded, his chin on his breast. That night without a word of explanation he left the house, declining Manfred's suggestion that he should walk with him and volunteering no information as to where he was going.

Gonsalez walked by the cliff road, across Babbacombe Downs and came to the doctor's house at nine o'clock that night. The doctor had a large house and maintained a big staff of servants, but amongst his other eccentricities was the choice of a gardener's cottage away from the house as his sleeping place at night.

It was only lately that the doctor had chosen this lonely lodging. He had been happy enough in the big old house which had been his father's, until he had heard voices whispering to him at night and the creak of boards and had seen shapes vanishing along the dark corridors, and then in his madness he had conceived the idea that his servants were conspiring against him and that he might any night be murdered in his bed. So he had the gardener turned out of his cottage, had refurnished the little house, and there, behind locked doors, he read and thought and slept the nights away. Gonsalez had heard of this peculiarity and approached the cottage with some caution, for a frightened man is more dangerous than a wicked man. He rapped at the door and heard a step across the flagged floor.

'Who is that?' asked a voice.

'It is I,' said Gonsalez and gave the name by which he was known.

After hesitation the lock turned and the door opened.

'Come in, come in,' said Viglow testily and locked the door behind him. 'You have come to congratulate me, I am sure. You must come to my wedding too, my friend. It will be a wonderful wedding, for there I shall make a speech and tell the story of my discovery. Will you have a drink? I have nothing here, but I can get it from the house. I have a telephone in my bedroom.'

Leon shook his head.

'I have been rather puzzling out your plan, Doctor,' he said, accepting the proffered cigarette, 'and I have been trying to connect those postal bags which I saw being loaded at the door of your laboratory with the discovery which you revealed this afternoon.'

Dr Viglow's narrow eyes were gleaming with merriment and he leant back in his chair and crossed his legs, like one preparing for a pleasant recital.

'I will tell you,' he said. 'For months I have been in correspondence with farming associations, both here and on the Continent. I have something of a European reputation,' he said, with that extraordinary immodesty which Leon had noticed before. 'In fact, I think that my treatment for phylloxera did more to remove the scourge from the vineyards of Europe than any other preparation.'

Leon nodded. He knew this to be the truth.

'So you see, my word is accepted in matters dealing with agriculture. But I found after one or two talks with our own stupid farmers that there is an unusual prejudice against destroying – ' he did not mention the dreaded name but shivered – 'and that of course I had to get round. Now that I am satisfied that my preparation is exact, I can release the packets in the post office. In fact, I was just about to telephone to the postmaster telling him that they could go off – they are all stamped and addressed – when you knocked at the door.'

'To whom are they addressed?' asked Leon steadily.

'To various farmers – some fourteen thousand in all in various parts of the country and Europe, and each packet has printed instructions in English, French, German and Spanish. I had to tell them that it was a new kind of fertiliser or they may not have been as enthusiastic in the furtherance of my experiment as I am.'

'And what are they going to do with these packets when they get them?' asked Leon quietly.

'They will dissolve them and spray a certain area of their land – I suggested ploughed land. They need only treat a limited area of earth,' he explained. 'I think these wretched beasts will carry infection quickly enough. I believe,' he leant forward and spoke impressively, 'that in six months there will not be one living in Europe or Asia.'

'They do not know that the poison is intended to kill – earth-worms?' asked Leon.

'No, I've told you,' snapped the other. 'Wait, I will telephone the postmaster.'

He rose quickly to his feet, but Leon was quicker and gripped his arm.

'My dear friend,' he said, 'you must not do this.'

Dr Viglow tried to withdraw his arm.

'Let me go,' he snarled. 'Are you one of those devils who are trying to torment me?'

In ordinary circumstances, Leon would have been strong enough to hold the man, but Viglow's strength was extraordinary and Gonsalez found himself thrust back into the chair. Before he could spring up, the man had passed through the door and slammed and locked it behind him.

The cottage was on one floor and was divided into two rooms by a wooden partition which Viglow had erected. Over the door was a fanlight, and pulling the table forward Leon sprang on to the top and with his elbow smashed the flimsy frame.

'Don't touch that telephone,' he said sternly. 'Do you hear?'

The doctor looked round with a grin. 'You are a friend of those devils!' he said, and his hand was on the receiver when Leon shot him dead.

* * *

Manfred came back the next morning from his walk and found Gonsalez pacing the lawn, smoking an extra long cigar.

'My dear Leon,' said Manfred as he slipped his arm in the other's. 'You did not tell me.'

'I thought it best to wait,' said Leon.

'I heard quite by accident,' Manfred went on. 'The story is that a burglar broke into the cottage and shot the doctor when he was telephoning for assistance. All the silverware in the outer room has been stolen. The doctor's watch and pocket-book have disappeared.'

'They are at this moment at the bottom of Babbacombe Bay,' said Leon. 'I went fishing very early this morning before you were awake.'

They paced the lawn in silence for a while and then: 'Was it necessary?' asked Manfred.

'Very necessary,' said Leon gravely. 'You have to realise first of all that although this man was mad, he had discovered not only a poison but an infection.'

'But, my dear fellow,' smiled Manfred, 'was an earthworm worth it?'

'Worth more than his death,' said Leon. 'There isn't a scientist in the world who does not agree that if the earthworm was destroyed the world would become sterile and the people of this world would be starving in seven years.'

Manfred stopped in his walk and stared down at his companion.

'Do you really mean that?'

Leon nodded.

'He is the one necessary creature in God's world,' he said soberly. 'It fertilises the land and covers the bare rocks with earth. It is the surest friend of mankind that we know, and now I am going down to the post office with a story which I think will be sufficiently plausible to recover those worm poisoners.'

Manfred mused a while, then he said: 'I'm glad in many ways – in every way,' he corrected. 'I rather liked that girl, and I'm sure that impossible person isn't so impossible.'

The Man who died Twice

The interval between Acts 2 and 3 was an unusually long one, and the three men who sat in the stage box were in such harmony of mind that none of them felt the necessity for making conversation. The piece was a conventional crook play and each of the three had solved the 'mystery' of the murder before the drop fell on the first act. They had reached the same solution (and the right one) without any great mental effort.

Fare, the Police Commissioner, had dined with George Manfred and Leon Gonsalez (he addressed them respectively as 'Señor Fuentes' and 'Señor Mandrelino' and did not doubt that they were natives of Spain, despite their faultless English) and the party had come on to the theatre.

Mr Fare frowned as at some unpleasant memory and heard a soft laugh. Looking up, he met the dancing eyes of Leon.

'Why do you laugh?' he asked, half smiling in sympathy.

'At your thoughts,' replied the calm Gonsalez.

'At my thoughts!' repeated the other, startled,

'Yes,' Leon nodded, 'you were thinking of the Four Just Men.'

'Extraordinary!' exclaimed Fare. 'It is perfectly true. What is it, telepathy?'

Gonsalez shook his head. As to Manfred, he was gazing abstractedly into the stalls.

'No, it was not telepathy,' said Leon, 'it was your facial expression.'

'But I haven't mentioned those rascals, how – '

'Facial expression,' said Leon, revelling in his pet topic, 'especially an expression of the emotions, comes into the category of primitive instincts – they are not "willed". For example, when a billiard player strikes a ball he throws and twists his body after the ball – you must have seen the contortions of a player who has missed his shot by a narrow margin? A man using scissors works his jaw, a rower cmoves his lips with every stroke of the oar. These are what we call "automatisms". Animals have these characteristics. A hungry dog approaching meat pricks his ears in the direction of his meal – '

'Is there a particular act of automatism produced by the thought of the Four Just Men?' asked the Commissioner, smiling.

Leon nodded.

'It would take long to describe, but I will not deceive you. I less read than guessed your thoughts by following them. The last line in the last act we saw was uttered by a ridiculous stage parson who says: "Justice! There is a justice beyond the law!" And I saw you frown. And then you looked across the stalls and nodded to the editor of the *Megaphone*. And I remembered that you had written an article on the Four Just Men for that journal – '

'A little biography on poor Falmouth who died the other day,' corrected Fare. 'Yes, yes, I see. You were right, of course. I was thinking of them and their pretensions to act as judges and executioners when the law fails to punish the guilty, or rather the guilty succeed in avoiding conviction.'

Manfred turned suddenly.

'Leon,' he spoke in Spanish, in which language the three had been conversing off and on during the evening. 'View the cavalier with the diamond in his shirt – what do you make of him?' The question was in English.

Leon raised his powerful opera glasses and surveyed the man whom his friend had indicated.

'I should like to hear him speak,' he said after a while. 'See how delicate his face is and how powerful are his jaws – almost prognathic, for the upper maxilla is distinctly arrested. Regard him, Señor, and tell me if you do not agree that his eyes are unusually bright?'

Manfred took the glasses and looked at the unconscious man.

'They are swollen – yes, I see they are bright.'

'What else do you see?'

'The lips are large and a little swollen too, I think,' said Manfred.

Leon took the glasses and turned to the Commissioner.

'I do not bet, but if I did I would wager a thousand pesetas that this man speaks with a harsh cracked voice.'

Fare looked from his companion to the object of their scrutiny and then back to Leon.

'You are perfectly right,' he said quietly. 'His name is Ballam and his voice is extraordinarily rough and harsh. What is he?'

'Vicious,' replied Gonsalez. 'My dear friend, that man is vicious, a bad man. Beware of the bright eyes and the cracked voice, Señor! They stand for evil!'

Fare rubbed his nose irritably, a trick of his.

'If you were anybody else I should be very rude and say that you knew him or had met him,' he said, 'but after your extraordinary demonstration the other day I realise there must be something in physiognomy.'

He referred to a visit which Leon Gonsalez and Manfred had paid to the record department of Scotland Yard. There, with forty photographs of criminals spread upon the table before him Gonsalez, taking them in order, had enumerated the crimes with which their names were associated. He only made four errors and even they were very excusable.

'Yes, Gregory Ballam is a pretty bad lot,' said the Commissioner thoughtfully. 'He has never been through our hands, but that is the luck of the game. He's as shrewd as the devil and it hurts me to see him with a nice girl like Genee Maggiore.'

'The girl who is sitting with him?' asked Manfred, interested.

'An actress,' murmured Gonsalez. 'You observe, my dear George, how she turns her head first to the left and then to the right at intervals, though there is no attraction in either direction. She has the habit of being seen – it is not vanity, it is merely a peculiar symptom of her profession.'

'What is his favourite vanity?' asked Manfred and the Commissioner smiled. 'You know our Dickens, eh?' he asked, for he thought of Manfred as a Spaniard. 'Well, it would be difficult to tell you what Gregory Ballam does to earn his respectable income,' he said more seriously. 'I think he is connected with a moneylender's business and runs a few profitable sidelines.'

'Such as – ' suggested Manfred.

Mr Fare was not, apparently, anxious to commit himself. 'I'll tell you in the strictest confidence,' he said. 'We believe, and have good cause to believe, that he has a hop joint which is frequented by wealthy people. Did you read last week about the man, John Bidworth, who shot a nursemaid in Kensington Gardens and then shot himself?'

Manfred nodded.

'He was quite a well-connected person, wasn't he?' he asked.

'He was very well connected,' replied Fare emphatically. 'So well connected that we did not want to bring his people into the case at all. He died the next day in hospital and the surgeons tell us that he was undoubtedly under the influence of some Indian drug and that in his few moments of consciousness he as much as told the surgeon in charge of the case that he had been on a jag the night before and had finished up in what he called an opium house, and remembered nothing further till he woke up in the hospital. He died without knowing that he had committed this atrocious crime. There is no doubt that under the maddening influence of the drug he shot the first person he saw.'

'Was it Mr Ballam's opium house?' asked Gonsalez, interested.

The curtain rose at that moment and conversation went on in a whisper.

'We don't know – in his delirium he mentioned Ballam's name. We have tried our best to find out. He has been watched. Places at which he has stayed any length of time have been visited, but we have found nothing to incriminate him.'

Leon Gonsalez had a favourite hour and a favourite meal at which he was at his brightest. That hour was at nine o'clock in the morning and the meal was breakfast. He put down his paper the next morning and asked:

'What is crime?'

'Professor,' said Manfred solemnly, 'I will tell you. It is the departure from the set rules which govern human society.'

'You are conventional,' said Gonsalez. 'My dear George, you are always conventional at nine o'clock in the morning! Now, had I asked you at midnight you would have told me that it is any act which wilfully offends and discomforts your neighbour. If I desired to give it a narrow and what they call in this country a legal interpretation I would add, "contrary to the law". There must be ten thousand crimes committed for every one detected. People associated crime only with those offences which are committed by a certain type of illiterate or semi-illiterate lunatic or half-lunatic, glibly dubbed a "criminal". Now, here is a villainous crime, a monumental crime. He is a man who is destroying the souls of youth and breaking hearts ruthlessly! Here is one who is dragging down men and women from the upward road and debasing them in their own eyes, slaying ambition and all beauty of soul and mind in order that he should live in a certain comfort, wearing a clean dress shirt every evening of his life and drinking expensive and unnecessary wines with his expensive and indigestible dinner.'

'Where is this man?' asked Manfred.

'He lives at 993 Jermyn Street, in fact he is a neighbour,' said Leon.

'You're speaking of Mr Ballam?'

'I'm speaking of Mr Ballam,' said Gonsalez gravely. 'Tonight I am going to be a foreign artist with large rolls of money in my pockets and an irresistible desire to be amused. I do not doubt that sooner or later Mr Ballam and I will gravitate together. Do I look like a detective, George?' he asked abruptly.

'You look more like a successful pianist,' said George and Gonsalez sniffed.

'You can even be offensive at nine o'clock in the morning,' he said.

There are two risks which criminals face (with due respect to the opinions of Leon Gonsalez, this word criminal is employed by the narrator) in the pursuit of easy wealth. There is the risk of detection and punishment which applies to the big as well as to the little delinquent. There is the risk of losing large sums of money invested for the purpose of securing even larger sums. The criminal who puts money in his business runs the least risk of detection. That is why only the poor and foolish come stumbling up the stairs which lead to the dock at the Old Bailey, and that is why the big men, who would be indignant at the very suggestion that they were in the category of law-breakers, seldom or never make their little bow to the Judge.

Mr Gregory Ballam stood for and represented certain moneyed interests which had purchased at auction three houses in Montague Street, Portland Place. They were three houses which occupied an island site. The first of these was let out in offices, the ground floor being occupied by a lawyer, the first floor by a wine and spirit merchant, the second being a very plain suite, dedicated to the business hours of Mr Gregory Ballam. This gentleman also rented the cellar, which by the aid of lime-wash and distemper had been converted into, if not a pleasant, at any rate a neat and cleanly storage place. Through this cellar you could reach (amongst other places) a brand-new garage, which had been built for one of Mr Ballam's partners, but in which Mr Ballam was not interested at all.

None but the workmen who had been employed in renovation knew that it was possible also to walk from one house to the other, either through the door in the cellar which had existed when the houses were purchased, or through a new door in Mr Ballam's office.

The third house, that at the end of the island site, was occupied by the International Artists' Club, and the police had never followed Mr Ballam there because Mr Ballam had never gone there, at least not by the front door. The Artists' Club had a 'rest room' and there were times when Mr Ballam had appeared, as if by magic, in that room, had met a select little party and conducted them through a well-concealed pass-door to the ground floor of the middle house.

The middle house was the most respectable looking of the three. It had neat muslin curtains at all its windows and was occupied by a venerable gentleman and his wife.

The venerable gentleman made a practice of going out to business every morning at ten o'clock, his shiny silk hat set jauntily on the side of his head, a furled umbrella under his arm and a button-hole in his coat. The police knew him by sight and local constables touched their helmets to him. In the days gone by when Mr Raymond, as he called himself, had a luxurious white beard and earned an elegant income by writing begging letters and interviewing credulous and sympathetic females, he did not have that name or the reputation which he enjoyed in Montague Street. But now he was clean-shaven and had the appearance of a retired admiral and he received £4 a week for going out of the house every morning at ten o'clock, with his silk hat set at a rakish angle, and his furled umbrella and his neat little boutonniere. He spent most of the day in the Guild-hall reading-room and came back at five o'clock in the evening as jaunty as ever.

And his day's work being ended, he and his hard-faced wife went to their little attic room and played cribbage and their language was certainly jaunty but was not venerable.

On the first floor, behind triple black velvet curtains, men and women smoked day and night. It was a large room, being two rooms which had been converted into one and it had been decorated under Mr Ballam's eye. In this room nothing but opium was smoked. If you had a fancy for hasheesh you indulged yourself in a basement apartment. Sometimes Mr Ballam himself came to take a whiff of the dream-herb, but he usually reserved these visits for such occasions as the introduction of a new and profitable client. The pipe had no ill-effect upon Mr Ballam. That was his boast. He boasted now to a new client, a rich Spanish artist who had been picked up by one of his jackals and piloted to the International Artists' Club.

'Nor on me,' said the newcomer, waving away a yellow-faced Chinaman who ministered to the needs of the smokers. 'I always bring my own smoke.'

Ballam leant forward curiously as the man took a silver box from his pocket and produced therefrom a green and sticky-looking pill.

'What is that?' asked Ballam curiously.

'It is a mixture of my own, *cannabis indica*, opium and a little Turkish tobacco mixed. It is even milder than opium and the result infinitely more wonderful.'

'You can't smoke it here,' said Ballam, shaking his head. 'Try the pipe, old man.'

But the 'old man' – he was really young in spite of his grey hair – was emphatic.

'It doesn't matter,' he said, 'I can smoke at home. I only came out of curiosity,' and he rose to go.

'Don't be in a hurry,' said Ballam hastily. 'See here, we've got a basement downstairs where the hemp pipes go – the smokers up here don't like the smell – I'll come down and try one with you. Bring your coffee.'

The basement was empty and selecting a comfortable divan Mr Ballam and his guest sat down.

'You can light this with a match, you don't want a spirit stove,' said the stranger.

Ballam, sipping his coffee, looked dubiously at the pipe which Gonsalez offered.

'There was a question I was going to ask you,' said Leon. 'Does running a show like this keep you awake at nights?'

'Don't be silly,' said Mr Ballam, lighting his pipe slowly and puffing with evident enjoyment. 'This isn't bad stuff at all. Keep me awake at nights? Why should it?'

'Well,' answered Leon. 'Lots of people go queer here, don't they? I mean it ruins people smoking this kind of stuff.'

'That's their look out,' said Mr Ballam comfortably. 'They get a lot of fun. There's only one life and you've got to die once.'

'Some men die twice,' said Leon soberly. 'Some men who under the influence of a noxious drug go *fantee* and wake to find themselves murderers. There's a drug in the East which the natives call *bal*. It turns men into raving lunatics.'

'Well, that doesn't interest me,' said Ballam impatiently. 'We must hurry up with this smoke. I've a lady coming to see me. Must keep an appointment, old man,' he laughed.

'On the contrary, the introduction of this drug into a pipe interests you very much,' said Leon, 'and in spite of Miss Maggiore's appointment – '

The other started.

'What the hell are you talking about?' he asked crossly.

'In spite of that appointment I must break the news to you that the drug which turns men into senseless beasts is more potent than any you serve in this den.'

'What's it to do with me?' snarled Ballam.

'It interests you a great deal,' said Leon coolly, 'because you are at this moment smoking a double dose!'

With a howl of rage Ballam sprang to his feet and what happened after that he could not remember. Only something seemed to split in his head, and a blinding light flashed before his eyes and then a whole century of time went past, a hundred years of moving time and an eternity of flashing lights, of thunderous noises, of whispering voices, of ceaseless troubled movement. Sometimes he knew he was talking and listened eagerly to hear what he himself had to say. Sometimes people spoke to him and mocked him and he had a consciousness that he was being chased by somebody.

How long this went on he could not judge. In his half-bemused condition he tried to reckon time but found he had no standard of measurement. It seemed years after that he opened his eyes with a groan, and put his hand to his aching head. He was lying in bed. It was a hard bed and the pillow was even harder. He stared up at the white-washed ceiling and looked round at the plain dis-tempered walls. Then he peered over the side of the bed and saw that the floor was of concrete. Two lights were burning, one above a table and one in a corner of the room where a man was sitting reading a newspaper. He was a curious-looking man and Ballam blinked at him.

'I am dreaming,' he said aloud and the man looked up.

'Hello! Do you want to get up?'

Ballam did not reply. He was still staring, his mouth agape. The man was in uniform, in a dark, tight-fitting uniform. He wore a cap on his head and a badge. Round his waist was a shiny black belt and then Ballam read the letters on the shoulder-strap of the tunic.

'A.W.,' he repeated, dazed. 'A.W.'

What did 'A.W.' stand for? And then the truth flashed on him.

Assistant Warder! He glared round the room. There was one window, heavily barred and covered with thick glass. On the wall was pasted a sheet of printed paper. He staggered out of bed and read, still open-mouthed: 'Regulations for His Majesty's Prisons.'

He looked down at himself. He had evidently gone to bed with his breeches and stockings on and his breeches were of coarse yellow material and branded with faded black arrows. He was in prison! How long had he been there?

'Are you going to behave today?' asked the warder curtly. 'We don't want any more of those scenes you gave us yesterday!'

'How long have I been here?' croaked Ballam.

'You know how long you've been here. You've been here three weeks, yesterday.'

'Three weeks!' gasped Ballam. 'What is the charge?'

'Now don't come that game with me, Ballam,' said the warder, not unkindly. 'You know I'm not allowed to have conversations with you. Go back and sleep. Sometimes I think you are as mad as you profess to be.'

'Have I been – bad?' asked Ballam.

'Bad?' The warder jerked up his head. 'I wasn't in the court with you, but they say you behaved in the dock like a man demented, and when the Judge was passing sentence of death – '

'My God!' shrieked Ballam and fell back on the bed, white and haggard. 'Sentenced to death!' He could hardly form the words. 'What have I done?'

'You killed a young lady, you know that,' said the warder. 'I'm surprised at you, trying to come it over me after the good friend I've been to you, Ballam. Why don't you buck up and take your punishment like a man?'

There was a calendar above the place where the warder had been sitting.

'Twelfth of April,' read Ballam and could have shrieked again, for it was the first day of March that he met that mysterious stranger. He remembered it all now. *Bal*! The drug that drove men mad.

He sprang to his feet.

'I want to see the Governor! I want to tell them the truth! I've been drugged!'

'Now you've told us all that story before,' said the warder with an air of resignation. 'When you killed the young lady – '

'What young lady?' shrieked Ballam. 'Not Maggiore! Don't tell me – '

'You know you killed her right enough,' said the warder. 'What's the good of making all this fuss? Now go back to bed, Ballam. You can't do any good by kicking up a shindy this night of all nights in the world.'

'I want to see the Governor! Can I write to him?'

'You can write to him if you like,' and the warder indicated the table.

Ballam staggered up to the table and sat down shakily in a chair. There was half a dozen sheets of blue note-paper headed in black: 'H.M. Prison, Wandsworth, S.W.1.'

He was in Wandsworth prison! He looked round the cell. It did not look like a cell and yet it did. It was so horribly bare and the door was heavy looking. He had never been in a cell before and of course it was different to what he had expected.

A thought struck him.

'When – when am I to be punished?' he said chokingly.

'Tomorrow!'

The word fell like a sentence of doom and the man fell forward, his head upon his arms and wept hysterically. Then of a sudden he began to write with feverish haste, his face red with weeping.

His letter was incoherent. It was about a man who had come to the club and had given him a drug and then he had spent a whole eternity in darkness seeing lights and being chased by people and hearing whispering voices. And he was not guilty. He loved Genee Maggiore. He would not have hurt a hair of her head.

He stopped here to weep again. Perhaps he was dreaming? Perhaps he was under the influence of this drug. He dashed his knuckles against the wall and the shock made him wince.

'Here, none of that,' said the warder sternly. 'You get back to bed.'

Ballam looked at his bleeding knuckles. It was true! It was no dream! It was true, true!

He lay on the bed and lost consciousness again and when he awoke the warder was still sitting in his place reading. He seemed to doze again for an hour, although in reality it was only for a few minutes, and every time he woke something within him said: 'This morning you die!'

Once he sprang shrieking from the bed and had to be thrown back.

'If you give me any more trouble I'll get another officer in and we'll tie you down. Why don't you take it like a man? It's no worse for you than it was for her,' said the warder savagely.

After that he lay still and he was falling into what seemed a longer sleep when the warder touched him. When he awoke he found his own clothes laid neatly by the side of the bed upon a chair and he dressed himself hurriedly.

He looked around for something.

'Where's the collar?' he asked trembling.

'You don't need a collar,' the warder's voice had a certain quality of sardonic humour.

'Pull yourself together,' said the man roughly. 'Other people have gone through this. From what I've heard you ran an opium den. A good many of your clients gave us a visit. They had to go through with it, and so must you.'

He waited, sitting on the edge of the bed, his face in his hands and then the door opened and a man came in. He was a slight man with a red beard and a mop of red hair.

The warder swung the prisoner round.

'Put your hands behind you,' he said and Ballam sweated as he felt the strap grip his wrists.

The light was extinguished. A cap was drawn over his face and he thought he heard voices behind him. He wasn't fit to die, he knew that. There always was a parson in a case like this. Someone grasped his arm on either side and he walked slowly forward through the door across a yard and through another door. It was a long way and once his knees gave under him but he stood erect. Presently they stopped.

'Stand where you are,' said a voice and he found a noose slipped round his neck and waited, waited in agony, minutes, hours it seemed. He took no account of time and could not judge it. Then he heard a heavy step and somebody caught him by the arm.

'What are you doing here, governor?' said a voice.

The bag was pulled from his head. He was in the street. It was night and he stood under the light of a street-lamp. The man regarding him curiously was a policeman.

'Got a bit of rope round your neck, too, somebody tied your hands. What is it – a hold-up case?' said the policeman as he loosened the straps. 'Or is it a lark?' demanded the representative of the law. 'I'm surprised at you, an old gentleman like you with white hair!'

Gregory Ballam's hair had been black less than seven hours before when Leon Gonsalez had drugged his coffee and had brought him through the basement exit into the big yard at the back of the club.

For here was a nice new garage as Leon had discovered when he prospected the place, and here they were left uninterrupted to play the comedy of the condemned cell with blue sheets of prison note-paper put there for the occasion and a copy of Prison Regulations which was donated quite unwittingly by Mr Fare, Commissioner of Police.

The Man who hated Amelia Jones

There was a letter that came to Leon Gonsalez, and the stamp bore the image and superscription of Alphonse XIII. It was from a placid man who had written his letter in the hour of siesta, when Cordova slept, and he had scribbled all the things which had come into his head as he sat in an orange bower overlooking the lordly Guadalquivir, now in yellow spate.

'It is from Poiccart,' said Leon.

'Yes?' replied George Manfred, half asleep in a big armchair before the fire.

That and a green-shaded reading lamp supplied the illumination to their comfortable Jermyn Street flat at the moment.

'And what,' said George, stretching himself, 'what does our excellent friend Poiccart have to say?'

'A blight has come upon his onions,' said Leon solemnly and Manfred chuckled and then was suddenly grave.

There was a time when the name of these three, with one who now lay in the Bordeaux cemetery, had stricken terror to the hearts of evil-doers. In those days the Four Just Men were a menace to the sleep of many cunning men who had evaded the law, yet had not evaded this ubiquitous organisation, which slew ruthlessly in the name of Justice.

Poiccart was growing onions! He sighed and repeated the words aloud.

'And why not?' demanded Leon. 'Have you read of the Three Musketeers?'

'Surely,' said Manfred, with a smile at the fire.

'In what book, may I ask?' demanded Leon.

'Why, in *The Three Musketeers*, of course,' replied Manfred in surprise.

'Then you did wrong,' said Leon Gonsalez promptly. 'To love the Three Musketeers, you must read of them in *The Iron Mask*. When one of them has grown fat and is devoting himself to his raiment, and one is a mere courtier of the King of France, and the other is old and full of sorrow for his love-sick child. Then they become human, my dear Manfred, just as Poiccart becomes human when he grows onions. Shall I read you bits?'

'Please,' said Manfred, properly abashed.

'H'm,' read Gonsalez, 'I told you about the onions, George. "I have some gorgeous roses. Manfred would love them . . . do not take too much heed of this new blood test, by which the American doctor professes that he can detect degrees of relationship . . . the new little pigs are doing exceedingly well. There is one that is exceptionally intelligent and contemplative. I have named him George." '

George Manfred by the fire squirmed in his chair and chuckled.

' "This will be a very good year for wine, I am told," ' Leon read on, ' "but the oranges are not as plentiful as they were last year . . . do you know that the finger-prints of twins are identical? Curiously enough the fingerprints of twins of the anthropoid ape are dissimilar. I wish you would get information on this subject . . . " '

He read on, little scraps of domestic news, fleeting excursions into scientific side-issues, tiny scraps of gossip – they filled ten closely written pages.

Leon folded the letter and put it in his pocket. 'Of course he's not right about the finger-prints of twins being identical. That was one of the illusions of the excellent Lombroso. Anyway the finger-print system is unsatisfactory.'

'I never heard it called into question,' said George in surprise. 'Why isn't it satisfactory?'

Leon rolled a cigarette with deft fingers, licked down the paper and lit the ragged end before he replied.

'At Scotland Yard, they have, let us say, one hundred thousand finger-prints. In Britain there are fifty million inhabitants. One hundred thousand is exactly one five-hundredth of fifty millions. Suppose you were a police officer and you were called to the Albert Hall where five hundred people were assembled and told that one of these had in his possession stolen property and you received permission to search them. Would you be content with searching one and giving a clean bill to the rest?'

'Of course not,' said Manfred, 'but I don't see what you mean.'

'I mean that until the whole of the country and every country in Europe adopts a system by which every citizen registers his finger-prints and until all the countries have an opportunity of exchanging those finger-prints and comparing them with their own, it is ridiculous to say that no two prints are alike.'

'That settles the finger-print system,' said Manfred, *sotto voce*.

'Logically it does,' said the complacent Leon, 'but actually it will not, of course.'

There was a long silence after this and then Manfred reached to a case by the side of the fireplace and took down a book.

Presently he heard the creak of a chair as Gonsalez rose and the soft 'pad' of a closing door. Manfred looked up at the clock and, as he knew, it was half past eight.

In five minutes Leon was back again. He had changed his clothing and, as Manfred had once said before, his disguise was perfect. It was not a disguise in the accepted understanding of the word, for he had not in any way touched his face, or changed the colour of his hair.

Only by his artistry he contrived to appear just as he wished to appear, an extremely poor man. His collar was clean, but frayed. His boots were beautifully polished, but they were old and patched. He did not permit the crudity of a heel worn down, but had fixed two circular rubber heels just a little too large for their foundations.

'You are an old clerk battling with poverty, and striving to the end to be genteel,' said Manfred.

Gonsalez shook his head.

'I am a solicitor who, twenty years ago, was struck off the rolls and ruined because I helped a man to escape the processes of the law. An ever so much more sympathetic role, George. Moreover, it brings people to me for advice. One of these nights you must come down to the public bar of the Cow and Compasses and hear me discourse upon the Married Woman's Property Act.'

'I never asked you what you were before,' said George. 'Good hunting, Leon, and my respectful salutations to Amelia Jones!'

Gonsalez was biting his lips thoughtfully and looking into the fire and now he nodded.

'Poor Amelia Jones?' he said softly.

'You're a wonderful fellow,' smiled Manfred, 'only you could invest a charwoman of middle age with the glamour of romance.'

Leon was helping himself into a threadbare overcoat.

'There was an English poet once – it was Pope, I think – who said that everybody was romantic who admired a fine thing, or did one. I rather think Amelia Jones has done both.'

The Cow and Compasses is a small public-house in Treet Road, Deptford. The gloomy thoroughfare was well-nigh empty, for it was a grey cold night when Leon turned into the bar. The uninviting weather may have been responsible for the paucity of clients that evening, for there were scarcely half a dozen people on the sanded floor when he made his way to the bar and ordered a claret and soda.

One who had been watching for him started up from the deal form on which she had been sitting and subsided again when he walked toward her with glass in hand.

'Well, Mrs Jones,' he greeted her, 'and how are you this evening?'

She was a stout woman with a white worn face and hands that trembled spasmodically.

'I am glad you've come, sir,' she said.

She held a little glass of port in her hand, but it was barely touched. It was on one desperate night when in an agony of terror and fear this woman had fled from her lonely home to the light and comfort of the public-house that Leon had met her. He was at the time pursuing with the greatest caution a fascinating skull which he had seen on the broad shoulders of a Covent Garden porter. He had tracked the owner to his home and to his place of recreation and was beginning to work up to his objective, which was to secure the history and the measurements of this unimaginative bearer of fruit, when the stout charwoman had drifted into his orbit. Tonight she evidently had something on her mind of unusual importance, for she made three lame beginnings before she plunged into the matter which was agitating her.

'Mr Lucas,' (this was the name Gonsalez had given to the *habitués* of the Cow and Compasses) 'I want to ask you a great favour. You've been very kind to me, giving me advice about my husband, and all that. But this is a big favour and you're a very busy gentleman, too.'

She looked at him appealingly, almost pleadingly.

'I have plenty of time just now,' said Gonsalez.

'Would you come with me into the country tomorrow?' she asked. 'I want you to – to – to see somebody.'

'Why surely, Mrs Jones,' said Gonsalez.

'Would you be at Paddington Station at nine o'clock in the morning? I would pay your fare,' she went on fervently. 'Of course, I shouldn't allow you to go to any expense – I've got a bit of money put by.'

'As to that,' said Leon, 'I've made a little money myself today, so don't trouble about the fare. Have you heard from your husband?'

'Not from him,' she shook her head, 'but from another man who has just come out of prison.'

Her lips trembled and tears were in her eyes.

'He'll do it, I know he'll do it,' she said, with a catch in her voice, 'but it's not me that I'm thinking of.'

Leon opened his eyes.

'Not you?' he repeated.

He had suspected the third factor, yet he had never been able to fit it in the scheme of this commonplace woman.

'No, sir, not me,' she said miserably. 'You know he hates me and you know he's going to do me in the moment he gets out, but I haven't told you why.'

'Where is he now?' asked Leon.

'Devizes Gaol, he's gone there for his discharge. He'll be out in two months.'

'And then he'll come straight to you, you think?'

She shook her head.

'Not he,' she said bitterly. 'That ain't his way. You don't know him, Mr Lucas. But nobody does know him like I do. If he'd come straight to me it'd be all right, but he's not that kind. He's going to kill me, I tell you, and I don't care how soon it comes. He wasn't called Bash Jones for nothing. I'll get it all right!' she nodded grimly. 'He'll just walk into the room and bash me without a word and that'll be the end of Amelia Jones. But I don't mind, I don't mind,' she repeated. 'It's the other that's breaking my heart and has been all the time.'

He knew it was useless to try to persuade her to tell her troubles, and at closing time they left the bar together.

'I'd ask you home only that might make it worse, and I don't want to get you into any kind of bother, Mr Lucas,' she said.

He offered his hand. It was the first time he had done so, and she took it in her big limp palm and shook it feebly.

'Very few people have shaken hands with Amelia Jones,' thought Gonsalez, and he went back to the flat in Jermyn Street to find Manfred asleep before the fire.

He was waiting at Paddington Station the next morning in a suit a little less shabby, and to his surprise Mrs Jones appeared dressed in better taste than he could have imagined was possible. Her clothes were plain but they effectively disguised the class to which she belonged. She took the tickets for Swindon and there was little conversation on the journey. Obviously she did not intend to unburden her mind as yet.

The train was held up at Newbury whilst a slow up-train shunted to allow a school special to pass. It was crowded with boys and girls who waved a cheery and promiscuous greeting as they passed.

'Of course!' nodded Leon. 'It is the beginning of the Easter holidays. I had forgotten.'

At Swindon they alighted and then for the first time the woman gave some indication as to the object of their journey.

'We've got to stay on this platform,' she said nervously. 'I'm expecting to see somebody, and I'd like you to see her, too, Mr Lucas.'

Presently another special ran into the station and the majority of the passengers in this train also were children. Several alighted at the junction, apparently to change for some other destination than London, and Leon was talking to the woman, who he knew was not listening, when he saw her face light up. She left him with a little gasp and walked quickly along the platform to greet a tall, pretty girl wearing the crimson and white hat-ribbon of a famous West of England school.

'Why, Mrs Jones, it is so kind of you to come down to see me. I wish you wouldn't take so much trouble. I should be only too happy to come to London,' she laughed. 'Is this a friend of yours?'

She shook hands with Leon, her eyes smiling her friendliness.

'It's all right, Miss Grace,' said Mrs Jones, agitated. 'I just thought I'd pop down and have a look at you. How are you getting on at school, miss?'

'Oh, splendidly,' said the girl. 'I've won a scholarship.'

'Isn't that lovely!' said Mrs Jones in an awe-stricken voice. 'You always was wonderful, my dear.'

The girl turned to Leon.

'Mrs Jones was my nurse, you know, years and years ago, weren't you, Mrs Jones?'

Amelia Jones nodded.

'How is your husband? Is he still unpleasant?'

'Oh, he ain't so bad, miss,' said Mrs Jones bravely. 'He's a little trying at times.'

'Do you know, I should like to meet him.'

'Oh no, you wouldn't, miss,' gasped Amelia. 'That's only your kind heart. Where are you spending your holidays, miss?' she asked.

'With some friends of mine at Clifton, Molly Walker, Sir George Walker's daughter.'

The eyes of Amelia Jones devoured the girl and Leon knew that all the love in her barren life was lavished upon this child she had nursed. They walked up and down the platform together and when her train came in Mrs Jones stood at the carriage door until it drew out from the station and then waited motionless looking after the express until it melted in the distance.

'I'll never see her again!' she muttered brokenly. 'I'll never see her again! Oh, my God!'

Her face was drawn and ghastly in its pallor and Leon took her arm.

'You must come and have some refreshment, Mrs Jones. You are very fond of that young lady?'

'Fond of her?' She turned upon him. 'Fond of her? She – she is my daughter!'

They had a carriage to themselves going back to Town and Mrs Jones told her story.

'Grace was three years old when her father got into trouble,' she said. 'He had always been a brute and I think he'd been under the eyes of the police since he was a bit of a kid. I didn't know this when I married him. I was nursemaid in a house that he'd burgled and I was discharged because I'd left the kitchen door ajar for him, not knowing that he was a thief. He did one long lagging and when he came out he swore he wouldn't go back to prison again, and the next time if there was any danger of an alarm being raised, he would make it a case of murder. He and another man got into touch with a rich bookmaker on Blackheath. Bash used to do his dirty work for him, but they quarrelled and Bash and his pal burgled the house and got away with nearly nine thousand pounds.

'It was a big race day and Bash knew there'd be a lot of money in notes that had been taken on the racecourse and that couldn't be traced. I thought he'd killed this man at first. It wasn't his fault that he hadn't. He walked into the room and bashed him as he lay in bed – that was Bash's way – that's how he got his name. He thought there'd be a lot of enquiries and gave me the money to look after. I had to put the notes into an old beer jar half full of sand, ram in the cork and cover the cork and the neck with candle-wax so that the water couldn't g et through, and then put it in the cistern which he could reach from one of the upstairs rooms at the back of the house. I was nearly mad with fear because I thought the gentleman had been killed, but I did as I was told and sunk the jar in the cistern. That night Bash and his mate were getting away to the north of England when they were arrested at Euston Station. Bash's friend was killed, for he ran across the line in front of an engine, but they caught Bash and the house was searched from end to end. He got fifteen years' penal servitude and he would have been out two years ago if he hadn't been a bad character in prison.

'When he was in gaol I had to sit down and think, Mr Lucas, and my first thought was of my child. I saw the kind of life that she was going to grow up to, the surroundings, the horrible slums, the fear of the police, for I knew that Bash would spend a million if he had it in a few weeks. I knew I was free of Bash for at least twelve years and I thought and I thought and at last I made up my mind.

'It was twelve months after he was in gaol that I dared get the money, for the police were still keeping their eye on me as the money had not been found. I won't tell you how I bought grand clothes so that nobody would suspect I was a working woman or how I changed the money.

'I put it all into shares. I'm not well educated, but I read the newspapers for months, the columns about money. At first I was puzzled and I could make no end to it, but after a while I got to understand and it was in an Argentine company that I invested the money, and I got a lawyer in Bermondsey to make a trust of it. She gets the interest every quarter and pays her own bills – I've never touched a penny of it. The next thing was to get my little girl out of the neighbourhood, and I sent her away to a home for small children – it broke my heart to part with her – until she was old enough to go into a school. I used to see her regularly and when, after my first visit, I found she had almost forgotten who I was, I pretended that I'd been her nurse – and that's the story.'

Gonsalez was silent.

'Does your husband know?'

'He knows I spent the money,' said the woman staring blankly out of the window. 'He knows that the girl is at a good school. He'll find out,' she spoke almost in a whisper. 'He'll find out!'

So that was the tragedy! Leon was struck dumb by the beauty of this woman's sacrifice. When he found his voice again, he asked:

'Why do you think he will kill you? These kind of people threaten.'

'Bash doesn't threaten as a rule,' she interrupted him. 'It's the questions he's been asking people who know me. People from Deptford who he's met in prison. Asking what I do at nights, what time I go to bed, what I do in the daytime. That's Bash's way.'

'I see,' said Leon. 'Has anybody given him the necessary particulars?' he asked.

She shook her head.

'They've done their best for me,' she said. 'They are bad characters and they commit crimes, but there's some good hearts amongst them. They have told him nothing.'

'Are you sure?'

'I'm certain. If they had he wouldn't be still asking. Why, Toby Brown came up from Devizes a month ago and told me Bash was there and was still asking questions about me. He'd told Toby that he'd never do another lagging and that he reckoned he'd be alive up to Midsummer Day if they caught him.'

Leon went up to his flat that night exalted.

'What have you been doing with yourself?' asked Manfred. 'I for my part have been lunching with the excellent Mr Fare.'

'And I have been moving in a golden haze of glory! Not my own, no, not my own, Manfred,' he shook his head, 'but the glory of Amelia Jones. A wonderful woman, George. For her sake I am going to take a month's holiday, during which time you can go back to Spain and see our beloved Poiccart and hear all about the onions.'

'I would like to go back to Madrid for a few days,' said Manfred thoughtfully. 'I find London particularly attractive, but if you really are going to take a holiday – where are you spending it, by the way?'

'In Devizes Gaol,' replied Gonsalez cheerfully, and Manfred had such faith in his friend that he offered no comment.

Leon Gonsalez left for Devizes the next afternoon. He arrived in the town at dusk and staggered unsteadily up the rise toward the market-place. At ten o'clock that night a police constable found him leaning against a wall at the back of the Bear Hôtel, singing foolish songs, and ordered him to move away. Whereupon Leon addressed him in language for which he was at the time (since he was perfectly sober) heartily ashamed. Therefore he did appear before a bench of magistrates the next morning, charged with being drunk, using abusive language and obstructing the police in the execution of their duty.

'This is hardly a case which can be met by imposing a fine,' said the staid chairman of the Bench. 'Here is a stranger from London who comes into this town and behaves in a most disgusting manner. Is anything known against the man?'

'Nothing, sir,' said the gaoler regretfully.

'You will pay a fine of twenty shillings or go to prison for twenty-one days.'

'I would much rather go to prison than pay,' said Leon truthfully.

So they committed him to the local gaol as he had expected. Twenty-one days later, looking very brown and fit, he burst into the flat and Manfred turned with outstretched hands.

'I heard you were back,' said Leon joyously. 'I've had a great time! They rather upset my calculations by giving me three weeks instead of a month, and I was afraid that I'd get back before you.'

'I came back yesterday,' said George and his eyes strayed to the sideboard.

Six large Spanish onions stood in a row and Leon Gonsalez doubled up with mirth. It was not until he had changed into more presentable garments that he told of his experience.

'Bash Jones had undoubtedly homicidal plans,' he said. 'The most extraordinary case of facial anamorphosis I have seen. I worked with him in the tailor's shop. He is coming out next Monday.'

'He welcomed you, I presume, when he discovered you were from Deptford?' said Manfred dryly.

Leon nodded.

'He intends to kill his wife on the third of the month, which is the day after he is released,' he said.

'Why so precise?' asked Manfred in surprise.

'Because that is the only night she sleeps in the house alone. There are usually two young men lodgers who are railwaymen and these do duty until three in the morning on the third of every month.'

'Is this the truth or are you making it up?' asked Manfred.

'I did make it up,' admitted Gonsalez. 'But this is the story I told and he swallowed it eagerly. The young men have no key, so they come in by the kitchen door which is left unlocked. The kitchen door is reached by a narrow passage which runs the length of Little Mill Street and parallel with the houses. Oh yes, he was frightfully anxious to secure information, and he told me that he would never come back to gaol again except for a short visit. An interesting fellow. I think he had better die,' said Leon, with some gravity. 'Think of the possibilities for misery, George. This unfortunate girl, happy in her friends, well-bred – '

'Would you say that,' smiled Manfred, 'with Bash for a father?'

'Well-bred, I repeat,' said Gonsalez firmly. 'Breeding is merely a quality acquired through life-long association with gentle-folk. Put the son of a duke in the slums and he'll grow up a peculiar kind of slum child, but a slum child nevertheless. Think of the horror of it. Dragging this child back to the kennels of Deptford, for that will be the meaning of it, supposing this Mr Bash Jones does not kill his wife. If he kills her then the grisly truth is out. No, I think we had better settle this Mr Bash Jones.'

'I agree,' said Manfred, puffing thoughtfully at his cigar, and Leon Gonsalez sat down at the table with Browning's poems open before him and read, pausing now and again to look thoughtfully into space as he elaborated the method by which Bash Jones should die.

On the afternoon of the third, Mrs Amelia Jones was called away by telegram. She met Leon Gonsalez at Paddington Station.

'You have brought your key with you, Mrs Jones?'

'Yes, sir,' said the woman in surprise, then, 'Do you know that my husband is out of prison?'

'I know, I know,' said Gonsalez, 'and because he is free I want you to go away for a couple of nights. I have some friends in Plymouth. They will probably meet you at the station and if they do not meet you, you must go to this address.'

He gave her an address of a boarding-house that he had secured from a Plymouth newspaper.

'Here is some money. I insist upon your taking it. My friends are very anxious to help you.'

She was in tears when he left her.

'You are sure you have locked up your house?' said Leon at parting.

'I've got the key here, sir.'

She opened her bag and he noticed that now her hands trembled all the time.

'Let me see,' said Leon taking the bag in his hand and peering at the interior in his short-sighted way. 'Yes, there it is.'

He put in his hand, brought it out apparently empty and closed the bag again.

'Goodbye, Mrs Jones,' he said, 'and don't lose courage.'

When dark fell Leon Gonsalez arrived in Little Mill Street carrying a bulky something in a black cloth bag. He entered the house unobserved, for the night was wet and gusty and Little Mill Street crouched over its scanty fires.

He closed the door behind him and with the aid of his pocket lamp found his way to the one poor bedroom in the tiny house. He turned down the cover, humming to himself, then very carefully he removed the contents of the bag, the most important of which was a large glass globe.

Over this he carefully arranged a black wig and searched the room for articles of clothing which might be rolled into a bundle. When he had finished his work, he stepped back and regarded it with admiration. Then he went downstairs, unlocked the kitchen door, and to make absolutely certain crossed the little yard and examined the fastening of the gate which led from the lane. The lock apparently was permanently out of order and he went back satisfied.

In one corner of the room was a clothes hanger, screened from view by a length of cheap cretonne. He had cleared this corner of its clothing to make up the bundle on the bed. Then he sat down in a chair and waited with the patience which is the peculiar attribute of the scientist.

The church bells had struck two when he heard the back gate creak, and rising noiselessly took something from his pocket and stepped behind the cretonne curtain. It was not a house in which one could move without sound, for the floor-boards were old and creaky and every stair produced a creak. But the man who was creeping from step to step was an artist and Leon heard no other sound until the door slowly opened and a figure came in.

It moved with stealthy steps across the room and stood for a few seconds by the side of the bulky figure in the bed. Apparently he listened and was satisfied. Then Leon saw a stick rise and fall.

Bash Jones did not say a word until he heard the crash of the broken glass. Then he uttered an oath and Leon heard him fumble in his pocket for his matches. The delay was fatal. The chlorine gas, compressed at a pressure of many atmospheres, surged up around him. He choked, turned to run and fell, and the yellow gas rolled over him in a thick and turgid cloud.

Leon Gonsalez stepped from his place of concealment and the dying man staring up saw two enormous glass eyes and the snout-like nozzle of the respirator and went bewildered to his death.

Leon collected the broken glass and carefully wrapped the pieces in his bag. He replaced the clothes with the most extraordinary care and put away the wig and tidied the room before he opened the window and the door. Then he went to the front of the house and opened those windows too. A south-wester was blowing and by the morning the house would be free from gas.

Not until he was in the back yard did he remove the gas mask he wore and place that too in the bag.

An hour later he was in his own bed in a deep, untroubled sleep.

Mrs Jones slept well that night, and in a dainty cubicle somewhere in the west of England a slim girlish figure in pyjamas snuggled into her pillow and sighed happily.

But Bash Jones slept soundest of all.

The Man who was Happy

On a pleasant evening in early summer, Leon Gonsalez descended from the top of a motor-omnibus at Piccadilly Circus and walking briskly down the Haymarket, turned into Jermyn Street apparently oblivious of the fact that somebody was following on his heels.

Manfred looked up from his writing as his friend came in, and nodded smilingly as Leon took off his light overcoat and made his way to the window overlooking the street.

'What are you searching for so anxiously, Leon?' he asked.

'Jean Prothero, of 75 Barside Buildings, Lambeth,' said Leon, not taking his eyes from the street below. 'Ah, there he is, the industrious fellow!'

'Who is Jean Prothero?'

Gonsalez chuckled.

'A very daring man,' evaded Leon, 'to wander about the West End at this hour.' He looked at his watch. 'Oh no, not so daring,' he said, 'everybody who is anybody is dressing for dinner just now.'

'A ladder larcenist?' suggested Manfred, and Leon chuckled again.

'Nothing so vulgar,' he said. 'By ladder larcenist I presume you mean the type of petty thief who puts a ladder against a bedroom window whilst the family are busy at dinner downstairs, and makes off with the odd scraps of jewellery he can find?'

Manfred nodded.

'That is the official description of this type of criminal,' he agreed.

Leon shook his head.

'No, Mr Prothero is interesting,' he said. 'Interesting for quite another reason. In the first place, he is a bald-headed criminal, or potential criminal, and as you know, my dear George, criminals are rarely bald. They are coarse-haired, and they are thin-haired: they have such personal eccentricities as parting their hair on the wrong side, but they are seldom bald. The dome of Mr Prothero's head is wholly innocent of hair of any kind. He is the second mate of a tramp steamer engaged in the fruit trade between the Canary Islands and Southampton. He has a very pretty girl for a wife and, curiously enough, a ladder larcenist for a brother-in-law, and I have excited his suspicion quite unwittingly. Incidentally,' he added as though it were a careless afterthought, 'he knows that I am one of the Four Just Men.'

Manfred was silent.

Then: 'How does he know that?' he asked quietly.

Leon had taken off his coat and had slipped his arms into a faded alpaca jacket; he did not reply until he had rolled and lit an untidy Spanish cigarette.

'Years ago, when there was a hue and cry after that pernicious organisation, whose name I have mentioned, an organisation which, in its humble way, endeavoured to right the injustice of the world and to mete out to evil-doers the punishment which the ponderous machinery of the Law could not inflict, you were arrested, my dear George, and consigned to Chelmsford Gaol. From there you made a miraculous escape, and on reaching the coast you and I and Poiccart were taken aboard the yacht of our excellent friend the Prince of the Asturias, who honoured us by acting as the fourth of our combination.'

Manfred nodded.

'On that ship was Mr Jean Prothero,' said Leon. 'How he came to be on the yacht of His Serene Highness I will explain at a later stage, but assuredly he was there. I never forget faces, George, but unfortunately I am not singular in this respect. Mr Prothero remembered me, and seeing me in Barside Buildings –'

'What were you doing in Barside Buildings?' asked Manfred with a faint smile.

'In Barside Buildings,' replied Leon impressively, 'are two men unknown to one another, both criminals, and both colour-blind!'

Manfred put down his pen and turned, prepared for a lecture on criminal statistics, for he had noticed the enthusiasm in Gonsalez's voice.

'By means of these two men,' said Leon joyously, 'I am able to refute the perfectly absurd theories which both Mantegazza and Scheml have expounded, namely, that criminals are never colour-blind. The truth is, my dear George, both these men have been engaged in crime since their early youth. Both have served terms of imprisonment, and what is more important, their fathers were colour-blind and criminals!'

'Well, what about Mr Prothero?' said Manfred, tactfully interrupting what promised to be an exhaustive disquisition upon optical defects in relation to congenital lawlessness.

'One of my subjects is Prothero's brother-in-law, or rather, half-brother to Mrs Prothero, her own father having been a blameless carpenter, and lives in the flat overhead. These flats are just tiny dwelling places consisting of two rooms and a kitchen. The builders of Lambeth tenements do not allow for the luxury of a bathroom. In this way I came to meet Mrs Prothero whilst overcoming the reluctance of her brother to talk about himself.'

'And you met Prothero, too, I presume,' said Manfred patiently.

'No, I didn't meet him, except by accident. He passed on the stairs and I saw him give me a swift glance. His face was in the shadow and I did not recognise him until our second meeting, which was today. He followed me home. As a matter of fact,' he added, 'I have an idea that he followed me yesterday, and only came today to confirm my place of residence.'

'You're a rum fellow,' said Manfred.

'Maybe I'll be rummer,' smiled Leon. 'Everything depends now,' he said thoughtfully, 'upon whether Prothero thinks that I recognised him. If he does – '

Leon shrugged his shoulders.

'Not for the first time have I fenced with death and overcome him,' he said lightly.

Manfred was not deceived by the flippancy of his friend's tone.

'As bad as that, eh?' he said, 'and more dangerous for him, I think,' he added quietly. 'I do not like the idea of killing a man because he has recognised us – that course does not seem to fit in with my conception of justice.'

'Exactly,' said Leon briskly, 'and there will be no need, I think. Unless, of course – ' he paused.

'Unless what?' asked Manfred.

'Unless Prothero really does love his wife, in which case it may be a very serious business.'

The next morning he strolled into Manfred's bedroom carrying the cup of tea which the servant usually brought, and George stared up at him in amazement.

'What is the matter with you, Leon, haven't you been to bed?'

Leon Gonsalez was dressed in what he called his 'pyjama outfit' – a grey flannel coat and trousers, belted at the waist, a silk shirt open at the neck and a pair of light slippers constituted his attire, and Manfred, who associated this costume with all-night studies, was not astonished when Leon shook his head.

'I have been sitting in the dining-room, smoking the pipe of peace,' he said.

'All night?' said Manfred in surprise. 'I woke up in the middle of the night and I saw no light.'

'I sat in the dark,' admitted Leon. 'I wanted to hear things.'

Manfred stirred his tea thoughtfully. 'Is it as bad as that? Did you expect – '

Leon smiled. 'I didn't expect what I got,' he said. 'Will you do me a favour, my dear George?'

'What is your favour?'

'I want you not to speak of Mr Prothero for the rest of the day. Rather, I wish you to discuss purely scientific and agricultural matters, as becomes an honest Andalusian farmer, and moreover to speak in Spanish.'

Manfred frowned.

'Why?' and then: 'I'm sorry, I can't get out of the habit of being mystified, you know, Leon. Spanish and agriculture it shall be, and no reference whatever to Prothero.'

Leon was very earnest and Manfred nodded and swung out of bed.

'May I talk of taking a bath?' he asked sardonically.

Nothing particularly interesting happened that day. Once Manfred was on the point of referring to Leon's experience, and divining the drift of his thought, Leon raised a warning finger.

Gonsalez could talk about crime, and did. He talked of its more scientific aspects and laid particular stress upon his discovery of the colour-blind criminal. But of Mr Prothero he said no word.

After they had dined that night, Leon went out of the flat and presently returned.

'Thank heaven we can now talk without thinking,' he said.

He pulled a chair to the wall and mounted it nimbly. Above his head was a tiny ventilator fastened to the wall with screws. Humming a little tune he turned a screwdriver deftly and lifted the little grille from its socket, Manfred watching him gravely.

'Here it is,' said Leon. 'Pull up a chair, George.'

'It' proved to be a small flat brown box four inches by four in the centre of which was a black vulcanite depression.

'Do you recognise him?' said Leon. 'He is the detectaphone – in other words a telephone receiver fitted with a microphonic attachment.'

'Has somebody been listening to all we've been saying?'

Leon nodded.

'The gentleman upstairs has had a dull and dreary day. Admitting that he speaks Spanish, and that I have said nothing which has not illuminated that branch of science which is my particular hobby,' he added modestly, 'he must have been terribly bored.'

'But – ' began Manfred.

'He is out now,' said Gonsalez. 'But to make perfectly sure – '

With deft fingers he detached one of the wires by which the box was suspended in the ventilator shaft.

'Mr Prothero came last night,' he explained. 'He took the room upstairs, and particularly asked for it. This I learnt from the head waiter – he adores me because I give him exactly three times the tip which he gets from other residents in these service flats, and because I tip him three times as often. I didn't exactly know what Prothero's game was, until I heard the tap-tap of the microphone coming down the shaft.'

He was busy re-fixing the grille of the ventilator – presently he jumped down.

'Would you like to come to Lambeth today? I do not think there is much chance of our meeting Mr Prothero. On the other hand, we shall see Mrs Prothero shopping at eleven o'clock in the London Road, for she is a methodical lady.'

'Why do you want me to see her?' asked Manfred.

He was not usually allowed to see the workings of any of Leon's schemes until the dramatic dénouement, which was meat and drink to him, was near at hand.

'I want you, with your wide knowledge of human nature, to tell me whether she is the type of woman for whom a bald-headed man would commit murder,' he said simply, and Manfred stared at him in amazement.

'The victim being – ?'

'Me!' replied Gonsalez, and doubled up with silent laughter at the blank look on Manfred's face.

It was four minutes to eleven exactly when Manfred saw Mrs Prothero. He felt the pressure of Leon's hand on his arm and looked.

'There she is,' said Leon.

A girl was crossing the road. She was neatly, even well-dressed for one of her class. She carried a market bag in one gloved hand, a purse in the other.

'She's pretty enough,' said Manfred.

The girl had paused to look in a jeweller's window and Manfred had time to observe her. Her face was sweet and womanly, the eyes big and dark, the little chin firm and rounded.

'What do you think of her?' said Leon.

'I think she's rather a perfect specimen of young womanhood,' said Manfred.

'Come along and meet her,' said the other, and took his arm.

The girl looked round at first in surprise, and then with a smile. Manfred had an impression of flashing white teeth and scarlet lips parted in amusement. Her voice was not the voice of a lady, but it was quiet and musical.

'Good morning, Doctor,' she said to Leon. 'What are you doing in this part of the world so early in the morning.'

'Doctor,' noted Manfred.

The adaptable Gonsalez assumed many professions for the purpose of securing his information.

'We have just come from Guy's Hospital. This is Dr Selbert,' he introduced Manfred. 'You are shopping, I suppose?'

She nodded.

'Really, there was no need for me to come out, Mr Prothero being away at the Docks for three days,' she replied.

'Have you seen your brother this morning?' asked Leon.

A shadow fell over the girl's face.

'No,' she said shortly.

Evidently, thought Manfred, she was not particularly proud of her relationship. Possibly she suspected his illicit profession, but at any rate she had no desire to discuss him, for she changed the subject quickly.

They talked for a little while, and then with an apology she left them and they saw her vanish through the wide door of a grocer's store.

'Well, what do you think of her?'

'She is a very beautiful girl,' said Manfred quietly.

'The kind of girl that would make a bald-headed criminal commit a murder?' asked Leon, and Manfred laughed.

'It is not unlikely,' he said, 'but why should he murder you?'

'*Nous verrons*,' replied Leon.

When they returned to their flat in the afternoon the mail had been and there were half a dozen letters. One bearing a heavy crest upon the envelope attracted Manfred's attention.

'Lord Pertham,' he said, looking at the signature. 'Who is Lord Pertham?'

'I haven't a Who's Who handy, but I seem to know the name,' said Leon. 'What does Lord Pertham want?'

'I'll read you the note,' said Manfred.

'Dear Sir,' [it read] 'Our mutual friend Mr Fare of Scotland Yard is dining with us tonight at Connaught Gardens, and I wonder whether you would come along? Mr Fare tells me that you are one of the cleverest criminologists of the century, and as it is a study which I have made particularly my own, I shall be glad to make your acquaintance.'

It was signed 'Pertham' and there was a postscript running –

'Of course, this invitation also includes your friend.'

Manfred rubbed his chin.

'I really do not want to dine fashionably tonight,' he said.

'But I do,' said Leon promptly. 'I have developed a taste for English cooking, and I seem to remember that Lord Pertham is an epicurean.'

Promptly at the hour of eight they presented themselves at the big house standing at the corner of Connaught Gardens and were admitted by a footman who took their hats and coats and showed them into a large and gloomy drawing-room.

A man was standing with his back to the fire – a tall man of fifty with a mane of grey hair, that gave him an almost leonine appearance.

He came quickly to meet them.

'Which is Mr Fuentes?' he asked, speaking in English.

'I am Signor Fuentes,' replied Manfred, with a smile, 'but it is my friend who is the criminologist.'

'Delighted to meet you both – but I have an apology to make to you;' he said, speaking hurriedly. 'By some mischance – the stupidity of one of my men – the letter addressed to Fare was not posted. I only discovered it half an hour ago. I hope you don't mind.'

Manfred murmured something conventional and then the door opened to admit a lady.

'I want to present you to her ladyship,' said Lord Pertham.

The woman who came in was thin and vinegary: a pair of pale eyes, a light-lipped mouth and a trick of frowning deprived her of whatever charm Nature had given to her.

Leon Gonsalez, who analysed faces automatically and mechanically, thought, 'Spite – suspicion – uncharity – vanity.'

The frown deepened as she offered a limp hand.

'Dinner is ready, Pertham,' she said, and made no attempt to be agreeable to her guests.

It was an awkward meal. Lord Pertham was nervous and his nervousness might have communicated itself to the two men if they had been anything but what they were. This big man seemed to be in terror of his wife – was deferential, even humble in her presence, and when at last she swept her sour face from the room he made no attempt to hide his sigh of relief.

'I am afraid we haven't given you a very good dinner,' he said. 'Her ladyship has had a little – er – disagreement with my cook.'

Apparently her ladyship was in the habit of having little disagreements with her cook, for in the course of the conversation which followed he casually mentioned certain servants in his household who were no longer in his employ. He spoke mostly of their facial characteristics, and it seemed to Manfred, who was listening as intently as his companion, that his lordship was not a great authority upon the subject. He spoke haltingly, made several obvious slips, but Leon did not correct him. He mentioned casually that he had an additional interest in criminals because his own life had been threatened.

'Let us go up and join my lady,' he said after a long and blundering exposition of some phase of criminology which Manfred could have sworn he had read up for the occasion.

They went up the broad stairs into a little drawing-room on the first floor. It was empty. His lordship was evidently surprised.

'I wonder – ' he began, when the door opened and Lady Pertham ran in. Her face was white and her thin lips were trembling.

'Pertham,' she said rapidly, 'I'm sure there's a man in my dressing-room.'

'In your dressing-room?' said Lord Pertham, and ran out quickly.

The two men would have followed him, but he stopped half-way up the stairs and waved them back.

'You had better wait with her ladyship,' he said. 'Ring for Thomas, my love,' he said.

Standing at the foot of the stairs they heard him moving about. Presently they heard a cry and the sound of a struggle. Manfred was half-way up the stairs when a door slammed above. Then came the sound of voices and a shot, followed by a heavy fall.

Manfred flung himself against the door from whence the sound came.

'It's all right,' said Lord Pertham's voice.

A second later he unlocked the door and opened it.

'I'm afraid I've killed this fellow.'

The smoking revolver was still in his hand. In the middle of the floor lay a poorly dressed man and his blood stained the pearl-grey carpet.

Gonsalez walked quickly to the body and turned it over. At the first sight he knew that the man was dead. He looked long and earnestly in his face, and Lord Pertham said: 'Do you know him?'

'I think so,' said Gonsalez quietly. 'He is my colour-blind criminal,' for he had recognised the brother of Mrs Prothero.

They walked home to their lodgings that night leaving Lord Pertham closeted with a detective-inspector, and Lady Pertham in hysterics.

Neither man spoke until they reached their flat, then Leon, with a sigh of content, curled up in the big armchair and pulled lovingly at an evil-smelling cigar.

'Leon!'

He took no notice.

'Leon!'

Leon shifted his head round and met George's eye.

'Did anything about that shooting tonight strike you as peculiar?'

'Several things,' said Leon.

'Such as?'

'Such as the oddness of the fate that took Slippery Bill – that was the name of my burglar – to Lord Pertham's house. It was not odd that he should commit the burglary, because he was a ladder larcenist, as you call him. By the way, did you look at the dead man's hand?' he asked, twisting round and peering across the table at Manfred.

'No, I didn't,' said the other in surprise.

'What a pity – you would have thought it still more peculiar. What are the things you were thinking of?'

'I was wondering why Lord Pertham carried a revolver. He must have had it in his pocket at dinner.'

'That is easily explained,' said Gonsalez. 'Don't you remember his telling us that his life had been threatened in anonymous letters?'

Manfred nodded.

'I had forgotten that,' he said. 'But who locked the door?'

'The burglar, of course,' said Leon and smiled. And by that smile Manfred knew that he was prevaricating. 'And talking of locked doors – ' and rose.

He went into his room and returned with two little instruments that looked like the gongs of electric bells, except that there was a prong sticking up from each.

He locked the sitting-room door and placed one of these articles on the floor, sticking the spike into the bottom of the door so that it was impossible to open without exercising pressure upon the bell. He tried it and there was a shrill peal.

'That's all right,' he said, and turned to examine the windows.

'Are you expecting burglars?'

'I am rather,' said Leon, 'and really I cannot afford to lose my sleep.'

Not satisfied with the fastening of the window he pushed in a little wedge, and performed the same office to the second of the windows looking upon the street.

Another door, leading to Manfred's room from the passage without, he treated as he had served the first.

In the middle of the night there was a frantic ring from one of the bells. Manfred leapt out of bed and switched on the light. His own door was fast and he raced into the sitting-room, but Gonsalez was there before him examining the little sentinel by the door. The door had been unlocked. He kicked away the alarm with his slippered foot.

'Come in, Lord Pertham,' he said. 'Let's talk this matter over.'

There was a momentary silence, then the sound of a slippered foot, and a man came in. He was fully dressed and hatless, and Manfred, seeing the bald head, gasped.

'Sit down and make yourself at home, and let me relieve you of that lethal weapon you have in your pocket, because this matter can be arranged very amicably,' said Leon.

It was undoubtedly Lord Pertham, though the great mop of hair had vanished, and Manfred could only stare as Leon's left hand slipped into the pocket of the midnight visitor and drew forth a revolver which he placed carefully on the mantelshelf.

Lord Pertham sank into a chair and covered his face with his hands. For a while the silence was unbroken.

'You may remember the Honourable George Fearnside,' began Leon, and Manfred started.

'Fearnside? Why, he was on the Prince's yacht – '

'He was on the Prince's yacht,' agreed Gonsalez, 'and we thoroughly believed that he did not associate us with escaping malefactors, but apparently he knew us for the Four Just Men. You came into your title about six years ago, didn't you, Pertham?'

The bowed figure nodded. Presently he sat up – his face was white and there were black circles about his eyes.

'Well, gentlemen,' he said, 'it seems that instead of getting you, you have got me. Now what are you going to do?'

Gonsalez laughed softly.

'For myself,' he said, 'I am certainly not going in the witness-box to testify that Lord Pertham is a bigamist and for many years has been leading a double life. Because that would mean I should also have to admit certain uncomfortable things about myself.'

The man licked his lips and then: 'I came to kill you,' he said thickly.

'So we gather,' said Manfred. 'What is this story, Leon?'

'Perhaps his lordship will tell us,' said Gonsalez.

Lord Pertham looked round for something.

'I want a glass of water,' he said, and it was Leon who brought it.

'It is perfectly true,' said Lord Pertham after a while. 'I recognised you fellows as two of the Four Just Men. I used to be a great friend of His Highness, and it was by accident that I was on board the yacht when you were taken off. His Highness told me a yarn about some escapade, but when I got to Spain and read the newspaper account of the escape I was pretty certain that I knew who you were. You probably know something about my early life, how I went before the mast as a common sailor and travelled all over the world. It was the kind of life which satisfied me more than any other, for I got to know people and places and to know them from an angle which I should never have understood in any other way. If you ever want to see the world, travel in the fo'c'sle,' he said with a half-smile.

'I met Martha Grey one night in the East End of London at a theatre. When I was a seaman I acted like a seaman. My father and I were not on the best of terms and I never wanted to go home. She sat by my side in the pit of the theatre and ridiculous as it may seem to you I fell in love with her.'

'You were then married?' said Leon, but the man shook his head.

'No,' he said quickly. 'Like a fool I was persuaded to marry her ladyship about three months later, after I had got sick of the sea and had come back to my own people. She was an heiress and it was a good match for me. That was before my father had inherited his cousin's money. My life with her ladyship was a hell upon earth. You saw her tonight and you can guess the kind of woman she is. I have too great a respect for women and live too much in awe of them to exercise any control over her viperish temper and it was the miserable life I lived with her which drove me to seek out Martha.

'Martha is a good girl,' he said, and there was a glitter in his eye as he challenged denial. 'The purest, the dearest, the sweetest woman that ever lived. It was when I met her again that I realised how deeply in love I was, and as with a girl of her character there was no other way – I married her.

'I had fever when I was on a voyage to Australia and lost all my hair. That was long before I met Martha. I suppose it was vanity on my part, but when I went back to my own life and my own people, as I did for a time after that, I had a wig made which served the double purpose of concealing my infirmity and preventing my being recognised by my former shipmates.

'As the little hair I had had gone grey I had the wig greyed too, had it made large and poetical – ' he smiled sadly, 'to make my disguise more complete. Martha didn't mind my bald head. God bless her!' he said softly, 'and my life with her has been a complete and unbroken period of happiness. I have to leave her at times to manage my own affairs and in those times I pretend to be at sea, just as I used to pretend to her ladyship that business affairs called me to America to explain my absence from her.'

'The man you shot was Martha's half-brother, of course,' said Gonsalez, and Lord Pertham nodded.

'It was just ill luck which brought him to my house,' he said, 'sheer bad luck. In the struggle my wig came off, he recognised me and I shot him,' he said simply. 'I shot him deliberately and in cold blood, not only because he threatened to wreck my happiness, but because for years he has terrorised his sister and has been living on her poor earnings.'

Gonsalez nodded.

'I saw grey hair in his hands and I guessed what had happened,' he said.

'Now what are you going to do?' asked the Earl of Pertham.

Leon was smoking now.

'What are you going to do?' he asked in retort. 'Perhaps you would like me to tell you?'

'I should,' said the man earnestly.

'You are going to take your bigamous wife abroad just as soon as this inquest is over, and you are going to wait a reasonable time and then persuade your wife to get a divorce. After which you will marry your Mrs Prothero in your own name,' said Gonsalez.

'Leon,' said Manfred after Fearnside had gone back to the room above, the room he had taken in the hope of discovering how much Gonsalez knew, 'I think you are a thoroughly unmoral person. Suppose Lady Pertham does not divorce his lordship?'

Leon laughed.

'There is really no need for her to divorce Lord Pertham,' he said, 'for his lordship told us a little lie. He married his Martha first, deserted her and went back to her. I happen to know this because I have already examined both registers, and I know there was a Mrs Prothero before there was a Lady Pertham.'

'You're a wonderful fellow, Leon,' said Manfred admiringly.

'I am,' admitted Leon Gonsalez.

The Man who loved Music

The most striking characteristics of Mr Homer Lynne were his deep and wide sympathies, and his love of Tschaikovsky's '1812'. He loved music generally, but his neighbours in Pennerthon Road, Hampstead, could testify with vehemence and asperity to his preference for that great battle piece. It had led from certain local unpleasantness to a police-court application, having as its object the suppression of Mr Homer Lynne as a public nuisance, and finally to the exchange of lawyers' letters and the threat of an action in the High Court.

That so sympathetic and kindly a gentleman should utterly disregard the feelings and desires of his neighbours, that he should have in his bedroom the largest gramophone that Hampstead had ever known, and a gramophone, moreover, fitted with an automatic arm, so that no sooner was the record finished than the needle was switched to the outer edge of the disc and began all over again, and that he should choose the midnight hour for his indulgence, were facts as strange as they were deplorable.

Mr Lynne had urged at the police court that the only method he had discovered for so soothing his nerves that he could ensure himself a night's sleep, was to hear that thunderous piece.

That Mr Lynne was sympathetic at least three distressed parents could testify. He was a theatrical agent with large interests in South America; he specialised in the collection of 'turns' for some twenty halls large and small, and the great artists who had travelled through the Argentine and Mexico, Chile and Brazil, had nothing but praise for the excellent treatment they had received at the hands of those Mr Lynne represented. It was believed, and was in truth, a fact, that he was financially interested in quite a number of these places of amusement, which may have accounted for the courtesy and attention which the great performers received on their tour.

He also sent out a number of small artists – microscopically small artists whose names had never figured on the play bills of Britain. They were chosen for their beauty, their sprightliness and their absence of ties.

'It's a beautiful country,' Mr Homer Lynne would say.

He was a grave, smooth man, clean-shaven, save for a sign of grey side-whiskers, and people who did not know him would imagine that he was a successful lawyer, with an ecclesiastical practice.

'It's a beautiful country,' he would say, 'but I don't know whether I like sending a young girl out there. Of course, you'll have a good salary, and live well – have you any relations?'

If the girl produced a brother or a father, or even a mother, or an intimate maiden aunt, Mr Lynne would nod and promise to write on the morrow, a promise which he fulfilled, regretting that he did not think the applicant would quite suit his purpose – which was true. But if she were isolated from these connections, if there were no relations to whom she would write, or friends who were likely to pester him with enquiries, her first-class passage was forthcoming – but not for the tour which the great artists followed, nor for the bigger halls where they would be likely to meet. They were destined for smaller halls, which were not so much theatre as cabaret.

Now and again, on three separate occasions to be exact, the applicant for an engagement would basely deceive him. She would say she had no relations, and lo! there would appear an inquisitive brother, or, as in the present case, a father.

On a bright morning in June, Mr Lynne sat in his comfortable chair, his hands folded, regarding gravely a nervous little man who sat on the other side of the big mahogany desk balancing his bowler hat on his knees.

'Rosie Goldstein,' said Mr Lynne thoughtfully, 'I seem to remember the name.'

He rang a bell and a dark young man answered.

'Bring me my engagement book, Mr Mandez,' said Mr Lynne.

'You see how it is, Mr Lynne,' said the caller anxiously – he was unmistakably Hebraic and very nervous. 'I hadn't any idea that Rosie had gone abroad until a friend of hers told me that she had come here and got an engagement.'

'I see,' said Mr Lynne. 'She did not tell you she was going.'

'No, sir.'

The dark young man returned with the book and Mr Lynne turned the pages leisurely, running his finger down a list of names.

'Here we are,' he said. 'Rosie Goldstein. Yes, I remember the girl now, but she told me she was an orphan.'

Goldstein nodded.

'I suppose she thought I'd stop her,' he said with a sigh of relief. 'But as long as I know where she is, I'm not so worried. Have you her present address?'

Lynne closed the book carefully and beamed at the visitor.

'I haven't her present address,' he said cheerfully, 'but if you will write her a letter and address it to me, I will see that it goes forward to our agents in Buenos Aires: they, of course, will be able to find her. You see, there are a large number of halls in connection with the circuit, and it is extremely likely that she may be performing up-country. It is quite impossible to keep track of every artist.'

'I understand that, sir,' said the grateful little Jew.

'She ought to have told you,' said the sympathetic Lynne shaking his head.

He really meant that she ought to have told him.

'However, we'll see what can be done.'

He offered his plump hand to the visitor, and the dark young man showed him to the door.

Three minutes later Mr Lynne was interviewing a pretty girl who had the advantage of stage experience – she had been a member of a beauty chorus in a travelling revue. And when the eager girl had answered questions relating to her stage experiences, which were few, Mr Lynne came to the real crux of the interview.

'Now what do your father and mother say about this idea of your accepting this engagement to go abroad?' he asked with his most benevolent smile.

'I have no father or mother,' said the girl, and Mr Lynne guessed from the momentary quiver of the lips that she had lost one of these recently.

'You have brothers, perhaps?'

'I have no brothers,' she answered, shaking her head. 'I haven't any relations in the world, Mr Lynne. You will let me go, won't you?' she pleaded.

Mr Lynne would let her go. If the truth be told, the minor 'artists' he sent to the South American continent were infinitely more profitable than the great performers whose names were household words in London.

'I will write you tomorrow,' he said conventionally.

'You will let me go?'

He smiled. 'You are certain to go, Miss Hacker. You need have no fear on the subject. I will send you on the contract – no, you had better come here and sign it.'

The girl ran down the stairs into Leicester Square, her heart singing. An engagement at three times bigger than the biggest salary she had ever received! She wanted to tell everybody about it, though she did not dream that in a few seconds she would babble her happiness to a man who at that moment was a perfect stranger.

He was a foreign-looking gentleman, well dressed and good-looking. He had the kind of face that appeals to children – an appeal that no psychologist has ever yet analysed.

She met him literally by accident. He was standing at the bottom of the stairs as she came down, and missing her footing she tell forward into his arms.

'I am ever so sorry,' she said with a smile.

'You don't look very sorry,' smiled the man. 'You look more like a person who had just got a very nice engagement to go abroad.'

She stared at him.

'However did you know that?'

'I know it because – well, I know,' he laughed, and apparently abandoning his intention of going upstairs, he turned and walked with her into the street.

'Yes, I am,' she nodded. 'I've had a wonderful opportunity. Are you in the profession?'

'No, I'm not in the profession,' said Leon Gonsalez, 'if you mean the theatrical profession, but I know the countries you're going to rather well. Would you like to hear something about the Argentine?'

She looked at him dubiously.

'I should very much,' she hesitated, 'but I – '

'I'm going to have a cup of tea, come along,' said Leon good-humouredly.

Though she had no desire either for tea or even for the interview (though she was dying to tell somebody) the magnetic personality of the man held her, and she fell in by his side. And at that very moment Mr Lynne was saying to the dark-skinned man:

'Fonsio! She's a beaut!' and that staid man kissed the bunched tips of his fingers ecstatically.

This was the third time Leon Gonsalez had visited the elegant offices of Mr Homer Lynne in Panton Street.

Once there was an organisation which was called the Four Just Men, and these had banded themselves together to execute justice upon those whom the law had missed, or passed by, and had earned for themselves a reputation which was world-wide. One had died, and of the three who were left, Poiccart (who had been called the brains of the four) was living quietly in Seville. To him had come a letter from a compatriot in Rio, a compatriot who did not identify him with the organisation of the Four Just Men, but had written vehemently of certain abominations. There had been an exchange of letters, and Poiccart had discovered that most of these fresh English girls who had appeared in the dance halls of obscure towns had been imported through the agency of the respectable Mr Lynne, and Poiccart had written to his friends in London.

'Yes, it's a beautiful country,' said Leon Gonsalez, stirring his tea thoughtfully. 'I suppose you're awfully pleased with yourself.'

'Oh, it's wonderful,' said the girl. 'Fancy, I'm going to receive £12 a week and my board and lodging. Why, I shall be able to save almost all of it.'

'Have you any idea where you will perform?'

The girl smiled.

'I don't know the country,' she said, 'and it's dreadfully ignorant of me, but I don't know one single town in the Argentine.'

'There aren't many people who do,' smiled Leon, 'but you've heard of Brazil, I suppose?'

'Yes, it's a little country in South America,' she nodded, 'I know that.'

'Where the nuts come from,' laughed Leon. 'No, it's not a little country in South America: it's a country as wide as from here to the centre of Persia, and as long as from Brighton to the equator. Does that give you any idea?'

She stared at him.

And then he went on, but confined himself to the physical features of the sub-continent. Not once did he refer to her contract – that was not his object. That object was disclosed, though not to her, when he said: 'I must send you a book. Miss Hacker: it will interest you if you are going to the Argentine. It is full of very accurate information.'

'Oh, thank you,' she said gratefully. 'Shall I give you my address?'

That was exactly what Leon had been fishing for. He put the scrap of paper she had written on into his pocket-book, and left her.

George Manfred, who had acquired a two-seater car, picked him up outside the National Gallery, and drove him to Kensington Gardens, the refreshment buffet of which, at this hour of the day, was idle. At one of the deserted tables Leon disclosed the result of his visit.

'It was singularly fortunate that I should have met one of the lambs.'

'Did you see Lynne himself?'

Leon nodded.

'After I left the girl I went up and made a call. It was rather difficult to get past the Mexican gentleman – Mandez I think his name is – into the sanctum but eventually Lynne saw me.'

He chuckled softly: 'I do not play on the banjo; I declare this to you, my dear George, in all earnestness. The banjo to me is a terrible instrument – '

'Which, means,' said Manfred with a smile, 'that you described yourself as a banjo soloist who wanted a job in South America.'

'Exactly,' said Leon, 'and I need hardly tell you that I was not engaged. The man is interesting, George.'

'All men are interesting to you, Leon,' laughed Manfred, putting aside the coffee he had ordered, and lighting a long, thin cigar.

'I should have loved to tell him that his true vocation was arson. He has the face of the true incendiary, and I tell you George, that Lombroso was never more accurate than when he described that type. A fair, clear, delicate skin, a plump, babylike face, hair extraordinarily fine: you can pick them out anywhere.'

He caressed his chin and frowned.

'Callous destruction of human happiness also for profit. I suppose the same type of mind would commit both crimes. It is an interesting parallel. I should like to consult our dear friend Poiccart on that subject.'

'Can he be touched by the law?' asked Manfred. 'Is there no way of betraying him?'

'Absolutely none,' said Leon shortly. 'The man is a genuine agent. He has the names of some of the best people on his books and they all speak loudly in his praise. The lie that is half a lie is easier to detect than the criminal who is half honest. If the chief cashier of the Bank of England turned forger, he would be the most successful forger in the world. This man has covered himself at every point. I had a talk with a Jewish gentleman – a pathetic old soul named Goldstein, whose daughter went abroad some seven or eight months ago. He has not heard from her, and he told me that Lynne was very much surprised to discover that she had any relations at all. The unrelated girl is his best investment.'

'Did Lynne give the old man her address?'

Leon shrugged his shoulders.

'There are a million square miles in the Argentine – where is she? Cordoba, Tucuman, Mendoza, San Louis, Santa Fé, Rio Cuarto, those are a few towns. And there are hundreds of towns where this girl may be dancing, towns which have no British or American Consul. It's rather horrible, George.'

Manfred looked thoughtfully across the green spaces in the park.

'If we could be sure,' said Gonsalez softly. 'It will take exactly two months to satisfy us, and I think it would be worth the money. Our young friend will leave by the next South American packet, and you, some time ago, were thinking of returning to Spain. I think I will take the trip.'

George nodded.

'I thought you would,' he said. 'I really can't see how we can act unless you do.'

Miss Lilah Hacker was amazed when she boarded the *Braganza* at Boulogne to discover that she had as fellow passenger the polite stranger who had lectured so entertainingly on the geography of South America.

To the girl her prospect was rosy and bright. She was looking forward to a land of promise, her hopes for the future were at zenith, and if she was disappointed a little that the agreeable Gonsalez did not keep her company on the voyage, but seemed for ever pre-occupied, that was a very unimportant matter.

It was exactly a month from the day she put foot on the *Braganza* that her hope and not a little of her faith in humanity were blasted by a stout Irishman whose name was Rafferty, but who had been born in the Argentine. He was the proprietor of a dance hall called 'La Plaza' in a cattle town in the interior. She had been sent there with two other girls wiser than she, to entertain the half-breed vaqueros who thronged the town at night, and for whom 'La Plaza' was the principal attraction.

'You've got to get out of them ways of yours,' said Rafferty, twisting his cigar from one side of his mouth to the other. 'When Señor Santiago wanted you to sit on his knee last night, you made a fuss, I'm told.'

'Of course, I did,' said the girl indignantly. 'Why, he's coloured!'

'Now see here,' said Mr Rafferty, 'there ain't no coloured people in this country. Do you get that? Mr Santiago is a gentleman and he's got stacks of money, and the next time he pays you a little attention, you've got to be pleasant, see?'

'I'll do nothing of the sort,' said the girl, pale and shaking, 'and I'm going straight back to Buenos Aires tonight.'

'Oh you are, are you?' Rafferty smiled broadly. 'That's an idea you can get out of your head, too.'

Suddenly he gripped her by the arm.

'You're going up to your room, now,' he said, 'and you're going to stay there till I bring you out tonight to do your show, and if you give me any of your nonsense – you'll be sorry!'

He pushed her through the rough unpainted door of the little cell which was termed bedroom, and he paused in the doorway to convey information (and there was a threat in the course of it) which left her white and staring.

She came down that night and did her performance and to her surprise and relief did not excite even the notice of the wealthy Mr Santiago, a half-bred Spaniard with a yellow face, who did not so much as look at her.

Mr Rafferty was also unusually bland and polite.

She went to her room that night feeling more comfortable. Then she discovered that her key was gone, and she sat up until one o'clock in the morning waiting for she knew not what. At that hour came a soft footfall in the passage; somebody tried the handle of her door, but she had braced a chair under the handle.

They pushed and the rickety chair creaked; then there was a sound like a stick striking a cushion, and she thought she heard somebody sliding against the wooden outer wall of the room. A tap came to her door.

'Miss Hacker,' the voice said. She recognised it immediately. 'Open the door quickly. I want to get you away.'

With a trembling hand she removed the chair, and the few little articles of furniture she had piled against the door, and opened it. By the light of the candle which was burning in her room she recognised the man who had been her fellow passenger on the *Braganza*.

'Come quietly,' he said. 'There is a back stair to the compound. Have you a cloak? Bring it, because you have a sixty-mile motor journey before we come to the railway . . .'

As she came through the door she saw the upturned toes of somebody who was lying in the passage, and with a shudder she realised that was the thumping sound she had heard.

They reached the big yard behind the 'Plaza' crowded with the dusty motor-cars of ranchers and their foremen, who had come into town for the evening, and passed out through the doorway. A big car was standing in the middle of the road, and to this he guided her. She threw one glance back at Rafferty's bar. The windows blazed with light, the sound of the orchestra came faintly through the still night air, then she dropped her head on her hands and wept.

Leon Gonsalez had a momentary pang of contrition, for he might have saved her all this.

* * *

It was two months exactly from the day he had left London, when he came running up the stairs of the Jermyn Street flat and burst in upon Manfred.

'You're looking fit and fine, Leon,' said George, jumping up and gripping his hand. 'You didn't write and I never expected that you would. I only got back from Spain two days ago.'

He gave the news from Seville and then: 'You proved the case?'

'To our satisfaction,' said Leon grimly. 'Though you would not satisfy the law that Lynne was guilty. It is, however, a perfectly clear case. I visited his agent when I was in Buenos Aires, and took the liberty of rifling his desk in his absence. I found several letters from Lynne and by their tone there can be no doubt whatever that Lynne is consciously engaged in this traffic.'

They looked at one another.

'The rest is simple,' said Manfred, 'and I will leave you to work out the details, my dear Leon, with every confidence that Mr Homer Lynne will be very sorry indeed that he departed from the safe and narrow way.'

There was no more painstaking, thorough or conscientious workman that Leon Gonsalez. The creation of punishment was to him a work of love. No General ever designed the battle with a more punctilious regard to the minutest detail than Leon.

Before the day was over he had combed the neighbourhood in which Mr Lynne lived of every vital fact. It was then that he learnt of Mr Lynne's passion for music. The cab which took Leon back to Jermyn Street did not go fast enough: he literally leapt into the sitting-room, chortling his joy.

'The impossible is possible, my dear George,' he cried, pacing about the apartment like a man demented. 'I thought I should never be able to carry my scheme into effect, but he loves music, George! He adores the tuneful phonograph!'

'A little ice water, I think,' suggested Manfred gently.

'No, no.' said Leon, 'I am not hot, I am cool: I am ice itself! And who would expect such good luck? Tonight we will drive to Hampstead and we will hear his concert.'

It was a long time before he gave a coherent account of what he had learnt. Mr Lynne was extremely unpopular in the neighbourhood, and Leon explained why.

Manfred understood better that night, when the silence of the sedate road in which Mr Lynne's detached house was situated was broken by the shrill sound of trumpets, and the rolling of drums, the clanging of bells, the simulated boom of cannon – all the barbarian musical interjection which has made '1812' so popular with unmusical people.

'It sounds like a real band,' said Manfred in surprise.

A policeman strolled along, and seeing the car standing before the house, turned his head with a laugh.

'It's an awful row, isn't it?'

'I wonder it doesn't wake everybody up,' suggested Manfred.

'It does,' replied the policeman, 'or it did until they got used to it. It's the loudest gramophone in the world, I should think: like one of those things you have at the bottom of the tube stairs, to tell the people to move on. A stentaphone, isn't it?'

'How long does this go on? All night?' asked Manfred.

'For about an hour, I believe,' said the policeman. 'The gentleman who lives in that house can't go to sleep without music. He's a bit artistic, I think.'

'He is,' said Leon grimly.

The next day he found out that four servants were kept in the establishment, three of whom slept on the premises. Mr Lynne was in the habit of returning home every evening at about ten o'clock, except on Fridays when he went out of Town.

Wednesday evening was the cook's night out, and it was also the night when Mr Lynne's butler and general factotum was allowed an evening off. There remained the housemaid, and even she presented no difficulty. The real trouble was that all these people would return to the house or the neighbourhood at eleven o'clock. Leon decided to make his appointment with Mr Lynne for Friday night, on which day he usually went to Brighton. He watched the genial man leave Victoria, and then he called up Lynne's house.

'Is that Masters?' he asked, and a man's voice answered him.

'Yes, sir,' was the reply.

'It is Mr Mandez here,' said Leon, imitating the curious broken English of Lynne's Mexican assistant. 'Mr Lynne is returning to the house tonight on very important business, and he does not want any of the servants to be there.'

'Indeed, sir,' said Masters and showed no surprise. Evidently these instructions had been given before. Leon had expected some difficulty here, and had prepared a very elaborate explanation which it was not necessary to give.

'He wouldn't like me to stay, sir?'

'Oh, no,' said Leon. 'Mr Lynne particularly said that nobody was to be in the house. He wants the side door and the kitchen door left unlocked,' he added as an afterthought. It was a brilliant afterthought if it came off, and apparently it did.

'Very good, sir,' said Masters.

Leon went straight from the telephone call-box, where he had sent the message, to the counter and wrote out a wire, addressed to Lynne, Hôtel Ritz, Brighton. The message ran –

The girl Goldstein has been discovered at Santa Fé. Terrible row. Police have been making enquiries. Have very important information for you. I am waiting for you at your house.

He signed it Mandez.

'He will get the wire at eight. There is a train back at nine. That should bring him to Hampstead by half past ten,' said Leon when he had rejoined Manfred who was waiting for him outside the post office. 'We will be there an hour earlier: that is as soon as it is dark.'

They entered the house without the slightest difficulty. Manfred left his two-seater outside a doctor's house, a place where an unattended car would not be noticed, and went on foot to Lynne's residence. It was a large detached house, expensively furnished, and as Leon had expected, the servants had gone. He located Lynne's room, a big apartment at the front of the house.

'There is his noise box,' said Leon pointing to a handsome cabinet near the window. 'Electrical, too. Where does that wire lead?'

He followed the flex to a point above the head of the bed, where it terminated in what looked like a hanging bell push.

Leon was momentarily puzzled and then a light dawned upon him.

'Of course, if he has this infernal noise to make him go to sleep, the bell push switches off the music and saves him getting out of bed.'

He opened the lid of the gramophone cabinet and examined the record.

'1812,' he chuckled. He lifted the needle from the disc, turned the switch and the green table revolved. Then he walked to the head of the bed and pushed the knob of the bell push. Instantly the revolutions stopped.

'That is it,' he nodded, and turned over the soundbox, letting the needle rest upon the edge of the record.

'That,' he pointed to a bronze rod which ran from the centre to the side of the disc and fitted to some adjustment in the sound-box, 'is the repeater. It is an American invention which I saw in Buenos Aires, but I haven't seen many on this side. When the record is finished the rod automatically transfers the needle to the beginning of the record.'

'So that it can go on and on and on,' said Manfred interested. 'I don't wonder our friend is unpopular.'

Leon was looking round the room for something and at last he found what he was seeking. It was a brass clothes peg fastened to a door which led to a dressing-room. He put all his weight on the peg but it held firm.

'Excellent,' he said, and opened his bag. From this he took a length of stout cord and skilfully knotted one end to the clothes hook. He tested it but it did not move. From the bag he took a pair of handcuffs, unlocked and opened them and laid them on the bed. Then he took out what looked to be a Field-Marshal's baton. It was about fourteen inches long, and fastened around were two broad strips of felt; tied neatly to the baton were nine pieces of cord which were fastened at one end to the cylinder. The cords were twice the length of the handle and were doubled over neatly and temporarily fastened to the handle by pieces of twine.

Leon looked at one end of the baton and Manfred saw a red seal.

'What on earth is that, Leon?'

Leon showed him the seal, and Manfred read: 'Prison Commission.'

'That,' said Leon, 'is what is colloquially known as the "cat". In other words, the "cat of nine tails". It is an authentic instrument which I secured with some difficulty.'

He cut the twine that held the cords to the handle and let the nine thongs fall straight. Manfred took them into his hands and examined them curiously. The cords were a little thinner than ordinary window line, but more closely woven: at the end of each thong there was a binding of yellow silk for about half an inch.

Leon took the weapon in his hands and sent the cords whistling round his head.

'Made in Pentonville Gaol,' he explained, 'and I'm afraid I'm not as expert as the gentleman who usually wields it.'

The dusk grew to darkness. The two men made their way downstairs and waited in the room leading from the hall.

At half past ten exactly they heard a key turn in the lock and the door close.

'Are you there, Mandez?' called the voice of Mr Lynne, and it sounded anxious.

He took three steps towards the door and then Gonsalez stepped out.

'Good evening, Mr Lynne,' he said.

The man switched on the light.

He saw before him a figure plainly dressed, but who it was he could not guess, for the intruder's face was covered by a white semi-diaphanous veil.

'Who are you? What do you want?' gasped Lynne.

'I want you,' said Leon shortly. 'Before we go any further, I will tell you this, Mr Lynne, that if you make an outcry, if you attempt to attract attention from outside, it will be the last sound you ever make.'

'What do you want of me?' asked the stout man shakily, and then his eyes fell upon Manfred similarly veiled and he collapsed into the hall chair.

Manfred gripped his arm and led him upstairs to his bedroom. The blinds were pulled and the only light came from a small table-lamp by the side of the bed.

'Take off your coat,' said Manfred.

Mr Lynne obeyed.

'Now your waistcoat.'

The waistcoat was discarded.

'Now I fear I shall have to have your shirt,' said Gonsalez.

'What are you going to do?' asked the man hoarsely.

'I will tell you later.'

The stout man, his face twitching, stood bare to the waist, and offered no resistance when Manfred snapped the handcuffs on him.

They led him to the door where the hat peg was, and deftly Leon slipped the loose end of the rope through the links and pulled his manacled hands tightly upwards.

'Now we can talk,' said Gonsalez. 'Mr Lynne, for some time you have been engaged in abominable traffic. You have been sending women, who sometimes were no more than children, to South America, and the penalties for that crime are, as you know, a term of imprisonment and this.'

He picked the baton from where he had placed it, and shook out the loose cords. Mr Lynne gazed at them over his shoulder, with a fascinated stare.

'This is colloquially known as the "cat of nine tails",' said Gonsalez, and sent the thongs shrilling round his head.

'I swear to you I never knew – ' blubbered the man. 'You can't prove it – '

'I do not intend proving it in public,' said Leon carefully. 'I am here merely to furnish proof to you that you cannot break the law and escape punishment.'

And then it was that Manfred started the gramophone revolving, and the blare of trumpets and the thunder of drums filled the room with strident harmony.

The same policeman to whom Manfred and Gonsalez had spoken a few nights previously paced slowly past the house and stopped to listen with a grin. So, too, did a neighbour.

'What a din that thing makes,' said the aggrieved householder.

'Yes it does,' admitted the policeman. 'I think he wants a new record. It sounds almost as though somebody was shrieking their head off, doesn't it?'

'It always sounds like that to me,' grumbled the neighbour, and went on.

The policeman smiled and resumed his beat, and from behind the windows of Mr Lynne's bedroom came the thrilling cadences of the 'Marseillaise' and the boom of guns, and a shrill thin sound of fear and pain for which Tschaikovsky was certainly not responsible.

The Man who was Plucked

On Sunday night Martaus Club is always crowded with the smartest of the smart people who remain in Town over the week-end. Martaus Club is a place of shaded lights, of white napery, of glittering silver and glass, of exotic flowers, the tables set about the walls framing a parallelogram of shining floor.

Young men and women, and older folks too, can be very happy in Martaus Club – at a price. It is not the size of the 'note' which Louis, the head waiter, initials, nor the amazing cost of wine, nor the half-a-crown strawberries, that breaks a man.

John Eden could have footed the bill for all he ate or drank or smoked in Martaus, and in truth the club was as innocent as it was gay. A pack of cards had never been found within its portals. Louis knew every face and the history behind the face, and could have told within a few pounds just what was the bank balance of every habitué. He did not know John Eden, who was the newest of members, but he guessed shrewdly.

John Eden had danced with a strange girl, which was unusual at Martaus, for you bring your own dancing partner, and never under any circumstances solicit a dance with a stranger.

But Welby was there. Jack knew him slightly, though he had not seen him for years. Welby was the mirror of fashion and apparently a person of some importance. When he came across to him, Jack felt rather like a country cousin. He had been eight years in South Africa, and he felt rather out of it, but Welby was kindness itself, and then and there insisted upon introducing him to Maggie Vane. A beautiful girl, beautifully gowned, magnificently jewelled – her pearl necklace cost £20,000 – she rather took poor Jack's breath away, and when she suggested that they should go to Bingley's, he would not have dreamt of refusing.

As he passed out through the lobby Louis, the head waiter, with an apology, brushed a little bit of fluff from his dress-coat, and said in a voice, inaudible save to Jack: 'Don't go to Bingley's', which was of course a preposterous piece of impertinence, and Jack glared at him.

He was at Bingley's until six o'clock in the morning, and left behind him cheques which would absorb every penny he had brought back from Africa, and a little more. He had come home dreaming of a little estate with a little shooting and a little fishing, and the writing of that book of his on big-game hunting, and all his dreams went out when the croupier, with a smile on his bearded lips, turned a card with a mechanical: '*Le Rouge gagnant et couleur*'.

He had never dreamt Bingley's was a gambling-house, and it certainly had not that appearance when he went in. It was only when this divine girl introduced him to the inner room, where they played *trente-et-quarante* and he saw how high the stakes were running, that he began to feel nervous. He sat by her side at the table and staked modestly and won. And continued to win – until he increased his stakes.

They were very obliging at Bingley's. They accepted cheques, and. indeed, had cheque forms ready to be filled in.

Jack Eden came back to the flat he had taken in Jermyn Street, which was immediately above that occupied by Manfred and Leon Gonsalez, and wrote a letter to his brother in India . . .

Manfred heard the shot and woke up. He came out into the sitting-room in his pyjamas to find Leon already there, looking at the ceiling, the whitewash of which was discoloured by a tiny red patch which was growing larger.

Manfred went out on to the landing and found the proprietor of the flats in his shirt and trousers, for he had heard the shot from his basement apartment.

'I thought it was in your room, sir,' he said, 'it must be in Mr Eden's apartment.'

Going up the stairs he explained that Mr Eden was a new arrival in the country. The door of his flat was locked, but the proprietor produced a key which opened it. The lights were burning in the sitting-room, and one glance told Manfred the story. A huddled figure was lying across the table, from which the blood was dripping and forming a pool on the floor.

Gonsalez handled the man scientifically.

'He is not dead,' he said. 'I doubt if the bullet has touched any vital organ.'

The man had shot himself in the breast; from the direction of the wound Gonsalez was fairly sure that the injuries were minor. He applied a first-aid dressing and together they lifted him on to a sofa.

Then when the wound was dressed, Gonsalez looked round and saw the tell-tale letter.

'Pinner,' he said, holding the letter up, 'I take it that you do not want to advertise the fact that somebody attempted to commit suicide in one of your flats?'

'That is the last thing in the world I want,' said the flat proprietor, fervently.

'Then I'm going to put this letter in my pocket. Will you telephone to the hospital and say there has been an accident. Don't talk about suicide. The gentleman has recently come back from South Africa; he was packing his pistol, and it exploded.'

The man nodded and left the room hurriedly.

Gonsalez went to where Eden was lying and it was at that moment the young man's eyes opened. He looked from Manfred to Gonsalez with a puzzled frown.

'My friend,' said Leon, in a gentle voice as he leant over the wounded man, 'you have had an accident, you understand? You are not fatally injured; in fact, I think your injury is a very slight one. The ambulance will come for you and you will go to a hospital and I will visit you daily.'

'Who are you?' whispered the man.

'I am a neighbour of yours,' smiled Leon.

'The letter!' Eden gasped the words and Leon nodded.

'I have it in my pocket,' he said, 'and I will restore it to you when you are recovered. You understand that you have had an accident?'

Eden nodded.

A quarter of an hour later the hospital ambulance rolled up to the door, and the would-be suicide was taken away.

'Now,' said Leon, when they were back in their own room, 'we will discover what all this is about,' and very calmly he slit open the envelope and read.

'What is it?' asked Manfred.

'Our young friend came back from South Africa with £7,000, which he had accumulated in eight years of hard work. He lost it in less than eight hours at a gambling-house which he does not specify. He has not only lost all the money he has but more, and apparently has given cheques to meet his debts.'

Leon scratched his chin.

'That necessitates a further examination of his room. I wonder if the admirable Mr Pinner will object?'

The admirable Mr Pinner was quite willing that Leon should anticipate the inevitable visit of the police. The search was made, and Leon found a cheque-book for which he had been looking, tucked away in the inside pocket of Jack Eden's dress-suit, and brought it down to his room.

'No names,' he said disappointedly. 'Just "cash" on every counter-foil. All, I should imagine, to the same person. He banks with the Third National Bank of South Africa, which has an office in Throg-morton Street.'

He carefully copied the numbers of the cheques – there were ten in all.

'First of all,' he said, 'as soon as the post office is open we will send a telegram to the bank stopping the payment of these. Of course he can be sued, but a gambling debt is not recoverable at law, and before that happens we shall see many developments.'

The first development came the next afternoon. Leon had given instructions that anybody who called for Mr Eden was to be shown up to him, and at three o'clock came a very smartly dressed young man who aspirated his h's with suspicious emphasis.

'Is this Mr Eden's flat?'

'No, it isn't,' said Gonsalez. 'It is the flat of myself and my friend who are acting for Mr Eden.'

The visitor frowned suspiciously at Leon.

'Acting for him?' he said. 'Well, you can perhaps give me a little information about some cheques that have been stopped. My gov-ernor went to get a special clearance this morning, and the bank refused payment. Does Mr Eden know all about this?'

'Who is your governor?' asked Leon pleasantly.

'Mr Mortimer Birn.'

'And his address?'

The young man gave it. Mr Mortimer Birn was apparently a bill-discounter, and had cashed the cheques for a number of people who did not want to pass them through their banks. The young man was very emphatic as to the cheques being the property of a large number of people.

'And they all came to Mr Birn. What a singular coincidence,' agreed Leon.

'I'd rather see Mr Eden, if you don't mind,' said the emissary of Mr Mortimer Birn, and his tone was unpleasant.

'You cannot see him because he has met with an accident,' said Leon. 'But I will see your Mr Birn.'

He found Mr Birn in a very tiny office in Glasshouse Street. The gentleman's business was not specified either on the door-plate or on the painted window, but Leon smelt 'money-lender' the moment he went into his office.

The outer office was unoccupied when he entered. It was a tiny dusty cupboard of a place with just room enough to put a diminutive table, and the space was further curtailed by a wooden partition, head high, which served to exclude the unfortunate person who occupied the room from draughts and immediate observation. A door marked private led to Mr Birn's holy of holies and from this room came the sound of loud voices.

Gonsalez listened.

' . . . come without telephoning, hey? She always comes in the morning, haven't I told you a hundred times?' roared one voice.

'She doesn't know me,' grumbled the other.

'She's only got to see your hair . . . '

It was at that moment that the young man who called at Jermyn Street came out of the room. Gonsalez had a momentary glimpse of two men. One was short and stout, the other was tall, but it was his bright red hair that caught Leon's eye. And then Mr Birn's clerk went back to the room and the voices ceased. When Gonsalez was ushered into the office, only the proprietor of the establishment was visible.

Birn was a stout bald man, immensely affable. He told Leon the same story as his clerk had told.

'Now, what is Eden going to do about these cheques?' asked Birn at last.

'I don't think he's going to meet them,' said Leon gently. 'You see, they are gambling debts.'

'They are cheques,' interrupted Birn, 'and a cheque is a cheque whether it's for a gambling debt or a sack of potatoes.'

'Is that the law?' asked Leon, 'and if it is, will you write me a letter to that effect, in which case you will be paid.'

'Certainly I will,' said Mr Birn. 'If that's all you want, I'll write it now.'

'Proceed,' said Leon, but Mr Birn did not write the letter. Instead he talked about his lawyers; grew virtuously indignant on the un-sportsmanlike character of people who repudiated debts of honour (how he came to be satisfied that the cheques represented gambling losses, he did not explain) and ended the interview a little apoplectically. And all the time Leon was speculating upon the identity of the third man he had seen and who had evidently left the room through one of the three doors which opened from the office.

Leon went down the narrow stairs into the street, and as he stepped on to the pavement, a little car drove up and a girl descended. She did not look at him, but brushing past ran up the stairs. She was alone, and had driven her own luxurious coupé. Gonsalez, who was interested, waited till she came out, which was not for twenty minutes, and she was obviously distressed.

Leon was curious and interested. He went straight on to the hospital where they had taken Eden, and found the young man sufficiently recovered to be able to talk.

His first words betrayed his anxiety and his contrition.

'I say, what did you do with that letter? I was a fool to – '

'Destroyed it,' said Leon, which was true. 'Now, my young friend, you've got to tell me something. Where was the gambling-house to which you went?'

It took a long time to persuade Mr John Eden that he was not betraying a confidence and then he told him the whole story from beginning to end.

'So it was a lady who took you there, eh?' said Leon thoughtfully.

'She wasn't in it,' said John Eden quickly. 'She was just a visitor like myself. She told me she had lost five hundred pounds.'

'Naturally, naturally,' said Leon. 'Is she a fair lady with very blue eyes, and has she a little car of her own?'

The man looked surprised.

'Yes, she drove me in her car,' he said, 'and she is certainly fair and has blue eyes. In fact, she's one of the prettiest girls I've ever seen. You needn't worry about the lady, sir,' he said shaking his head. 'Poor girl, she was victimised, if there was any victimisation.'

'196 Paul Street, Mayfair, I think you said.'

'I'm certain it was Paul Street, and almost as sure it was 196,' said Eden. 'But I hope you're not going to take any action against them, because it was my own fault. Aren't you one of the two gentlemen who live in the flat under me?' he asked suddenly.

Leon nodded.

'I suppose the cheques have been presented and some of them have come back.'

'They have not been presented yet, or at any rate they have not been honoured,' said Leon. 'And had you shot yourself, my young friend, they would not have been honoured at all, because your bank would have stopped payment automatically.'

Manfred dined alone that night. Leon had not returned, and there had been no news from him until eight o'clock, when there came a District Messenger with a note asking Manfred to give the bearer his dress clothes and one or two articles which he mentioned.

Manfred was too used to the ways of Leon Gonsalez to be greatly surprised. He packed a small suitcase, sent the messenger boy off with it and he himself spent the evening writing letters.

At half past two he heard a slight scuffle in the street outside, and Leon came in without haste, and in no wise perturbed, although he had just emerged from a rough-and-tumble encounter with a young man who had been watching the house all the evening for his return.

He was not in evening dress, Manfred noticed, but was wearing the clothes he had on when he went out in the morning.

'You got your suitcase all right?'

'Oh yes, quite,' replied Leon.

He took a short stick from his trousers pocket, a stick made of rhinoceros hide, and called in South Africa a 'sjambok'. It was about a foot and a half in length, but it was a formidable weapon and was one of the articles which Leon had asked for. He examined it in the light.

'No, I didn't cut his scalp,' he said. 'I was afraid I had.'

'Who was this?'

Before he replied, Leon put out the light, pulled back the curtains from the open window and looked out. He came back, replaced the curtains, and put the light on again.

'He has gone away, but I do not think we have seen the last of that crowd,' he said.

He drank a glass of water, sat down by the table and laughed.

'Do you realise, my dear Manfred,' he said, 'that we have a friend in Mr Fare, the Police Commissioner, and that he occasionally visits us?'

'I realise that very well,' smiled Manfred. 'Why, have you seen him?'

Leon shook his head.

'No, only other people have seen him and have associated me with the Metropolitan Constabulary. I had occasion to interview our friend Mr Bingley, and he and those who are working with him are perfectly satisfied that I am what is known in London as a "split", in other words a detective, and it is generally believed that I am engaged in the business of suppressing gambling-houses. Hence the mild attention I have received and hence the fact, as I recognised when I was on my way back to Jermyn Street today – luckily I had forgotten to tell the cabman where to stop and he passed the watchers before I could stop him – that I am under observation.'

He described his visit to the hospital and his interview with Mr Birn.

'Birn, who of course is Bingley, is the proprietor of three, and probably more, big gambling-houses in London, at least he is the financial power behind them. I should not imagine that he himself frequents any of them. The house in Mayfair was, of course, shut up tonight and I did not attempt to locate it. They were afraid that our poor friend would inform the police. But oh, my dear Manfred, how can I describe to you the beauties of that lovely house in Bayswater Road, where all that is fashionable and wealthy in London gathers every night to try its luck at baccarat?'

'How did you get there?' asked Manfred.

'I was taken,' replied Gonsalez simply. 'I went to dinner at Martaus Club. I recognised Mr Welby and greeted him as an old friend. I think he really believed that he had met me before I went to the Argentine and made my pile, and of course, he sat down with me and we drank liqueurs, and he introduced me to a most beautiful girl, with a most perfectly upholstered little run-about.'

'You weren't recognised?'

Leon shook his head.

'The moustache which I put on my face was indistinguishable from the real thing,' he said not without pride. 'I put it on hair by hair, and it took me two hours to manufacture. When it was done you would not have recognised me. I danced with the beautiful Margaret and – ' He hesitated.

'You made love to her,' said Manfred admiringly.

Leon shrugged.

'My dear Manfred, it was necessary,' he said solemnly. 'And was it not fortunate that I had in my pocket a diamond ring which I had brought back from South America – it cost me 110 guineas in Regent Street this afternoon – and how wonderful that it should fit her. She wasn't feeling at her best, either, until that happened. That was the price of my admission to the Bayswater establishment. She drove me there in her car. It was a visit not without profit,' he said modestly. He put his hand in his pocket and pulled out a stiff bundle of notes.

Manfred was laughing softly.

Leon was the cleverest manipulator of cards in Europe. His long delicate fingers, the amazing rapidity with which he could move them, his natural gift for palming, would have made his fortune either as a conjurer or a card-sharper.

'The game was baccarat and the cards were dealt from a box by an intelligent croupier,' explained Leon. 'Those which were used were thrown into a basin. Those in the stack were, of course, so carefully arranged that the croupier knew the sequence of them all. To secure a dozen cards from the basin was a fairly simple matter. To stroll from the room and rearrange them so that they were alternately against and for the bank, was not difficult, but to place them on the top of those he was dealing – My dear Manfred, I was an artist!'

Leon did not explain what form his artistry took, nor how he directed the attention of croupier and company away from the 'deck' for that fraction of a second necessary – the croupier seldom took his hands from the cards – but the results of his enterprise were to be found in the thick stack of notes which lay on the table.

He took off his coat and put on his old velvet jacket, pacing the room with his hands in his pockets.

'Margaret Vane,' he said softly. 'One of God's most beautiful works, George, flawless, gifted, and yet if she is what she appears, something so absolutely loathsome that . . . '

He shook his head sadly.

'Does she play a big part, or is she just a dupe?' asked Manfred.

Leon did not answer at once.

'I'm rather puzzled,' he said slowly. He related his experience in Mr, Birn's office, the glimpse of the red-haired man and Mr Birn's fury with him.

'I do not doubt that the "she" to whom reference was made was Margaret Vane. But that alone would not have shaken my faith in her guilt. After I left the Bayswater house I decided that I would discover where she was living. She had so skilfully evaded any question on this matter which I had put to her that I grew suspicious. I hired a taxi-cab and waited, sitting inside. Presently her car came out and I followed her. Mr Birn has a house in Fitzroy Square and it was to there she drove. A man was waiting outside to take her car, and she went straight into the house, letting herself in. It was at this point that I began to think that Birn and she were much better friends than I had thought.

'I decided to wait, and stopped the car on the other side of the Square. In about a quarter of an hour the girl came out, and to my surprise, she had changed her clothes. I dismissed the cab and followed on foot. She lives at 803 Gower Street.'

'That certainly is puzzling,' agreed Manfred. 'The thing does not seem to dovetail, Leon.'

'That is what I think,' nodded Leon. 'I am going to 803 Gower Street tomorrow morning.'

Gonsalez required very little sleep and at ten o'clock in the morning was afoot.

The report he brought back to Manfred was interesting.

'Her name is Elsie Chaucer, and she lives with her father, who is paralysed in both legs. They have a flat, one servant and a nurse, whose business it is to attend to the father. Nothing is known of them except that they have seen better times. The father spends the day with a pack of cards, working out a gambling system, and probably that explains their poverty. He is never seen by visitors, and the girl is supposed to be an actress – that is, supposed by the landlady. It is rather queer,' said Gonsalez thoughtfully. 'The solution is, of course, in Birn's house and in Birn's mind.'

'I think we will get at that, Leon.'

Leon nodded.

'So I thought,' said he. 'Mr Birn's establishment does not present any insuperable difficulties.'

Mr Birn was at home that night. He was at home most nights. Curled up in a deep armchair, he puffed at a long and expensive cigar, and read the *London Gazette* which was to him the most interesting piece of literature which the genius of Caxton had made possible.

At midnight his housekeeper came in. She was a middle-aged Frenchwoman and discreet.

'All right?' queried Mr Birn lazily.

'No, monsieur, I desire that you should speak to Charles.'

Charles was Mr Birn's chauffeur, and between Charles and Madame was a continuous feud.

'What has Charles been doing?' asked Mr Birn with a frown.

'He is admitted every evening to the kitchen for supper,' explained madame, 'and it is an order that he should close the door after he goes out. But, m'sieur, when I went this evening at eleven o'clock to bolt the door, it was not closed. If I had not put on the lights and with my own eyes have seen it, the door would have been open, and we might have been murdered in our beds.'

'I'll talk to him in the morning,' growled Mr Birn. 'You've left the door of mademoiselle's room unfastened?'

'Yes, m'sieur, the key is in the lock.'

'Good night,' said Mr Birn resuming his study.

At half past two he heard the street door close gently and a light footstep passed through the hall. He looked up at the clock, threw away the end of his cigar and lit another before he rose and went heavily to a wall safe. This he unlocked and took out an empty steel box, which he opened and placed on the table. Then he resumed his chair.

Presently came a light tap at the door.

'Come in,' said Mr Birn.

The girl who was variously called Vane and Chaucer came into the room. She was neatly but not richly dressed. In many ways the plainness of her street costume enhanced her singular beauty and Mr Birn gazed approvingly upon her refreshing figure.

'Sit down, Miss Chaucer,' he said, putting out his hand for the little linen bag she carried.

He opened it and took out a rope of pearls and examined every gem separately.

'I haven't stolen any,' she said contemptuously.

'Perhaps you haven't,' said Mr Birn, 'but I've known some funny things to happen.'

He took the diamond pin, the rings, the two diamond and emerald bracelets, and each of these he scrutinised before he returned them to the bag and put the bag into the steel box.

He did not speak until he had placed them in the safe.

'Well, how are things going tonight?' he asked.

She shrugged her shoulders.

'I take no interest in gambling,' she said shortly and Mr Birn chuckled.

'You're a fool,' he said frankly.

'I wish I were no worse than that,' said Elsie Chaucer bitterly. 'You don't want me any more, Mr Birn?'

'Sit down,' he ordered. 'Who did you find tonight?'

For a moment she did not reply.

'The man whom Welby introduced last night,' she said.

'The South American?' Mr Birn pulled a long face. 'He wasn't very profitable. I suppose you know that? We lost about four thousand pounds.'

'Less the ring,' said the girl.

'The ring he gave you? Well, that's worth about a hundred, and I'll be lucky to get sixty for it,' said Mr Birn with a shrug. 'You can keep that ring if you like.'

'No thank you, Mr Birn,' said the girl quietly. 'I don't want those kinds of presents.'

'Come here,' said Birn suddenly, and reluctantly she came round the table and stood before him.

He rose and took her hand.

'Elsie,' he said, 'I've got very fond of you and I've been a good friend of yours, you know. If it hadn't been for me what would have happened to your father? He'd have been hung! That would have been nice for you, wouldn't it?'

She did not reply but gently disengaged her hand.

'You needn't put away those jewels and fine clothes every night, if you're sensible,' he went on, 'and – '

'Happily I am sensible, if by sensible you mean sane,' said the girl, 'and now I think I'll go if you don't mind, Mr Birn. I'm rather tired.'

'Wait,' he said.

He walked to the safe, unlocked it again and took out an oblong parcel wrapped in brown paper, fastened with tapes and sealed.

'There's a diamond necklace inside there,' he said. 'It's worth eight thousand pounds if it's worth a penny. I'm going to put it in my strong box at the bank tomorrow, unless – '

'Unless – ' repeated the girl steadily.

'Unless you want it,' said Mr Birn. 'I'm a fool with the ladies.'

She shook her head.

'Does it occur to you, Mr Birn,' she said quietly, 'that I could have had many necklaces if I wanted them? No, thank you. I am looking forward to the end of my servitude.'

'And suppose I don't release you?' growled Mr Birn as he put back the package in the safe and locked the door. 'Suppose I want you for another three years? How about that? Your father's still liable to arrest. No man can kill another, even if he's only a croupier, without hanging for it.'

'I've paid for my father's folly, over and over again,' said the girl in a low voice. 'You don't know how I hate this life, Mr Birn. I feel worse than the worst woman in the world! I spend my life luring men to ruin – I wish to God I had never made the bargain. Sometimes I think I will tell my father just what I am paying for his safety, and let him decide whether my sacrifice is worth it!'

A momentary look of alarm spread on the man's face.

'You'll do nothing of the kind,' he said sharply. 'Just as you've got into our ways! I was only joking about asking you to stay on. Now, my dear,' he said with an air of banter, 'you'd better go home and get your beauty sleep.'

He walked with her to the door, saw her down the steps and watched her disappear in the darkness of the street, then he came back to lock up for the night. He drank up the half glass of whisky he had left and made a wry face.

'That's a queer taste,' he said, took two steps towards the passage and fell in a heap.

The man who had slipped into the room when he had escorted Elsie Chaucer to the door came from behind the curtain and stooping, loosened his collar. He stepped softly into the dimly lit passage and beckoned somebody, and Manfred came from the shadows, noiselessly, for he was wearing rubber over-boots.

Manfred glanced down at the unconscious man and then to the dregs in the whisky glass.

'Butyl chloride, I presume?'

'No more and no less,' said the practical Leon, 'in fact the "knock-out-drop" which is so popular in criminal circles.'

He searched the man, took out his keys, opened the safe and removing the sealed packet, he carried it to the table. Then he looked thoughtfully at the prostrate man.

'He will only be completely under the "drop" for five minutes, Manfred, but I think that will be enough.'

'Have you stopped to consider what will be the pathological results of "twilight sleep" on top of butyl?' asked Manfred. 'I saw you blending the hyocine with the morphia before we left Jermyn Street and I suppose that is what you are using?'

'I did not look it up,' replied Gonsalez carelessly, 'and if he dies, shall I weep? Give him another dose in half an hour, George. I will return by then.'

He took from his pocket a small black case, and opened it; the hypodermic syringe it contained was already charged, and rolling back the man's sleeve, he inserted the needle and pressed home the piston.

* * *

Mr Birn woke the next morning with a throbbing headache.

He had no recollection of how he had got to bed, yet evidently he had undressed himself, for he was clad in his violet pyjamas. He rang the bell and got on to the floor, and though the room spun round him, he was able to hold himself erect.

The bell brought his housekeeper.

'What happened to me last night?' he asked, and she looked astounded.

'Nothing, sir. I left you in the library.'

'It is that beastly whisky,' grumbled Mr Birn.

A cold bath and a cup of tea helped to dissipate the headache, but he was still shaky when he went into the room in which he had been sitting the night before.

A thought had occurred to him. A terrifying thought. Suppose the whisky had been drugged (though what opportunity there had been for drugging his drink he could not imagine) and somebody had broken in! . . .

He opened the safe and breathed a sigh of relief. The package was still there. It must have been the whisky, he grumbled, and declining breakfast, he ordered his car and was driven straight to the bank.

When he reached his office, he found the hatchet-faced young man in a state of agitation.

'I think we must have had burglars here last night, Mr Birn.'

'Burglars?' said Mr Birn alarmed. And then with a laugh, 'well, they wouldn't get much here. But what makes you think they have been?'

'Somebody has been in the room, that I'll swear,' said the young man. 'The safe was open when I came and one of the books had been taken out and left on your table.'

A slow smile dawned on Mr Birn's face.

'I wish them luck,' he said.

Nevertheless he was perturbed, and made a careful search of all his papers to see if any important documents had been abstracted. His promissory notes were at the bank, in that same large box wherein was deposited the necklace which had come to him for the settlement of a debt.

Just before noon his clerk came in quickly.

'That fellow is here,' he whispered.

'Which fellow?' growled Mr Birn.

'The man from Jermyn Street who stopped the payment of Eden's cheques.'

'Ask him in,' said Mr Birn. 'Well, sir,' he said jovially, 'have you thought better about settling those debts?'

'Better and better,' said Gonsalez. 'I can speak to you alone, I suppose?'

Birn signalled his assistant to leave them.

'I've come to settle all sorts of debts. For example, I've come to settle the debt of a gentleman named Chaucer.'

The gambling-house keeper started.

'A very charming fellow, Chaucer. I've been interviewing him this morning. Some time ago he had a shock which brought on a stroke of paralysis. He's not been able to leave his room in consequence for some time.'

'You're telling me a lot I don't want to hear about.' said Mr Birn briskly.

'The poor fellow is under the impression that he killed a red-haired croupier of yours. Apparently he was gambling and lost his head, when he saw your croupier taking a bill.'

'My croupier,' said the other with virtuous indignation. 'What do you mean? I don't know what a croupier is.'

'He hit him over the head with a money-rake. You came to Chaucer the next day and told him your croupier was dead, seeking to extract money from him. You soon found he was ruined. You found also he had a very beautiful daughter, and it occurred to you that she might be of use to you in your nefarious schemes, so you had a little talk with her and she agreed to enter your service in order to save her father from ruin and possibly imprisonment.'

'This is a fairy story you're telling me, is it?' said Birn, but his face had gone a pasty white and the hand that took the cigar from his lips trembled.

'To bolster up your scheme,' Gonsalez went on, 'you inserted an advertisement in the death column of *The Times* and also you sent to the local newspaper a very flowery account of Mr Jinkins's funeral, which was also intended for Chaucer and his daughter.'

'It's Greek to me,' murmured Mr Birn with a pathetic attempt at a smile.

'I interviewed Mr Chaucer this morning and was able to assure him that Jinkins is very much alive and is living at Brighton, and is running a little gambling-house – a branch of your many activities. And by the way, Mr Birn, I don't think you will see Elsie Chaucer again.'

Birn was breathing heavily. 'You know a hell of a lot,' he began, but something in Leon's eyes stopped him.

'Birn,' said Gonsalez softly. 'I am going to ruin you – to take away every penny of the money you have stolen from the foolish men who patronise your establishments.'

'Try it on,' said Birn shakily. 'There's a law in this country! Go and rob the bank, and you'd have little to rob,' he added with a grin. 'There's two hundred thousand pounds' worth of securities in my bank – gilt-edged ones, Mr Clever! Go and ask the bank manager to hand them over to you. They're in Box 65,' he jeered. 'That's the only way you can ruin me, my son.'

Leon rose with a shrug.

'Perhaps I'm wrong,' he said. 'Perhaps after all you will enjoy your ill-gotten gains.'

'You bet your life I will.' Mr Birn relit his cigar.

He remembered the conversation that afternoon when he received an urgent telephone message from the bank. What the manager said took him there as fast as a taxi could carry him.

'I don't know what's the matter with your strong box,' said the bank manager, 'but one of my clerks who had to go into the vault said there was an extraordinary smell, and when we looked at the box, we found a stream of smoke coming through the keyhole.'

'Why didn't you open it?' screamed Birn, fumbling for his key.

'Partly because I haven't a key, Mr Birn,' said the bank manager intelligently.

With shaking hands the financier inserted the key and threw back the lid. A dense cloud of acrid yellow smoke came up and nearly stifled him . . . all that remained of his perfectly good securities was a black, sticky mess; a glass bottle, a few dull gems and nothing . . .

* * *

'It looks to me,' said the detective officer who investigated the circumstance, 'as though you must have inadvertently put in a package containing a very strong acid. What the acid is our analysts are working on now. It must have either leaked out or burst.'

'The only package there,' wailed Mr Birn, 'was a package containing a diamond necklace.'

'The remnants of which are still there,' said the detective. 'You are quite sure nobody could get at that package and substitute a destroying agent? It could easily be made. A bottle such as we found – a stopper made of some easily consumed material and there you are! Could anybody have opened the package and slipped the bottle inside?'

'Impossible, impossible,' moaned the financier.

He was sitting with his face in his hands, weeping for his lost affluence, for though a few of the contents of that box could be replaced, there were certain American bonds which had gone for ever and promissory notes by the thousandwhich would never be signed again.

The Man who would not Speak

But for the fact that he was already the possessor of innumerable coats-of-arms, quarterings, family mottoes direct and affiliated, Leon Gonsalez might have taken for his chief motto the tag *'homo sum, nihil humani a me alienum puto.'* For there was no sphere of human activity which did not fascinate him. Wherever crowds gathered, wherever man in the aggregate was to be seen at his best or worst, there was Gonsalez to be found, oblivious to the attractions which had drawn the throng together, intensely absorbed in the individual members of the throng themselves.

Many years ago four young men, wealthy and intensely sincere, had come together with a common purpose inspired by one common ideal. There had been, and always will be, such combinations of enthusiasts. Great religious revivals, the creation of missions and movements of sociological reform, these and other developments have resulted from the joining together of fiery young zealots.

But the Four Just Men had as their objective the correction of the law's inequalities. They sought and found the men whom the wide teeth of the legal rake had left behind, and they dealt out their justice with terrible swiftness.

None of the living three (for one had died at Bordeaux) had departed from their ideals, but it was Leon who retained the appearance of that youthful enthusiasm which had brought them together.

He sought for interests in all manner of places, and it is at the back of the grand-stand on Hurst Park racecourse that he first saw 'Spaghetti' Jones. It is one of the clear laws of coincidence, that if, in reading a book, you come across a word which you have not seen before, and which necessitates a reference to the dictionary, that same word will occur within three days on some other printed page. This law of the Inexplicable Recurrences applies equally to people, and Leon, viewing the bulk of the big man, had a queer feeling that they were destined to meet again – Leon's instincts were seldom at fault.

Mr Spaghetti Jones was a tall, strong and stoutly built man, heavy eyed and heavy jawed. He had a long dark moustache which curled at the ends, and he wore a green and white bow tie that the startling pink of his shirt might not be hidden from the world. There were diamond rings on his fat fingers, and a cable chain across his figured waistcoat. He was attired in a very bright blue suit, perfectly tailored, and violently yellow boots encased his feet, which were small for a man of his size. In fact, Mr Spaghetti Jones was a model of what Mr Spaghetti Jones thought a gentleman should be.

It was not his rich attire, nor his greatness of bulk, which ensured for him Leon's fascinated interest. Gonsalez had strolled to the back of the stand whilst the race was in progress, and the paddock was empty. Empty save for Mr Jones and two men, both smaller and both more poorly dressed than he.

Leon had taken a seat near the ring where the horses paraded, and it happened that the party strolled towards him. Spaghetti Jones made no attempt to lower his voice. It was rich and full of volume, and Leon heard every word. One of the men appeared to be quarrelling: the other, after a vain attempt to act as arbitrator, had subsided into silence.

'I told you to be at Lingfield, and you weren't there,' Mr Jones was saying gently.

He was cleaning his nails with a small penknife, Leon saw, and apparently his attention was concentrated on the work of beautification.

'I'm not going to Lingfield, or to anywhere else, for you, Jones.' said the man angrily.

He was a sharp, pale-faced man, and Leon knew from the note in his voice that he was frightened, and was employing this blustering manner to hide his fear.

'Oh, you're not going to Lingfield or anywhere else, aren't you?' repeated Spaghetti Jones.

He pushed his hat to the back of his head, and raised his eyes momentarily, and then resumed his manicuring.

'I've had enough of you and your crowd,' the man went on. 'We're blooming slaves, that's what we are! I can make more money running alone, now do you see?'

'I see,' said Jones. 'But, Tom, I want you to be at Sandown next Thursday. Meet me in the ring – '

'I won't, I won't,' roared the other, red of face. 'I've finished with you, and all your crowd!'

'You're a naughty boy,' said Spaghetti Jones almost kindly.

He slashed twice at the other's face with his little penknife, and the man jumped back with a cry.

'You're a naughty boy,' said Jones, returning to the contemplation of his nails, 'and you'll be at Sandown when I tell you.'

With that he turned and walked away.

The man called Tom pulled out a handkerchief and dabbed his bleeding face. There were two long shallow gashes – Mr Jones knew to an nth of an inch how deeply he could go in safety – but they were ugly and painful.

The wounded man glared after the retreating figure, and showed his discoloured teeth in an ugly grin, but Leon knew that he would report for duty at Sandown as he was ordered.

The sight was immensely interesting to Leon Gonsalez.

He came back to the flat in Jermyn Street full of it.

Manfred was out visiting his dentist, but the moment he came into the doorway Leon babbled forth his discovery.

'Absolutely the most amazing fellow I've seen in my life, George!' he cried enthusiastically. 'A gorgeous atavism – a survival of the age of cruelty such as one seldom meets. You remember that shepherd we found at Escorial? He was the nearest, I think. This man's name is Spaghetti Jones,' he went on, 'he is the leader of a racecourse gang which blackmails bookmakers. His nickname is derived from the fact that he has Italian blood and lives in the Italian quarter, and I should imagine from the general asymmetry of the face, and the fullness of his chin, that there is a history of insanity, and certainly epilepsy, on the maternal side of his family.'

Manfred did not ask how Leon had made these discoveries. Put Leon on the track of an interesting 'subject' and he would never leave it until it was dissected fibre by fibre and laid bare for his examination.

'He has a criminal record – I suppose?'

Gonsalez laughed, delighted.

'That is where you're wrong, my dear Manfred. He has never been convicted, and probably never will be. I found a poor little bookmaker in the silver ring – the silver ring is the enclosure where smaller bets are made than in Tattersall's reservation – who has been paying tribute to Caesar for years. He was a little doleful and maudlin, otherwise he would not have told me what he did. I drove him to a public-house in Cobham, far from the madding crowd, and he drank gin (which is the most wholesome drink obtainable in this country, if people only knew it) until he wept, and weeping unbuttoned his soul.'

Manfred smiled and rang the bell for dinner.

'The law will lay him low sooner or later: I have a great faith in English law,' he said. 'It misses far fewer times than any other law that is administered in the world.'

'But will it?' said Leon doubtfully. 'I'd like to talk with the courteous Mr Fare about this gentleman.'

'You'll have an opportunity,' said Manfred, 'for we are dining with him tomorrow night at the Metropolitan Restaurant.'

Their credentials as Spanish criminologists had served them well with Mr Fare and they in turn had assisted him – and Fare was thankful.

It was after the Sunday night dinner, when they were smoking their cigars, and most of the diners at the Metropolitan had strayed out into the dancing-room, that Leon told his experience.

Fare nodded.

'Oh yes. Spaghetti Jones is a hard case,' he said. 'We have never been able to get him, although he has been associated with some pretty unpleasant crimes. The man is colossal. He is brilliantly clever, in spite of his vulgarity and lack of education: he is remorseless, and he rules his little kingdom with a rod of iron. We have never been able to get one man to turn informer against him, and certainly he has never yet been caught with the goods.'

He flicked the ash of his cigar into his saucer, and looked a long time thoughtfully at the grey heap.

'In America the Italians have a Black Hand organisation. I suppose you know that? It is a system of blackmail, the operations of which, happily, we have not seen in this country. At least, we hadn't seen it until quite recently. I have every reason to believe that Spaghetti Jones is the guiding spirit in the one authentic case which has been brought to our notice.'

'Here in London?' said Manfred in surprise. 'I hadn't the slightest idea they tried that sort of thing in England.'

The Commissioner nodded.

'It may, of course, be a fake, but I've had some of my best men on the track of the letter-writers for a month, without getting any nearer to them. I was only wondering this morning, as I was dressing, whether I could not interest you gentlemen in a case where I confess we are a little at sea. Do you know the Countess Vinci?'

To Leon's surprise Manfred nodded.

'I met her in Rome, about three years ago,' he said. 'She is the widow of Count Antonio Vinci, is she not?'

'She is a widow with a son aged nine,' said the Commissioner, 'and she lives in Berkeley Square. A very wealthy lady and extremely charming. About two months ago she began to receive letters, which had no signature, but in its stead, a black cross. They were written in beautiful script writing, and that induced a suspicion of Spaghetti Jones who, in his youth, was a sign-writer.'

Leon nodded his head vigorously.

'Of course, it is impossible to identify that kind of writing,' he said admiringly. 'By "script" I suppose you mean writing which is actually printed? That is a new method, and a particularly ingenious one, but I interrupted you, sir. Did these letters ask for money?'

'They asked for money and threatened the lady as to what would happen if she failed to send to an address which was given. And here the immense nerve of Jones and his complicity was shown. Ostensibly Jones carries on the business of a newsagent. He has a small shop in Netting Hill, where he sells the morning and evening papers, and is a sort of local agent for racing tipsters whose placards you sometimes see displayed outside newspaper shops. In addition, the shop is used as an accommodation address – '

'Which means,' said Manfred, 'that people who do not want their letters addressed to their houses can have them sent there?'

The Commissioner nodded.

'They charge twopence a letter. These accommodation addresses should, of course, be made illegal, because they open the way to all sorts of frauds. The cleverness of the move is apparent: Jones receives the letter, ostensibly on behalf of some client, the letter is in his hands, he can open it or leave it unopened so that if the police call – as we did on one occasion – there is the epistle intact! Unless we prevent it reaching his shop we are powerless to keep the letter under observation. As a matter of fact, the name of the man to whom the money was to be sent, according to the letter which the Countess received, was "H. Frascati, care of John Jones". Jones, of course, received the answer to the Countess's letter, put the envelope with dozens of other letters which were waiting to be claimed, and when our man went in in the evening, after having kept observation of the shop all day, he was told that the letter had been called for, and as, obviously, he could not search everybody who went in and out of the shop in the course of the day, it was impossible to prove the man's guilt.'

'A wonderful scheme!' said the admiring Gonsalez. 'Did the Countess send money?'

'She sent £200 very foolishly,' said Fare with a shake of his head, 'and then when the next demand came she informed the police. A trap letter was made up and sent to Jones's address, with the result as I have told you. She received a further note, demanding immediate payment, and threatening her and her boy, and a further trap letter was sent; this was last Thursday: and from a house on the opposite side of the road two of our officers kept observation, using field-glasses, which gave them a view of the interior of the shop. No letter was handed over during the day by Jones, so in the evening we raided the premises, and there was that letter on the shelf with the others, unopened, and we looked extremely foolish,' said the Commissioner with a smile. He thought awhile. 'Would you like to meet the Countess Vinci?' he asked.

'Very much indeed,' said Gonsalez quickly, and looked at his watch.

'Not tonight,' smiled the Commissioner. 'I will fix an interview for you tomorrow afternoon. Possibly you two ingenious gentlemen may think of something which has escaped our dull British wits.'

On their way back to Jermyn Street that night, Leon Gonsalez broke the silence with a startling question.

'I wonder where one could get an empty house with a large bathroom and a very large bath?' he asked thoughtfully.

'Why ever – ?' began Manfred, and then laughed. 'I'm getting old, I think, Leon,' he said as they turned into the flat. 'There was a time when the amazing workings of your mind did not in any way surprise me. What other characteristics must this ideal home of yours possess?'

Leon scientifically twirled his hat across the room so that it fell neatly upon a peg of the hat-rack.

'How is that for dexterity, George?' he asked in self-admiration. 'The house – oh well, it ought to be a little isolated, standing by itself in its own grounds, if possible. Well away from the road, and the road not often frequented. I should prefer that it was concealed from observation by bushes or trees.'

'It sounds as if you're contemplating a hideous crime,' said Manfred good-humouredly.

'Not I,' corrected Leon quickly, 'but I think our friend Jones is a real nasty fellow.' He heaved a big sigh. 'I'd give anything for his head measurements,' he said inconsequently.

Their interview with the Countess Vinci was a pleasant one. She was a tall, pretty woman, of thirty-four, the 'grande dame' to her finger-tips.

Manfred, who was human, was charmed by her; for Leon Gonsalez she was too normal to be really interesting.

'Naturally I'm rather worried,' she said. 'Philip is not very strong, though he is not delicate.'

Later the boy came in, a straight, little fellow with an olive skin and brown eyes, self-possessed and more intelligent than Manfred had expected from his years. With him was his governess, a pretty Italian girl.

'I trust Beatrice more than I trust your police,' said the Countess when the girl had taken her charge back to his lessons. 'Her father is an officer in the Sicilian police, and she has lived practically all her life under threat of assassination.'

'Does the boy go out?' asked Manfred.

'Once a day, in the car,' said the Countess. 'Either I take him or Beatrice and I, or Beatrice alone.'

'Exactly what do they threaten?' asked Gonsalez.

'I will show you one of their letters,' said the Countess.

She went to a bureau, unlocked it, and came back with a stout sheet of paper. It was of excellent quality and the writing was in copper-plate characters:

You will send us a thousand pounds on the first of March, June, September and December. The money should be in bank-notes and should be sent to H. Frascati, care of J. Jones, 194 Notting Hill Crescent. It will cost you more to get your boy back than it will cost you to keep him with you.

Gonsalez held the paper to the light, then carried it to the window for a better examination.

'Yes,' he said as he handed it back. 'It would be difficult to trace the writer of that. The best expert in the world would fail.'

'I suppose you can suggest nothing,' said the Countess, shaking her head in anticipation, as they rose to go.

She spoke to Manfred, but it was Gonsalez who answered.

'I can only suggest, madame,' he said, 'that if your little boy does disappear you communicate with us immediately.'

'And my dear Manfred,' he said when they were in the street, 'that Master Philip *will* disappear is absolutely certain. I'm going to take a cab and drive round London looking for that house of mine.'

'Are you serious, Leon?' asked Manfred, and the other nodded.

'Never more serious in my life,' he said soberly. 'I will be at the flat in time for dinner.'

It was nearly eight o'clock, an hour after dinner-time, when he came running up the stairs of the Jermyn Street establishment, and burst into the room.

'I have got – ' he began, and then saw Manfred's face. 'Have they taken him?'

Manfred nodded.

'I had a telephone message an hour ago,' he said.

Leon whistled.

'So soon,' he was speaking to himself. And then: 'How did it happen?'

'Fare has been here. He left just before you came,' said Manfred. 'The abduction was carried out with ridiculous ease. Soon after we left, the governess took the boy out in the car, and they followed their usual route, which is across Hampstead Heath to the country beyond. It is their practice to go a few miles beyond the Heath in the direction of Beacon's Hill and then to turn back.'

'Following the same route every day was, of course, sheer lunacy,' said Leon. 'Pardon me.'

'The car always turns at the same point,' said Manfred, 'and that is the fact which the abductors had learnt. The road is not especially wide, and to turn the big Rolls requires a little manoeuvring. The chauffeur was engaged in bringing the car round, when a man rode up on a bicycle, a pistol was put under the chauffeur's nose, and at the same time two men, appearing from nowhere, pulled open the door of the car, snatched away the revolver which the governess carried, and carried the screaming boy down the road to another car, which the driver of the Vinci car had seen standing by the side of the road, but which apparently had not aroused his suspicion.'

'The men's faces, were they seen?'

Manfred shook his head.

'The gentleman who held up the chauffeur wore one of those cheap theatrical beards which you can buy for a shilling at any toyshop, and in addition a pair of motor goggles. Both the other men seemed to be similarly disguised. I was just going to the Countess when you came. If you'll have your dinner, Leon – '

'I want no dinner,' said Leon promptly.

Commissioner Fare was at the house in Berkeley Square when they called, and he was endeavouring vainly to calm the distracted mother.

He hailed the arrival of the two men with relief.

'Where is the letter?' said Leon immediately he entered the room.

'What letter?'

'The letter they have sent stating their terms.'

'It hasn't arrived yet,' said the other in a low voice. 'Do you think that you can calm the Countess? She is on the verge of hysteria.'

She was lying on a sofa deathly white, her eyes closed, and two maidservants were endeavouring to rouse her. She opened her eyes at Manfred's voice, and looked up.

'Oh my boy, my boy?' she sobbed, and clasped his hands in both of hers. 'You will get him back, please. I will give anything, anything. You cannot name a sum that I will not pay!'

It was then that the butler came into the room bearing a letter on a salver.

She sprang up, but would have fallen had not Manfred's arm steadied her.

'It is from – them,' she cried wildly and tore open the envelope with trembling fingers.

The message was a longer one:

Your son is in a place which is known only to the writer. The room is barred and locked and contains food and water sufficient to last for four days. None but the writer knows where he is or can find him. For the sum of twenty-five thousand pounds his hiding place will be sent to the Countess, and if that sum is not forthcoming, he will be left to starve.

'I must send the money immediately,' cried the distraught lady. 'Immediately! Do you understand? My boy – my boy! . . . '

'Four days,' murmured Leon, and his eyes were bright. 'Why it couldn't be better!'

Only Manfred heard him.

'Madam,' said Mr Fare gravely, 'if you send twenty-five thousand pounds what assurance have you that the boy will be restored? You are a very rich woman. Is it not likely that this man, when he gets your money, will make a further demand upon you?'

'Besides which,' interrupted Leon, 'it would be a waste of money. I will undertake to restore your boy in two days. Perhaps in one, it depends very much upon whether Spaghetti Jones sat up late last night.'

*   *   *

Mr Spaghetti Jones was nicknamed partly because of his association with the sons and daughters of Italy, and partly because, though a hearty feeder, he invariably finished his dinner, however many courses he might have consumed, with the Italian national dish.

He had dined well at his favourite restaurant in Soho, sitting aloof from the commonplace diners, and receiving the obsequious services of the restaurant proprietor with a complacency which suggested that it was no more than his right.

He employed a tooth-pick openly, and then paying his bill, he sauntered majestically forth and hailed a taxi-cab. He was on the point of entering it when two men closed in, one on each side of him.

'Jones,' said one sharply.

'That's my name,' said Mr Jones.

'I am Inspector Jetheroe from Scotland Yard, and I shall take you into custody on a charge of abducting Count Philip Vinci.'

Mr Jones stared at him.

Many attempts had been made to bring him to the inhospitable shelter which His Majesty's Prisons afford, and they had all failed.

'You have made a bloomer, haven't you?' he chuckled, confident in the efficiency of his plans.

'Get into that cab,' said the man shortly, and Mr Jones was too clever and experienced a juggler with the law to offer any resistance.

Nobody would betray him – nobody could discover the boy, he had not exaggerated in that respect. The arrest meant no more than a visit to the station, a few words with the inspector and at the worst a night's detention.

One of his captors had not entered the cab until he had a long colloquy with the driver, and Mr Jones, seeing through the window the passing of a five-pound note, wondered what mad fit of generosity had overtaken the police force.

They drove rapidly through the West End, down Whitehall, and to Mr Jones's surprise, did not turn into Scotland Yard, but continued over Westminster Bridge.

'Where are you taking me?' he asked.

The man who sat opposite him, the smaller man who had spoken to the cabman, leant forward and pushed something into Mr Jones's ample waistcoat, and glancing down he saw the long black barrel of an automatic pistol, and he felt a momentary sickness.

'Don't talk – yet,' said the man.

Try as he did, Jones could not see the face of either detective. Passing, however, under the direct rays of an electric lamp, he had a shock. The face of the man opposite to him was covered by a thin white veil which revealed only the vaguest outlines of a face. And then he began to think rapidly. But the solutions to his difficulties came back to that black and shining pistol in the other's hands.

On through New Cross, Lewisham, and at last the cab began the slow descent of Blackheath Hill. Mr Jones recognised the locality as one in which he had operated from time to time with fair success.

The cab reached the Heath Road, and the man who was sitting by his side opened the window and leant out, talking to the driver. Suddenly the car turned through the gateway of a garden and stopped before the uninviting door of a gaunt, deserted house.

'Before you get out,' said the man with the pistol, 'I want you to understand that if you talk or shout or make any statement to the driver of this cab, I shall shoot you through the stomach. It will take you about three days to die, and you will suffer pains which I do not think your gross mind can imagine.'

Mr Jones mounted the steps to the front door and passed meekly and in silence into the house. The night was chilly and he shivered as he entered the comfortless dwelling. One of the men switched on an electric lamp, by the light of which he locked the door. Then he put the light out, and they found their way up the dusty stairs with the assistance of a pocket lamp which Leon Gonsalez flashed before him.

'Here's your little home,' said Leon pleasantly, and opening the door, turned a switch.

It was a big bathroom. Evidently Leon had found his ideal, thought Manfred, for the room was unusually large, so large that a bed could be placed in one corner, and had been so placed by Mr Gonsalez. George Manfred saw that his friend had had a very busy day. The bed was a comfortable one, and with its white sheets and soft pillows looked particularly inviting.

In the bath, which was broad and deep, a heavy Windsor chair had been placed, and from one of the taps hung a length of rubber hosing.

These things Mr Jones noticed, and also marked the fact that the window had been covered with blankets to exclude the light.

'Put out your hands,' said Leon sharply, and before Spaghetti Jones realised what was happening, a pair of handcuffs had been snapped on his wrists, a belt had been deftly buckled through the connecting links, and drawn between his legs.

'Sit down on that bed. I want you to see how comfortable it is,' said Leon humorously.

'I don't know what you think you're doing,' said Mr Jones in a sudden outburst of rage, 'but by God you'll know all about it! Take that veil off your face and let me see you.'

'I'd rather you didn't,' said Leon gently. 'If you saw my face I should be obliged to kill you, and that I have no desire to do. Sit down.'

Mr Jones obeyed wonderingly, and his wonder increased when Leon began to strip his patent shoes and silk socks, and to roll up the legs of his trousers.

'What is the game?' asked the man fearfully.

'Get on to that chair.' Gonsalez pointed to the chair in the bath. 'It is an easy Windsor chair – '

'Look here,' began Jones fearfully.

'Get in,' snapped Leon, and the big fellow obeyed.

'Are you comfortable?' asked Leon politely.

The man glowered at him.

'You'll be uncomfortable before I'm through with you,' he said.

'How do you like the look of that bed?' asked Leon. 'It looks rather cosy, eh?'

Spaghetti Jones did not answer, and Gonsalez tapped him lightly on the shoulder.

'Now, my gross friend, will you tell me where you have hidden Philip Vinci?'

'Oh, that is it, is it?' grinned Mr Jones. 'Well, you can go on asking!'

He glared down at his bare feet, and then from one to the other of the two men.

'I don't know anything about Philip Vinci,' he said. 'Who is he?'

'Where have you hidden Philip Vinci?'

'You don't suppose if I knew where he was I'd tell you, do you?' sneered Jones.

'If you know, you certainly will tell me,' answered Leon quietly, 'but I fancy it is going to be a long job. Perhaps in thirty-six hours' time? George, will you take the first watch? I'm going to sleep on that very comfortable bed, but first,' he groped at the back of the bath and found a strap and this he passed round the body of his prisoner, buckling it behind the chair, 'to prevent you falling off,' he said pleasantly.

He lay down on the bed and in a few minutes was fast asleep. Leon had that gift of sleeping at will, which has ever been the property of great commanders.

Jones looked from the sleeper to the veiled man who lounged in an easy chair facing him. Two eyes were cut in the veil, and the watcher had a book on his knee and was reading.

'How long is this going on?' he demanded.

'For a day or two,' said Manfred calmly. 'Are you very much bored? Would you like to read?'

Mr Jones growled something unpleasant, and did not accept the offer. He could only think and speculate upon what their intentions were. He had expected violence, but apparently no violence was intended. They were merely keeping him prisoner till he spoke. But he would show them! He began to feel tired. Suddenly his head drooped forward, till his chin touched his breast. 'Wake up,' said Manfred shortly.

He awoke with a start.

'You're not supposed to sleep,' explained Manfred.

'Ain't I?' growled the prisoner. 'Well, I'm going to sleep!' and he settled himself more easily in the chair.

He was beginning to doze when he experienced an acute discomfort and drew up his feet with a yell. The veiled man was directing a stream of ice-cold water upon his unprotected feet, and Mr Jones was now thoroughly awake. An hour later he was nodding again, and again the tiny hose-pipe was directed to his feet, and again Manfred produced a towel and dried them as carefully as though Mr Jones were an invalid.

At six o'clock in the morning, red-eyed and glaring, he watched Manfred rouse the sleeping Leon and take his place on the bed.

Again and again nature drew the big man's chin down to his chest, and again and again the icy stream played maddeningly upon him and he woke with a scream.

'Let me sleep, let me sleep!' he cried in helpless rage, tugging at the strap. He was half-mad with weariness, his eyes were like lead.

'Where is Philip Vinci?' demanded the inexorable Leon.

'This is torture, damn you – ' screamed the man.

'No worse for you than for the boy locked up in a room with four days' supply of food. No worse than slitting a man's face with a penknife, my primitive friend. But perhaps you do not think it is a serious matter to terrify a little child.'

'I don't know where he is, I tell you,' said Spaghetti hoarsely.

'Then we shall have to keep you awake till you remember,' replied Leon, and lit a cigarette.

Soon after he went downstairs and returned with coffee and biscuits for the man, and found him sleeping soundly.

His dreams ended in a wail of agony.

'Let me sleep, please let me sleep,' he begged with tears in his eyes.

'I'll give you anything if you'll let me sleep!'

'You can sleep on that bed – and it's a very comfortable bed too – ' said Leon, 'but first we shall learn where Philip Vinci is.'

'I'll see you in hell before I'll tell you,' screamed Spaghetti Jones.

'You will wear your eyes out looking for me,' answered Leon politely. 'Wake up!'

At seven o'clock that evening a weeping, whimpering, broken man, moaned an address, and Manfred went off to verify this information.

'Now let me sleep!'

'You can keep awake till my friend comes back,' said Leon.

At nine o'clock George Manfred returned from Berkeley Square, having released a frightened little boy from a very unpleasant cellar in Notting Hill, and together they lifted the half-dead man from the bath and unlocked the handcuffs.

'Before you sleep, sit here,' said Manfred, 'and sign this.'

'This' was a document which Mr Jones could not have read even if he had been willing. He scrawled his signature, and crawling on to the bed was asleep before Manfred pulled the clothes over him. And he was still asleep when a man from Scotland Yard came into the room and shook him violently.

Spaghetti Jones knew nothing of what the detective said; had no recollection of being charged or of hearing his signed confession read over to him by the station sergeant. He remembered nothing until they woke him in his cell to appear before a magistrate for a preliminary hearing.

'It's an extraordinary thing, sir,' said the gaoler to the divisional surgeon. 'I can't get this man to keep awake.'

'Perhaps he would like a cold bath.' said the surgeon helpfully.

The Man who was Acquitted

'Have you ever noticed,' said Leon Gonsalez, looking up from his book and taking off the horn-rimmed glasses he wore when he was reading, 'that poisoners and baby-farmers are invariably mystics?'

'I haven't noticed many baby-farmers – or poisoners for the matter of that,' said Manfred with a little yawn. 'Do you mean by "mystic" an ecstatic individual who believes he can communicate directly with the Divine Power?'

Leon nodded.

'I've never quite understood the association of a superficial but vivid form of religion with crime,' said Leon, knitting his forehead. 'Religion, of course, does not develop the dormant criminality in a man's ethical system; but it is a fact that certain criminals develop a queer form of religious exaltation. Ferri, who questioned 200 Italian murderers, found that they were all devout: Naples, which is the most religious city in Europe, is also the most criminal. Ten per cent of those inmates of British prisons who are tattooed are marked with religious symbols.'

'Which only means that when a man of low intelligence submits to the tattoo artist, he demands pictures of the things with which he is familiar,' said Manfred, and took up the paper he was reading. Suddenly he dropped the journal on his knees.

'You're thinking of Dr Twenden,' he said and Leon inclined his head slowly.

'I was,' he confessed.

Manfred smiled.

'Twenden was acquitted with acclamation and cheered as he left the Exeter Assize Court,' he said, 'and yet he was guilty!'

'As guilty as a man can be – I wondered if your mind was on the case, George. I haven't discussed it with you.'

'By the way, was he religious?' asked Manfred.

'I wouldn't say that,' said the other, shaking his head. 'I was thinking of the pious letter of thanks he wrote, and which was published in the Baxeter and Plymouth newspapers – it was rather like a sermon.

What he is in private life I know no more than the account of the trial told me. You think he poisoned his wife?'

'I am sure,' said Manfred quietly. 'I intended discussing the matter with you this evening.'

The trial of Dr Twenden had provided the newspaper sensation of the week. The doctor was a man of thirty: his wife was seventeen years his senior and the suggestion was that he had married her for her money – she had a legacy of £2,000 a year which ceased at her death. Three months before this event she had inherited £63,000 from her brother, who had died in Johannesburg.

Twenden and his wife had not been on the best of terms, one of the subjects of disagreement being her unwillingness to continue paying his debts. After her inheritance had been transferred to her, she sent to Torquay, to her lawyer, the draft of a will in which she left the income from £12,000 to her husband, providing he did not marry again. The remainder of her fortune she proposed leaving to her nephew, one Jacley, a young civil engineer in the employ of the Plymouth Corporation.

The lawyer drafted her bequests and forwarded a rough copy for her approval before the will was engrossed. That draft arrived at Newton Abbot where the doctor and his wife were living (the doctor had a practice there) and was never seen again. A postman testified that it had been delivered at the 8 o'clock 'round' on a Saturday. That day the doctor was called into consultation over a case of viper bite. He returned in the evening and dined with his wife. Nothing happened that was unusual. The doctor went to his laboratory to make an examination of the poison sac which had been extracted from the reptile.

In the morning Mrs Twenden was very ill, showed symptoms which could be likened to blood-poisoning and died the same night.

It was found that in her arm was a small puncture such as might be made by a hypodermic needle, such a needle as, of course, the doctor possessed – he had in fact ten.

Suspicion fell upon him immediately. He had not summoned any further assistance besides that which he could give, until all hope of saving the unfortunate woman had gone. It was afterwards proved that the poison from which the woman had died was snake venom.

In his favour was the fact that no trace of the poison was found in either of the three syringes or the ten needles in his possession. It was his practice, and this the servants and another doctor who had ordered the treatment testified, to give his wife a subcutaneous injection of a new serum for her rheumatism.

This he performed twice a week and on the Saturday the treatment was due.

He was tried and acquitted. Between the hour of his arrest and his release he had acquired the popularity which accumulates about the personality of successful politicians and good-looking murderers, and he had been carried from the Sessions House shoulder high through a mob of cheering admirers, who had discovered nothing admirable in his character, and were not even aware of his existence, till the iron hand of the law closed upon his arm.

Possibly the enthusiasm of the crowd was fanned to its high temperature by the announcement the accused man had made in the dock – he had defended himself.

'Whether I am convicted or acquitted, not one penny of my dear wife's money will I touch. I intend disposing of this accursed fortune to the poor of the country. I, for my part, shall leave this land for a distant shore and in a strange land, amidst strangers, I will cherish the memory of my dear wife, my partner and my friend.'

Here the doctor broke down.

'A distant shore,' said Manfred, recalling the prisoner's passionate words. 'You can do a lot with sixty-three thousand pounds on a distant shore.'

The eyes of Leon danced with suppressed merriment.

'It grieves me, George, to hear such cynicism. Have you forgotten that the poor of Devonshire are even now planning how the money will be spent?'

Manfred made a noise of contempt, and resumed his reading, but his companion had not finished with the subject.

'I should like to meet Twenden,' he said reflectively. 'Would you care to go to Newton Abbot, George? The town itself is not particularly beautiful, but we are within half an hour's run of our old home at Babbacombe.'

This time George Manfred put away his paper definitely.

'It was a particularly wicked crime,' he said gravely. 'I think I agree with you, Leon. I have been thinking of the matter all the morning, and it seems to call for some redress. But,' he hesitated, 'it also calls for some proof. Unless we can secure evidence which did not come before the Court, we cannot act on suspicion.'

Leon nodded.

'But if we prove it,' he said softly, 'I promise you, Manfred, a most wonderful scheme.'

That afternoon he called upon his friend, Mr Fare of Scotland Yard, and when the Commissioner heard his request, he was less surprised than amused.

'I was wondering how long it would be before you wanted to see our prisons, Señor,' he said. 'I can arrange that with the Commissioners. What prison would you like to see?'

'I wish to see a typical county prison,' said Leon. 'What about Baxeter?'

'Baxeter,' said the other in surprise. 'That's rather a long way from London. It doesn't differ very materially from Wandsworth, which is a few miles from this building, or Pentonville, which is our headquarters prison.'

'I prefer Baxeter,' said Leon. 'The fact is I am going to the Devonshire coast, and I could fill in my time profitably with this inspection.'

The order was forthcoming on the next day. It was a printed note authorising the Governor of H. M. Prison, Baxeter, to allow the bearer to visit the prison between the hours of ten and twelve in the morning, and two and four in the afternoon.

They broke their journey at Baxeter, and Leon drove up to the prison, a prettier building than most of its kind. He was received by the Deputy Governor and a tall, good-looking chief warder, an ex-Guardsman, who showed him round the three wings, and through the restricted grounds of the gaol.

Leon rejoined his companion on the railway station just in time to catch the Plymouth express which would carry them to Newton Abbot.

'A thoroughly satisfactory visit,' said Leon. 'In fact, it is the most amazingly convenient prison I have ever been in.'

'Convenient to get into or convenient to get away from?' asked Manfred.

'Both,' said Leon.

They had not engaged rooms at either of the hôtels. Leon had decided, if it was possible, to get lodgings near to the scene of the tragedy, and in this he was successful. Three houses removed from the corner house where Doctor Twenden was in residence he discovered furnished lodgings were to let.

A kindly rosy-faced Devonshire woman was the landlady, and they were the only tenants, her husband being a gunner on one of His Majesty's ships, and he was at sea. She showed them a bright sitting-room and two bedrooms on the same floor. Manfred ordered tea, and when the door closed on the woman, he turned to behold Leon standing by the window gazing intently at the palm of his left hand, which was enclosed, as was the other, in a grey silk glove.

Manfred laughed.

'I don't usually make comments on our attire, my dear Leon,' he said, 'and remembering your Continental origin, it is remarkable that you commit so few errors in dress – from an Englishman's point of view,' he added.

'It's queer, isn't it,' said Leon, still looking at his palm.

'But I've never seen you wearing silk gloves before,' Manfred went on curiously. 'In Spain it is not unusual to wear cotton gloves, or even silk – '

'The finest silk,' murmured Leon, 'and I cannot bend my hand in it.'

'Is that why you've been carrying it in your pocket,' said Manfred in surprise, and Gonsalez nodded.

'I cannot bend my hand in it,' he said, 'because in the palm of my hand is a stiff copper-plate and on that plate is half an inch thickness of plastic clay of a peculiarly fine texture.'

'I see,' said Manfred slowly.

'I love Baxeter prison,' said Leon, 'and the Deputy Governor is a dear young man: his joy in my surprise and interest when he showed me the cells was delightful to see. He even let me examine the master key of the prison, which naturally he carried, and if, catching and holding his eye, I pressed the business end of the key against the palm of my gloved hand, why it was done in a second, my dear George, and there was nothing left on the key to show him the unfair advantage I had taken.'

He had taken a pair of folding scissors from his pocket and dexterously had opened them and was soon cutting away the silk palm of the glove.

' "How wonderful," said I, "and that is the master key!" and so we went on to see the punishment cell and the garden and the little unkempt graves where the dead men lie who have broken the law, and all the time I had to keep my hand in my pocket, for fear I'd knock against something and spoil the impression. Here it is.'

The underside of the palm had evidently been specially prepared for the silk came off easily, leaving a thin grey slab of slate-coloured clay in the centre of which was clearly the impression of a key.

'The little hole at the side is where you dug the point of the key to get the diameter?' said Manfred, and Leon nodded.

'This is the master key of Baxeter Gaol, my dear Manfred,' he said with a smile, as he laid it upon the table. 'With this I could walk in – no, I couldn't.' He stopped suddenly and bit his lip.

'You are colossal,' said Manfred admiringly.

'Aren't I,' said Leon with a wry face. 'Do you know there is one door we can't open?'

'What is that?'

'The big gates outside. They can only be opened from the inside. H'm.'

He laid his hat carefully over the clay mould when the landlady came in with the tray.

Leon sipped his tea, staring vacantly at the lurid wallpaper, and Manfred did nor interrupt his thoughts.

Leon Gonsalez had ever been the schemer of the Four Just Men, and he had developed each particular of his plan as though it were a story he was telling himself.

His extraordinary imagination enabled him to foresee every contingency. Manfred had often said that the making of the plan gave Leon as much pleasure as its successful consummation.

'What a stupid idiot I am,' he said at last. 'I didn't realise that there was no keyhole in the main gate of a prison – except of course Dartmoor.'

Again he relapsed into silent contemplation of the wall, a silence broken by cryptic mutterings. 'I send the wire . . . It must come, of course, from London . . . They would send down if the wire was strong enough. It must be five men – no five could go into a taxi – six . . . If the door of the van is locked, but it won't be . . . If it fails then I could try the next night.'

'What on earth are you talking about?' asked Manfred good-humouredly.

Leon woke with a start from his reverie.

'We must first prove that this fellow is guilty,' he said, 'and we'll have to start on that job tonight. I wonder if our good landlady has a garden.'

The good landlady had one. It stretched out for two hundred yards at the back of the house, and Leon made a survey and was satisfied.

'The doctor's place?' he asked innocently, as the landlady pointed out this object of interest. 'Not the man who was tried at Baxeter?'

'The very man,' said the woman triumphantly. 'I tell you, it caused a bit of a sensation round here.'

'Do you think he was innocent?'

The landlady was not prepared to take a definite standpoint.

'Some think one thing and some think the other,' she replied, in the true spirit of diplomacy. 'He's always been a nice man, and he attended my husband when he was home last.'

'Is the doctor staying in his house?'

'Yes, sir,' said the woman. 'He's going abroad soon.'

'Oh yes, he is distributing that money, isn't he? I read something about it in the newspapers – the poor are to benefit, are they not?'

The landlady sniffed.

'I hope they get it,' she said significantly.

'Which means that you don't think they will,' smiled Manfred, strolling back from an inspection of her early chrysanthemums.

'They may,' said the cautious landlady, 'but nothing has happened yet. The vicar went to the doctor yesterday morning, and asked him whether a little of it couldn't be spared for the poor of Newton Abbot. We've had a lot of unemployment here lately, and the doctor said "Yes he would think about it", and sent him a cheque for fifty pounds from what I heard.'

'That's not a great deal,' said Manfred. 'What makes you think he is going abroad?'

'All his trunks are packed and his servants are under notice, that's how I came to know,' said the landlady. 'I don't think it's a bad thing. Poor soul, she didn't have a very happy life.'

The 'poor soul' referred to was apparently the doctor's wife, and when asked to explain, the landlady knew no more than that people had talked, that there was probably nothing in it, and why shouldn't the doctor go motoring on the moor with pretty girls if he felt that way inclined.

'He had his fancies,' said the landlady.

Apparently those 'fancies' came and went through the years of his married life.

'I should like to meet the doctor,' said Leon, but she shook her head.

'He won't see anyone, not even his patients, sir,' she said.

Nevertheless Leon succeeded in obtaining an interview. He had judged the man's character correctly thus far, and he knew he would not refuse an interview with a journalist.

The servant took Leon's name, closing the front door in his face while she went to see the doctor, and when she came back it was to invite him in.

He found the medical gentleman in his study, and the dismantled condition of the room supported Mrs Martin's statement that he was leaving the town at an early date. He was in fact engaged in destroying old business letters and bills when Leon arrived.

'Come in,' grumbled the doctor. 'I suppose if I didn't see you, you'd invent something about me. Now what do you want?'

He was a good-looking young man with regular features, a carefully trimmed black moustache and tiny black side-whiskers.

'Light-blue eyes I do not like,' said Leon to himself, 'and I should like to see you without a moustache.'

'I've been sent down from London to ask to what charities you are distributing your wife's money, Dr Twenden,' said Leon, with the brisk and even rude directness of a London reporter.

The doctor's lips curled.

'The least they can do is to give me a chance to make up my mind,' he said. 'The fact is, I've got to go abroad on business, and whilst I'm away I shall carefully consider the merits of the various charity organisations of Devon to discover which are the most worthy and how the money is to be distributed.'

'Suppose you don't come back again?' asked Leon cruelly. 'I mean, anything might happen; the ship may sink or the train smash – what happens to the money then?'

'That is entirely my affair,' said the doctor stiffly, and closing his eyes, arched his eyebrows for a second as he spoke. 'I really don't wish to reopen this matter. I've had some very charming letters from the public, but I've had abusive ones too. I had one this morning saying that it was a pity that the Four Just Men were not in existence! The Four Just Men!' he smiled contemptuously, 'as though I should have cared a snap of my fingers for that kind of cattle!'

Leon smiled too.

'Perhaps it would be more convenient if I saw you tonight,' he suggested.

The doctor shook his head.

'I'm to be the guest-of honour of a few friends of mine,' he said, with a queer air of importance, 'and I shan't be back until half past eleven at the earliest.'

'Where is the dinner to be held? That might make an interesting item of news,' said Leon.

'It's to be held at the Lion Hôtel. You can say that Sir John Murden is in the chair, and that Lord Tussborough has promised to attend. I can give you the list of the people who'll be there.'

'The dinner engagement is a genuine one,' thought Leon with satisfaction.

The list was forthcoming, and pocketing the paper with due reverence, Gonsalez bowed himself out. From his bedroom window that evening he watched the doctor, splendidly arrayed, enter a taxi and drive away. A quarter of an hour later the servant, whom Leon had seen, came out pulling on her gloves. Gonsalez watched her for a good quarter of an hour, during which time she stood at the corner of the street. She was obviously waiting for something or somebody. What it was he saw. The Torquay bus passed by, stopped, and she mounted it.

After dinner he had a talk with the landlady and brought the conversation back to the doctor's house.

'I suppose it requires a lot of servants to keep a big house like that going.'

'He's only got one now, sir: Milly Brown, who lives in Torquay. She is leaving on Saturday. The cook left last week. The doctor has all his meals at the hôtel.'

He left Manfred to talk to the landlady – and Manfred could be very entertaining.

Slipping through the garden he reached a little alleyway at the back of the houses. The back gate giving admission to the doctor's garden was locked, but the wall was not high. He expected that the door of the house would be fastened, and he was not surprised when he found it was locked. A window by the side of the door was, however, wide open: evidently neither the doctor nor his maid expected burglars. He climbed through the window on to the kitchen sink, through the kitchen and into the house, without difficulty. His search of the library into which he had been shown that afternoon was a short one. The desk had no secret drawers, and most of the papers had been burnt. The ashes overflowed the grate on to the tiled hearth. The little laboratory, which had evidently been a creamery when the house was in former occupation, yielded nothing, nor did any of the rooms.

He had not expected that in this one search he would make a discovery, remembering that the police had probably ransacked the house after the doctor's arrest and had practically been in occupation ever since.

He went systematically and quickly through the pockets of all the doctor's clothing that he found in the wardrobe of his bedroom, but it produced nothing more interesting than a theatre programme.

'I'm afraid I shan't want that key,' said Leon regretfully, and went downstairs again. He turned on his pocket lamp: there might be other clothing hanging in the hall, but he found the rack was empty.

As he flashed the light around, the beam caught a large tin letter-box fastened to the door. He lifted up the yellow lid and at first saw nothing. The letter-box looked as if it had been home-made. It was, as he had seen at first, of grained and painted tin that had been shaped roughly round a wooden frame; he saw the supports at each corner. One was broken. He put in his hand, and saw that what he thought had been the broken ends of the frame, was a small square packet standing bolt upright: it was now so discoloured by dust that it seemed to be part of the original framework. He pulled it out, tearing the paper cover as he did so; it had been held in its place by the end of a nail which had been driven into the original wood, which explained why it had not fallen over when the door had been slammed. He blew the dust from it; the package was addressed from the Pasteur Laboratory. He had no desire to examine it there, and slipped it into his pocket, getting out of the house by the way he had come in, and rejoining Manfred just when that gentleman was beginning to get seriously worried, for Leon had been three hours in the house.

'Did you find anything?' asked Manfred when they were alone.

'This,' said Leon. He pulled the packet out of his pocket and explained where he had found it.

'The Pasteur Institute,' said Manfred in surprise. 'Of course,' he said suddenly, 'the serum which the doctor used to inject into his wife's arm. Pasteur are the only people who prepare that. I remember reading as much in the account of the trial.'

'And which he injected twice a week, if I remember rightly,' said Leon, 'on Wednesdays and Saturdays, and the evidence was that he did not inject it on the Wednesday before the murder. It struck me at the time as being rather curious that nobody asked him when he was in the witness box why he had omitted this injection.'

He cut along the paper and pulled it apart: inside was an oblong wooden box, about which was wrapped a letter. It bore the heading of the laboratory, directions, and was in French.

Sir [it began],
We despatch to you immediately the serum Number 47 which you desire, and we regret that through the fault of a subordinate,

this was not sent you last week. We received your telegram today that you are entirely without serum, and we will endeavour to expedite the delivery of this.

'Entirely without serum,' repeated Gonsalez. He took up the wrapping-paper and examined the stamp. 'Paris, the 14th September,' he said, 'and here's the receiving stamp, Newton Abbot the 16th September, 7 a.m.'

He frowned.

'This was pushed through the letter-box on the morning of the 16th,' he said slowly. 'Mrs Twenden was injected on the evening of the 15th. The 16th was a Sunday, and there's an early post. Don't you see, Manfred?'

Manfred nodded.

'Obviously he could not have injected serum because he had none to inject, and this arrived when his wife was dying. It is, of course, untouched.'

He took out a tiny tube and tapped the seal.

'H'm,' said Leon, 'I shall want that key after all. Do you remember, Manfred, he did not inject on Wednesday: why? because he had no serum. He was expecting the arrival of this, and it must have gone out of his mind. Probably we shall discover that the postman knocked, and getting no answer on the Sunday morning, pushed the little package through the letter-box, where by accident it must have fallen into the corner where I discovered it.'

He put down the paper and drew a long breath.

'And now I think I will get to work on that key,' he said.

Two days later Manfred came in with news.

'Where is my friend?'

Mrs Martin, the landlady, smiled largely.

'The gentleman is working in the greenhouse, sir. I thought he was joking the other day when he asked if he could put up a vice on the potting bench, but, lord, he's been busy ever since!'

'He's inventing a new carburettor,' said Manfred, devoutly hoping that the lady had no knowledge of the internal-combustion engine.

'He's working hard, too, sir; he came out to get a breath of air just now, and I never saw a gentleman perspire so! He seems to be working with that file all the day.'

'You mustn't interrupt him,' began Manfred.

'I shouldn't dream of doing it,' said the landlady indignantly.

Manfred made his way to the garden, and his friend, who saw him coming – the greenhouse made an ideal workshop for Leon, for he could watch his landlady's approach and conceal the key he had been filing for three days – walked to meet him.

'He is leaving today, or rather tonight,' said Manfred. 'He's going to Plymouth: there he will catch the Holland-American boat to New York.'

'Tonight?' said Leon in surprise. 'That cuts me rather fine. By what train?'

'That I don't know,' said Manfred.

'You're sure?'

Manfred nodded.

'He's giving it out that he's leaving tomorrow, and is slipping away tonight. I don't think he wants people to know of his departure. I discovered it through an indiscretion of the worthy doctor's. I was in the post office when he was sending a wire. He had his pocket-book open on the counter, and I saw some labels peeping out. I knew they were steamship labels, and I glimpsed the printed word "Rotterdam", looked up the newspapers, and saw that the *Rotterdam* was leaving tomorrow. When I heard that he had told people that he was leaving Newton Abbot tomorrow I was certain.'

'That's all to the good,' said Leon. 'George, we're going to achieve the crowning deed of our lives. I say "we", but I'm afraid I must do this alone – though you have a very important role to play.'

He chuckled softly and rubbed his hands.

'Like every other clever criminal he has made one of the most stupid of blunders. He has inherited his wife's money under an old will, which left him all her possessions, with the exception of £2,000 which she had on deposit at the bank, and this went to her nephew, the Plymouth engineer. In his greed Twenden is pretty certain to have forgotten this legacy. He's got all the money in a Torquay bank. It was transferred from Newton Abbot a few days ago and was the talk of the town. Go to Plymouth, interview young Jacley, see his lawyer, if he has one, or any lawyer if he hasn't, and if the two thousand pounds has not been paid, get him to apply for a warrant for Twenden's arrest. He is an absconding trustee under those circumstances, and the Justices will grant the warrant if they know the man is leaving by the *Rotterdam* tomorrow.'

'If you were an ordinary man, Leon,' said Manfred, 'I should think that your revenge was a little inadequate.'

'It will not be that,' said Leon quietly.

At nine-thirty, Dr Twenden, with his coat collar turned up and the brim of a felt hat hiding the upper part of his face, was entering a first-class carriage at Newton Abbot, when the local detective-sergeant whom he knew tapped him on the shoulder.

'I want you, Doctor.'

'Why, Sergeant?' demanded the doctor, suddenly white.

'I have a warrant for your arrest,' said the officer.

When the charge was read over to the man at the police station he raved like a lunatic.

'I'll give you the money now, now! I must go tonight. I'm leaving for America tomorrow.'

'So I gather,' said the Inspector dryly. 'That is why you're arrested, Doctor.'

And they locked him in the cells for the night.

The next morning he was brought before the Justices. Evidence was taken, the young nephew from Plymouth made his statement, and the Justices conferred.

'There is *prima facie* evidence here of intention to defraud, Dr Twenden,' said the chairman at last. 'You are arrested with a very large sum of money and letters of credit in your possession, and it seems clear that it was your intention to leave the country. Under those circumstances we have no other course to follow, but commit you to take your trial at the forthcoming session.'

'But I can have bail: I insist upon that,' said the doctor furiously.

'There will be no bail,' was the sharp reply, and that afternoon he was removed by taxi-cab to Baxeter prison.

The Sessions were for the following week, and the doctor again fumed in that very prison from which he had emerged if not with credit, at least without disaster.

On the second day of his incarceration the Governor of Baxeter Gaol received a message.

Six star men transferred to you will arrive at Baxeter Station 10.15. Arrange for prison van to meet.

It was signed 'Imprison', which is the telegraphic address of the Prison Commissioner.

It happened that just about then there had been a mutiny in one of the London prisons, and the deputy governor, beyond expressing his surprise as to the lateness of the hour, arranged for the prison van to be at Baxeter station yard to meet the batch of transfers.

The 10.15 from London drew into the station, and the warders waiting on the platform walked slowly down the train looking for a carriage with drawn blinds But there were no prisoners on the train, and there was no other train due until four o'clock in the morning.

'They must have missed it,' said one of the warders. 'All right, Jerry,' this to the driver. He slammed the door of the Black Maria which had been left open, and the van lumbered out of the station yard.

Slowly up the slope and through the black prison gates: the van turned through another gate to the left, a gate set at right angles to the first, and stopped before the open doors of a brick shed isolated from the prison.

The driver grumbled as he descended and unharnessed his horses.

'I shan't put the van in the shed tonight,' he said. 'Perhaps you'll get some of the prisoners to do it tomorrow.'

'That will be all right,' said the warder, anxious to get away.

The horses went clopping from the place of servitude, there was a snap of locks as the gates were closed, and then silence.

So far all was well from one man's point of view. A roaring south-wester was blowing down from Dartmoor round the angles of the prison, and wailing through the dark, deserted yard.

Suddenly there was a gentle crack, and the door of the Black Maria opened. Leon had discovered that his key could not open yet another door. He had slipped into the prison van when the warders were searching the train, and had found some difficulty in getting out again. No men were coming from London, as he knew, but he was desperately in need of that Black Maria. It had piloted him to the very spot he wished to go. He listened. There was no sound save the wind, and he walked cautiously to a little glass-covered building, and plied his master key. The lock turned, and he was inside a small recess where the prisoners were photographed. Through another door and he was in a store-room. Beyond that lay the prison wards. He had questioned wisely and knew where the remand cells were to be found.

A patrol would pass soon, he thought, looking at his watch, and he waited till he heard footsteps go by the door. The patrol would now be traversing a wing at right angles to the ward, and he opened the door and stepped into the deserted hall. He heard the feet of the patrol man receding and went softly up a flight of iron stairs to the floor above and along the cell doors. Presently he saw the man he wanted. His key went noiselessly into the cell door and turned. Doctor Twenden blinked up at him from his wooden bed.

'Get up,' whispered Gonsalez, 'and turn round.'

Numbly the doctor obeyed.

Leon strapped his hands behind him and took him by the arm, stopping to lock the cell door. Out through the store-room into the little glass place, then before the doctor knew what had happened, he slipped a large silk handkerchief over his mouth.

'Can you hear me?'

The man nodded.

'Can you feel that?'

'That' was a something sharp that stabbed his left arm. He tried to wriggle his arm away.

'You will recognise the value of a hypodermic syringe, you better than any,' said the voice of Gonsalez in his ear. 'You murdered an innocent woman, and you evaded the law. A few days ago you spoke of the Four Just Men. I am one of them!'

The man stared into the darkness at a face he could not see.

'The law missed you, but we have not missed you. Can you understand?'

The head nodded more slowly now.

Leon released his grip of the man's arm, and felt him slipping to the floor. There he lay whilst Gonsalez went into the shed, pulled up the two traps that hung straightly in the pit until they clicked together, and slipped the end of the rope he had worn round his waist over the beam . . .

Then he went back to the unconscious man.

In the morning when the warders came to the coach house, which was also the execution shed, they saw a taut rope. The track was open, and a man was at the end of the rope, very still. A man who had escaped the gallows of the law, but had died at the hands of justice.

THE END

THE THREE JUST MEN

Chapter 1

The firm of Oberzohn

'£520 p.a. Wanted at once, Laboratory Secretary (lady). Young; no previous experience required, but must have passed recognized examination which included physics and inorganic (elementary) chemistry. Preference will be given to one whose family has some record in the world of science. Apply by letter, Box 9754, *Daily Megaphone*. If applicant is asked to interview advertiser, fare will be paid from any station within a hundred and fifty miles of London.'

A good friend sent one of the issues containing this advertisement to Heavytree Farm and circled the announcement with a blue pencil.

Mirabelle Leicester found the newspaper on the hall settee when she came in from feeding the chickens, and thought that it had been sent by the Alington land agent who was so constantly calling her attention to the advertisers who wished to buy cheap farms. It was a practice of his. She had the feeling that he resented her presence in the country, and was anxious to replace her with a proprietor less poverty-stricken.

Splitting the wrapper with a dusty thumb, she turned naturally to the advertisement pages, having the agent in mind. Her eyes went rapidly down the 'Wanted to Buy' column. There were several 'gentlemen requiring small farm in good district', but none that made any appeal to her, and she was wondering why the parsimonious man had spent tuppence-ha'penny on postage and paper when the circled paragraph caught her eye.

'Glory!' said Mirabelle, her red lips parted in excited wonder.

Aunt Alma looked up from her press-cutting book, startled as Mirabelle dashed in.

'Me!' she said dramatically, and pointed a finger at the advertisement. 'I am young – I have no experience – I have my higher certificate – and daddy was something in the world of science. And, Alma, we are exactly a hundred and forty miles from London town!'

'Dear me!' said Aunt Alma, a lady whose gaunt and terrifying appearance was the terror of tradesmen and farm hands, although a milder woman never knitted stockings.

'Isn't it wonderful? This solves all our problems. We leave the farm to Mark, open the flat in Bloomsbury . . . we can afford one or even two theatres a week . . . '

Alma read the announcement for the second time.

'It seems good,' she said with conventional caution, 'though I don't like the idea of your working, my dear. Your dear father . . . '

'Would have whisked me up to town and I should have had the job by tonight,' said Mirabelle definitely.

But Alma wasn't sure. London was full of pitfalls and villainy untold lurked in its alleys and dark passages. She herself never went to London except under protest.

'I was there years ago when those horrible Four Just Men were about, my dear,' she said, and Mirabelle, who loved her, listened to the oft-told story. 'They terrorized London. One couldn't go out at night with the certainty that one would come back again alive . . . and to think that they have had a free pardon! It is simply encouraging crime.'

'My dear,' said Mirabelle (and this was her inevitable rejoinder), 'they weren't criminals at all. They were very rich men who gave up their lives to punishing those whom the law let slip through its greasy old fingers. And they were pardoned for the intelligence work they did in the war – one worked for three months in the German War Office – and there aren't four at all: there are only three. I'd love to meet them – they must be dears!'

When Aunt Alma made a grimace, she was hideous. Mirabelle averted her eyes.

'Anyway, they are not in London now, darling,' she said, 'and you will be able to sleep soundly at nights.'

'What about the snake?' asked Miss Alma Goddard ominously.

Now if there was one thing which no person contemplating a visit to London wished to be reminded about, it was the snake.

Six million people rose from their beds every morning, opened their newspapers and looked for news of the snake. Eighteen daily newspapers never passed a day without telling their readers that the scare was childish and a shocking commentary on the neurotic tendencies of the age; they also published, at regular intervals, intimate particulars of the black mamba, its habits and its peculiar deadliness, and maintained quite a large staff of earnest reporters to 'work on the story'.

The black mamba, most deadly of all the African snakes, had escaped from the Zoo one cold and foggy night in March. And there should have been the end of him – a three-line paragraph, followed the next day by another three-line paragraph detailing how the snake was found dead on the frozen ground – no mamba could live under a temperature of 75 Fahrenheit. But the second paragraph never appeared. On the 2nd of April a policeman found a man huddled up in a doorway in Orme Place. He proved to be a well-known and apparently wealthy stockbroker, named Emmett. He was dead. In his swollen face were found two tiny punctured wounds, and the eminent scientist who was called into consultation gave his opinion that the man had died from snake-bite: an especially deadly snake. The night was chilly; the man had been to a theatre alone. His chauffeur stated that he had left his master in the best of spirits on the doorstep. The key found in the dead man's hand showed that he was struck before the car had turned. When his affairs were investigated he was found to be hopelessly insolvent. Huge sums drawn from his bank six months before had disappeared.

London had scarcely recovered from this shocking surprise when the snake struck again. This time in the crowded street, and choosing a humble victim, though by no means a blameless one. An ex-convict named Sirk, a homeless down-and-out, was seen to fall by a park-keeper near the Achilles statue in Hyde Park. By the time the keeper reached him he was dead. There was no sign of a snake – nobody was near him. This time the snake had made his mark on the wrist – two little punctured wounds near together.

A month later the third man fell a victim. He was a clerk of the Bank of England, a reputable man who was seen to fall forward in a subway train, and, on being removed to hospital, was discovered to have died – again from snake-bite.

So that the snake became a daily figure of fear, and its sinister fame spread even so far afield as Heavytree Farm.

'Stuff!' said Mirabelle, yet with a shiver. 'Alma, I wish you wouldn't keep these horrors in your scrapbook.'

'They are Life,' said Alma soberly, and then: 'When d'you take up your appointment?' she asked, and the girl laughed.

'We will make a beginning right away – by applying for the job,' she said practically. 'And you needn't start packing your boxes for a very long time!'

An hour later she intercepted the village postman and handed him a letter.

And that was the beginning of the adventure which involved so many lives and fortunes, which brought the Three Just men to the verge of dissolution, and one day was to turn the heart of London into a battlefield.

Two days after the letter was dispatched came the answer, typewritten, surprisingly personal, and in places curiously worded. There was an excuse for that, for the heading on the note-paper was

OBERZOHN & SMITTS
Merchants and Exporters

On the third day Mirabelle Leicester stepped down from a 'bus in the City Road and entered the unimposing door of Romance, and an inquisitive chauffeur who saw her enter followed and overtook her in the lobby.

'Excuse me, madame – are you Mrs Carter?'

Mirabelle did not look like Mrs Anybody.

'No,' she said, and gave her name.

'But you're the lady from Hereford . . . you live with your mother at Telford Park . . . ?'

The man was so agitated that she was not annoyed by his insistence. Evidently he had instructions to meet a stranger and was fearful of missing her.

'You have made a mistake – I live at Heavytree Farm, Daynham – with my aunt.'

'Is she called Carter?'

She laughed.

'Miss Alma Goddard – now are you satisfied?'

'Then you're not the lady, miss; I'm waiting to pick her up.'

The chauffeur withdrew apologetically.

The girl waited in the ornate ante-room for ten minutes before the pale youth with the stiff, upstanding hair and the huge rimless spectacles returned. His face was large, expressionless, unhealthy. Mirabelle had noted as a curious circumstance that every man she had seen in the office was of the same type. Big heavy men who gave the impression that they had been called away from some very urgent work to deal with the triviality of her inquiries. They were speechless men who glared solemnly at her through thick lenses and nodded or shook their heads according to the requirements of the moment. She expected to meet foreigners in the offices of Oberzohn & Smitts; German, she imagined, and was surprised later to discover that both principals and staff were in the main Swedish.

The pale youth, true to the traditions of the house, said nothing: he beckoned her with a little jerk of his head, and she went into a larger room, where half a dozen men were sitting at half a dozen desks and writing furiously, their noses glued short-sightedly to the books and papers which engaged their attention. Nobody looked up as she passed through the waist-high gate which separated the caller from the staff. Hanging upon the wall between two windows was a map of Africa with great green patches. In one corner of the room were stacked a dozen massive ivory tusks, each bearing a hanging label. There was the model of a steamship in a case on a window-ledge, and on another a crudely carved wooden idol of native origin.

The youth stopped before a heavy rosewood door and knocked. When a deep voice answered, he pushed open the door and stood aside to let her pass. It was a gigantic room – that was the word which occurred to her as most fitting, and the vast space of it was emphasized by the almost complete lack of furniture. A very small ebony writing-table, two very small chairs and a long and narrow black cupboard fitted into a recess were all the furnishings she could see. The high walls were covered with a golden paper. Four bright-red rafters ran across the black ceiling – the floor was completely covered with a deep purple carpet. It seemed that there was a rolled map above the fireplace – a long thin cord came down from the cornice and ended in a tassel within reach.

The room, with its lack of appointments, was so unexpected a vision that the girl stood staring from walls to roof, until she observed her guide making urgent signs, and then she advanced towards the man who stood with his back to the tiny fire that burnt in the silver fireplace.

He was tall and grey; her first impression was of an enormously high forehead. The sallow face was long, and nearer at hand, she saw, covered by innumerable lines and furrows. She judged him to be about fifty until he spoke, and then she realized that he was much older.

'Miss Mirabelle Leicester?'

His English was not altogether perfect; the delivery was queerly deliberate and he lisped slightly.

'Pray be seated. I am Dr Eruc Oberzohn. I am not German. I admire the Germans, but I am Swedish. You are convinced?'

She laughed, and when Mirabelle Leicester laughed, less suscept-ible men than Dr Eruc Oberzohn had forgotten all other business. She was not very tall – her slimness and her symmetrical figure made her appear so. She had in her face and in her clear grey eyes something of the countryside; she belonged to the orchards where the apple-blossom lay like heavy snow upon the bare branches; to the cold brooks that ran noisily under hawthorn hedges. The April sunlight was in her eyes and the springy velvet of meadows everlastingly under her feet.

To Dr Oberzohn she was a girl in a blue tailor-made costume. He saw that she wore a little hat with a straight brim that framed her face just above the lift of her curved eyebrows. A German would have seen these things, being a hopeless sentimentalist. The doctor was not German; he loathed their sentimentality.

'Will you be seated? You have a scientific training?'

Mirabelle shook tier head.

'I haven't,' she confessed ruefully, 'but I've passed in the subjects you mentioned in your advertisement.'

'But your father – he was a scientist?'

She nodded gravely.

'But not a great scientist,' he stated. 'England and America do not produce such men. Ah, tell me not of your Kelvins, Edisons, and Newtons! They were incomplete, dull men, ponderous men – the fire was not there.'

She was somewhat taken aback, but she was amused as well. His calm dismissal of men who were honoured in the scientific world was so obviously sincere.

'Now talk to me of yourself.' He seated himself in the hard, straight-backed chair by the little desk.

'I'm afraid there is very little I can tell you, Dr Oberzohn. I live with my aunt at Heavytrec Farm in Gloucester, and we have a flat in Doughty Court. My aunt and I have a small income – and I think that is all.'

'Go on, please,' he commanded. 'Tell me of your sensations when you had my letter – I desire to know your mind. That is how I form all opinions; that is how I made my immense fortune. By the analysis of the mind.'

She had expected many tests; an examination in elementary science; a typewriting test possibly (she dreaded this most); but she never for one moment dreamt that the flowery letter asking her to call at the City Road offices of Oberzohn & Smitts would lead to an experiment in psycho-analysis.

'I can only tell you that I was surprised,' she said, and the tightening line of her mouth would have told him a great deal if he were the student of human nature he claimed to be. 'Naturally the salary appeals to me – ten pounds a week is such a high rate of pay that I cannot think I am qualified – '

'You are qualified.' His harsh voice grew more strident as he impressed this upon her. 'I need a laboratory secretary. You are qualified' – he hesitated, and then went on – 'by reason of distinguished parentage. Also – ' he hesitated again for a fraction of a second – 'also because of general education. Your duties shall commence soon!' He waved a long, thin hand to the door in the corner of the room. 'You will take your position at once,' he said.

The long face, the grotesquely high forehead, the bulbous nose and wide, crooked mouth all seemed to work together when he spoke. At one moment the forehead was full of pleats and furrows – at the next, comparatively smooth. The point of his nose dipped up and down at every word, only his small, deep-set eyes remained steadfast, unwinking. She had seen eyes like those before, brown and pathetic. Of what did they remind her? His last words brought her to the verge of panic.

'Oh, I could not possibly start today,' she said in trepidation.

'Today, or it shall be never,' he said with an air of finality.

She had to face a crisis. The salary was more than desirable; it was necessary. The farm scarcely paid its way, for Alma was not the best of managers. And the income grew more and more attenuated. Last year the company in which her meagre fortune was invested had passed a dividend and she had to give up her Swiss holiday.

'I'll start now.' She had to set her teeth to make this resolve.

'Very good; that is my wish.'

He was still addressing her as though she were a public meeting. Rising from his chair, he opened the little door and she went into a smaller room. She had seen laboratories, but none quite so beautifully fitted as this – shelf upon shelf of white porcelain jars, of cut-glass bottles, their contents engraved in frosted letters; a bench that ran the length of the room, on which apparatus of every kind was arranged in order. In the centre of the room ran a long, glass-topped table, and here, in dustproof glass, were delicate instruments, ranging from scales which she knew could be influenced by a grain of dust, to electrical machines, so complicated that her heart sank at the sight of them.

'What must I do?' she asked dismally.

Everything was so beautifully new; she was sure she would drop one of those lovely jars . . . all the science of the school laboratory had suddenly drained out of her mind, leaving it a blank.

'You will do.' Remarkably enough, the doctor for the moment seemed as much at a loss as the girl. 'First – quantities. In every jar or bottle there is a quantity. How much? Who knows? The last secretary was careless, stupid. She kept no book. Sometimes I go for something – it is not there! All gone. That is very regrettable.'

'You wish me to take stock?' she asked, her hopes reviving at the simplicity of her task.

There were measures and scales enough. The latter stood in a line like a platoon of soldiers ranged according to their size. Everything was very new, very neat. There was a smell of drying enamel in the room as though the place had been newly painted.

'That is all,' said the long-faced man. He put his hand in the pocket of his frock-coat and took out a large wallet. From this he withdrew two crisp notes.

'Ten pounds,' he said briefly. 'We pay already in advance. There is one more thing I desire to know,' he said. 'It is of the aunt. She is in London?'

Mirabelle shook her head.

'No, she is in the country. I expected to go back this afternoon, and if I was – successful, we were coming to town tomorrow.'

He pursed his thickish lips; she gazed fascinated at his long forehead rippled in thought.

'It will be a nervous matter for her if you stay in London tonight – no?'

She smiled and shook her head.

'No. I will stay at the flat; I have often stayed there alone, but even that will not be necessary. I will wire asking her to come up by the first train.'

'Wait.' He raised a pompous hand and darted back to his room. He returned with a packet of telegraph forms. 'Write your telegram,' he commanded. 'A clerk shall dispatch it at once.'

Gratefully she took the blanks and wrote her news and request.

'Thank you,' she said.

Mr Oberzohn bowed, went to the door, bowed again, and the door closed behind him.

Fortunately for her peace of mind, Mirabelle Leicester had no occasion to consult her employer or attempt to open the door. Had she done so, she would have discovered that it was locked. As for the telegram she had written, that was a curl of black ash in his fire.

Chapter 2

The three men of Curzon Street

No. 233, Curzon Street, was a small house. Even the most enthusiastic of agents would not, if he had any regard to his soul's salvation, describe its dimensions with any enthusiasm. He might enlarge upon its bijou beauties, refer reverently its historical association, speak truthfully of its central heating and electric installation, but he would, being an honest man, convey the impression that No. 233 was on the small side.

The house was flanked by two modern mansions, stone-fronted, with metal and glass doors that gave out a blur of light by night. Both overtopped the modest roof of their neighbour by many storeys – No. 233 had the appearance of a little man crushed in a crowd and unable to escape, and there was in its mild frontage the illusion of patient resignation and humility.

To that section of Curzon Street wherein it had its place, the house was an offence and was, in every but a legal sense, a nuisance. A learned Chancery judge to whom application had been made on behalf of neighbouring property owners, ground landlords and the like, had refused to grant the injunction for which they had pleaded, 'prohibiting the said George Manfred from carrying on a business, to wit the Triangle Detective Agency, situate at the aforesaid number two hundred and thirty-three Curzon Street in the City of Westminster in the County of Middlesex'.

In a judgment which occupied a third of a column of *The Times* he laid down the dictum that a private detective might be a professional rather than a business man – a dictum which has been, and will be, disputed to the end of time.

So the little silver triangle remained fixed to the door and he continued to interview his clients – few in number, for he was most careful to accept only those who offered scope for his genius.

A tall, strikingly handsome man, with the face of a patrician and the shoulders of an athlete, Curzon Street – or such of the street as took the slightest notice of anything – observed him to be extremely well dressed on all occasions. He was a walking advertisement for a Hanover Street tailor who was so fashionable that he would have died with horror at the very thought of advertising at all. Car folk held up at busy crossings glanced into his limousine, saw the clean-cut profile and the tanned, virile face, and guessed him for a Harley Street specialist. Very few people knew him socially. Dr Elver, the Scotland Yard surgeon, used to come up to Curzon Street at times and give his fantastic views on the snake and its appearances, George Manfred and his friends listening in silence and offering no help. But apart from Elver and an Assistant Commissioner of Police, a secretive man, who dropped in at odd moments to smoke a pipe and talk of old times, the social callers were few and far between.

His chauffeur-footman was really better known than he. At the mews where he garaged his car, they called him 'Lightning', and it was generally agreed that this thin-faced, eager-eyed man would sooner or later meet the end which inevitably awaits all chauffeurs who take sharp corners on two wheels at sixty miles an hour: some of the critics had met the big Spanz on the road and had reproached him after-wards, gently or violently, according to the degree of their scare.

Few knew Mr Manfred's butler, a dark-browed foreigner, rather stout and somewhat saturnine. He was a man who talked very little even to the cook and the two housemaids who came every morning at eight and left the house punctually at six, for Mr Manfred dined out most nights.

He advertised only in the more exclusive newspapers, and not in his own name; no interviews were granted except by appointment, so that the arrival of Mr Sam Barberton was in every sense an irregularity.

He knocked at the door just as the maids were leaving, and since they knew little about Manfred and his ways except that he liked poached eggs and spinach for breakfast, the stranger was allowed to drift into the hall, and here the taciturn butler, hastily summoned from his room, found him.

The visitor was a stubby, thick-set man with a brick-red face and a head that was both grey and bald. His dress and his speech were equally rough. The butler saw that he was no ordinary artisan because his boots were of a kind known as *veldtschoen*. They were of undressed leather, patchily bleached by the sun.

'I want to see the boss of this Triangle,' he said in a loud voice, and, diving into his waistcoat pocket, brought out a soiled newspaper cutting.

The butler took it from him without a word. It was the *Cape Times* – he would have known by the type and the spacing even if on the back there had not been printed the notice of a church bazaar at Wynberg. The butler studied such things.

'I am afraid that you cannot see Mr Manfred without an appointment,' he said. His voice and manner were most expectedly gentle in such a forbidding man.

'I've got to see him, if I sit here all night,' said the man stubbornly, and symbolized his immovability by squatting down in the hall chair.

Not a muscle of the servant's face moved. It was impossible to tell whether he was angry or amused.

'I got this cutting out of a paper I found on the *Benguella* – she docked at Tilbury this afternoon – and I came straight here. I should never have dreamt of coming at all, only I want fair play for all concerned. That Portuguese feller with a name like a cigar – Villa, that's it! – he said, "What's the good of going to London when we can settle everything on board ship?" But half-breed Portuguese! My God, I'd rather deal with bushmen! Bushmen are civilized – look here.'

Before the butler realized what the man was doing, he had slipped off one of his ugly shoes. He wore no sock or stocking underneath, and he upturned the sole of his bare foot for inspection. The flesh was seamed and puckered into red weals, and the butler knew the cause.

'Portuguese,' said the visitor tersely as he resumed his shoe. 'Not niggers – Portugooses – half-bred, I'll admit. They burnt me to make me talk, and they'd have killed me only one of those hell-fire American traders came along – full of fight and fire-water. He brought me into the town.'

'Where was this?' asked the butler.

'Mosamades: I went ashore to look round, like a fool. I was on a Woerman boat that was going up to Boma. The skipper was a Hun, but white – he warned me.'

'And what did they want to know from you?'

The caller shot a suspicious glance at his interrogator.

'Are you the boss?' he demanded.

'No – I'm Mr Manfred's butler. What name shall I tell him?'

'Barberton – Mister Samuel Barberton. Tell him I want certain things found out. The address of a young lady by the name of Miss Mirabelle Leicester. And I'll tell your governor something too. This Portugoose got drunk one night, and spilled it about the fort they've got in England. Looks like a house but it's a fort: he went there . . . '

No, he was not drunk; stooping to pick up an imaginary match-stalk, the butler's head had come near the visitor; there was a strong aroma of tobacco but not of drink.

'Would you very kindly wait?' he asked, and disappeared up the stairs.

He was not gone long before he returned to the first landing and beckoned Mr Barberton to come. The visitor was ushered into a room at the front of the house, a small room, which was made smaller by the long grey velvet curtains that hung behind the empire desk where Manfred was standing.

'This is Mr Barberton, sir,' said the butler, bowed, and went out, closing the door.

'Sit down, Mr Barberton.' He indicated a chair and seated himself. 'My butler tells me you have quite an exciting story to tell me – you are from the Cape?'

'No, I'm not,' said Mr Barberton. 'I've never been at the Cape in my life.'

The man behind the desk nodded.

'Now, if you will tell me – '

'I'm not going to tell you much,' was the surprisingly blunt reply. 'It's not likely that I'm going to tell a stranger what I wouldn't even tell Elijah Washington – and he saved my life!'

Manfred betrayed no resentment at this cautious attitude. In that room he had met many clients who had shown the same reluctance to accept him as their confidant. Yet he had at the back of his mind the feeling that this man, unlike the rest, might remain adamant to the end: he was curious to discover the real object of the visit.

Barberton drew his chair nearer the writing-table and rested his elbows on the edge.

'It's like this, Mr What's-your-name. There's a certain secret which doesn't belong to me, and yet does in a way. It is worth a lot of money. Mr Elijah Washington knew that and tried to pump me, and Villa got a gang of Kroomen to burn my feet, but I've not told yet. What I want you to do is to find Miss Mirabelle Leicester; and I want to get her quick, because there's only about two weeks, if you understand me, before this other crowd gets busy – Villa is certain to have cabled 'em, and according to him they're hot!'

Mr Manfred leant back in his padded chair, the glint of an amused smile in his grey eyes.

'I take it that what you want us to do is find Miss Leicester?'

The man nodded energetically.

'Have you the slightest idea as to where she is to be found? Has she any relations in England?'

'I don't know,' interrupted the man. 'All I know is that she lives here somewhere, and that her father died three years ago, on the twenty-ninth of May – make a note of that: he died in England on the twenty-ninth of May.'

That was an important piece of information, and it made the search easy, thought Manfred.

'And you're going to tell me about the fort, aren't you?' he said, as he looked up from his notes.

Barberton hesitated.

'I was,' he admitted, 'but I'm not so sure that I will now, until I've found this young lady. And don't forget,' – he rapped the table to emphasize his words – 'that crowd is hot!'

'Which crowd?' asked Manfred good-humouredly. He knew many 'crowds', and wondered if it was about one which was in his mind that the caller was speaking.

'The crowd I'm talking about,' said Mr Barberton, who spoke with great deliberation and was evidently weighing every word he uttered for fear that he should involuntarily betray his secret.

That seemed to be an end of his requirements, for he rose and stood a little awkwardly, fumbling in his inside pocket.

'There is nothing to pay,' said Manfred, guessing his intention. 'Perhaps, when we have located your Miss Mirabelle Leicester, we shall ask you to refund our out-of-pocket expenses.'

'I can afford to pay – ' began the man.

'And we can afford to wait.' Again the gleam of amusement in the deep eyes.

Still Mr Barberton did not move.

'There's another thing I meant to ask you. You know all that's happening in this country?'

'Not quite everything,' said the other with perfect gravity.

'Have you ever heard of the Four Just Men?'

It was a surprising question. Manfred bent forward as though he had not heard aright.

'The Four – ?'

'The Four Just Men – three, as a matter of fact. I'd like to get in touch with those birds.'

Manfred nodded.

'I think I have heard of them,' he said.

'They're in England now somewhere. They've got a pardon: I saw that in the *Cape Times* – the bit I tore the advertisement from.'

'The last I heard of them, they were in Spain,' said Manfred, and walked round the table and opened the door. 'Why do you wish to get in touch with them?'

'Because,' said Mr Barberton impressively, 'the crowd are scared of 'em – that's why.'

Manfred walked with his visitor to the landing.

'You have omitted one important piece of information,' he said with a smile, 'but I did not intend your going until you told me. What is your address?'

'Petworth Hôtel, Norfolk Street.'

Barberton went down the stairs; the butler was waiting in the hall to show him out, and Mr Barberton, having a vague idea that something of the sort was usual in the houses of the aristocracy, slipped a silver coin in his hand. The dark-faced man murmured his thanks: his bow was perhaps a little lower, his attitude just a trifle more deferential.

He closed and locked the front door and went slowly up the stairs to the office room. Manfred was sitting on the empire table, lighting a cigarette. The chauffeur-valet had come through the grey curtains to take the chair which had been vacated by Mr Barberton.

'He gave me half a crown – generous fellow,' said Poiccart, the butler. 'I like him, George.'

'I wish I could have seen his feet,' said the chauffeur, whose veritable name was Leon Gonsalez. He spoke with regret. 'He comes from West Sussex, and there is insanity in his family. The left parietal is slightly recessed and the face is asymmetrical.'

'Poor soul!' murmured Manfred, blowing a cloud of smoke to the ceiling. 'It's a great trial introducing one's friends to you, Leon.'

'Fortunately, you have no friends,' said Leon, reaching out and taking a cigarette from the open gold case on the table. 'Well, what do you think of our Mr Barberton's mystery?'

George Manfred shook his head.

'He was vague, and, in his desire to be diplomatic, incoherent. What about your own mystery, Leon? You have been out all day . . . have you found a solution?'

Gonsalez nodded.

'Barberton is afraid of something,' said Poiccart, a slow and sure analyst. 'He carried a gun between his trousers and his waistcoat – you saw that?'

George nodded.

'The question is, who or which is the crowd? Question two is, where and who is Miss Mirabelle Leicester? Question three is, why did they burn Barberton's feet? . . . and I think that is all.'

The keen face of Gonsalez was thrust forward through a cloud of smoke.

'I will answer most of them and propound two more,' he said. 'Mirabelle Leicester took a job today at Oberzohn's – laboratory secretary!'

George Manfred frowned.

'Laboratory? I didn't know that he had one.'

'He hadn't till three days ago – it was fitted in seventy-two hours by experts who worked day and night; the cost of its installation was sixteen hundred pounds – and it came into existence to give Oberzohn an excuse for engaging Mirabelle Leicester. You sent me out to clear up that queer advertisement which puzzled us all on Monday – I have cleared it up. It was designed to bring our Miss Leicester into the Oberzohn establishment. We all agreed when we discovered who was the advertiser, that Oberzohn was working for something – I watched his office for two days, and she was the only applicant for the job – hers the only letter they answered. Oberzohn lunched with her at the Ritz-Carlton – she sleeps tonight in Chester Square.'

There was a silence which was broken by Poiccart.

'And what is the question you have to propound?' he asked mildly.

'I think I know,' said Manfred, and nodded. 'The question is: how long has Mr Samuel Barberton to live?'

'Exactly,' said Gonsalez with satisfaction. 'You are beginning to understand the mentality of Oberzohn!'

Chapter 3
The vendetta

The man who that morning walked without announcement into Dr Oberzohn's office might have stepped from the pages of a catalogue of men's fashions. He was, to the initiated eye, painfully new. His lemon gloves, his dazzling shoes, the splendour of his silk hat, the very correctness of his handkerchief display, would have been remarkable even in the Ascot paddock on Cup day. He was good-looking, smooth, if a trifle plump, of face, and he wore a tawny little moustache and a monocle. People who did not like Captain Monty Newton – and their names were many – said of him that he aimed at achieving the housemaid's conception of a guardsman. They did not say this openly, because he was a man to be propitiated rather than offended. He had money, a place in the country, a house in Chester Square, and an assortment of cars. He was a member of several good clubs, the committees of which never discussed him without offering the excuse of wartime courtesies for his election. Nobody knew how he made his money, or, if it were inherited, whose heir he was. He gave extravagant parties, played cards well, and enjoyed exceptional luck, especially when he was the host and held the bank after one of the splendid dinners he gave in his Chester Square mansion.

'Good morning, Oberzohn – how is Smitts?'

It was his favourite jest, for there was no Smitts, and had been no Smitts in the firm since '96.

The doctor, peering down at the telegram he was writing, looked up.

'Good morning, Captain Newton,' he said precisely. Newton passed to the back of him and read the message he was writing. It was addressed to 'Miss Alma Goddard, Heavytree Farm, Daynham, Gloucester,' and the wire ran:

Have got the fine situation. Cannot expeditiously return tonight.
I am sleeping at our pretty flat in Doughty Court. Do not come
up until I send for you – Miss Mirabelle Leicester

'She's here, is she?' Captain Newton glanced at the laboratory door. 'You're not going to send that wire? "Miss Mirabelle Leicester" "Expeditiously return!" She'd tumble it in a minute. Who is Alma Goddard?'

'The aunt,' said Oberzohn. 'I did not intend the dispatching until you had seen it. My English is too correct.'

He made way for Captain Newton, who, having taken a sheet of paper from the rack on which to deposit with great care his silk hat, and having stripped his gloves and deposited them in his hat, sat down in the chair from which the older man had risen, pulled up the knees of his immaculate trousers, tore off the top telegraph form, and wrote under the address:

Have got the job. Hooray! Don't bother to come up, darling, until I am settled. Shall sleep at the flat as usual. Too busy to write. Keep my letters – Mirabelle

'That's real,' said Captain Newton, surveying his work with satisfaction. 'Push it off.'

He got up and straddled his legs before the fire.

'The hard part of the job may be to persuade the lady to come to Chester Square,' he said.

'My own little house – ' began Oberzohn.

'Would scare her to death,' said Newton with a loud laugh. 'That dog-kennel! No, it is Chester Square or nothing. I'll get Joan or one of the girls to drop in this afternoon and chum up with her. When does the *Benguella* arrive?'

'This afternoon: the person has booked rooms by radio at the Petworth Hôtel.'

'Norfolk Street . . . humph! One of your men can pick him up and keep an eye on him. Lisa? So much the better. That kind of trash will talk for a woman. I don't suppose he has seen a white woman in years. You ought to fire Villa – crude beast! Naturally the man is on his guard now.'

'Villa is the best of my men on the coast,' barked Oberzohn fiercely. Nothing so quickly touched the raw places of his amazing vanity as a reflection upon his organizing qualities.

'How is trade?' Captain Newton took a long ebony holder from his tail pocket, flicked out a thin platinum case and lit a cigarette in one uninterrupted motion.

'Bat!' When Dr Oberzohn was annoyed the purity of his pronunciation suffered. 'There is nothing but expense!'

Oberzohn & Smitts had once made an enormous income from the sale of synthetic alcohol. They were, amongst other things, coast traders. They bought rubber and ivory, paying in cloth and liquor. They sold arms secretly, organized tribal wars for their greater profit, and had financed at least two Portuguese revolutions nearer at home. And with the growth of their fortune, the activities of the firm had extended. Guns and more guns went out of Belgian and French workshops. To Kurdish insurrectionaries, to ambitious Chinese generals, to South American politicians, planning to carry their convictions into more active fields. There was no country in the world that did not act as host to an O. & S. agent – and agents can be very expensive. Just now the world was alarmingly peaceful. A revolution had failed most dismally in Venezuela, and Oberzohn & Smitts had not been paid for two ship-loads of lethal weapons ordered by a general who, two days after the armaments were landed, had been placed against an adobe wall and incontinently shot to rags by the soldiers of the Government against which he was in rebellion.

'But that shall not matter.' Oberzohn waved bad trade from the considerable factors of life. 'This shall succeed: and then I shall be free to well punish – '

'To punish well,' corrected the purist, stroking his moustache. 'Don't split your infinitives, Eruc – it's silly. You're thinking of Manfred and Gonsalez and Poiccart? Leave them alone. They are nothing!'

'Nothing!' roared the doctor, his sallow face instantly distorted with fury. 'To leave them alone, is it? Of my brother what? Of my brother in heaven, sainted martyr . . . !'

He spun round, gripped the silken tassel of the cord above the fireplace, and pulled down, not a map, but a picture. It had been painted from a photograph by an artist who specialized in the gaudy banners which hang before every booth at every country fair. In this setting the daub was a shrieking incongruity; yet to Dr Oberzohn it surpassed in beauty the masterpieces of the Prado. A full-length portrait of a man in a frock-coat. He leaned on a pedestal in the attitude which cheap photographers believe is the acme of grace. His big face, idealized as it was by the artist, was brutal and stupid. The carmine lips were parted in a simper. In one hand he held a scroll of paper, in the other a Derby hat which was considerably out of drawing.

'My brother!' Dr Oberzohn choked. 'My sainted Adolph . . . murdered! By the so-called Three Just Men . . . my brother!'

'Very interesting,' murmured Captain Newton, who had not even troubled to look up. He flicked the ash from his cigarette into the fireplace and said no more.

Adolph Oberzohn had certainly been shot dead by Leon Gonsalez: there was no disputing the fact. That Adolph, at the moment of his death, was attempting to earn the generous profits which come to those who engage in a certain obnoxious trade between Europe and the South American states, was less open to question. There was a girl in it: Leon followed his man to Porto Rico, and in the Café of the Seven Virtues they had met. Adolph was by training a gunman and drew first – and died first. That was the story of Adolph Oberzohn: the story of a girl whom Leon Gonsalez smuggled back to Europe belongs elsewhere. She fell in love with her rescuer and frightened him sick.

Dr Oberzohn let the portrait roll up with a snap, blew his nose vigorously, and blinked the tears from his pale eyes.

'Yes, very sad, very sad,' said the captain cheerfully. 'Now what about this girl? There is to be nothing rough or raw, you understand, Eruc? I want the thing done sweetly. Get that bug of the Just Men out of your mind – they are out of business. When a man lowers himself to run a detective agency he's a back number. If they start anything we'll deal with them scientifically, eh? Scientifically!'

He chuckled with laughter at this good joke. It was obvious that Captain Newton was no dependant on the firm of Oberzohn & Smitts. If he was not the dominant partner, he dominated that branch which he had once served in a minor capacity. He owed much to the death of Adolph – he never regretted the passing of that unsavoury man.

'I'll get one of the girls to look her over this afternoon – where is your telephone pad – the one you write messages received?'

The doctor opened a drawer of his desk and took out a little memo pad, and Newton found a pencil and wrote:

To Mirabelle Leicester, care Oberzohn (phone) London. Sorry I can't come up tonight. Don't sleep at flat alone. Have wired Joan Newton to put you up for night. She will call – Alma.

'There you are,' said the gallant captain, handing the pad to the other. 'That message came this afternoon. All telegrams to Oberzohn come by 'phone – never forget it!'

'Ingenious creature!' Dr Oberzohn's admiration was almost reverential.

'Take her out to lunch . . . after lunch, the message. At four o'clock, Joan or one of the girls. A select dinner. Tomorrow the office . . . gently, gently. Bull-rush these schemes and your plans die the death of a dog.'

He glanced at the door once more.

'She won't come out, I suppose?' he suggested. 'Deuced awkward if she came out and saw Miss Newton's brother!'

'I have locked the door,' said Dr Oberzohn proudly.

Captain Newton's attitude changed: his face went red with sudden fury. 'Then you're a – you're a fool. Unlock the door when I've gone – and keep it unlocked! Want to frighten her?'

'It was my idea to risk nothing,' pleaded the long-faced Swede.

'Do as I tell you.'

Captain Newton brushed his speckless coat with the tips of his fingers. He pulled on his gloves, fitted his hat with the aid of a small pocket-mirror he took from his inside pocket, took up his clouded cane and strolled from the room.

'Ingenious creature,' murmured Dr Oberzohn again, and went in to offer the startled Mirabelle an invitation to lunch.

Chapter 4

The snake strikes

The great restaurant, with its atmosphere of luxury and wealth, had been a little overpowering. The crowded tables, the soft lights, the very capability and nonchalance of the waiters, were impressive. When her new employer had told her that it was his practice to take the laboratory secretary to lunch, 'for I have not other time to speak of business things,' she accepted uncomfortably. She knew little of office routine, but she felt that it was not customary for principals to drive their secretaries from the City Road to the Ritz-Carlton to lunch expensively at that resort of fashion and the epicure. It added nothing to her self-possession that her companion was an object of interest to all who saw him. The gay luncheon parties forgot their dishes and twisted round to stare at the extraordinary-looking man with the high forehead.

At a little table alone she saw a man whose face was tantalizingly familiar. A keen, thin face with eager, amused eyes. Where had she seen him before? Then she remembered: the chauffeur had such a face – the man who had followed her into Oberzohn's when she arrived that morning. It was absurd, of course; this man was one of the leisured class, to whom lunching at the Ritz-Carlton was a normal event. And yet the likeness was extraordinary.

She was glad when the meal was over. Dr Oberzohn did not talk of 'business things'. He did not talk at all, but spent his time shovelling incredible quantities of food through his wide slit of a mouth. He ate intently, noisily – Mirabelle was glad the band was playing, and she went red with suppressed laughter at the whimsical thought; and after that she felt less embarrassed.

No word was spoken as the big car sped citywards. The doctor had his thoughts and ignored her presence. The only reference he made to the lunch was as they were leaving the hôtel, when he had condescended to grunt a bitter complaint about the quality of English-made coffee. He allowed her to go back to her weighing and measuring without displaying the slightest interest in her progress.

And then came the crowning surprise of the afternoon – it followed the arrival of a puzzling telegram from her aunt. She was weighing an evil-smelling mass of powder when the door opened and there floated into the room a delicate-looking girl, beautifully dressed. A small face framed in a mass of little golden-brown curls smiled a greeting. 'You're Mirabelle Leicester, aren't you? I'm Joan Newton – your aunt wired me to call on you.'

'Do you know my aunt?' asked Mirabelle in astonishment. She had never heard Alma speak of the Newtons, but then, Aunt Alma had queer reticences. Mirabelle had expected a middle-aged dowd – it was amazing that her unprepossessing relative could claim acquaintance with this society butterfly.

'Oh yes – we know Alma very well,' replied the visitor. 'Of course, I haven't seen her since I was quite a little girl – she's a dear.'

She looked round the laboratory with curious interest.

'What a nasty-smelling place!' she said, her nose up-turned. 'And how do you like old – er – Mr Oberzohn?'

'Do you know him?' asked Mirabelle, astounded at the possibility of this coincidence.

'My brother knows him – we live together, my brother and I, and he knows everybody. A man about town has to, hasn't he, dear?'

'Man about town' was an expression that grated a little; Mirabelle was not of the 'dearing' kind. The combination of errors in taste made her scrutinize the caller more closely. Joan Newton was dressed beautifully but not well. There was something . . . Had Mirabelle a larger knowledge of life, she might have thought that the girl had been dressed to play the part of a lady by somebody who wasn't quite sure of the constituents of the part. Captain Newton she did not know at the time, or she would have guessed the dress authority.

'I'm going to take you back to Chester Square after Mr Oberzohn – such a funny name, isn't it? – has done with you. Monty insisted upon my bringing the Rolls. Monty is my brother; he's rather classical.'

Mirabelle wondered whether this indicated a love of the Greek poets or a passion for the less tuneful operas. Joan (which was her real name) meant no more than classy: it was a favourite word of hers; another was 'morbid'.

Half an hour later the inquisitive chauffeur put his foot on the starter and sent his car on the trail of the Rolls, wondering what Mirabelle Leicester had in common with Joan Alice Murphy, who had brought so many rich young men to the green board in Captain Newton's beautiful drawing-room, where stakes ran high and the captain played with such phenomenal luck.

* * *

'And there you are,' said Gonsalez complacently. 'I've done a very good day's work. Oberzohn has gone back to his rabbit-hutch to think up new revolutions – Miss Mirabelle Leicester is to be found at 307, Chester Square. Now the point is, what do we do to save the valuable life of Mr Sam Barberton?'

Manfred looked grave. 'I hardly like the thought of the girl spending the night in Newton's house,' he said.

'Why allow her to remain there?' asked Poiccart in his heavy way.

'Exactly!' Leon nodded.

George Manfred looked at his watch.

'Obviously the first person to see is friend Barberton,' he said, 'If we can prevail on him to spend the evening with us, the rest is a simple matter – '

The telephone bell rang shrilly and Leon Gonsalez monopolized the instrument.

'Gloucester? Yes.' He covered the receiver with his hand. 'I took the liberty of asking Miss Alma Goddard to ring me up . . . her address I discovered very early in the day: Heavytree Farm, Daynham, near Gloucester . . . yes, yes, it is Mr Johnson speaking. I wanted to ask you if you would take a message to Miss Leicester . . . oh, she isn't at home?' Leon listened attentively, and, after a few minutes: 'Thank you very much. She is staying at Doughty Court? She wired you . . . oh, nothing very important. I – er – am her old science master and I saw an advertisement . . . oh, she has seen it, has she?'

He hung up the receiver.

'Nothing to go on,' he said. 'The girl has wired to say she is delighted with her job. The aunt is not to come up until she is settled, and Mirabelle is sleeping at Doughty Court.'

'And a very excellent place too,' said Manfred. 'When we've seen Mr Barberton I shouldn't be surprised if she didn't sleep there after all.'

Petworth Hôtel in Norfolk Street was a sedate residential hostel, greatly favoured by overseas visitors, especially South Africans. The reception clerk thought Mr Barberton was out: the hall porter was sure.

'He went down to the Embankment – he said he'd like to see the river before it was dark,' said that confidant of so many visitors.

Manfred stepped into the car by Leon's side – Poiccart seldom went abroad, but sat at home piecing together the little jigsaw puzzles of life that came to Curzon Street for solution. He was the greatest of all the strategists: even Scotland Yard brought some of its problems for his inspection.

'On the Embankment?' Manfred looked up at the blue and pink sky. The sun had gone down, but the light of day remained. 'If it were darker I should be worried . . . stop, there's Dr Elver.'

The little police surgeon who had passed them with a cheery wave of his hand turned and walked back.

'Well, Children of the Law' – he was inclined to be dramatic – 'on what dread errand of vengeance are you bound?'

'We are looking for a man named Barberton to ask him to dinner,' said Manfred, shaking hands.

'Sounds tame to me: has he any peculiarities which would appeal to me?'

'Burnt feet,' said Leon promptly. 'If you would like to learn how the coastal intelligence department extract information from unwilling victims, come along.'

Elver hesitated. He was a man burnt up by the Indian suns, wizened like a dried yellow apple, and he had no interest in the world beyond his work.

'I'll go with you,' he said, stepping into the car. 'And if your Barberton man fails you, you can have me as a guest. I like to hear you talking. One cannot know too much of the criminal mind! And life is dull since the snake stopped biting!'

The car made towards Blackfriars Bridge, and Manfred kept watch of the sidewalk. There was no sign of Barberton, and he signalled Leon to turn and come back. This brought the machine to the Embankment side of the broad boulevard. They had passed under Waterloo Bridge and were nearing Cleopatra's Needle when Gonsalez saw the man they were seeking.

He was leaning against the parapet, his elbows on the coping and his head sunk forward as though he were studying the rush of the tide below. The car pulled up near a policeman who was observing the lounger thoughtfully. The officer recognized the police surgeon and saluted.

'Can't understand that bird, sir,' he said. 'He's been standing there for ten minutes. I'm keepin' an eye on him, because he looks to me like a suicide who's thinkin' it over!'

Manfred approached the man, and suddenly, with a shock, saw his face. It was set in a grin – the eyes were wide open, the skin a coppery red.

'Elver! Leon!'

As Leon sprang from the car, Manfred touched the man's shoulder and he fell limply to the ground. In a second the doctor was on his knees by the side of the still figure.

'Dead,' he said laconically, and then: 'Good God!'

He pointed to the neck, where a red patch showed.

'What is that?' asked Manfred steadily.

'The snake!' said the doctor.

Chapter 5
The golden woman

Barberton had been stricken down in the heart of London, under the very eyes of the policeman, it proved.

'Yes, sir, I've had him under observation for a quarter of an hour. I saw him walking along the Embankment, admiring the view, long before he stopped here.'

'Did anybody go near him to speak to him?' asked Dr Elver, looking up.

'No, sir, he stood by himself. I'll swear that nobody was within two yards of him. Of course, people have been passing to and fro, but I have been looking at him all the time, and I've not seen man or woman within yards of him, and my eyes were never off him.'

A second policeman had appeared on the scene, and he was sent across to Scotland Yard in Manfred's car for the ambulance and the police reserves necessary to clear and keep in circulation the gathering crowd. These returned simultaneously, and the two friends watched the pitiable thing lifted into a stretcher, and waited until the white-bodied vehicle had disappeared with its sad load before they returned to their machine.

Gonsalez took his place at the wheel; George got in by his side. No word was spoken until they were back at Curzon Street. Manfred went in alone, whilst his companion drove the machine to the garage. When he returned, he found Poiccart and George deep in discussion.

'You were right, Raymond.' Leon Gonsalez stripped his thin coat and threw it on a chair. 'The accuracy of your forecasts is almost depressing. I am waiting all the time for the inevitable mistake, and I am irritated when this doesn't occur. You said the snake would reappear, and the snake has reappeared. Prophesy now for me, O seer!'

Poiccart's heavy face was gloomy; his dark eyes almost hidden under the frown that brought his bushy eyebrows lower.

'One hasn't to be a seer to know that our association with Barberton will send the snake wriggling towards Curzon Street,' he said. 'Was it Gurther or Pfeiffer?'

Manfred considered.

'Pfeiffer, I think. He is the steadier of the two. Gurther has brain-storms; he is on the neurotic side. And that nine-thonged whip of yours, Leon, cannot have added to his mental stability. No, it was Pfeiffer, I'm sure.'

'I suppose the whip unbalanced him a little,' said Leon. He thought over this aspect as though it were one worth consideration. 'Gurther is a sort of Jekyll and Hyde, except that there is no virtue to him at all. It is difficult to believe, seeing him dropping languidly into his seat at the opera, that this exquisite young man in his private moments would not change his linen more often than once a month, and would shudder at the sound of a running bath-tap! That almost sounds as though he were a morphia fiend. I remember a case in '99 . . . but I am interrupting you?'

'What precautions shall you take, Leon?' asked George Manfred.

'Against the snake?' Leon shrugged his shoulders. 'The old military precaution against Zeppelin raids; the precaution the farmer takes against a plague of wasps. You cannot kneel on the chest of the *vespa vulgaris* and extract his sting with an anaesthetic. You destroy his nest – you bomb his hangar. Personally, I have never feared dissolution in any form, but I have a childish objection to being bitten by a snake.'

Poiccart's saturnine face creased for a moment in a smile. 'You've no objection to stealing my theories,' he said drily, and the other doubled up in silent laughter.

Manfred was pacing the little room, his hands behind him, a thick Egyptian cigarette between his lips.

'There's a train leaves Paddington for Gloucester at ten forty-five,' he said. 'Will you telegraph to Miss Goddard, Heavytree Farm, and ask her to meet the train with a cab? After that I shall want two men to patrol the vicinity of the farm day and night.'

Poiccart pulled open a drawer of the desk, took out a small book and ran his finger down the index.

'I can get this service in Gloucester,' he said. 'Gordon, Williams, Thompson and Elfred – they're reliable people and have worked for us before.'

Manfred nodded.

'Send them the usual instructions by letter. I wonder who will be in charge of this Barberton case? If it's Meadows, I can work with him. On the other hand, if it's Arbuthnot, we shall have to get our information by subterranean methods.'

'Call Elver,' suggested Leon, and George pulled the telephone towards him.

It was some time before he could get into touch with Dr Elver, and then he learnt, to his relief, that the redoubtable Inspector Meadows had complete charge.

'He's coming up to see you,' said Elver. 'As a matter of fact, the chief was here when I arrived at the Yard, and he particularly asked Meadows to consult with you. There's going to be an awful kick at the Home Secretary's office about this murder. We had practically assured the Home Office that there would be no repetition of the mysterious deaths and that the snake had gone dead for good.'

Manfred asked a few questions and then hung up.

'They are worried about the public – you never know what masses will do in given circumstances. But you can gamble that the English mass does the same thing – Governments hate intelligent crowds. This may cost the Home Secretary his job, poor soul! And he's doing his best.'

A strident shout in the street made him turn his head with a smile.

'The late editions have got it – naturally. It might have been committed on their doorstep.'

'But why?' asked Poiccart 'What was Barberton's offence?'

'His first offence,' said Leon promptly, without waiting for Manfred to reply, 'was to go in search of Miss Mirabelle Leicester. His second and greatest was to consult with us. He was a dead man when he left the house.'

The faint sound of a bell ringing sent Poiccart down to the hall to admit an unobtrusive, middle-aged man, who might have been anything but what he was: one of the cleverest trackers of criminals that Scotland Yard had known in thirty years. A sandy-haired, thin-faced man, who wore pince-nez and looked like an actor, he had been a visitor to Curzon Street before, and now received a warm welcome. With little preliminary he came to the object of his call, and Manfred told him briefly what had happened, and the gist of his conversation with Barberton.

'Miss Mirabelle Leicester is – ' began Manfred.

'Employed by Oberzohn – I know,' was the surprising reply. 'She came up to London this morning and took a job as laboratory assistant. I had no idea that Oberzohn & Smitts had a laboratory on the premises.'

'They hadn't until a couple of days ago,' interrupted Leon. 'The laboratory was staged especially for her.'

Meadows nodded, then turned to Manfred. 'He didn't give you any idea at all why he wanted to meet Miss Leicester?'

George shook his head.

'No, he was very mysterious indeed on that subject,' he said.

'He arrived by the *Benguella*, eh?' said Meadows, making a note. 'We ought to get something from the ship before they pay off their stewards. If a man isn't communicative on board ship, he'll never talk at all! And we may find something in his belongings. Would you like to come along, Manfred?'

'I'll come with pleasure,' said George gravely. 'I may help you a little – you will not object to my making my own interpretation of what we see?'

Meadows smiled.

'You will be allowed your private mystery,' he said.

A taxi set them down at the Petworth Hôtel in Norfolk Street, and they were immediately shown up to the room which the dead man had hired but had not as yet occupied. His trunk, still strapped and locked, stood on a small wooden trestle, his overcoat was hanging behind the door; in one corner of the room was a thick hold-all, tightly strapped, and containing, as they subsequently discovered, a weather-stained mackintosh, two well-worn blankets and an air pillow, together with a collapsible canvas chair, also showing considerable signs of usage. This was the object of their preliminary search.

The lock of the trunk yielded to the third key which the detective tried. Beyond changes of linen and two suits, one of which was practically new and bore the tab of a store in St Paul de Loanda, there was very little to enlighten them. They found an envelope full of papers, and sorted them out one by one on the bed. Barberton was evidently a careful man; he had preserved his hôtel bills, writing on their backs brief but pungent comments about the accommodation he had enjoyed or suffered. There was an hôtel in Lobuo which was full of vermin; there was one at Mossamedes of which he had written: 'Rats ate one boot. Landlord made no allowance. Took three towels and pillow-slip.'

'One of the Four Just Men in embryo,' said Meadows dryly.

Manfred smiled.

On the back of one bill were closely written columns of figures: '126, 1315, 107, 1712, about 24,' etc. Against a number of these figures the word 'about' appeared, and Manfred observed that invariably this qualification marked one of the higher numbers. Against the 107 was a thick pencil mark.

There were amongst the papers several other receipts. In St Paul he had bought a 'pistol automatic of precision' and ammunition for the same. The 'pistol automatic of precision' was not in the trunk.

'We found it in his pocket,' said Meadows briefly. 'That fellow was expecting trouble, and was entitled to, if it is true that they tortured him at Mosamodes.'

'Moss-AM-o-dees,' Manfred corrected the mispronunciation. It almost amounted to a fad in him that to hear a place miscalled gave him a little pain.

Meadows was reading a letter, turning the pages slowly.

'This is from his sister: she lives at Brightlingsea, and there's nothing in it except . . . ' He read a portion of the letter aloud.

' . . . thank you for the books. The children will appreciate them. It must have been like old times writing them – but I can under- stand how it helped pass the time. Mr Lee came over and asked if I had heard from you. He is wonderful.'

The letter was in an educated hand.

'He didn't strike me as a man who wrote books,' said Meadows, and continued his search.

Presently he unfolded a dilapidated map, evidently of Angola. It was rather on the small scale, so much so that it took in a portion of the Kalahari Desert in the south, and showed in the north the undulations of the rolling Congo.

'No marks of any bind,' said Meadows, carrying the chart to the window to examine it more carefully. 'And that, I think, is about all – unless this is something.'

'This' was wrapped in a piece of cloth, and was fastened to the bottom and the sides of the trunk by two improvised canvas straps. Meadows tried to pull it loose and whistled.

'Gold,' he said. 'Nothing else can weigh quite as heavily as this.'

He lifted out the bundle eventually, unwrapped the covering, and gazed in amazement on the object that lay under his eyes. It was an African *bete*, a nude, squat idol, rudely shaped, the figure of a native woman.

'Gold?' said Manfred incredulously, and tried to lift it with his finger and thumb. He took a firmer grip and examined the discovery closely.

There was no doubt that it was gold, and fine gold. His thumb-nail made a deep scratch in the base of the statuette. He could see the marks where the knife of the inartistic sculptor had sliced and carved.

Meadows knew the coast fairly well: he had made many trips to Africa and had stopped off at various ports en route.

'I've never seen anything exactly like it before,' he said, 'and it isn't recent workmanship either. When you see this' – he pointed to a physical peculiarity of the figure – 'you can bet that you've got something that's been made at least a couple of hundred years, and probably before then. The natives of West and Central Africa have not worn toe-rings, for example, since the days of the Caesars.'

He weighed the idol in his hand.

'Roughly ten pounds,' he said. 'In other words, eight hundred pounds' worth of gold.'

He was examining the cloth in which the idol had been wrapped, and uttered an exclamation.

'Look at this,' he said.

Written on one corner, in indelible pencil, were the words:

'Second shelf up left Gods lobby sixth.'

Suddenly Manfred remembered.

'Would you have this figure put on the scales right away?' he said. 'I'm curious to know the exact weight.'

'Why?' asked Meadows in surprise, as he rang the bell.

The proprietor himself, who was aware that a police search was in progress, answered the call, and, at the detective's request, hurried down to the kitchen and returned in a few minutes with a pair of scales, which he placed on the table. He was obviously curious to know the purpose for which they were intended, but Inspector Meadows did not enlighten him, standing pointedly by the door until the gentleman had gone.

The figure was taken from under the cloth where it had been hidden whilst the scales were being placed, and put in one shallow pan on the machine.

'Ten pounds seven ounces,' nodded Manfred triumphantly. 'I thought that was the one!'

'One what?' asked the puzzled Meadows.

'Look at this list.'

Manfred found the hôtel bill with the rows of figures and pointed to the one which had a black cross against it.

'107,' he said. 'That is our little fellow, and the explanation is fairly plain. Barberton found some treasure-house filled with these statues. He took away the lightest. Look at the figures! He weighed them with a spring balance, one of those which register up to 21 lb. Above that he had to guess – he puts "about 24", "about 22".'

Meadows looked at his companion blankly, but Manfred was not deceived. That clever brain of the detective was working.

'Not for robbery – the trunk is untouched. They did not even burn his feet to find the idol or the treasure house: they must have known nothing of that It was easy to rob him – or, if they knew of his gold idol, they considered it too small loot to bother with.'

He looked slowly round the apartment. On the mantelshelf was a slip of brown paper like a pipe-spill. He picked it up, looked at both sides, and, finding the paper blank, put it back where he had found it. Manfred took it down and absently drew the strip between his sensitive finger-tips.

'The thing to do,' said Meadows, taking one final look round, 'is to find Miss Leicester.'

Manfred nodded.

'That is one of the things,' he said slowly. 'The other, of course, is to find Johnny.'

'Johnny?' Meadows frowned suspiciously. 'Who is Johnny?' he asked.

'Johnny is my private mystery.' George Manfred was smiling. 'You promised me that I might have one!'

Chapter 6

In Chester Square

When Mirabelle Leicester went to Chester Square, her emotions were a curious discord of wonder, curiosity and embarrassment. The latter was founded on the extraordinary effusiveness of her companion, who had suddenly, and with no justification, assumed the position of dearest friend and lifelong acquaintance. Mirabelle thought the girl was an actress: a profession in which sudden and violent friendships are not a rare occurrence. She wondered why Aunt Alma had not made an effort to come to town, and wondered more that she had known of Alma's friendship with the Newtons. That the elder woman had her secrets was true, but there was no reason why she should have refrained from speaking of a family who were close enough friends to be asked to chaperon her in town.

She had time for thought, for Joan Newton chattered away all the time, and if she asked a question, she either did not wait for approval, or the question was answered to her own satisfaction before it was put.

Chester Square, that dignified patch of Belgravia, is an imposing quarter. The big house into which the girl was admitted by a footman had that air of luxurious comfort which would have appealed to a character less responsive to refinement than Mirabelle Leicester's. She was ushered into a big drawing-room which ran from the front to the back of the house, and did not terminate even there, for a large, cool conservatory, bright with flowers, extended a considerable distance.

'Monty isn't back from the City yet,' Joan rattled on. 'My dear! He's awfully busy just now, what with stocks and shares and things like that.'

She spoke as though 'stocks and shares and things like that' were phenomena which had come into existence the day before yesterday for the occupation of Monty Newton.

'Is there a boom?' asked Mirabelle with a smile, and the term seemed to puzzle the girl.

'Ye-es, I suppose there is. You know what the Stock Exchange is, my dear? Everybody connected with it is wealthy beyond the dreams of avarice. The money they make is simply wicked! And they can give a girl an awfully good time – theatres, parties, dresses, pearls – why, Monty would think nothing of giving a string of pearls to a girl if he took a liking to her!'

In truth Joan was walking on very uncertain ground. Her instructions had been simple and to the point. 'Get her to Chester Gardens, make friends with her, and don't mention the fact that I know Oberzohn.' What was the object of bringing Mirabelle Leicester to the house, what was behind this move of Monty's, she did not know. She was merely playing for safety, baiting the ground, as it were, with her talk of good times and vast riches, in case that was required of her. For she, no less than many of her friends, entertained a wholesome dread of Monty Newton's disapproval, which usually took a definite unpleasant shape.

Mirabelle was laughing softly.

'I didn't know that stockbrokers were so rich,' she said dryly, 'and I can assure you that some of them aren't!'

She passed tactfully over the *gaucherie* of the pearls that Monty would give to any girl who took his fancy. By this time she had placed Joan: knew something of her upbringing, guessed pretty well the extent of her intelligence, and marvelled a little that a man of the unknown Mr Newton's position should have allowed his sister to come through the world without the benefit of a reasonably good education.

'Come up to your room, my dear,' said Joan. 'We've got a perfectly topping little suite for you, and I'm sure you'll be comfortable. It's at the front of the house, and if you can get used to the milkmen yowling about the streets before they're aired, you'll have a perfectly topping time.'

When Mirabelle inspected the apartment she was enchanted. It fulfilled Joan's vague description. Here was luxury beyond her wildest dreams. She admired the silver bed and the thick blue carpet, the silken panelled walls, the exquisite fittings, and stood in rapture before the entrance of a little bathroom, with its silver and glass, its shaded lights and marble walls.

'I'll have a cup of tea sent up to you, my dear. You'll want to rest after your horrible day at that perfectly terrible factory, and I wonder you can stand Oberzohn, though they tell me he's quite a nice man . . .'

She seemed anxious to go, and Mirabelle was no less desirous of being alone.

'Come down when you feel like it,' said Joan at parting, and ran down the stairs, reaching the hall in time to meet Mr Newton, who was handing his hat and gloves to his valet.

'Well, is she here?'

'She's here all right,' said Joan, who was not at all embarrassed by the presence of the footman. 'Monty, isn't she a bit of a fool? She couldn't say boo to a goose. What is the general scheme?'

He was brushing his hair delicately in the mirror above the hall-stand.

'What's what scheme?' he asked, after the servant had gone, as he strolled into the drawing-room before her.

'Bringing her here – is she sitting into a game?'

'Don't be stupid,' said Monty without heat, as he dropped wearily to a low divan and drew a silken cushion behind him. 'Nor inquisitive,' he added. 'You haven't scared her, have you?'

'I like that!' she said indignantly.

She was one of those ladies who speak more volubly and with the most assurance when there is a mirror in view, and she had her eyes fixed upon herself all the time she was talking, patting a strand of hair here and there, twisting her head this way and that to get a better effect, and never once looking at the man until he drew attention to himself.

'Scared! I'll bet she's never been to such a beautiful house in her life! What is she, Monty? A typist or something? I don't understand her.'

'She's a lady,' said Monty offensively. 'That's the type that'll always seem like a foreign language to you.'

She lifted one shoulder delicately.

'I don't pretend to be a lady, and what I am, you've made me,' she said, and the reproach was mechanical. He had heard it before, not only from her, but from others similarly placed. 'I don't think it's very kind to throw my education up in my face, considering the money I've made for you.'

'And for yourself.' He yawned. 'Get me some tea.'

'You might say "please" now and again,' she said resentfully, and he smiled as he took up the evening paper, paying her no more attention, until she had rung the bell with a vicious jerk and the silver tray came in and was deposited on a table near him.

'Where are you going tonight?'

His interest in her movements was unusual, and she was flattered.

'You know very well, Monty, where I'm going tonight,' she said reproachfully. 'You promised to take me, too. I think you'd look wonderful as a Crusader – one of them – those old knights in armour.'

He nodded, but not to her comment.

'I remember, of course – the Arts Ball.'

His surprise was so well simulated that she was deceived.

'Fancy your forgetting! I'm going as Cinderella, and Minnie Gray is going as a pierrette – '

'Minnie Gray isn't going as anything,' said Monty, sipping his tea. 'I've already telephoned to her to say that the engagement is off. Miss Leicester is going with you.'

'But, Monty – ' protested the girl.

'Don't "but Monty" me,' he ordered. 'I'm telling you! Go up and see this girl, and put it to her that you've got a ticket for the dance.'

'But her costume, Monty! The girl hasn't got a fancy dress. And Minnie – '

'Forget Minnie, will you? Mirabelle Leicester is going to the Arts Ball tonight.' He tapped the tray before him to emphasize every word. 'You have a ticket to spare, and you simply can't go alone because I have a very important business engagement and your friend has failed you. Her dress will be here in a few minutes: it is a bright green domino with a bright red hood.'

'How perfectly hideous!' She forgot for the moment her disappointment in this outrage. 'Bright green! Nobody has a complexion to stand that!'

Yet he ignored her.

'You will explain to Miss Leicester that the dress came from a friend who, through illness or any cause you like to invent, is unable to go to the dance – she'll jump at the chance. It is one of the events of the year and tickets are selling at a premium.'

She asked him what that meant, and he explained patiently.

'Maybe she'll want to spend a quiet evening – have one of those headaches,' he went on. 'If that is so, you can tell her that I've got a party coming to the house tonight, and they will be a little noisy. Did she want to know anything about me?'

'No, she didn't,' snapped Joan promptly. 'She didn't want to know about anything. I couldn't get her to talk. She's like a dumb oyster.'

Mirabelle was sitting by the window, looking down into the square, when there was a gentle tap at the door and Joan came in.

'I've got wonderful news for you,' she said.

'For me?' said Mirabelle in surprise.

Joan ran across the room, giving what she deemed to be a surprisingly life-like representation of a young thing full of innocent joy.

'I've got an extra ticket for the Arts Ball tonight. They're selling at a – they're very expensive. Aren't you a lucky girl!'

'I?' said Mirabelle in surprise. 'Why am I the lucky one?'

Joan rose from the bed and drew back from her reproachfully.

'You surely will come with me? If you don't, I shan't able to go at all. Lady Mary and I were going together . . . now she's sick!'

Mirabelle opened her eyes wider.

'But I can't go, surely. It is a fancy dress ball, isn't it? I read something about it in the papers. And I'm awfully tired tonight.'

Joan pouted prettily.

'My dear, if you lay down for an hour you'd be fit. Besides, you couldn't sleep here early tonight. Monty's having one of his men parties, and they're a noisy lot of people – though thoroughly respectable,' she added hastily.

Poor Joan had a mission outside her usual range.

'I'd love to go' – Mirabelle was anxious not to be a kill-joy – 'if I could get a dress.'

'I've got one,' said the girl promptly, and ran out of the room.

She returned very quickly, and threw the domino on the bed.

'It's not pretty to look at, but it's got this advantage, that you can wear almost anything underneath.'

'What time does the ball start?' Mirabelle, examining her mind, found that she was not averse to going; she was very human, and a fancy dress ball would be a new experience.

'Ten o'clock,' said Joan. 'We can have dinner before Monty's friends arrive. You'd like to see Monty, wouldn't you? He's downstairs – such a gentleman, my dear!'

The girl could have laughed.

A little later she was introduced to the redoubtable Monty, and found his suave and easy manner a relief after the jerky efforts of the girl to be entertaining. Monty had seen most parts of the world and could talk entertainingly about them all. Mirabelle rather liked him, though she thought he was something of a fop, yet was not sorry when she learned that, so far from having friends to dinner, he did not expect them to arrive until after she and Joan had left.

The meal put her more at her ease. He was a polished man of the world, courteous to the point of pomposity; he neither said nor suggested one thing that could offend her; they were half-way through dinner when the cry of a newsboy was heard in the street. Through the dining-room window she saw the footman go down the steps and buy a newspaper. He glanced at the stop-press space and came back slowly up the stairs reading. A little later he came into the room, and must have signalled to her host, for Monty went out immediately and she heard their voices in the passage. Joan was uneasy.

'I wonder what's the matter?' she asked, a little irritably. 'It's very bad manners to leave ladies in the middle of dinner – '

At that moment Monty came back. Was it imagination on her part, or had he gone suddenly pale? Joan saw it, and her brows met, but she was too wise to make a comment upon his appearance.

Mr Newton seated himself in his place with a word of apology and poured out a glass of champagne. Only for a second did his hand tremble, and then, with a smile, he was his old self.

'What is wrong, Monty?'

'Wrong? Nothing,' he said curtly, and took up the topic of conversation where he had laid it down before leaving the room.

'It isn't that old snake, is it?' asked Joan with a shiver. 'Lord! that unnerves me! I never go to bed at night without looking under, or turning the clothes right down to the foot! They ought to have found it months ago if the police – '

At this point she caught Monty Newton's eye, cold, menacing, malevolent, and the rest of her speech died on her lips.

Mirabelle went upstairs to dress, and Joan would have followed but the man beckoned her.

'You're a little too talkative, Joan,' he said, more mildly than she had expected. 'The snake is not a subject we wish to discuss at dinner. And listen!' He walked into the passage and looked round, then came back and closed the door. 'Keep that girl near you.'

'Who is going to dance with me?' she asked petulantly. 'I like having a hell of a lively night!'

'Benton will be there to look after you, and one of the "Old Guard" – '

He saw the frightened look in her face and chuckled. 'What's the matter, you fool?' he asked good-humouredly. 'He'll dance with the girl.'

'I wish those fellows weren't going to be there,' she said uneasily, but he went on, without noticing her:

'I shall arrive at half-past eleven. You had better meet me near the entrance to the American bar. My party didn't turn up, you understand. You'll get back here at midnight.'

'So soon?' she said in dismay. 'Why, it doesn't end till – '

'You'll be back here at midnight,' he said evenly. 'Go into her room, clear up everything she may have left behind. You understand? Nothing is to be left.'

'But when she comes back she'll – '

'She'll not come back,' said Monty Newton, and the girl's blood ran cold.

Chapter 7

'Moral suasion'

'Here's a man wants to see you, governor.'

It was a quarter-past nine. The girls had been gone ten minutes, and Montague Newton had settled himself down to pass the hours of waiting before he had to dress. He put down the patience cards he was shuffling.

'A man to see me? Who is he, Fred?'

'I don't know: I've never seen him before. Looks to me like a "busy".'

A detective! Monty's eyebrows rose, but not in trepidation. He had met many detectives in the course of his chequered career and had long since lost his awe of them.

'Show him in,' he said with a nod.

The slim man in evening dress who came softly into the room was a stranger to Monty, who knew most of the prominent figures in the world of criminal detection. And yet his face was in some way familiar.

'Captain Newton?' he asked.

'That is my name.' Newton rose with a smile.

The visitor looked slowly round towards the door through which the footman had gone.

'Do your servants always listen at the keyhole?' he asked, in a quiet, measured tone, and Newton's face went a dusky red. In two strides he was at the door and had flung it open, just in time to see the disappearing heels of the footman.

'Here, you!' He called the man back, a scowl on his face. 'If you want to know anything, will you come in and ask?' he roared. 'If I catch you listening at my door, I'll murder you!'

The man with a muttered excuse made a hurried escape.

'How did you know?' growled Newton, as he came back into the room and slammed the door behind him.

'I have an instinct for espionage,' said the stranger, and went on, without a break: 'I have called for Miss Mirabelle Leicester.'

Newton's eyes narrowed.

'Oh, you have, have you?' he said softly. 'Miss Leicester is not in the house. She left a quarter of an hour ago.'

'I did not see her come out of the house.'

'No, the fact is, she went out by way of the mews. My – er – ' he was going to say 'sister' but thought better of it – 'my young friend – '

'Flash Jane Smith,' said the stranger. 'Yes?'

Newton's colour deepened. He was rapidly reaching the point when his sang-froid, nine-tenths of his moral assets, was in danger of deserting him.

'Who are you, anyway?' he asked.

The stranger wetted his lips with the tip of his tongue, a curiously irritating action of his, for some inexplicable reason.

'My name is Leon Gonsalez,' he said simply.

Instinctively the man drew back. Of course! Now he remembered, and the colour had left his cheeks, leaving him grey. With an effort he forced a smile.

'One of the redoubtable Four Just Men? What extraordinary birds you are!' he said. 'I remember ten-fifteen years ago, being scared out of my life by the very mention of your name – you came to punish where the law failed, eh?'

'You must put that in your reminiscences,' said Leon gently. 'For the moment I am not in an autobiographical mood.'

But Newton could not be silenced.

'I know a man' – he was speaking slowly, with quiet vehemence – 'who will one day cause you a great deal of inconvenience, Mr Leon Gonsalez: a man who never forgets you in his prayers. I won't tell you who he is.'

'It is unnecessary. You are referring to the admirable Oberzohn. Did I not kill his brother . . . ? Yes, I thought I was right. He was the man with the oxycephalic head and the queerly prognathic jaw. An interesting case: I would like to have had his measurements, but I was in rather a hurry.'

He spoke almost apologetically for his haste.

'But we're getting away from the subject, Mr Newton. You say this young lady has left your house by the mews, and you were about to suggest she left in the care of Miss – I don't know what you call her. Why did she leave that way?'

Leon Gonsalez had something more than an instinct for espionage: he had an instinct for truth, and he knew two things immediately: first, that Newton was not lying when he said the girl had left the house; secondly, that there was an excellent, but not necessarily a sinister, reason for the furtive departure.

'Where has she gone?'

'Home,' said the other laconically. 'Where else should she go?'

'She came to dinner . . . intending to stay the night?'

'Look here, Gonsalez,' interrupted Monty Newton savagely. 'You and your gang were wonderful people twenty years ago, but a lot has happened since then – and we don't shiver at the name of the Three Just Men. I'm not a child – do you get that? And you're not so very terrible at close range. If you want to complain to the police – '

'Meadows is outside. I persuaded him to let me see you first,' said Leon, and Newton started.

'Outside?' incredulously.

In two strides he was at the window and had pulled aside the blind. On the other side of the street a man was standing on the edge of the sidewalk, intently surveying the gutter. He knew him at once.

'Well, bring him in,' he said.

'Where has this young lady gone? That is all I want to know.'

'She has gone home, I tell you.'

Leon went to the door and beckoned Meadows; they spoke together in low tones, and then Meadows entered the room and was greeted with a stiff nod from the owner of the house.

'What's the idea of this, Meadows – sending this bird to cross-examine me?'

'This bird came on his own,' said Meadows coldly, 'if you mean Mr Gonsalez? I have no right to prevent any person from cross-examining you. Where is the young lady?'

'I tell you, she has gone home. If you don't believe me, search the house – either of you.'

He was not bluffing: Leon was sure of that. He turned to the detective.

'I personally have no wish to trouble this gentleman any more.'

He was leaving the room when, from over his shoulder: 'That snake is busy again, Newton.'

'What snake are you talking about?'

'He killed a man tonight on the Thames Embankment. I hope it will not spoil Lisa Marthon's evening.'

Meadows, watching the man, saw him change colour.

'I don't know what you mean,' he said loudly.

'You arranged with Lisa to pick up Barberton tonight and get him talking. And there she is, poor girl, all dressed to kill, and only a dead man to vamp – only a murdered man.' He turned suddenly, and his voice grew hard. 'That is a good word, isn't it, Newton – murder?'

'I didn't know anything about it.'

As Newton's hand came towards the bell: 'We can show ourselves out,' said Leon.

He shut the door behind him, and presently there was a slam of the outer door. Monty got to the window too late to see his unwelcome guests depart, and went up to his room to change, more than a little perturbed in mind.

The footman called him from the hall.

'I'm sorry about that affair, sir. I thought it was a "busy".'

'You think too much, Fred' – Newton threw the words down at his servitor with a snarl. 'Go back to your place – which is the servants' hall. I'll ring you if I want you.'

He resumed his progress up the stairs and the man turned sullenly away.

He opened the door of his room, switched on the light, had closed the door and was half-way to his dressing-table, when an arm like steel closed round his neck, he was jerked suddenly backward on to the floor, and looked up into the inscrutable face of Gonsalez.

'Shout and you die!' whispered a voice in his ear.

Newton lay quiet.

'I'll fix you for this,' he stammered.

The other shook his head.

'I think not, if by "fixing" me you mean you're going to complain to the police. You've been under my watchful eye for quite a long time, Monty Newton, and you'll be amazed to learn that I've made several visits to your house. There is a little wall safe behind that curtain' – he nodded towards the corner of the room – 'would you be surprised to learn that I've had the door open and every one of its documentary contents photographed?'

He saw the fear in the man's eyes as he snapped a pair of aluminium handcuffs of curious design about Monty's wrists. With hardly an effort he lifted him, heavy as he was, threw him on the bed, and, having locked the door, returned, and, sitting on the bed, proceeded first to strap his ankles and then leisurely to take off his prisoner's shoes.

'What are you going to do?' asked Monty in alarm.

'I intend finding out where Miss Leicester has been taken,' said Gonsalez, who had stripped one shoe and, pulling off the silken sock, was examining the man's bare foot critically. 'Ordinary and strictly legal inquiries take time and fail at the end – unfortunately for you, I have not a minute to spare.'

'I tell you she's gone home.'

Leon did not reply. He pulled open a drawer of the bureau, searched for some time, and presently found what he sought: a thin silken scarf. This, despite the struggles of the man on the bed, he fastened about his mouth.

'In Mosamodes,' he said – 'and if you ever say that before my friend George Manfred, be careful to give its correct pronunciation: he is rather touchy on the point – some friends of yours took a man named Barberton, whom they subsequently murdered, and tried to make him talk by burning his feet. He was a hero. I'm going to see how heroic you are.'

'For God's sake don't do it!' said the muffled voice of Newton.

Gonsalez was holding a flat metal case which he had taken from his pocket, and the prisoner watched him, fascinated, as he removed the lid, and snapped a cigar-lighter close to its blackened surface. A blue flame rose and swayed in the draught.

'The police force is a most excellent institution,' said Leon. He had found a silver shoe-horn on the table and was calmly heating it in the light of the flame, holding the rapidly warming hook with a silk handkerchief. 'But unfortunately, when you are dealing with crimes of violence, moral suasion and gentle treatment produce nothing more poignant in the bosom of your adversary than a sensation of amused and derisive contempt. The English, who make a god of the law, gave up imprisoning thugs and flogged them, and there are few thugs left. When the Russian gunmen came to London, the authorities did the only intelligent thing – they held back the police and brought up the artillery, having only one desire, which was to kill the gunmen at any expense. Violence fears violence. The gunman lives in the terror of the gun – by the way, I understand the old guard is back in full strength?'

When Leon started in this strain he could continue for hours.

'I don't know what you mean,' mumbled Monty.

'You wouldn't.' The intruder lifted the blackened, smoking shoe-horn, brought it as near to his face as he dared.

'Yes, I think that will do,' he said, and came slowly towards the bed.

The man drew up his feet in anticipation of pain, but a long hand caught him by the ankles and drew them straight again.

'They've gone to the Arts Ball.' Even through the handkerchief the voice sounded hoarse.

'The Arts Ball?' Gonsalez looked down at him, and then, throwing the hot shoe-horn into the fire-place, he removed the gag. 'Why have they gone to the Arts Ball?'

'I wanted them out of the way tonight.'

'Is Oberzohn likely to be at the Arts Ball?'

'Oberzohn?' The man's laugh bordered on the hysteric.

'Or Gurther?'

This time Mr Newton did not laugh.

'I don't know who you mean,' he said.

'We'll go into that later,' replied Leon lightly, pulling the knot of the handkerchief about the ankles. 'You may get up now. What time do you expect them back?'

'I don't know. I told Joan not to hurry, as I was meeting somebody here tonight.'

Which sounded plausible. Leon remembered that the Arts Ball was a fancy dress affair, and there was some reason for the departure from the mews instead of from the front of the house. As though he were reading his thoughts, Newton said: 'It was Miss Leicester's idea, going through the back. She was rather shy . . . she was wearing a domino.'

'Colour?'

'Green, with a reddish hood.'

Leon looked at him quickly.

'Rather distinctive. Was that the idea?'

'I don't know what the idea was,' growled Newton, sitting on the edge of the bed and pulling on a sock. 'But I do know this, Gonsalez,' he said, with an outburst of anger which was half fear; 'that you'll be sorry you did this to me!'

Leon walked to the door, turned the key and opened it.

'I only hope that you will not be sorry I did not kill you,' he said, and was gone.

Monty Newton waited until from his raised window he saw the slim figure pass along the sidewalk and disappear round a corner, and then he hurried down, with one shoe on and one off, to call New Cross 93.

Chapter 8

The house of Oberzohn

In a triangle two sides of which were expressed by the viaducts of converging railroads and the base by the dark and sluggish waters of the Grand Surrey Canal, stood the gaunt ruins of a store in which had once been housed the merchandise of the O. & S. Company. A Zeppelin in passing had dropped an incendiary bomb at random, and torn a great ugly gap in the roof. The fire that followed left the iron frames of the windows twisted and split; the roof by some miracle remained untouched except for the blackened edges about the hole through which the flames had rushed to the height of a hundred feet.

The store was flush with the canal towing-path; barges had moored here, discharging rubber in bales, palm nut, nitrates even, and had restocked with Manchester cloth and case upon case of Birmingham-made geegaws of brass and lacquer.

Mr Oberzohn invariably shipped his spirituous cargoes from Hamburg, since Germany is the home of synthesis. In the centre of the triangle was a red-brick villa, more unlovely than the factory, missing as it did that ineffable grandeur, made up of tragedy and pathos, attaching to a burnt-out building, however ugly it may have been in its prime.

The villa was built from a design in Mr Oberzohn's possession, and was the exact replica of the house in Sweden where he was born. It had high, gabled ends at odd and unexpected places. The roof was shingled with grey tiles; there were glass panels in the curious-looking door, and iron ornaments in the shape of cranes and dogs flanking the narrow path through the rank nettle and dock which constituted his garden.

Here he dwelt, in solitude, yet not in solitude, for two men lived in the house, and there was a stout Swedish cook and a very plain Danish maid, a girl of vacant countenance, who worked from sun-up to midnight without complaint, who seldom spoke and never smiled. The two men were somewhere in the region of thirty. They occupied the turret rooms at each end of the building, and had little community of interest. They sometimes played cards together with an old and greasy pack, but neither spoke more than was necessary. They were lean, hollow-faced men, with a certain physiognomical resemblance. Both had thin, straight lips; both had round, staring, dark eyes filled with a bright but terrifying curiosity.

'They look,' reported Leon Gonsalez, when he went to examine the ground, 'as if they are watching pigs being killed and enjoying every minute of it. Iwan Pfeiffer is one, Sven Gurther is the other. Both have escaped the gallows or the axe in Germany; both have convictions against them. They are typical German-trained criminals, as pitiless as wolves. Dehumanized.'

The 'Three', as was usual, set the machinery of the law in motion, and found that the hands of the police were tied. Only by stretching the law could the men be deported, and the law is difficult to stretch. To all appearance they offended in no respect. A woman, by no means the most desirable of citizens, laid a complaint against one. There was an investigation – proof was absent; the very character of the complainant precluded a conviction, and the matter was dropped – by the police.

Somebody else moved swiftly.

One morning, just before daybreak, a policeman patrolling the tow-path heard a savage snarl and looked round for the dog. He found instead, up one of those narrow entries leading to the canal bank, a man. He was tied to the stout sleeper fence, and his bare back showed marks of a whip. Somebody had held him up at night as he prowled the bank in search of amusement, had tied and flogged him. Twenty-five lashes: an expert thought the whip used was the official cat-o'-nine-tails.

Scotland Yard, curious, suspicious, sought out the Three Just Men. They had alibis so complete as to be unbreakable. Sven Gurther went unavenged – but he kept from the tow-path thereafter.

In this house of his there were rooms which only Dr Oberzohn visited. The Danish maid complained to the cook that when she had passed the door of one as the doctor came out, a blast of warm, tainted air had rushed out and made her cough for an hour. There was another room in which from time to time the doctor had installed a hotchpotch of apparatus. Vulcanizing machines, electrical machines (older and more used than Mirabelle had seen in her brief stay in the City Road), a liquid air plant, not the most up-to-date but serviceable.

He was not, curiously enough, a doctor in the medical sense. He was not even a doctor of chemistry. His doctorate was in Literature and Law. These experiments of his were hobbies – hobbies that he had pursued from his childhood.

On this evening he was sitting in his stuffy parlour reading a close-printed and closer-reasoned volume of German philosophy, and thinking of something else. Though the sun had only just set, the blinds and curtains were drawn; a wood fire crackled in the grate, and the bright lights of three half-watt lamps made glaring radiance.

An interruption came in the shape of a telephone call. He listened, grunting replies.

'So!' he said at last, and spoke a dozen words in his strange English.

Putting aside his book, he hobbled in his velvet slippers across the room and pressed twice upon the bell-push by the side of the fire-place. Gurther came in noiselessly and stood waiting.

He was grimy, unshaven. The pointed chin and short upper lip were blue. The V of his shirt visible above the waistcoat was soiled and almost black at the edges. He stood at attention, smiling vacantly, his eyes fixed at a point above the doctor's head.

Dr Oberzohn lifted his eyes from his book.

'I wish you to be a gentleman of club manner tonight,' he said. He spoke in that hard North-German tongue which the Swede so readily acquires.

'*Ja*, Herr Doktor!'

The man melted from the room.

Dr Oberzohn for some reason hated Germans. So, for the matter of that, did Gurther and Pfeiffer, the latter being Polish by extraction and Russian by birth. Gurther hated Germans because they stormed the little jail at Altostadt to kill him after the dogs found Frau Siedlitz's body. He would have died then but for the green police, who scented a Communist rising, scattered the crowd and sent Gurther by road to the nearest big town under escort. The two escorting policemen were never seen again. Gurther reappeared mysteriously in England two years after, bearing a veritable passport. There was no proof even that he was Gurther – Leon knew, Manfred knew, Poiccart knew.

There had been an alternative to the whipping.

'It would be a simple matter to hold his head under water until he was drowned,' said Leon.

They debated the matter, decided against this for no sentimental or moral reason – none save expediency. Gurther had his whipping and never knew how near to the black and greasy water of the canal he had been.

Dr Oberzohn resumed his book – a fascinating book that was all about the human soul and immortality and time. He was in the very heart of an analysis of eternity when Gurther reappeared dressed in the 'gentleman-club manner'. The dress-coat fitted perfectly; shirt and waistcoat were exactly the right cut. The snowy shirt, the braided trousers, the butterfly bow, and winged collar . . .

'That is good.' Dr Oberzohn went slowly over the figure. 'But the studs should be pearl – not enamel. And the watch-chain is *démodé* – it is not worn. The gentleman-club manner does not allow of visible ornament Also I think a moustache . . . ?'

'*Ja*, Herr Doktor!'

Gurther, who was once an actor, disappeared again. When he returned the enamel studs had gone: there were small pearls in their place, and his white waistcoat had no chain across. And on his upper lip had sprouted a small brown moustache, so natural that even Oberzohn, scrutinizing closely, could find no fault with it. The doctor took a case from his pocket, fingered out three crisp notes.

'Your hands, please?'

Gurther took three paces to the old man, halted, clicked his heels and held out his hands for inspection.

'Good! You know Leon Gonsalez? He will be at the Arts Ball. He wears no fancy dress. He was the man who whipped you.'

'He was the man who whipped me,' said Gurther without heat.

There was a silence, Dr Oberzohn pursing his lips.

'Also, he did that which brands him as an infamous assassin . . . I think . . . yes, I think my dear Gurther . . . there will be a girl also, but the men of my police will be there to arrange such matters. Benton will give you instructions. For you, only Gonsalez.'

Gurther bowed stiffly.

'I have implored the order,' he said, bowed again and withdrew. Later, Dr Oberzohn heard the drone of the little car as it bumped and slithered across the grass to the road. He resumed his book: this matter of eternity was fascinating.

*   *   *

The Arts Ball at the Corinthian Hall was one of the events of the season, and the tickets, issued exclusively to the members of three clubs, were eagerly sought by society people who could not be remotely associated with any but the art of living.

When the girl came into the crowded hall, she looked around in wonder. The balconies, outlined in soft lights and half-hidden with flowers, had been converted into boxes; the roof had been draped with blue and gold tissue; at one end of the big hall was a veritable bower of roses, behind which one of the two bands was playing. Masks in every conceivable guise were swinging rhythmically across the polished floor. To the blasé, there was little difference between the Indians, the pierrots and the cavaliers to be seen here and those they had seen a hundred times on a hundred different floors.

As the girl gazed round in wonder and delight, forgetting all her misgivings, two men, one in evening dress, the other in the costume of a brigand, came from under the shadow of the balcony towards them.

'Here are our partners,' said Joan, with sudden vivacity. 'Mirabelle, I want you to know Lord Evington.'

The man in evening dress stroked his little moustache, clicked his heels and bent forward in a stiff bow. He was thin-faced, a little pallid, unsmiling. His round, dark eyes surveyed her for a second, and then:

'I'm glad to meet you, Miss Leicester,' he said, in a high, harsh voice, that had just the trace of a foreign accent.

This struck the girl with as much surprise as the cold kiss he had implanted upon her hand, and, as if he read her thoughts, he went on quickly: 'I have lived so long abroad that England and English manners are strange to me. Won't you dance? And had you not better mask? I must apologise to you for my costume.' He shrugged his shoulders. 'But there was no gala dress available.'

She fixed the red mask, and in another second she was gliding through the crowd and was presently lost to view.

'I don't understand it all, Benton.'

Joan was worried and frightened. She had begun to realize that the game she played was something different . . . her part more sinister than any role she had yet filled. To jolly along the gilded youth to the green tables of Captain Monty Newton was one thing; but never before had she seen the gang working against a woman.

'I don't know,' grumbled the brigand, who was not inaptly arrayed. 'There's been a hurry call for everybody.' He glanced round uneasily as though he feared his words might be overheard. 'All the guns are here – Defson, Cuccini, Jewy Stubbs . . . '

'The guns?' she whispered in horror, paling under her rouge. 'You mean . . . ?'

'The guns are out: that's all I know,' he said doggedly. 'They started drifting in half an hour before you came.'

Joan was silent, her heart racing furiously. Then Monty had told her the truth. She knew that somewhere behind Oberzohn, behind Monty Newton, was a force perfectly dovetailed into the machine, only one cog of which she had seen working. These card parties of Monty's were profitable enough, but for a long time she had had a suspicion that they were the merest side-line. The organization maintained a regular corps of gunmen, recruited from every quarter of the globe. Monty Newton talked sometimes in his less sober moments of what he facetiously described as the 'Old Guard'. How they were employed, on what excuse, for what purpose, she had never troubled to think. They came and went from England in batches. Once Monty had told her that Oberzohn's people had gone to Smyrna, and he talked vaguely of unfair competition that had come to the traders of the O. & S. outfit. Afterwards she read in the paper of a 'religious riot' which resulted in the destruction by fire of a great block of business premises. After that Monty spoke no more of competition. The Old Guard returned to England, minus one of its number, who had been shot in the stomach in the course of this 'religious riot'. What particular faith he possessed in such a degree as to induce him to take up arms for the cause, she never learned. She knew he was dead, because Monty had written to the widow, who lived in the Bronx.

Joan knew a lot about Monty's business, for an excellent reason. She was with him most of the time; and whether she posed as his niece or daughter, his sister, or some closer relationship, she was undoubtedly the nearest to a confidante he possessed.

'Who is that man with the moustache – is he one?' she asked.

'No; he's Oberzohn's man – for God's sake don't tell Monty I told you all this! I got orders tonight to put him wise about the girl.'

'What about her . . . what are they doing with her?' she gasped in terror.

'Let us dance,' said Benton, and half guided, half carried her into the throng. They had reached the centre of the floor when, with no warning, every light in the hall went out.

Chapter 9

Before the lights went out

The band had stopped, a rustle of hand-clapping came from the hot dancers, and almost before the applause had started the second band struck up 'Kulloo'.

Mirabelle was not especially happy. Her partner was the most correct of dancers, but they lacked just that unity of purpose, the oneness of interest which makes all the difference between the ill- and the well-matched.

'May we sit down?' she begged. 'I am rather hot.'

'Will the gracious lady come to the little hall?' he asked. 'It is cooler there, and the chairs are comfortable.'

She looked at him oddly.

' "Gracious lady" is a German expression – why do you use it, Lord Evington? I think it is very pretty,' she hastened to assure him.

'I lived for many years in Germany,' said Mr Gurther. 'I do not like the German people – they are so stupid.'

If he had said 'German police' he would have been nearer to the truth; and had he added that the dislike was mutual, he might have gained credit for his frankness.

At the end of the room, concealed by the floral decorations of the bandstand, was a door which led to a smaller room, ordinarily separated from the main hall by folding doors which were seldom opened. Tonight the annexe was to be used as a conservatory. Palms and banked flowers were everywhere. Arbours had been artificially created, and there were cosy nooks, half-hidden by shrubs, secluded seats and tables, all that ingenuity could design to meet the wishes of sitters-out.

He stood invitingly at the entrance of a little grotto, dimly illuminated by one Chinese lantern.

'I think we will sit in the open,' said Mirabelle, and pulled out a chair.

'Excuse me.'

Instantly he was by her side, the chair arranged, a cushion found, and she sank down with a sigh of relief. It was early yet for the loungers: looking round, she saw that, but for a solitary waiter fastening his apron with one eye upon possible customers, they were alone.

'You will drink wine . . . no? An orangeade? Good!' He beckoned the waiter and gave his order. 'You must excuse me if I am a little strange. I have been in Germany for many years – except during the war, when I was in France.'

Mr Gurther had certainly been in Germany for many years, but he had never been in France. Nor had he heard a shot fired in the war. It is true that an aerial bomb had exploded perilously near the prison at Mainz in which he was serving ten years for murder, but that represented his sole warlike experience.

'You live in the country, of course?'

'In London: I am working with Mr Oberzohn.'

'So: he is a good fellow. A gentleman.'

She had not been very greatly impressed by the doctor's breeding, but it was satisfying to hear a stranger speak with such heartiness of her new employer. Her mind at the moment was on Heavytree Farm: the cool parlour with its chintzes – a room, at this hour, fragrant with the night scents of flowers which came stealing through the open casement. There was a fox-terrier, Jim by name, who would be wandering disconsolately from room to room, sniffing unhappily at the hall door. A lump came up into her throat. She felt very far from home and very lonely. She wanted to get up and run back to where she had left Joan and tell her that she had changed her mind and must go back to Gloucester that night . . . she looked impatiently for the waiter. Mr Gurther was fiddling with some straws he had taken from the glass container in the centre of the table. One end of the straws showed above the edge of the table, the others were thrust deep in the wide-necked little bottle he had in the other hand. The hollow straws held half an inch of the red powder that filled the bottle.

'Excuse!'

The waiter put the orangeades on the table and went away to get change. Mirabelle's eyes were wistfully fixed on a little door at the end of the room. It gave to the street, and there were taxicabs which could get her to Paddington in ten minutes.

When she looked round he was stirring the amber contents of her glass with a spoon. Two straws were invitingly protruding from the foaming orangeade. She smiled and lifted the glass as he fitted a cigarette into his black holder.

'I may smoke – yes?'

The first taste she had through the straws was one of extreme bitterness. She made a wry face and put down the glass.

'How horrid!'

'Did it taste badly . . . ?' he began, but she was pouring out water from a bottle.

'It was most unpleasant – '

'Will you try mine, please?' He offered the glass to her and she drank. 'It may have been something in the straw.' Here he was telling her the fact.

'It was . . . '

The room was going round and round, the floor was rising up and down like the deck of a ship in a stormy sea. She rose, swayed, and caught him by the arm.

'Open the little door, waiter, please – the lady is faint.'

The waiter turned to the door and threw it open. A man stood there – just outside the door. He wore over his dinner dress a long cloak in the Spanish style. Gurther stood staring, a picture of amused dismay, his cigarette still unlit. He did not move his hands. Gonsalez was waiting there, alert . . . death grinning at him . . . and then the room went inky black. Somebody had turned the main switch.

Chapter 10

When the lights went out

Five, ten minutes passed before the hall-keeper tripped and stumbled and cursed his way to the smaller room and, smashing down the hired flowers, he passed through the wreckage of earthen pots and tumbled mould to the control. Another second and the rooms were brilliantly lit again – the band struck up a two-step and fainting ladies were escorted to the decent obscurity of their retiring rooms.

The manager of the hall came flying into the annexe.

'What happened – the main fuse gone?'

'No,' said the hall-keeper sourly, 'some fool turned over the switch.'

The agitated waiter protested that nobody had been near the switch-box.

'There was a lady and gentleman here, and another gentleman outside.' He pointed to the open door.

'Where are they now?'

'I don't know. The lady was faint.'

The three had disappeared when the manager went out into a small courtyard that led round the corner of the building to a side street. Then he came back on a tour of inspection.

'Somebody did it from the yard. There's a window open – you can reach the switch easily.'

The window was fastened and locked.

'There is no lady or gentleman in the yard,' he said. 'Are you sure they did not go into the big hall?'

'In the dark – maybe.'

The waiter's nervousness was understandable. Mr Gurther had given him a five-pound note and the man had not as yet delivered the change. Never would he return to claim it if all that his keen ears heard was true.

Four men had appeared in the annexe: one shut the door and stood by it. The three others were accompanied by the manager, who called Phillips, the waiter.

'This man served them,' he said, troubled. Even the most innocent do not like police visitations. 'What was the gentleman like?'

Phillips gave a brief and not inaccurate description.

'That is your man, I think, Herr Fluen?'

The third of the party was bearded and plump; he wore a Derby hat with evening dress.

'That is Gurther,' he nodded. 'It will be a great pleasure to meet him. For eight months the Embassy has been striving for his extradition. But our people at home . . . !'

He shrugged his shoulders. All properly constituted officials behave in such a manner when they talk of Governments.

'The lady now' – Inspector Meadows was patently worried – 'she was faint, you say. Had she drunk anything?'

'Orangeade – there is the glass. She said there was something nasty in the straws. These.'

Phillips handed them to the detective. He wetted his fin from them, touched his tongue and spat out quickly.

'Yes,' he said, and went out by the little door.

Gonsalez, of course: but where had he gone, and how, with a drugged girl on his hands and the Child of the Snake? Gurther was immensely quick to strike, and an icy-hearted man: the presence of a woman would not save Leon.

'When the light went out – ' began the waiter, and the trouble cleared from Mr Meadows's face.

'Of course – I had forgotten that,' he said softly. 'The lights went out!'

All the way back to the Yard he was trying to bring something from the back of his mind – something that was there, the smooth tip of it tantalizingly displayed, yet eluding every grasp. It had nothing to do with the lights – nor Gonsalez, nor yet the girl. Gurther? No. Nor Manfred? What was it? A name had been mentioned to him that day – it had a mysterious significance. A golden idol! He picked up the end of the thought . . . Johnny! Manfred's one mystery. That was the dust which lay on all thought. And now that he remembered he was disappointed. It was so ridiculously unimportant a matter to baffle him.

He left his companions at the corner of Curzon Street and went alone to the house. There was a streak of light showing between the curtains in the upstairs room. The passage was illuminated – Poiccart answered his ring at once.

'Yes, George and Leon were here a little time back – the girl? No, they said nothing about a girl. They looked rather worried, I thought. Miss Leicester, I suppose? Won't you come in?'

'No, I can't wait. There's a light in Manfred's room.'

The ghost of a smile lit the heavy face and faded as instantly.

'My room also,' he said. 'Butlers take vast liberties in the absence of their masters. Shall I give a message to George?'

'Ask him to call me at the Yard.'

Poiccart closed the door on him; stopped in the passage to arrange a salver on the table and hung up a hat. All this Meadows saw through the fanlight and walking-stick periscope which is so easily fitted and can be of such value. And seeing, his doubts evaporated.

Poiccart went slowly up the stairs into the little office room, pulled back the curtains and opened the window at the top. The next second, the watching detective saw the light go out and went away.

'I'm sorry to keep you in the dark,' said Poiccart.

The men who were in the room waited until the shutters were fast and the curtains pulled across, and then the light flashed on. White of face, her eyes closed, her breast scarcely moving, Mirabelle Leicester lay on the long settee. Her domino was a heap of shimmering green and scarlet on the floor, and Leon was gently sponging her face, George Manfred watching from the back of the settee, his brows wrinkled.

'Will she die?' he asked bluntly.

'I don't know: they sometimes die of that stuff,' replied Leon cold-bloodedly. 'She must have had it pretty raw. Gurther is a crude person.'

'What was it?' asked George.

Gonsalez spread out his disengaged hand in a gesture of uncertainty.

'If you can imagine morphia with a kick in it, it was that. I don't know. I hope she doesn't die: she is rather young – it would be the worst of bad luck.'

Poiccart stirred uneasily. He alone had within his soul what Leon would call 'a trace' of sentiment.

'Could we get Elver?' he asked anxiously, and Leon looked up with his boyish smile. 'Growing onions in Seville has softened you, Raymondo *mio*!' He never failed in moments of great strain to taunt the heavy man with his two years of agricultural experiment, and they knew that the gibes were deliberately designed to steady his mind. 'Onions are sentimental things – they make you cry: a vegetable *muchos simpatico*! This woman is alive!'

Her eyelids had fluttered twice. Leon lifted the bare arm, inserted the needle of a tiny hypodermic and pressed home the plunger.

'Tomorrow she will feel exactly as if she had been drunk,' he said calmly, 'and in her mouth will be the taste of ten rank cigars. Oh, señorinetta, open thy beautiful eyes and look upon thy friends!'

The last sentence was in Spanish. She heard: the lids fluttered and rose.

'You're a long way from Heavytree Farm, Miss Leicester.'

She looked up wonderingly into the kindly face of George Manfred.

'Where am I?' she asked faintly, and closed her eyes again with a grimace of pain.

'They always ask that – just as they do in books,' said Leon oracularly. 'If they don't say "Where am I?" they ask for their mothers. She's quite out of danger.'

One hand was on her wrist, another at the side of her neck.

'Remarkably regular. She has a good head – mathematical probably.'

'She is very beautiful,' said Poiccart in a hushed voice.

'All people are beautiful – just as all onions are beautiful. What is the difference between a lovely maid and the ugliest of duennas – what but a matter of pigmentation and activity of tissue? Beneath that, an astounding similarity of the circulatory, sustentacular, motorvascular – '

'How long have we got?' Manfred interrupted him, and Leon shook his head.

'I don't know – not long, I should think. Of course, we could have told Meadows and he'd have turned out police reserves, but I should like to keep them out of it.'

'The Old Guard was there?'

'Every man jack of them – those tough lads! They will be here just as soon as the Herr Doktor discovers what is going forward. Now, I think you can travel. I want her out of the way.'

Stooping, he put his hands under her and lifted her. The strength in his frail body was a never-ending source of wonder to his two friends.

They followed him down the stairs and along the short passage, down another flight to the kitchen. Manfred opened a door and went out into the paved yard. There was a heavier door in the boundary wall. He opened this slowly and peeped out. Here was the inevitable mews. The sound of an engine running came from a garage near by. Evidently somebody was on the look out for them. A long-bodied car drew up noiselessly and a woman got out. Beside the driver at the wheel sat two men.

'I think you'll just miss the real excitement,' said Gonsalez, and then to the nurse he gave a few words of instruction and closed the door on her.

'Take the direct road,' he said to the driver. 'Swindon – Gloucester. Good night.'

'Good night, sir.'

He watched anxiously as the machine swung into the main road. Still he waited, his head bent. Two minutes went by, and the faint sound of a motor-horn, a long blast and a short, and he sighed.

'They're clear of the danger zone,' he said.

Plop!

He saw the flash, heard the smack of the bullet as it struck the door, and his hand stiffened. There was a thudding sound – a scream of pain from a dark corner of the mews and the sound of voices. Leon drew back into the yard and bolted the door.

'He had a new kind of silencer. Oberzohn is rather a clever old bird. But my air pistol against their gun for noiselessness.'

'I didn't expect the attack from that end of the mews.' Manfred was slipping a Browning back to his pocket.

'If they had come from the other end the car would not have passed – I'd like to get one of those silencers.'

They went into the house. Poiccart had already extinguished the passage light.

'You hit your man – does that thing kill?'

'By accident – it is possible. I aimed at his stomach: I fear that I hit him in the head. He would not have squealed for a stomach wound. I fear he is alive.'

He felt his way up the stairs and took up the telephone. Immediately a voice said, 'Number?'

'Give me 8877 Treasury.'

He waited, and then a different voice asked: 'Yes – Scotland Yard speaking.'

'Can you give me Mr Meadows?'

Manfred was watching him frowningly.

'That you, Meadows? . . . They have shot Leon Gonsalez – can you send police reserves and an ambulance?'

'At once.'

Leon hung up the receiver, hugging himself.

'The idea being – ?' said Poiccart.

'These people are clever.' Leon's voice was charged with admiration. 'They haven't cut the wires – they've simply tapped it at one end and thrown it out of order on the exchange side.'

'Phew!' Manfred whistled. 'You deceived me – you were talking to Oberzohn?'

'Captain Monty and Lew Cuccini. They may or may not be deceived, but if they aren't, we shall know all about it.'

He stopped dead. There was a knock on the front door, a single, heavy knock. Leon grinned delightedly.

'One of us is now supposed to open an upper window cautiously and look out, whereupon he is instantly gunned. I'm going to give these fellows a scare.'

He ran up the stairs to the top floor, and on the landing, outside an attic door, pulled at a rope. A fire ladder lying flat against the ceiling came down, and at the same time a small skylight opened. Leon went into the room, and his pocket-lamp located what he needed: a small papier-mache cylinder, not unlike a seven-pound shell. With this on his arm, he climbed up the ladder on to the roof, fixed the cylinder on a flat surface, and, striking a match, lit a touch-paper. The paper sizzled and spluttered, there was a sudden flash and 'boom!' a dull explosion, and a white ball shot up into the sky, described a graceful curve and burst into a shower of brilliant crimson stars. He waited till the last died out; then, with the hot cylinder under his arm, descended the ladder, released the rope that held it in place, and returned to his two friends.

'They will imagine a secret arrangement of signals with the police,' he said; 'unless my knowledge of their psychology is at fault, we shall not be bothered again.'

Ten minutes later there was another knock at the door, peremptory, almost official in its character.

'This,' said Leon, 'is a policeman to summon us for discharging fireworks in the public street!'

He ran lightly down into the hall and without hesitation pulled open the door. A tall, helmeted figure stood on the doorstep, note-book in hand.

'Are you the gentleman that let off that rocket – ' he began.

Leon walked past him, and looked up and down Curzon Street. As he had expected, the Old Guard had vanished.

Gurther

Monty Newton dragged himself home, a weary angry man, and let himself in with his key. He found the footman lying on the floor of the hall asleep, his greatcoat pulled over him, and stirred him to wakefulness with the toe of his boot.

'Get up,' he growled. 'Anybody been here?'

Fred rose, a little dazed, rubbing his eyes.

'The old man's in the drawing-room,' he said, and his employer passed on without another word.

As he opened the door, he saw that all the lights in the drawing-room were lit. Dr Oberzohn had pulled a small table near the fire, and before this he sat bolt upright, a tiny chess-board before him, immersed in a problem. He looked across to the newcomer for a second and then resumed his study of the board, made a move . . .

'Ach!' he said in tones of satisfaction. 'Leskina was wrong! It is possible to mate in five moves!'

He pushed the chessmen into confusion and turned squarely to face Newton.

'Well, have you concluded these matters satisfactorily?'

'He brought up the reserves,' said Monty, unlocking a tantalus on a side table and helping himself liberally to whisky. 'They got Cuccini through the jaw. Nothing serious.'

Dr Oberzohn laid his bony hands on his knees.

'Gurther must be disciplined,' he said. 'Obviously he has lost his nerve; and when a man loses his nerve also he loses his sense of time. And his timing – how deplorable! The car had not arrived; my excellent police had not taken position . . . deplorable!'

'The police are after him: I suppose you know that?' Newton looked over his glass.

Dr Oberzohn nodded.

'The extradition so cleverly avoided is now accomplished. But Gurther is too good a man to be lost. I have arranged a hiding-place for him. He is of many uses.'

'Where did he go?'

Dr Oberzohn's eyebrows wrinkled up and down.

'Who knows?' he said. 'He has the little machine. Maybe he has gone to the house – the green light in the top window will warn him and he will move carefully.'

Newton walked to the window and looked out. Chester Square looked ghostly in the grey light of dawn. And then, out of the shadows, he saw a figure move and walk slowly towards the south side of the square. 'They're watching this house,' he said, and laughed.

'Where is my young lady?' asked Oberzohn, who was staring glumly into the fire.

'I don't know . . . there was a car pulled out of the mews as one of our men "closed" the entrance. She has probably gone back to Heavytree Farm, and you can sell that laboratory of yours. There is only one way now, and that's the rough way. We have time – we can do a lot in six weeks. Villa is coming this morning – I wish we'd taken that idol from the trunk. That may put the police on to the right track.'

Dr Oberzohn pursed his lips as though he were going to whistle, but he was guilty of no such frivolity.

'I am glad they found him,' he said precisely. 'To them it will be a scent. What shall they think, but that the unfortunate Barberton had come upon an old native treasure-house? No, I do not fear that.' He shook his head. 'Mostly I fear Mr Johnson Lee and the American, Elijah Washington.'

He put his hand into his jacket pocket and took out a thin pad of letters. 'Johnson Lee is for me difficult to understand. For what should a gentleman have to do with this boor that he writes so friendly letters to him?'

'How did you get these?'

'Villa took them: it was one of the intelligent actions also to leave the statue.'

He passed one of the letters across to Newton. It was addressed 'Await arrival, Poste Restante, Mosamedes.' The letter was written in a curiously round, boyish hand. Another remarkable fact was that it was perforated across the page at regular intervals, and upon the lines formed by this perforation Mr Johnson Lee wrote –

Dear B, [the letter ran] 'I have instructed my bankers to cable you £500. I hope this will carry you through and leave enough to pay your fare home. You may be sure that I shall not breathe a word, and your letters, of course, nobody in the house can read but me. Your story is amazing and I advise you to come home at once and see Miss Leicester.

Your friend,

Johnson Lee

The note-paper was headed 'Rath Hall, January 13th'.

'They came to me today. If I had seen them before, there would have been no need for the regrettable happening.'

He looked thoughtfully at his friend. 'They will be difficult: I had that expectation,' he said; and Monty knew that he referred to the Three Just Men. 'Yet they are mortal also – remember that, my Newton: they are mortal also.'

'As we are,' said Newton gloomily

'That is a question,' said Oberzohn, 'so far as I am concerned.'

Dr Oberzohn never jested; he spoke with the greatest calm and assurance. The other man could only stare at him.

Although it was light, a green lamp showed clearly in the turret room of the doctor's house as he came within sight of the ugly place. And, seeing that warning, he did not expect to be met in the passage by Gurther. The man had changed from his resplendent kit and was again in the soiled and shabby garments he had discarded the night before.

'You have come, Gurther?'

'*Ja*, Herr Doktor.'

'To my parlour!' barked Dr Oberzohn, and marched ahead.

Gurther followed him and stood with his back to the door, erect, his chin raised, his bright, curious eyes fixed on a point a few inches above his master's head.

'Tell me now.' The doctor's ungainly face was working ludicrously.

'I saw the man and struck, Herr Doktor, and then the lights went out and I went to the floor, expecting him to shoot . . . I think he must have taken the gracious lady. I did not see, for there was a palm between us. I returned at once to the greater hall, and walked through the people on the floor. They were very frightened.'

'You saw them?'

'Yes, Herr Doktor,' said Gurther. 'It is not difficult for me to see in the dark. After that I ran to the other entrance, but they were gone.'

'Come here.'

The man took two stilted paces towards the doctor and Oberzohn struck him twice in the face with the flat of his hand. Not a muscle of the man's face moved: he stood erect, his lips framed in a half-grin, his curious eyes staring straight ahead.

'That is for bad time, Gurther. Nobody saw you return?'

'No, Herr Doktor, I came on foot.'

'You saw the light?'

'Yes, Herr Doktor, and I thought it best to be here.'

'You were right,' said Oberzohn. 'March!'

He went into the forbidden room, turned the key, and passed into the super-heated atmosphere. Gurther stood attentively at the door. Presently the doctor came out, carrying a long case covered with baize under his arm. He handed it to the waiting man, went into the room, and, after a few minutes' absence, returned with a second case, a little larger.

'March!' he said.

Gurther followed him out of the house and across the rank, weed-grown 'garden' towards the factory. A white mist had rolled up from the canal, and factory and grounds lay under the veil.

He led the way through an oblong gap in the wall where once a door had stood, and followed a tortuous course through the blackened beams and twisted girders that littered the floor. Only a half-hearted attempt had been made to clear up the wreckage after the fire, and the floor was ankle-deep in charred shreds of burnt cloth. Near the far end of the building, Oberzohn stopped, put down his box and pushed aside the ashes with his foot until he had cleared a space about three feet square. Stooping, he grasped an iron ring and pulled, and a flagstone came up with scarcely an effort, for it was well counter-weighted. He took up the box again and descended the stone stairs, stopping only to turn on a light.

The vaults of the store had been practically untouched by the fire. There were shelves that still carried dusty bales of cotton goods. Oberzohn was in a hurry. He crossed the stone floor in two strides, pulled down the bar of another door, and, walking into the darkness, deposited his box on the floor.

The electric power of the factory had, in the old days, been carried on two distinct circuits, and the connection with the vaults was practically untouched by the explosion.

They were in a smaller room now, fairly comfortably furnished. Gurther knew it well, for it was here that he had spent the greater part of his first six months in England. Ventilation came through three small gratings near the roof. There was a furnace, and, as

Gurther knew, an ample supply of fuel in one of the three cellars that opened into the vault.

'Here will you stay until I send for you,' said Oberzohn. 'Tonight, perhaps, after they have searched. You have a pistol?'

'*Ja*, Herr Doktor.'

'Food, water, bedding – all you need.' Oberzohn jerked open another of the cellars and took stock of the larder. 'Tonight I may come for you – tomorrow night – who knows? You will light the fire at once.' He pointed to the two baize-covered boxes. 'Good morning, Gurther.'

'Good morning, Herr Doktor.'

Oberzohn went up to the factory level, dropped the trap and his foot pushed back the ashes which hid its presence, and with a cautious look round he crossed the field to his house. He was hardly in his study before the first police car came bumping along the lane.

Chapter 12
Leon theorizes

Making inquiries, Detective-Inspector Meadows discovered that, on the previous evening at eight o'clock, two men had called upon Barberton. The first of these was described as tall and rather aristocratic in appearance. He wore dark, horn-rimmed spectacles. The hôtel manager thought he might have been an invalid, for he walked with a stick. The second man seemed to have been a servant of some kind, for he spoke respectfully to the visitor.

'No, he gave no name, Mr Meadows,' said the manager. 'I told him of the terrible thing which had happened to Mr Barberton, and he was so upset that I didn't like to press the question.'

Meadows was on his circuitous way to Curzon Street when he heard this, and he arrived in time for breakfast. Manfred's servants regarded it as the one eccentricity of an otherwise normal gentleman that he invariably breakfasted with his butler and chauffeur. This matter had been discussed threadbare in the tiny servants' hall, and it no longer excited comment when Manfred telephoned down to the lower regions and asked for another plate.

The Triangle were in cheerful mood. Leon Gonsalez was especially bright and amusing, as he invariably was after such a night as he had spent.

'We searched Oberzohn's house from cellar to attic,' said Meadows when the plate had been laid.

'And of course you found nothing. The elegant Gurther?'

'He wasn't there. That fellow will keep at a distance if he knows that there's a warrant out for him. I suspect some sort of signal. There was a very bright green light burning in one of those ridiculous Gothic turrets.'

Manfred stifled a yawn. 'Gurther went back soon after midnight,' he said, 'and was there until Oberzohn's return.'

'Are you sure?' asked the astonished detective.

Leon nodded, his eyes twinkling. 'After that, one of those infernal river mists blotted out observation,' he said, 'but I should imagine Herr Gurther is not far away. Did you see his companion, Pfeiffer?'

Meadows nodded. 'Yes, he was cleaning boots when I arrived.'

'How picturesque!' said Gonzalez. 'I think he will have a valet the next time be goes to prison, unless the system has altered since your days, George?'

George Manfred, who had once occupied the condemned cell in Chelmsford Prison, smiled.

'An interesting man, Gurther,' mused Gonsalez. 'I have a feeling that he will escape hanging. So you could not find him? I found him last night. But for the lady, who was both an impediment and an interest, we might have put a period to his activities.' He caught Meadows's eye. 'I should have handed him to you, of course.'

'Of course,' said the detective dryly.

'A remarkable man, but nervous. You are going to see Mr Johnson Lee?'

'What made you say that?' asked the detective in astonishment, for he had not as yet confided his intention to the three men.

'He will surprise you,' said Leon. 'Tell me, Mr Meadows: when you and George so thoroughly and carefully searched Barberton's box, did you find anything that was suggestive of his being a cobbler, let us say – or a bookbinder?'

'I think in his sister's letter there was a reference to the books he had made. I found nothing particular except an awl and a long oblong of wood which was covered with pinpricks. As a matter of fact, when I saw it my first thought was that, living the kind of life he must have done in the wilderness, it was rather handy to be able to repair his own shoes. The idea of bookbinding is a new one.'

'I should say he never bound a book in his life, in the ordinary sense of the word,' remarked Manfred; 'and as Leon says, you will find Johnson Lee a very surprising man.'

'Do you know him?'

Manfred nodded gravely.

'I have just been on the telephone to him,' he said. 'You'll have to be careful of Mr Lee, Meadows. Our friend the snake may be biting his way, and will, if he hears a breath of suspicion that he was in Barberton's confidence.'

The detective put down his knife and fork.

'I wish you fellows would stop being mysterious,' he said, half annoyed, half amused. 'What is behind this business? You talk of the snake as though you could lay your hands on him.'

'And we could,' they said in unison.

'Who is he?' challenged the detective.

'The Herr Doktor,' smiled Gonsalez.

'Oberzohn?'

Leon nodded.

'I thought you would have discovered that by connecting the original three murders together – and murders they were. First – ' he ticked the names off on his fingers – 'we have a stockbroker. This gentleman was a wealthy speculator who occasionally financed highly questionable deals. Six months before his death he drew from the bank a very large sum of money in notes. By an odd coincidence the bank clerk, going out to luncheon, saw his client and Oberzohn driving past in a taxicab, and as they came abreast he saw a large blue envelope go into Oberzohn's pocket. The money had been put into a blue envelope when it was drawn. The broker had financed the doctor, and when the scheme failed and the money was lost, he not unnaturally asked for its return. He trusted Oberzohn not at all; carried his receipt about in his pocket, and never went anywhere unless he was armed – that fact did not emerge at the inquest, but you know it is true.'

Meadows nodded.

'He threatened Oberzohn with exposure at a meeting they had in Winchester Street, on the day of his death. That night he returns from a theatre or from his club, and is found dead on the doorstep. No receipt is found. What follows?

'A man, a notorious blackmailer, homeless and penniless, was walking along the Bayswater Road, probably looking for easy money, when he saw the broker's car going into Orme Place. He followed on the off-chance of begging a few coppers. The chauffeur saw him. The tramp, on the other hand, must have seen something else. He slept the next night at Rowton House, told a friend, who had been in prison with him, that he had a million pounds as good as in his hand . . .'

Meadows laughed helplessly.

'Your system of investigation is evidently more thorough than ours!'

'It is complementary to yours,' said George quietly. 'Go on, Leon.'

'Now what happened to our friend the burglar? He evidently saw somebody in Orme Place whom he either recognized or trailed to his home. For the next day or two he was in and out of public telephone booths, though no number has been traced. He goes to Hyde Park, obviously by appointment – and the snake bites!'

'There was another danger to the confederacy. The bank clerk, learning of the death of the client, is troubled. I have proof that he called Oberzohn on the 'phone. If you remember, when the broker's affairs were gone into, it was found that he was almost insolvent. A large sum of money had been drawn out of the bank and paid to "X". The certainty that he knew who "X" was worried this decent bank clerk, and he called Oberzohn, probably to ask him why he had not made a statement. On the day he telephoned the snake man, that day he died.'

The detective was listening in silent wonder. 'It sounds like a page out of a sensational novel,' he said, 'yet it hangs together.'

'It hangs together because it is true.' Poiccart's deep voice broke into the conversation. 'This has been Oberzohn's method all his life. He is strong for logic, and there is no more logical action in the world than the destruction of those who threaten your safety and life.'

Meadows pushed away his plate, his breakfast half eaten. 'Proof,' he said briefly.

'What proof can you have, my dear fellow?' scoffed Leon.

'The proof is the snake,' persisted Meadows. 'Show me how he could educate a deadly snake to strike, as he did, when the victim was under close observation, as in the case of Barberton, and I will believe you.'

The Three looked at one another and smiled together. 'One of these days I will show you,' said Leon. 'They have certainly tamed their snake! He can move so quickly that the human eye cannot follow him. Always he bites on the most vital part, and at the most favourable time. He struck at me last night, but missed me. The next time he strikes – ' he was speaking slowly and looking at the detective through the veriest slits of his half-closed eyelids – 'the next time he strikes, not all Scotland Yard on the one side, nor his agreeable company of gunmen on the other, will save him!'

Poiccart rose suddenly. His keen ears had heard the ring of a bell, and he went noiselessly down the stairs.

'The whole thing sounds like a romance to me.' Meadows was rubbing his chin irritably. 'I am staring at the covers of a book whilst you are reading the pages. I suppose you devils; have the A and Z of the story?'

Leon nodded.

'Why don't you tell me?'

'Because I value your life,' said Leon simply. 'Because I wish – we all wish – to keep the snake's attention upon ourselves.'

Poiccart came back at that moment and put his head in the door.

'Would you like to see Mr Elijah Washington?' he asked, and they saw by the gleam in his eyes that Mr Elijah Washington was well worth meeting.

He arrived a second or two later, a tall, broad-shouldered man with a reddish face. He wore pince-nez, and behind the rimless glasses his eyes were alive and full of bubbling laughter. From head to foot he was dressed in white; the cravat which flowed over the soft silk shirt was a bright yellow; the belt about his waist as bright as scarlet.

He stood beaming upon the company, his white panama crushed under his arm, both huge hands thrust into his trousers pockets.

'Glad to know you folks,' he greeted them in a deep boom of a voice. 'I guess Mr Barberton told you all about me. That poor little guy! Listen: he was a he-man all right, but kinder mysterious. They told me I'd find the police chief here – Captain Meadows?'

'Mister,' said the inspector, 'I'm that man.'

Washington put out his huge paw and caught the detective's hand with a grip that would have been notable in a boa constrictor.

'Glad to know you! My name is Elijah Washington – the Natural History Syndicate, Chicago.'

'Sit down, Mr Washington.' Poiccart pushed forward a chair.

'I want to tell you gentlemen that this Barberton was murdered. Snake? Listen, I know snakes – brought up with 'um! Snakes are my hobby: I know 'um from egg-eaters to "tigers" – *notechis sentatus*, moccasins, copperheads, corals, mamba, *fer de lance* – gosh! snakes are just common objects like flies. An' I tell you boys right here and now, that there ain't a snake in this or the next world that can climb up a parapet, bite a man and get away with it with a copper looking on.'

He beamed from one to the other: he was almost paternal.

'I'd like to have shown you folks a worse-than-mamba,' he said regretfully, 'but carrying round snakes in your pocket is just hot dog: it's like a millionaire wearin' diamond ear-rings just to show he can afford 'em. I liked that little fellow; I'm mighty sorry he's dead, but if any man tells you that a snake bit him, go right up to him, hit him on the nose, and say "Liar!" '

'You will have some coffee?' Manfred had rung the bell.

'Sure I will: never have got used to this tea-drinking habit. I'm on the wagon too: got scared up there in the back-lands of Angola – '

'What were you doing there?' asked Leon.

'Snakes,' said the other briefly. 'I represent an organization that supplies specimens to zoos and museums. I was looking for a flying snake – there ain't such a thing, though the natives say there is. I got a new kinder cobra – *viperidae crotalinae* – and yet not!'

He scratched his head, bringing his scientific perplexity into the room. Leon's heart went out to him.

He had met Barberton by accident. Without shame he confessed that he had gone to a village in the interior for a real solitary jag, and returning to such degree of civilization as Mossamedes represented, he found a group of Portuguese breeds squatting about a fire at which the man's feet were toasting.

'I don't know what he was – a prospector, I guess. He was one of those what-is-its you meet along that coast. I've met his kind most everywhere – as far south as Port Nottosh. In Angola there are scores: they go native at the end.'

'You can tell us nothing about Barberton?'

Mr Elijah Washington shook his head.

'No, sir: I know him same as I might know you. It got me curious when I found out the why of the torturing: he wouldn't tell where it was.'

'Where what was?' asked Manfred quickly, and Washington was surprised.

'Why, the writing they wanted to get. I thought maybe he'd told you. He said he was coming right along to spill all that part of it. It was a letter he'd found in a tin box – that was all he'd say.'

They looked at one another.

'I know no more about it than that,' Mr Washington added, when he saw Gonsalez' lips move. 'It was just a letter. Who it was from, why, what it was about, he never told me. My first idea was that he'd been flirting round about here, but divorce laws are mighty generous and they wouldn't trouble to get evidence that way. A man doesn't want any documents to get rid of his wife. I dare say you folks wonder why I've come along.' Mr Washington raised his steaming cup of coffee, which must have been nearly boiling, and drank it at one gulp. 'That's fine,' he said, 'the nearest to coffee I've had since I left home.'

He wiped his lips with a large and vivid silk handkerchief.

'I've come along, gentleman, because I've got a pretty good idea that I'd be useful to anybody who's snake-hunting in this little dorp.'

'It's rather a dangerous occupation, isn't it?' said Manfred quietly. Washington nodded.

'To you, but not to me,' he said. 'I am snake-proof.'

He pulled up his sleeve: the forearm was scarred and pitted with old wounds.

'Snakes,' he said briefly. 'That's cobra.' He pointed proudly. 'When that snake struck, my boys didn't wait for anything, they started dividing my kit. Sort of appointed themselves a board of executors and joint heirs of the family estate.'

'But you were very ill?' said Gonsalez.

Mr Washington shook his head.

'No, sir, not more than if a bee bit me, and not so much as if a wasp had got in first punch. Some people can eat arsenic, some people can make a meal of enough morphia to decimate a province. I'm snake-proof – been bitten ever since I was five.'

He bent over towards them, and his jolly face went suddenly serious. 'I'm the man you want,' he said.

'I think you are,' said Manfred slowly.

'Because this old snake ain't finished biting. There's a graft in it somewhere, and I want to find it. But first I want to vindicate the snake. Anybody who says a snake's naturally vicious doesn't understand. Snakes are timid, quiet, respectful things, and don't want no trouble with nobody. If a snake sees you coming, he naturally lights out for home. When momma snake's running around with her family, she's naturally touchy for fear you'd tread on any of her boys and girls, but she's a lady, and if you give her time she'll Maggie 'um and get 'um into the parlour where the foot of white man never trod.'

Leon was looking at him with a speculative eye.

'It is queer to think,' he said, speaking half to himself, 'that you may be the only one of us who will be alive this day week!'

Meadows, not easily shocked, felt a cold shiver run down his spine.

Chapter 13

Mirabelle goes home

The prediction that Leon Gonsalez had made was not wholly fulfilled, though he himself had helped to prevent the supreme distress
he prophesied. When Mirabelle Leicester awoke in the morning, her
head was thick and dull, and for a long time she lay between sleeping
and waking, trying to bring order to the confusion of her thoughts,
her eyes on the ceiling towards a gnarled oak beam which she had
seen before somewhere; and when at last she summoned sufficient
energy to raise herself on her elbow, she looked upon the very
familiar surroundings of her own pretty little room.

Heavytree Farm! What a curious dream she had had! A dream
filled with fleeting visions of old men with elongated heads, of dance
music and a crowded ball-room, of a slightly over-dressed man who
had been very polite to her at dinner. Where did she dine? She sat up
in bed, holding her throbbing head.

Again she looked round the room and slowly, out of her dreams,
emerged a few tangible facts. She was still in a state of bewilderment
when the door opened and Aunt Alma came in, and the unprepossessing face of her relative was accentuated by her look of anxiety.

'Hullo, Alma!' said Mirabelle dully. 'I've had such a queer dream.'

Alma pressed her lips tightly together as she placed a tray on a
table by the side of the bed.

'I think it was about that advertisement I saw.' And then, with a
gasp: 'How did I come here?'

'They brought you,' said Alma. 'The nurse is downstairs having
her breakfast. She's a nice woman and keeps press-cuttings.'

'The nurse?' asked Mirabelle in bewilderment.

'You arrived here at three o'clock in the morning in a motor-car.
You had a nurse with you.' Alma enumerated the circumstances in
chronological order. 'And two men. First one of the men got out and
knocked at the door. I was worried to death. In fact, I'd been worried
all the afternoon, ever since I had your wire telling me not to come
up to London.'

'But I didn't send any such wire,' replied the girl.

'After I came down, the man – he was really a gentleman and very pleasantly spoken – told me that you'd been taken ill and a nurse had brought you home. They then carried you, the two men and the nurse, upstairs and laid you on the bed, and nurse and I undressed you. I simply couldn't get you to wake up: all you did was to talk about the orangeade.'

'I remember! It was so bitter, and Lord Evington let me drink some of his. And then I . . . I don't know what happened after that,' she said, with a little grimace.

'Mr Gonsalez ordered the car, got the nurse from a nursing home,' explained Alma.

'Gonsalez! Not my Gonsalez – the – the Four Just Men Gonsalez?' she asked in amazement.

'I'm sure it was Gonsalez: they made no secret about it. You can see the gentleman who brought you: he's about the house somewhere. I saw him in Heavytree Lane not five minutes ago, strolling up and down and smoking. A pipe,' added Alma.

The girl got out of bed; her knees were curiously weak under her, but she managed to stagger to the window, and, pushing open the casement still farther, looked out across the patchwork quilt of colour. The summer flowers were in bloom; the delicate scents came up on the warm morning air, and she stood for a moment, drinking in great draughts of the exquisite perfume, and then, with a sigh, turned back to the waiting Alma.

'I don't know how it all happened and what it's about, but my word, Alma, I'm glad to be back! That dreadful man . . . ! We lunched at the Ritz-Carlton . . . I never want to see another restaurant or a ball-room or Chester Square, or anything but old Heavytree!'

She took the cup of tea from Alma's hand, drank greedily, and put it down with a little gasp.

'That was wonderful! Yes, the tea was too, but I'm thinking about Gonsalez. If it should be he!'

'I don't see why you should get excited over a man who's committed I don't know how many murders.'

'Don't be silly, Alma!' scoffed the girl. 'The Just Men have never murdered, any more than a judge and jury murder.'

The room was still inclined to go round, and it was with the greatest difficulty that she could condense the two Almas who stood before her into one tangible individual.

'There's a gentleman downstairs: he's been waiting since twelve.'

And when she asked, she was to learn, to her dismay, that it was half-past one.

'I'll be down in a quarter of an hour,' she said recklessly. 'Who is it?'

'I've never heard of him before, but he's a gentleman,' was the unsatisfactory reply. 'They didn't want to let him come in.'

'Who didn't?'

'The gentlemen who brought you here in the night.'

Mirabelle stared at her.

'You mean . . . they're guarding the house?'

'That's how it strikes me,' said Alma bitterly. 'Why they should interfere with us, I don't know. Anyway, they let him in. Mr Johnson Lee.'

The girl frowned.

'I don't know the name,' she said.

Alma walked to the window.

'There's his car,' she said, and pointed.

It was just visible, standing at the side of the road beyond the box hedge, a long-bodied Rolls, white with dust. The chauffeur was talking to a strange man, and from the fact that he was smoking a pipe Mirabelle guessed that this was one of her self-appointed custodians.

She had her bath, and with the assistance of the nurse, dressed and came shakily down the stairs. Alma was waiting in the brick-floored hall.

'He wants to see you alone,' she said in a stage whisper. 'I don't know whether I ought to allow it, but there's evidently something wrong. These men prowling about the house have got thoroughly on my nerves.'

Mirabelle laughed softly as she opened the door and walked in. At the sound of the door closing, the man who was sitting stiffly on a deep settee in a window recess got up. He was tall and bent, and his dark face was lined. His eyes she could not see; they were hidden behind dark green glasses, which were turned in her direction as she came across the room to greet him.

'Miss Mirabelle Leicester?' he asked, in the quiet, modulated voice of an educated man. He took her hand in his.

'Won't you sit down?' she said, for he remained standing after she had seated herself.

'Thank you.' He sat down gingerly, holding between his knees the handle of the umbrella he had brought into the drawing-room. 'I'm afraid my visit may be inopportune, Miss Leicester,' he said. 'Have you by any chance heard about Mr Barberton?'

Her brows wrinkled in thought. 'Barberton? I seem to have heard the name.'

'He was killed yesterday on the Thames Embankment.'

Then she recollected.

'The man who was bitten by the snake?' she asked in horror.

The visitor nodded.

'It was a great shock to me, because I have been a friend of his for many years, and had arranged to call at his hôtel on the night of his death.' And then abruptly he turned the conversation in another and a surprising direction. 'Your father was a scientist, Miss Leicester?'

She nodded.

'Yes, he was an astronomer, an authority upon meteors.'

'Exactly. I thought that was the gentleman. I have only recently had his book read to me. He was in Africa for some years?'

'Yes,' she said quietly, 'he died there. He was studying meteors for three years in Angola. You probably know that a very large number of shooting stars fall in that country. My father's theory was that it was due to the ironstone mountains which attract them – so he set up a little observatory in the interior.' Her lips trembled for a second. 'He was killed in a native rising,' she said.

'Do you know the part of Angola where be had his observatory?'

She shook her head.

'I'm not sure. I have never been in Africa, but perhaps Aunt Alma may know.'

She went out to find Alma waiting in the passage, in conversation with the pipe-smoker. The man withdrew hastily at the sight of her.

'Alma, do you remember what part of Angola father had his observatory?' she asked.

Alma did not know off-hand, but one of her invaluable scrapbooks contained all the information that the girl wanted, and she carried the book to Mr Lee.

'Here are the particulars,' she said, and laid the book open before them.

'Would you read it for me?' he requested gently, and she read to him the three short paragraphs which noted that Professor Leicester had taken up his residence in Bishaka.

'That is the place,' interrupted the visitor. 'Bishaka! You are you sure that Mr Barberton did not communicate with you?'

'With me?' she said in amazement 'No – why should he?'

He did not answer, but sat for a long time, turning the matter over in his mind.

'You're perfectly certain that nobody sent you a document, probably in the Portuguese language, concerning –' he hesitated – 'Bishaka?'

She shook her head, and then, as though he had not seen the gesture, he asked the question again.

'I'm certain,' she said. 'We have very little correspondence at the farm, and it isn't possible that I could overlook anything so remarkable.'

Again he turned the problem over in his mind.

'Have you any documents in Portuguese or in English . . . any letters from your father about Angola?'

'None,' she said. 'The only reference my father ever made to Bishaka was that he was getting a lot of information which he thought would be valuable, and that he was a little troubled because his cameras, which he had fixed in various parts of the country to cover every sector of the skies, were being disturbed by wandering prospectors.'

'He said that, did he?' asked Mr Lee eagerly. 'Come now, that explains a great deal!'

In spite of herself she laughed. 'It doesn't explain much to me, Mr Lee,' she said frankly. And then, in a more serious tone: 'Did Barberton come from Angola?'

'Yes, Barberton came from that country,' he said in a lower voice. 'I should like to tell you,' – he hesitated – 'but I am rather afraid.'

'Afraid to tell me? Why?'

He shook his head.

'So many dreadful things have happened recently to poor Barberton and others, that knowledge seems a most dangerous thing. I wish I could believe that it would not be dangerous to you,' he added kindly, 'and then I could speak what is in my mind and relieve myself of a great deal of anxiety.' He rose slowly. 'I think the best thing I can do is to consult my lawyer. I was foolish to keep it from him so long. He is the only man I can trust to search my documents.'

She could only look at him in astonishment

'But surely you can search your own documents?' she said good-humouredly.

'No, I'm afraid I can't. Because – ' he spoke with the simplicity of a child – 'I am blind.'

'Blind?' gasped Mirabelle, and the man laughed gently.

'I am pretty capable for a blind man, am I not? I can walk across a room and avoid all the furniture. The only thing I cannot do is to read – at least, read the ordinary print. I can read Braille: poor Barberton taught me. He was a school-master,' he explained, 'at a blind school near Brightlingsea. Not a particularly well-educated man, but a marvellously quick writer of Braille. We have corresponded for years through that medium. He could write a Braille letter almost as quickly as you can with pen and ink.'

Her heart was full of pity for the man: he was so cheery, so confident, and withal so proud of his own accomplishments, that pity turned to admiration. He had the ineffable air of obstinacy which is the possession of so many men similarly stricken, and she began to realize that self-pity, that greatest of all afflictions which attends blindness, had been eliminated from his philosophy.

'I should like to tell you more,' he said, as he held out his hand. 'Probably I will dictate a long letter to you tomorrow, or else my lawyer will do so, putting all the facts before you. For the moment, however, I must be sure of my ground. I have no desire to raise in your heart either fear or – hope. Do you know a Mr Manfred?'

'I don't know him personally,' she said quickly. 'George Manfred?'

He nodded.

'Have you met him?' she asked eagerly. 'And Mr Poiccart, the Frenchman?'

'No, not Mr Poiccart. Manfred was on the telephone to me very early this morning. He seemed to know all about my relationships with my poor friend. He knew also of my blindness. A remarkable man, very gentle and courteous. It was he who gave me your address. Perhaps,' he roused, 'it would be advisable if I first consulted him.'

'I'm sure it would!' she said enthusiastically. 'They are wonderful. You have heard of them, of course, Mr Lee – the Four Just Men?'

He smiled.

'That sounds as though you admire them,' he said. 'Yes, I have heard of them. They are the men who, many years ago, set out to regularize the inconsistencies of the English law, to punish where no punishment is provided by the code. Strange I never associated them . . .'

He meditated upon the matter in silence for a long while, and then: 'I wonder,' he said, but did not tell her what he was wondering.

She walked down the garden path with him into the road-way and stood chatting about the country and the flowers that he had never seen, and the weather and such trivialities as people talk about when their minds are occupied with more serious thoughts which they cannot share, until the big limousine pulled up and he stepped into its cool interior. He had the independence which comes to the educated blind and gently refused the offer of her guidance, an offer she did not attempt to repeat, sensing the satisfaction he must have had in making his way without help. She waved her hand to the car as it moved off, and so naturally did his hand go up in salute that for a moment she thought he had seen her.

So he passed out of her sight, and might well have passed out of her life, for Mr Oberzohn had decreed that the remaining hours of blind Johnson Lee were to be few.

But it happened that the Three Men had reached the same decision in regard to Mr Oberzohn, only there was some indecision as to the manner of his passing. Leon Gonsalez had original views.

Chapter 14
The pedlar

The man with the pipe was standing within half a dozen paces of her. She was going back through the gate, when she remembered Aunt Alma's views on the guardianship.

'Are you waiting here all day?' she asked.

'Till this evening, miss. We're to be relieved by some men from Gloucester – we came from town, and we're going back with the nurse, if you can do without her?'

'Who placed you here?' she asked.

'Mr Gonsalez. He thought it would be wise to have somebody around.'

'But why?'

The big man grinned.

'I've known Mr Gonsalez many years,' he said. 'I'm a police pensioner, and I can remember the time when I'd have given a lot of money to lay my hands on him – but I've never asked him why, miss. There is generally a good reason for everything he does.'

Mirabelle went back into the farmhouse, very thoughtful. Happily, Alma was not inquisitive; she was left alone in the drawing-room to reconstruct her exciting yesterday.

Mirabelle harboured very few illusions. She had read much, guessed much, and in the days of her childhood had been in the habit of linking cause to effect. The advertisement was designed especially for her: that was her first conclusion. It was designed to bring her into the charge of Oberzohn. For now she recognized this significant circumstance: never once, since she had entered the offices of Oberzohn & Smitts, until the episode of the orangeade, had she been free to come and go as she wished. He had taken her to lunch, he had brought her back; Joan Newton had been her companion in the drive from the house, and from the house to the hall; and from then on she did not doubt that Oberzohn's surveillance had continued, until . . .

Dimly she remembered the man in the cloak who had stood in the rocking doorway. Was that Gonsalez? Somehow she thought it must have been. Gonsalez, watchful, alert – why? She had been in danger – was still in danger. Though why anybody should have picked unimportant her was the greatest of all mysteries.

In some inexplicable way the death of Barberton had been associated with that advertisement and the attention she had received from Dr Oberzohn and his creatures. Who was Lord Evington? She remembered his German accent and his 'gracious lady', the curious click of his heels and his stiff bow. That was a clumsy subterfuge which she ought to have seen through from the first. He was another of her watchers. And the drugged orangeade was his work. She shuddered. Suppose Leon Gonsalez, or whoever it was, had not arrived so providentially, where would she be at this moment?

Walking to the window, she looked out, and the sight of the two men just inside the gate gave her a sense of infinite relief and calm; and the knowledge that she, for some reason, was under the care and protection of this strange organization about which she had read, thrilled her.

She walked into the vaulted kitchen, to find the kitchen table covered with fat volumes, and Aunt Alma explaining to the interested nurse her system of filing. Two subjects interested that hard-featured lady: crime and family records. She had two books filled with snippings from country newspapers relating to the family of a distant cousin who had been raised to a peerage during the war. She had another devoted to the social triumphs of a distant woman, Goddard, who had finally made a sensational appearance as petitioner in the most celebrated divorce suit of the age. But crime, generally speaking, was Aunt Alma's chief preoccupation. It was from these voluminous cuttings that Mirabelle had gained her complete knowledge of the Four Just Men and their operations. There were books packed with the story of the Ramon murder, arranged with loving care in order of time, for chronology was almost a vice in Alma Goddard. Only one public sensation was missing from her collection, and she was explaining the reason to the nurse as Mirabelle came into the kitchen.

'No, my dear,' she was saying, 'there is nothing about The Snake. I won't have anything to do with that: it gives me the creeps. In fact, I haven't read anything that has the slightest reference to it.'

'I've got every line,' said the nurse enthusiastically. 'My brother is a reporter on the *Megaphone*, and he says this is the best story they've had for years – '

Mirabelle interrupted this somewhat gruesome conversation to make inquiries about luncheon. Her head was steady now and she had developed an appetite.

The front door stood open, and as she turned to go into the dining-room to get her writing materials, she heard an altercation at the gate. A third man had appeared: a grimy-looking pedlar who carried a tray before him, packed with all manner of cheap buttons and laces. He was a middle-aged man with a ragged beard, and despite the warmth of the day, was wearing a long overcoat that almost reached to his heels.

'You may or you may not be,' the man with the pipe was saying, 'but you're not going in here.'

'I've served this house for years,' snarled the pedlar. 'What do you mean by interfering with me? You're not a policeman.'

'Whether I'm a policeman or a dustman or a postman,' said the patient guard, 'you don't pass through this gate – do you understand that?'

At this moment the pedlar caught sight of the girl at the door and raised his battered hat with a grin. He was unknown to the girl; she did not remember having seen him at the house before. Nor did Alma, who came out at that moment.

'He's a stranger here, but we're always getting new people up from Gloucester,' she said. 'What does he want to sell?'

She stalked out into the garden, and at the sight of her the grin left the pedlar's face.

'I've got some things I'd like to sell to the young lady, ma'am,' he said.

'I'm not so old, and I'm a lady,' replied Alma sharply. 'And how long is it since you started picking and choosing your customers?'

The man grumbled something under his breath, and without waiting even to display his wares, shuffled off along the dusty road, and they watched him until he was out of sight.

Heavytree Farm was rather grandly named for so small a property. The little estate followed the road to Heavytree Lane, which formed the southern boundary of the property. The lane itself ran at an angle to behind the house, where the third boundary was formed by a hedge dividing the farmland from the more pretentious estate of a local magnate. It was down the lane the pedlar turned.

'Excuse me, ma'am,' said the companion of the man with the pipe.

He opened the gate, walked in, and, making a circuit of the house, reached the orchard behind. Here a few outhouses were scattered, and, clearing these, he came to the meadow, where Mira-belle's one cow ruminated in the lazy manner of her kind. Half-hidden by a thick-boled apple-tree, the watcher waited, and pres-ently, as he expected, he saw a head appear through the boundary hedge. After an observation the pedlar sprang into the meadow and stood, taking stock of his ground. He had left his tray and his bag, and, running with surprising swiftness for a man of his age, he gained a little wooden barn, and, pulling open the door, disappeared into its interior. By this time the guard had been joined by his companion and they had a short consultation, the man with the pipe going back to his post before the house, whilst the other walked slowly across the meadow until he came to the closed door of the barn.

Wise in his generation, he first made a circuit of the building, and discovered there were no exits through the blackened gates. Then, pulling both doors open wide:

'Come out, bo'!' he said.

The barn was empty, except for a heap of hay that lay in one corner and some old and wheel-less farm-wagons propped up on three trestles awaiting the wheelwright's attention.

A ladder led to a loft, and the guard climbed slowly. His head was on a level with the dark opening, when: 'Put up your hands!'

He was looking into the adequate muzzle of an automatic pistol.

'Come down, bo'!'

'Put up your hands,' hissed the voice in the darkness, 'or you're a dead man!'

The watcher obeyed, cursing his folly that he had come alone.

'Now climb up.'

With some difficulty the guard brought himself up to the floor level.

'Step this way, and step lively,' said the pedlar. 'Hold your hands out.'

He felt the touch of cold steel on his wrist, heard a click.

'Now the other hand.'

The moment he was manacled, the pedlar began a rapid search.

'Carry a gun, do you?' he sneered, as he drew a pistol from the man's hip pocket. 'Now sit down.'

In a few seconds the discomfited guard was bound and gagged. The pedlar, crawling to the entrance of the loft, looked out between a crevice in the boards. He was watching, not the house, but the hedge through which he had climbed. Two other men had appeared there, and he grunted his satisfaction. Descending into the barn, he pulled away the ladder and let it fall on the floor, before he came out into the open and made a signal.

The second guard had made his way back by the short cut to the front of the house, passing through the garden and in through the kitchen door. He stopped to shoot the bolt, and the girl, coming into the kitchen, saw him.

'Is anything wrong?' she asked anxiously.

'I don't know, miss.' He was looking at the kitchen windows: they were heavily barred. 'My mate has just seen that pedlar go into the barn.'

She followed him to the front door. He had turned to go, but, changing his mind, came back, and she saw him put his hand into his hip pocket and was staggered to see him produce a long-barrelled Browning.

'Can you use a pistol, miss?'

She nodded, too surprised to speak, and watched him as he jerked back the jacket and put up the safety catch.

'I want to be on the safe side, and I'd feel happier if you were armed.'

There was a gun hanging on the wall and he took it down.

'Have you any shells for this?' he asked.

She pulled open the drawer of the hall-stand and took out a card-board carton.

'They may be useful,' he said.

'But surely, Mr – '

'Digby.' He supplied his name.

'Surely you're exaggerating? I don't mean that you're doing it with any intention of frightening me, but there isn't any danger to us?'

'I don't know. I've got a queer feeling – had it all morning. How far is the nearest house from here?'

'Not half a mile away,' she said.

'You're on the phone?'

She nodded.

'I'm scared, maybe. I'll just go out into the road and have a look round. I wish that fellow would come back,' he added fretfully.

He walked slowly up the garden path and stood for a moment leaning over the gate. As he did so, he heard the rattle and asthmatic wheezing of an ancient car, and saw a tradesman's trolley come round a corner of Heavytree Lane. Its pace grew slower as it got nearer to the house, and opposite the gate it stopped altogether. The driver, getting down with a curse, lifted up the battered tin bonnet, and, groping under the seat, brought out a long spanner. Then, swift as thought, he half turned and struck at Digby's head. The girl heard the sickening impact, saw the watcher drop limply to the path, and in another second she had slammed the door and thrust home the bolts.

She was calm; the hand that took the revolver from the hall-table did not tremble.

'Alma!' she called, and Alma came running downstairs.

'What on earth – ?' she began, and then saw the pistol in Mirabelle's hands.

'They are attacking the house,' said the girl quickly. 'I don't know who "they" are, but they've just struck down one of the men who was protecting us. Take the gun, Alma.'

Alma's face was contorted, and might have expressed fear or anger or both. Mirabelle afterwards learnt that the dominant emotion was one of satisfaction to find herself in so war-like an environment.

Running into the drawing-room, the girl pushed open the window, which commanded a view of the road. The gate was unfastened and two men, who had evidently been concealed inside the trolley, were lifting the unconscious man, and she watched, with a calm she could not understand in herself, as they threw him into the interior and fastened the tailboard. She counted four in all, including the driver, who was climbing back to his seat. One of the newcomers, evidently the leader, was pointing down the road towards the lane, and she guessed that he was giving directions as to where the car should wait, for it began to go backwards almost immediately and with surprising smoothness, remembering the exhibition it had given of decrepitude a few minutes before.

The man who had given instructions came striding down the path towards the door.

'Stop!'

He looked round with a start into the levelled muzzle of a Browning, and his surprise would, in any other circumstances, have been comical.

'It's all right, miss – ' he began.

'Put yourself outside that gate,' said Mirabelle coolly.

'I wanted to see you . . . very important – '

Bang!

Mirabelle fired a shot, aimed above his head, towards the old poplar. The man ducked and ran. Clear of the gate he dropped to the cover of a hedge, where his men already were, and she heard the murmur of their voices distinctly, for the day was still, and the far-off chugging of the trolley's engine sounded close at hand. Presently she saw a head peep round the hedge.

'Can I have five minutes' talk with you?' asked the leader loudly.

He was a thick-set, bronzed man, with a patch of lint plastered to his face, and she noted unconsciously that he wore gold ear-rings.

'There's no trouble coming to you,' he said, opening the gate as he spoke. 'You oughtn't to have fired, anyway. Nobody's going to hurt you – '

He had advanced a yard into the garden as he spoke.

Bang, bang!

In her haste she had pressed butt and trigger just a fraction too long, and, startled by the knowledge that another shot was coming, her hand jerked round, and the second shot missed his head by the fraction of an inch. He disappeared in a flash, and a second later she saw their hats moving swiftly above the box. They were running towards the waiting car.

'Stay here, Alma!'

Alma Goddard nodded grimly, and the girl flew up the stairs to her room. From this elevation she commanded a better view. She saw them climb into the van, and in another second the limp body of the guard was thrown out into the hedge; then, after a brief space of time, the machine began moving and, gathering speed, disappeared in a cloud of dust on the Highcombe Road.

Mirabelle came down the stairs at a run, pulled back the bolts and flew out and along the road towards the still figure of the detective. He was lying by the side of the ditch, his head a mass of blood, and she saw that he was still breathing. She tried to lift him, but it was too great a task. She ran back to the house. The telephone was in the hall: an old-fashioned instrument with a handle that had to be turned, and she had not made two revolutions before she realized that the wire had been cut.

Alma was still in the parlour, the gun gripped tight in her hand, a look of fiendish resolution on her face.

'You must help me to get Digby into the house,' she said. 'Where is he?'

Mirabelle pointed, and the two women, returning to the man, half lifted, half dragged him back to the hall. Laying him down on the brick floor, the girl went in search of clean linen. The kitchen, which was also the drying place for Alma's more intimate laundry, supplied all that she needed. Whilst Alma watched unmoved the destruction of her wardrobe, the girl bathed the wound and the frightened nurse (who had disappeared at the first shot) applied a rough dressing. The wound was an ugly one, and the man showed no signs of recovering consciousness.

'We shall have to send Mary into Gloucester for an ambulance,' said Mirabelle. 'We can't send nurse – she doesn't know the way.'

'Mary,' said Alma calmly, 'is at this moment having hysterics in the larder. I'll harness the dog-cart and go myself. But where is the other man?'

Mirabelle shook her head.

'I don't like to think what has happened to him,' she said. 'Now, Alma, do you think we can get him into the drawing-room?'

Together they lifted the heavy figure and staggered with it into the pretty little room, laying him at last upon the settee under the window.

'He can rest there till we get the ambulance,' began Mirabelle, and a chuckle behind her made her turn with a gasp.

It was the pedlar, and in his hand he held the pistol which she had discarded.

'I only want you – ' he nodded to the girl. 'You other two women can come out here.' He jerked his head to the passage. Under the stairs was a big cupboard and he pulled the door open invitingly. 'Get in here. If you make a noise, you'll be sorry for yourselves.'

Alma's eyes wandered longingly to the gun she had left in the corner, but before she could make a move he had placed himself between her and the weapon.

'Inside,' said the pedlar, and Mirabelle was not much surprised when Aunt Alma meekly obeyed.

He shut the door on the two women and fastened the latch.

'Now, young lady, put on your hat and be lively!'

He followed her up the stairs into her room and watched her while she found a hat and a cloak. She knew only that it was a waste of time even to temporize with him. He, for his part, was so exultant at his success that he grew almost loquacious.

'I suppose you saw the boys driving away and you didn't remember that I was somewhere around. Was that you doing the shooting?'

She did not answer.

'It couldn't have been Lew, or you'd have been dead,' he said. He was examining the muzzle of the pistol. 'It was you all right.' He chuckled. 'Ain't you the game one! Sister, you ought to be – '

He stopped dead, staring through the window. He was paralysed with amazement at the sight of a bare-headed Aunt Alma flying along the Gloucester Road. With an oath he turned to the girl.

'How did she get out? Have you got anybody here? Now speak up.'

'The cupboard under the stairs leads to the wine cellar,' said Mirabelle coolly, 'and there are two ways out of the wine cellar. I think Aunt Alma found one of them.'

With an oath, he took a step towards her, gripped her by the arm and jerked her towards the door.

'Lively!' he said, and dragged her down the stairs through the hall, into the kitchen.

He shot back the bolts, but the lock of the kitchen door had been turned.

'This way.' He swore cold-bloodedly, and, her arm still in his powerful grip, he hurried along the passage and pulled open the door.

It was an unpropitious moment. A man was walking down the path, a half smile on his face, as though he was thinking over a remembered jest. At the sight of him the pedlar dropped the girl's arm and his hand went like lightning to his pocket.

'When will you die?' said Leon Gonsalez softly. 'Make a choice, and make it quick!'

And the gun in his hand seemed to quiver with homicidal eagerness.

Chapter 15

Two 'accidents'

The pedlar, his face twitching, put up his shaking hands.

Leon walked to him, took the Browning from his moist grip and dropped it into his pocket.

'Your friends are waiting, of course?' he said pleasantly.

The pedlar did not answer.

'Cuccini too? I thought I had incapacitated him for a long time.'

'They've gone,' growled the pedlar.

Gonsalez looked round in perplexity.

'I don't want to take you into the house. At the same time, I don't want to leave you here,' he said. 'I almost wish you'd drawn that gun of yours,' he added regretfully. 'It would have solved so many immediate problems.'

This particular problem was solved by the return of the dishevelled Alma and the restoration to her of her gun.

'I would so much rather you shot him than I,' said Leon earnestly. 'The police are very suspicious of my shootings, and they never wholly believe that they are done in self-defence.'

With a rope he tied the man, and tied him uncomfortably, wrists to ankles. That done, he made a few inquiries and went swiftly out to the barn, returning in a few minutes with the unhappy guard.

'It can't be helped,' said Leon, cutting short the man's apologies. 'The question is, where are the rest of the brethren?'

Something zipped past him: it had the intensified hum of an angry wasp, and a second later he heard a muffled 'Plop!' In a second he was lying flat on the ground, his Browning covering the hedge that hid Heavytree Lane.

'Run to the house,' he called urgently. 'They won't bother about you.' And the guard, nothing loth, sprinted for the cover of walls.

Presently Leon located the enemy, and at a little distance off he saw the flat top of the covered trolley. A man walked invitingly across the gap in the hedge, but Gonsalez held his fire, and presently the manoeuvre was repeated. Obviously they were trying to concentrate his mind upon the gap whilst they were moving elsewhere. His eyes swept the meadow boundary – running parallel, he guessed, was a brook or ditch which would make excellent cover.

Again the man passed leisurely across the gap. Leon steadied his elbow, and glanced along the sight. As he did so, the man reappeared.

Crack!

Gonsalez aimed a foot behind him. The man saw the flash and jumped back, as he had expected. In another second he was writhing on the ground with a bullet through his leg.

Leon showed his teeth in a smile and switched his body round to face the new point of attack. It came from the spot that he had expected: a little rise of ground that commanded his position.

The first bullet struck the turf to his right with an angry buzz, sent a divot flying heavenward, and ricocheted with a smack against a tree. Before the raised head could drop to cover, Gonsalez fired; fired another shot to left and right, then, rising, raced for the shelter of the tree, and reached it in time to see three heads bobbing back to the road. He waited, covering the gap, but the people who drew the wounded man out of sight did not show themselves, and a minute later he saw the trolley moving swiftly down the by-road, and knew that danger was past.

The firing had attracted attention. He had not been back in the house a few minutes before a mounted policeman, his horse in a lather, came galloping up to the gate and dismounted. A neighbouring farm had heard the shots and telephoned to constabulary headquarters. For half an hour the mounted policeman took notes, and by this time half the farmers in the neighbourhood, their guns under their arms, had assembled in Mirabelle's parlour.

She had not seen as much of the redoubtable Leon as she could have wished, and when they had a few moments to themselves she seized the opportunity to tell him of the call which Lee had made that morning. Apparently he knew all about it, for he expressed no surprise, and was only embarrassed when she showed a personal interest in himself and his friends.

It was not a very usual experience for him, and he was rather annoyed with himself at this unexpected glimpse of enthusiasm and hero-worship, sane as it was, and based, as he realized, upon her keen sense of justice.

'I'm not so sure that we've been very admirable really,' he said. 'But the difficulty is to produce at the moment a judgement which would be given from a distance of years. We have sacrificed everything which to most men would make life worth living, in our desire to see the scales held fairly.'

'You are not married, Mr Gonsalez?'

He stared into the frank eyes. 'Married! Why, no,' he said, and she laughed.

'You talk as though that were a possibility that had never occurred to you.'

'It hasn't,' he admitted. 'By the very nature of our work we are debarred from that experience. And is it an offensive thing to say that I have never felt my singleness to be a deprivation?'

'It is very rude,' she said severely, and Leon was laughing to himself all the way back to town as at a great joke that improved upon repetition.

'I think we can safely leave her for a week,' he reported, on his return to Curzon Street. 'No, nothing happened. I was held up in a police trap near Newbury for exceeding the speed limit They said I was doing fifty, but I should imagine it was nearer eighty. Meadows will get me out of that. Otherwise, I must send the inevitable letter to the magistrate and pay the inevitable fine. Have you done anything about Johnson Lee?'

Manfred nodded. 'Meadows and the enthusiastic Mr Washington have gone round to see him. I have asked Washington to go because – ' he hesitated – 'the snake is a real danger, so far as he is concerned. Elijah Washington promises to be a very real help. He is afraid of nothing, and has undertaken to stay with Lee and to apply such remedies for snake-bites as he knows.'

He was putting on his gloves as he spoke, and Leon Gonsalez looked at him with a critical admiration.

'Are you being presented at Court, or are you taking tea with a duchess?'

'Neither. I'm calling upon friend Oberzohn.'

'The devil you are!' said Leon, his eyebrows rising.

'I have taken the precaution of sending him a note, asking him to keep his snakes locked up,' said Manfred, 'and as I have pointedly forwarded the carbon copy of the letter, to impress the fact that another exists and may be brought in evidence against him, I think I shall leave Oberzohn & Smitts' main office without hurt. If you are not too tired, Leon, I would rather prefer the Buick to the Spanz.'

'Give me a quarter of an hour,' said Leon, and went up to his room to make himself tidy.

It was fifteen minutes exactly when the Buick stopped at the door, and Manfred got into the saloon. There was no partition between driver and passenger, and conversation was possible.

'It would have been as well if you'd had Brother Newton there,' he suggested.

'Brother Newton will be on the spot: I took the precaution of sending him a similar note,' said Manfred. 'I shouldn't imagine they'll bring out their gunmen.'

'I know two, and possibly three, they won't bring out.' Gonsalez grinned at the traffic policeman who waved him into Oxford Street. 'That Browning of mine throws high, Manfred: I've always had a suspicion it did. Pistols are queer things, but this may wear into my hand.' He talked arms and ammunition until the square block of Oberzohn & Smitts came into sight. 'Good hunting!' he said, as he got out, opened the saloon door and touched his hat to Manfred as he alighted.

He got back into his seat, swung the little car round in a circle, and sat on the opposite side of the road, his eyes alternately on the entrance and on the mirror which gave him a view of the traffic approaching him from the rear.

Manfred was not kept in the waiting-room for more than two minutes. At the end of that time, a solemn youth in spectacles, with a little bow, led him across the incurious office into the presence of the illustrious doctor.

The old man was at his desk. Behind him, his debonair self, Monty Newton, a large yellow flower in his buttonhole, a smile on his face. Oberzohn got up like a man standing to attention.

'Mr Manfred, this is a great honour,' he said, and held out his hand stiffly.

An additional chair had been placed for the visitor: a rich-looking tapestried chair, to which the doctor waved the hand which Manfred did not take.

'Good morning, Manfred.' Newton removed his cigar and nodded genially. 'Were you at the dance last night?'

'I was there, but I didn't come in,' said Manfred, seating himself. 'You did not turn up till late, they tell me?'

'It was of all occurrences the most unfortunate,' said Dr Oberzohn, and Newton laughed.

'I've lost his laboratory secretary and he hasn't forgiven me,' he said almost jovially. 'The girl he took on yesterday. Rather a stunner in the way of looks. She didn't wish to go back to the country where she came from, so my sister offered to put her up for the night in Chester Square. I'm blessed if she didn't lose herself at the dance, and we haven't seen her since!'

'It was a terrible thing,' said Oberzohn sadly. 'I regard her as in my charge. For her safety I am responsible. You, I trust, Mr Newton – '

'I don't think I should have another uneasy moment if I were you, doctor,' said Manfred easily. 'The young lady is back at Heavytree Farm. I thought that would surprise you. And she is still there: that will surprise you more, if you have not already heard by telephone that your Old Guard failed dismally to – er – bring her back to work. I presume that was their object?'

'My old guard, Mr Manfred?' Oberzohn shook his head in bewilderment. 'This is beyond my comprehension.'

'Is your sister well?' asked Manfred blandly.

Newton shrugged his shoulders.

'She is naturally upset. And who wouldn't be? Joan is a very tender-hearted girl.'

'She has been that way for years,' said Manfred offensively. 'May I smoke?'

'Will you have one of my cigarettes?' Manfred's grave eyes fixed the doctor in a stare that held the older man against his will.

'I have had just one too many of your cigarettes,' he said. His words came like a cold wind. 'I do not want any more, Herr Doktor, or there will be vacancies in your family circle. Who knows that, long before you compound your wonderful elixir, you may be called to normal immortality?'

The yellow face of Oberzohn had turned to a dull red.

'You seem to know as much about me, Mr Manfred, as myself,' he said in a husky whisper.

Manfred nodded.

'More. For whilst you are racing against time to avoid the end of a life which does not seem especially worthy of preservation, and whilst you know not what day or hour that end may come, I can tell you to the minute.' The finger of his gloved hand pointed the threat.

All trace of a smile had vanished from Monty Newton's face. His eyes did not leave the caller's.

'Perhaps you shall tell me.' Oberzohn found a difficulty in speaking. Rage possessed him, and only his iron will choked down the flames from view.

'The day that injury comes to Mirabelle Leicester, that day you go out – you and those who are with you!'

'Look here, Manfred, there's a law in this country – ' began Monty
Newton hotly.

'I am the law.' The words rang like a knell of fate. 'In this matter
I am judge, jury, hangman. Old or young, I will not spare,' he said
evenly.

'Are you immortal too?' sneered Monty.

Only for a second did Manfred's eyes leave the old man's face.

'The law is immortal,' he said. 'If you dream that, by some cleverly
concerted coup, you can sweep me from your path before I grow
dangerous, be sure that your sweep is clean.'

'You haven't asked me to come here to listen to this stuff, have
you?' asked Newton, and though his words were bold, his manner
aggressive, there were shadows on his face which were not there
when Manfred had come into the room – shadows under his eyes and
in his cheeks where plumpness had been.

'I've come here to tell you to let up on Miss Leicester. You're after
something that you cannot get, and nobody is in a position to give
you. I don't know what it is – I will make you a present of that piece
of information. But it's big – bigger than any prize you've ever gone
after in your wicked lives. And to get that, you're prepared to sacrifice innocent lives with the recklessness of spendthrifts who think
there is no bottom to their purse. The end is near!'

He rose slowly and stood by the table, towering over the stiff-
backed doctor.

'I cannot say what action the police will take over this providential
snake-bite, Oberzohn, but I'll make you this offer: I and my friends
will stand out of the game and leave Meadows to get you in his
own way. You think that means you'll go scot-free? But it doesn't.
These police are like bull-dogs: once they've got a grip of you, they'll
never let go.'

'What is the price you ask for this interesting service?' Newton was
puffing steadily at his cigar, his hands clasped behind him, his feet
apart, a picture of comfort and well-being.

'Leave Miss Leicester alone. Find a new way of getting the money
you need so badly.'

Newton laughed.

'My dear fellow, that's a stupid thing to say. Neither Oberzohn nor
I are exactly poor.'

'You're bankrupt, both of you,' said Manfred quietly. 'You are in
the position of gamblers when the cards have run against you for a
long time. You have no reserve, and your expenses are enormous.

Find another way, Newton – and tell your sister – ' he paused by the door, looking down into the white lining of his silk hat – 'I'd like to see her at Curzon Street tomorrow morning at ten o'clock.'

'Is that an order?' asked Newton sarcastically.

Manfred nodded.

'Then let me tell you,' roared the man, white with passion, 'that I take no orders for her or for me. Got swollen heads since you've had your pardon, haven't you? You look out for me, Manfred. I'm not exactly harmless.'

He felt the pressure of the doctor's foot upon his and curbed his temper.

'All right,' he growled, 'but don't expect to see Joan.'

He added a coarse jest, and Manfred raised his eyes slowly and met his.

'You will be hanged by the State or murdered by Oberzohn – I am not sure which,' he said simply, and he spoke with such perfect confidence that the heart of Monty Newton turned to water.

Manfred stood in the sidewalk and signalled, and the little car came swiftly and noiselessly across. Leon's eyes were on the entrance. A tall man standing in the shadow of the hall was watching. He was leaning against the wall in a negligent attitude, and for a second Leon was startled.

'Get in quickly!'

Leon almost shouted the words back, and Manfred jumped into the machine, as the chauffeur sent the car forward, with a jerk that strained every gear.

'What on – ?' began Manfred, but the rest of his words were lost in the terrific crash which followed.

The leather hood of the machine was ripped down at the back, a splinter of glass struck Leon's cap and sliced a half-moon neatly. He jammed on the brakes, threw open the door of the saloon and leaped out. Behind the car was a mass of wreckage; a great iron casting lay split into three pieces amidst a tangle of broken packing-case. Leon looked up; immediately above the entrance to Oberzohn & Smitts' was a crane, which had swung out with a heavy load just before Manfred came out. The steel wire hung loosely from the derrick. He heard excited voices speaking from the open doorway three floors above, and two men in large glasses were looking down and gabbling in a language he did not understand.

'A very pretty accident. We might have filled half a column in the evening newspapers if we had not moved.'

'And the gentleman in the hall – what was he doing?'

Leon walked back through the entrance: the man had disappeared, but near where he had been standing was a small bell-push which, it was obvious, had recently been fixed, for the wires ran loosely on the surface of the wall and were new.

He came back in time to see a policeman crossing the road.

'I wish to find out how this accident occurred, constable,' he said. 'My master was nearly killed.'

The policeman looked at the ton of debris lying half on the sidewalk, half on the road, then up at the slackened hawser.

'The cable has run off the drum, I should think.'

'I should think so,' said Leon gravely.

He did not wait for the policeman to finish his investigations, but went home at a steady pace, and made no reference to the 'accident' until he had put away his car and had returned to Curzon Street.

'The man in the hall was put there to signal when you were under the load – certain things must not happen,' he said. 'I am going out to make a few inquiries.'

Gonsalez knew one of Oberzohn's staff: a clean young Swede, with that knowledge of English which is normal in Scandinavian countries; and at nine o'clock that night he drifted into a Swedish restaurant in Dean Street and found the young man at the end of his meal. It was an acquaintance – one of many – that Leon had assiduously cultivated. The young man, who knew him as Mr Heinz – Leon spoke German remarkably well – was glad to have a companion with whom he could discuss the inexplicable accident of the afternoon.

'The cable was not fixed to the drum,' he said. 'It might have been terrible: there was a gentleman in a motor-car outside, and he had only moved away a few inches when the case fell. There is bad luck in that house. I am glad that I am leaving at the end of the week.'

Leon had some important questions to put, but he did not hurry, having the gift of patience to a marked degree. It was nearly ten when they parted, and Gonsalez went back to his garage, where he spent a quarter of an hour.

At midnight, Manfred had just finished a long conversation with the Scotland Yard man who was still at Brightlingsea, when Leon came in, looking very pleased with himself. Poiccart had gone to bed, and Manfred had switched out one circuit of lights when his friend arrived.

'Thank you, my dear George,' said Gonsalez briskly. 'It was very good of you, and I did not like troubling you, but – '

'It was a small thing,' said Manfred with a smile, 'and involved merely the changing of my shoes. But why? I am not curious, but why did you wish me to telephone the night watchman at Oberzohn's to be waiting at the door at eleven o'clock for a message from the doctor?'

'Because,' said Leon cheerfully, rubbing his hands, 'the night watchman is an honest man; he has a wife and six children, and I was particularly wishful not to hurt anybody. The building doesn't matter: it stands, or stood, isolated from all others. The only worry in my mind was the night watchman. He was at the door – I saw him.'

Manfred asked no further questions. Early the next morning he took up the paper and turned to the middle page, read the account of the 'Big Fire in City Road' which completely gutted the premises of Messrs Oberzohn & Smitts; and, what is more, he expected to read it before he had seen the paper.

'Accidents are accidents,' said Leon the philosopher that morning at breakfast. 'And that talk I had with the clerk last night told me a lot: Oberzohn has allowed his fire insurance to lapse!'

Chapter 16
Rath Hall

In one of the forbidden rooms that was filled with the apparatus which Dr Oberzohn had accumulated for his pleasure and benefit, was a small electrical furnace which was the centre of many of his most interesting experiments. There were, in certain known drugs, constituents which it was his desire to eliminate. Dr Oberzohn believed absolutely in many things that the modern chemist would dismiss as fantastical.

He believed in the philosopher's stone, in the transmutation of base metals to rare; he had made diamonds, of no great commercial value, it is true; but his supreme faith was that somewhere in the *materia medica* was an infallible elixir which would prolong life far beyond the normal span. It was to all other known properties as radium is to pitch-blende. It was something that only the metaphysician could discover, only the patient chemist could materialize. Every hour he could spare he devoted himself to his obsession; and he was in the midst of one of his experiments when the telephone bell called him back to his study. He listened, every muscle of his face moving, to the tale of disaster that Monty Newton wailed. 'It is burning still? Have you no fire-extinguishing machinery in London?'

'Is the place insured or is it not?' asked Monty for the second time.

Dr Oberzohn considered. 'It is not,' he said. 'But this matter is of such small importance compared with the great thing which is coming, that I shall not give it a thought.'

'It was incendiary,' said Newton angrily. 'The fire brigade people are certain of it. That cursed crowd are getting back on us for what happened this afternoon.'

'I know of nothing that happened this afternoon,' said Dr Oberzohn coldly. 'You know of nothing either. It was an accident which we all deplored. As to this man . . . we shall see.'

He hung up the telephone receiver very carefully, went along the passage, down a steep flight of dark stairs, and into a basement kitchen. Before he opened the door he heard the sound of furious voices, and he stood for a moment surveying the scene with every feeling of satisfaction. Except for two men, the room was empty. The servants used the actual kitchen at the front of the house, and this place was little better than a scullery. On one side of the deal table stood Gurther, white as death, his round eyes red with rage. On the other, the short, stout Russian Pole, with his heavy pasty face and baggy eyes; his little moustache and beard bristling with anger. The cards scattered on the table and the floor told the Herr Doktor that this was a repetition of the quarrel which was so frequent between them.

'*Schweinhund*!' hissed Gurther. 'I saw you palm the King as you dealt. Thief and robber of the blind – '

'You German dog! You – '

They were both speaking in German. Then the doctor saw the hand of Gurther steal down and back.

'Gurther!' he called, and the man spun round. 'To my parlour – march!'

Without a word, the man strode past him, and the doctor was left with the panting Russian.

'Herr Doktor, this Gurther is beyond endurance!' His voice trembled with rage. 'I would sooner live with a pig than this man, who is never normal unless he is drugged.'

'Silence!' shouted Oberzohn, and pointed to the chair. 'You shall wait till I come,' he said.

When he came back to his room, he found Gurther standing stiffly to attention.

'Now, Gunther,' he said – he was almost benevolent as he patted the man on the shoulder – 'this matter of Gonsalez must end. Can I have my Gurther hiding like a worm in the ground? No, that cannot be. Tonight I will send you to this man, and you are so clever that you cannot fail. He whipped you, Gurther – tied you up and cruelly beat you – always remember that, my brave fellow – he beat you till you bled. Now you shall see the man again. You will go in a dress for-every-occasion,' he said. 'The city-clerk manner. You will watch him in your so clever way, and you shall strike – it is permitted.'

'*Ja*, Herr Doktor.'

He turned on his heels and disappeared through the door. The doctor waited till he heard him going up the stairs, and then he rang for Pfeiffer. The man came in sullenly. He lacked all the precision of the military Gurther; yet, as Oberzohn knew, of the two he was the more alert, the more cunning.

'Pfeiffer, it has come to me that you are in some danger. The police wish to take you back to Warsaw, where certain unpleasant things happened, as you well know. And I am told – ' he lowered his voice – 'that a friend of ours would be glad to see you go, *hein*?'

The man did not raise his sulky eyes from the floor, did not answer, or by any gesture or movement of body suggest that he had heard what the older man had said.

'Gurther goes tomorrow, perhaps on our good work, perhaps to speak secretly to his friends in the police – who knows? He has work to do: let him do it, Pfeiffer. All my men will be there – at a place called Brightlingsea. You also shall go. Gurther would rob a blind man? Good! You shall rob one also. As for Gurther, I do not wish him back. I am tired of him: he is a madman. All men are mad who sniff that white snuff up their foolish noses – eh, Pfeiffer?'

Still the awkward-looking man made no reply.

'Let him do his work: you shall not interfere, until – it is done.'

Pfeiffer was looking at him now, a cold sneer on his face.

'If he comes back, I do not,' he said. 'This man is frightening me. Twice the police have been here – three times . . . you remember the woman. The man is a danger, Herr Doktor. I told you he was the day you brought him here.'

'He can dress in the gentleman-club manner,' said the doctor gently.

'Pshaw!' said the other scornfully. 'Is he not an actor who has postured and painted his face and thrown about his legs for so many marks a week?'

'If he does not come back I shall be relieved,' murmured the doctor. 'Though it would be a mistake to leave him so that these cunning men could pry into our affairs.'

Pfeiffer said nothing: he understood his instructions; there was nothing to be said. 'When does he go?'

'Early tomorrow, before daylight. You will see him, of course.'

He said something in a low tone, that only Pfeiffer heard. The shadow who stood in stockinged feet listening at the door only heard two words. Gurther grinned in the darkness; his bright eyes grew luminous. He heard his companion move towards the door and sped up the stairs without a sound.

*   *   *

Rath Hall was a rambling white building of two storeys, set in the midst of a little park, so thickly wooded that the house was invisible from the road; and since the main entrance to the estate was a very commonplace gate, without lodge or visible drive beyond, Gonsalez would have missed the place had he not recognized the man who was sitting on the moss-grown and broken wall who jumped down as Leon stopped his car.

'Mr Meadows is at the house, sir. He said he expected you.'

'And where on earth is the house?' asked Leon Gonsalez, as he went into reverse.

For answer the detective opened the gate wide and Leon sent his car winding between the trees, for close at hand he recognized where a gravel drive had once been, and, moreover, he saw the tracks of cars in the soft earth. He arrived just as Mr Johnson Lee was taking his two guests in to dinner; and Meadows was obviously glad to see him. He excused himself, and took Leon aside into the hall, where they could not be overheard.

'I have had your message,' he said. 'The only thing that happened out of the ordinary is that the servants have an invitation to a big concert at Brightlingsea. You expected that?'

Leon nodded.

'Yes: I hope Lee will let them go. I prefer that they should be out of the way. A crude scheme – but Oberzohn does these things. Has anything else happened?'

'Nothing. There have been one or two queer people around.'

'Has he showed you the letters he had from Barberton?'

To his surprise the inspector answered in the affirmative.

'Yes, but they are worse than Greek to me. A series of tiny protuberances on thick brown paper. He keeps them in his safe. He read some of the letters to me: they were not very illuminating.'

'But the letter of letters?' asked Leon anxiously. 'That which Lee answered – by the way, you know that Mr Lee wrote all his letters between perforated lines?'

'I've seen the paper,' nodded the detective. 'No, I asked him about that, but apparently he is not anxious to talk until he has seen his lawyer, who is coming down tonight. He should have been here, in fact, in time for dinner.'

They passed into the dining-room together. The blind man was waiting patiently at the head of the table, and with an apology Leon took the place that had been reserved for him. He sat with his back to the wall, facing one of the three long windows that looked out upon the park. It was a warm night and the blinds were up, as also was the middle window that faced him. He made a motion to Mr Washington, who sat opposite him, to draw a little aside, and the American realized that he wished an uninterrupted view of the park.

'Would you like the window closed?' asked Mr Lee, leaning forward and addressing the table in general. 'I know it is open,' he said with a little laugh, 'because I opened it! I am a lover of fresh air.'

They murmured their agreement and the meal went on without any extraordinary incident. Mr Washington was one of those adaptable people who dovetail into any environment in which they find themselves. He was as much at home at Rath Hall as though he had been born and bred in the neighbourhood. Moreover, he had a special reason for jubilation: he had found a rare adder when walking in the woods that morning, and spent ten minutes explaining in what respect it differed from every other English adder.

'Is it dead?' asked Meadows nervously.

'Kill it?' said the indignant Mr Washington. 'Why' should I kill it? I saw a whole lot of doves out on the lawn this morning – should I kill 'em? No, sir! I've got none of those mean feelings towards snakes. I guess the Lord sent snakes into this world for some other purpose than to be chased and killed every time they're seen. I sent him up to London today by train to a friend of mine at the Zoological Gardens. He'll keep him until I'm ready to take him back home.'

Meadows drew a long sigh.

'As long as he's not in your pocket,' he said.

'Do you mind?'

Leon's voice was urgent as he signalled Washington to move yet farther to the left, and when the big man moved his chair, Leon nodded his thanks. His eyes were on the window and the darkening lawn. Not once did he remove his gaze.

'It's an extraordinary thing about Poole, my lawyer,' Mr Lee was saying. 'He promised faithfully he'd be at Rath by seven o'clock. What is the time?'

Meadows looked at his watch.

'Half-past eight,' he said. He saw the cloud that came over the face of the blind owner of Rath Hall.

'It is extraordinary! I wonder if you would mind – '

His foot touched a bell beneath the table and his butler came in.

'Will you telephone to Mr Poole's house and ask if he has left?'

The butler returned in a short time.

'Yes, sir, Mr Poole left the house by car at half-past six.'

Johnson Lee sat back in his chair.

'Half-past six? He should have been here by now.'

'How far away does he live?'

'About fifteen miles. I thought he might have come down from London rather late. That is extraordinary.'

'He may have had tyre trouble,' said Leon, not shifting his fixed stare.'

'He could have telephoned.'

'Did anyone know he was coming – anybody outside your own household?' asked Gonsalez.

The blind man hesitated.

'Yes, I mentioned the fact to the post office this morning. I went in to get my letters, and found that one I had written to Mr Poole had been returned through a mistake on my part. I told the postmaster that he was coming this evening and that there was no need to forward it.'

'You were in the public part of the post office?'

'I believe I was.'

'You said nothing else, Mr Lee – nothing that would give any idea of the object of this visit?'

Again his host hesitated. 'I don't know. I'm almost afraid that I did,' he confessed. 'I remember telling the postmaster that I was going to talk to Mr Poole about poor Barberton – Mr Barberton was very well known in this neighbourhood.'

'That is extremely unfortunate,' said Leon.

He was thinking of two things at the same time: the whereabouts of the missing lawyer, and the wonderful cover that the wall between the window and the floor gave to any man who might creep along out of sight until he got back suddenly to send the snake on its errand of death.

'How many men have you got in the grounds, by the way, Meadows?'

'One, and he's not in the grounds but outside on the road. I pull him in at night, or rather in the evening, to patrol the grounds, and he is armed.' He said this with a certain importance. An armed English policeman is a tremendous phenomenon that few have seen.

'Which means that he has a revolver that he hasn't fired except at target practice,' said Leon. 'Excuse me – I thought I heard a car.'

He got up noiselessly from the table, went round the back of Mr Lee, and, darting to the window, looked out. A flower-bed ran close to the wall, and beyond that was a broad gravel drive. Between gravel and flowers was a wide strip of turf. The drive continued some fifty feet to the right before it turned under an arch of rambler roses. To the left it extended for less than a dozen feet, and from this point a path parallel the side of the house ran into the drive.

'Do you hear it?' asked Lee.

'No, sir, I was mistaken.'

Leon dipped his hand into his side pocket, took out a handful of something that looked like tiny candles wrapped in coloured paper. Only Meadows saw him scatter them left and right, and he was too discreet to ask why. Leon saw the inquiring lift of his eyebrows as he came back to his seat, but was wilfully dense. Thereafter, he ate his dinner with only an occasional glance towards the window.

'I'm not relying entirely upon my own lawyer's advice,' said Mr Lee. 'I have telegraphed to Lisbon to ask Dr Pinto Caillao to come to England, and he may be of greater service even than Poole, though where – ' The butler came in at this moment.

'Mrs Poole has just telephoned, sir. Her husband has had a bad accident: his car ran into a tree trunk which was lying across the road near Lawley. It was on the other side of the bend, and he did not see it until too late.'

'Is he very badly hurt?'

'No, sir, but he is in the Cottage Hospital. Mrs Poole says he is fit to travel home.'

The blind man sat open-mouthed.

'What a terrible thing to have happened!' he began.

'A very lucky thing for Mr Poole,' said Leon cheerfully. 'I feared worse than that – '

From somewhere outside the window came a 'snap!' – the sound that a Christmas cracker makes when it is exploded. Leon got up from the table, walked swiftly to the side of the window and jumped out. As he struck the earth, he trod on one of the little bon-bons he had scattered and it cracked viciously under his foot.

There was nobody in sight. He ran swiftly along the grass-plot, slowing his pace as came to the end of the wall, and then jerked round, gun extended stiffly. Still nobody. Before him was a close-growing box hedge, in which had been cut an opening. He heard the crack of a signal behind him, guessed that it was Meadows, and presently the detective joined him. Leon put his fingers to his lips, leapt the path to the grass on the other side, and dodged behind a tree until he could see straight through the opening in the box hedge. Beyond was a rose-garden, a mass of pink and red and golden blooms.

Leon put his hand in his pocket and took out a black cylinder, fitting it, without taking his eyes from the hedge opening, to the muzzle of his pistol. Meadows heard the dull thud of the explosion before he saw the pistol go up. There was a scatter of leaves and twigs and the sound of hurrying feet. Leon dashed through the opening in time to see a man plunge into a plantation.

'*Plop!*'

The bullet struck a tree not a foot from the fugitive.

'That's that!' said Leon, and took off his silencer. 'I hope none of the servants heard it, and most of all that Lee, whose hearing is unfortunately most acute, mistook the shot for something else.'

He went back to the window, stopping to pick up such of his crackers as had not exploded.

'They are useful things to put on the floor of your room when you're expecting to have your throat cut in the middle of the night,' he said pleasantly. 'They cost exactly two dollars a hundred, and they've saved my life more often than I can count. Have you ever waited in the dark to have your throat cut?' he asked. 'It happened to me three times, and I will admit that it is not an experience that I am anxious to repeat. Once in Bohemia, in the city of Prague; once in New Orleans, and once in Ortona.'

'What happened to the assassins?' asked Meadows with a shiver.

'That is a question for the theologian, if you will forgive the well-worn jest,' said Leon. 'I think they are in hell, but then I'm prejudiced.'

Mr Lee had left the dining-table and was standing at the front door, leaning on his stick; and with him an interested Mr Washington.

'What was the trouble?' asked the old man in a worried voice. 'It is a great handicap not being able to see things. But I thought I heard a shot fired.'

'Two,' said Leon promptly. 'I hoped you hadn't heard them. I don't know who the man was, Mr Lee, but he certainly had no right in the grounds, and I scared him off.'

'You must have used a silencer: I did not hear the shots fully. Did you catch a view of the man's face?'

'No, I saw his back,' he said. Leon thought it was unnecessary to add that a man's back was as familiar to him as his face. For when he studied his enemies, his study was a very thorough and complete one. Moreover, Gurther ran with a peculiar swing of his shoulder.

He turned suddenly to the master of Rath Hall. 'May I speak with you privately for a few minutes, Mr Lee?' he asked. He had taken a sudden resolution.

'Certainly,' said the other courteously, and tapped his way into the hall and into his private study.

For ten minutes Leon was closeted with him. When he came out, Meadows had gone down to his man at the gate, and Washington was standing disconsolately alone. Leon took him by the arm and led him on to the lawn.

'There's going to be real trouble here tonight,' he said, and told him the arrangement he had made with Mr Johnson Lee. 'I've tried to persuade him to let me see the letter which is in his safe, but he is like rock on that matter, and I'd hate to burgle the safe of a friend. Listen.'

Elijah Washington listened and whistled.

'They stopped the lawyer coming,' Gonsalez went on, 'and now they're mortally scared if, in his absence, the old man tells us what he intended keeping for his lawyer.'

'Meadows is going to London, isn't he?'

Leon nodded slowly.

'Yes, he is going to London – by car. Did you know all the servants were going out tonight?'

Mr Washington stared at him.

'The women, you mean?'

'The women and the men,' said Leon calmly. 'There is an excellent concert at Brightlingsea tonight, and though they will be late for the first half of the performance, they will thoroughly enjoy the latter portion of the programme. The invitation is not mine, but it is one I thoroughly approve.'

'But does Meadows want to go away when the fun is starting?'

Apparently Inspector Meadows was not averse from leaving at this critical moment. He was, in fact, quite happy to go.

Mr Washington's views on police intelligence underwent a change for the worse.

'But surely he had better stay?' said the American. 'If you're expecting an attack . . . they are certain to marshal the whole of their forces?'

'Absolutely certain,' said the calm Gonsalez 'Here is the car.'

The Rolls came out from the back of the house at that moment and drew up before the door.

'I don't like leaving you,' said Meadows, as he swung himself up by the driver's side and put his bag on the seat.

'Tell the driver to avoid Lawley like the plague,' said Leon. 'There's a tree down, unless the local authorities have removed it – which is very unlikely.'

He waited until the tail lights of the machine had disappeared into the gloom, then he went back to the hall.

'Excuse me, sir,' said the butler, struggling into his great-coat as he spoke. 'Will you be all right – there is nobody left in the house to look after Mr Lee. I could stay – '

'It was Mr Lee's suggestion you should all go,' said Gonsalez briefly. 'Just go outside and tell me when the lights of the char-a-banc come into view. I want to speak to Mr Lee before you go.'

He went into the library and shut the door behind him. The waiting butler heard the murmur of his voice and had some qualms of conscience. The tickets had come from a local agency; he had never dreamt that, with guests in the house, his employer would allow the staff to go in its entirety.

It was not a char-a-banc but a big closed bus that came lumbering up the apology for a drive, and swept round to the back of the house, to the annoyance of the servants, who were gathered in the hall.

'Don't bother, I will tell him,' said Leon. He seemed to have taken full charge of the house, an unpardonable offence in the eyes of well-regulated servants.

He disappeared through a long passage leading into the myst-erious domestic regions, and returned to announce that the driver had rectified his error and was coming to the front entrance: an unnecessary explanation, since the big vehicle drew up as he was telling the company.

'There goes the most uneasy bunch of festive souls it has ever been my misfortune to see,' he said, as the bus, its brakes squeaking, went down the declivity towards the unimposing gate. 'And yet they'll have the time of their lives. I've arranged supper for them at the Beech Hôtel, and although they are not aware of it, I am removing them to a place where they'd give a lot of money to be – if they hadn't gone!'

'That leaves you and me alone,' said Mr Washington glumly, but brightened up almost at once. 'I can't say that I mind a rough house, with or without gun-play,' he said. He looked round the dark hall a little apprehensively. 'What about fastening the doors behind?' he asked.

'They're all right,' said Leon. 'It isn't from the back that danger will come. Come out and enjoy the night air . . . it is a little too soon for the real trouble.'

But here, for once, he was mistaken.

Elijah Washington followed him into the park, took two paces, and suddenly Leon saw him stagger. In a second he was by the man's side, bent and peering, his glasses discarded on the grass.

'Get me inside,' said Washington's voice. He was leaning heavily upon his companion.

With his arm round his waist, taking half his weight, Leon pushed the man into the hall but did not close the door. Instead, as the American sat down with a thud upon a hall seat, Leon fell to the ground, and peered along the artificial sky-line he had created. There was no movement, no sign of any attacker. Then and only then did he shut the door and drop the bar, and pushing the study door wide, carried the man into the room and switched on the lights.

'I guess something got me then,' muttered Washington.

His right cheek was red and swollen, and Leon saw the tell-tale bite; saw something else. He put his hand to the cheek and examined his finger-tips.

'Get me some whisky, will you? – about a gallon of it.'

He was obviously in great pain and sat rocking himself to and fro.

'Gosh! This is awful!' he groaned. 'Never had any snake that bit like this!'

'You're alive, my friend, and I didn't believe you when you said you were snake-proof.'

Leon poured out a tumbler of neat whisky and held it to the American's lips.

'Down with Prohibition!' murmured Washington, and did not take the glass from his lips until it was empty. 'You can give me another dose of that – I shan't get pickled,' he said.

He put his hand up to his face and touched the tiny wound gingerly – 'It is wet,' he said in surprise.

'What did it feel like?'

'Like nothing so much as a snake-bite,' confessed the expert.

Already his face was puffed beneath the eyes, and the skin was discoloured black and blue.

Leon crossed to the fire-place and pushed the bell, and Washington watched him in amazement.

'Say, what's the good of ringing? The servants have gone.'

There was a patter of feet in the hall, the door was flung open and George Manfred came in, and behind him the startled visitor saw Meadows and a dozen men.

'For the Lord's sake!' he said sleepily.

'They came in the char-a-banc, lying on the floor,' explained Leon, 'and the only excuse for bringing a char-a-banc here was to send the servants to that concert.'

'You got Lee away?' asked Manfred.

Leon nodded.

'He was in the car that took friend Meadows, who transferred to the char-a-banc somewhere out of sight of the house.'

Washington had taken a small cardboard box from his pocket and was rubbing a red powder gingerly upon the two white-edged marks, groaning the while.

'This is certainly a snake that's got the cobra skinned to death and a rattlesnake's bite ain't worse than a dog nip,' he said. 'Mamba nothing! I know the mamba; he is pretty fatal, but not so bad as this.'

Manfred looked across to Leon.

'Gurther?' he asked simply, and Gonsalez nodded.

'It was intended for me obviously, but, as I've said before, Gurther is nervous. And it didn't help him any to be shot up.'

'Do you fellows mind not talking so loud?' He glanced at the heavy curtains that covered the windows. Behind these the shutters had been fastened, and Dr Oberzohn was an ingenious man.

Leon took a swift survey of the visitor's feet; they wore felt slippers.

'I don't think I can improve upon the tactics of the admirable Miss Leicester,' he said, and went up to Mr Lee's bedroom, which was in the centre of the house and had a small balcony, the floor of which was formed by the top of the porch.

The long French windows were open and Leon crawled out into the darkness and took observation through the pillars of the balustrade. They were in the open now, making no attempt to conceal their presence. He counted seven, until he saw the cigarette of another near the end of the drive. What were they waiting for? he wondered. None of them moved; they were not even closing on the house. And this inactivity puzzled him. They were awaiting a signal. What was it to be? Whence would it come?

He saw a man come stealthily across the lawn . . . one or two? His eyes were playing tricks. If there were two, one was Gurther. There was no mistaking him. For a second he passed out of view behind a pillar of the balcony. Leon moved his head . . . Gurther had fallen! He saw him stumble to his knees and tumble flat upon the ground. What did that mean?

He was still wondering when he heard a soft scraping, and a deep-drawn breath, and tried to locate the noise. Suddenly, within a few inches of his face, a hand came up out of the darkness and gripped the lower edge of the balcony.

Swiftly, noiselessly, Gonsalez wriggled back to the room, drew erect in the cover of the curtains and waited. His hand touched something: it was a long silken cord by which the curtains were drawn. Leon grinned in the darkness and made a scientific loop.

The intruder drew himself up on to the parapet, stepped quietly across, then tiptoed to the open window. He was not even suspicious, for the French windows had been open all the evening. Without a sound, he stepped into the room and was momentarily silhouetted against the starlight reflected in the window.

'Hatless,' thought Leon. That made things easier. As the man took another stealthy step, the noose dropped over his neck, jerked tight and strangled the cry in his throat. In an instant he was lying flat on the ground with a knee in his back. He struggled to rise, but Leon's fist came down with the precision of a piston-rod, and he went suddenly quiet.

Gonsalez loosened the slip-knot, and, flinging the man over his shoulder, carried him out of the room and down the stairs. He could only guess that this would be the only intruder, but left nothing to chance, and after he had handed his prisoner to the men who were waiting in the hall, he ran back to the room, to find, as he had expected, that no other adventurer had followed the lead. They were still standing at irregular intervals where he had seen them last. The signal was to come from the house. What was it to be? he wondered.

He left one of his men on guard in the room and went back to the study, to find that the startled burglar was an old friend. Lew Cuccini was looking from one of his captors to the other, a picture of dumbfounded chagrin. But the most extraordinary discovery that Leon made on his return to the study was that the American snake-charmer was his old cheerful self, and, except for his un-sightly appearance, seemed to be none the worse for an ordeal which would have promptly ended the lives of ninety-nine men out of a hundred. 'Snake-proof – that's me. Is this the guy that did it?' He pointed to Cuccini.

'Where is Gurther?' asked Manfred,

Cuccini grinned up into his face.

'You'd better find out, boss,' he said. 'He'll fix you. As soon as I shout – '

'Cuccini – ' Leon's voice was gentle. The point of the long-bladed knife that he held to the man's neck was indubitably sharp.

Cuccini shrank back. 'You will not shout. If you do, I shall cut your throat and spoil all these beautiful carpets – that is a genuine silken Bokhara, George. I haven't seen one in ten years.' He nodded to the soft-hued rug on which George Manfred was standing. 'What is the signal, Cuccini?' turning his attention again to the prisoner. 'And what happens when you give the signal?'

'Listen,' said Cuccini, 'that throat-cutting stuff don't mean anything to me. There's no third degree in this country, and don't forget it.'

'You have never seen my ninety-ninth degree.' Leon smiled like a delighted boy. 'Put something in his mouth, will you?'

One of the men tied a woollen scarf round Cuccini's head.

'Lay him on the sofa.'

He was already bound hand and foot and helpless.

'Have you any wax matches? Yes, here are some.' Leon emptied a cut-glass container into the palm of his hand and looked round at the curious company. 'Now, gentlemen, if you will leave me alone for exactly five minutes, I will give Mr Cuccini an excellent imitation of the persuasive methods of Gian Visconti, an excellent countryman of his, and the inventor of the system I am about to apply.'

Cuccini was shaking his head furiously. A mumble of unintelligible sounds came from behind the scarf.

'Our friend is not unintelligent. Any of you who say that Signer Cuccini is unintelligent will incur my severest displeasure,' said Leon.

They sat the man up and he talked brokenly, hesitatingly.

'Splendid,' said Leon, when he had finished. 'Take him into the kitchen and give him a drink – you'll find a tap above the kitchen sink.'

'I've often wondered, Leon,' said George, when they were alone together, 'whether you would ever carry out those horrific threats of yours of torture and malignant savagery?'

'Half the torture of torture is anticipation,' said Leon easily, lighting a cigarette with one of the matches he had taken from the table, and carefully guiding the rest back into the glass bowl. 'Any man versed in the art of suggestive descriptions can dispense with thumbscrews and branding irons, little maidens and all the ghastly apparatus of criminal justice ever employed by our ancestors. I, too, wonder,' he mused, blowing a ring of smoke to the ceiling, 'whether I could carry my threats into execution – I must try one day.' He nodded pleasantly, as though he were promising himself a great treat.

Manfred looked at his watch.

'What do you intend doing – giving the signal?' Gonsalez nodded. 'And then?'

'Letting them come in. We may take refuge in the kitchen. I think it would be wiser.'

George Manfred nodded. 'You're going to allow them to open the safe?'

'Exactly,' said Leon. 'I particularly wish that safe to be opened, and since Mr Lee demurs, I think this is the best method. I had that in my mind all the time. Have you seen the safe, George? I have. Nobody but an expert could smash it. I have no tools. I did not provide against such a contingency, and I have scruples. Our friends have tools – and no scruples!'

'And the snake – is there any danger?'

Leon snapped his fingers.

'The snake has struck for the night, and will strike no more! As for Gurther – '

'He owes you something.'

Leon sent another ring up and did not speak until it broke on the ceiling.

'Gurther is dead,' he said simply. 'He has been lying on the lawn in front of the house for the past ten minutes.'

Chapter 17

Written in Braille

Leon briefly related the scene he had witnessed from the balcony.

'It was undoubtedly Gurther,' he said. 'I could not mistake him. He passed out of view for a second behind one of the pillars, and when I looked round he was lying flat on the ground.'

He threw his cigarette into the fire-place.

'I think it is nearly time,' he said. He waited until Manfred had gone, and, going to the door, moved the bar and pulled it open wide.

Stooping down, he saw that the opening of the door had been observed, for one of the men was moving across the lawn in the direction of the house. From his pocket he took a small electric lamp and sent three flickering beams into the darkness. To his surprise, only two men walked forward to the house. Evidently Cuccini was expected to deal with any resistance before the raid occurred.

The house had been built in the fifteenth century, and the entrance hall was a broad, high barn of a place. Some Georgian architect, in the peculiar manner of his kind, had built a small minstrel gallery over the dining-room entrance and immediately facing the study. Leon had already explored the house and had found the tiny staircase that led to this architectural monstrosity. He had no sooner given the signal than he dived into the dining-room, through the tall door, and was behind the thick curtains at the back of the narrow gallery when the first two men came in. He saw them go straight into the study and push open the door. At the same time a third man appeared under the porch, though he made no attempt to enter the hall.

Presently one of those who had gone into the study came out and called Cuccini by name. When no answer came, he went grumbling back to his task. What that task was, Leon could guess, before the peculiarly acrid smell of hot steel was wafted to his sensitive nostrils.

By crouching down he could see the legs of the men who were working at the safe. They had turned on all the lights, and apparently expected no interruption. The man at the door was joined by another man.

'Where is Lew?'

In the stillness of the house the words, though spoken in a low tone, were audible.

'I don't know – inside somewhere. He had to fix that dago.'

Leon grinned. This description of himself never failed to tickle him.

One of the workers in the library came out at this point.

'Have you seen Cuccini?'

'No,' said the man at the door.

'Go in and find him. He ought to be here.'

Cuccini's absence evidently made him uneasy, for though he returned to the room he was out again in a minute, asking if the messenger had come back. Then, from the back of the passage, came the searcher's voice: 'The kitchen's locked.'

The safe-cutter uttered an expression of amazement.

'Locked? What's the idea?'

He came to the foot of the stairs and bellowed up: 'Cuccini!'

Only the echo answered him.

'That's queer.' He poked his head in the door of the study. 'Rush that job, Mike. There's some funny business here.' And over his shoulder, 'Tell the boys to get ready to jump.'

The man went out into the night and was absent some minutes, to return with an alarming piece of news.

'They've gone, boss. I can't see one of them.'

The 'boss' cursed him, and himself went into the grounds on a visit of inspection. He came back in a hurry, ran into the study, and Leon heard his voice: 'Stand ready to clear.'

'What about Cuccini?'

'Cuccini will have to look after himself . . . got it, Mike?'

The deep voice said something. There followed the sound of a crack, as though something of iron had broken. It was the psychological moment. Leon parted the curtains and dropped lightly to the floor.

The man at the door turned in a flash at the sound.

'Put 'em up!' he said sharply.

'Don't shoot.' Leon's voice was almost conversational in its calmness. 'The house is surrounded by police.'

With an oath the man darted out of the door, and at that instant came the sound of the first shot, followed by desultory firing from the direction of the road. The second guard had been the first to go. Leon ran to the door, slammed it tight and switched on the lights as the two men came from the study. Under the arm of one was a thick pad of square brown sheets. He dropped his load and put up his hands at the sight of the gun; but his companion was made of harder material, and, with a yell, he leapt at the man who stood between him and freedom. Leon twisted aside, advanced his shoulder to meet the furious drive of the man's fist; then, dropping his pistol, he stooped swiftly and tackled him below the knees. The man swayed, sought to recover his balance and fell with a crash on the stone floor. All the time his companion stood dazed and staring, his hands waving in the air.

There was a knock at the outer door. Without turning his back upon his prisoners, Leon reached for the bar and pulled it up. Manfred came in.

'The gentleman who shouted "Cuccini" scared them. I think they've got away. There were two cars parked on the road.'

His eyes fell upon the brown sheets scattered on the floor and he nodded.

'I think you have all you want, Leon,' he said.

The detectives came crowding in at that moment and secured their prisoners whilst Leon Gonsalez and his friend went out on to the lawn to search for Gurther.

The man lay as he had fallen, on his face, and as Leon flashed his lamp upon the figure, he saw that the snake had struck behind the ear.

'Gurther?' frowned Leon.

He turned the figure on its back and gave a little gasp of surprise, for there looked up to the starry skies the heavy face of Pfeiffer.

'Pfeiffer! I could have sworn it was the other! There has been some double-crossing here. Let me think.' He stood for fully a minute, his chin on his hand. 'I could have understood Gurther; he was becoming a nuisance and a danger to the old man. Pfeiffer, the more reliable of the two, hated him. My first theory was that Gurther had been put out by order of Oberzohn.'

'Suppose Gurther heard that order, or came to know of it?' asked Manfred quietly.

Leon snapped his fingers.

'That is it! We had a similar case a few years ago, you will remember, George? The old man gave the "out" order to Pfeiffer – and Gurther got his blow in first. Shrewd fellow!'

When they returned to the house, the three were seated in a row in Johnson Lee's Library. Cuccini, of course, was an old acquaintance. Of the other two men, Leon recognized one, a notorious gunman whose photograph had embellished the pages of *Hue and Cry* for months.

The third, and evidently the skilled workman of the party, for he it was whom they had addressed as 'Mike' and who had burnt out the lock of Lee's safe, was identified by Meadows as Mike Selwyn, a skilful burglar and bank-smasher, who had, according to his statement, only arrived from the Continent that afternoon in answer to a flattering invitation which promised considerable profit to himself.

'And why I left Milan,' he said bitterly, 'where the graft is easy and the money's good, I'd like you to tell me!'

The prisoners were removed to the nearest secure lock-up, and by the time Lee's servants returned from their dance, all evidence of an exciting hour had disappeared, except that the blackened and twisted door of the safe testified to the sinister character of the visitation.

Meadows returned as they were gathering together the scattered sheets. There were hundreds of them, all written in Braille characters, and Manfred's sensitive fingers were skimming their surface.

'Oh, yes,' he said, in answer to a question that was put to him, 'I knew Lee was blind, the day we searched Barberton's effects. That was my mystery.' He laughed. 'Barberton expected a call from his old friend and had left a message for him on the mantelpiece. Do you remember that strip of paper? It ran: "Dear Johnny, I will be back in an hour." These are letters – ' he indicated the papers.

'The folds tell me that,' said Meadows. 'You may not get a conviction against Cuccini; the two burglars will come up before a judge, but to charge Cuccini means the whole story of the snake coming out, and that means a bigger kick than I'm prepared to laugh away – I am inclined to let Cuccini go for the moment.'

Manfred nodded. He sat with the embossed sheets on his knee.

'Written from various places,' he went on.

It was curious to see him, his fingers running swiftly along the embossed lines, his eyes fixed on vacancy.

'So far I've learnt nothing, except that in his spare time Barberton amused himself by translating native fairy stories into English and putting them into Braille for use in the blind school. I knew, of course, that he did that, because I'd already interviewed his sister, who is the mistress of the girls' section.'

He had gone through half a dozen letters when he rose from the table and walked across to the safe.

'I have a notion that the thing we're seeking is not here,' he said. 'It is hardly likely that he would allow a communication of that character to be jumbled up with the rest of the correspondence.'

The safe door was open and the steel drawer at the back had been pulled out. Evidently it was from this receptacle that the letters had been taken. Now the drawer was empty. Manfred took it out and measured the depth of it with his finger.

'Let me see,' said Gonsalez suddenly.

He groped along the floor of the safe, and presently he began to feel carefully along the sides.

'Nothing here,' he said. He drew out half a dozen account books and a bundle of documents which at first glance Manfred had put aside as being personal to the owner of Rath Hall. These were lying on the floor amidst the mass of molten metal that had burnt deep holes in the carpet. Leon examined the books one by one, opening them and running his nail along the edge of the pages. The fourth, a weighty ledger, did not open so easily – did not, indeed, open at all. He carried it to the table and tried to pull back the cover. 'Now, how does this open?'

The ledger covers were of leather; to all appearance a very ordinary book, and Leon was anxious not to disturb so artistic a camouflage. Examining the edge carefully, he saw a place where the edges had been forced apart. Taking out a knife, he slipped the thin blade into the aperture. There was a click and the cover sprang up like the lid of a box.

'And this, I think, is what we are looking for,' said Gonsalez.

The interior of the book had been hollowed out, the edges being left were gummed tight, and the receptacle thus formed was packed close with brown papers; brown, except for one, which was written on a large sheet of foolscap, headed:

'Bureau of the Ministry of Colonies, Lisbon.'

Barberton had superimposed upon this long document his Braille writing, and now one of the mysteries was cleared up.

'Lee said he had never received any important documents,' said Manfred, 'and, of course, he hadn't, so far as he knew. To him this was merely a sheet of paper on which Braille characters were inscribed. Read this, Leon.'

Leon scanned the letter. It was dated 'July 21st, 1912', and bore, in the lower left-hand corner, the seal of the Portuguese Colonial Office. He read it through rapidly and at the end looked up with a sigh of satisfaction.

'And this settles Oberzohn and Co., and robs them of a fortune, the extent of which I think we shall discover when we read Barberton's letter.'

He lit a cigarette and scanned the writing again, whilst Meadows, who did not understand Leon's passion for drama, waited with growing impatience.

'Illustrious Senhor,' [began Leon, reading] 'I have this day had the honour of placing before His Excellency the President, and the Ministers of the Cabinet, your letter dated May 15th, 1912. By a letter dated January 8th, 1911, the lands marked Ex. 275 on the Survey Map of the Biskara district were conceded to you, Illustrious Senhor, in order to further the cause of science – a cause which is very dear to the heart of His Excellency the President. Your further letter, in which you complain, Illustrious Senhor, that the incursion of prospectors upon our land is hampering your scientific work, and your request that an end may be put to these annoyances by the granting to you of an extension of the concession, so as to give you title to all mineral found in the aforesaid area, Ex. 275 on the Survey Map of Biskara, and thus making the intrusion of prospectors illegal, has been considered by the Council, and the extending concession is hereby granted, on the following conditions: The term of the concession shall be for twelve years, as from the 14th day of June, 1912, and shall be renewable by you, your heirs or nominees, every twelfth year, on payment of a nominal sum of 1,000 milreis. In the event of the concessionaire, his heirs or nominees, failing to apply for a renewal on the 14th day of June, 1924, the mineral rights of the said area, Ex. 275 on the Survey Map of Biskara, shall be open to claim in accordance with the laws of Angola – '

Leon sat back.

'Fourteenth of June?' he said, and looked up. 'Why, that is next week – five days! We've cut it rather fine, George.'

'Barberton said there were six weeks,' said Manfred. 'Obviously he made the mistake of timing the concession from July 21st – the date of the letter. He must have been the most honest man in the world; there was no other reason why he should have communicated with Miss Leicester. He could have kept quiet and claimed the rights for himself. Go on, Leon.'

'That is about all,' said Leon, glancing at the tail of the letter. 'The rest is more or less flowery and complimentary and has reference to the scientific work in which Professor Leicester was engaged. Five days – phew!' he whistled.

'We may now find something in Barberton's long narrative to give us an idea of the value of this property.' Manfred turned the numerous pages. 'Do any of you gentlemen write shorthand?'

Meadows went out into the hall and brought back an officer. Waiting until he had found pencil and paper, Leon began the extraordinary story of William Barberton – most extraordinary because every word had been patiently and industrially punched in the Braille characters.

Chapter 18
The story of Mont d'Or

'Dear Friend Johnny,

'I have such a lot to tell you that I hardly know where to begin. I've struck rich at last, and the dream I've often talked over with you has come true. First of all, let me tell you that I have come upon nearly £50,000 worth of wrought gold. We've been troubled round here with lions, one of which took away a carrier of mine, and at last I decided to go out and settle accounts with this fellow. I found him six miles from the camp and planted a couple of bullets into him without killing him, and decided to follow up his spoor. It was a mad thing to do, trailing a wounded lion in the jungle, and I didn't realize how mad until we got out of the bush into the hills and I found Mrs Lion waiting for me. She nearly got me too. More by accident than anything else, I managed to shoot her dead at the first shot, and got another pot at her husband as he was slinking into a cave which was near our tent.

'As I had gone so far, I thought I might as well go the whole hog, especially as I'd seen two lion cubs playing around the mouth of the cave, and bringing up my boys, who were scared to death, I crawled in, to find, as I expected, that the old lion was nearly gone, and a shot finished him. I had to kill the cubs: they were too young to be left alone, and too much of a nuisance to bring back to camp. This cave had been used as a lair years; it was full of bones, human amongst them.

'But what struck me was the appearance of the roof, which, I was almost certain, had been cut out by hand. It was like a house, and there was a cut door in the rock at the back. I made a torch and went through on a tour of inspection, and you can imagine my surprise when I found myself in a little room with a line of stone niches or shelves. There were three lines on each side. Standing on these at intervals there were little statuettes. They were so covered with dust that I thought they were stone, until I tried to take one down to examine it; then I knew by its weight that it was gold, as they all were.

'I didn't want my boys to know about my find, because they are a treacherous lot, so I took the lightest, after weighing them all with a spring balance, and made a note where I'd taken it from. You might think that was enough of a find for one man in a lifetime, but my luck had set in. I sent the boys back and ordered them to break camp and join me on top of the Thaba. I called it the Thaba, because it is rather like a hill I know in Basutoland, and is one of two.

'The camp was moved up that night; it was a better pitch than any we had had. There was water, plenty of small game, and no mosquitoes. The worst part of it was the terrific thunderstorms which come up from nowhere, and until you've seen one in this ironstone country you don't know what a thunderstorm is like! The hill opposite vas slightly smaller than the one I had taken as a camp, and between was a shallow valley, through which ran a small shallow river – rapids would be a better word.

'Early the next morning I was looking round through my glasses, and saw what I thought was a house on the opposite hill. I asked my head-man who lived there, and he told me that it was once the house of the Star Chief; and I remembered that somebody told me, down in Mossamedes, that an astronomer had settled in this neighbourhood and had been murdered by the natives. I thought I would go over and have a look at the place. The day being cloudy and not too hot, I took my gun and a couple of boys and we crossed the river and began climbing the hill. The house was, of course, in ruins; it had only been a wattle hut at the best of times. Part of it was covered with vegetation, but out of curiosity I searched round, hoping to pick up a few things that might be useful to me, more particularly kettles, for my boys had burnt holes in every one I had. I found a kettle, and then, turning over a heap of rubbish which I think must have been his bed, I found a little rusty tin box and broke it open with my stick. There were a few letters which were so faded that I could only read a word here and there, and in a green oilskin, a long letter from the Portuguese Government.'

(It was at this point, either by coincidence or design, that the narrative continued on the actual paper to which he referred.)

'I speak Portuguese and can read it as easily as English, and the only thing that worried me about it was that the concession gave Professor Leicester all rights to my cave. My first idea was to burn it, but then I began to realize what a scoundrelly business that would be, and I took the letters out into the sun and tried to find if he had any relations, hoping that I'd be able to fix it up with them to take at any rate 50 per cent. of my find. There was only one letter that helped me. It was written in a child's hand and was evidently from his daughter. It had no address, but there was the name – "Mirabelle Leicester".

'I put it in my pocket with the concession and went on searching, but found nothing more. I was going down the hill towards the valley when it struck me that perhaps this man had found gold, and the excuse for getting the concession was a bit of artfulness. I sent a boy back to the camp for a pick, a hammer and a spade, and when he returned I began to make a cutting in the side of the hill. There was nothing to guide me – no outcrop, such as you usually find near a true reef – but I hadn't been digging for an hour before I struck the richest bed of conglomerate I've ever seen. I was either dreaming, or my good angel had at last led me to the one place in the hill where gold could be found. I had previously sent the boys back to camp and told them to wait for me, because, if I did strike metal, I did not want the fact advertised all over Angola, where they've been looking for gold for years.

'Understand, it was not a reef in the ordinary sense of the word, it was all conglomerate, and the wider I made my cutting, the wider the bed appeared, I took the pick to another part of the hill and dug again, with the same result – conglomerate. It was as though nature had thrown up a huge golden hump in the earth. I covered both cuttings late that night and went back to camp. (I was stalked by a leopard in the low bush, but managed to get him.)

'Early next morning, I started off and tried another spot, and with the same result; first three feet of earth, then about six inches of shale, and then conglomerate. I tried to work through the bed, thinking that it might be just a skin, but I was saved much exertion by coming upon a deep rift in the hill about twenty feet wide at the top and tapering down to about fifty feet below the ground level. This gave me a section to work on, and as near as I can judge, the conglomerate bed is something over fifty feet thick and I'm not so sure that it doesn't occur again after an interval of twenty feet or more, for I dug more shale and had a showing of conglomerate at the very bottom of the ravine.

'What does this mean, Johnny? It means that we have found a hill of gold; not solid gold, as in the storybooks, but gold that pays ounces and probably pounds to the ton. How the prospectors have missed it all these years I can't understand, unless it is that they've made their cuttings on the north side of the hill, where they have found nothing but slate and sandstone. The little river in the valley must be feet deep in alluvial, for I panned the bed and got eight ounces of pure gold in an hour – and that was by rough-and-ready methods. I had to be careful not to make the boys too curious, and I am breaking camp tomorrow, and I want you to cable or send me £500 to Mossamedes. The statuette I'm bringing home is worth all that. I would bring more, only I can't trust these Angola boys; a lot of them are mission boys and can read Portuguese, and they're too friendly with a half-breed called Villa, who is an agent of Oberzohn & Smitts; the traders and I know these people to be the most unscrupulous scoundrels on the coast.

'I shall be at Mossamedes about three weeks after you get this letter, but I don't want to get back to the coast in a hurry, otherwise people are going to suspect I have made a strike.'

Leon put the letter down.

'There is the story in a nutshell, gentlemen,' he said. 'I don't, for one moment, believe that Mr Barberton showed Villa the letter. It is more likely that one of the educated natives he speaks about saw it and reported it to Oberzohn's agent. Portuguese is the lingua franca of that part of the coast. Barberton was killed to prevent his meeting the girl and telling her of his find – incidentally, of warning her to apply for a renewal of the concession. It wasn't even necessary that they should search his belongings to recover the letter, because once they knew of its existence and the date which Barberton had apparently confounded with the date the letter was written, their work was simply to prevent an application to the Colonial Office at Lisbon. It was quite different after Barberton was killed, when they learnt or guessed that the letter was in Mr Lee's possession.'

Meadows agreed.

'That was the idea behind Oberzohn's engagement of Mirabelle Leicester?'

'Exactly, and it was also behind the attack upon Heavytree Farm. To secure this property they must get her away and keep her hidden either until it is too late for her to apply for a renewal, or until she has been bullied or forced into appointing a nominee.'

'Or married,' said Leon briskly. 'Did that idea occur to you? Our tailor-made friend, Monty Newton, may have had matrimonial intentions. It would have been quite a good stroke of business to secure a wife and a large and auriferous hill at the same time. This, I think, puts a period to the ambitions of Herr Doktor Oberzohn.'

He got up from the table and handed the papers to the custody of the detective, and turned with a quizzical smile to his friend.

'George, do you look forward with any pleasure to a two hundred and fifty miles' drive?'

'Are you the chauffeur?' asked George.

'I am the chauffeur,' said Leon cheerfully. 'I have driven a car for many years and I have not been killed yet. It is unlikely that I shall risk my precious life and yours tonight. Come with me and I promise never to hit her up above sixty except on the real speedways.'

Manfred nodded.

'We will stop at Oxley and try to get a 'phone call through to Gloucester,' said Leon. 'This line is, of course, out of order. They would do nothing so stupid as to neglect the elementary precaution of disconnecting Rath Hall.'

At Oxley the big Spanz pulled up before the dark and silent exterior of the inn, and Leon, getting down, brought the half-clad landlord to the door and explained his mission, and also learned that two big cars had passed through half an hour before, going in the direction of London.

'That was the gang. I wonder how they'll explain to their paymaster their second failure?'

His first call was to the house in Curzon Street, but there was no reply. 'Ring them again,' said Leon. 'You left Poiccart there?'

Manfred nodded.

They waited for five minutes; still there was no reply.

'How queer!' said Manfred. 'It isn't like Poiccart to leave the house. Get Gloucester.'

At this hour of the night the lines are comparatively clear, and in a very short time he heard the Gloucester operator's voice, and a few seconds later the click that told them they were connected with Heavytree Farm. Here there was some delay before the call was answered.

It was not Mirabelle Leicester nor her aunt who spoke. Nor did he recognize the voice of Digby, who had recovered sufficiently to return to duty.

'Who is that?' asked the voice sharply. 'Is that you, sergeant?'

'No, it is Mr Meadows,' said Leon mendaciously.

'The Scotland Yard gentleman?' It was an eager inquiry.

'I'm Constable Kirk, of the Gloucester Police. My sergeant's been trying to get in touch with you, sir.'

'What is the matter?' asked Leon, a cold feeling at his heart.

'I don't know, sir. About half an hour ago, I was riding past here – I'm one of the mounted men – and I saw the door wide open and all the lights on, and when I came in there was nobody up. I woke Miss Goddard and Mr Digby, but the young lady was not in the house.'

'Lights everywhere?' asked Leon quickly.

'Yes, sir – in the parlour at any rate.'

'No sign of a struggle?'

'No, sir; but a car passed me three miles from the house and it was going at a tremendous rate. I think she may have been in that. Mr Digby and Miss Goddard have just gone into Gloucester.'

'All right, officer. I am sending Mr Gonsalez down to see you,' said Leon, and hung up the receiver.

'What is it?' asked George Manfred, who knew that something was wrong by his friend's face.

'They've got Mirabelle Leicester after all,' said Leon. 'I'm afraid I shall have to break my promise to you, George. That machine of mine is going to travel before daybreak!'

Chapter 19

At Heavytree Farm

It had been agreed that, having failed in their attack, and their energies for the moment being directed to Rath Hall, an immediate return of the Old Guard to Heavytree Farm was unlikely. This had been Meadows's view, and Leon and his friend were of the same mind. Only Poiccart, that master strategist, working surely with a queer knowledge of his enemies' psychology, had demurred from this reasoning; but as he had not insisted upon his point of view, Heavytree Farm and its occupants had been left to the care of the local police and the shaken Digby.

Aunt Alma offered to give up her room to the wounded man, but he would not hear of this, and took the spare bedroom, an excellent position for a defender, since it separated Mirabelle's apartment from the pretty little room which Aunt Alma used as a study and sleeping-place.

The staff of Heavytree Farm consisted of an ancient cowman, a cook and a maid, the latter of whom had already given notice and left on the afternoon of the attack. She had, as she told Mirabelle in all seriousness, a weak heart.

'And a weak head too!' snapped Alma. 'I should not worry about your heart, my girl, if I were you.'

'I was top of my class at school,' bridled the maid, touched to the raw by this reflection upon her intelligence.

'It must have been a pretty small class,' retorted Alma.

A new maid had been found, a girl who had been thrilled by the likelihood that the humdrum of daily labour would be relieved by exciting events out of the ordinary, and before evening the household had settled down to normality. Mirabelle was feeling the reaction and went to bed early that night, waking as the first slant of sunlight poured through her window. She got up, feeling, she told herself, as well as she had felt in her life. Pulling back the chintz curtains, she looked out upon a still world with a sense of happiness and relief beyond measure. There was nobody in sight. Pools of mist lay in the hollows, and from one white farmstead, far away on the slope of the hill, she saw that blue smoke was rising. It was a morning to remember, and, to catch its spirit the better, she dressed hastily and went down into the garden. As she walked along the path she heard a window pulled open and the bandaged head of Mr Digby appeared.

'Oh, it's you, is it, miss?' he said with relief, and she laughed.

'There is nothing more terrible in sight than a big spider,' she said, and pointed to a big flat fellow, who was already spinning his web between the tall hollyhocks. And the first of the bees was abroad.

'If anybody had come last night I shouldn't have heard them,' he confessed. 'I slept like a dead man.' He touched his head gingerly. 'It smarts, but the ache is gone,' he said, not loth to discuss his infirmities. 'The doctor said I had a narrow escape; he thought there was a fracture. Would you like me to make some tea, miss, or shall I call the servant?'

She shook her head, but he had already disappeared, and came seeking her in the garden ten minutes later, with a cup of tea in his hand. He told her for the second time that he was a police pensioner and had been in the employ of Gonsalez for three years. The Three paid well, and had, she learned to her surprise, considerable private resources.

'Does it pay them – this private detective business?'

'Lord bless your heart, no, miss!' He scoffed at the idea. 'They are very rich men. I thought everybody knew that. They say Mr Gonsalez was worth a million even before the war.'

This was astonishing news.

'But why do they do this – ' she hesitated – 'this sort of thing?'

'It is a hobby, miss,' said the man vaguely. 'Some people run race-horses, some own yachts – these gentlemen get a lot of pleasure out of their work and they pay well,' he added.

Men in the regular employ of the Three Just Men not only received a good wage, but frequently a bonus which could only be described as colossal. Once, after they had rounded up and destroyed a gang of Spanish bank robbers, they had distributed £1,000 to every man who was actively employed. He hinted rather than stated that this money had formed part of the loot which the Three had recovered, and did not seem to think that there was anything improper in this distribution of illicit gains.

'After all, miss,' he said philosophically, 'when you collect money like that, it's impossible to give it back to the people it came from.

This Diego had been holding up banks for years, and banks are not like people – they don't feel the loss of money.'

'That's a thoroughly immoral view,' said Mirabelle, intent upon her flower-picking.

'It may be, miss,' agreed Digby, who had evidently been one of the recipients of bounty, and took a complacent and a tolerant view. 'But a thousand pounds is a lot of money.'

The day passed without event. From the early evening papers that came from Gloucester she learned of the fire at Oberzohn's, and did not connect the disaster with anything but an accident. She was not sorry. The fire had licked out one ugly from the past. Incidentally it had destroyed a crude painting which was to Dr Oberzohn more precious than any that Leonardo had painted or Raphael conceived, but this she did not know.

It was just before the dinner hour that there came the first unusual incident of the day. Mirabelle was standing by the garden gate, intent upon the glories of the evening sky, which was piled high with red and slate-coloured cumuli. The glass was falling and a wet night was promised. But the loveliness of that lavish colouring held her. And then she became dimly aware that a man was coming towards the house from the direction of Gloucester. He walked in the middle of the road slowly, as though he, too, were admiring the view and there was no need to hurry. His hands were behind him, his soft felt hat at the back of his head. A stocky-looking man, but his face was curiously familiar. He turned his unsmiling eyes in her direction, and, looking again at his strong features, at the tiny grey-black moustache under his aquiline nose, she was certain she had seen him before. Perhaps she had passed him in the street, and had retained a subconscious mental picture of him.

He slowed his step until, when he came abreast of her, he stopped.

'This is Heavytree Lane?' he asked, in a deep musical voice.

'No – the lane is the first break in the hedge,' she smiled. 'I'm afraid it isn't much of a road – generally it is ankle-deep in mud.'

He looked past her to the house; his eyes ranged the windows, dropped for a moment upon a climbing clematis, and came back to her.

'I don't know Gloucestershire very well,' he said, and added: 'You have a very nice house.'

'Yes,' she said in surprise.

'And a garden.' And then, innocently: 'Do you grow onions?'

She stared at him and laughed.

'I think we do – I am not sure. My aunt looks after the kitchen garden.'

His sad eyes wandered over the house again.

'It is a very nice place,' he said, and, lifting his hat, went on.

Digby was out: he had gone for a gentle walk, and, looking up the road after the stranger, she saw the guard appear round a bend in the road, and saw him stop and speak to the stranger. Apparently they knew one another, for they shook hands at meeting, and after a while Digby pointed down the road to where she was standing, and she saw the man nod. Soon after the stranger went out of view. Who could he be? Was it an additional guard that the three men had put to protect her? When Digby came up to her, she asked him. 'That gentleman, miss? He is Mr Poiccart.'

'Poiccart?' she said, delighted. 'Oh, I wish I had known!'

'I was surprised to see him,' said the guard. 'As a matter of fact, he's the one of the three gentlemen I've met the most. He's generally in Curzon Street, even when the others are away.'

Digby had nothing to say about Poiccart except that he was a very quiet gentleman and took no active part in the operations of the Three Just Men.

'I wonder why he wanted to know about onions?' asked the girl thoughtfully. 'That sounded awfully mysterious.'

It would not have been so mysterious to Leon.

The house retired to bed soon after ten, Alma going the rounds, and examining the new bolts and locks which had been attached that morning to every door which gave ingress to the house.

Mirabelle was unaccountably tired, and was asleep almost as soon as her head touched the pillow.

She heard in her dreams the swish of the rain beating against her window, lay for a long time trying to energise herself to rise and shut the one open window where the curtains were blowing in. Then came the heavier patter against a closed pane, and something rattled on the floor of her room. She sat up. It could not be hail, although there was a rumble of thunder in the distance.

She got out of bed, pulled on her dressing-gown, went to the window, and had all her work to stifle a scream. Somebody was standing on the path below . . . a woman! She leaned out.

'Who is it?' she asked.

'It is me – I – Joan!' There was a sob in the voice of the girl. Even in that light Mirabelle could see that the girl was drenched. 'Don't wake anybody. Come down – I want you.'

'What is wrong?' asked Mirabelle in a low voice.

'Everything . . . everything!'

She was on the verge of hysteria. Mirabelle lit a candle and crossed the room, went downstairs softly, so that Alma should not be disturbed. Putting the candle on the table, she unbarred and unbolted the door, opened it, and as she did so, a man slipped through the half-opened door, his big hands smothering the scream that rose to her lips.

Another man followed and, lifting the struggling girl, carried her into the drawing-room. One of the men took a small iron bottle from his pocket, to which ran a flexible rubber tube ending in a large red cap. Her captor removed his hands just as long as it took to fix the cap over her face. A tiny faucet was turned. Mirabelle felt a puff on her face, a strangely sweet taste, and then her heart began to beat thunderously. She thought she was dying, and writhed desperately to free herself.

* * *

'She's all right,' said Monty Newton, lifting an eyelid for a second. 'Get a blanket.' He turned fiercely to the whimpering girl behind him. 'Shut up, you!' he said savagely. 'Do you want to rouse the whole house?'

A woebegone Joan was whimpering softly, tears running down her face, her hands clasping and unclasping in the agony of her mind.

'You told me you weren't going to hurt her!' she sobbed.

'Get out,' he hissed, and pointed to the door. She went meekly.

A heavy blanket was wrapped round the unconscious girl, and, lifting her between them, the two men went out into the rain, where the old trolley was waiting, and slid her along the straw-covered floor. In another second the trolley moved off, gathering speed.

By this time the effect of the gas had worn off and Mirabelle had regained consciousness. She put out a hand and touched a woman's knee. 'Who is that – Alma?'

'No,' said a miserable voice, 'it's Joan.'

'Joan? Oh, yes, of course . . . why did you do it? – how wicked!'

'Shut up!' Monty snarled. 'Wait until you get to – where you're going before you start these "whys" and "wherefores".'

Mirabelle was deathly sick and bemused, and for the next hour she was too ill to feel even alarmed. Her head was going round and round, and ached terribly, and the jolting of the truck did not improve matters in this respect.

Monty, who was sitting with his back to the truck's side, was smoking. He cursed now and then, as some unusually heavy jolt flung him forward. They passed through the heart of the storm: the flicker of lightning was almost incessant and the thunder was deafening. Rain was streaming down the hood of the trolley, rendering it like a drum.

Mirabelle fell into a sleep and woke feeling better. It was still dark, and she would not have known the direction they were taking, only the driver took the wrong turning coming through a country town, and by the help of the lightning she saw what was indubitably the stand of a race-track, and a little later saw the word 'Newbury.' They were going towards London, she realized.

At this hour of the morning there was little or no traffic, and when they turned on to the new Great West Road a big car went whizzing past at seventy miles an hour and the roar of it woke the girl. Now she could feel the trolley wheels skidding on tram-lines. Lights appeared with greater frequency. She saw a store window brilliantly illuminated, the night watchman having evidently forgotten to turn off the lights at the appointed hour.

Soon they were crossing the Thames. She saw the red and green lights of a tug, and black upon near black a string of barges in mid-stream. She dozed again and was jerked wide awake when the trolley swayed and skidded over a surface more uneven than any. Once its wheels went into a pothole and she was flung violently against the side. Another time it skidded and was brought up with a crash against some obstacle. The bumping grew more gentle, and then the machine stopped, and Monty jumped down and called to her sharply.

Her head was clear now, despite its throbbing. She saw a queer-shaped house, all gables and turrets, extraordinarily narrow for its height. It seemed to stand in the middle of a field. And yet it was in London: she could see the glow of furnace fires and hear the deep boom of a ship's siren as it made its way down the river on the tide.

She had not time to take observations, for Monty fastened to her arm and she squelched through the mud up a flight of stone steps into a dimly lit hall. She had a confused idea that she had seen little dogs standing on the side of the steps, and a big bird with a long bill, but these probably belonged to the smoke dreams which the gas had left.

Monty opened a door and pushed her in before him, and she stared into the face of Dr Oberzohn.

He wore a black velvet dressing-gown that had once been a regal garment but was now greasy and stained. On his egg-shaped head he had an embroidered smoking-cap. His feet were encased in warm velvet slippers. He put down the book he had been reading, rubbed his glasses on one velvet sleeve, and then: 'So!' he said.

He pointed to the remains of a fire.

'Sit down, Mirabelle Leicester, and warm yourself. You have come quickly, my friend.' – he addressed Monty.

'I'm black and blue all over,' growled Newton. 'Why couldn't we have a car?'

'Because the cars were engaged, as I told you.'

'Did you – ' began Newton quickly, but the old man glanced significantly at the girl, shivering before the fire and warming her hands mechanically.

'I will answer, but you need not ask, in good time. This is not of all moments the most propitious. Where is your woman?'

He had forgotten Joan, and went out to find her shivering in the passage.

'Do you want her?' he asked, poking his head in the door.

'She shall go with this girl. You will explain.'

'Where are you going to put her?'

Oberzohn pointed to the floor.

'Here? But – '

'No, no. My friend, you are too quick to see what is not meant. The gracious lady shall live in a palace – I have a certain friend who will no longer need it.'

His face twitched in the nearest he ever approached to a smile. Groping under the table, he produced a pair of muddy Wellingtons, kicked off his slippers and pulled on the boots with many gasps and jerks.

'All that they need is there: I have seen to it. March!'

He led the way out of the room, pulling the girl to her feet, and Newton followed, Joan bringing up the rear. Inside the factory, Oberzohn produced a small hand torch from his pocket and guided them through the debris till he came to that part of the floor where the trap was. With his foot he moved the covering of rubbish, pulled up the trap and went down.

'I can't go down there, Monty, I can't!' said Joan's agitated voice. 'What are you going to do with us? My God! if I'd known – '

'Don't be a fool,' said Newton roughly. 'What have you got to be afraid of? There's nothing here. We want you to look after her for a day or two. You don't want her to go down by herself: she'd be frightened to death.'

Her teeth chattering, Joan stumbled down the steps behind him. Certainly the first view of her new quarters was reassuring. Two little trestle beds had been made; the underground room had been swept clean, and a new carpet laid on the floor. Moreover, the apartment was brilliantly lit, and a furnace gave almost an uncomfortable warmth which was nevertheless very welcome, for the temperature had dropped 20° since noon.

'In this box there are clothes of all varieties, and expensive to purchase,' said Oberzohn, pointing to a brand-new trunk at the foot of one of the beds. 'Food you will have in plenty – bread and milk newly every day. By night you shall keep the curtain over the ventilator.' On the wall was a small black curtain about ten inches square.

Monty took her into the next apartment and showed her the washplace. There was even a bath, a compulsory fixture under the English Factory Act in a store of this description, where, in the old days, men had to handle certain insanitary products of the Coast.

'But how do we get out, Monty? Where do we get exercise?'

'You'll come out tomorrow night: I'll see to that,' he said, dropping his voice. 'Now listen, Joan: you've got to be a sensible girl and help me. There's money in this – bigger money than you've ever dreamed of. And when we've got this unpleasant business over, I'm taking you away for a trip round the world.'

It was the old promise, given before, never fulfilled, always hoped for. But this time it did not wholly remove her uneasiness.

'But what are you going to do with the girl?' she asked.

'Nothing; she will be kept here for a week. I'll swear to you that nothing will happen to her. At the end of a week she's to be released without a hair of her head being harmed.'

She looked at him searchingly. As far as she was able to judge, he was speaking the truth. And yet –

'I can't understand it – ' she shook her head, and for once Monty Newton was patient with her.

'She's the owner of a big property in Africa, and that we shall get, if things work out right,' he said. 'The point is that she must claim within a few days. If she doesn't, the property is ours.'

Her face cleared.

'Is that all?' She believed him, knew him well enough to detect his rare sincerity. 'That's taken a load off my mind, Monty. Of course I'll stay and look after her for you – it makes it easier to know that nothing will happen. What are those baize things behind the furnace – they look like boxes?'

He turned on her quickly.

'I was going to tell you about those,' he said. 'You're not to touch them under any circumstances. They belong to the old man and he's very stuffy about such things. Leave them just as they are. Let him touch them and nobody else. Do you understand?'

She nodded, and, to his surprise, pecked his cheek with her cold lips.

'I'll help you, boy,' she said tremulously. 'Maybe that trip will come off after all, if – '

'If what?'

'Those men – the men you were talking about – the Four Just Men, don't they call themselves? They scare me sick, Monty! They were the people who took her away before, and they'll kill us – even Oberzohn says that. They're after him. Has he – ' she hesitated – 'has he killed anybody? That snake stuff . . . you're not in it, are you, Monty?'

She looked more like a child than a sophisticated woman, clinging to his arm, her blue eyes looking pleadingly into his.

'Stuff! What do I know about snakes?' He disengaged himself and came back to where Oberzohn was waiting, a figure of patience.

The girl was lying on the bed, her face in the crook of her arm, and he was gazing at her, his expression inscrutable.

'That is all, then. Good night, gracious ladies.'

He turned and marched back towards the step and waved his hand. Monty followed. The girl heard the thud of the trap fall, the scrape of the old man's boots, and then a rumbling sound, which she did not immediately understand. Later, when in a panic she tried the trap, she found that a heavy barrel had been put on top, and that it was immovable.

Chapter 20

Gurther reports

Dr Oberzohn had not been to bed for thirty-five years. It was his practice to sleep in a chair, and alternate his dozes with copious draughts from his favourite authors. Mostly the books were about the soul, and free will, and predestination, with an occasional dip into Nietzsche by way of light recreation. In ordinary circumstances he would have had need for all the philosophy he could master; for ruin had come. The destruction of his store, which, to all intents and purposes, was uninsured, would have been the crowning stroke of fate but for the golden vision ahead.

Villa, that handsome half-breed, had arrived in England and had been with the doctor all the evening. At that moment he was on his way to Liverpool to catch the Coast boat, and he had left with his master a record of the claims that had already been pegged out on Monto Doro, as he so picturesquely renamed the new mountain. There were millions there; uncountable wealth. And between the Herr Doktor and the achievement of this colossal fortune was a life which he had no immediate desire to take. The doctor was a bachelor; women bored him. Yet he was prepared to take the extreme step if by so doing he could doubly ensure his fortune. Mirabelle dead gave him one chance; Mirabelle alive and persuaded, multiplied that chance by a hundred.

He opened the book he was reading at the last page and took out the folded paper. It was a special licence to marry, and had been duly registered at the Greenwich Registrar's Office since the day before the girl had entered his employment. This was his second and most powerful weapon. He could have been legally married on this nearly a week ago. It was effective for two months at least, and only five days separated him from the necessity of a decision. If the time expired, Mirabelle could live. It was quite a different matter, killing in cold blood a woman for whom the police would be searching, and with whose disappearance his name would be connected, from that other form of slaying he favoured: the striking

down of strange men in crowded thoroughfares. She was not for
the snake – as yet.

He folded the paper carefully, put it back in the book and turned
the page, when there was a gentle tap at the door and he sat up.

'Come in, Pfeiffer. March!'

The door opened slowly and a man sidled into the room, and at the
sight of him Dr Oberzohn gasped.

'Gurther!' he stammered, for once thrown out of his stride.

Gurther smiled and nodded, his round eyes fixed on the tassel of
the Herr Doktor's smoking-cap.

'You have returned – and failed?'

'The American, I think, is dead, Herr Doktor,' said the man in
staccato tone. 'The so excellent Pfeiffer is also – dead!'

The doctor blinked twice.

'Dead?' he said gratingly. 'Who told you this?'

'I saw him. Something happened . . . to the snake. Pfeiffer was
bitten.'

The old man's hard eyes fixed him.

'So!' he said softly.

'He died very quickly – in the usual manner,' jerked Gurther, still
with that stupid smile.

'So!' said the doctor again. 'All then was failure, and out of it comes
an American, who is nothing, and Pfeiffer, who is much – dead!'

'God have him in His keeping!' said Gurther, not lowering or
raising his eyes. 'And all the way back I thought this, Herr Doktor –
how much better that it should be Pfeiffer and not me. Though my
nerves are so bad.'

'So!' said the doctor for the fourth time, and held out his hand.

Gurther slipped his fingers into his waistcoat pocket and took out a
gold cigarette-case. The doctor opened it and looked at the five
cigarettes that reposed, at the two halves of the long holder neatly
lying in their proper place, closed the case with a snap and laid it on
the table.

'What shall I do with you, Gurther? Tomorrow the police will
come and search this house.'

'There is the cellar, Herr Doktor: it is very comfortable there. I
would prefer it.'

Dr Oberzohn made a gesture like a boy wiping something from a
slate.

'That is not possible: it is in occupation,' he said. 'I must find a new
place for you.' He stared and mused. 'There is the boat,' he said.

Gurther's smile did not fade.

The boat was a small barge, which had been drawn up into the private dock of the O. & S. factory, and had been rotting there for years, the playing-ground of rats, the doss-house of the homeless. The doctor saw what was in the man's mind.

'It may be comfortable. I will give you some gas to kill the rats, and it will only be for five-six days.'

'*Ja*, Herr Doktor.'

'For tonight you may sleep in the kitchen. One does not expect – '

There was a thunderous knock on the outer door. The two men looked at one another, but still Gurther grinned.

'I think it is the police,' said the doctor calmly.

He got to his feet, lifted the seat of a long hard-looking sofa, disclosing a deep cavity, and Gurther slipped in, and the seat was replaced. This done, the doctor waddled to the door and turned the key.

'Good morning, Inspector Meadows,'

'May I come in?' said Meadows.

Behind him were two police officers, one in uniform.

'Do you wish to see me? Certainly.' He held the door cautiously open and only Meadows came in, and preceded the doctor into his study.

'I want Mirabelle Leicester,' said Meadows curtly. 'She was abducted from her home in the early hours of this morning, and I have information that the car which took her away came to this house. There are tracks of wheels in the mud outside.'

'If there are car tracks, they are mine,' said the doctor calmly. He enumerated the makes of machines he possessed. 'There is another matter: as to cars having come here in the night, I have a sense of hearing, Mr Inspector Meadows, and I have heard many cars in Hangman's Lane – but not in my ground. Also, I'm sure you have not come to tell me of abducted girls, but to disclose to me the miscreant who burnt my store. That is what I expected of you.'

'What you expect of me and what you will get will be entirely different propositions,' said Meadows unpleasantly. 'Now come across, Oberzohn! We know why you want this girl – the whole plot has been blown. You think you'll prevent her from making a claim on the Portuguese Government for the renewal of a concession granted in June, 1912, to her father.'

If Dr Oberzohn was shocked to learn that his secret was out, he did not show it by his face. Not a muscle moved.

'Of such matters I know nothing. It is a fantasy, a story of fairies. Yet it must be true, Mr Inspector Meadows, if you say it. No: I think you are deceived by the criminals of Curzon Street, W. Men of blood and murder, with records that are infamous. You desire to search my house? It is your privilege.' He waved his hand. 'I do not ask you for the ticket of search. From basement to attic the house is yours.'

He was not surprised when Meadows took him at his word, and, going out into the hall, summoned his assistants. They visited each room separately, the old cook and the half-witted Danish girl accepting this visitation as a normal occurrence: they had every excuse to do so, for this was the second time in a fortnight that the house had been visited by the police.

'Now I'll take a look at your room, if you don't mind,' said Meadows.

His quick eyes caught sight of the box ottoman against the wall, and the fact that the doctor was sitting thereon added to his suspicions.

'I will look in here, if you please,' he said.

Oberzohn rose and the detective lifted the lid. It was empty. The ottoman had been placed against the wall, at the bottom of which was a deep recess. Gurther had long since rolled through the false back.

'You see – nothing,' said Oberzohn. 'Now perhaps you would like to search my factory? Perhaps amongst the rafters and the burnt girders I may conceal a something. Or the barge in my slipway? Who knows what I may place amongst the rats?'

'You're almost clever,' said Meadows, 'and I don't profess to be a match for you. But there are three men in this town who are! I'll be frank with you, Oberzohn. I want to put you where I can give you a fair trial, in accordance with the law of this country, and I shall resist, to the best of my ability, any man taking the law into his own hands. But whether you're innocent or guilty, I wouldn't stand in your shoes for all the money in Angola!'

'So?' said the doctor politely.

'Give up this girl, and I rather fancy that half your danger will be at an end. I tell you, you're too clever for me. It's a stupid thing for a police officer to say, but I can't get at the bottom of your snake. They have.'

The old man's brows worked up and down.

'Indeed?' he said blandly. 'And of which snake do you speak?'

Meadows said nothing more. He had given his warning: if Ober-zohn did not profit thereby, he would be the loser.

Nobody doubted, least of all he, that, in defiance of all laws that man had made, independent of all the machinery of justice that human ingenuity had devised, inevitable punishment awaited Ober-zohn and was near at hand.

Chapter 21

The account book

It was five o'clock in the morning when the mud-spattered Spanz dropped down through the mist and driving rain of the Chiltern Hills and struck the main Gloucester Road, pulling up with a jerk before Heavytree Farm. Manfred sprang out, but before he could reach the door, Aunt Alma had opened it, and by the look of her face he saw that she had not slept that night.

'Where is Digby?' he asked.

'He's gone to interview the Chief Constable,' said Alma. 'Come in, Mr Gonsalez.'

Leon was wet from head to foot: there was not a dry square centimetre upon him. But he was his old cheerful self as he stamped into the hall, shaking himself free of his heavy mackintosh.

'Digby, of course, heard nothing, George.'

'I'm the lightest sleeper in the world,' said Aunt Alma, 'but I heard not a sound. The first thing I knew was when a policeman came up and knocked at my door and told me that he'd found the front door open.'

'No clue was left at all?'

'Yes,' said Aunt Alma. They went into the drawing-room and she took up from the table a small black bottle with a tube and cap attached. 'I found this behind the sofa. She'd been lying on the sofa; the cushions were thrown on the floor and she tore the tapestry in her struggle.'

Leon turned the faucet, and, as the gas hissed out, sniffed.

'The new dental gas,' he said. 'But how did they get in? No window was open or forced?'

'They came in at the door: I'm sure of that. And they had a woman with them,' said Aunt Alma proudly.

'How do you know?'

'There must have been a woman,' said Aunt Alma. 'Mirabelle would not have opened the door except to a woman, without waking either myself or Mr Digby.'

Leon nodded, his eyes gleaming.

'Obviously,' he said.

'And I found the marks of a woman's foot in the passage. It is dried now, but you can still see it.'

'I have already seen it,' said Leon. 'It is to the left of the door: a small pointed shoe and a rubber heel. Miss Leicester opened the door to the woman, the men came in, and the rest was easy. You can't blame Digby,' he said appealingly to George.

He was the friend at court of every agent, but this time Manfred did not argue with him.

'I blame myself,' he said. 'Poiccart told me – '

'He was here,' said Aunt Alma.

'Who – Poiccart? asked Manfred, surprised, and Gonsalez slapped his knee.

'That's it, of course! What fools we are! We ought to have known why this wily old fox had left his post. What time was he here?'

Alma told him all the circumstances of the visit.

'He must have left the house immediately after us,' said Leon, with a wide grin of amusement, 'caught the five o'clock train for Gloucester, taxied across.'

'And after that?' suggested Manfred.

Leon scratched his chin.

'I wonder if he's back?' He took up the telephone and put a trunk call through to London. 'Somehow I don't think he is. Here's Digby, looking as if he expected to be summarily executed.'

The police pensioner was indeed in a mournful and pathetic mood.

'I don't know what you'll think of me, Mr Manfred – ' he began.

'I've already expressed a view on that subject.' George smiled faintly. 'I'm not blaming you, Digby. To leave a man who has been knocked about as you have been without an opposite number was the height of folly. I didn't expect them back so soon. As a matter of fact, I intended putting four men on from today. You've been making inquiries?'

'Yes, sir. The car went through Gloucester very early in the morning and took the Swindon road. It was seen by a cyclist policeman; he said there was a fat roll of tarpaulin lying on the tent of the trolley.'

'No sign of anybody chasing it in a car, or on a motor-bicycle?' asked Manfred anxiously.

Poiccart had recently taken to motor-cycling.

'No, sir.'

'You saw Mr Poiccart?'

'Yes, he was just going back to London. He said he wanted to see the place with his own eyes.'

George was disappointed. If it had been a visit of curiosity, Poiccart's absence from town was understandable. He would not have returned at the hour he was rung up.

Aunt Alma was cooking a hasty breakfast, and they had accepted her offering gratefully, for both men were famished; and they were in the midst of the meal when the London call came through.

'Is that you, Poiccart?'

'That is I,' said Poiccart's voice. 'Where are you speaking from?'

'Heavytree Farm. Did you see anything of Miss Leicester?'

There was a pause.

'Has she gone?'

'You didn't know?'

Another pause.

'Oh, yes, I knew; in fact, I accompanied her part of the way to London, and was bumped off when the trolley struck a refuge on the Great West Road. Meadows is here: he has just come from Oberzohn's. He says he has found nothing.'

Manfred thought for a while.

'We will be back soon after nine,' he said.

'Leon driving you?' was the dry response.

'Yes – in spite of which we shall be back at nine.'

'That man has got a grudge against my driving,' said Leon, when Manfred reported the conversation. 'I knew it was he when Digby described the car and said there was a fat roll of mackintosh on the top. "Fat roll" is not a bad description. Do you know whether Poiccart spoke to Miss Leicester?'

'Yes, he asked her if she grew onions.' – a reply which sent Leon into fits of silent laughter.

Breakfast was over and they were making their preparations for departure, when Leon asked unexpectedly: 'Has Miss Leicester a writing-table of her own?'

'Yes, in her room,' said Alma, and took him up to show him the old bureau.

He opened the drawers without apology, took out some old letters, turned them over, reading them shamelessly. Then he opened the blotter. There were several sheets of blank paper headed 'Heavytree Farm,' and two which bore her signature at the bottom. Alma explained that the bank account of the establishment was in Mirabelle's name, and, when it was necessary to draw cash, it was a rule of the bank that it should be accompanied by a covering letter – a practice which still exists in some of the old West-country banking establishments. She unlocked a drawer that he had not been able to open and showed him a cheque-book with three blank cheques signed with her name.

'That banker has known me since I was so high,' said Alma scornfully. 'You wouldn't think there'd be so much red-tape.'

Leon nodded.

'Do you keep any account books?'

'Yes, I do,' said Alma in surprise. 'The household accounts, you mean?'

'Could I see one?'

She went out and returned with a thin ledger, and he made a brief examination of its contents. Wholly inadequate, thought Alma, considering the trouble she had taken and the interest he had shown.

'That's that,' he said. 'Now, George, *en voiture!*'

'Why did you want to see the account book?' asked Manfred as they bowled up the road.

'I am naturally commercial-minded,' was the unsatisfactory reply. 'And, George, we're short of juice. Pray like a knight in armour that we sight a filling station in the next ten minutes.'

If George had prayed, the prayer would have been answered: just as the cylinders started to miss they pulled up the car before a garage, and took in a supply which was more than sufficient to carry them to their destination. It was nine o'clock exactly when the car stopped before the house. Poiccart, watching the arrival from George's room, smiled grimly at the impertinent gesture of the chauffeur.

Behind locked doors the three sat in conference.

'This has upset all my plans,' said Leon at last. 'If the girl was safe, I should settle with Oberzohn tonight.'

George Manfred stroked his chin thoughtfully. He had once worn a trim little beard, and had never got out of that beard-stroking habit of his.

'We think exactly alike. I intended suggesting that course,' he said gravely.

'The trouble is Meadows. I should like the case to have been settled one way or the other, and for Meadows to be out of it altogether. One doesn't wish to embarrass him. But the urgency is very obvious. It would have been very easy,' said Leon, a note of regret in his gentle voice. 'Now of course it is impossible until the girl is safe. But for that – ' he shrugged his shoulders – 'tomorrow friend Oberzohn would have experienced a sense of lassitude. No pain . . . just a little tiredness. Sleep, coma – death on the third day. He is an old man, and one has no desire to hurt the aged. There is no hurt like fear. As for Gurther, we will try a more violent method, unless Oberzohn gets him first. I sincerely hope he does.'

'This is news to me. What is this about Gurther?' asked Poiccart. Manfred told him.

'Leon is right now,' Poiccart nodded. He rose from the table and unlocked the door. 'If any of you men wish to sleep, your rooms are ready; the curtains are drawn, and I will wake you at such and such an hour.'

But neither was inclined for sleep. George had to see a client that morning: a man with a curious story to tell. Leon wanted a carburettor adjusted. They would both sleep in the afternoon, they said.

The client arrived soon after. Poiccart admitted him and put him in the dining-room to wait before he reported his presence.

'I think this is your harem man,' he said, and went downstairs to show up the caller.

He was a commonplace-looking man with a straggling, fair moustache and a weak chin.

'Debilitated or degenerate,' he suggested.

'Probably a little of both,' assented Manfred, when the butler had announced him.

He came nervously into the room and sat down opposite to Manfred.

'I tried to get you on the 'phone last night,' he complained, 'but I got no answer.'

'My office hours are from ten till two!' said George good-humouredly. 'Now will you tell me again this story of your sister?'

The man leaned back in the chair and clasped his knees, and began in a sing-song voice, as though he were reciting something that he had learned by heart.

'We used to live in Turkey. My father was a merchant of Constantinople, and my sister, who went to school in England, got extraordinary ideas, and came back a most violent pro-Turk. She is a very pretty girl and she came to know some of the best Turkish families, although my father and I were dead against her going about with these people. One day she went to call on Hymer Pasha, and that night she didn't come back. We went to the Pasha's house and asked for her, but he told us she had left at four o'clock. We then consulted the police, and they told us, after they had made investigations, that she had been seen going on board a ship which left for Odessa the same night. I hadn't seen her for ten years, until I went down to the Gringo Club, which is a little place in the East End – not high class, you understand, but very well conducted. There was a cabaret show after midnight, and whilst I was sitting there, thinking about going home – very bored, you understand, because that sort of thing doesn't appeal to me – I saw a girl come out from behind a curtain dressed like a Turkish woman, and begin a dance. She was in the middle of the dance when her veil slipped off. It was Marie! She recognized me at once, and darted through the curtains. I tried to follow her, but they held me back.'

'Did you go to the police?' asked Manfred.

The man shook his head.

'No, what is the use of the police?' he went on in a monotonous tone. 'I had enough of them in Constantinople, and I made up my mind that I would get outside help. And then somebody told me of you, and I came along. Mr Manfred, is it impossible for you to rescue my sister? I'm perfectly sure that she is being detained forcibly and against her will.'

'At the Gringo Club?' asked Manfred.

'Yes,' he nodded.

'I'll see what I can do,' said George. 'Perhaps my friends and I will come down and take a look round some evening. In the meantime will you go back to your friend Dr Oberzohn and tell him that you have done your part and I will do mine? Your little story will go into my collection of Unplausible Inventions!'

He touched a bell and Poiccart came in.

'Show Mr Liggins out, please. Don't hurt him – he may have a wife and children, though it is extremely unlikely.'

The visitor slunk from the room as though he had been whipped.

The door had scarcely closed upon him when Poiccart called Leon down from his room.

'Son,' he said, 'George wants that man trailed.'

Leon peeped out after the retiring victim of Turkish tyranny.

'Not a hard job,' he said. 'He has flat feet!'

Poiccart returned to the consulting-room. 'Who is he?' he asked.

'I don't know. He's been sent here either by Oberzohn or by friend Newton, the general idea being to bring us all together at the Gringo Club – which is fairly well known to me – on some agreeable evening. A bad actor! He has no tone. I shouldn't be surprised if Leon finds something very interesting about him.'

'He's been before, hasn't he?'

Manfred nodded.

'Yes, he was here the day after Barberton came. At least, I had his letter the next morning and saw him for a few moments in the day. Queer devil, Oberzohn! And an industrious devil,' he added. 'He sets everybody moving at once, and of course he's right. A good general doesn't attack with a platoon, but with an army, with all his strength, knowing that if he fails to pierce the line at one point he may succeed at another. It's an interesting thought, Raymond, that at this moment there are probably some twenty separate and independent agencies working for our undoing. Most of them ignorant that their efforts are being duplicated. That is Oberzohn's way – always has been his way. It's the way he has started revolutions, the way he has organized religious riots.'

After he had had his bath and changed, he announced his intention of calling at Chester Square.

'I'm rather keen on meeting Joan Newton again, even if she has returned to her normal state of Jane Smith.'

Miss Newton was not at home, the maid told him when he called. Would he see Mr Montague Newton, who was not only at home, but anxious for him to call, if the truth be told, for he had seen his enemy approaching.

'I shall be pleased,' murmured Manfred, and was ushered into the splendour of Mr Newton's drawing-room.

'Too bad about Joan,' said Mr Newton easily. 'She left for the Continent this morning.'

'Without a passport?' smiled Manfred.

A little slip on the part of Monty, but how was Manfred to know that the authorities had, only a week before, refused the renewal of her passport pending an inquiry into certain irregularities? The suggestion had been that other people than she had travelled to and from the Continent armed with this individual document.

'You don't need a passport for Belgium,' he lied readily. 'Anyway, this passport stuff's a bit overdone. We're not at war now.'

'All the time we're at war,' said Manfred. 'May I sit down?'

'Do. Have a cigarette?'

'Let me see the brand before I accept,' said Manfred cautiously, and the man guffawed as at a great joke.

The visitor declined the offer of the cigarette-case and took one from a box on the table.

'And is Jane making the grand tour?' he asked blandly.

'Jane's run down and wants a rest.'

'What's the matter with Aylesbury?'

He saw the man flinch at the mention of the women's convict establishment, but he recovered instantly. 'It is not far enough out, and I'm told that there are all sorts of queer people living round there. No, she's going to Brussels and then on to Aix-la-Chapelle, then prob-ably to Spa – I don't suppose I shall see her again for a month or two.'

'She was at Heavytree Farm in the early hours of this morning,' said Manfred, 'and so were you. You were seen and recognized by a friend of mine – Mr Raymond Poiccart. You travelled from Heavytree Farm to Oberzohn's house in a Ford trolley.'

Not by a flicker of an eyelid did Monty Newton betray his dismay.

'That is bluff,' he said. 'I didn't leave this house last night. What happened at Heavytree Farm?'

'Miss Leicester was abducted. You are surprised, almost agitated, I notice.'

'Do you think I had anything to do with it?' asked Monty steadily.

'Yes, and the police share my view. A provisional warrant was issued for your arrest this morning. I thought you ought to know.'

Now the man drew back, his face went from red to white, and then to a deeper red again. Manfred laughed softly.

'You've got a guilty conscience, Newton,' he said, 'and that's half-way to being arrested. Where is Jane?'

'Gone abroad, I tell you.'

He was thrown off his balance by this all too successful bluff and had lost some of his self-possession.

'She is with Mirabelle Leicester: of that I'm sure,' said Manfred. 'I've warned you twice, and it is not necessary to warn you a third time. I don't know how far deep you're in these snake murders: a jury will decide that sooner or later. But you're dead within six hours of my learning that Miss Leicester has been badly treated. You know that is true, don't you?'

Manfred was speaking very earnestly.

'You're more scared of us than you are of the law, and you're right, because we do not put our men to the hazard of a jury's intelligence. You get the same trial from us as you get from a judge who knows all the facts. You can't beat an English judge, Newton.'

The smile returned and he left the room. Fred, near at hand, waiting in the passage but at a respectful distance from the door, let him out with some alacrity.

Monty Newton turned his head sideways, caught a fleeting glimpse of the man he hated – hated worse than he hated Leon Gonsalez – and then called harshly for his servant.

'Come here,' he said, and Fred obeyed. 'They'll be sending round to make inquiries, and I want you to know what to tell them,' he said. 'Miss Joan went away this morning to the Continent by the eight-fifteen. She's either in Brussels or Aix-la-Chapelle. You're not sure of the hôtel, but you'll find out. Is that clear to you?'

'Yes, sir.'

Fred was looking aimlessly about the room.

'What's the matter with you?'

'I was wondering where the clock is.'

'Clock?' Now Monty Newton heard it himself. The tick-tick-tick of a cheap clock, and he went livid. 'Find it,' he said hoarsely, and even as he spoke his eyes fell upon the little black box that had been pushed beneath the desk, and he groped for the door with a scream of terror.

Passers-by in Chester Square saw the door flung open and two men rush headlong into the street. And the little American clock, which Manfred had purchased a few days before, went on ticking out the time, and was still ticking merrily when the police experts went in and opened the box. It was Manfred's oldest jest, and never failed.

Chapter 22

In the store cellar

It was impossible that Mirabelle Leicester could fail to realize the serious danger in which she stood. Why she had incurred the enmity of Oberzohn, for what purpose this man was anxious to keep her under his eye, she could not even guess. It was a relief to wake up in the early morning, as she did, and find Joan sleeping in the same room; for though she had many reasons for mistrusting her, there was something about this doll-faced girl that made an appeal to her.

Joan was lying on the bed fully dressed, and at the sound of the creaking bed she turned and got up, fastening her skirt.

'Well, how do you like your new home?' she asked, with an attempt at joviality, which she was far from feeling, in spite of Monty's assurances.

'I've seen better,' said Mirabelle coolly.

'I'll bet you have!' Joan stretched and yawned; then, opening one of the cupboards, took a shovelful of coal and threw it into the furnace, clanging the iron door. 'That's my job,' she said humorously, 'to keep you warm.'

'How long am I going to be kept here?'

'Five days,' was the surprising answer.

'Why five?' asked Mirabelle curiously.

'I don't know. Maybe they'll tell you,' said Joan.

She fixed a plug in the wall and turned on the small electric fire. Disappearing, she came back with a kettle which she placed on top of the ring.

'The view's not grand, but the food's good,' she said, with a gaiety that Mirabelle was now sure was forced.

'You're with these people, of course – Dr Oberzohn and Newton?'

'Mister Newton,' corrected Joan. 'Yes, I'm his fiancée. We're going to be married when things get a little better,' she said vaguely, 'and there's no use in your getting sore with me because I helped to bring you here. Monty's told me all about it. They're going to do you no harm at all.'

'Then why – ' began Mirabelle.

'He'll tell you,' interrupted Joan, 'sooner or later. The old man, or – or – well, Monty isn't in this: he's only obliging Oberzohn.'

With one thing Mirabelle agreed: it was a waste of time to indulge in recriminations or to reproach the girl for her supreme treachery. After all, Joan owed nothing to her, and had been from the first a tool employed for her detention. It would have been as logical for a convict to reproach the prison guard.

'How do you come to be doing this sort of thing?' she asked, watching the girl making tea.

'Where do you get "this sort of thing" from?' demanded Joan. 'If you suppose that I spend my life chaperoning females, you've got another guess coming. Scared, aren't you?'

She looked across at Mirabelle and the girl shook her head.

'Not really.'

'I should be,' confessed Joan. 'Do you mind condensed milk? There's no other. Yes, I should be writhing under the table, knowing something about Oberzohn.'

'If I were Oberzohn,' said Mirabelle with spirit, 'I should be hiding in a deep hole where the Four Just Men would not find me.'

'Four Just Men!' sneered the girl, and then her face changed. 'Were they the people who whipped Gurther?'

Mirabelle had not heard of this exploit, but she gave them credit with a nod.

'Is that so? Does Gurther know they're friends of yours?' she asked significantly.

'I don't know Gurther.'

'He's the man who danced with you the other night – Lord – I forget what name we gave him. Because, if he does know, my dear,' she said slowly, 'you've got two people to be extremely careful with. Gurther's half mad. Monty has always said so. He dopes too, and there are times when he's not a man at all but a low-down wolf. I'm scared of him – I'll admit it. There aren't Four Just Men, anyway,' she went off at a tangent. 'There haven't been more than three for years. One of them was killed in Bordeaux. That's a town I'd hate to be killed in,' said Joan irreverently.

An interval of silence followed whilst she opened an airtight tin and took out a small cake, and, putting it on the table, cut it into slices.

'What are they like?' she asked. Evidently the interval had been filled with thoughts of the men from Curzon Street. 'Monty says they're just bluff, but I'm not so sure that Monty tells me all he thinks. He's so scared that he told me to call and see them, just because they gave him an order – which isn't like Monty. They've killed people, haven't they?'

Mirabelle nodded.

'And got away with it? They must be clever.' Joan's admiration was dragged from her. 'Where do they get their money?'

That was always an interesting matter to Joan.

When the girl explained, she was really impressed. That they could kill and get away with it was wonderful; that they were men of millions placed them in a category apart.

'They'll never find you here,' said Joan. 'There's nobody living knows about this vault. There used to be eight men working here, sorting monkey hides, and every one of them's dead. Monty told me. He said this place is below the canal level, and Oberzohn can flood it in five minutes. Monty thinks the old man had an idea of running a slush factory here.'

'What is a slush factory?' asked Mirabelle, open-mouthed.

'Phoney – snide – counterfeit. Not English, but Continental work. He was going to do that if things had gone really bad, but of course you make all the difference.'

Mirabelle put down her cup.

'Does he expect to make money out of me?' she said, trying hard not to laugh.

The girl nodded solemnly.

'Does he think I have a great deal of money?'

'He's sure.'

Joan was sure too. Her tone said that plainly enough.

Mirabelle sat down on the bed, for the moment too astonished to speak. Her own financial position was no mystery. She had been left sufficient to bring her in a small sum yearly, and with the produce of the farm had managed to make both ends meet. It was the failure of the farm as a source of profit which had brought her to her new job in London. Alma had also a small annuity; the farm was the girl's property, but beyond these revenues she had nothing. There was not even a possibility that she was an heiress. Her father had been a comparatively poor man, and had been supported in his numerous excursions to various parts of the world in search of knowledge by the scientific societies to which he was attached; his literary earnings were negligible; his books enjoyed only a very limited sale. She could trace her ancestry back for seven generations; knew of her uncles and

aunts, and they did not include a single man or woman who, in the
best traditions of the story-books, had gone to America and made an
immense fortune.

'It is absurd,' she said. 'I have no money. If Mr Oberzohn puts me
up to ransom, it will have to be something under a hundred!'

'Put you up to ransom?' said Joan. 'I don't get you there. But
you're rich all right – I can tell you that. Monty says so, and Monty
wouldn't lie to me.'

Mirabelle was bewildered. It seemed almost impossible that a man
of Oberzohn's intelligence and sources of information could make
such a mistake. And yet Joan was earnest.

'They must have mistaken me for somebody else,' she said, but
Joan did not answer. She was sitting up in a listening attitude, and
her eyes were directed towards the iron door which separated their
sleeping apartment from the larger vault. She had heard the creak of
the trap turning and the sound of feet coming down the stairs.

Mirabelle rose as Oberzohn came in. He wore his black dressing-
gown, his smoking-cap was at the back of his head, and the muddy
Wellington boots which he had pulled over his feet looked incongruous, and would at any other time have provoked her to laughter.
He favoured her with a stiff nod.

'You have slept well, gracious lady?' he said, and to her amazement
took her cold hand in his and kissed it.

She felt the same feeling of revulsion and unreality as had overcome
her that night at the dance when Gurther had similarly saluted her.

'It is a nice place, for young people and for old.' He looked round
the apartment with satisfaction. 'Here I should be content to spend
my life reading my books, and giving my mind to thought, but – ' he
spread his hands and shrugged – 'what would you? I am a business
man, with immense interests in every part of the world. I am rich,
too, beyond your dreams! I have stores in every part of the world,
and thousands of men and women on my pay-roll.'

Why was he telling her all this, she wondered, reciting the facts in
a monotonous voice. Surely he had not come down to emphasize the
soundness of his financial position?

'I am not very much interested in your business, Mr Oberzohn,'
she said; 'but I want to know why I am being detained here. Surely, if
you're so rich, you do not want to hold me to ransom?'

'To ransom?' His forehead went up and down. 'That is foolish
talk. Did she tell you?' He pointed at the girl, and his face went as
black as thunder.

'No, I guessed,' said Mirabelle quickly, not wishing to get her companion into bad odour.

'I do not hold you to ransom. I hold you, lovely lady, because you are good for my eyes. Did not Heine say, "The beauty of women is a sedative to the soul"? You should read Heine: he is frivolous, but in his stupidity there are many clever thoughts. Now tell me, lovely lady, have you all you desire?'

'I want to go out,' she said. 'I can't stay in this underground room without danger to my health.'

'Soon you shall go.' He bowed stiffly again, and shuffled across the floor to the furnace. Behind this were the two baize-covered boxes, and one he lifted tenderly. 'Here are secrets such as you should not pry into,' he said in his awkward English. 'The most potent of chemicals, colossal in power. The ignorant would touch them and they would explode – you understand?'

He addressed Mirabelle, who did not understand but made no answer.

'They must be kept warm for that reason. One I take, the other I leave. You shall not touch it – that is understood? My good friend has told you?' He brought his eyes to Joan.

'I understand all right,' she said. 'Listen, Oberzohn: when am I going out for a walk? This place is getting on my nerves already.'

'Tonight you shall exercise with the lovely lady. I myself will accompany you.'

'Why am I here, Mr Oberzohn?' Mirabelle asked again.

'You are here because you are in danger,' said Oberzohn, holding the green box under his arm. 'You are in very great danger.' He nodded with every word. 'There are certain men, of all the most infamous, who have a design upon your life. They are criminal, cunning and wise – but not so cunning or wise as Dr Oberzohn. Because I will not let you fall into their hands I keep you here, young miss. Good morning.'

Again he bowed stiffly and went out, the iron door clanging behind him. They heard him climbing the stairs, the thud of the trap as it fell, and the rumble which Joan, at any rate, knew was made by the cement barrel being rolled to the top of the trap.

'Pleasant little fellow, isn't he?' said Joan bitterly. 'Him and his chemicals!' She glared down at the remaining box. 'If I were sure it wouldn't explode, I should smash it to smithereens!' she said.

Later she told the prisoner of Oberzohn's obsession; of how he spent time and money in his search for the vital elixir.

'Monty thinks he'll find it,' she said seriously. 'Do you know, that old man has had an ox stewed down to a pint? There used to be a king in Europe – I forget his name – who had the same stuff, but not so strong. Monty says that Oberzohn hardly ever takes a meal – just a teaspoonful of this dope and he's right for the day. And Monty says . . . '

For the rest of that dreary morning the girl listened without hearing to the wise sayings and clever acts of Monty; and every now and again her eyes strayed to the baize-covered box which contained 'the most potent chemicals', and she wondered whether, in the direst extremity, she would be justified in employing these dread forces for her soul's salvation.

Chapter 23
The courier

Elijah Washington came up to London for a consultation. With the exception of a blue contusion beneath his right eye, he was none the worse for his alarming experience.

Leon Gonsalez had driven him to town, and on the way up the big man had expressed views about snake-bite which were immensely interesting to the man at the wheel. 'I've figured it out this way: there is no snake at all. What happens is that these guys have extracted snake venom – and that's easy, by making a poison-snake bite on something soft – and have poisoned a dart or a burr with the venom. I've seen that done in Africa, particularly up in the Ituri country, and it's pretty common in South America. The fellow just throws or shoots it, and just where the dart hits, he gets snake-poisoning right away.'

'That is an excellent theory,' said Leon, 'only – no dart or burr has ever been found. It was the first thing the police looked for in the case of the stockbroker. They had the ground searched for days. And it was just the same in the case of the tramp and the bank clerk, just the same in the case of Barberton. A dart would stick some time and would be found in the man's clothing or near the spot where he was struck down. How do you account for that?'

Mr Washington very frankly admitted that he couldn't account for it at all, and Leon chuckled.

'I can,' he said. 'In fact, I know just how it's done.'

'Great snakes!' gasped Washington in amazement. 'Then why don't you tell the police?'

'The police know – now,' said Leon. 'It isn't snake-bite – it is nicotine poisoning.'

'How's that?' asked the startled man, but Leon had his joke to himself.

After a consultation which had lasted most of the night they had brought Washington from Rath Hall, and on the way Leon hinted gently that the Three had a mission for him and hoped he would accept.

'You're much too good a fellow to be put into an unnecessarily dangerous position,' he said; 'and even if you weren't, we wouldn't lightly risk your blessed life; but the job we should ask you to do isn't exactly a picnic.'

'Listen!' said Mr Washington with sudden energy. 'I don't want any more snakes – not that kind of snake! I've felt pain in my time, but nothing like this! I know it must have been snake venom, but I'd like to meet the little wriggler who brews the brand that was handed to me, and maybe I'd change my mind about collecting him – alive!'

Leon agreed silently, and for the next few moments was avoiding a street car on one side, a baker's cart on another, and a blah woman who was walking aimlessly in the road, apparently with no other intention than of courting an early death, this being the way of blah women.

'Phew!' said Mr Washington, as the car skidded on the greasy road. 'I don't know whether you're a good driver or just naturally under the protection of Providence.'

'Both,' said Leon, when he had straightened the machine. 'All good drivers are that.'

Presently he continued.

'It is snake venom all right, Mr Washington; only snake venom that has been most carefully treated by a man who knows the art of concentration of its bad and the extraction of its harmless constituents. My theory is that certain alkaloids are added, and it is possible that there has been a blending of two different kinds of poison. But you're right when you say that no one animal carries in his poison sac that particular variety of death-juice. If it is any value to you, we are prepared to give you a snake-proof certificate!'

'I don't want another experience of that kind,' Elijah Washington warned him; but Leon turned the conversation to the state of the road and the problems of traffic control.

There had been nothing seen or heard of Mirabelle, and Meadows's activities had for the moment been directed to the forthcoming inquest on Barberton. Nowadays, whenever he reached Scotland Yard, he moved in a crowd of reporters, all anxious for news of further developments. The Barberton death was still the livest topic in the newspapers: the old scare of the snake had been revived and in some degree intensified. There was not a journal which did not carry columns of letters to the editor denouncing the inactivity of the policed Were they, asked one sarcastic correspondent, under the hypnotic influence of the snake's eyes? Could they not, demanded another, give up trapping speeders on the Lingfield road and bring their mighty brains to the elucidation of a mystery that was to cause every household in London the gravest concern? The Barberton murder was the peg on which every letter-writing faddist had a novel view to hang, and Mr Meadows was not at that time the happiest officer in the force.

'Where is Lee?' asked Washington as they came into Curzon Street.

'He's in town for the moment, but we are moving him to the North of England, though I don't think there is any danger to him, now that Barberton's letters are in our possession. They would have killed him yesterday to prevent our handling the correspondence. Today I should imagine he has no special importance in the eyes of Oberzohn and Company. And here we are!'

Mr Washington got out stiffly and was immediately admitted by the butler. The three men went upstairs to where George Manfred was wrestling with a phase of the problem. He was not alone; Digby, his head swathed in bandages, sat, an unhappy man, on the edge of a chair and answered Leon's cheery greeting with a mournful smile.

'I'm sending Digby to keep observation on Oberzohn's house; and especially do I wish him to search that old boat of his.'

He was referring to an ancient barge which lay on the mud at the bottom of Mr Oberzohn's private dock. From the canal there was a narrow waterway into the little factory grounds. It was so long since the small cantilever bridge which covered the entrance had been raised, that locals regarded the bridge floor as part of the normal bank of the canal. But behind the green water-gates was a concrete dock large enough to hold one barge, and here for years a decrepit vessel had wallowed, the hunting-ground of rats and the sleeping-place of the desperately homeless.

'The barge is practically immovable: I've already reported on that,' said Leon.

'It certainly has that appearance, and yet I would like a search,' replied Manfred. 'You understand that this is night duty, and I have asked Meadows to notify the local inspector that you will be on duty – I don't want to be pulled out of my bed to identify you at the Peckham police station. It isn't a cheerful job, but you might be able to make it interesting by finding your way into his grounds. I don't think the factory will yield much, but the house will certainly be a profitable study to an observer of human nature.'

'I hope I do better this time, Mr Manfred,' said Digby, turning to go. 'And, if you don't mind, I'll go by day and take a look at the place. I don't want to fall down this time!'

George smiled as he rose and shook the man's hand at parting. 'Even Mr Gonsalez makes mistakes,' he said maliciously, and Leon looked hurt.

Manfred tidied some papers on his desk and put them into a drawer, waiting for Poiccart's return. When he had come: 'Now, Mr Washington, we will tell you what we wish you to do. We wish you to take a letter to Lisbon. Leon has probably hinted something to that effect, and it is now my duty to tell you that the errand is pretty certain to be an exceedingly dangerous one, but you are the only man I know to whom I could entrust this important document. I feel I cannot allow you to undertake this mission without telling you that the chances are heavily against your reaching Portugal.'

'Bless you for those cheerful words,' said Washington blankly. 'The only thing I want to be certain about is, am I likely to meet Mr Snake?'

Manfred nodded, and the American's face lengthened.

'I don't know that even that scares me,' he said at last, 'especially now that I know that the dope they use isn't honest snake-spit at all but a synthesized poison. It was having my confidence shaken in snakes that rattled me. When do you want me to go?'

'Tonight.'

Mr Washington for the moment was perplexed, and Manfred continued: 'Not by the Dover-Calais route. We would prefer that you travelled by Newhaven-Dieppe. Our friends are less liable to be on the alert, though I can't even guarantee that. Oberzohn spends a lot of money in espionage. This house has been under observation for days. I will show you.'

He walked to the window and drew aside the curtain.

'Do you see a spy?' he asked, with a twinkle in his eye.

Mr Washington looked up and down the street.

'Sure!' he said. 'That man at the corner smoking a cigar – '

'Is a detective officer from Scotland Yard,' said Manfred. 'Do you see anybody else?'

'Yes,' said Washington after a while, 'there's a man cleaning windows on the opposite side of the road: he keeps looking across here.'

'A perfectly innocent citizen,' said Manfred.

'Well, he can't be in any of those taxis, because they're empty.' Mr Washington nodded to a line of taxis drawn up on the rank in the centre of the road.

'On the contrary, he is in the first taxi on the rank – he is the driver! If you went out and called a cab, he would come to you. If anybody else called him, he would be engaged. His name is Clarke, he lives at 43, Portlington Mews; he is an ex-convict living apart from his wife, and he receives seven pounds a week for his services, ten pounds every time he drives Oberzohn's car, and all the money he makes out of his cab.'

He smiled at the other's astonishment.

'So the chances are that your movements will be known; even though you do not call the cab, he will follow you. You must be prepared for that. I'm putting all my cards on the table, Mr Washington, and asking you to do something which, if you cannot bring yourself to agree, must be done by either myself, Poiccart or Gonsalez. Frankly, none of us can be spared.'

'I'll go,' said the American. 'Snake or no snake, I'm for Lisbon. What is my route?'

Poiccart took a folded paper from his pocket.

'Newhaven, Dieppe, Paris. You have a reserved compartment on the Sud Express; you reach Valladolid late tomorrow night, and change to the Portuguese mail. Unless I can fix an aeroplane to meet you at Irun. We are trying now. Otherwise, you should be in Lisbon at two o'clock on the following afternoon. He had better take the letter now, George.'

Manfred unlocked the wall safe and took out a long envelope. It was addressed to 'Senhor Alvaz Manuel y Cintra, Minister of Colonies,' and was heavily sealed.

'I want you to place this in Senhor Cintra's hands. You'll have no difficulty there because you will be expected,' he said. 'Will you travel in that suit?'

The American thought.

'Yes, that's as good as any,' he said.

'Will you take off your jacket?'

Mr Washington obeyed, and with a small pair of scissors Manfred cut a slit in the lining and slipped the letter in. Then, to the American's astonishment, Leon produced a rolled housewife, threaded a needle with extraordinary dexterity, and for the next five minutes the snake-hunter watched the deft fingers stitching through paper and lining. So skilfully was the slit sewed that Elijah

Washington had to look twice to make sure where the lining had been cut.

'Well, that beats the band!' he said. 'Mr Gonsalez, I'll send you my shirts for repair!'

'And here is something for you to carry.' It was a black leather portfolio, well worn. To one end was attached a steel chain terminating in a leather belt. 'I want you to put this round your waist, and from now on to carry this wallet. It contains nothing more important than a few envelopes imposingly sealed, and if you lose it no great harm will come.'

'You think they'll go for the wallet?' Manfred nodded.

'One cannot tell, of course, what Oberzohn will do, and he's as wily as one of his snakes. But my experience has been,' he said, 'that the cleverer the criminal, the bigger the fool and the more outrageous his mistakes. You will want money.'

'Well, I'm not short of that,' said the other with a smile. 'Snakes are a mighty profitable proposition. Still, I'm a business man . . . '

For the next five minutes they discussed financial details, and he was more than surprised to discover the recklessness with which money was disbursed.

He went out, with a glance from the corner of his eye at the taximan, whose hand was raised inquiringly, but, ignoring the driver, he turned and walked towards Regent Street, and presently found a wandering taxi of an innocuous character, and ordered the man to drive to the Ritz-Carlton, where rooms had been taken for him.

He was in Regent Street before he looked round through the peep-hole, and, as Manfred had promised him, the taxi was following, its flag down to prevent chance hiring. Mr Washington went up to his room, opened the window and looked out: the taxi had joined a nearby rank. The driver had left his box.

'He's on the 'phone,' muttered Mr Washington, and would have given a lot of money to have known the nature of the message.

Chapter 24

On the night mail

A man of habit, Mr Oberzohn missed his daily journey to the City Road. In ordinary circumstances the loss would have been a paralysing one, but of late he had grown more and more wedded to his deep armchair and his ponderous volumes; and though the City Road had been a very useful establishment in many ways, and was ill replaced by the temporary building which his manager had secured, he felt he could almost dispense with that branch of his business altogether.

Oberzohn & Smitts was an institution which had grown out of nothing. The energy of the partners, and especially the knowledge of African trading conditions which the departed Smitts possessed, had produced a nourishing business which ten years before could have been floated for half a million pounds.

Orders still came in. There were up-country stores to be restocked; new, if unimportant, contracts to be fulfilled; there was even a tentative offer under consideration from one of the South American States for the armaments of a political faction. But Mr Oberzohn was content to mark time, in the faith that the next week would see him superior to these minor considerations and in a position, if he so wished, to liquidate his business and sell his stores and his trade. There were purchasers ready, but the half million pounds had dwindled to a tenth of that sum, which outstanding bills would more than absorb. As Manfred had said, his running expenses were enormous. He had agents in every central Government office in Europe, and though they did not earn their salt, they certainly drew more than condiment for their services.

He had spent a busy morning in his little workshop-laboratory, and had settled himself down in his chair, when a telegraph messenger came trundling his bicycle across the rough ground, stopped to admire for a second the iron dogs which littered the untidy strip of lawn, and woke the echoes of this gaunt house with a thunderous knock. Mr Oberzohn hurried to the door. A telegram to this address must necessarily be important. He took the telegram, slammed the door in the messenger's face and hurried back to his room, tearing open the envelope as he went.

There were three sheets of misspelt writing, for the wire was in Portuguese and telegraph operators are bad guessers. He read it through carefully, his lips moving silently, until he came to the end, then he started reading all over again, and, for a better under-standing of its purport, he took a pencil and paper and translated the message into Swedish. He laid the telegram face downwards on the table and took up his book, but he was not reading. His busy mind slipped from Lisbon to London, from Curzon Street to the factory, and at last he shut his book with a bang, got up, and opening the door, barked Gurther's name. That strange man came downstairs in his stockinged feet, his hair hanging over his eyes, an unpleasant sight. Dr Oberzohn pointed to the room and the man entered.

For an hour they talked behind locked doors, and then Gurther came out, still showing his teeth in a mechanical smile, and went up the stairs two at a time. The half-witted Danish maid, passing the door of the doctor's room, heard his gruff voice booming into the telephone, but since he spoke a language which, whilst it had some relation to her own, was subtly different, she could not have heard the instructions, admonitions, orders and suggestions which he fired in half a dozen different directions, even if she had heard him clearly.

This done, Dr Oberzohn returned to his book and a midday refreshment, spooning his lunch from a small cup at his side con-taining a few fluid ounces of dark red liquid. One half of his mind was pursuing his well-read philosophers; the other worked at feverish speed, conjecturing and guessing, forestalling and baffling the minds that were working against him. He played a game of mental chess, all the time seeking for a check, and when at last he had discovered one that was adequate, he put down his book and went out into his garden, strolling up and down inside the wire fence, stopping now and again to pick a flower from a weed, or pausing to examine a rain-filled pothole as though it were the star object in a prize landscape.

He loved this ugly house, knew every brick of it, as a feudal lord might have known the castle he had built, the turret, the flat roof with its high parapet, that commanded a view of the canal bank on the one side and the railway arches left and right. They were railway arches which had a value to him. Most of them were blocked up, having been converted into lock-up garages and sheds, and through only a few could ingress be had. One, under which ran the muddy lane – why it was called Hangman's Lane nobody knew; another that gave to some allotments on the edge of his property; and a third through which he also could see daylight, but which spanned no road at all.

An express train roared past in a cloud of steam, and he scanned the viaduct with benignant interest. And then he performed his daily tour of inspection. Turning back into the house, he climbed the stairs to the third floor, opened a little door that revealed an extra flight of steps, and emerged on to the roof. At each corner was a square black shed, about the height of a man's chest. The doors were heavily padlocked, and near by each was a stout black box, equally weatherproof. There were other things here: great, clumsy wall-plugs at regular intervals. Seeing them, it might be thought that Mr Oberzohn contemplated a night when, in the exultation of achievement, he would illuminate his ungainly premises. But up till now that night had not arrived, and in truth the only light usable was one which at the moment was dismantled in the larger of the four sheds.

From here he could look down upon the water cutting into the factory grounds; and the black bulk of the barge, which filled the entire width of the wharf, seemed so near that he could have thrown a stone upon it. His idle interest was in the sluggish black water that oozed through the gates. A slight mist lay upon the canal; a barge was passing down towards Deptford, and he contemplated the straining horse that tugged the barge rope with a mind set upon the time when he, too, might use the waterway in a swifter craft.

London lay around him, its spires and chimneys looming through the thin haze of smoke. Far away the sun caught the golden ball of St Paul's and added a new star to the firmament. Mr Oberzohn hated London – only this little patch of his had beauty in his eyes. Not the broad green parks and the flowering rhododendrons; not the majestic aisles of pleasure which the rich lounger rode or walked, nor the streets of stone-fronted stores, nor the pleasant green of suburban roads – he loved only these God-forgotten acres, this slimy wilderness in which he had set up his habitation.

He went downstairs, locking the roof door behind him, and, passing Gurther's room, knocked and was asked to enter. The man sat in his singlet; he had shaved once, but now the keen razor was going across his skin for the second time. He turned his face, shining with cream, and grinned round at the intruder, and with a grunt the doctor shut the door and went downstairs, knowing that the man was for the moment happy; for nothing pleased Gurther quite so much as 'dressing up'.

The doctor stood at the entrance of his own room, hesitating between books and laboratory, decided upon the latter, and was busy for the next two hours. Only once he came out, and that was to bring from the warm room the green baize box which contained 'the most potent of chemicals, colossal in power'.

* * *

The Newhaven-Dieppe route is spasmodically popular. There are nights when the trains to Paris are crowded; other nights when it is possible to obtain a carriage to yourself; and it happened that this evening, when Elijah Washington booked his seat, he might, if it had been physically possible, have sat in one compartment and put his feet on the seat in another.

Between the two great branches of the Anglo-Saxon race there is one notable difference. The Englishman prefers to travel in solitude and silence. His ideal journey is one from London to Constantinople in a compartment that is not invaded except by the ticket collector; and if it is humanly possible that he can reach his destination without having given utterance to anything more sensational than an agreement with some other passenger's comment on the weather, he is indeed a happy man. The American loves company; he has the acquisitiveness of the Latin, combined with the rhetorical virtues of the Teuton. Solitude makes him miserable; silence irritates him. He wants to talk about large and important things, such as the future of the country, the prospects of agriculture and the fluctuations of trade, about which the average Englishman knows nothing, and is less interested. The American has a town pride, can talk almost emotionally about a new drainage system and grow eloquent upon a municipal balance sheet. The Englishman does not cultivate his town pride until he reaches middle age, and then only in sufficient quantities to feel disappointed with the place of his birth after he has renewed its acquaintance.

Mr Washington found himself in an empty compartment, and, grunting his dissatisfaction, walked along the corridor, peeping into one cell after another in the hope of discovering a fellow-countryman in a similar unhappy plight. His search was fruitless and he returned to the carriage in which his bag and overcoat were deposited, and settled down to the study of an English humorous newspaper and a vain search for something at which any intelligent man could laugh.

The doors of the coach were at either end, and most passengers entering had to pass the open entrance of Mr Washington's compartment. At every click of the door he looked up, hoping to find a congenial soul. But disappointment awaited him, until a lady hesitated by the door. It was a smoking carriage, but Washington, who was a man of gallant character, would gladly have sacrificed his cigar for the pleasure of her society. Young, he guessed, and a widow. She was in black, an attractive face showed through a heavy veil.

'Is this compartment engaged?' she asked in a low voice that was almost a whisper.

'No, madam.' Washington rose, hat in hand.

'Would you mind?' she asked in a soft voice.

'Why, surely! Sit down, ma'am,' said the gallant American. 'Would you like the corner seat by the window?'

She shook her head, and sat down near the door, turning her face from him.

'Do you mind my smoking?' asked Washington, after a while.

'Please smoke,' she said, and again turned her face away.

'English,' thought Mr Washington in disgust, and hunched himself for an hour and a half of unrelieved silence.

A whistle blew, the train moved slowly from the platform, and Elijah Washington's adventurous journey had begun.

They were passing through Croydon when the girl rose, and, leaning out, closed the little glass-panelled door.

'You should let me do that,' said Elijah reproachfully, and she murmured something about not wishing to trouble him, and he relapsed into his seat.

One or two of the men who passed looked in, and evidently this annoyed her, for she reached and pulled down the spring blind which partially hid her from outside observation, and after the ticket collector had been and punched the slips, she lowered the second of the three blinds.

'Do you mind?' she asked.

'Sure not, ma'am,' said Elijah, without any great heartiness. He had no desire to travel alone with a lady in a carriage so discreetly curtained. He had heard of cases . . . and by nature he was an extremely cautious man.

The speed of the train increased; the wandering passengers had settled down. The second of the ticket inspections came as they were rushing through Redhill, and Mr Washington thought uncomfortably that there was a significant look in the inspector's face as he glanced first at the drawn blinds, then from the lady to himself.

She affected a perfume of a peculiarly pleasing kind. The carriage was filled with this subtle fragrance. Mr Washington smelt it above the scent of his cigar. Her face was still averted; he wondered if she had gone to sleep, and, growing weary of his search for humour, he put down the paper, folded his hands and closed his eyes, and found himself gently drifting to that medley of the real and unreal which is the overture of dreams.

The lady moved; he looked at her out of the corner of his half-closed eyes. She had moved round so as to half face him. Her veil was still down, her white gloves were reflectively clasped on her knees. He shut his eyes again, until another movement brought him awake. She was feeling in her bag.

Mr Washington was awake now – as wide awake as he had ever been in his life. In stretching out her hand, the lady had pulled short her sleeve, and there was a gap of flesh between the glove and the wrist of her blouse, and on her wrist was hair!

He shifted his position slightly, grunted as in his sleep, and dropped his hand to his pocket, and all the time those cold eyes were watching him through the veil.

Lifting the bottom of the veil, she put the ebony holder between her teeth and searched the bag for a match. Then she turned appealingly to him as though she had sensed his wakefulness. As she rose, Washington rose too, and suddenly he sprang at her and flung her back against the door. For a moment the veiled lady was taken by surprise, and then there was a flash of steel.

From nowhere a knife had come into her hand and Washington gripped the wrist and levered it over, pushing the palm of his hand under the chin. Even through the veil he could feel the bristles, and knew now, if he had not known before, that he had to deal with a man. A live, active man, rendered doubly strong by the knowledge of his danger. Gurther butted forward with his head, but Washington saw the attack coming, shortened his arm and jabbed full at the face behind the veil. The blow stopped the man only for an instant, and again he came on, and this time the point of the knife caught the American's shoulder, and ripped the coat to the elbow. It needed this to bring forth Elijah Washington's mental and physical reserves. With a roar he gripped the throat of his assailant and threw him with such violence against the door that it gave, and the 'widow in mourning' crashed against the panel of the outer corridor. Before he could reach the attacker, Gurther had turned and sped along the corridor to the door of the coach. In a second he had flung it open and had dropped to the footboard. The train was slowing to take Horsham Junction, and the cat eyes waited until he saw a good fall, and let go. Staring back into the darkness, Washington saw nothing, and then the train inspector came along.

'It was a man in woman's clothes,' he said, a little breathlessly, and they went back to search the compartment, but Mr Gurther had taken bag and everything with him, and the only souvenir of his presence was the heel of a shoe that had been torn off in the struggle.

Chapter 25

Gurther returns

The train was going at thirty miles an hour when Gurther dropped on to a ridge of sand by the side of the track, and in the next second he was sliding forward on his face. Fortunately for him the veil, though torn, kept his eyes free. Stumbling to his feet, he looked round. The level-crossing gates should be somewhere here. He had intended jumping the train at this point, and Oberzohn had made arrangements accordingly. A signalman, perched high above the track, saw the figure and challenged.

'I've lost my way,' said Gurther. 'Where is the level-crossing?'

'A hundred yards farther on. Keep clear of those metals – the Eastbourne express is coming behind.'

If Gurther had had his way, he would have stopped long enough to remove a rail for the sheer joy of watching a few hundred of the hated people plunged to destruction. But he guessed that the car was waiting, went sideways through the safety gates into a road which was fairly populous. There were people about who turned their heads and looked in amazement at the bedraggled woman in black, but he had got beyond worrying about his appearance.

He saw the car with the little green light which Oberzohn invariably used to mark his machines from others, and, climbing into the cab (as it was), sat down to recover his breath. The driver he knew as one of the three men employed by Oberzohn, one of whom Mr Washington had seen that morning.

The journey back to town was a long one, though the machine, for a public vehicle, was faster than most. Gurther welcomed the ride. Once more he had failed, and he reasoned that this last failure was the most serious of all. The question of Oberzohn's displeasure did not really arise. He had travelled far beyond the point when the Swede's disapproval meant very much to him. But there might be a consequence more serious than any. He knew well with what instructions Pfeiffer had been primed on the night of the attack at Rath House – only Gurther had been quicker, and his snake had bitten first. Dr Oberzohn had no illusions as to what happened, and if he had tactfully refrained from making reference to the matter, he had his purpose and reasons. And this night journey with Elijah Washington was one of them.

There was no excuse; he had none to offer. His hand wandered beneath the dress to the long knife that was strapped to his side, and the touch of the worn handle was very reassuring. For the time being he was safe; until another man was found to take Pfeiffer's place Oberzohn was working single-handed and could not afford to dispense with the services of this, the last of his assassins.

It was past eleven when he dismissed the taxi at the end of the long lane, and, following the only safe path, came to the unpainted door that gave admission to Oberzohn's property. And the first words of his master told him that there was no necessity for explanation.

'So you did not get him, Gurther?'

'No, Herr Doktor.'

'I should not have sent you.' Oberzohn's voice was extraordinarily mild in all the circumstances. 'That man you cannot kill – with the snake. I have learned since you went that he was bitten at the blind man's house, yet lives! That is extraordinary. I would give a lot of money to test his blood. You tried the knife?'

'*Ja*, Herr Doktor.' He lifted his veil, stripped off hat and wig in one motion. The rouged and powdered face was bruised; from under the brown wig was a trickle of dried blood.

'Good! You have done as well as you could. Go to your room, Gurther – march!'

Gurther went upstairs, and for a quarter of an hour was staring at his grinning face in the glass, as with cream and soiled towel he removed his make-up.

Oberzohn's very gentleness was a menace. What did it portend? Until that evening neither Gurther nor his dead companion had been taken into the confidence of the two men who directed their activities. He knew there were certain papers to be recovered; he knew there were men to be killed; but what value were the papers, or why death should be directed to this unfortunate or that, he neither knew nor cared. His duty had been to obey, and he had served a liberal paymaster well and loyally. That girl in the underground room? Gurther had many natural explanations for her imprisonment. And yet none of them fitted the conditions. His cogitations were wasted time. That night, for the first time, the doctor took him into his confidence.

He had finished dressing and was on his way to his kitchen when the doctor stood at the doorway and called him in.

'Sit down, Gurther.' He was almost kind. 'You will have a cigar? These are excellent.'

He threw a long, thin, black cheroot, and Gurther caught it between his teeth and seemed absurdly pleased with his trick.

'The time has come when you must know something, Gurther,' said the doctor. He took a fellow to the weed the man was smoking, and puffed huge clouds of rank smoke into the room. 'I have for a friend – who? Herr Newton?' He shrugged his shoulders. 'He is a very charming man, but he has no brains. He is the kind of man, Gurther, who would live in comfort, take all we gave him by our cleverness and industry, and never say thank you! And in trouble what will he do, Gurther? He will go to the police – yes, my dear friend, he will go to the police!'

He nodded. Gurther had heard the same story that night when he had crept soft-footed to the door and had heard the doctor discuss certain matters with the late Mr Pfeiffer.

'He would, without a wink of his eyelash, without a snap of his hand, send you and me to death, and would read about our execution with a smile, and then go forth and eat his plum-pudding and roast beef! That is our friend Herr Newton! You have seen this with your own eyes?'

'*Ja*, Herr Doktor!' exclaimed the obedient Gurther.

'He is a danger for many reasons,' Oberzohn proceeded deliberately. 'Because of these three men who have so infamously set themselves out to ruin me, who burnt down my house, and who whipped you, Gurther – they tied you up to a post and whipped you with a whip of nine tails. You have not forgotten, Gurther?'

'*Nein*, Herr Doktor!' Indeed, Gurther had not forgotten, though the vacant smirk on his face might suggest that he had a pleasant memory of the happening.

'A fool in an organization,' continued the doctor oracularly, 'is like a bad plate on a ship, or a weak link in a chain. Let it snap, and what happens? You and I die, my dear Gurther. We go up before a stupid man in a white wig and a red cloak, and he hands us to another man who puts a rope around our necks, drops us through a hole in the ground – all because we have a stupid man like Herr Montague Newton to deal with.'

'*Ja*, Herr Doktor,' said Gurther as his master stopped. He felt that this comment was required of him.

'Now, I will tell you the whole truth.' The doctor carefully knocked off the ash of his cigar into the saucer of his cup. 'There is a fortune for you and for me, and this girl that we have in the quiet place can give it to us. I can marry her, or I can wipe her out, so! If I marry her, it would be better, I think, and this I have arranged.'

And then, in his own way, he told the story of the hill of gold, concealing nothing, reserving nothing – all that he knew, all that Villa had told him.

'For three-four days now she must be here. At the end of that time nothing matters. The letter to Lisbon – of what value is it? I was foolish when I tried to stop it. She has made no nominee, she has no heirs, she has known nothing of her fortune, and therefore is in no position to claim the renewal of the concession.'

'Herr Doktor, will you graciously permit me to speak?'

The doctor nodded.

'Does the Newton know this?'

'The Newton knows all this,' said the doctor.

'Will you graciously permit me to speak again, Herr Doktor? What was this letter I was to have taken, had I not been overcome by misfortune?'

Oberzohn examined the ceiling.

'I have thought this matter from every angle,' he said, 'and I have decided thus. It was a letter written by Gonsalez to the Secretary or the Minister of the Colonies, asking that the renewal of the concession should be postponed. The telegram from my friend at the Colonial Office in Lisbon was to this effect.' He fixed his glasses, fumbled in his waistcoat and took out the three-page telegram. 'I will read it to you in your own language –

'Application has been received from Leon Gonsalez, asking His Excellency to receive a very special letter which arrives in two days. The telegram does not state the contents of the letter, but the Minister has given orders for the messenger to be received. The present Minister is not favourable to concessions granted to England or Englishmen.'

He folded the paper.

'Which means that there will be no postponement, my dear Gurther, and this enormous fortune will be ours.'

Gurther considered this point and for a moment forgot to smile, and looked what he was in consequence: a hungry, discontented wolf of a man.

'Herr Doktor, graciously permit me to ask you a question?'

'Ask,' said Oberzohn magnanimously.

'What share does Herr Newton get? And if you so graciously honoured me with a portion of your so justly deserved gains, to what extent would be that share?'

The other considered this, puffing away until the room was a mist of smoke.

'Ten thousand English pounds,' he said at last.

'Gracious and learned doctor, that is a very small proportion of many millions,' said Gurther gently.

'Newton will receive one half,' said the doctor, his face working nervously, 'if he is alive. If misfortune came to him, that share would be yours, Gurther, my brave fellow! And with so much money a man would not be hunted. The rich and the noble would fawn upon him; he would have his lovely yacht and steam about the summer seas everlastingly, huh?'

Gurther rose and clicked his heels.

'Do you desire me again this evening?'

'No, no, Gurther.' The old man shook his head. 'And pray remember that there is another day tomorrow, and yet another day after. We shall wait and hear what our friend has to say. Good night, Gurther.'

'Good night, Herr Doktor.'

The doctor looked at the door for a long time after his man had gone and took up his book. He was deep in the chapter which was headed, in the German tongue: 'The Subconscious Activity of the Human Intellect in Relation to the Esoteric Emotions'. To Dr Oberzohn this was more thrilling than the most exciting novel.

Chapter 26

In captivity

The second day of captivity dawned unseen, in a world that lay outside the brick roof and glazed white walls of Mirabelle Leicester's prison-house. She had grown in strength and courage, but not so her companion, Joan, who had started her weary vigil with an almost cheerful gaiety, had sunk deeper and deeper into depression as the hours progressed, and Mirabelle woke to the sound of a woman's sobs, to find the girl sitting on the side of her bed, her head in her wet hands.

'I hate this place!' she sobbed. 'Why does he keep me here? God! If I thought the hound was double-crossing me . . . ! I'll go mad if they keep me here any longer. I will, Leicester!' she screamed.

'I'll make some tea,' said Mirabelle, getting out of bed and finding her slippers.

The girl sat throughout the operation huddled in a miserable heap, and by and by her whimpering got on Mirabelle's nerves.

'I don't know why you should be wretched,' she said. 'They're not after your money!'

'You can laugh – and how you can, I don't know,' sobbed the girl, as she took the cup in her shaking hands. 'I know I'm a fool, but I've never been locked up – like this before. I didn't dream he'd break his word. He swore he'd come yesterday. What time is it?'

'Six o'clock,' said Mirabelle.

It might as well have been eight or midday, for all she knew to the contrary.

'This is a filthy place,' said the hysterical girl. 'I think they're going to drown us all . . . or that thing will explode – ' she pointed to the green baize box – 'I know it! I feel it in my blood. That beast Gurther is here somewhere, ugh? He's like a slimy snake. Have you ever seen him?'

'Gurther? You mean the man who danced with me?'

'That's he. I keep telling you who he is,' said Joan impatiently. 'I wish we could get out of here.'

She jumped up suddenly.

'Come and see if you can help me lift the trap.'

Mirabelle knew it was useless before she set forth on the quest for freedom. Their united efforts failed to move the stone, and Joan was on the point of collapse when they came back to their sleeping-room.

'I hope Gurther doesn't know that those men are friends of yours,' she said, when she became calmer.

'You told me that yesterday. Would that make any difference?'

'A whole lot,' said Joan vehemently. 'He's got the blood of a fish, that man! There's nothing he wouldn't do. Monty ought to be flogged for leaving us here at his mercy. I'm not scared of Oberzohn – he's old. But the other fellow dopes, and goes stark, staring mad at times. Monty told me one night that he was – ' she choked – 'a killer. He said that these German criminals who kill people are never satisfied with one murder, they go on and on until they've got twenty or thirty! He says that the German prisons are filled with men who have the murder habit.'

'He was probably trying to frighten you.'

'Why should he?' said the girl, with unreasonable anger. 'And leave him alone! Monty is the best in the world. I adore the ground he walks on!'

Very wisely, Mirabelle did not attempt to traverse this view.

It was only when her companion had these hysterical fits that fear was communicated to her. Her faith was completely and wholeheartedly centred on the three men – upon Gonsalez. She wondered how old he was. Sometimes he looked quite young, at others an elderly man. It was difficult to remember his face; he owed so much to his expression, the smile in his eyes, to the strange, boyish eagerness of gesture and action which accompanied his speech. She could not quite understand herself; why was she always thinking of Gonsalez, as a maid might think of a lover? She went red at the thought. He seemed so apart, so aloof from the ordinary influences of women. Suppose she had committed some great crime and had escaped the vigilance of the law, would he hunt her down in the same remorseless, eager way, planning to cut off every avenue of her escape until he shepherded her into a prison cell? It was a horrible thought, and she screwed up her eyes tight to blot out the mental picture she had made.

It would have given her no ordinary satisfaction to have known how often Gonsalez's thoughts strayed to the girl who had so strangely come into his life. He spent a portion of his time that morning in his bedroom, fixing to the wall a large railway map which took in the south of England and the greater part of the Continent. A red-ink line marked the route from London to Lisbon, and he was fixing a little green flag on the line just south of Paris when Manfred strolled into the room and surveyed his work.

'The Sud Express is about there,' he said, pointing to the last of the green flags, 'and I think our friend will have a fairly pleasant and uneventful journey as far as Valladolid – where I have arranged for Miguel Garcia, an old friend of mine, to pick him up and shadow him on the westward journey – unless we get the 'plane. I'm expecting a wire any minute. By the way, the Dieppe police have arrested the gentleman who tried to bump him overboard in mid-Channel, but the man who snatched at his portfolio at the Gare St Lazare is still at liberty.'

'He must be getting quite used to it now,' said Manfred coolly, and laughed to himself.

Leon turned. 'He's a good fellow,' he said with quick earnestness. 'We couldn't have chosen a better man. The woman on the train, of course, was Gurther. He is the only criminal I've ever known who is really efficient at disguising himself.'

Manfred lit his pipe; he had lately taken to this form of smoking. 'The case grows more and more difficult every day. Do you realize that?'

Leon nodded. 'And more dangerous,' he said. 'By the laws of average, Gurther should get one of us the next time he makes an attempt. Have you seen the papers?'

Manfred smiled.

'They're crying for Meadows's blood, poor fellow! Which shows the extraordinary inconsistency of the public. Meadows has only been in one snake case. They credit him with having fallen down on the lot.'

'They seem to be in remarkable agreement that the snake deaths come into the category of wilful murder,' said Gonsalez as they went down the stairs together.

Meadows had been talking to the reporters. Indeed, that was his chief offence from the viewpoint of the official mind. For the first article in the code of every well-constituted policeman is, 'Thou shalt not communicate to the Press.'

Leon strolled aimlessly about the room. He was wearing his chauffeur's uniform, and his hands were thrust into the breeches pockets. Manfred, recognizing the symptoms, rang the bell for Poiccart, and that quiet man came from the lower regions.

'Leon is going to be mysterious,' said Manfred dryly.

'I'm not really,' protested Leon, but he went red. It was one of his most charming peculiarities that he had never forgotten how to blush. 'I was merely going to suggest that there's a play running in London that we ought to see. I didn't know that "The Ringer" was a play until this morning, when I saw one of Oberzohn's more genteel clerks go into the theatre, and, being naturally of an inquisitive turn of mind, followed him. A play that interests Oberzohn will interest me, and should interest you, George,' he said severely, 'and certainly should interest Meadows – it is full of thrilling situations! It is about a criminal who escapes from Dartmoor and comes back to murder his betrayer. There is one scene which is played in the dark, that ought to thrill you – I've been looking up the reviews of the dramatic critics, and as they are unanimous that it is not an artistic success, and is, moreover, wildly improbable, it ought to be worth seeing. I always choose an artistic success when I am suffering from insomnia,' he added cruelly.

'Oberzohn is entitled to his amusements, however vulgar they may be.'

'But this play isn't vulgar,' protested Leon, 'except in so far as it is popular. I found it most difficult to buy a seat. Even actors go to see the audience act.'

'What seat did he buy?'

'Box A,' said Leon promptly, 'and paid for it with real money. It is the end box on the prompt side – and before you ask me whence I gained my amazing knowledge of theatrical technique, I will answer that even a child in arms knows that the prompt side is the left-hand side facing the audience.'

'For tonight?'

Leon nodded.

'I have three stalls,' he said and produced them from his pocket. 'If you cannot go, will you give them to the cook? She looks like a woman who would enjoy a good cry over the sufferings of the tortured heroine. The seats are in the front row, which means that you can get in and out between the acts without walking on other people's knees.'

'Must I go?' asked Poiccart plaintively. 'I do not like detective plays, and I hate mystery plays. I know who the real murderer is before the curtain has been up ten minutes, and that naturally spoils my evening.'

'Could you not take a girl?' asked Leon outrageously. 'Do you know any who would go?'

'Why not take Aunt Alma?' suggested Manfred, and Leon accepted the name joyously.

Aunt Alma had come to town at the suggestion of the Three, and had opened up the Doughty Court flat.

'And really she is a remarkable woman, and shows a steadiness and a courage in face of the terrible position of our poor little friend, which is altogether praiseworthy. I don't think Mirabelle Leicester is in any immediate danger. I think I've said that before. Oberzohn merely wishes to keep her until the period of renewal has expired. How he will escape the consequences of imprisoning her, I cannot guess. He may not attempt to escape them, may accept the term of imprisonment which will certainly be handed out to him, as part of the payment he must pay for his millions.'

'Suppose he kills her?' asked Poiccart.

For a second Leon's face twitched.

'He won't kill her,' he said quietly. 'Why should he? We know that he has got her – the police know. She is a different proposition from Barberton, an unknown man killed nobody knew how, in a public place. No, I don't think we need cross that bridge, only . . . ' He rubbed his hands together irritably. 'However, we shall see. And in the meantime I'm placing a lot of faith in Digby, a shrewd man with a sense of his previous shortcomings. You were wise there, George.'

He was looking at the street through the curtains.

'Tittlemouse is at his post, the faithful hound!' he said, nodding towards the solitary taxicab that stood on the rank. 'I wonder whether he expects – '

Manfred saw a light creep into his eyes.

'Will you want me for the next two hours?' Leon asked quickly, and was out of the room in a flash.

Ten minutes later, Poiccart and George were talking together when they heard the street door close, and saw Leon stroll to the edge of the pavement and wave his umbrella. The taxi-driver was suddenly a thing of quivering excitement. He leaned down, cranked his engine, climbed back into his seat and brought the car up quicker than any taxicab driver had ever moved before.

'New Scotland Yard,' said Leon, and got into the machine.

The cab passed through the forbidding gates of the Yard and dropped him at the staff entrance.

'Wait here,' said Leon, and the man shifted uncomfortably.

'I've got to be back at my garage – ' he began.

'I shall not be five minutes,' said Leon.

Meadows was in his room, fortunately.

'I want you to pull in this man and give him a dose of the third degree you keep in this country,' said Leon. 'He carries a gun; I saw that when he had to get down to crank up his cab in Piccadilly Circus. The engine stopped.'

'What do you want to know?'

'All that there is to be known about Oberzohn. I may have missed one or two things. I've seen him outside the house. Oberzohn employs him for odd jobs and occasionally he acts as the old man's chauffeur. In fact, he drove the machine the day Miss Leicester lunched with Oberzohn at the Ritz-Carlton. He may not have a cabman's licence, and that will make it all the easier for you.'

A few minutes later, a very surprised and wrathful man was marched into Cannon Row and scientifically searched. Leon had been right about the revolver; it was produced and found to be loaded, and his excuse that he carried the weapon as a protection following upon a recent murder of a cab-driver had not the backing of the necessary permit. In addition – and this was a more serious offence – he held no permit from Scotland Yard to ply for hire on the streets, and his badge was the property of another man.

'Put him inside,' said Meadows, and went back to report to the waiting Leon. 'You've hit the bull's-eye first time. I don't know whether he will be of any use to us, but I don't despise even the smallest fish.'

Whilst he was waiting, Leon had been engaged in some quick thinking.

'The man has been at Greenwich lately. One of my men saw him there twice, and I needn't say that he was driving Oberzohn.'

'I'll talk to him later and telephone you,' said Meadows, and Leon Gonsalez went back to Curzon Street, one large smile.

'You have merely exchanged a spy you know for a spy you don't know,' said George Manfred, 'though I never question these freakish acts of yours, Leon. So often they have a trick of turning up trumps. By the way, the police are raiding the Gringo Club in the Victoria Dock Road tonight, and they may be able to pick up a few of Mr Oberzohn's young gentlemen who are certain to be regular users of the place.'

The telephone bell rang shrilly, and Leon took up the receiver, and recognized Meadows's voice.

'I've got a queer story for you,' said the inspector immediately.

'Did he talk?' asked the interested Leon.

'After a while. We took a finger-print impression, and found that he was on the register. More than that, he is a ticket-of-leave man. As an ex-convict we can send him back to finish his unexpired time. I promised to say a few words for him, and he spilt everything. The most interesting item is that Oberzohn is planning to be married.'

'To be married? Who is this?' asked Manfred, in surprise. 'Oberzohn?'

Leon nodded.

'Who is the unfortunate lady?' asked Leon.

There was a pause, and then: 'Miss Leicester.'

Manfred saw the face of his friend change colour, and guessed.

'Does he know when?' asked Leon in a different voice.

'No. The licence was issued over a week ago, which means that Oberzohn can marry any morning he likes to bring along his bride. What's the idea, do you think?'

'Drop in this evening and either I or George will tell you,' said Leon.

He put the telephone on the hook very carefully.

'That is a danger I had not foreseen, although it was obviously the only course Oberzohn could take. If he marries her, she cannot be called in evidence against him. May I see the book, George?'

Manfred unlocked the wall safe and brought back a small ledger. Leo Gonsalez turned the pages thoughtfully.

'Dennis – he has done good work for us, hasn't he?' he asked.

'Yes, he's a very reliable man. He owes us, amongst other things, his life. Do you remember, his wife was – '

'I remember.' Leon scribbled the address of a man who had proved to be one of the most trustworthy of his agents.

'What are you going to do?' asked Manfred.

'I've put Dennis on the doorstep of the Greenwich registrar's office from nine o'clock in the morning until half-past three in the afternoon, and he will have instructions from me that, the moment he sees Oberzohn walk out of a cab with a lady, he must push him firmly but gently under the wheels of the cab and ask the driver politely to move up a yard.'

Leon in his more extravagantly humorous moods was very often in deadly earnest.

Chapter 27

Mr Newton's dilemma

The most carefully guided streaks of luck may, in spite of all precautions, overflow into the wrong channel, and this had happened to
Mr Montague Newton, producing an evening that was financially
disastrous and a night from which sleep was almost banished. He had
had one of his little card parties; but whether it was the absence of
Joan, and the inadequacy of her fluffy-haired substitute, or whether
the wine had disagreed with one of the most promising victims, the
result was the same. They had played *chemin de fer*, and the gilded
pigeon, whose feathers seemed already to be ornamenting the head-
dress of Monty Newton, had been successful, and when he should
have been signing cheques for large amounts, he was cashing his
counters with a reluctant host.

The night started wrong with Joan's substitute, whose name was
Lisa. She had guided to the establishment, via an excellent dinner at
Mero's, the son of an African millionaire. Joan, of course, would
have brought him alone, but Lisa, less experienced, had allowed a
young-looking friend of the victim to attach himself to the party, and
she had even expected praise for her perspicacity and enterprise in
producing two birds for the stone which Mr Newton so effectively
wielded, instead of one.

Monty did not resent the presence of the newcomer, and rather
took the girl's view, until he learnt that Lisa's 'find' was not, as she
had believed, an officer of the Guards, but a sporting young lawyer
with a large criminal practice, and one who had already, as a junior,
conducted several prosecutions for the Crown. The moment his
name was mentioned, Monty groaned in spirit. He was, moreover,
painfully sober. His friend was not so favourably situated.

That was the first of the awkward things to happen. The second was
the bad temper of the player, who, when the bank was considerably
over £3,000, had first of all insisted upon the cards being reshuffled,
and then he had gone banquo – the game being baccarat. Even this
contretemps might have been overcome, but after he had expressed

his willingness to 'give it', the card which Monty had so industriously palmed slipped from his hand to the table, and though the fact was unnoticed by the players, the lawyer's attention being diverted at the moment, it was impossible to recover that very valuable piece of pasteboard. And Monty had done a silly thing. Instead of staging an artistic exhibition of annoyance at remarks which the millionaire's son had made, he decided to take a chance on the natural run of the cards. And he had lost. On top of that, the slightly inebriated player had decided that when a man had won a coup of £3,000 it was time to stop playing. So Monty experienced the mortification of paying out money, and accompanying his visitor to the door with a smile that was so genial and so full of good-fellowship that the young gentleman was compelled to apologize for his boorishness.

'Come along some other night and give me my revenge,' said Monty.

'You bet I will! I'm going to South Africa tomorrow, but I shall be back early next year, and I'll look you up.'

Monty watched him going down the steps and hoped he would break his neck.

He was worried about Joan – more worried than he thought it was possible for him to be about so light a girl. She was necessary to him in many ways. Lisa was a bungling fool, he decided, though he sent her home without hurting her feelings. She was a useful girl in many ways, and nothing spoils a tout quicker than constant nagging.

He felt very lonely in the house, and wandered from room to room, irritated with himself that the absence of this featherbrained girl, who had neither the education nor the breed of his own class, should make such a big difference. And it did; he had to admit as much to himself. He hated the thought of that underground room. He knew something of her temperament, and how soon her experience would get on her nerves. In many respects he wished he did not feel that way about her, because she had a big shock coming, and it was probably because he foresaw this hurt that he was anxious to make the present as happy as he could for her.

After he had done what he was to do, there was no reason in the world why they should be bad friends, and he would give her a big present. Girls of that class soon forget their miseries if the present is large enough. Thus he argued, tossing from side to side in his bed, and all the time his thoughts playing about that infernal cellar. What she must be feeling! He did not worry at all about Mirabelle, because – well, she was a principal in the case. To him, Joan was the real victim.

Sleep did not come until daybreak, and he woke in his most irritable frame of mind. He had promised the girl he would call and see her, though he had privately arranged with Oberzohn not to go to the house until the expiry of the five days.

By lunch-time he could stand the worry no longer, and, ordering his car, drove to a point between New Cross and Bermondsey, walking on foot the remainder of the distance. Mr Oberzohn expected the visit. He had a shrewd knowledge of his confederate's mental outfit, and when he saw this well-dressed man picking a dainty way across the littered ground, he strolled out on the steps to meet him.

'It is curious you should have come,' he said.

'Why didn't you telephone?' growled Newton. This was his excuse for the visit.

'Because there are human machines at the end of every wire,' said Oberzohn. 'If they were automatic and none could listen, but you and I, we would talk and talk and then talk! All day long would I speak with you and find it a pleasure. But not with Miss This and Miss That saying, "One moment, if you please", and saying to the Scotland Yard man, "Now you cut in"!'

'Is Gurther back?'

'Gurther is back,' said the doctor soberly.

'Nothing happened to that bird? At least, I saw nothing in the evening papers.'

'He has gone to Lisbon,' replied the doctor indifferently. 'Perhaps he will get there, perhaps he will not – what does it matter? I should like to see the letter, because it is data, and data has an irresistible charm for a poor old scientist. You will have a drink?'

Monty hesitated, as he always did when Oberzohn offered him refreshment. You could never be sure with Oberzohn.

'I'll have a whisky,' he said at last, 'a full bottle – one that hasn't been opened. I'll open it myself.'

The doctor chuckled unevenly.

'You do not trust?' he said. 'I think you are wise. For who is there in this world of whom a man can say, "He is my friend. To the very end of my life I will have confidence in him."?'

Monty did not feel that the question called for an answer.

He took the whisky bottle to the light, examined the cork and drove in the corkscrew.

'The soda water – that also might be poisoned,' said Dr Oberzohn pleasantly.

At any other time he would not have made that observation. That he said it at all betrayed a subtle but ominous change in their relationship. If Monty noticed this, he did not say a word, but filled his glass and sat down on the sofa to drink. And all the time the doctor was watching him interestedly.

'Yes, Gurther is back. He failed, but you must excuse failure in a good man. The perfect agent has yet to be found, and the perfect principal also. The American, Washington, had left Paris when I last heard of him. He is to be congratulated. If I myself lived in Paris I should always be leaving. It is a frivolous city.'

Monty lit a cigar, and decided to arrive at the object of his visit by stages. For he had come to perform two important duties. He accounted as a duty a call upon Joan. No less was it a duty, and something of a relief also, to make his plan known to his partner.

'How are the girls?' he asked.

'They are very happy,' said Dr Oberzohn, who had not resumed his seat, but stood in an attitude somewhat reminiscent of Gurther, erect, staring, motionless. 'Always my guests are happy.'

'In that dog-hole?' said the other contemptuously. 'I don't want Joan to be here.'

The Herr Doktor shrugged.

'Then take her away, my friend,' he said. 'Why should she stay, if you are unhappy because this woman is not with you? She serves no purpose. Possibly she is fretting. By all means – I will bring her to you.' He moved to the door.

'Wait a moment,' said Monty. 'I'll see her later and take her out perhaps, but I don't want her to be away permanently. Somebody ought to stay with that girl.'

'Why? Am I not here?' asked Oberzohn blandly.

'You're here, and Gurther's here.' Monty was looking out of the window and did not meet the doctor's eyes. 'Especially Gurther. That's why I think that Mirabelle Leicester should have somebody to look after her. Has it ever struck you that the best way out of this little trouble is – marriage?'

'I have thought that,' said the doctor. 'You also have thought it? This is wonderful! You are beginning to think.'

The change of tone was noticeable enough now. Monty snapped round at the man who had hitherto stood in apparent awe of him and his judgments.

'You can cut that sarcasm right out, Oberzohn,' he said, and, without preamble: 'I'm going to marry that girl.'

Oberzohn said nothing to this.

'She's not engaged; she's got no love affairs at all. Joan told me, and Joan is a pretty shrewd girl. I don't know how I'm going to fix it, but I guess the best thing I can do is to pretend that I am a real friend and get her out of your cellar. She'll be so grateful that maybe she will agree to almost anything. Besides, I think I made an impression the first time I saw her. And I've got a position to offer her, Oberzohn: a house in the best part of London – '

'My house,' interrupted Oberzohn's metallic voice.

'Your house? Well, our house, let us say. We're not going to quarrel about terms.'

'I also have a position to offer her, and I do not offer her any other man's.'

Oberzohn was looking at him wide-eyed, a comical figure; his elongated face seemed to stand out in the gloom like a pantomime mask.

'You?' Monty could hardly believe his ears.

'I, Baron Eruc Oberzohn.'

'A baron, are you?' The room shook with Monty's laughter. 'Why, you damned old fool, you don't imagine she'd marry you, do you?'

Oberzohn nodded.

'She would do anythings what I tell her.' In his agitation his English was getting a little ragged. 'A girl may not like a mans, but she might hate something worse – you understand? A woman says death is nothing, but a woman is afeard of death, isn't it?'

'You're crazy,' said Monty scornfully.

'I am crazy, am I? And a damned old fool also – yes? Yet I shall marry her.'

There was a dead silence, and then Oberzohn continued the conversation, but on a much calmer note.

'Perhaps I am what you call me, but it is not a thing worthy for two friends to quarrel. Tomorrow you shall come here, and we will discuss this matter like a business proposition, *hein*?'

Monty examined him as though he were a strange insect that had wandered into his ken.

'You're not a Swede, you're German,' he said. 'That baron stuff gave you away.'

'I am from the Baltic, but I have lived many years in Sweden,' said Oberzohn shortly. 'I am not German: I do not like them.'

More than this he would not say. Possibly he shared Gurther's repugnance towards his sometime neighbours.

'We shall not quarrel, anyway,' he continued. 'I am a fool, you are a fool, we are all fools. You wish to see your woman?'

'I wish to see Joan,' said Monty gruffly. 'I don't like that "your woman" line of yours.'

'I will go get her. You wait.'

Again the long boots came from under the table, were dragged on to the doctor's awkward feet, and Monty watched him from the window as he crossed to the factory and disappeared.

He was gone five minutes before he came out again, alone. Monty frowned. What was the reason for this?

'My friend,' panted Oberzohn, to whom these exertions were becoming more and more irksome, 'it is not wise.'

'I want to see her – ' began Monty.

'Gently, gently; you shall see her. But on the canal bank Gurther has also seen a stranger, who has been walking up and down, pretending to fish. Who can fish in a canal, I ask you?'

'What is he to do with it?'

'Would it be wise to bring her in daylight, I ask you again? Do not the men think that your – that this girl is in Brussels?'

This had not occurred to Monty.

'I have an idea for you. It is a good idea. The brain of old fool Oberzohn sometimes works remarkably. This morning a friend sent to me a ticket for a theatre. Now you shall take her tonight. There is always a little fog when the sun is setting and you can leave the house in a car. Presently I will send a man to attract this watcher's attention, and then I will bring her to the house and you can call for her.'

'I will wait for her.' Monty was dogged on this point.

And wait he did, until an hour later a half-crazy girl came flying into the room and into his arms.

Dr Oberzohn witnessed the reunion unmoved.

'That is a pretty scene for me,' he said, 'for one to be so soon married,' and he left them alone.

*   *   *

'Monty, I can't possibly go back to that beastly place tonight. She'll have to stay by herself. And she's not a bad kid, Monty, but she doesn't know she's worth a lot of money.'

'Have you been talking to her?' he asked angrily. 'I told you – '

'No, I've only just asked her a few questions. You can't be in a poky hole like that, thrown together day and night, without talking, can you? Monty, you're absolutely sure nothing can happen to her?'

Monty cleared his throat.

'The worst thing that can happen to her,' he said, 'is to get married.'

She opened her eyes at this.

'Does somebody want to marry her?'

'Oberzohn,' he said.

'That old thing!' she scoffed.

Again he found a difficulty in speaking.

'I have been thinking it over, honey,' he said. 'Marriage doesn't mean a whole lot to anybody.'

'It'll mean a lot to me,' she said quietly.

'Suppose I married her?' he blurted.

'You!' She stepped back from him in horror.

'Only just a . . . well, this is the truth, Joan. It may be the only way to get her money. Now you're in on this graft, and you know what you are to me. A marriage – a formal marriage – for a year or two, and then a divorce, and we could go away together, man and wife.'

'Is that what he meant?' She jerked her head to the door. 'About "married so soon"?'

'He wants to marry her himself.'

'Let him,' she said viciously. 'Do you think I care about money? Isn't there any other way of getting it?'

He was silent. There were too many other ways of getting it for him to advance a direct negative.

'Oh, Monty, you're not going to do that?'

'I don't know what I'm going to do yet,' he said.

'But not that?' she insisted, clinging to him by his coat.

'We'll talk about it tonight. The old man's got us tickets for the theatre. We'll have a bit of dinner up West and go on, and it really doesn't matter if anybody sees us, because they know very well you're not in Brussels. What is that queer scent you've got?'

Joan laughed, forgetting for the moment the serious problem which faced her.

'Joss-sticks,' she said. 'The place got so close and stuffy, and I found them in the pantry with the provisions. As a matter of fact, it was a silly thing to do, because we had the place full of smoke. It's gone now, though. Monty, you do these crazy things when you're locked up,' she said seriously. 'I don't think I can go back again.'

'Go back tomorrow,' he almost pleaded. 'It's only for two or three days, and it means a lot to me. Especially now that Oberzohn has ideas.'

'You're not going to think any more about – about marrying her, are you?'

'We'll talk of it tonight at dinner. I thought you'd like the idea of the graft,' he added untruthfully.

Joan had to return to her prison to collect some of her belongings. She found the girl lying on the bed, reading, and Mirabelle greeted her with a smile.

'Well, is your term of imprisonment ended?'

Joan hesitated. 'Not exactly. Do you mind if I'm not here tonight?'

Mirabelle shook her head. If the truth be told, she was glad to be alone. All that day she had been forced to listen to the plaints and weepings of this transfigured girl, and she felt that she could not well stand another twenty-four hours.

'You're sure you won't mind being alone?'

'No, of course not. I shall miss you,' added Mirabelle, more in truth than in compliment. 'When will you return?'

The girl made a little grimace. 'Tomorrow.'

'You don't want to come back, naturally? Have you succeeded in persuading your – your friend to let me out too?'

Joan shook her head.

'He'll never do that, my dear, not till . . . ' She looked at the girl. 'You're not engaged, are you?'

'I? No. Is that another story they've heard?' Mirabelle got up from the bed, laughing. 'An heiress, and engaged?'

'No, they don't say you were engaged.' Joan hastened to correct the wrong impression. There was genuine admiration in her voice when she said: 'You're wonderful, kid! If I were in your shoes I'd be quaking. You're just as cheerful as though you were going to the funeral of a rich aunt!'

She did not know how near to a breakdown her companion had been that day, and Mirabelle, who felt stronger and saner now, had no desire to tell her.

'You're rather splendid,' Joan nodded. 'I wish I had your pluck.'

And then, impulsively, she came forward and kissed the girl.

'Don't feel too sore at me,' she said, and was gone before Mirabelle could make a reply.

The doctor was waiting for her in the factory.

'The spy has walked up to the canal bridge. We can go forward,' he said. 'Besides – ' he had satisfaction out of this – 'he cannot see over high walls.'

'What is this story about marrying Mirabelle Leicester?'

'So he has told you? Also did he tell you that – that he is going to marry her?'

'Yes, and I'll tell you something, doctor. I'd rather he married her than you.'

'So!' said the doctor.

'I'd rather anybody else married her, except that snake of yours.'

Oberzohn looked round sharply. She had used the word quite innocently, without any thought of its application, and uttered an 'Oh!' of dismay when she realized her mistake.

'I meant Gurther,' she said.

'Well, I know you meant Gurther, young miss,' he said stiffly.

To get back to the house they had to make a half-circle of the factory and pass between the canal wall and the building itself. The direct route would have taken them into a deep hollow into which the debris of years had been thrown, and which now Nature, in her kindness, had hidden under a green mantle of wild convolvulus. It was typical of the place that the only beautiful picture in the grounds was out of sight.

They were just turning the corner of the factory when the doctor stopped and looked up at the high wall, which was protected by a *cheval de frise* of broken glass. All except in one spot, about two feet wide, where not only the glass but the mortar which held it in place had been chipped off. There were fragments of the glass, and, on the inside of the wall, marks of some implement on the hard surface of the mortar.

'So!' said the doctor.

He was examining the scratches on the wall.

'Wait,' he ordered, and hurried back into the factory, to return, carrying in each hand two large rusty contraptions which he put on the ground.

One by one he forced open the jagged rusty teeth until they were wide apart and held by a spring catch. She had seen things like that in a museum. They were man-traps – relics of the barbarous days when trespass was not only a sin but a crime.

He fixed the second of the traps on the path between the factory and the wall.

'Now we shall see,' he said. 'Forward!'

Monty was waiting for her impatiently. The Rolls had been turned out in her honour, and the sulky-looking driver was already in his place at the wheel.

'What is the matter with that chauffeur?' she asked, as they bumped up the lane towards easier going. 'He looks so happy that I shouldn't be surprised to hear that his mother was hanged this morning.'

'He's sore with the old man,' explained Monty. 'Oberzohn has two drivers. They do a little looking round in the morning. The other fellow was supposed to come back to take over duty at three o'clock, and he hasn't turned up. He was the better driver of the two.'

The chauffeur was apparently seeking every pothole in the ground, and in the next five minutes she was alternately clutching the support of the arm-strap and Monty. They were relieved when at last the car found a metal road and began its noiseless way towards the lights. And then her hand sought his, and for a moment this beautiful flower which had grown in such foul soil, bloomed in the radiance of a love common to every woman, high and low, good and bad.

Chapter 28

At Frater's

Manfred suggested an early dinner at the Lasky, where the soup was to his fastidious taste. Leon, who had eaten many crumpets for tea – he had a weakness for this indigestible article of diet – was prepared to dispense with the dinner, and Poiccart had views, being a man of steady habits. They dined at the Lasky, and Leon ordered a baked onion, and expatiated upon the two wasted years of Poiccart's life, employing a wealth of imagery and a beauty of diction worthy of a better subject.

Manfred looked at his watch.

'Where are they dining?' he asked.

'I don't know yet,' said Leon. 'Our friend will be here in a few minutes: when we go out he will tell us. You don't want to see her?'

Manfred shook his head.

'No,' he said.

'I'm going to be bored,' complained Poiccart.

'Then you should have let me bring Alma,' said Leon promptly.

'Exactly.' Raymond nodded his sober head. 'I have the feeling that I am saving a lady from an unutterably dreary evening.'

There was a man waiting for them when they came out of the restaurant – a very uninteresting-looking man who had three sentences to say *sotto voce* as they stood near him, but apparently in ignorance of his presence.

'I did not wish to go to Mero's,' said Manfred, 'but as we have the time, I think it would be advisable to stroll in that direction. I am curious to discover whether this is really Oberzohn's little treat, or whether the idea emanated from the unadmirable Mr Newton.'

'And how will you know, George?' asked Gonsalez.

'By the car. If Oberzohn is master of the ceremonies, we shall find his machine parked somewhere in the neighbourhood. If it is Newton's idea, then Oberzohn's limousine, which brought them from South London, will have returned, and Newton's car will be in its place.'

Mero's was one of the most fashionable of dining clubs, patronized not only by the élite of society, but having on its books the cream of the theatrical world. It was situated in one of those quiet, old-world squares which are to be found in the very heart of London, enjoying, for some mysterious reason, immunity from the hands of the speculative property owner. The square retained the appearance it had in the days of the Georges; and though some of the fine mansions had been given over to commerce and the professions, and the lawyer and the manufacturer's agent occupied the drawing-rooms and bedrooms sacred to the bucks and beauties of other days, quite a large number of the houses remained in private occupation.

There was nothing in the fascia of Mero's to advertise its character. The club premises consisted of three of these fine old dwellings. The uninitiated might not even suspect that there was communication between the three houses, for the old doorways and doorsteps remained untouched, though only one was used.

They strolled along two sides of the square before, amidst the phalanx of cars that stood wheel to wheel, their backs to the railings of the centre gardens, they saw Oberzohn's car. The driver sat with his arms folded on the wheel, in earnest conversation with a pale-faced man, slightly and neatly bearded, and dressed in faultless evening dress. He was evidently a cripple: one shoulder was higher than the other; and when he moved, he walked painfully with the aid of a stick.

Manfred saw the driver point up the line of cars, and the lame gentleman limped in the direction the chauffeur had indicated and stopped to speak to another man in livery. As they came abreast of him, they saw that one of his boots had a thick sole, and the limp was explained.

'The gentleman has lost his car,' said Manfred, for now he was peering short-sightedly at the number-plates.

The theft of cars was a daily occurrence. Leon had something to say on the potentialities of that branch of crime. He owned to an encyclopaedic knowledge of the current fashions in wrongdoing, and in a few brief sentences indicated the extent of these thefts.

'Fifty a week are shipped to India and the Colonies, after their numbers are erased and another substituted. In some cases the "knockers off", as they call the thieves, drive them straightway into the packing-cases which are prepared for every make of car; the ends are nailed up, and they are waiting shipment at the docks before the owner is certain of his loss. There are almost as many stolen cars in India, South Africa and Australia as there are honest ones!'

They walked slowly past the decorous portals of Mero's, and caught a glimpse, through the curtained windows, of soft table lamps burning, of bare-armed women and white-shirted men, and heard faintly the strains of an orchestra playing a Viennese waltz.

'I should like to see our Jane,' said Gonsalez. 'She never came to you, did she?'

'She came, but I didn't see her,' said Manfred. 'From the moment she leaves the theatre she must not be left.'

Leon nodded.

'I have already made that arrangement,' he said. 'Digby – '

'Digby takes up his duty at midnight,' said Manfred. 'He has been down to Oberzohn's place to get the lie of the land: he thought it advisable that he should study the topography in daylight, and I agreed. He might get himself into an awkward tangle if he started exploring the canal bank in the dark hours. Summer or winter, there is usually a mist on the water.'

They reached Frater's theatre so early that the queues at the pit door were still unadmitted, and Leon suggested that they make a circuit of this rambling house of entertainment. It stood in Shaftesbury Avenue and occupied an island site. On either side two narrow streets flanked the building, whilst the rear formed the third side of a small square, one of which was taken up by a County Council dwelling, mainly occupied by artisans. From the square a long passageway led to Cranbourn Street; whilst, in addition to the alley which opened just at the back of the theatre, a street ran parallel to Shaftesbury Avenue from Charing Cross Road to Rupert Street.

The theatre itself was one of the best in London, and although it had had a succession of failures, its luck had turned, and the new mystery play was drawing all London.

'That is the stage door,' said Leon – they had reached the square – 'and those are emergency exits – ' he pointed back the way they had come – 'which are utilized at the end of a performance to empty the theatre.'

'Why are you taking such an interest in the theatre itself?' asked Poiccart.

'Because,' said Gonsalez slowly, 'I am in agreement with George. We should have found Newton's car parked in Fitzreeve Gardens – not Oberzohn's. And the circumstances are a little suspicious.'

The doors of the pit and gallery were open now; the queues were moving slowly to the entrances; and they watched the great building swallow up the devotees of the drama, before they returned to the front of the house.

Cars were beginning to arrive, at first at intervals, but, as the hour of the play's beginning approached, in a ceaseless line that made a congestion and rendered the traffic police articulate and occasionally unkind. It was short of the half-hour after eight when Manfred saw Oberzohn's glistening car in the block, and presently it pulled up before the entrance of the theatre. First Joan and then Monty Newton alighted and passed out of view.

Gonsalez thought he had never seen the girl looking quite as radiantly pretty. She had the colouring and the shape of youth, and though the more fastidious might object to her daring toilette, the most cantankerous could not cavil at the pleasing effect.

'It is a great pity – ' Leon spoke in Spanish – 'a thousand pities! I have the same feeling when I see a perfect block of marble placed in the hands of a tombstone-maker to be mangled into ugliness!'

Manfred put out his hand and drew him back into the shadow. A cab was dropping the lame man. He got out with the aid of a link-man, paid the driver, and limped into the vestibule. It was not a remarkable coincidence: the gentleman had evidently come from Mero's, and as all London was flocking to the drama, there was little that was odd in finding him here. They saw that he went up into the dress circle, and later, when they took their places in the stalls, Leon, glancing up, saw the pale, bearded face and noted that he occupied the end seat of the front row.

'I've met that man somewhere,' he said, irritated. 'Nothing annoys me worse than to forget, not a face, but where I have seen it!'

Did Gurther but know, he had achieved the height of his ambition: he had twice passed under the keen scrutiny of the cleverest detectives in the world, and had remained unrecognized.

Chapter 29

Work for Gurther

Gurther was sleeping when he was called for duty, but presented himself before his director as bright and alert as though he had not spent a sleepless night, nor yet had endured the strain of a midnight train jump.

'Once more, my Gurther, I send you forth.' Dr Oberzohn was almost gay. 'This time to save us all from the Judas treachery of one we thought was our friend. Tonight the snake must bite, and bite hard, Gurther. And out into the dark goes the so-called Trusted! And after that, my brave boy, there shall be nothing to fear.'

He paused for approval, and got it in a snapped agreement.

'Tonight we desire from you a *chef d'oeuvre*, the supreme employment of your great art, Gurther; the highest expression of genius! The gentleman-club manner will not do. They may look for you and find you. Better it should be, this time, that you –'

'Herr Doktor, will you graciously permit me to offer a humble suggestion?' said Gurther eagerly.

The doctor nodded his head slowly.

'You may speak, Gurther,' he said. 'You are a man of intelligence; I would not presume to dictate to an artist.'

'Let me go for an hour, perhaps two hours, and I will return to you with a manner that is unique. Is it graciously permitted, Herr Doktor?'

'March!' said the doctor graciously, waving his hand to the door.

Nearly an hour and a half passed before the door opened and a gentleman came in who for a moment even the doctor thought was a stranger. The face had an unearthly ivory pallor; the black brows, the faint shadows beneath the eyes that suggested a recent illness, the close-cropped black beard in which grey showed – these might not have deceived him. But the man was obviously the victim of some appalling accident of the past. One shoulder was hunched, the hand that held the stick was distorted out of shape, and as he moved, the clump of his club foot advertised his lameness.

'Sir, you desire to see me – ?' began the doctor, and then stared open-mouthed. 'It is not . . . !'

Gurther smiled.

'Herr Doktor, are you condescendingly pleased?'

'Colossal!' murmured Oberzohn, gazing in amazement. 'Of all accomplishments this is supreme! Gurther, you are an artist. Some day we shall buy a theatre for you in Unter den Linden, and you shall thrill large audiences.'

'Herr Doktor, this is my own idea; this I have planned for many months. The boots I made myself; even the coat I altered – ' he patted his deformed shoulder proudly.

'An eyeglass?'

'I have it,' said Gurther promptly.

'The cravat – is it not too proper?'

Gurther fingered his tie.

'For the grand habit I respectfully claim that the proper tie is desirable, if you will graciously permit.'

The Herr Doktor nodded.

'You shall go with God, Gurther,' he said piously, took a golden cigarette-case from his pocket and handed it to the man. 'Sit down, my dear friend.'

He rose and pointed to the chair he had vacated.

'In my own chair, Gurther. Nothing is too good for you. Now here is the arrangement . . . '

Step by step he unfolded the time-table, for chronology was almost as great a passion with this strange and wicked man as it was with Aunt Alma.

So confident was Gurther of his disguise that he had gone in the open to speak to Oberzohn's chauffeur, and out of the tail of his eye he had seen Manfred and Gonsalez approaching. It was the supreme test and was passed with credit to himself.

He did not dine at Mero's; Gurther never ate or drank when he was wearing a disguise, knowing just how fatal that occupation could be. Instead, he had called a taxi, and had killed time by being driven slowly round and round the Outer Circle of Regent's Park.

Gurther was doing a great deal of thinking in these days, and at the cost of much physical discomfort had curtailed his pernicious prac-tices, that his head might be clear all the time. For if he were to live, that clear head of his was necessary.

The prisoner in the cellar occupied his thoughts. She had an importance for two reasons: she was a friend of the men whom he hated with a cold and deadly malignity beyond description; she represented wealth untold, and the Herr Doktor had even gone to the length of planning a marriage with her. She was not to be killed, not to be hurt; she was so important that the old man would take the risks attendant upon a marriage. There must be an excellent reason for that, because Dr Oberzohn had not a very delicate mind.

He seemed to remember that, by the English law, a wife could not give evidence against her husband. He was not sure, but he had a dim notion that Pfeiffer had told him this: Pfeiffer was an educated man and had taken high honours at the gymnasium.

Gurther was not well read. His education had been of a scrappy character, and once upon a time he had been refused a leading part because of his provincial accent. That fault he had corrected in prison, under the tuition of a professor who was serving a life sentence for killing two women; but by the time Gurther had been released, he was a marked man, and the stage was a career lost to him for ever.

Oberzohn possessed advantages which were not his. He was the master; Gurther was the servant. Oberzohn could determine events by reason of his vast authority, and the strings which he pulled in every part of the world. Even Gurther had accepted this position of blind, obedient servant, but now his angle had shifted, even as Oberzohn's had moved in relation to Montague Newton. Perhaps because of this. The doctor, in curtailing one confidence, was enlarging another, and in the enlargement his prestige suffered.

Gurther was now the confidant, therefore the equal, and logically, the equal can always become the superior. He had dreamed dreams of a life of ease, a gratification of his sense of luxury without the sobering thought that somewhere round the corner was waiting a man ready to tap him on the shoulder . . . a white palace in a flowery land, with blue swimming pools, and supple girls who called him Master. Gurther began to see the light.

Until he had taken his seat in the theatre, he had not so much as glimpsed the man and the woman in the end box.

Joan was happy – happier than she remembered having been. Perhaps it was the reaction from her voluntary imprisonment. Certainly it was Monty's reluctant agreement to a change of plans which so exalted her. Monty had dropped the thin pretence of an accommodation marriage; and once he was persuaded to this, the last hindrance to enjoyment was dissipated. Let Oberzohn take the girl if he wanted her; take, too, such heavy responsibility as followed.

Monty Newton would get all that he wanted without the risk. Having arrived at this decision, he had ordered another bottle of champagne to seal the bargain, and they left Mero's club a much happier couple than they had been when they entered.

'As soon as we've carved up this money, we'll get away out of England,' he told her as they were driving to the theatre. 'What about Buenos Ayres for the winter, old girl?'

She did not know where Buenos Ayres was, but she gurgled her delight at the suggestion, and Monty expatiated upon the joys of the South American summer, the beauties of B.A., its gaieties and amusements.

'I don't suppose there'll be any kick coming,' he said, 'but it wouldn't be a bad scheme if we took a trip round the world, and came back in about eighteen months' time to settle down in London. My hectic past would have been forgotten by then – why, I might even get into Parliament.'

'How wonderful!' she breathed, and then: 'What is this play about, Monty?'

'It's a bit of a thrill, the very play for you – a detective story that will make your hair stand on end.'

She had all the gamin's morbid interest in murder and crime, and she settled down in the box with a pleasant feeling of anticipation, and watched the development of the first act.

The scene was laid in a club, a low-down resort where the least desirable members of society met, and she drank in every word, because she knew the life, had seen that type of expensively dressed woman who swaggered on to the stage and was addressed familiarly by the club proprietor. She knew that steady-eyed detective when he made his embarrassing appearance. The woman was herself. She even knew the cadaverous wanderer who approached stealthily at the door: a human wolf that fled at the sight of the police officer.

The three who sat in the front row of the stalls – how Leon Gonsalez secured these tickets was one of the minor mysteries of the day – saw her, and one at least felt his heart ache.

Monty beamed his geniality. He had taken sufficient wine to give him a rosy view of the world, and he was even mildly interested in the play, though his chief pleasure was in the girl's enchantment. He ordered ices for her after the first interval.

'You're getting quite a theatre fan, kiddie,' he said. 'I must take you to some other shows. I had no idea you liked this sort of thing.'

She drew a long breath and smiled at him.

'I like anything when I'm with you,' she said, and they held hands foolishly, till the house lights dimmed and the curtain rose upon a lawyer's office.

The lawyer was of the underworld: a man everlastingly on the verge of being struck off the rolls. He had betrayed a client with whom he had had dealings, and the man had gone to prison for a long term, but had escaped. Now the news had come that he had left Australia and was in London, waiting his opportunity to destroy the man whose treachery was responsible for his capture.

Here was a note to which the heart of the girl responded. Even Monty found himself leaning forward, as the old familiar cant terms of his trade came across the footlights.

'It is quite all right,' he said, at the second interval, 'only – ' he hesitated – 'isn't it a bit too near the real thing? After all, one doesn't come to the theatre to see . . . '

He stopped, realizing that conditions and situations familiar to him were novel enough to a fashionable audience which was learning for the first time that a 'busy' was a detective, and that a police informer went by the title of 'nose'.

The lights up, he glanced round the house, and suddenly he started and caught her arm.

'Don't look for a moment,' he said, averting his eyes, 'then take a glance at the front row. Do you see anybody you know?'

Presently she looked.

'Yes, that is the fellow you hate so much, isn't it – Gonsalez?'

'They're all there – the three of them,' said Monty. 'I wonder – ' he was troubled at the thought – 'I wonder if they're looking for you?'

'For me? They've nothing on me, Monty.'

He was silent.

'I'm glad you're not going back to that place tonight. They'll trail you sure – sure!'

He thought later that it was probably a coincidence that they were there at all. They seemed to show no interest in the box, but were chattering and talking and laughing to one another. Not once did their eyes come up to his level, and after a while he gained in confidence, though he was glad enough when the play was resumed.

There were two scenes in the act: the first was a police station, the second the lawyer's room. The man was drunk, and the detective had come to warn him that The Ringer was after him. And then suddenly the lights on the stage were extinguished and the whole house was in the dark. It was part of the plot. In this darkness, and in the very presence of the police, the threatened man was to be murdered. They listened in tense silence, the girl craning her head forward, trying to pierce the dark, listening to the lines of intense dialogue that were coming from the blackness of the stage. Somebody was in the room – a woman, and they had found her. She slipped from the stage detective's grasp and vanished, and when the lights went up she was gone.

'What has happened, Monty?' she whispered.

He did not answer.

'Do you think- ?'

She looked round at him. His head was resting on the plush-covered ledge of the box. His face, turned towards her, was grey; the eyes were closed, and his teeth showed in a hideous grin.

She screamed.

'Monty! Monty!'

She shook him. Again her scream rang through the house. At first the audience thought that it was a woman driven hysterical by the tenseness of the stage situation, and then one or two people rose from their stalls and looked up.

'Monty! Speak to me! He's dead, he's dead!'

Three seats in the front row had emptied. The screams of the hysterical girl made it impossible for the scene to proceed, and the curtain came down quickly.

The house was seething with excitement. Every face was turned towards the box where she knelt by the side of the dead man, clasping him in her arms, and the shrill agony in her voice was unnerving.

The door of the box swung open, and Manfred dashed in. One glance he gave at Monty Newton, and he needed no other.

'Get the girl out,' he said curtly.

Leon tried to draw her from the box, but she was a shrieking fury.

'You did it, you did it! . . . Let me go to him!'

Leon lifted her from her feet, and, clawing wildly at his face, she was carried from the box.

The manager was running along the passage, and Leon sent him on with a jerk of his head. And then a woman in evening dress came from somewhere.

'May I take her?' she said, and the exhausted girl collapsed into her arms.

Gonsalez flew back to the box. The man was lying on the floor, and the manager, standing at the edge of the box, was addressing the audience.

'The gentleman has fainted, and I'm afraid his friend has become a little hysterical. I must apologize to you, ladies and gentlemen, for this interruption. If you will allow us a minute to clear the box, the play will be resumed. If there is a doctor in the house, I should be glad if he would come.'

There were two doctors within reach, and in the passage, which was now guarded by a commissionaire, a hasty examination was made. They examined the punctured wound at the back of the neck and then looked at one another.

'This is The Snake,' said one.

'The house musn't know,' said Manfred. 'He's dead, of course?'

The doctor nodded.

Out in the passage was a big emergency exit door, and this the manager pushed open, and, running out into the street, found a cab, into which all that was mortal of Monty Newton was lifted.

Whilst this was being done, Poiccart returned.

'His car has just driven off,' he said. 'I saw the number-plate as it turned into Lisle Street.'

'How long ago?' asked Gonsalez quickly.

'At this very moment.'

Leon pinched his lip thoughtfully.

'Why didn't he wait, I wonder?'

He went back through the emergency door, which was being closed, and passed up the passage towards the entrance. The box was on the dress-circle level, and the end of a short passage brought him into the circle itself.

And then the thought of the lame man occurred to him, and his eyes sought the first seat in the front row, which was also the seat nearest to the boxes. The man had gone.

As he made this discovery, George emerged from the passage.

'Gurther!' said Leon. 'What a fool I am! But how clever!'

'Gurther?' said Manfred in amazement. 'Do you mean the man with the club foot?'

Leon nodded.

'He was not alone, of course,' said Gonsalez. 'There must have been two or three of the gang here, men and women – Oberzohn works these schemes out with the care and thoroughness of a general. I wonder where the management have taken the girl?'

He found the manager discussing the tragedy with two other men, one of whom was obviously associated with the production, and he signalled him aside.

'The lady? I suppose she's gone home. She's left the theatre.'

'Which way did she go?' asked Gonsalez, in a sudden panic.

The manager called a linkman, who had seen a middle-aged woman come out of the theatre with a weeping girl, and they had gone down the side-street towards the little square at the back of the playhouse.

'She may have taken her home to Chester Square,' said Manfred. His voice belied the assumption of confidence.

Leon had not brought his own machine, and they drove to Chester Square in a taxi. Fred, the footman, had neither heard nor seen the girl, and nearly fainted when he learned of the tragic ending to his master's career.

'Oh, my God!' he groaned. 'And he only left here this afternoon . . . dead, you say?'

Gonsalez nodded.

'Not – not The Snake?' faltered the man.

'What do you know about the snake?' demanded Manfred sternly.

'Nothing, except – well, the snake made him nervous, I know. He told me today that he hoped he'd get through the week without a snake-bite.'

He was questioned closely, but although it was clear that he knew something of his master's illicit transactions, and that he was connected in business with Oberzohn, the footman had no connection with the doctor's gang. He drew a large wage and a percentage of profits from the gaming side of the business, and confessed that it was part of his duties to prepare stacks of cards and pass them to his master under cover of bringing in the drinks. But of anything more sinister he knew nothing.

'The woman, of course, was a confederate, who had been planted to take charge of the girl the moment the snake struck. I was in such a state of mind,' confessed Leon, 'that I do not even remember what she looked like. I am a fool – a double-distilled idiot! I think I must be getting old. There's only one thing for us to do, and that is to get back to Curzon Street – something may have turned up.'

'Did you leave anybody in the house?'

Leon nodded. 'Yes, I left one of our men, to take any 'phone messages that came through.'

They paid off the taxi before the house, and Leon sprinted to the garage to get the car. The man who opened the door to them was he who had been tied up by the pedlar at Heavy-tree Farm, and his first words came as a shock to Manfred: 'Digby's here, sir.'

'Digby?' said the other in surprise. 'I thought he was on duty?'

'He's been here since just after you left, sir. If I'd known where you had gone, I'd have sent him to you.'

Digby came out of the waiting-room at that moment, ready to apologize.

'I had to see you, sir, and I'm sorry I'm away from my post.'

'You may not be missing much,' said Manfred unsmilingly. 'Come upstairs and tell me all about it.'

Digby's story was a strange one. He had gone down that afternoon to the canal bank to make a reconnaissance of ground which was new to him.

'I'm glad I did too, because the walls have got broken glass on top. I went up into the Old Kent Road and bought a garden hoe, and prised the mortar loose, so that if I wanted, I could get over. And then I climbed round the water-gate and had a look at that barge of his. There was nobody about, though I think they spotted me afterwards. It is a fairly big barge, and, of course, in a terrible state, but the hold is full of cargo – you know that, sir?'

'You mean there is something in the barge?'

Digby nodded.

'Yes, it has a load of some kind. The after part, where the bargee's sleeping quarters are, is full of rats and water, but the fore part of the vessel is water-tight, and it holds something heavy too. That is why the barge is down by its head in the mud. I was in the Thames police and I know a lot about river craft.'

'Is that what you came to tell me?'

'No, sir, it was something queerer than that. After I'd given the barge a look over and tried to pull up some of the boards – which I didn't manage to do – I went along and had a look at the factory. It's not so easy to get in, because the entrance faces the house, but to get to it you have to go half round the building, and that gives you a certain amount of cover. There was nothing I could see in the factory itself. It was in a terrible mess, full of old iron and burnt-out boxes. I was coming round the back of the building,' he went on impressively, 'when I smelt a peculiar scent.'

'A perfume?'

'Yes, sir, it was perfume, but stronger – more like incense. I thought at first it might be an old bale of stuff that had been thrown out, or else I was deceiving myself. I began poking about in the rubbish heaps – but they didn't smell of scent! Then I went back into the building again, but there was no smell at all. It was very strong when I returned to the back of the factory, and then I saw a little waft of smoke come out of a ventilator close to the ground. My first idea was that the place was on fire, but when I knelt down, it was this scent.'

'Joss-sticks?' said Poiccart quickly.

'That's what it was!' said the detective. 'Like incense, yet not like it. I knelt down and listened at the grating, and I'll swear that I heard voices. They were very faint.'

'Men's?'

'No, women's.'

'Could you see anything?'

'No, sir, it was a blind ventilator; there was probably a shaft there – in fact, I'm sure there was, because I pushed a stone through one of the holes and heard it drop some distance down.'

'There may be an underground room there,' said Poiccart, 'and somebody's burnt joss-sticks to sweeten the atmosphere.'

'Under the factory? It's not in the plans of the building. I've had them from the surveyor's office and examined them,' said George, 'although surveyors' plans aren't infallible. A man like Oberzohn would not hesitate to break so unimportant a thing as a building law!'

Leon came in at that moment, heard the story and was in complete agreement with Poiccart's theory.

'I wondered at the time we saw the plans whether we ought to accept that as conclusive,' he said. 'The store was built at the end of 1914, when architects and builders took great liberties and pleaded the exigencies of the war.'

Digby went on with his story.

'I was going back to the barge to get past the water-gate, but I saw the old man coming down the steps of the house, so I climbed the wall, and very glad I was that I'd shifted that broken glass, or I should never have got over.'

Manfred pulled his watch from his pocket with a frown. They had lost nearly an hour of precious time with their inquiries in Chester Square.

'I hope we're not too late,' he said ominously. 'Now Leon . . . '

But Leon had gone down the stairs in three strides.

Chapter 30

Joan a prisoner

Dazed with grief, not knowing, not seeing, not caring, not daring to think, Joan suffered herself to be led quickly into the obscurity of the side-street, and did not even realize that Oberzohn's big limousine had drawn up by the sidewalk.

'Get in,' said the woman harshly.

Joan was pushed through the door and guided to a seat by somebody who was already in the machine.

She collapsed in a corner moaning as the door slammed and the car began to move.

'Where are we going? Let me get back to him!'

'The gracious lady will please restrain her grief,' said a hateful voice, and she swung round and stared unseeingly to the place whence the voice had come.

The curtains of the car had been drawn; the interior was as black as pitch.

'You – you beast!' she gasped. 'It's you, is it? . . . Gurther! You murdering beast!'

She struck at him feebly, but he caught her wrist.

'The gracious lady will most kindly restrain her grief,' he said suavely. 'The Herr Newton is not dead. It was a little trick in order to baffle certain interferers.'

'You're lying, you're lying!' she screamed, struggling to escape from those hands of steel. 'He's dead! You know he's dead, and you killed him! You snake-man!'

'The gracious lady must believe me,' said Gurther earnestly. They were passing through a public part of the town and at any moment a policeman might hear her shrieks. 'If Herr Newton had not pretended to be hurt, he would have been arrested . . . he follows in the next car.'

'You're trying to quieten me,' she said, 'but I won't be quiet.'

And then a hand came over her mouth and pressed her head back against the cushions. She struggled desperately, but two fingers slid up her face and compressed her nostrils. She was being suffocated. She struggled to free herself from the tentacle hold of him, and then slipped into unconsciousness.

Gurther felt the straining figure go limp and removed his hands. She did not feel the prick of the needle on her wrist, though the drugging was clumsily performed in the darkness and in a car that was swaying from side to side. He felt her pulse, his long fingers pressed her throat and felt the throb of the carotid artery; propping her so that she could not fall, Herr Gurther sank back luxuriously into a corner of the limousine and lit a cigar.

The journey was soon over. In a very short time they were bumping down Hangman's Lane and turned so abruptly into the factory grounds that one of the mudguards buckled to the impact of the gate-post.

* * *

It must have been two hours after the departure of her companion, when Mirabelle, lying on her bed, half dozing, was wakened by her book slipping to the floor, and sat up quickly to meet the apprising stare of the man whom, of all men in the world, she disliked most cordially. Dr Oberzohn had come noiselessly into the room and under his arm was a pile of books.

'I have brought these for you,' he said, in his booming voice, and stacked them neatly on the table.

She did not answer.

'Novels of a frivolous kind, such as you will enjoy,' he said, unconscious of offence. 'I desired the seller of the books to pick them for me. Fiction stories of adventure and of amorous exchanges. These will occupy your mind, though to me they would be the merest rubbish and nonsense.'

She stood silently, her hands clasped behind her, watching him. He was neater than usual, had resumed the frock-coat he wore the day she had first met him – how long ago that seemed! – his collar was stiffly white, and if his cravat was more gorgeous than is usually seen in a man correctly arrayed, it had the complementary value of being new.

He held in his hands a small bouquet of flowers tightly packed, their stems enclosed in silver foil, a white paper frill supplying an additional expression of gentility.

'These are for you.' He jerked out his hand towards her.

Mirabelle looked at the flowers, but did not take them. He seemed in no way disconcerted, either by her silence, or by the antagonism which her attitude implied, but, laying the flowers on top of the books, he clasped his hands before him and addressed her. He was nervous, for some reason; the skin of his forehead was furrowing and smoothing with grotesque rapidity. She watched the contortions, fascinated.

'To every man,' he began, 'there comes a moment of domestic allurement. Even to the scientific mind, absorbed in its colossal problems, there is this desire for family life and for the haven of rest which is called marriage.'

He paused, as though he expected her to offer some comment upon his platitude.

'Man alone,' he went on, when she did not speak, 'has established an artificial and unnatural convention that, at a certain age, a man should marry a woman of that same age. Yet it has been proved by history that happy marriages are often between a man who is in the eyes of the world old, and a lady who is youthful.'

She was gazing at him in dismay. Was he proposing to her? The idea was incredible, almost revolting. He must have read in her face the thoughts that were uppermost in her mind, the loathing, the sense of repulsion which filled her, yet he went on, unabashed: 'I am a man of great riches. You are a girl of considerable poverty. But because I saw you one day in your poor house, looking, gracious lady, like a lily growing amidst foul weeds, my heart went out to you, and for this reason I brought you to London, spending many thousands of pounds in order to give myself the pleasure of your company.'

'I don't think you need go any farther, Dr Oberzohn,' she said quietly, 'if you're proposing marriage, as I think you are.'

He nodded emphatically.

'Such is my honourable intention,' he said.

'I would never marry you in any circumstances,' she said. 'Not even if I had met you under the happiest conditions. The question of your age' – she nearly added 'and of your appearance,' but her natural kind-ness prevented that cruel thrust, though it would not have hurt him in the slightest degree – 'has nothing whatever to do with my decision. I do not even like you, and have never liked you, Mr Oberzohn.'

'Doctor,' he corrected, and in spite of her woeful plight she could have laughed at this insistence upon the ceremonial title.

'Young miss, I cannot woo you in the way of my dear and sainted brother, who was all for ladies and had a beautiful manner.'

She was amazed to hear that he had a brother at all – and it was almost a relief to know that he was dead.

'Martyred, at the hands of wicked and cunning murderers, slain in his prime by the assassin's pistol . . . ' His voice trembled and broke. 'For that sainted life I will some day take vengeance.'

It was not wholly curiosity that impelled her to ask who killed him.

'Leon Gonsalez.' The words in his lips became the grating of a file. 'Killed . . . murdered! And even his beautiful picture destroyed in that terrible fire. Had he saved that, my heart would have been soft towards him.' He checked himself, evidently realizing that he was getting away from the object of his call. 'Think over this matter, young lady. Read the romantic books and the amorous books, and then perhaps you will not think it so terrible a fate to drift at moonlight through the canals of Venice, with the moon above and the gondoliers.'

He wagged his head sentimentally.

'There is no book which will change my view, doctor,' she said. 'I cannot understand why you propose such an extraordinary course, but I would rather die than marry you.'

His cold eyes filled her with a quick terror.

'There are worse things than death, which is but sleep – many worse things, young miss. Tomorrow I shall come for you, and we will go into the country, where you will say "yes" and "no" according to my desire. I have many – what is the word? – certificates for marriage, for I am too clever a man to leave myself without alternatives.'

(This was true; he had residential qualifications in at least four counties, and at each he had given legal notice of his intended marriage.)

'Not tomorrow or any other day. Nothing would induce me.'

His eyebrows went almost to the top of his head.

'So!' he said, with such significance that her blood ran cold. 'There are worse men than the Herr Doktor – ' he raised a long finger warningly – 'terrible men with terrible minds. You have met Gurther?'

She did not answer this.

'Yes, yes, you danced with him. A nice man, is he not, to ladies? Yet this same Gurther . . . I will tell you something.'

He seated himself on a corner of the table and began talking, until she covered her ears with her hands and hid her white face from him.

'They would have killed him for that,' he said, when her hands came down, 'but Gurther was too clever, and the poor German peasants too stupid. You shall remember that, shall you not?'

He did not wait for her answer. With a stiff bow he strutted out of the room and up the stairs. There came the thud of the trap falling and the inevitable rumble of the concrete barrel.

He had some work to do, heavy work for a man who found himself panting when he climbed stairs. And though four of his best and most desperate men were waiting in his parlour drinking his whisky and filling the little room with their rank cigar smoke, he preferred to tackle this task which he had already begun as soon as night fell, without their assistance or knowledge.

On the edge of the deep hole in his grounds, where the wild convolvulus grew amidst the rusty corners of discarded tins and oil barrels, was a patch of earth that yielded easily to the spade. When the factory had been built, the depression had been bigger, but the builders had filled in half the hole with the light soil that they had dug out of the factory's foundations.

He took his spade, which he had left in the factory, and, skirting the saucer-shaped depression, he reached a spot where a long trench had already been dug. Taking off his fine coat and waistcoat, unfastening cravat and collar and carefully depositing them upon the folded coat, he continued his work, stopping now and again to wipe his streaming brow.

He had to labour in the dark, but this was no disadvantage; he could feel the edges of the pit. In an hour the top of the trench was level with his chin, and, stooping to clear the bottom of loose soil, he climbed up with greater difficulty than he had anticipated, and it was only after the third attempt that he managed to reach the top, out of breath and short of temper.

He dressed again, and with his electric torch surveyed the pit he had made and grunted his satisfaction.

He was keenly sensitive to certain atmospheres, and needed no information about the change which had come over his subordinates. In their last consultation Gurther had been less obsequious, had even smoked in his presence without permission – absentmindedly, perhaps, but the offence was there. And Dr Oberzohn, on the point of smacking his face for his insolence, heard a warning voice within himself which had made his hand drop back at his side. Or was it the look he saw on Gurther's face? The man was beyond the point where he could discipline him in the old Junker way. For although Dr Oberzohn condemned all things Teutonic, he had a sneaking reverence for the military caste of that nation.

He left the spade sticking in a heap of turned earth. He would need that again, and shortly. Unless Gurther failed. Somehow he did not anticipate a failure in this instance. Mr Monty Newton had not yet grown suspicious, would not be on his guard. His easy acceptance of the theatre tickets showed his mind in this respect.

The four men in his room rose respectfully as he came in. The air was blue with smoke, and Lew Cuccini offered a rough apology. He had been released that morning from detention, for Meadows had found it difficult to frame a charge which did not expose the full activities of the police, and the part they were playing in relation to Mirabelle Leicester. Evidently Cuccini had been reproaching, in his own peculiar way and in his own unprincipled language, the cowardice of his three companions, for the atmosphere seemed tense when the doctor returned. Yet, as was subsequently proved, the appearance of discord was deceptive; might indeed have been staged for their host's benefit.

'I've just been telling these birds – ' began Cuccini.

'Oh, shut up, Lew!' growled one of his friends. 'If that crazy man hadn't been shouting your name, we should not have gone back! He'd have wakened the dead. And our orders were to retire at the first serious sign of an alarm. That's right, doctor, isn't it?'

'Sure it's right,' said the doctor blandly. 'Never be caught – that is a good motto. Cuccini was caught.'

'And I'd give a year of my life to meet that Dago again,' said Cuccini, between his teeth.

He was delightfully inconsistent, for he came into the category, having been born in Milan, and had had his early education in the Italian quarter of Hartford, Connecticut.

'He'd have tortured me too . . . he was going to put lighted wax matches between my fingers – '

'And then you spilled it!' accused one of the three hotly. 'You talk about us bolting!'

'Silence!' roared the doctor. 'This is unseemly! I have forgiven everything. That shall be enough for you all. I will hear no other word.'

'Where is Gurther?' Cuccini asked the question.

'He has gone away. Tonight he leaves for America. He may return – who knows? But that is the intention.'

'Snaking?' asked somebody, and there was a little titter of laughter.

'Say, doctor, how do you work that stunt?' Cuccini leaned forward, his cigar between his fingers, greatly intrigued. 'I saw no snakes down at Rath Hall, and yet he was bitten, just as that Yankee was bitten – Washington.'

'He will die,' said the doctor complacently. He was absurdly jealous for the efficacy of his method.

'He was alive yesterday, anyway. We shadowed him to the station.'

'Then he was not bitten – no, that is impossible. When the snake bites – ' Oberzohn raised his palms and gazed piously at the ceiling – 'after that there is nothing. No, no, my friend, you are mistaken.'

'I tell you I'm not making any mistake,' said the other doggedly. 'I was in the room, I tell you, soon after they brought him in, and I heard one of the busies say that his face was all wet.'

'So!' said Oberzohn dully. 'That is very bad.'

'But how do you do it, doctor? Do you shoot or sump'n?'

'Let us talk about eventual wealth and happiness,' said the doctor. 'Tonight is a night of great joy for me. I will sing you a song.'

Then, to the amazement of the men and to their great unhappiness, he sang, in a thin reedy old voice, the story of a young peasant who had been thwarted in love and had thrown himself from a cliff into a seething waterfall. It was a lengthy song, intensely sentimental, and his voice held few of the qualities of music. The gang had never been set a more difficult job than to keep straight faces until he had finished.

'Gee! You're some artist, doctor!' said the sycophantic Cuccini, and managed to get a simulation of envy into his voice.

'In my student days I was a great singer,' said the doctor modestly.

Over the mantelpiece was a big, old clock, with a face so faded that only a portion of the letters remained. Its noisy ticking had usually a sedative effect on the doctor. But its main purpose and value was its accuracy. Every day it was corrected by a message from Greenwich, and as Oberzohn's success as an organizer depended upon exact timing, it was one of his most valuable assets.

He glanced up at the clock now, and that gave Cuccini his excuse.

'We'll be getting along, doctor,' he said. 'You don't want anything tonight? I'd like to get a cut at that Gonsalez man. You won't leave me out if there's anything doing?'

Oberzohn rose and went out of the room without another word, for he knew that the rising of Cuccini was a signal that not only was the business of the day finished, but also that the gang needed its pay.

Every gang-leader attended upon Mr Oberzohn once a week with his pay-roll, and it was usually the custom for the Herr Doktor to bring his cash-box into the room and extract sufficient to liquidate his indebtedness to the leader. It was a big box, and on pay-day, as this was, filled to the top with bank-notes and Treasury bills. He brought it back now, put it on the table, consulted the little slip that Cuccini offered to him, and, taking out a pad of notes, fastened about by a rubber band, he wetted his finger and thumb.

'You needn't count them,' said Cuccini. 'We'll take the lot.'

The doctor turned to see that Cuccini was carelessly holding a gun in his hand.

'The fact is, doctor,' said Cuccini coolly, 'we've seen the red light, and if we don't skip now, while the skipping's good, there's going to be no place we can stay comfortable in this little island, and I guess we'll follow Gurther.'

One glance the doctor gave at the pistol and then he resumed his counting, as though nothing had happened.

'Twenty, thirty, forty, fifty . . . '

'Now quit that,' said Cuccini roughly. 'I tell you, you needn't count.'

'My friend, I prefer to know what I am going to lose. It is a pardonable piece of curiosity.'

He raised his hand to the wall, where a length of cord hung, and pulled it gently, without taking his eyes from the bank-notes.

'What are you doing? Put up your hands!' hissed Cuccini.

'Shoot, I beg.' Oberzohn threw a pad of notes on the table. 'There is your pay.' He slammed down the lid of the box. 'Now you shall go, if you can go! Do you hear them?' He raised his hand, and to the strained ears of the men came a gentle rustling sound from the passage outside as though somebody were dragging a piece of parchment along the floor. 'Do you hear? You shall go if you can,' said the doctor again, with amazing calmness.

'The snakes!' breathed Cuccini, going white, and the hand that held the pistol shook.

'Shoot them, my friend,' sneered Oberzohn. 'If you see them, shoot them. But you will not see them, my brave man. They will be – where? No eyes shall see them come or go. They may lie behind a picture, they may wait until the door is opened, and then . . . !'

Cuccini's mouth was dry.

'Call 'em off, doctor,' he said tremulously.

'Your gun – on the table.'

Still the rustling was audible. Cuccini hesitated for a second, then obeyed, and took up the notes.

The other three men were huddled together by the fireplace, the picture of fear.

'Don't open the door, doc,' said Cuccini, but Oberzohn had already gripped the handle and turned it.

They heard another door open and the click of the passage light as it had come on. Then he returned.

'If you go now, I shall not wish to see you again. Am I not a man to whom all secrets are known? You are well aware!'

Cuccini looked from the doctor to the door.

'Want us to go?' he asked, troubled.

Oberzohn shrugged.

'As you wish! It was my desire that you should stay with me tonight – there is big work and big money for all of you.'

The men were looking at one another uneasily.

'How long do you want us to stay?' asked Cuccini.

'Tonight only; if you would not prefer . . . '

Tonight would come the crisis. Oberzohn had realized this since the day dawned for him.

'We'll stay – where do we sleep?'

For answer Oberzohn beckoned them from the room and they followed him into the laboratory. In the wall that faced them was a heavy iron door that opened into a concrete storehouse, where he kept various odds and ends of equipment, oil and spirit for his cars, and the little gas engine that worked a small dynamo in the laboratory and gave him, if necessary a lighting plant independent of outside current.

There were three long windows heavily barred and placed just under the ceiling.

'Looks like the condemned cell to me,' grumbled Cuccini suspiciously.

'Are the bolts on the inside of a condemned cell?' asked Oberzohn. 'Does the good warden give you the key as I give you?'

Cuccini took the key.

'All right,' he said ungraciously, 'there are plenty of blankets here, boys – I guess you want us where the police won't look, eh?'

'That is my intention,' replied the doctor.

Dr Oberzohn closed the door on them and re-entered his study, his big mouth twitching with amusement. He pulled the cord again and closed the ventilator he had opened. It was only a few days before that he had discovered that there were dried leaves in the ventilator shaft, and that the opening of the inlet made them rustle, disturbingly for a man who was engaged in a profound study of the lesser known, and therefore the more highly cultured, philosophers.

Chapter 31

The things in the box

He heard the soft purr of engines, and, looking through the hall window, saw the dim lights of the car approaching the house, and turned out the hall lamp. There he waited in the darkness, till the door of the limousine opened and Gurther jumped out. 'I respectfully report that it is done, Herr Doktor,' he said.

Oberzohn nodded.

'The woman of Newton – where is she?'

'She is inside. Is it your wish that I should bring her? She was very troublesome, Herr Doktor, and I had to use the needle.'

'Bring her in. You – !' he barked to the chauffeur. 'Help our friend.'

Together they lifted the unconscious girl, but carried her no farther than the steps. At this point Oberzohn decided that she must return to the prison. First they sent the chauffeur away; the car was garaged at New Cross (it was one of Oberzohn's three London depots), where the man also lived. After he had gone, they carried Joan between them to the factory, taking what, to Gurther, seemed an unnecessarily circuitous route. If it was necessary, it was at least expedient, for the nearest way to the factory led past the yawning hole that the doctor had dug with such labour.

There was no mistaking Oberzohn's arrival this time. The trap went up with a thud, and Mirabelle listened, with a quickly beating heart, to the sound of feet coming down the stone stairs. There were two people, and they were walking heavily. Somehow she knew before she saw their burden that it was Joan. She was in evening dress, her face as white as chalk and her eyes closed; the girl thought she was dead when she saw them lay her on the bed.

'You have given her too much, Gurther,' said Oberzohn.

Gurther? She had not recognized him. It was almost impossible to believe that this was the dapper young man who had danced with her at the Arts Ball.

'I had to guess in the dark, Herr Doktor,' said Gurther.

They were talking in German, and Mirabelle's acquaintance with that language was very slight. She saw Gurther produce a small flat case from his pocket, take out a little phial, and shake into the palm of his hand a small brown capsule. This he dissolved in a tiny tube which, with the water he used, was also extracted from the case. Half filling a minute syringe, he sent the needle into Joan's arm. A pause, and then: 'Soon she will wake, with your kind permission, Herr Doktor,' said Gurther.

Mirabelle was not looking at him, but she knew that his hot eyes were fixed on her, that all the time except the second he was operating, he was looking at her; and now she knew that this was the man to be feared. A cold hand seemed to grip at her heart.

'That will do, Gurther.' Oberzohn's voice was sharp. He, too, had interpreted the stare. 'You need not wait.'

Gurther obediently stalked from the room, and the doctor followed. Almost before the trap had fastened down she was by the girl's side, with a basin of water and a wet towel. The second the water touched her face, Joan opened her eyes and gazed wildly up at the vaulted ceiling, then rolling over from the bed to her knees, she struggled to her feet, swayed and would have fallen, had not Mirabelle steadied her.

'They've got him! They've got my boy . . . killed him like a dog!'

'What – Mr – Mr Newton?' gasped Mirabelle, horrified.

'Killed him – Monty – Monty!'

And then she began to scream and run up and down the room like a thing demented. Mirabelle, sick at heart, almost physically sick at the sight, caught her and tried to calm her, but she was distracted, half mad. The drug and its antidote seemed to have combined to take away the last vestige of restraint. It was not until she fell, exhausted, that Mirabelle was able to drag her again to the bed and lay her upon it.

Montague Newton was dead! Who had killed him? Who were the 'they'? Then she thought of Gurther in his strange attire; white dress-front crumpled, even his beard disarranged in the struggle he had had with the overwrought woman.

In sheer desperation she ran up the steps and tried the trap, but it was fast. She must get away from here – must get away at once. Joan was moaning pitiably, and the girl sat by her side, striving to calm her. She seemed to have passed into a state of semi-consciousness; except for her sobs, she made no sound and uttered no intelligible word. Half an hour passed – the longest and most dreadful half-hour in Mirabelle Leicester's life. And then she heard a sound. It had penetrated even to the brain of this half-mad girl, for she opened her eyes wide, and, gripping Mirabelle, drew herself up.

'He's coming,' she said, white to the lips, 'coming . . . the Killer is coming!'

'For God's sake don't talk like that!' said Mirabelle, beside herself with fear.

There it was, in the outer room; a stealthy shuffle of feet. She stared at the closed door, and the strain of the suspense almost made her faint. And then she saw the steel door move slowly, and first a hand came through, the edge of a face . . . Gurther was leering at her. His beard was gone, and his wig; he was collarless, and had over his white shirt the stained jacket that was his everyday wear.

'I want you.' He was talking to Mirabelle. Her tongue clave to the roof of her mouth, but she did not speak.

'My pretty little lady – ' he began, and then, with a shriek, Joan leapt at him.

'Murderer, murderer . . . ! Beast!' she cried, striking wildly at his face. With a curse, he tried to throw her off, but she was clinging to him; a bestial lunatic thing, hardly human.

He flung her aside at last, and then he put up his hand to guard his face as she leapt at him again. This time she went under his arm and was through the door in a flash. He heard the swift patter of her feet on the stairs, and turned in pursuit. The trap was open. He stumbled and tripped in the dark across the floor of the gaunt factory. Just as she reached the open, he grabbed at her and missed. Like a deer she sped, but he was fleeter-footed behind her; and suddenly his hand closed about her throat.

'You had better go out, my friend,' he said, and tightened his grip.

As she twisted to avoid him, he put out his foot. There was a grating snap, something gripped his legs, and the excruciating pain of it was agonizing. He loosened his hold of her throat, but held her arm tightly. With all his strength he threw her against the wall and she fell in a heap. Then, leaning down, he forced apart the cruel jagged teeth of the mantrap on to which he had put his foot, and drew his leg clear. He was bleeding; his trouser leg was torn to ribbons. He stopped only long enough to drag the girl to her feet, and, throwing her across his shoulder as though she were a sack, he went back into the factory, down the stairs, and threw her on to the bed with such violence that the spring supports broke. It had a strange effect upon the dazed woman, but this he did not see, for he had turned to Mirabelle.

'My little lady, I want you!' he breathed.

Blood was trickling down from his wounded calf, but he did not feel the pain any more; felt nothing, save the desire to hurt those who hunted him; wanted nothing but the materialization of crude and horrid dreams.

She stood, frozen, paralysed, incapable of movement. And then his hand came under her chin and he lifted her face; and she saw the bright, hungry eyes devouring her, saw the thin lips come closer and closer, could not move; had lost all sentient impressions, and could only stare into the eyes of this man-snake, hypnotized by the horror of the moment.

And then a raging fury descended upon him. Narrow fingers tore at his face, almost blinding him. He turned with a howl of rage, but the white-faced Joan had flown to the furnace and taken up a short iron bar that had been used to rake the burning coals together. She struck at him and missed. He dodged past her and she flung the bar at him, and again missed him. The iron struck the green box, behind the furnace, there was a sound of smashing glass. He did not notice this, intent only upon the girl, and Mirabelle closed her eyes and heard only the blow as he struck her.

When she looked again, Joan was lying on the bed and he was tying one of her hands to the bed-rail with a strap which he had taken from his waist. Then Mirabelle saw a sight that released her pent speech. He heard her scream and grinned round at her . . . saw where she was looking and looked too.

Something was coming from the broken green box! A black, spade-shaped head, with bright, hard eyes that seemed to survey the scene in a malignant stare. And then, inch by inch, a thick shining thing, like a rubber rope, wriggled slowly to the floor, coiled about upon itself, and raised its flat head. 'Oh, God, look!'

He turned about at the sight, that immovable grin of his upon his face, and said something in a guttural tongue. The snake was motionless, its baleful gaze first upon the sinking girl, then upon the man.

Gurther's surprise was tragic; it was as though he had been con-fronted with some apparition from another world. And then his hand went to his hip pocket; there was a flash of light and a deaf-ening explosion that stunned her. The pistol dropped from his hand and fell with a clatter to the floor, and she saw his arm was stiffly extended, and protruding from the cuff of his coat a black tail that wound round and round his wrist. It had struck up his sleeve. The cloth about his biceps was bumping up and down erratically.

He stood straightly erect, grinning, the arm still outflung, his astonished eyes upon the coil about his wrist. And then, slowly his other hand came round, gripped the tail and pulled it savagely forth. The snake turned with an angry hiss and tried to bite back at him; but raising his hand, he brought the head crashing down against the furnace. There was a convulsive wriggle as the reptile fell among the ashes.

'*Gott in himmel*!' whispered Gurther, and his free hand went up to his arm and felt gingerly. 'He is dead, gracious lady. Perhaps there is another?'

He went, swaying as he walked, to the green box, and put in his hand without hesitation. There was another – a bigger snake, roused from its sleep and angry. He bit twice at the man's wrist, but Gurther laughed, a gurgling laugh of pure enjoyment. For already he was a dead man; that he knew. And it had come to him, at the moment and second of his dissolution, when the dread gates of judgment were already ajar, that he should go to his Maker with this clean space in the smudge of his life.

'Go, little one,' he said, grinning into the spade-face. 'You have no more poison; that is finished!'

He put the writhing head under his heel, and Mirabelle shut her eyes and put her hands to her ears. When she looked again, the man was standing by the door, clinging to the post and slipping with every frantic effort to keep himself erect. He grinned at her again; this man of murder, who had made his last kill.

'Pardon, gracious lady,' he said thickly, and went down on his knees, his head against the door, his body swaying slowly from side to side, and finally tumbled over.

She heard Oberzohn's harsh voice from the floor above. He was calling Gurther, and presently he appeared in the doorway, and there was a pistol in his hand.

'So!' he said, looking down at the dying man.

And then he saw the snake, and his face wrinkled. He looked from Mirabelle to the girl on the bed, went over and examined her, but did not attempt to release the strap. It was Mirabelle who did that; Mirabelle who sponged the bruised face and loosened the dress.

So doing, she felt a hand on her shoulder.

'Come,' said Oberzohn.

'I'm staying here with Joan, until – '

'You come at once, or I will give you to my pretty little friends.' He pointed to the two snakes on the floor who still moved spasmodically.

She had to step past Gurther, but that seemed easier than passing those wriggling, shining black ropes; and, her hand in his, she stumbled up the dark steps and eventually into the clean, sweet air of the night.

He was dressed for a journey; she had noticed that when he appeared. A heavy cloth cap was on his curious-shaped head, and he looked less repulsive with so much of his forehead hidden. Though the night was warm, he wore an overcoat.

They were passing between the wall and the factory when he stopped and put his hand before her mouth. He had heard voices, low voices on the other side of the wall, and presently the scrape of something. Without removing his hand from her face, he half dragged, half pushed her until they were clear of the factory.

She thought they were going back to the house, which was in darkness, but instead, he led her straight along the wall, and presently she saw the bulk of the barge.

'Stay, and do not speak,' he said, and began to turn a rusty wheel. With a squeak and a groan the water-gates opened inwards. What did he intend doing? There was no sign of a boat, only this old dilapidated barge. She was presently to know.

'Come,' he said again. She was on the deck of the barge, moving forward to its bow, which pointed towards the open gate and the canal beyond.

She heard him puff and groan as he strained at a rope he had found, and then, looking down, she saw the front of the barge open, like the two water-gates of a lock. Displaying remarkable agility, he lowered himself over the edge; he seemed to be standing on something solid, for again he ordered her to join him.

'I will not go,' she said breathlessly, and turning, would have fled, but his hand caught her dress and dragged at her.

'I will drown you here, woman,' he, said, and she knew that the threat would have a sequel.

Tremblingly she lowered herself over the edge until her foot touched something hard and yet yielding. He was pushing at the barge with all his might, and the platform beneath her grew in space. First the sharp nose and then the covered half-deck of the fastest motor-boat that Mr Oberzohn's money could buy, or the ingenuity of builders could devise. The old barge was a boat-house, and this means of escape had always been to his hand. It was for this reason that he lived in a seemingly inaccessible spot.

The men who had been on the canal bank were gone. The propellers revolving slowly, the boat stole down the dark waters, after a short time slipped under a bridge over which street-cars were passing, and headed for Deptford and the river.

Dr Oberzohn took off his overcoat and laid it tenderly inside the shelter of the open cabin, tenderly because every pocket was packed tight with money.

To Mirabelle Leicester, crouching in the darkness of that sheltered space, the time that passed had no dimension. Once an authoritative voice hailed them from the bank. It was a policeman; she saw him after the boat had passed. A gas-lamp showed the glitter of his metal buttons. But soon he was far behind.

Deptford was near when they reached a barrier which neither ingenuity nor money could pass; a ragged night-bird peered down curiously at the motor-boat. 'You can't get through here, guv'nor,' he said simply. 'The lock doesn't open until high tide.'

'When is this high tide?' asked Oberzohn breathlessly.

'Six o'clock tomorrow morning,' said the voice.

For a long time he was stricken to inactivity by the news, and then he sent his engines into reverse and began circling round.

'There is one refuge for us, young miss,' he said. 'Soon we shall see it. Now I will tell you something. I desire so much to live. Do you also?'

She did not answer.

'If you cry out, if you will make noises, I will kill you – that is all,' he said; and the very simplicity of his words, the lack of all emphasis behind the deadly earnestness, told her that he would keep his word.

Chapter 32

The search

' 'Ware man-traps,' said Gonsalez.

The white beam of his lamp had detected the ugly thing. He struck at it with his stick, and with a vicious snap it closed.

'Here's one that's been sprung,' he said, and examined the teeth. 'And, what's more, it has made a catch! There's blood here.'

Manfred and Digby were searching the ground cautiously. Then Manfred heard the quick intake of his breath, and he stooped again, picked up a strip of braided cloth.

'A man's,' he said, and his relief betrayed his fear. 'Somebody in evening dress, and quite recent.' He looked at his finger. 'The blood is still wet.'

Digby showed him the ventilator grating through which he had smelt the incense, and when Leon stooped, the faint aroma still remained.

'We will try the factory first. If that draws blank, we'll ask Dr Oberzohn's guidance, and if it is not willingly given I shall persuade him.' And in the reflected light of the lamp George Manfred saw the hard Leon he knew of old. 'This time I shall not promise: my threat will be infinitely milder than my performance.'

They came to the dark entry of the factory, and Manfred splashed his light inside.

'You'll have to walk warily here,' he said,

Progress was slow, for they did not know that a definite path existed between the jagged ends of broken iron and debris. Once or twice Leon stopped to stamp on the floor; it gave back a hollow sound.

The search was long and painfully slow: a quarter of an hour passed before Leon's lamp focused on the upturned flagstone and the yawning entrance of the vault. He was the first to descend, and, as he reached the floor, he saw silhouetted in the light that flowed from the inner room, a man, as he thought, crouching in the doorway, and covered him.

'Put up your hands!' he said.

The figure made no response, and Manfred ran to the shape. The face was in the shadow, but he brought his own lamp down and recognized the set grin of the dead man.

Gurther!

So thus he had died, in a last effort to climb out for help.

'The Snake,' said Manfred briefly. 'There are no marks on his face, so far as I can see.'

'Do you notice his wrist, George?'

Then, looking past the figure, Gonsalez saw the girl lying on the bed, and recognized Joan before he saw her face. Halfway across the room he slipped on something. Instinctively he knew it was a snake and leapt around, his pistol balanced.

'Merciful heaven! Look at this!'

He stared from the one reptile to the other.

'Dead!' he said. 'That explains Gurther.'

Quickly he unstrapped Joan's wrists and lifted up her head, listening, his ear pressed to the faintly fluttering heart. The basin and the sponge told its own story. Where was Mirabelle?

There was another room, and a row of big cupboards, but the girl was in no place that he searched.

'She's gone, of course,' said Manfred quietly. 'Otherwise, the trap would not have been open. We'd better get this poor girl out of the way and search the grounds. Digby, go to – '

He stopped. If Oberzohn were in the house, they must not take the risk of alarming him.

But the girl's needs were urgent. Manfred picked her up and carried her out into the open, and, with Leon guiding them, they came, after a trek which almost ended in a broken neck for Leon, to within a few yards of the house.

'I presume,' said Gonsalez, 'that the hole into which I nearly dived was dug for a purpose, and I shouldn't be surprised to learn it was intended that the late Mr Gurther should find a permanent home there. Shall I take her?'

'No, no,' said Manfred, 'go on into the lane. Poiccart should be there with the car by now.'

'Poiccart knows more about growing onions than driving motor-cars.' The gibe was mechanical; the man's heart and mind were on Mirabelle Leicester.

They had to make a circuit of the stiff copper-wire fence which surrounded the house, and eventually reached Hangman's Lane just as the headlamps of the Spanz came into view.

'I will take her to the hospital and get in touch with the police,' said Manfred. 'I suppose there isn't a nearby telephone?'

'I shall probably telephone from the house,' said Leon gravely.

From where he stood he could not tell whether the door was open or closed. There was no transom above the door, so that it was impossible to tell whether there were lights in the passage or not. The house was in complete darkness.

He was so depressed that he did not even give instructions to Poiccart, who was frankly embarrassed by the duty which had been imposed upon him, and gladly surrendered the wheel to George.

They lifted the girl into the tonneau, and, backing into the gate, went cautiously up the lane – Leon did not wait to see their departure, but returned to the front of the house.

The place was in darkness. He opened the wire gate and went silently up the steps. He had not reached the top before he saw that the door was wide open. Was it a trap? His lamp showed him the switch: he turned on the light and closed the door behind him, and, bending his head, listened.

The first door on the right was Oberzohn's room. The door was ajar, but the lamps were burning inside. He pushed it open with the toe of his boot, but the room was empty.

The next two doors he tried on that floor were locked. He went carefully down to the kitchens and searched them both. They were tenantless. He knew there was a servant or two on the premises, but one thing he did not know, and this he discovered in the course of his tour, was that Oberzohn had no bedroom. One of the two rooms above had evidently been occupied by the servants. The door was open, the room was empty and in some confusion; a coarse night-dress had been hastily discarded and left on the tumbled bedclothes. Oberzohn had sent his servants away in a hurry – why?

There was a half-smoked cigarette on the edge of a deal wash-stand. The ash lay on the floor. In a bureau every drawer was open and empty, except one, a half-drawer filled with odd scraps of cloth. Probably the cook or the maid smoked. He found a packet of cigarettes under one pillow to confirm this view, and guessed they had gone to bed leisurely with no idea that they would be turned into the night.

He learned later that Oberzohn had bundled off his servants at ten minutes' notice, paying them six months' salary as some salve for the indignity.

Pfeiffer's room was locked; but now, satisfied that the house was empty, he broke the flimsy catch, made a search but found nothing. Gurther's apartment was in indescribable disorder. He had evidently changed in a hurry. His powder puffs and beards, crêpe hair and spirit bottles, littered the dressing-table. He remembered, with a pang of contrition, that he had promised to telephone the police, but when he tried to get the exchange he found the line was dead: a strange circumstance, till he discovered that late that evening Meadows had decided to cut the house from all telephonic communication, and had given orders accordingly.

It was a queerly built house: he had never realized its remarkable character until he had examined it at these close quarters. The walls were of immense thickness: that fact was brought home to him when he had opened the window of the maid's room to see if Digby was in sight. The stairs were of concrete, the shutters which covered the windows of Oberzohn's study were steel-faced. He decided, pending the arrival of the police, to make an examination of the two locked rooms. The first of these he had no difficulty in opening. It was a large room on the actual ground level, and was reached by going down six steps. A rough bench ran round three sides of this bare apartment, except where its continuity broke to allow entrance to a further room. The door was of steel and was fastened.

The room was dusty but not untidy. Everything was in order. The various apparatus was separated by a clear space. In one corner he saw a gas engine and dynamo covered with dust. There was nothing to be gained here. The machine which interested him most was one he knew all about, only he had not guessed the graphite moulds. The contents of a small blue bottle, tightly corked, and seemingly filled with discoloured swabs of cotton-wool, however, revived his interest. With a glance round the laboratory, he went out and tried the second of the locked doors.

This room, however, was well protected, both in the matter of stoutness of door and complication of locks. Leon tried all his keys, and then used his final argument. This he carried in a small leather pouch in his hip pocket; three steel pieces that screwed together and ended in a bright claw. Hammering the end of the jemmy with his fist, he forced the claw between door and lintel, and in less than a minute the lock had broken, and he was in the presence of the strangest company that had ever been housed.

Four electric radiators were burning. The room was hot and heavy, and the taint of it caught his throat, as it had caught the throat of the

Danish servant. He put on all the lights – and they were many – and then began his tour.

There were two lines of shelves, wide apart, and each supporting a number of boxes, some of which were wrapped in baize, some of which, however, were open to view. All had glass fronts, all had steel tops with tiny air-holes, and in each there coiled, in its bed of wool or straw, according to its requirements, one or two snakes. There were cobras, puff-adders, two rattlesnakes, seemingly dead, but, as he guessed, asleep; there was a South American *fer-de-lance*, that most unpleasant representative of his species; there were little coral snakes, and, in one long box, a whole nest of queer little things that looked like tiny yellow lobsters, but which he knew as scorpions.

He was lifting a baize cover when: 'Don't move, my friend! I think I can promise you more intimate knowledge of our little family.'

Leon turned slowly, his hands extended. Death was behind him, remorseless, unhesitating. To drop his hand to his pocket would have been the end for him – he had that peculiar instinct which senses sincerity, and when Dr Oberzohn gave him his instructions he had no doubt whatever that his threat was backed by the will to execute.

Oberzohn stood there, and a little behind him, white-faced, open-eyed with fear, Mirabelle Leicester.

Digby – where was he? He had left him in the grounds.

The doctor was examining the broken door and grunted his annoyance.

'I fear my plan will not be good,' he said, 'which was to lock you in this room and break all those glasses, so that you might become better acquainted with the Quiet People. That is not to be. Instead, march!'

What did he intend? Leon strolled out nonchalantly, but Oberzohn kept his distance, his eyes glued upon those sensitive hands that could move so quickly and jerk and fire a gun in one motion.

'Stop!'

Leon halted, facing the open front door and the steps.

'You will remember my sainted brother, Señor Gonsalez, and of the great loss which the world suffered when he was so vilely murdered?'

Leon stood without a quiver. Presently the man would shoot. At any second a bullet might come crashing on its fatal errand. This was a queer way to finish so full a life. He knew it was coming, had only one regret; that this shaken girl should be called upon to witness such a brutal thing. He wanted to say goodbye to her, but was afraid of frightening her.

'You remember that so sainted brother?' Oberzohn's voice was raucous with fury. Ahead of him the light fell upon a face.

'Digby! Stay where you are!' shouted Leon.

The sound of the explosion made him jump. He saw the brickwork above the doorway splinter, heard a little scuffle, and turned, gun in hand. Oberzohn had pulled the girl in front of him so that she afforded a complete cover: under her arm he held his pistol.

'Run!' she screamed.

He hesitated a second. Again the pistol exploded and a bullet ricochetted from the door. Leon could not fire. Oberzohn so crouched that nothing but a trick shot could miss the girl and hit him. And then, as the doctor shook free the hand that gripped his wrist, he leapt down the steps and into the darkness. Another second and the door slammed. He heard the thrust of the bolts and a clang as the great iron bar fell into its place. Somehow he had a feeling as of a citadel door being closed against him.

* * *

Dr Oberzohn had returned unobserved, though the night was clear. Passing through the open water-gate he had tied up to the little quay and landed his unwilling passenger. Digby, according to instructions, had been making a careful circuit of the property, and at the moment was as far away from the barge as it was humanly possible to be. Unchallenged, the doctor had worked his way back to the house. The light in the hall warned him that somebody was there. How many? He could not guess.

'Take off your shoes,' he growled in Mirabelle's ear, and she obeyed.

Whatever happened, he must not lose touch of her, or give her an opportunity to escape. Still grasping her arm with one hand and his long Mauser pistol in the other, he went softly up the steps, got into the hall and listened, locating the intruder instantly.

It all happened so quickly that Mirabelle could remember nothing except the desperate lunge she made to knock up the pistol that had covered the spine of Leon Gonsalez. She stood dumbly by, watching this horrible old man fasten the heavy door, and obediently preceded him from room to room. She saw the long cases in the hot room and shrank back. And then began a complete tour of the house. There were still shutters to be fastened, peep-holes to be opened up. He screwed up the shutters of the servants' room, and then, with a hammer, broke the thumb-piece short.

'You will stay here,' he said. 'I do not know what they will do. Perhaps they will shoot. I also am a shooter!'

Not satisfied with the lock that fastened her door, he went into his workshop, found a staple, hook and padlock, and spent the greater part of an hour fixing this additional security. At last he had finished, and could put the situation in front of four very interested men.

He unlocked the door of the concrete annexe and called the crest-fallen gunmen forth, and in a very few words explained the situation and their danger.

'For every one of you the English police hold warrants,' he said. 'I do not bluff, I know. This afternoon I was visited by the police. I tell you I do not bluff you – me they cannot touch, because they know nothing, can prove nothing. At most I shall go to prison for a few years, but with you it is different.'

'Are they waiting outside?' asked one suspiciously. 'Because, if they are, we'd better move quick.'

'You do not move, quick or slow,' said Oberzohn. 'To go out from here means certain imprisonment for you all. To stay, if you follow my plan, means that every one of you may go free and with money.'

'What's the idea?' asked Cuccini. 'Are you going to fight them?'

'Sure I am going to fight them,' nodded Oberzohn. 'That is my scheme. I have the young miss upstairs; they will not wish to do her any harm. I intend to defend this house.'

'Do you mean you're going to hold it?' asked one of the staggered men.

'I will hold it until they are tired, and make terms.'

Cuccini was biting his nails nervously.

'Might as well be hung for a sheep as a lamb, boss,' he growled. 'I've got an idea you've roped us into this.'

'You may rope yourself out of it!' snapped Oberzohn. 'There is the door – go if you wish. There are police there; make terms with them. A few days ago you were in trouble, my friend. Who saved you? The doctor Oberzohn. There is life imprisonment for every one of you, and I can hold this house myself. Stay with me, and I will give you a fortune greater than any you have dreamt about. And, more than this, at the end you shall be free.'

'Where's Gurther?'

'He has been killed – by accident.' Oberzohn's face was working furiously. 'By accident he died,' he said, and told the truth uncon-vincingly. 'There is nothing now to do but to make a decision.'

Cuccini and his friends consulted in a whisper.

'What do we get for our share?' he asked, and Oberzohn mentioned a sum which staggered them.

'I speak the truth,' he said. 'In two days I shall have a gold-mine worth millions.'

The habit of frankness was on him, and he told them the story of the golden hill without reservations. His agents at Lisbon had already obtained from the Ministry an option upon the land and its mineral rights. As the clock struck twelve on June 14, the goldfield of Biskara automatically passed into his possession.

'On one side you have certain imprisonment, on the other you have great moneys and happiness.'

'How long will we have to stay here?' asked Cuccini.

'I have food for a month, even milk. They will not cut the water because of the girl. For the same reason they will not blow in the door.'

Again they had a hasty consultation and made their decision.

'All right, boss, we'll stay. But we want that share-out put into writing.'

'To my study,' said Oberzohn promptly, 'march!'

He was half-way through writing the document when there came a thunderous knock on the door and he got up, signalling for silence. Tiptoeing along the passage, he came to the door.

'Yes – who is that?' he asked.

'Open, in the name of the law!' said a voice, and he recognized Meadows. 'I have a warrant for your arrest, and if necessary the door will be broken in.'

'So!' said Oberzohn, dropped the muzzle of his pistol until it rested on the edge of the little letter-slit and fired twice.

Chapter 33

The siege

Bur Meadows had already been warned to keep clear of the letter-box, and the bullets eventually reached one of the railway viaducts, to the embarrassment of a road ganger who happened to be almost in the line of fire.

Meadows slipped down the steps to cover. Inside the wire fence a dozen policemen were waiting. 'Sergeant, go back to the station in the police car and bring arms,' he said. 'This is going to be a long job.'

Gonsalez had made a very careful reconnaissance of the ground, and from the first had recognized the difficulties which lay ahead of the attacking party. The wall rose sheer without any break; such windows as were within reach were heavily shuttered; and even the higher windows, he guessed, had been covered. The important problem in his mind was to locate the room in which the girl was imprisoned, and making a mental review of the house, he decided that she was either in the servants' apartment or in that which had held Gurther. By the light of the lantern he made a rapid sketch plan of the floors he had visited.

Meadows had gone away to telephone to police headquarters. He had decided to re-establish telephone connection with the doctor, and when this was done, he called the house and Oberzohn's voice answered him.

The colloquy was short and unsatisfactory. The terms which the doctor offered were such as no self-respecting Government could accept. Immunity for himself and his companions (he insisted so strongly upon this latter offer that Meadows guessed, accurately, that the gang were standing around the instrument).

'I don't want your men at all. So far as I am concerned, they can go free,' said Meadows. 'Ask one of them to speak on the 'phone.'

'Oh, indeed, no,' said Oberzohn. 'It is ridiculous to ask me that.'

He hung up at this point and explained to the listening men that the police had offered him freedom if he would surrender the gang.

'As I already told you,' he said in conclusion, 'that is not the way of Dr Oberzohn. I will gain nothing at the expense of my friends.'

A little later, when Cuccini crept into the room to call police head-quarters and confirm this story of the doctor, he found that not only had the wire been cut, but a yard of the flex had been removed. Dr Oberzohn was taking no risks.

The night passed without any further incident. Police reserves were pouring into the neighbourhood; the grounds had been isol-ated, and even the traffic of barges up and down the canal prohibited. The late editions of the morning newspapers had a heavily head-lined paragraph about the siege of a house in the New Cross area, and when the first reporters arrived a fringe of sightseers had already gathered at every police barrier. Later, special editions, with fuller details, begun to roll out of Fleet Street; the crowd grew in density, and a high official from Scotland Yard, arriving soon after nine, ordered a further area to be cleared, and with some difficulty the solid wedge of humanity at the end of Hangman's Lane was slowly pushed back until the house was invisible to them. Even here, a passageway was kept for police cars and only holders of passes were allowed to come within the prohibited area.

The three men, with the police chief, had taken up their head-quarters in the factory, from which the body of Gurther had been removed in the night. The Deputy Commissioner, who came on the spot at nine and examined the dead snakes, was something of a herpetologist, and pronounced them to be veritable *fers-de-lance*, a view from which Poiccart differed.

'They are a species of African tree snakes that the natives call mamba. There are two, a black and a green. Both of these are the black type.'

'The Zoo mamba?' said the official, remembering the sensational disappearance of a deadly snake which had preceded the first of the snake mysteries.

'You will probably find the bones of the Zoo mamba in some mole run in Regent's Park – he must have been frozen to death the night of his escape,' said Poiccart. 'It was absolutely impossible that at that temperature he could live. I have made a very careful inspection of the land, and adjacent to the Zoological Gardens is a big stretch of earth which is honeycombed by moles. No, this was imported, and the rest of his menagerie was imported.'

The police chief shook his head.

'Still, I'm not convinced that a snake could have been responsible for these deaths,' he said, and went over the ground so often covered.

The three listened in polite silence, and offered no suggestion.

The morning brought news of Washington's arrival in Lisbon. He had left the train at Irun, Leon's agent in Madrid having secured a relay of aeroplanes, and the journey from Irun to Lisbon had been completed in a few hours. He was now on his way back.

'If he makes the connections he will be here tonight,' he told Manfred. 'I rather think he will be a very useful recruit to our forces.'

'You're thinking of the snakes in the house?'

Leon nodded.

'I know Oberzohn,' he said simply, and George Manfred thought of the girl, and knew the unspoken fears of his friend were justified.

The night had not been an idle one for Oberzohn and his companions. With the first light of dawn they had mounted to the roof, and, under his direction, the gunmen had dismantled the four sheds which stood at each corner of the parapet. Unused to the handling of such heavy metal, the remnants of the Old Guard gazed in awe upon the tarnished jackets of the Maxim guns that were revealed.

Oberzohn understood the mechanism of the machines so thoroughly that in half an hour he had taught his crew the method of handling and sighting. In the larger shed was a collapsible tripod, which was put together, and on this he mounted a small but powerful searchlight and connected it up with one of the plugs in the roof.

He pointed to them the three approaches to the house: the open railway arches and the long lane, at the end of which the crowd at that moment was beginning to gather.

'From only these places can the ground be approached,' he said, 'and my little quick-firers cover them!'

Just before eleven there came down Hangman's Lane, drawn by a motor tractor, a long tree-trunk, suspended about the middle by chains, and Oberzohn, examining it carefully through his field-glasses, realized that no door in the world could stand against the attack of that battering-ram. He took up one of the dozen rifles that lay on the floor, sighted it carefully, resting his elbow on the parapet, and fired.

He saw the helmet of a policeman shoot away from the head of the astonished man, and fired again. This time he was more successful, for a policeman who was directing the course of the tractor crumpled up and fell in a heap.

A shrill whistle blew; the policemen ran to cover, leaving the machine unattended. Again he fired, this time at the driver of the tractor. He saw the man scramble down from his seat and run for the shelter of the fence.

A quarter of an hour passed without any sign of activity on the part of his enemies, and then eight men, armed with rifles, came racing across the ground towards the wire barrier. Oberzohn dropped his rifle, and, taking a grip of the first machine-gun in his hand, sighted it quickly. The staccato patter of the Maxim awakened the echoes. One man dropped; the line wavered. Again the shrill whistle, and they broke for cover, dragging their wounded companion with them.

'I was afraid of that,' said Leon, biting his knuckles – sure evidence of his perturbation.

He had put a ladder against the wall of the factory, and now he climbed up on to the shaky roof and focused his glasses.

'There's another Maxim on this side,' he shouted down. And then, as he saw a man's head moving above the parapet, he jerked up his pistol and fired. He saw the stone splinters fly up and knew that it was not bad practice at four hundred yards. The shot had a double effect; it made the defenders cautious and aroused in them the necessary quantity of resentment.

He was hardly down before there was a splutter from the roof, and the whine and snap of machine-gun bullets; one slate tile shivered and its splinters leapt high in the air and dropped beside his hand.

The presence of the girl was the only complication. Without her, the end of Oberzohn and his companions was inevitable. Nobody realized this better than the doctor, eating a huge ham sandwich in the shelter of the parapet – an unusual luxury, for he ate few solids.

'This will be very shocking for our friends of Curzon Street,' he said. 'At this moment they bite their hands in despair.' (He was nearly right here.)

He peeped over the parapet. There was no policeman in sight. Even the trains that had roared at regular intervals along the viaduct had ceased to run, traffic being diverted to another route.

At half-past twelve, looking through a peep-hole, he saw a long yellow line of men coming down Hangman's Lane, keeping to the shelter of the fence.

'Soldiers,' he said, and for a second his voice quavered.

Soldiers they were. Presently they began to trickle into the grounds, one by one, each man finding his own cover. Simultaneously there came a flash and a crack from the nearest viaduct. A bullet smacked against the parapet and the sound of the ricochet was like the hum of a bee.

Another menace had appeared simultaneously; a great, lumbering, awkward vehicle, that kept to the middle of the lane and turned its ungainly nose into the field. It was a tank, and Oberzohn knew that only the girl's safety stood between him and the dangling noose.

He went down to see her, unlocked the door, and found her, to his amazement, fast asleep. She got up at the sound of the key in the lock, and accepted the bread and meat and water he brought her without a word.

'What time is it?'

Oberzohn stared at her.

'That you should ask the time at such a moment!' he said.

The room was in darkness but for the light he had switched on.

'It is noon, and our friends have brought soldiers. Ach! how important a woman you are, that the whole army should come out for you!'

Sarcasm was wasted on Mirabelle.

'What is going to happen – now?'

'I do not know.' He shrugged his shoulders. 'They have brought a diabolical instrument into the grounds. They may use it, to give them cover, so that the door may be blown in. At that moment I place you in the snake-room. This I shall tell our friends very quickly.'

She gazed at him in horror.

'You wouldn't do anything so wicked, Mr Oberzohn!'

Up and down went the skin of his forehead.

'That I shall tell them and that I shall do,' he said, and locked her in with this comfortless assurance.

He went into his study and, fastening the door, took two strands of wire from his pocket and repaired the broken telephone connections.

'I wish to speak to Meadows,' he said to the man who answered him – a police officer who had been stationed at the exchange to answer any call from this connection.

'I will put you through to him,' was the reply.

For a moment the doctor was surprised that Meadows was not at the exchange. He did not know then that a field telephone line had been organized, and that the factory headquarters of the directing staff was in communication with the world.

It was not Meadows, but another man who answered him, and by his tone of authority Oberzohn guessed that some higher police official than Meadows was on the spot.

'I am the doctor Oberzohn,' he barked. 'You have brought a tank machine to attack me. If this approaches beyond the wire fence, I shall place the woman Leicester in the home of the snakes, and there I will bind her and release my little friends to avenge me.'

'Look here – ' began the officer, but Oberzohn hung up on him.

He went out and locked the door, putting the key in his pocket. His one doubt was of the loyalty of his companions. But here, strangely enough, he underrated their faith in him. The very mildness of the attack, the seeming reluctance of the soldiers to fire, had raised their hopes and spirits; and when, a quarter of an hour later, they saw the tank turn and go out into Hangman's Lane, they were almost jubilant.

'You're sure that he will carry out his threat?' asked the police chief.

'Certain,' said Leon emphatically. 'There is nothing on earth that will stop Oberzohn. You will force the house to find a man who has died by his own hand, and – ' he shuddered at the thought. 'The only thing to be done is to wait for the night. If Washington arrives on time, I think we can save Miss Leicester.'

From the roof Dr Oberzohn saw that the soldiers were digging a line of trenches, and sent a spatter of machine-gun bullets in their direction. They stopped their work for a moment to look round, and then went on digging, as though nothing had happened.

The supply of ammunition was not inexhaustible, and he determined to reserve any further fire until the attack grew more active. Looking over the top of the parapet to examine the ground immediately below, something hot and vicious snicked his ear. He saw the brickwork of the chimney behind him crumble and scatter, and, putting up his hand, felt blood.

'You'd better keep down, Oberzohn,' said Cuccini, crouching in the shelter of the parapet. 'They nearly got you then. They're firing from that railway embankment. Have you had a talk with the boss of these birds?'

'They are weakening,' said Oberzohn promptly. 'Always they are asking me if I will surrender the men; always I reply, "Never will I do anything so dishonourable." '

Cuccini grunted, having his own views of the doctor's altruism.

Late in the afternoon, a flight of aeroplanes appeared in the west: five machines flying in V formation. None of the men on the roof recognized the danger, standing rather in the attitude and spirit of sightseers. The machines were flying low; with the naked eye Cuccini could read their numbers long before they came within a hundred yards of the house. Suddenly the roof began to spout little fountains of asphalt. Oberzohn screamed a warning and darted to the stairway, and three men followed him out. Cuccini lay spread-eagled where he fell, two machine-gun bullets through his head.

The fighting machines mounted, turned and came back. Standing on the floor below, Oberzohn heard the roar of their engines as they passed, and went incautiously to the roof, to discover that the guns of flying machines fire equally well from the tail. He was nearer to death then than he had ever been. One bullet hit the tip of his finger and sliced it off neatly. With a scream of pain he half fell, half staggered to safety, spluttering strange oaths in German.

The aeroplanes did not return. He waited until their noise had died away before he again ventured to the roof, to find the sky clear. Cuccini was dead, and it was characteristic of his three friends that they should make a thorough search of his pockets before they heaved the body over the parapet.

Oberzohn left the three on the roof, with strict instructions that they were to dive to cover at the first glint of white wings, and went down into his study. The death of Cuccini was in some ways a blessing. The man was full of suspicion; his heart was not in the fight, and the aeroplane gunner had merely anticipated the doctor's own plan.

Cuccini was a Latin, who spoke English well and wrote it badly. He had a characteristic hand, which it amused Oberzohn to copy, for the doctor was skilful with his pen. All through the next three hours he wrote, breaking off his labours at intervals to visit the guard on the roof. At last he had finished, and Cuccini's sprawling signature was affixed to the bottom of the third page. Oberzohn called down one of the men.

'This is the statement of Cuccini which he left. Will you put your name to his signature?'

'What is it?' asked the man surlily.

'It is a letter which the good Cuccini made – what generosity! In this he says that he alone was to blame for bringing you here, and nobody else. Also that he kept you by threats.'

'And you?' asked the man.

'Also me,' said Oberzohn, unabashed. 'What does it matter? Cuccini is dead. May he not in his death save us all? Come, come, my good friend, you are a fool if you do not sign. After that, send down our friends that they may also sign.'

A reluctant signature was fixed, and the other men came one by one, and one by one signed their names, content to stand by the graft which the doctor indicated, exculpating themselves from all responsibility in the defence.

Dusk fell and night came blackly, with clouds sweeping up from the west and a chill rain falling. Gonsalez, moodily apart from his companions, watched the dark bulk of the house fade into the background with an ever-increasing misery. What these men did after did not matter – to them. A policeman had been killed, and they stood equally guilty of murder in the eyes of the law. They could now pile horror upon horror, for the worst had happened. His only hope was that they did not know the inevitability of their punishment.

No orders for attack had been given. The soldiers were standing by, and even the attack by the aeroplanes had been due to a mis-apprehension of orders. He had seen Cuccini's body fall, and as soon as night came he determined to approach the house to discover if there was any other way in than the entrance by the front door.

The aeroplanes had done something more than sweep the roof with their guns. Late in the evening there arrived by special mess-enger telescopic photographs of the building, which the military commander and the police chief examined with interest.

Leon was watching the house when he saw a white beam of light shoot out and begin a circular sweep of the grounds. He expected this; the meaning of the connections in the wall was clear. He knew, too, how long that experiment would last. A quarter of an hour after the searchlight began its erratic survey of the ground, the lamp went out, the police having disconnected the current. But it was only for a little while, and in less than an hour the light was showing again.

'He has power in the house – a dynamo and a gas engine,' ex-plained Gonsalez.

Poiccart had been to town and had returned with a long and heavy steel cylinder, which Leon and Manfred carried between them into the open and left. They were sniped vigorously from the roof, and although the firing was rather wild, the officer in charge of the operations forbade any further movement in daylight.

At midnight came the blessed Washington. They had been wait-ing for him with eagerness, for he, of all men, knew something that they did not know. Briefly, Leon described the snake-room and its contents. He was not absolutely certain of some of the species, but his description was near enough to give the snake expert an idea of the species.

'Yes, sir, they're all deadly,' said Washington, shaking his head. 'I guess there isn't a thing there, bar the scorps, who wouldn't put a grown man to sleep in five minutes – ten minutes at the most.'

They showed him the remains of the dead snake and he instantly recognized the kind, as the zoological expert had done in the afternoon.

'That's mamba. He's nearly the deadliest of all. You didn't see a fellow with a long bill-shaped head? You did? Well, that's *fer-de-lance*, and he's almost as bad. The little red fellows were corals . . . '

Leon questioned him more closely.

'No, sir, they don't leap – that's not their way. A tree snake will hang on to something overhead and get you as you pass, and they'll swing from the floor, but their head's got to touch the floor first. The poor little fellow that killed Gurther was scared, and when they're scared they'll lash up at you – I've known a man to be bitten in the throat by a snake that whipped up from the ground. But usually they're satisfied to get your leg.'

Leon told him his plan.

'I'll come along with you,' said Washington without hesitation.

But this offer neither of the three would accept. Leon had only wanted the expert's opinion. There were scores of scientists in London, curators of museums and keepers of snakes, who could have told him everything there was to be known about the habits of the reptile in captivity. He needed somebody who had met the snake in his native environment.

An hour before daylight showed in the sky, there was a council of war, Leon put his scheme before the authorities, and the plan was approved. He did not wait for the necessary orders to be given, but, with Poiccart and Manfred, went to the place where they had left the cylinder, and, lifting it, made their slow way towards the house. In addition, Leon carried a light ladder and a small bag full of tools.

The rays of the searchlight were moving erratically, and for a long time did not come in their direction. Suddenly they found themselves in a circle of dazzling light and fell flat on their faces. The machine-gun spat viciously, the earth was churned up under the torrent of bullets, but none of the men was hit; and, more important, the cylinder was not touched.

Then suddenly, from every part of the ground, firing started. The target was the searchlight, and the shooting had not gone on for more than a minute before the light went out, so jerkily that it was obvious that one bullet at least had got home.

'Now,' said Manfred, and, lifting up the cylinder, they ran. Poiccart put his hand on the fence wire and was hurled back. The top wire was alive, but evidently the doctor's dynamo was not capable of generating a current that would be fatal. Leon produced an insulated wire cutter and snipped off a six-foot length, earthing the broken ends of the wire. They were now under the shadow of the wall of the house, and out of danger so far as bullets were concerned.

Leon planted his ladder against the window under which they stopped, and in a second had broken the glass, turned the catch and sent up the sash. From his bag he produced a small diamond drill and began to work through the thick steel plate. It was a terribly arduous job, and after ten minutes' labour he handed over the work to Manfred, who mounted in his place.

* * *

Whatever damage had been done to the searchlight had now been repaired, and its beam had concentrated on the spot where they had been last seen. This time no fusillade greeted its appearance, and Oberzohn was surprised and troubled by the inaction.

The light came into the sky, the walls grew grey and all objects sharply visible, when he saw the tank move out of the lane where it had been standing all the previous day, turn into the field, and slowly move towards the house. He set his teeth in a grin and, darting down the stairs, flung himself against the door of the girl's room, and his agitation was such that for a time he could not find the keyhole of the two locks that held the door secure.

It opened with a crash, and he almost fell into the room in his eagerness. Mirabelle Leicester was standing by the bed, her face white as death. Yet her voice was steady, almost unconcerned, when she asked:'What do you want?'

'You!' he hissed. 'You, my fine little lady – you are for the snakes!'

He flung himself upon her, though she offered no resistance, threw her back on the bed and snapped a pair of rusty handcuffs on her wrists. Pulling her to her feet, he dragged her from the room and down the stairs. He had some difficulty in opening the door of the snake-room, for he had wedged it close. The door was pushed open at last: the radiators were no longer burning. He could not afford the power. But the room was stiflingly hot, and when he turned on the lights, and she saw the long line of boxes, her knees gave way under her, and she would have fallen had he not put his arm about her waist. Dragging a heavy chair to the centre of the room, he pushed her down into it.

'Here you wait, my friend!' he yelled. 'You shall wait . . . but not long!'

On the wall there were three long straps which were used for fastening the boxes when it was necessary to travel with them. In a second one thong was about her and buckled tight to the back of the chair. The second he put under the seat and fastened across her knee.

'Goodbye, gracious lady!'

The rumble of the tank came to him in that room. But he had work to do. There was no time to open the boxes. The glass fronts might easily be broken. He ran along the line, hitting the glass with the barrel of his Mauser. The girl, staring in horror, saw a green head come into view through one opening; saw a sinuous shape slide gently to the floor. And then he turned out the lights, the door was slammed, and she was left alone in the room of terror.

Oberzohn was no sooner in the passage than the first bomb exploded at the door. Splinters of wood flew past him, as he turned and raced up the stairs, feeling in his pocket as he went for the precious document which might yet clear him.

Boom!

He had not locked the door of the snake-room; Leon had broken the hasp. Let them go in, if they wished. The front door was not down yet. From the landing above he listened over the balustrade. And then a greater explosion than ever shook the house, and after an interval of silence he heard somebody running along the passage and shake at the snake-room door.

Too late now! He grinned his joy, went up the last flight to the roof, to find his three men in a state of mutiny, the quelling of which was not left to him. The glitter of a bayonet came through the door opening, a khaki figure slipped on to the roof, finger on trigger.

'Hands up, you!' he said, in a raucous Cockney voice.

Four pairs of hands went upward.

Manfred followed the second soldier and caught the doctor by the arm.

'I want you, my friend,' he said, and Oberzohn went obediently down the stairs.

They had to pass Gurther's room: the door was open, and Manfred pushed his prisoner inside, as Poiccart and Leon ran up the stairs.

'The girl's all right. The gas killed the snakes the moment they touched the floor, and Brother Washington is dealing with the live ones,' said Leon rapidly.

He shut the door quickly. The doctor was alone for the first time in his life with the three men he hated and feared.

'Oberzohn, this is the end,' said Manfred.

That queer grimace that passed for a smile flitted across the puckered face of the doctor.

'I think not, my friends,' he said. 'Here is a statement by Cuccini. I am but the innocent victim, as you will see. Cuccini has confessed to all and has implicated his friends. I would not resist – why should I? I am an honest, respectable man, and a citizen of a great and friendly country. Behold!'

He showed the paper. Manfred took it from his hand but did not read it.

'Also, whatever happens, your lady loses her beautiful hill of gold.' He found joy in this reflection. 'For tomorrow is the last day – '

'Stand over there, Oberzohn,' said Manfred, and pushed him against the wall. 'You are judged. Though your confession may cheat the law, you will not cheat us.'

And then the doctor saw something and he screamed his fear. Leon Gonsalez was fixing a cigarette to the long black holder he had found in Gurther's room.

'You hold it thus,' said Leon, 'do you not?' He dipped the cigarette down and pressed the small spring that was concealed in the black ebonite. 'The holder is an insulated chamber that holds two small icy splinters – I found the mould in your laboratory, Herr Doktor. They drop into the cigarette, which is a metal one, and then . . . '

He lifted it to his lips and blew. None saw the two tiny icicles fly. Only Oberzohn put his hand to his cheek with a strangled scream, glared for a second, and then went down like a heap of rags.

Leon met Inspector Meadows on his way up.

'I'm afraid our friend has gone,' he said. 'He has cheated the hangman of ten pounds.'

'Dead?' said Meadows. 'Suicide?'

'It looks like a snake-bite to me,' said Leon carelessly, as he went down to find Mirabelle Leicester, half laughing, half crying, whilst an earnest Elijah Washington was explaining to her the admirable domestic qualities of snakes.

'There's five thousand dollars' worth dead,' he said, in despair, 'but there's enough left to start a circus!'

Chapter 34
The death tube

Later Manfred explained to an interested police chief.

'Oberzohn secured the poison by taking a snake and extracting his venom – a simple process: you have but to make him angry, and he will bite on anything. The doctor discovered a way of blending these venoms to bring out the most deadly qualities of them all – it sounds fantastic, and, from the scientists' point of view, unlikely. But it is nevertheless the fact. The venom was slightly diluted with water and enough to kill a dozen people was poured into a tiny mould and frozen.'

'Frozen?' said the chief, in astonishment.

Manfred nodded.

'There is no doubt about it,' he said. 'Snake venom does not lose its potency by being frozen, and this method of moulding their darts was a very sane one, from their point of view. It was only necessary for a microscopic portion of the splinter to pierce the flesh. Sufficient instantly melted to cause death, and if the victim rubbed the place where he had been struck, it was more certain that he would rub some of the venom, which had melted on his cheek, into the wound. Usually they died instantly. The cigarette holders that were carried by Gurther and the other assassin, Pfeiffer, were blowpipes, the cigarette a hollow metal fake. By the time they blew their little ice darts, it was in a half-molten condition and carried sufficient liquid poison to kill, even if the skin was only punctured. And, of course, all that did not enter the skin melted before there could be any examination by the police. That is why you never found darts such as the bush-men use, slithers of bamboo, thorns from trees. Oberzohn had the simplest method of dealing with all opposition: he sent out his snake-men to intercept them, and only once did they fail – when they aimed at Leon and caught that snake-proof man, Elijah Washington!'

'What about Miss Leicester's claim to the goldfields of Biskara?'

Manfred smiled.

'The renewal has already been applied for and granted. Leon found at Heavytree Farm some blank sheets of note-paper signed with the girl's name. He stole one during the aunt's absence and filled up the blank with a formal request for renewal. I have just had a wire to say that the lease is extended.'

He and Poiccart had to walk the best part of the way to New Cross before they could find a taxicab. Leon had gone on with the girl. Poiccart was worried about something, and did not speak his mind until the providential cab appeared on the scene and they were trundling along the New Cross Road.

'My dear George, I am a little troubled about Leon,' he said at last. 'It seems almost impossible to believe, but – '

'But what?' asked Manfred good-humouredly, and knowing what was coming.

'You don't believe,' said Poiccart in a hushed voice, as though he were discussing the advent of some world cataclysm – 'you don't believe that Leon is in love, do you?'

Manfred considered for a moment.

'Such things happen, even to just men,' he said, and Poiccart shook his head sadly.

'I have never contemplated such an unhappy contingency,' he said, and Manfred was laughing to himself all the way back to town.

THE END

AGAIN THE THREE

The characters in this book are entirely imaginary and have no relation to any living person.

The Rebus

As *The Megaphone* once said, in its most pessimistic and wondering mood, recording rather than condemning the strangeness of the time:

Even The Four Just Men have become a respectable institution. Not more than fifteen years ago we spoke of them as 'a criminal organization'; rewards were offered for their arrest . . . today you may turn into Curzon Street and find a silver triangle affixed to the sedate door which marks their professional headquarters . . . The hunted and reviled have become a most exclusive detective agency . . . We can only hope that their somewhat drastic methods of other times have been considerably modified.

It is sometimes a dangerous thing to watch a possible watcher.

'What is Mr Lewis Lethersohn afraid of?' asked Manfred, as he cracked an egg at breakfast. His handsome, clean-shaven face was tanned a teak-brown, for he was newly back from the sun and snows of Switzerland.

Leon Gonsalez sat opposite, absorbed in *The Times*; at the end of the table was Raymond Poiccart, heavy-featured and saturnine. Other pens than mine have described his qualities and his passion for growing vegetables.

He raised his eyes to Gonsalez.

'Is he the gentleman who has had this house watched for the past month?' he asked.

A smile quivered on Leon's lips as he folded the newspaper neatly.

'He is the gentleman – I'm interviewing him this morning,' he said. 'In the meantime, the sleuth hounds have been withdrawn – they were employed by the Ottis Detective Agency.'

'If he is watching us, he has a bad conscience,' said Poiccart, nodding slowly. 'I shall be interested to hear all about this.'

Mr Lewis Lethersohn lived in Lower Berkeley Street – a very large and expensive house. The footman who opened the door to Leon was arrayed in a uniform common enough in historical films but rather out of the picture in Lower Berkeley Street. Mulberry and gold and knee breeches . . . Leon gazed at him with awe.

'Mr Lethersohn will see you in the library,' said the man – he seemed, thought Leon, rather conscious of his own magnificence.

A gorgeous house this, with costly furnishings and lavish decorations. As he mounted the wide stairs he had a glimpse of a beautiful woman passing across the landing. One disdainful glance she threw in his direction and passed, leaving behind her the faint fragrance of some exotic perfume.

The room into which he was shown might have been mistaken for a bedroom, with its bric-a-brac and its beauty of appointments.

Mr Lethersohn rose from behind the Empire writing table and offered a white hand. He was thin, rather bald, and there was a suggestion of the scholar in his lined face.

'Mr Gonsalez?' His voice was thin and not particularly pleasant. 'Won't you sit down? I had your inquiry – there seems to be some mistake.'

He had resumed his own seat. Though he might endeavour to cover up his uneasiness by this cold attitude of his, he could not quite hide his perturbation.

'I know you, of course – but it is ridiculous that I should set men to watch your house. Why?'

Gonsalez was watching him intently.

'That is what I have come to learn,' he said, 'and I think it would be fairest to tell you that there is no doubt that you are watching us. We know the agency you employed – we know the fees you have paid and the instructions you have given. The only question is, why?'

Mr Lethersohn moved uncomfortably and smiled. 'Really . . . I suppose there is no wisdom in denying that I did employ detectives. The truth is, the Four Just Men is rather a formidable organization – and – er – well, I am a rich man . . .'

He was at a loss how to go on.

The interview ended lamely with polite assurances on either side. Leon Gonsalez went back to Curzon Street a very thoughtful man.

'He's afraid of somebody consulting us, and the detective people have been employed to head off that somebody. Now who?'

The next evening brought the answer.

It was a grey April night, chill and moist. The woman who walked slowly down Curzon Street, examining the numbers on the doors, was an object of suspicion to the policeman standing on Claridge's corner. She was in the region of thirty, rather slim, under the worn and soddened coat. Her face was faded and a little pinched. 'Pretty once,' mused Leon Gonsalez, observing her from behind the net curtain that covered the window. 'A working woman without a thought beyond keeping her body and soul together.'

He had time enough to observe her, since she stood for a long time by the kerb, looking up and down the street hopelessly.

'Notice the absence of any kind of luring finery – and this is the hour when even the poorest find a scarf or a pair of gloves.'

Manfred rose from the table where he had been taking his frugal meal and joined the keen-faced observer.

'Provincial, I think,' said Leon thoughtfully. 'Obviously a stranger to the West End – she's coming here!'

As he was speaking, the woman had turned, made a brief scrutiny of the front door . . . They heard the bell ring.

'I was mistaken – she hadn't lost her way; she was plucking up courage to ring – and if she isn't Lethersohn's *bête noire* I'm a Dutchman!'

He heard Poiccart's heavy tread in the passage – Poiccart played butler quite naturally. Presently he came in and closed the door behind him.

'You will be surprised,' he said in his grave way. That was peculiarly Poiccart – to say mysterious things gravely.

'About the lady? I refuse to be surprised.' Leon was vehement. 'She has lost something – a husband, a watch, something. She has the "lost" look – an atmosphere of vague helplessness surrounds her. The symptoms are unmistakable!'

'Ask her to come in,' said Manfred, and Poiccart retired.

A second later Alma Stamford was ushered into the room.

That was her name. She came from Edgware and she was a widow . . . Long before she came to the end of preliminaries Poiccart's promised surprise had been sprung, for this woman, wearing clothes that a charwoman would have despised, had a voice which was soft and educated. Her vocabulary was extensive and she spoke of conditions which could only be familiar to one who had lived in surroundings of wealth.

She was the widow of a man who – they gathered – had not been in his lifetime the best of husbands. Rich beyond the ordinary meaning of the term, with estates in Yorkshire and Somerset, a fearless rider to hounds, he had met his death in the hunting field.

'My husband had a peculiar upbringing,' she said. 'His parents died at an early age and he was brought up by his uncle. He was a terrible old man who drank heavily, was coarse to the last degree, and was jealous of outside interference. Mark saw practically nobody until, in the last year of the old man's life, he brought in a Mr Lethersohn, a young man a little older than Mark, to act as tutor – for Mark's education was terribly backward. My husband was twenty-one when his uncle died, but he retained a gentleman to act for him as companion and secretary.'

'Mr Lewis Lethersohn,' said Leon promptly, and she gasped.

'I can't guess how you know, but that is the name. Although we weren't particularly happy,' she went on, 'my husband's death was a terrible shock. But almost as great a shock was his will. In this he left one half of his fortune to Lethersohn, the other half to me at the expiration of five years from his death, provided that I carried out the conditions of the will. I was not to marry during that period, I was to live at a house in Harlow and never to leave the Harlow district. Mr Lethersohn was given absolute power as sole executor to dispose of property for my benefit. I have lived in Harlow until this morning.'

'Mr Lethersohn is of course married?' said Leon, his bright eyes fixed on the lady.

'Yes – you know him?'

Leon shook his head.

'I only know that he is married and very much in love with his wife.'

She was astounded at this.

'You must know him. Yes, he married just before Mark was killed. A very beautiful Hungarian girl – he is half Hungarian and I believe he adores her. I heard that she was very extravagant – I only saw her once.'

'What has happened at Harlow?' It was the silent, watchful Poiccart who asked the question.

He saw the woman's lips tremble.

'It has been a nightmare,' she said with a break in her voice. 'The house was a beautiful little place – miles from Harlow really, and off the main road. There I have been for two years practically a prisoner. My letters have been opened, I have been locked in my room every night by one of the two women Mr Lethersohn sent to look after me, and men have been patrolling the grounds day and night.'

'The suggestion is that you are not quite right in your head?' asked Manfred.

She looked startled at this.

'You don't think so?' she asked quickly, and, when he shook his head: 'Thank God for that! Yes, that was the story they told. I wasn't supposed to see newspapers, though I had all the books I wanted. One day I found a scrap of paper with the account of a bank fraud which you gentlemen had detected, and there was a brief account of your past. I treasured that because it had your address in the paragraph. To escape seemed impossible – I had no money, it was impossible to leave the grounds. But they had a woman who came to do the rough work twice a week. I think she came from the village. I managed to enlist her sympathy, and yesterday she brought me these clothes. Early this morning I changed, dropped out of my bedroom window and passed the guard. Now I come to my real mystery.'

She put her hand into the pocket of her wet coat and took out a small package. This she unwrapped.

'My husband was taken to the cottage hospital after his accident; he died early the next morning. He must have recovered consciousness unknown to the nurses, for the top of the sheet was covered with little drawings. He had made them with an indelible pencil attached to his temperature chart and hanging above his head – he must have reached up for it and broken it off.'

She spread out the square of soiled linen on the table.

'Poor Mark was very fond of drawing the figures that children and idle people who have no real knowledge of art love to scribble.'

'How did you get this?' asked Leon.

'The matron cut it off for me.'

Manfred frowned. 'The sort of things a man might draw in his delirium,' he said.

'On the contrary,' said Leon coolly, 'it is as clear as daylight to me. Where were you married?'

'At the Westminster Registry Office.'

Leon nodded.

'Take your mind back: was there anything remarkable about the marriage – did your husband have a private interview with the registrar?'

She opened her big blue eyes at this.

'Yes – Mr Lethersohn and my husband interviewed him in his private office.'

Leon chuckled, but was serious again instantly.

'One more question. Who drew up the will? A lawyer?'

She shook her head.

'My husband – it was written in his own hand from start to finish. He wrote rather a nice hand, very easily distinguishable from any other.'

'Were there any other conditions imposed upon you in your husband's will?'

She hesitated, and the watchers saw a dark flush pass over her face.

'Yes . . . it was so insulting that I did not tell you. It was this – and this was the main condition – that I should not at any time attempt to establish the fact that I was legally married to Mark. That was to me inexplicable – I can't believe that he was ever married before, but his early life was so remarkable that anything may have happened.'

Leon was smiling delightedly. In such moments he was as a child who had received a new and entrancing toy.

'I can relieve your mind,' he said, to her amazement. 'Your husband was never married before!'

Poiccart was studying the drawings.

'Can you get the plans of your husband's estates?' he asked, and Leon chuckled again.

'That man knows everything, George!' he exclaimed. 'Poiccart, *mon vieux*, you are superb!' He turned quickly to Mrs Stamford. 'Madam, you need rest, a change of clothing, and – protection. The first and the last are in this house, if you dare be our guest. The second I will procure for you in an hour – together with a temporary maid.'

She looked at him, a little bewildered . . . Five minutes later, an embarrassed Poiccart was showing her to her room, and a nurse of Leon's acquaintance was hurrying to Curzon Street with a bulging suitcase – Leon had a weakness for nurses, and knew at least a hundred by name.

Late as was the hour, he made several calls – one as far as Strawberry Hill, where a certain assistant registrar of marriages lived.

It was eleven o'clock that night when he rang the bell at the handsome house in Upper Berkeley Street. Another footman admitted him.

'Are you Mr Gonsalez? Mr Lethersohn has not returned from the theatre, but he telephoned asking you to wait in the library.'

'Thank you,' said Leon gratefully, though there was no need for gratitude, for he it was who had telephoned.

He was bowed into the ornate sanctum and left alone.

The footman had hardly left the room before Leon was at the Empire desk, turning over the papers rapidly. But he found what he sought on the blotting-pad, face downwards.

A letter addressed to a firm of wine merchants complaining of some deficiency in a consignment of champagne. He read this through rapidly – it was only half finished – folded the paper and put it into his pocket.

Carefully and rapidly he examined the drawers of the table: two were locked – the middle drawer was, however, without fastening. What he found interested him and gave him some little occupation. He had hardly finished before he heard a car stop before the house and, looking through the curtains, saw a man and woman alight.

Dark as it was, he recognized his unconscious host, and he was sitting demurely on the edge of a chair when Lethersohn burst into the room, his face white with fury.

'What the hell is the meaning of this?' he demanded as he slammed the door behind him. 'By God, I'll have you arrested for impersonating me – '

'You guessed that I had telephoned – that was almost intelligent,' smiled Leon Gonsalez.

The man swallowed.

'Why are you here – I suppose it concerns the poor woman who escaped from a mental hospital today – I only just heard before I went out . . . '

'So we gathered from the fact that your watchers have been on duty again tonight,' said Leon, 'but they were a little too late.'

The man's face went a shade paler.

'You've seen her?' he asked jerkily. 'And I suppose she told you a cock and bull story about me?'

Leon took from his pocket a piece of discoloured linen and held it up.

'You've not seen this?' he asked. 'When Mark Stamford died, this drawing was found on his sheet. He could draw these strange little things, you know that?'

Lewis Lethersohn did not answer.

'Shall I tell you what this is – it is his last will.

'That's a lie!' croaked the other.

'His last will,' nodded Leon sternly. 'Those three queer rhomboids are rough plans of his three estates. That house is a pretty fair picture of the Southern Bank premises and the little circles are money.'

Lethersohn was staring at the drawing.

'No court would accept that foolery,' he managed to say.

Leon showed his teeth in a mirthless grin..

'Nor the "awl" which means "all," nor the four strokes which stand as "for," nor the "Margaret," nor the final "Mark"? he asked.

With an effort Lethersohn recovered his composure. 'My dear man, the idea is fantastical – he wrote a will with his own hand – '

Leon stood with his head thrust forward. So far Lethersohn got, when: 'He couldn't write!' he said softly, and Lethersohn turned pale. 'He could draw these pictures but he couldn't write his own name. If Mrs Stamford had seen the registrar's certificate she would have seen that it was signed with a cross – that is why you put in the little bit about her not attempting to prove her marriage – why you kept her prisoner at Harlow in case she made independent inquiries.'

Suddenly Lethersohn flew to his desk and jerked open a drawer. In a second an automatic appeared in his hand. Running back to the door, he flung it open.

'Help . . . murder!' he shouted.

He swung round on the motionless Gonsalez and, levelling his gun, pulled the trigger. A click – and no more.

'I emptied the magazine,' said Leon coolly, 'so the little tragedy you so carefully staged has become a farce. Shall I telephone to the police or will you?'

Scotland Yard men arrested Lewis Lethersohn as he was stepping on to the boat at Dover.

'There may be some difficulty in proving the will,' said Manfred, reading the account in the evening newspapers; 'but the jury will not take long to put friend Lewis in his proper place . . .'

Later, when they questioned Leon – Poiccart was all for pinning down his psychology – he condescended to explain.

'The rebus told me he could not write – the fact that the will did not instruct Mrs Stamford to marry Lewis showed me that he was married and loved his wife. The rest was ridiculously easy.'

The Happy Travellers

Of the three men who had their headquarters in Curzon Street, George Manfred was by far the best looking. His were the features and poise of an aristocrat. In a crowd he stood out by himself, not alone because of his height, but the imponderable something which distinguishes breeding.

'George looks like a racehorse in a herd of Shetland ponies!' said the enthusiastic Leon Gonsalez on one occasion. Which was very nearly true.

Yet it was Leon who attracted the average woman, and even women above the average. It was fatal to send him to deal with a case in which women were concerned, not because he himself was given to philandering, but because it was as certain as anything could be that he would come back leaving at least one sighing maiden to bombard him with letters ten pages long.

Which really made him rather unhappy.

'I'm old enough to be their father,' he wailed on one occasion, 'and as I live I said no more than "Good morning" to the wench. Had I held her hand or chanted a canto or two into her pink ear, I would stand condemned. But, George, I swear – '

But George was helpless with laughter.

Yet Leon could act the perfect lover. Once in Cordova he paid court to a certain *señorita* – three knife scars on his right breast testify to the success of his wooing. As to the two men who attacked him, they are dead, for by his courting he lured into the open the man for whom the police of Spain and France were searching.

And he was especially effusive one spring morning to a slim and beautiful dark-eyed lady whom he met in Hyde Park. He was on foot, when he saw her walking past slowly and unattended. A graceful woman of thirty with a faultless skin and grey eyes that were almost black.

It was by no accident that they met, for Leon had been studying her movements for weeks.

'This is an answer to prayer, beautiful lady,' he said, and his extravagance was the more facile since he spoke in Italian.

She laughed softly, gave him one swift, quizzical glance from under the long lashes, and signalled him to replace the hat that was now in his hand.

'Good morning, Signor Carrelli,' she smiled, and gave him a small gloved hand. She was simply but expensively dressed. The only jewels she wore were the string of pearls about her white throat.

'I see you everywhere,' she said. 'You were dining at the Carlton on Monday night, and before that I saw you in a box at a theatre, and yesterday afternoon I met you!'

Leon showed his white teeth in a delighted smile.

'That is true, illustrious lady,' he said, 'but you make no reference to my searching London to find somebody who would introduce me. Nor do you pity my despair as I followed you, feasting my eyes upon your beauty, or my sleepless nights – '

All this he said with the fervour of a love-sick youth, and she listened without giving evidence of disapproval.

'You shall walk with me,' she said, in the manner of a queen conveying an immense privilege.

They strolled away from the crowd towards the open spaces of the park, and they talked of Rome and the hunting season, of runs on Campagna and the parties of Princess Leipnitz-Savalo – Leon read the society columns of the Roman press with great assiduity and remembered all that he read.

They came at last to a place of trees and comfortable garden chairs. Leon paid the watchful attendant, and, after he had strolled away: 'How beautiful it is to sit alone with divinity!' he began ecstatically. 'For I tell you this, signorita . . . '

'Tell me something else, Mr Leon Gonsalez,' said the lady, and this time she spoke in English and her voice had the qualities of steel and ice. 'Why are you shadowing me?'

If she expected to confound him it was because she did not know her Leon.

'Because you are an extremely dangerous lady, Madame Koskina,' he said coolly, 'and all the more dangerous because the Lord has given you kissable lips and a graceful body. How many impressionable young attachés of embassies have discovered these charms in you!'

She laughed at this and was seemingly well pleased.

'You have been reading,' she said. 'No, my dear Mr Gonsalez, I am out of politics – they bore me. Poor Ivan is in Russia struggling with the work of the Economic Commission and living in dread because of his well-known liberal views, and I am in London, which is delightfully capitalistic and comfortable! Believe me, Leningrad is no place for a lady!'

Isola Koskina had been Isola Caprevetti before she married a dashing young Russian attaché. She had been a revolutionary from birth; and now she had developed a zeal for revolution that amounted to fanaticism.

Leon smiled.

'There are worse places for a lady even than Leningrad. I should be grieved indeed, my dear Isola, to see you making coarse shirts in Aylesbury convict establishment.'

She looked at him steadily, insolently.

'That is a threat, and threats bore me. In Italy I have been threatened with . . . all sorts of dreadful things if I ever showed myself on the wrong side of the Simplon Pass. And really I am the most inoffensive person in the world, Monsieur Gonsalez. You are, of course, employed by the Government – how eminently respectable! Which government?'

Leon grinned, but was serious again in a second.

'The Italian frontiers are practically closed since the last attempt,' he said. 'You and your friends are causing everybody an immense amount of trouble. Naturally the Government are concerned. They do not wish to wake up one morning and find that they are implicated, and that some successful assassin made a jump from – England, shall we say?'

The lady shrugged her pretty shoulders. 'How very dramatic! And therefore poor Isola Koskina must be watched by detectives and reformed murderers – I suppose you and your precious comrades are reformed?'

The smile on the thin face of Leon Gonsalez widened. 'If we were not, signorita, what would happen? Should I be sitting here talking pretty-pretty talk with you? Would you not be picked out of the Thames at Limehouse all cold and clammy some morning, and lie on the slab till a coroner's jury returned a verdict of "Found drowned"?'

He saw the colour leave her face: fear came to her eyes. 'You had better threaten Ivan – ' she began.

'I will cable him: he is not in Leningrad but living in Berlin under the name of Petersohn – Martin Lutherstrasse 904. How easy it would be if we were not reformed! A dead man in a gutter and a policeman searching his pockets for a card of identity – '

She rose hurriedly; her very lips were bloodless.

'You do not amuse me,' she said and, turning from him, walked quickly away.

Leon made no attempt to follow her. It was two days after this encounter that the letter came. Many people wrote to the Just Men, a few abusively, quite a number fatuously. But now and again there could be extracted from the morning correspondence quite a pretty little problem. And the dingy letter with its finger-marks and creases was quite worth the amount that the postman charged them – for it came unstamped. The address was:

Four Just Men
Curzon Street
May Fair
West End, London

The writing was that of an illiterate, and the letter went:

Dear Sir

You are surposed to go in for misteries well hear is a mistery. I was a boiler makers mate in Hollingses but now out of work and one Sunday I was photoed by a foren lady she come in front of me with a camra and took me. There was a lot of chaps in the park but she only took me. Then she ast me my name and address and ast me if I knew a clergyman. And when I said yes she wrote down the name of the Rev J. Crewe, and then she said shed send me a picture dear sir she didn't send me a pictur but ast me to joyne the Happy Travlers to go to Swizzleland Rome, etc. and nothing to pay all expences payed also loss of time (Ten £) and soots of close everything done in stile. Well dear sir I got ready and she did everything close ten £ &. also she got tickets &c. But now the lady says I got to go to Devonshire not that I mind. Now dear sir thats a mistery because I just met a gentleman from Leeds and has had his photo took and joyned the Happy Travlers and hes going to Cornwall and this lady who took the picture of him ast him if he knew a clergyman and wrote it down. Now what is the mistery is it something to do with religion?

Yours Sincerely, T. Barger

George Manfred read the ill-spelt scrawl and threw the letter across the breakfast table to Leon Gonsalez.

'Read me that riddle, Leon,' he said.

Leon read and frowned.

' "Happy Travellers", eh? That's odd.'

The letter went to Raymond, who studied it with an expressionless face.

'Eh, Raymond?' Leon asked, his eyes alight.

'I think so,' said Raymond, nodding slowly.

'Will you let me into your "mistery"?' asked Manfred.

Leon chuckled.

'No mystery at all, my dear George. I will see this T. Barger, whose name is surely "Thomas" and will learn certain particulars as, for example, the colour of his eyes and the testimonial he has received from the Foreign Secretary.'

'Mistery on mistery,' murmured George Manfred as he sipped his coffee – though in truth the matter was no longer a mystery to him. The reference to the Foreign Secretary was very illuminating.

'As to the lady – ' said Leon, and shook his head.

His big Bentley created a mild sensation in the street where T. Barger lived. It was situated near the East India Dock, and T. Barger – whose front name was surprisingly Theophilus – proved to be a tall, dark man of thirty with a small black moustache and rather heavy black eyebrows. He was obviously wearing his new 'soot' and had expended at least a portion of his 'ten £' on alcoholic refreshment, for he was in a loud and confident mood.

'I'm leavin' tomorrow,' he said thickly, 'for Torquay – everything paid. Travellin' like a swell . . . first class. You one of them Justers!'

Leon induced him to go into the house.

'It's a myst'ry to me,' said Mr Barger, 'why she done it. Happy Trav'ler – that's what I am. She might have took me abroad – I'd like to have seen them mountains, but she says if I don't speak the Swiss language I'd be out of it. Anyway, what's the matter with Torquay?'

'The other man is going to Cornwall?'

Mr Barger nodded solemnly. 'An' his mate's goin' to Somerset – funny meetin' him at all . . . ' He explained the coincidence, which had to do with a public-house where Mr Barger had called for a drink.

'What was his name?'

'Rigson – Harry Rigson. I told him mine, he told me his. The other man? Harry's pal? I call him Harry – we're like pals – now let me think, mister . . . '

Leon let him think.

'Funny name . . Coke . . . no, Soke . . . Lokely! That's it – Joe Lokely.'

Leon asked a few more questions which were seemingly irrelevant but were not.

'Of course I had to be passed by the committee,' said the communicative Theophilus. 'Accordin' to Harry, this lady photoed a friend of his but he didn't pass.'

'I see,' said Leon. 'What time do you leave for Devonshire?'

'Tomorrow mornin' – seven o'clock. Bit early, ain't it? But this lady says that Happy Travellers must be early risers. Harry's goin' by the same train but in another coach . . . '

Leon went back to Curzon Street well satisfied. The question he had to decide was: was Isola an early riser too?

'I hardly think so,' said Raymond Poiccart. 'She would not take the risk – especially if she knows that she is watched.'

That night Scotland Yard was a very hive of industry, and Leon Gonsalez did without sleep. Fortunately Isola had been under police observation, and the Yard knew every district in England she had visited for the past month. By midnight two thousand ministers of religion had been awakened from their sleep by local police and asked to furnish certain particulars.

Isola went to a dinner and dance that night and her partner was a very nice young man, tall and dark of face. She chose the L'Orient, which is the most exclusive and plutocratic of night clubs. Men and women turned to admire or criticize her beauty as she entered, a radiant figure in a scarlet dress with a dull gold stole. The colours set off the glories of her lovely face, and there was sinuous grace in every movement.

They had reached the dessert when suddenly she laid two fingers on the table-cloth.

'Who is it?' asked her companion carelessly as he saw the danger signal.

'The man I told you about – he is at the table immediately opposite.'

Presently the dark young man looked. 'So that is the famous Gonsalez! A wisp of a man that I could break – '

'A wisp of a man who has broken giants, Emilio,' she interrupted. 'Have you heard of Saccoriva – was he not a giant? That man killed him – shot him down in his own headquarters when there was a guard of revolutionary brethren within call – and escaped!'

'He is anti-revolutionary?' Emilio was impressed.

She shook her head. 'Comrade Saccoriva was very foolish – with women. It was over some girl he had taken – and left. He is looking this way: I will call him over.'

Leon rose lazily at the signal and came across the crowded dance floor.

'Signorita, you will never forgive me!' he said in despair. 'Here am I watching you again! And yet I only came here because I was bored.'

'Bore me also,' she said with her sweetest smile, and then, remembering her companion: 'This is Herr Halz from Leipzig.'

Leon's eyes twinkled.

'Your friends change their nationalities as often as they change their names,' he said. 'I remember Herr Halz of Leipzig when he was Emilio Cassini of Turin!'

Emilio shifted uncomfortably, but Isola was amused.

'This man is omniscient! Dance with me, Señor Gonsalez, and promise that you will not murder me!'

They went twice round the dance floor before Leon spoke. 'If I had your face and figure and youth, I should have a good time and not bother with politics,' he said.

'And if I had your wisdom and cunning I should remove tyrants from their high positions,' she retorted, her voice quivering.

That was all that was said. Going out into the vestibule, Leon discovered the girl and her escort waiting. It was raining heavily and Isola's car could not be found.

'May I drop you, gracious lady?' Leon's smile was most entrancing. 'I have a poor car but it is at your disposition.'

Isola hesitated.

'Thank you,' she said.

Leon, ever the soul of politeness, insisted on taking one of the seats that put his back to the driver. It was not his own car. Usually he was very nervous about other drivers, but tonight he did not mind.

They crossed Trafalgar Square.

'The man is taking the wrong turning,' said Isola with quick vehemence.

'This is the right road to Scotland Yard,' said Leon. 'We call this the Way of the Happy Traveller – keep your hand away from your pocket, Emilio. I have killed men on less provocation, and I have been covering you ever since we left the club!'

* * *

In the early hours of the morning telegrams were despatched to police headquarters at Folkestone and Dover:

Arrest and detain Theophilus Barger, Joseph Lokely, Harry Rigson – [here followed five other names] – travelling to the Continent by boat either today or tomorrow.

There was no need to give instructions about Isola. For a perfect lady, her behaviour was indefensible.

'She blotted her copybook,' said Leon sadly. 'I've never seen a Happy Traveller less happy when we got her to Scotland Yard.'

Considering the matter at the morning conference which was part of the daily routine in Curzon Street, Manfred was inclined to regard the plot as elementary.

'If you speak disparagingly of my genius and power of deduction I shall burst into tears,' said Leon. 'Raymond thinks I was clever – I will not have that verdict challenged. George, you're getting old and grouchy.'

'The detection was clever,' Manfred hastened to placate his smiling friend.

'And the scheme was clever,' insisted Leon, 'and terribly like Isola. One of these days she'll do something awfully original and be shot. Obviously, what she set out to do was to collect seven men who bore some resemblance to the members of her murder gang. When she had found them, she made them get passports – that of course is why she asked if they knew a clergyman, for a padre's signature on the photograph and application form is as good as a lawyer's. Seven poor innocent men with passports which she handed over to her friends while the happy travellers were sent into out-of-the-way places. She was heading the gang into Italy – all the passports were visaed for that country.'

'Tell me,' said Manfred, 'did they arrest the spurious T. Barger at Dover?'

Leon shook his head.

'The man who was to have travelled with T. Barger's passport was one Emilio Cassini – I spotted the likeness immediately. Isola was very abusive – but I quietened her by suggesting that her husband might like to know something about her friendship with Emilio . . . I have been watching Isola for a long time and I have seen things.'

The Abductor

It was a year since Lord Geydrew invoked the aid of the Just Men who lived at the sign of the Triangle in Curzon Street. He was a narrow-headed man; the first time they met with him, Poiccart hazarded the opinion that he was constitutionally mean. The last time they met it was not so much an opinion as stark knowledge, for his lordship had most boldly repudiated the bill of expenses that Poiccart had rendered – even though Manfred and Gonsalez had risked their lives to recover the lost Geydrew diamond.

The Three did not take him to court. Not one of them had need of money. Manfred was satisfied with the experience; Poiccart was cock-a-hoop because a theory of his had worked home; Gonsalez found his consolation in the shape of the client's head.

'The most interesting recession of the parietal and malformation of the occiput I have ever seen,' he said enthusiastically.

The Just Men shared one extraordinary gift – a prodigious memory for faces and an extraordinary facility for attaching those faces to disreputable names. There was, however, no credit due for remembering the head of his lordship.

Manfred was sitting in his small room overlooking Curzon Street one night in spring, and he was in his most thoughtful mood when Poiccart – who invariably undertook the job of butler – came hobbling in to announce Lord Geydrew.

'Not the Geydrew of Gallat Towers?' Manfred could be massively ironical. 'Has he come to pay his bill?'

'God knows,' said Poiccart piously. 'Do peers of the realm pay their bills? For the moment I am less concerned about the peerage than I am about my ankle – really, Leon is a careless devil. I had to take a taxi . . . '

Manfred chuckled. 'He will be penitent and interesting,' he said; 'as for his lordship. Show him up.'

Lord Geydrew came in a little nervously, blinking at the bright light that burnt on Manfred's table. Evidently he was unusually agitated. The weak mouth was tremulous, he opened and closed his eyes with a rapidity for which the bright light was not wholly responsible. His long, lined face was twitching spasmodically; from time to time he thrust his fingers through the scanty, reddish-grey hair.

'I hope, Mr Manfred, there is no – um – er – '

He fumbled in his pocket, produced an oblong slip of paper and pushed it across the desk. Manfred looked and wondered. Poiccart, forgetful of his role as butler, watched interestedly. Besides, there was no need to pretend that he was anything but what he was.

Lord Geydrew looked from one to the other.

'I was hoping your friend – um – '

'Mr Gonsalez is out: he will be back later in the evening,' said Manfred, wondering what was coming.

Then his lordship collapsed with a groan, and let his head fall upon the arms that lay on the desk.

'Oh, my God!' he wailed . . . 'The most terrible thing . . . It doesn't bear thinking about.'

Manfred waited patiently. Presently the older man looked up.

'I must tell you the story from the beginning, Mr Manfred,' he said. 'My daughter Angela – you may have met her?'

Manfred shook his head.

'She was married this morning. To Mr Guntheimer, a very wealthy Australian banker and an immensely nice fellow.' He shook his head and dabbed his eyes with a handkerchief.

Light was beginning to dawn on Manfred.

'Mr Guntheimer is considerably older than my daughter,' his lordship went on, 'and I will not conceal from you the fact that Angela has certain objections to the match. In fact, she had very stupidly arrived at some sort of understanding with young Sidworth – good family and all that, but not a penny in the world . . . It would have been madness.'

Manfred now understood quite clearly.

'We had to hurry the marriage, since Guntheimer is leaving for Australia much earlier than he expected. Happily my daughter gave way to my legitimate wishes and they were married this morning at a registrar's office and were due to leave for the Isle of Wight by the three o'clock train.

'We did not go to see her off, and the only account I have of the occurrence was from the mouth of my son-in-law. He said that he was walking up to his reserved compartment, when suddenly he missed my daughter from his side. He looked round, retraced his steps, but could see nothing of her. Thinking that she might have gone ahead, he returned to the compartment, but it was empty. He then went back beyond the barrier: she was not in sight, but a porter whom he had engaged to carry his luggage and who followed him, said that he had seen her in earnest conversation with an elderly man and that they walked into the booking hall together and disappeared. Another porter on duty in the courtyard of the station saw them get into a car and drive off.'

Manfred was jotting down his notes on his blotting-pad. Poiccart never lifted his eyes from the visitor.

'The story the porter tells – the outside porter, I mean, went on his lordship, 'is that my daughter seemed reluctant to go, and that she was almost thrust into the car, which had to pass him. As the car came abreast, the man was pulling down the blinds, and the porter says that he has no doubt that my daughter was struggling with him.'

'With the elderly man?' said Manfred.

Lord Geydrew nodded.

'Mr Manfred' – his voice was a wail – 'I am not a rich man, and perhaps I would be wise to leave this matter in the hands of the police. But I have such extraordinary faith in your intelligence and acumen – I think you will find that cheque right – and in spite of your exorbitant charges I wish to engage you. She is my only daughter . . . ' His voice broke.

'Did the porter take the number of the car?'

Lord Geydrew shook his head. 'No,' he said. 'Naturally I wish to keep this out of the press – '

'I'm afraid you've failed,' said Manfred, and took a paper from a basket that was at his side, pointing out a paragraph in the stop press.

REPORTED ABDUCTION OF BRIDE

It is reported that a bride, just before leaving Waterloo on her honeymoon trip, was forcibly abducted by an elderly man. Scotland Yard have been notified.

'Porters will talk,' said Manfred, leaning back in his chair. 'Have the police a theory?'

'None,' snapped his lordship.

'Has Mr Sidworth been interviewed?'

Lord Geydrew shook his head vigorously.

'Naturally that was the first thought I had. Sidworth, I thought, has persuaded this unfortunate girl – '

'Is he an elderly man?' asked Manfred, with a twinkle in his eye which only Poiccart understood.

'Of course he isn't,' snapped his lordship. 'I told you he was young. At the present moment he's staying with some very dear friends of mine at Newbury – I think he took the marriage rather badly. At any rate, my friend says that he has not left Kingshott Manor all day, and that he has not once used the telephone.'

Manfred rubbed his shapely nose thoughtfully.

'And Mr Guntheimer – ?'

'Naturally he's distracted. I have never known a man so upset. He's almost mad with grief. Can you gentlemen give me any hope?'

He looked from one to the other, and his lean face brightened at Manfred's nod.

'Where is Mr Guntheimer staying?' asked Poiccart, breaking his silence.

'At the Gayborough Hôtel,' said Lord Geydrew.

'Another point – what was his present to the bride?' asked Manfred.

His visitor looked surprised, and then: 'A hundred thousand pounds,' he said impressively. 'Mr Guntheimer doesn't believe in our old method of settlement. I may say that his cheque for that amount is in my pocket now.'

'And your present to the bride?' asked Manfred.

Lord Geydrew showed some signs of impatience.

'My dear fellow, you're on the wrong track. Angela was not spirited away for purposes of property. The jewel case containing her diamonds was carried by Guntheimer. She had nothing of value in her possession except for a few odd pounds in her handbag.'

Manfred rose.

'I think that is all I want to ask you, Lord Geydrew. Unless I'm greatly mistaken, your daughter will come back to you in twenty-four hours.'

Poiccart showed the comforted man to his car, and returned to find Manfred reading the sporting column in an evening newspaper.

'Well?' asked Poiccart.

'A curious case and one in which my soul revels.' He put down the paper and stretched himself. 'If Leon comes in, will you ask him to await my return unless there is something urgent takes him elsewhere?' He lifted his head. 'I think that is him,' he said, at the sound of squealing brakes.

Poiccart shook his head.

'Leon is more noiseless,' he said, and went down to admit an agitated young man.

Mr Harry Sidworth was that type of youth for which Manfred had a very soft spot. Lank of body, healthy of face, he had all the incoherence of his age.

'I say, are you Mr Manfred?' he began, almost before he got into the room. 'I've been to that old devil's house and his secretary told me to come here, though for the Lord's sake don't tell anybody he said so!'

'You're Mr Sidworth, of course?'

The young man nodded vigorously. His face was anxious, his air wild; he was too young to hide his evident distress.

'Isn't it too terrible for words – ' he began.

'Mr Sidworth – ' Manfred fixed him with a kindly eye – 'you've come to ask me about your Angela, and I'm telling you, as I told Lord Geydrew, that I'm perfectly certain that she will come back to you unharmed. There's one thing I might ask – how long has she known her husband?'

The young man made a wry face.

'That's a hateful word to me,' he groaned. 'Guntheimer? About three months. He isn't a bad fellow. I've nothing against him, except that he got Angela. Old Geydrew thought I'd taken her away. He rang up the people I was staying with, and that was the first news I had that she'd disappeared. It's the most ghastly thing that's ever happened to me.'

'Have you heard from her lately?' asked Manfred.

Sidworth nodded. 'Yes, this morning,' he said dolefully. 'Just a little note thanking me for my wedding present. I gave her a jewel case – '

'A what?' asked Manfred sharply, and the young man, surprised at his vehemence, stared at him.

'A jewel case – my sister bought one about a month ago, and Angela was so taken with it that I had an exact copy made.'

Manfred was looking at him absently.

'Your sister?' he said slowly. 'Where does your sister live?'

'Why, she's at Maidenhead,' said the young man, surprised.

Manfred looked at his watch.

'Eight o'clock,' he said. 'This is going to be rather an amusing evening.'

The clocks were striking the half-hour after ten when the telephone in Mr Guntheimer's private suite buzzed softly. Guntheimer ceased his restless pacing and went to the instrument.

'I can't see anybody,' he said. 'Who?' He frowned. 'All right, I'll see him.'

It had been raining heavily and Manfred apologized for his wet raincoat and waited for an invitation to remove it. But apparently Mr Guntheimer was too preoccupied with his unhappy thoughts to be greatly concerned about his duties as host.

He was a tall, good-looking man, rather haggard of face now, and the hand that stroked the iron-grey moustache trembled a little.

'Geydrew told me he was going to see you – what is your explanation of this extraordinary happening, Mr Manfred?'

Manfred smiled.

'The solution is a very simple one, Mr Guntheimer,' he said. 'It is to be found in the pink diamond.'

'In the what?' asked the other, startled.

'Your wife has a rather nice diamond brooch,' said Manfred. 'Unless I am misinformed, the third from the end of the bar is of a distinctly pinkish hue. It is, or was, the property of the Rajah of Komitar, and on its topmost facet you will find an Arabic word, meaning "Happiness".'

Guntheimer was gazing at him open-mouthed.

'What has that to do with it?'

Again Manfred smiled.

'If there is a pink diamond and it is inscribed as I say, I can find your wife, not in twenty-four but in six hours.'

Guntheimer fingered his chin thoughtfully.

'That matter's easily settled,' he said. 'My wife's jewels are in the hôtel safe. Just wait.'

He was gone five minutes and returned carrying a small scarlet box. He put this on the table and opened it with a key which he took from his pocket. Lifting the lid, he took out a pad of wash-leather and revealed a trayful of glittering jewels.

'There's no brooch there,' he said after a search; he pulled out the tray and examined the padded bottom of the box.

There were brooches and bars of all kinds. Manfred pointed to one, and this was inspected – but there was no pink diamond; nor was there in any other brooch.

'Is that the best you can do in the way of detective work?' demanded Mr Guntheimer as he closed and locked the box. 'I thought that tale was a little fantastic . . . '

Crash! A stone came hurtling through the window, smashing the glass, and fell on the carpet. With an oath Guntheimer spun round.

'What was that?'

He grabbed the jewel box that was on the table and ran to the window. Outside the window was a small balcony which ran the length of the building.

'Somebody standing on the balcony must have thrown that,' said Guntheimer.

The sound of smashing glass had been heard in the Corridor, and two hôtel servants came in and examined the damage without, however, offering a solution to the mystery.

Manfred waited until the distracted bridegroom had locked away the jewel box in a strong trunk, and by this time Guntheimer was in a better humour.

'I've heard about you fellows,' he said, 'and I know you're pretty clever; otherwise, I should have thought that story of the pink diamond was all bunkum. Perhaps you will tell me what the Rajah of Who-was-it has to do with Angela's disappearance?'

Manfred was biting his lip thoughtfully.

'I don't wish to alarm you,' he said slowly. 'But has it occurred to you, Mr Guntheimer, that you may share her fate?'

Again that quick turn and look of apprehension.

'I don't quite understand you.'

'I wondered if you would,' said Manfred and, holding out his hand, he left his astonished host staring after him.

When he got to Curzon Street he found Gonsalez, his head in one deep armchair, his feet on another. Apparently Poiccart, who had reached home first, had told him of the callers, for he was holding forth on women.

'They are wilful, they are unreasonable,' he said bitterly. 'You remember, George, that woman at Cordova, how we saved her life from her lover and how we barely saved our own at her infuriated hands – there should be a law prohibiting women from possessing firearms. Here is a case in point. Tomorrow the newspapers will tell you the harrowing story of a bride torn from the arms of her handsome bridegroom. The old ladies of Bayswater will shed tears over the tragedy, knowing nothing of the aching heart of Mr Harry Sidworth or the great inconvenience to which this strange and tragic happening has put George Manfred, Raymond Poiccart, and Leon Gonsalez.'

Manfred opened the safe in a corner of the room and put into it something he had taken from his pocket. Characteristically, Gonsalez asked no questions, and it was remarkable and significant that nobody discussed the pink diamond.

The following morning passed uneventfully, save that Leon had much to say about the hardness of the drawing-room sofa, where he had spent the night, and the three men had finished lunch and were sitting smoking over their coffee, when a ring of the bell took Poiccart into the hall.

'Geydrew, full of bad tidings,' said George Manfred, as the sound of a voice came to them.

Lord Geydrew it was, shrill with his tremendous information.

'Have you heard the news? . . . Guntheimer has disappeared! The waiter went to his room this morning, could get no answer, opened the door with his key and walked in. The bed had not been slept in . . . all his luggage was there, and on the floor – '

'Let me guess,' said Manfred, and held his forehead. 'The jewel case was smashed to smithereens, without a single jewel in it! Or was it – '

But Lord Geydrew's face told him that his first guess was accurate.

'How did you know?' he gasped. 'It wasn't in the papers – my God, this is awful!'

In his agitation, he did not notice that Leon Gonsalez had slipped from the room, and only missed him when he turned to find the one man in whom, for some extraordinary reason, he had faith.

('Geydrew never did trust you or me,' said George afterwards.)

'I'm ashamed to confess it,' smiled Manfred. 'That was sheer guess-work. The jewel case had the appearance of being jumped on – I don't wonder!'

'But – but – ' stammered the nobleman, and at that minute the door opened and he stood amazed.

A smiling girl was there, and in another instant was in his arms.

'Here's your Angela,' said Leon, with great coolness, 'and with all due respect to everybody, I shan't be sorry to sleep in my own bed tonight. George, that sofa must be sent back to the brigands who supplied it.'

But George was at the safe, lifting out a red leather jewel case.

* * *

It was a long time before Geydrew was calm enough to hear the story.

'My friend Leon Gonsalez,' said Manfred, 'has a wonderful memory for faces – so have we all, for the matter of that. But Leon is specially gifted. He was waiting at Waterloo to drive friend Poiccart home. Raymond had been to Winchester to see a surgeon friend of ours over a matter of a sprained leg. Whilst Leon was waiting he saw Guntheimer and your daughter and instantly recognized Guntheimer whose other name is Lanstry, or Smith, or Malikin. Guntheimer's graft is bigamy, and Leon happens to know him rather well. A few inquiries made of the porter, and he discovered, not the identity of your daughter, but that this man had married that day. He approached Angela with a cock and bull story that some mysterious body was waiting to see her outside the station. I will not say that she imagined that mysterious body was Harry Sidworth, but at any rate she went very willingly. She showed some little fight when friend Leon pushed her into the car and drove away with her – '

'Anybody who has tried to drive a car and control an infuriated and terrified lady will sympathize with me,' broke in Leon.

'By the time Miss Angela Geydrew reached Curzon Street she was in full possession of the facts as Leon knew them,' Manfred went on. 'Leon's one object was to postpone the honeymoon until he could get somebody to identify Guntheimer. The young lady told us nothing about her jewel case, but we all guessed the hundred-thousand-pound cheque, presented too late to be banked; before it could be cleared, Guntheimer would be well out of the country with any loot he was able to gather – in this case the family diamonds – and of course it would have been pretty easy to arrest him last night. When your lordship called yesterday Leon was out finishing his investigations. Before he returned, I learnt where I could get a duplicate jewel box, and with Poiccart made a call on friend bigamist. Poiccart was on the balcony, listening, and at an agreed word signal he smashed the window, which gave me just the opportunity I wanted to change the jewel boxes. Later, I presume, Mr Guntheimer opened the box, found it was empty, realized the game was up and fled.'

'But how did you induce him to show you the jewel box?' asked Lord Geydrew.

Manfred smiled cryptically. The tale of the pink diamond was too crude to be repeated.

The Third Coincidence

Leon Gonsalez, like the famous scientist, had an unholy knack of collecting coincidences. He had, too, strange faiths, and believed that if a man saw a pink cow with one horn in the morning, he must, by the common workings of a certain esoteric law, meet another pink cow with one horn later in the day.

'Coincidences, my dear George,' he said, 'are inevitabilities – not accidents.'

Manfred murmured something in reply – he was studying the dossier of one William Yape, of whom something may be told at a later period.

'Now here is a coincidence.' Leon was in no sense abashed, for it was after dinner, the hour of the day when he was most confident. 'This morning I took the car for a run to Windsor – she was a trifle sticky yesterday – and at Langley what did I find? A gentleman sitting before an inn, very drunk. He was, I imagined, an agricultural labourer in his best Sunday suit, and it was remarkable that he wore a diamond ring worth five hundred pounds. He had, he told me, been to Canada, and had stayed at the Château Fronteuse – which is an expensive hôtel.'

Poiccart was interested.

'And the coincidence?'

'If George will listen.' Manfred looked up with a groan. 'Thank you. Hardly had I begun questioning this inebriated son of the soil when a Rolls drove up, and there stepped down a rather nice-looking gentleman who also wore a diamond ring on his little finger.'

'Sensation,' said George Manfred, and went back to his dossier.

'I shall be offended if you do not listen. Imagine the agriculturist suddenly jumping to his feet as if he had seen a ghost. "Ambrose!" he gasped. I tell you his face was the colour of milk. Ambrose – if he will pardon the liberty – could not have heard him, and passed into the inn. The labourer went stumbling away – it is remarkable that one's head sobers so much more quickly than one's legs – as though the devil was after him.

'I went into the inn and found Ambrose drinking tea – a man who drinks tea at eleven o'clock in the morning has lived either in South Africa or Australia. It proved to be South Africa. An alluvial diamond digger, an ex-soldier and a most gentlemanly person, though not very communicative. After he had gone I went in search of the labourer – overtook him as he entered a most flamboyant villa.'

'Which, with your peculiar disregard for the sacredness of the Englishman's home, you entered.'

Leon nodded.

'Truth is in you,' he said. 'Imagine, my dear George, a suburban villa so filled with useless furniture that you could hardly find a place to sit. Satin-covered settees, pseudo-Chinese cabinets, whatnots and wherefores crowding space. Ridiculous oil paintings, painted by the yard, in heavy gold frames, simpering enlargements of photographs covering hideous wallpaper – and two ladies, expensively dressed, bediamonded but without an "h" between them; common as the dirt on my shoes, shrill, ugly, coarse.

'As I entered the hall on the trail of the labourer I heard him say: "He wasn't killed – he's back," and a woman say: "Oh, my God!" And then the second woman said: "He must be killed – it was in the list on New Year's Day!" – after which I was so busy explaining my presence that further enlightenment was out of the question.'

George Manfred had tied his dossier neatly with a strip of red tape, and now he leaned back in his chair.

'You took the number of the Ambrose car, of course?'

Leon nodded.

'And he wore a diamond ring?'

'A lady's – it was on his little finger. A not very magnificent affair. It was the sort of dress ring that a girl would wear.'

Poiccart chuckled. 'Now we sit down and wait for the third coincidence,' he said. 'It is inevitable.'

A few minutes later Leon was on his way to Fleet Street, for he was a man whose curiosity was insatiable. For two hours, in the office of a friendly newspaper, he pored over the casualty lists that were published on four New Year's Days, looking for a soldier whose first name was 'Ambrose'.

'The Three Just Men,' said the Assistant Commissioner cheerfully, 'are now so eminently respectable that we give them police protection.'

* * *

You must allow for the fact that this was after dinner, when even an Assistant Commissioner grows a little expansive, especially when he is host in his nice house in Belgravia. You must also allow for the more interesting fact that one of the famous organization had been seen outside Colonel Yenford's house that very night.

'They are strange devils – why they should be watching this place beats me; if I'd known I should have asked the fellow in!'

Lady Irene Belvinne looked at one of the portraits on the wall: she seemed scarcely interested in the Three Just Men. Yet every word Colonel Yenford spoke was eagerly stored in her memory.

A beautiful woman of thirty-five, the widow of a man who had held Cabinet rank, she might claim to be especially favoured. She had been the wife of a many-times millionaire who had left her his entire fortune; she had the lineless face and serene poise of one who had never known care . . .

'I don't exactly know what they do.' Her voice was a soft drawl. 'Are they detectives? Of course, I know what they were.'

Who did not know what that ruthless trio were in the days when every hand was against them? When swift death followed their threat, when a whole world of secret lawbreakers trembled at their names.

'They're tame enough now,' said somebody. 'They wouldn't have played their monkey tricks today, eh, Yenford?'

Colonel Yenford was not so confident.

'It's strange,' mused Irene. 'I didn't think of them.'

She was so wholly absorbed in her thoughts that she did not realize she was speaking aloud.

'Why on earth should you think about them?' demanded Yenford, a little astonished.

She started at this and changed the subject.

It was past midnight when she reached her beautiful flat in Piccadilly, and all the staff except her maid had gone to bed. At the sound of a key turning in the lock the maid came flying into the hall, and with a sinking of heart Irene Belvinne knew that something was wrong.

'She's been waiting since nine, m'lady,' said the girl in a low voice. Irene nodded.

'Where is she?' she asked.

'I put her in the study, madam.'

Handing her coat to the maid, the woman walked up the broad passage, opened a door and entered the library. The woman who had been sitting on the hide-covered settee rose awkwardly at the sight of the radiant woman who entered. The visitor was poorly dressed, had a long, not too clean face, and a mouth that drooped pathetically. She looked up slyly from under her lowered lids, and though her tone was humble it also held a suggestion of menace.

'He's terribly bad again tonight, m'lady,' she said. 'We had all our work cut out to keep him in bed. He wanted to come here, he said, him being delirious. The doctor says that we ought to get him away to – ' her eyes rose quickly and fell again ' – South Africa.'

'It was Canada last time,' said Irene steadily. 'That was rather an expensive trip, Mrs Dennis.'

The woman mumbled something, rubbing her hands still more nervously.

'I'm sure I'm worried to death about the whole business, me being his aunt, and I'm sure I can't afford no five thousand pounds to take him to South Africa – '

Five thousand pounds! Irene was aghast at the demand. The Canadian trip had cost three thousand, but the original request was for one.

'I should like to see him myself,' she said with sudden determination.

Again that swift, sly look.

'I wouldn't let you come and see him, me lady, unless you brought a gentleman. I'd say your 'usband, but I know he's no more. I wouldn't take the responsibility, I wouldn't indeed. That's why I never tell you where we're living, in case you was tempted, me lady. He'd think no more of cutting your throat than he would of looking at you!'

A smile of contempt hardened the beautiful face.

'I am not so sure that really terrifies me,' said Irene quietly. 'You want five thousand pounds – when do you sail?'

'Next Saturday, me lady,' said the woman eagerly. 'And Jim say you was to pay the money in notes.'

Irene nodded.

'Very well,' she said. 'But you mustn't come here again unless I send for you.'

'Where shall I get the money, me lady?'

'Here at twelve o'clock tomorrow. And won't you please make yourself a little more presentable when you call?'

The woman grinned.

'I ain't got your looks or your clothes, me lady,' she sneered. 'Every penny piece I earn goes on poor Jim, a-trying to save his life, when if he had his rights he'd have millions.'

Irene walked to the door and opened it, waited in the passage until the maid had shut out the unprepossessing visitor.

'Open the windows and air the room,' said Irene.

She went upstairs and sat down before her dressing table, eyeing her reflection thoughtfully.

Then, of a sudden, she got up and crossed the room to the telephone. She lifted the receiver and then realized that she did not know the number. A search of the book gave her the information she wanted. The Triangle Detective Agency had their headquarters in Curzon Street. But they would be in bed by now, she thought; and even if the members of this extraordinary confederation were not, would they be likely to interest themselves at this late hour?

She had hardly given the number before she was through. She heard the rattle of the receiver as it was raised, and the distinctive tinkle of a guitar; then an eager voice asked her who she was.

'Lady Irene Belvinne,' she said. 'You don't know me, but – '

'I know you very well. Lady Irene.' She could almost detect the unknown smiling as he answered. 'You dined at Colonel Yenford's tonight and left the house at twelve minutes to twelve. You told your chauffeur to go back by way of Hyde Park . . . '

The guitar had ceased. She heard a distant voice say: 'Listen to Leon: he's being all Sherlock Holmes.' And then a laugh. She smiled in sympathy.

'Do you want to see me?' This was Leon Gonsalez speaking, then.

'When can I?' she asked.

'Now. I'll come right away, if you're in any serious trouble – I have an idea that you are.'

She hesitated. An immediate decision was called for and she set her teeth.

'Very well. Will you come? I'll wait up for you.'

In her nervousness she dropped the receiver down while he was answering her.

Five minutes later the maid admitted a slim, good-looking man. He wore a dark suit, and was strangely like a Chancery barrister she knew. On her part the greeting was awkward, for the interval had been too short for her to make up her mind what she should tell him, and how she should begin.

It was in the library tainted, to her sensitive nostrils, with her late frowsy visitor, that she made her confession, and he listened with an expressionless face.

' . . . I was very young – that is my only excuse; and he was a very handsome, very attractive young man . . . and a chauffeur isn't a servant . . . I mean, one can be quite good friends with him, as one couldn't be with – well, with other servants.'

He nodded.

'It was an act of lunacy, and nasty, and everything you can say. When my father sent him away I thought my heart would break.'

'Your father knew?' asked Gonsalez gravely.

She shook her head.

'No. Father was rather quick-tempered, and he bullied Jim for some fault that was not his – that was the end of it. I had one letter and then I heard no more until two or three years after I was married, when I got a letter from this woman, saying that her nephew was consumptive and she knew what – good friends we'd been.'

To her surprise her visitor was smiling, and at first she was hurt.

'You have told me only what I've guessed,' he said to her amazement.

'You guessed . . . but you didn't know – '

He interrupted her brusquely.

'Was your second marriage happy, Lady Irene? I am not being impertinent.'

She hesitated.

'It was quite happy. My husband was nearly thirty years older than I – why do you ask?'

Leon smiled again.

'I am a sentimentalist – which is a shocking confession for one who boasts of his scientific mind. I am a devourer of love stories, both in fiction and in life. This Jim was not unpleasant?'

She shook her head.

'No,' she said, and then added simply: I loved him – I love him still. That is the ghastly part of it. It is dreadful to think of him lying ill with this dreadful aunt looking after him – '

'Landlady,' broke in Leon calmly. 'He had no relations.'

She was on her feet now, staring at him.

'What do you know?'

He had a gesture which was almost mesmeric in its calming effect.

'I went to Colonel Yenford's house tonight – I happened to learn that you were his guest and I wanted to see your mouth. I'm sorry if I am being mysterious, but I judge women by their mouths – the test is infallible. That is why I knew the hour you left.'

Irene Belvinne was frowning at him.

'I don't understand, Mr Gonzalez,' she began. 'What has my mouth to do with the matter?'

He nodded slowly.

'If you had a certain type of mouth I should not have been interested – as it is . . . '

She waited, and presently he spoke.

'You will find James Ambrose Clynes in his suite at the Piccadilly Hôtel. The dress ring you gave him is on his little finger, and your photograph is the only one in his room.'

He put out his hand and steadied her as, white and shaking, she sank into a chair.

'He's a very rich man and a very nice man . . . and a very stupid man, or he would have come to see you.'

* * *

A car drew up before an ornate villa in the village of Langley and a poorly-dressed woman got down. The door was opened by a thickset man and the two passed into the over-furnished parlour. On the face of Mrs Dennis was a smile of satisfaction.

'It's all right – she'll part,' she said, throwing off her old coat.

The coarse-looking man with the diamond ring turned to his other sister.

'As soon as we get the money it's Canada for us,' he said ominously. 'I won't have another fright like I had on Tuesday – why were you so late, Maria?'

'A tyre burst on the Great West Road,' she said, rubbing her hands at the fire. 'What are you worrying about, Saul? We've done nothing. It ain't as though we ever threatened her. That'd be crime. Just askin' her to help a poor feller who's ill, that ain't crime.'

They discussed the pros and cons of this for nearly an hour. Then came the knock at the door.

It was the man who went out to interview the visitor . . .

'If I don't come in,' said Leon Gonsalez pleasantly, 'the police will. There will be a warrant issued tomorrow morning and you will be held on a charge of conspiring to defraud.'

A few seconds later he was questioning a trembling audience . . .

Poiccart and George Manfred were waiting up for him when he returned in the early hours of the morning.

'Rather a unique case,' said Leon, glancing through his notes. 'Our Ambrose, a well-educated man, had a love affair with the Earl of Carslake's daughter. He loses his job – because he loves the girl he decides not to communicate with her. He goes into the Army and, before he is sent overseas, he writes to his landlady, asks her to take out a sealed envelope, full of letters from Irene and burn them. By the time she gets these instructions, Ambrose is reported killed. The landlady, Mrs Dennis, with the inquisitiveness of her class, opens the envelope and learns enough to be able to blackmail this unfortunate girl. But Ambrose isn't dead – he is discharged from the army on account of wounds and, accepting the invitation of a South African soldier, goes to the Cape, where he makes good.

'In the meantime the Dennises wax rich. They pretend that "Jim", as they called him, is desperately ill, trusting that Irene has not heard of his death. By this means, and on the threat of telling her husband, they extract nearly twenty thousand pounds.'

'What shall we do to them?' asked Poiccart.

Leon took something from his pocket – a glittering diamond ring. 'I took this as payment for my advice,' he said.

George smiled.

'And your advice, Leon?'

'Was to get out of the country before Ambrose found them,' said Leon.

The Slane Mystery

The killing of Bernard Slane was one of those mysteries which delight the Press and worry the police. Mr Slane was a rich stock-broker, a bachelor and a good fellow. He had dined at a Pall Mall club and, his car being in the garage for repairs, he took a taxi and ordered the driver to take him to his flat in Albert Palace Mansions. The porter of the mansions had taken the elevator to the fifth floor at the time Mr Slane arrived.

The first intimation that there was anything wrong was when the porter came down to find the taxi-driver standing in the hall, and asked him what he wanted.

'I've just brought a gentleman here – Mr Slane, who lives at Number Seven,' said the driver. 'He hadn't got any change so he's gone in to get it.'

This was quite likely, because Slane lived on the first floor and invariably used the stairs. They chatted together, the porter and the driver, for some five minutes, and then the porter undertook to go up and collect the money for the fare.

Albert Palace Mansions differed from every other apartment-house of its kind in that, on the first and the most expensive floor, there was one small flat consisting of four rooms, which was occupied by Slane.

A light showed through the transom, but then it had been burning all the evening. The porter rang the bell and waited, rang it again, knocked – without, however, getting an answer. He returned to the driver.

'He must have gone to sleep – how was he?' he asked.

By his question he meant to inquire whether the stockbroker was quite sober. It is a fact that Slane drank rather heavily, and had come home more than once in a condition which necessitated the help of the night porter to get him to bed.

The driver, whose name was Reynolds, admitted his passenger had had as much as, and probably more than, was good for him. Again the porter attempted to get a reply from the flat and, when this failed, he paid the driver out of his own pocket, four shillings and sixpence.

The porter was on duty all night, and made several journeys up and down his shaft. Through the open grille on the first floor he commanded a view of No 7. His statement was that he saw nothing of Mr Slane that night, that it was impossible for the stockbroker to have left the building without his seeing him.

At half past five the next morning a policeman patrolling Green Park saw a man sitting huddled up on a garden chair. He wore a dinner jacket, and his attitude was so suspicious that the policeman stepped over the rails and crossed the stretch of grass which intervened between the pathway and the chair which was placed near a clump of rhododendrons. He came up to the man, to find his fears justified. The man was dead; he had been terribly battered with some blunt instrument, and a search of the pockets revealed his identity as Bernard Slane.

Near the spot was an iron gateway set in the rails leading to the Mall, and the lock of this was discovered to be smashed. Detectives from Scotland Yard were at once on the spot; the porter of Albert Palace Mansions was questioned; and a call was sent round, asking the driver Reynolds to call at the Yard. He was there by twelve o'clock, but could throw no light on the mystery.

Reynolds was a respectable man without any record against him, and was a widower who lived over a garage near Dorset Square, Baker Street.

'A most amusing crime,' said Leon Gonsalez, his elbows on the breakfast table, his head between his hands.

'Why amusing?' asked George.

Leon read on, his lips moving, a trick of his, as he devoured every printed line. After a while he leaned back in his chair and rubbed his eyes.

'It is amusing,' he said, 'because of the hôtel bill that was found in the dead man's pocket.'

He put his finger on a paragraph and Manfred drew the paper towards him and read.

The police discovered in the right hand pocket of the murdered man's overcoat a bloodstained paper which proved to be an hôtel bill, issued by the Plage Hôtel, Ostend, five years ago. The bill was made out in the name of Mr and Mrs Wilbraham and was for 7,500 francs.

Manfred pushed the paper back.

'Isn't the mystery why this half-drunken man left his flat and went back to Green Park, some considerable distance from Albert Palace Mansions?' he asked.

Leon, who was staring blankly at the farther wall, shook his head slowly; and then, in his characteristic way, went off at a tangent.

'There's a lot to be said for the law which prohibited the publication of certain details in divorce cases,' he said, 'but I believe that the circumstances which surrounded the visit of Mr and Mrs Wilbraham to the Plage would have been given the fullest publicity if the case had come into court.'

'Do you suspect a murder of revenge?'

Leon shrugged his shoulders and changed the subject. George Manfred used to say that Leon had the most amazing pigeon-hole of a mind that it had been his fortune to meet with. Very seldom indeed did he have to consult the voluminous notes and data he had collected during his life, and which made one room in that little house uninhabitable.

There was a man at Scotland Yard, Inspector Meadows, who was on the friendliest terms with the Three. It was his practice to smoke a pipe, indeed many pipes, of evenings in the little Curzon Street house. He came that night, rather full of the Slane mystery.

'Slane was a pretty rapid sort,' he said. 'From the evidence that was found in his house, it is clear that he was the one man in London who ought not to be a bachelor if about two dozen women had their rights! By the way, we've traced Mr and Mrs Wilbraham. Wilbraham was of course Slane. The lady isn't so easy to find; one of his pick-ups, I suppose – '

'And yet the only girl he was willing to marry,' said Gonsalez.

'How did you know that?' asked the startled detective.

Leon chuckled.

'The bill was obviously sent to give the husband evidence. The husband, either because he was willing to give his wife another chance or because he was a Roman Catholic, did not divorce her. Now tell me – ' he leaned forward over the table and beamed on the detective – 'when the taxi drew up before the door of Albert Palace Mansions, did Slane immediately alight? – I can tell you he didn't.'

'You've been making inquiries,' said the other suspiciously. 'No, he waited there. The driver, being a tactful individual, thought it best to keep him inside until the people who were in the hall had gone up in the lift – which is visible from the door.'

'Exactly. Was it the driver's idea or Slane's'?

'The driver's,' said Meadows. 'Slane was half asleep when the man pulled him out.'

'One more question: when the elevator man took this party to the fifth floor, did he come down immediately?'

The Inspector shook his head.

'No, he stayed up there talking to the tenants. He heard Slane's door slam, and that was the first intimation he had that somebody had come in.'

Leon jerked back into his chair, a delighted smile on his face.

'What do you think, Raymond?' He addressed the saturnine Poiccart.

'What do you think?' said the other.

Meadows looked from Poiccart to Gonsalez.

'Have you any theory as to why Slane went out again?'

'He didn't go out again,' said the two men in unison.

Meadows caught George Manfred's smiling eyes.

'They're trying to mystify you. Meadows, but what they say is true. Obviously he didn't go out again.'

He rose and stretched himself.

'I'm going to bed; and I'd like to bet you fifty pounds that Leon finds the murderer tomorrow, though I won't swear that he will hand him over to Scotland Yard.'

At eight o'clock next morning, when, with a cigarette in his mouth, Reynolds, the taxi-driver, was making a final inspection of his cab before taking it out for the day, Leon Gonsalez walked into the mews.

Reynolds was a man of forty, a quiet, good-looking fellow. He had a soft voice and was courteous in a particularly pleasing way.

'You're not another detective, are you?' he asked, smiling ruefully. 'I've answered as many foolish questions as I care to answer.'

'Is this your own cab?' Leon nodded to the shining vehicle.

'Yes, that's mine,' said the driver. 'Cab-owning is not the gold mine some people think it is. And if you happen to get mixed up in a case like this, your takings fall fifty per cent.'

Very briefly Leon explained his position.

'The Triangle Agency – oh, yes, I remember: you're the Four Just Men, aren't you? Good Lord! Scotland Yard haven't put you on the job?'

'I'm on the job for my own amusement,' said Leon, giving smile for smile. 'There are one or two matters which weren't quite clear to me, and I wondered if you would mind telling me something that the police don't seem to know.'

The man hesitated, and then: 'Come up to my room,' he said, and led the way up the narrow stairs.

The room was surprisingly well furnished. There were one or two old pieces, Leon noticed, which must have been worth a lot of money. On a gate-legged table in the centre of the room was a suitcase and near the table a trunk. The driver must have noticed his eyes rest on these, for he said quickly: 'They belong to a customer of mine. I'm taking them to the station.'

From where he stood, Leon could see they were addressed to the Tetley cloak room to be called for; he made no comment on this, but his observation evidently disconcerted his host for his manner changed.

'Now, Mr Gonsalez, I'm a working man, so I'm afraid I can't give you very much time. What is it you want to know?'

'I particularly wish to know,' said Leon, 'whether the day you brought Slane to his house had been a very busy one for you?'

'It was fairly profitable,' said the other. 'I've already given the police an account of my fares, including the hospital case – but I suppose you know that.'

'Which hospital case was this?'

The man hesitated.

'I don't want you to think I'm boasting about doing a thing like that – it was just humanity. A woman was knocked down by a bus in Baker Street: I picked her up and took her to the hospital.'

'Was she badly hurt?'

'She died.' His voice was curt.

Leon looked at him thoughtfully. Again his eyes roved to the trunk.

'Thank you,' he said. 'Will you come to Curzon Street tonight at nine o'clock? Here's my address.' He took a card from his pocket.

'Why?' There was a note of defiance in the voice.

'Because I want to ask you something that I think you'll be glad to answer,' said Leon.

His big car was waiting at the end of the mews, and he set it flying in the direction of the Walmer Street hospital. He learnt there no more than he expected, and returned to Curzon Street, a very silent and uninformative man.

At nine o'clock that night came Reynolds, and for an hour he and Leon Gonsalez were closeted together in the little room downstairs. Happily, Meadows did not consider it necessary to call. It was not until a week afterwards that he came with a piece of information that surprised only himself.

'It was rather a rum thing – that driver who took Slane back to his flat has disappeared – sold his taxi and cleared out. There's nothing to associate him with the murder or I should get a warrant for him. He has been straightforward from the very first.'

Manfred politely agreed. Poiccart was staringly vacant. Leon Gonsalez yawned and was frankly bored with all mysteries.

* * *

'It's very curious,' said Gonsalez, when he condescended to tell the full story, 'that the police never troubled to investigate Slane's life at Tetley. He had a big house there for some years. If they had, they couldn't have failed to hear the story of young Doctor Grain and his beautiful wife, who ran away from him. She and Slane disappeared together; and of course he was passionately fond of her and was ready to marry her. But then, Slane was the type who was passionately fond of people for about three months, and unless the marriage could be arranged instantly the unfortunate girl had very little chance of becoming his wife.

'The doctor offered to take his wife back, but she refused, and disappeared out of his life. He gave up the practice of medicine, came to London, invested his savings in a small garage, went broke, as all garage proprietors do unless they're backed with good capital, and having to decide whether he'd go back to the practice of medicine and pick up all that he'd lost in the years he'd been trying to forget his wife, he chose what to him was the less strenuous profession of cab-driver. I know another man who did exactly the same thing: I will tell you about him one of these days.

'He never saw his wife again, though he frequently saw Slane. Reynolds, or Grain, as I will call him, had shaved off his moustache and generally altered his appearance, and Slane never recognized him. It became an obsession of Grain's to follow his enemy about, to learn of his movements, his habits. The one habit he did discover, and which proved to be Slane's undoing, was his practice of dining at the Real Club in Pall Mall every Wednesday evening and of leaving the club at eleven-thirty on those occasions.

'He put his discovery to no use, nor did he expect he would, until the night of the murder. He was driving somewhere in the northwest district when he saw a woman knocked down by a bus and he himself nearly ran over the prostrate figure. Stopping his cab, he jumped down and, to his horror, as he picked her up, he found himself gazing into the emaciated face of his wife. He lifted her into the cab, drove full pelt to the nearest hospital. It was while they were in the waiting-room, before the house surgeon's arrival, that the dying woman told him, in a few broken, half-delirious words, the story of her downward progress . . . She was dead before they got her on to the operating table – mercifully, as it proved.

'I knew all this before I went to the hospital and found that some unknown person had decided that she should be buried at Tetley and had made the most lavish arrangements for her removal. I guessed it before I saw Grain's suitcase packed ready for that tragedy. He left the hospital, a man mad with hate. It was raining heavily. He crawled down Pall Mall, and luck was with him, for just as the porter came out to find an empty taxi, Grain pulled up before the door.

'On the pretext of a tyre burst he stopped in the Mall, forced open one of the gates that led to the park, and waited until no pedestrian was in sight before he dragged the half-drunken man into the gardens . . . He was sober enough before Grain finished his story. Grain swears that he gave him the chance of his life, but Slane pulled a gun on him, and he had to kill him in self-defence. That may or may not be true.

'He never lost his nerve. Reaching his cab without observation, he drove to Albert Palace Mansions, waited until the lift had risen, and then ran up the stairs. He had taken Slane's bunch of keys, and on the way had selected that which he knew would open the door. His first intention was to search the flat for everything that betrayed the man's association with his wife; but he heard the porter up above saying good night and, slamming the door, raced downstairs in time to be there when the man reached the ground floor.'

'We're not telling the police of this, of course?' said Manfred gravely.

Poiccart at the other end of the table burst into a loud guffaw.

'It's so good a story that the police would never believe it,' he said.

The Marked Cheque

The man who called at the little house in Curzon Street was in a rage, and anxious to say something that would hurt his late employer.

He had also a personal grievance against Mr Jens, the butler.

'Mr Storn took me on as a second footman, and it looked like being a good job, but I couldn't hit it off with the rest of the staff. But was it fair to chuck me out without a minute's warning because I happened to let drop a word in Arabic – ?'

'Arabic?' asked Leon Gonsalez in surprise. 'Do you speak Arabic?'

Tenley, the dismissed footman, grinned.

'About a dozen words: I was with the Army in Egypt after the war, and I picked up a few phrases. I was polishing the silver salver in the hall, and I happened to say "That's good" in Arabic; and I heard Mr Storn's voice behind me.

'"You clear out," he said, and before I knew what had happened, I was walking away from the house with a month's salary.'

Gonsalez nodded.

'Very interesting,' he said, 'but why have you come to us?'

He had asked the same question many times of inconsequential people who had come to the House of the Silver Triangle, with their trifling grievances.

'Because there's a mystery there,' said the man vaguely. Perhaps he had cooled down a little by now, and was feeling rather uncomfortable. 'Why was I fired for my Arabic? What's the meaning of the picture in Storn's private room – the men being hung?'

Leon sat upright. 'Men being hanged? What is that?'

'It's a photograph. You can't get it, because it's in the panelling and you have to open one of the panels. But I went in one day and he'd left the panel ajar . . . Three men hanging from a sort of gibbet an' a lot of Turks looking on. That's a funny thing for a gentleman to have in his house.'

Leon was silent for a while.

'I don't know that that is an offence. It is certainly odd. Is there anything I can do for you?'

Apparently nothing. The man left a little sheepishly, and Leon carried the news to his partner. He remembered afterwards that he had heard nothing of the grievance against the butler.

'The only thing I learnt about Storn is that he is extraordinarily mean, that he runs his house in Park Lane with a minimum number of staff, that he pays those the smallest wages possible. He is of Armenian origin and made his money out of oilfields which he acquired by very dubious means.

'As to the three hanged men, that is rather gruesome, but it might be worse. I have seen photographs in the house of the idle rich that would make your hair stand on end, my dear Poiccart. At any rate, the morbid interest of a millionaire in a Turkish execution is not extraordinary.'

'If I were an Armenian,' said Manfred, 'they would be my chief hobby; I should have a whole gallery of 'em!'

And there ended the matter of the morbid millionaire who lived meanly and underpaid his servants.

Early in April, Leon read in the newspaper that Mr Storn had gone to Egypt for a short holiday.

By every test, Ferdinand Storn was a desirable acquaintance. He was immensely rich; he was personally attractive in a dark, long-nosed way; and to such people as met him intimately – and they were few – he could talk Art and Finance with equal facility. So far as was known, he had no enemies. He lived at Burson House, Park Lane, a small, handsome residence which he had purchased from the owner, Lord Burson, for £150,000. He spent most of his time either there or at Felfry Park, his beautiful country house in Sussex. The Persian and Oriental Oil Trust, of which he was the head, had its offices in a magnificent building in Moorgate Street, and here he was usually to be found between ten o'clock in the morning and three o'clock in the afternoon.

This Trust, despite its titled board, was a one-man affair, and conducted, amongst other things, the business of bankers. Storn held most of the shares, and was popularly supposed to derive an income of something like a quarter of a million a year. He had few personal friends, and was a bachelor.

It was just short of a month after Leon had read the news that a big car drew up at the door of the Triangle, and a stout, prosperous-looking man got out and rang the bell. He was a stranger to Leon, who interviewed him, and was apparently loth to state his business, for he hummed and hawed and questioned until Leon, a little impatiently, asked him point-blank who he was and what was his object.

'Well, I'll tell you, Mr Gonsalez,' said the stout man. 'I am the General Manager of the Persian and Oriental Oil – '

'Storn's company?' asked Leon, his interest awakened.

'Storn's company. I suppose I really ought to go to the police with my suspicions, but a friend of mine has such faith in you and what he calls the Three Just Men, that I thought I had better see you first.'

'Is it about Mr Storn?' asked Leon.

The gentleman, who proved to be Mr Hubert Grey, the Managing Director of the Trust, nodded.

'You see, Mr Gonsalez, I am in rather a peculiar position. Mr Storn is a very difficult man, and I should lose my job if I made him look ridiculous.'

'He's abroad, isn't he?' asked Leon.

'He's abroad,' agreed the other soberly. 'He went abroad, as a matter of fact, quite unexpectedly; that is to say, it was unexpected by the office. In fact he had an important Board meeting the day he left, which he should have attended, but on that morning I got a letter from him saying that he had to go to Egypt on a matter which affected his personal honour. He asked me not to communicate with him, or even to announce the fact that he had left London. Unfortunately, one of my clerks very foolishly told a reporter who had called that day that Mr Storn had left.

'A week after he had gone, he sent us a letter from an hôtel in Rome, enclosing a cheque for eighty-three thousand pounds, and arranging that this cheque should be honoured when a gentleman called, which he did the next day.'

'An Englishman?' asked Leon.

Mr Grey shook his head. 'No, he was a foreigner of some kind; a rather dark-looking man. The money was paid over to him.

'A few days later we had another letter from Mr Storn, written from the Hôtel de Russie, Rome. This letter told us that a further cheque had been sent to Mr Kraman, which was to be honoured. This was for one hundred and seven thousand pounds and a few odd shillings. He gave us instructions as to how the money was to be paid, and asked us to telegraph to him at an hôtel in Alexandria the moment the cheque was honoured. This I did. The very next day there came a second letter written from the Hôtel Mediterraneo in Naples – I will let you have copies of all these – telling us that a third cheque was to be paid without fail, but to a different man, a Mr

Rezzio, who would call at the office. This was for one hundred and twelve thousand pounds, which very nearly exhausted Mr Storn's cash balance, although of course he has large reserves at the bank. I might say that Mr Storn is a man who is rather eccentric in the matter of large deposit reserves. Very little of his money is locked up in shares. Look here – ' he took a note-case from his pocket and produced a cheque form – 'this money has been paid, but I've brought you along the cheque to see.'

Leon took it in his hand. It was written in characteristic writing, and he examined the signature.

'There is no question of this being a forgery?'

'None whatever,' said Grey emphatically. 'The letter, too, was in his own handwriting. But what puzzled me about the cheque were the queer marks on the back.'

They were indistinguishable to Leon until he took them to the window, and then saw a line of faint pencil marks which ran along the bottom of the cheque.

'I suppose I can't keep this cheque for a day or two?' asked Leon.

'Certainly. The signature, as you see, has been cancelled out, and the money has been paid.'

Leon examined the cheque again. It was drawn on the Ottoman Oil Bank, which was apparently a private concern of Storn's.

'What do you imagine has happened?' he asked.

'I don't know, but I'm worried.'

Grey's troubled frown showed the extent of that worry.

'I don't know why I should be, but I've got an uncomfortable feeling at the back of my mind that there is a swindle somewhere.'

'Have you cabled to Alexandria?'

Mr Grey smiled. 'Naturally; and I have had a reply. It struck me that you might have agents in Egypt, in which case it might be a simple matter for you to discover whether there is anything wrong. The main point is that I don't wish Mr Storn to know that I've been making inquiries. I'll pay any reasonable expenditure you incur, and I'm quite sure that Mr Storn will agree that I have done the right thing.'

After the departure of his visitor, Leon interviewed Manfred.

'It may, of course, be a case of blackmail,' said George softly. 'But you will have to start at Storn's beginnings if you want to get under whatever mystery there is.'

'So I think,' said Gonsalez; and a few minutes afterwards went out of the house.

He did not return till midnight. He brought back an amazing amount of information about Mr Storn.

'About twelve years ago he was an operator in the service of the Turco Telegraph Company. He speaks eight Oriental languages, and was well-known in Istanbul. Does that tell you anything, George?'

Manfred shook his head.

'It tells me nothing yet, but I am waiting to be thrilled.'

'He was mixed up with the revolutionary crowd, the under-strappers who pulled the strings in the days of Abdul Ahmid, and there is no doubt that he got his Concession through these fellows.'

'What Concession?' asked Manfred.

'Oil land, large tracts of it. When the new Government came into power, the Concession was formed, though I suspect our friend paid heavily for the privilege. His five partners, however, were less fortunate. Three of them were accused of treason against the Government, and were hanged.'

'The photograph,' nodded Manfred. 'What happened to the other two?'

'The other two were Italians, and they were sent to prison in Asia Minor for the rest of their lives. When Storn came to London, it was as sole proprietor of the Concession, which he floated with a profit of three million pounds.'

The next morning Leon left the house early, and at ten o'clock was ringing the bell at Burson House.

The heavy-jowled butler who opened the door regarded him with suspicion, but was otherwise deferential.

'Mr Storn is abroad, and won't be back for some weeks, sir.'

'May I see Mr Storn's secretary?' asked Leon in his blandest manner.

'Mr Storn never has a secretary at his house; you will find the young lady at the offices of the Persian Oil Trust.'

Leon felt in his pocket and produced a card.

'I am one of the Bursons,' he said, 'and as a matter of fact my father was born here. Some months ago when I was in London I asked Mr Storn if he would give me permission to look over the house.'

The card contained a scribbled line, signed 'Ferdinand Storn', giving permission to the bearer to see the house at any hour 'when I am out of town.' It had taken Leon the greater part of an hour to forge that permit.

'I am afraid I cannot let you in, sir,' said the butler, barring the passage. 'Mr Storn told me before he went that I was to admit no strangers.'

'What is today?' asked Leon suddenly.

'Thursday, sir,' said the man.

Leon nodded. 'Cheese day,' he said.

Only for the fraction of a second was the man confused.

'I don't know what you mean, sir,' he said gruffly, and almost shut the door in the face of the caller.

Gonsalez made a circuit of the house. It stood with another upon an island site.

When he had finished, he went home, an amused and almost excited man, to give instructions to Raymond Poiccart who, amongst his other qualifications, had a very wide circle of criminal friends. There was not a big gangster in London that he did not know. He was acquainted with the public house in London where the confidence men and the safe smashers met: he could at any moment gather the gossip of the prisons, and was probably better acquainted with the secret news of the underworld than any man at Scotland Yard. Him Leon sent on a news-gathering mission, and in a small public house off Lambeth Walk, Poiccart learned of the dark philanthropist who had found employment for at least three ex-convicts.

Leon was sitting alone when he returned, examining with a powerful lens the odd marks on the back of the cheque.

Before Poiccart could retail his news, Leon reached for a telephone directory.

'Grey, of course, has left his office, but unless I am mistaken this is his private address,' he said, as his fingers stopped on one of the pages. A maid answered his call. Yes, Mr Grey was at home. Presently the Managing Director's voice came through.

'Mr Grey – who would handle the cheques which you have received from Storn; I mean who is the official?'

'The accountant,' was the reply.

'Who gave the accountant his job – you?'

A pause.

'No – Mr Storn. He used to be in the Eastern Telegraph Company – Mr Storn met him abroad.'

'And where is the accountant to be found?' asked Leon eagerly.

'He's on his holidays. He left before the last cheque came. But I can get him.'

Leon's laugh was one of sheer delight.

'You needn't worry – I knew he wasn't at the office,' he said, and hung up on the astonished manager.

'Now, my dear Poiccart, what did you find?'

He listened intently till his friend had finished, and then: 'Let us go to Park Lane – and bring a gun with you,' he said. 'We will call at Scotland Yard en route.'

It was ten o'clock when the butler opened the door. Before he could frame a question, a big detective gripped him and pulled him into the street.

The four plain-clothes officers who accompanied Leon flocked into the hall. A surly-faced footman was arrested before he could shout a warning. At the very top of the house, in a small windowless apartment that had once been used as a box-room, they found an emaciated man whom even his Managing Director, hastily summoned to the scene, failed to identify as the millionaire. The two Italians who kept guard on him and watched him through a hole broken through the wall from an adjoining room gave no trouble.

One of them, he who had carefully planted Burson House full of ex-convict servants, was very explicit.

'This man betrayed us, and we should have hanged like Hatim Effendi and Al Shiri and Maropulos the Greek, only we bribed witnesses,' he said. 'We were partners in the oilfields, and to rob us he manufactured evidence that we were conspiring against the Government. My friend and I broke prison and came back to London. I was determined he should pay us the money he owed us, and I knew that we could never get it from a Court of Law.'

*   *   *

'It was a very simple matter, and I really am ashamed of myself that I did not understand those marks at the back of the cheque at first glance,' explained Leon over the supper-table that night. 'Our Italian friend was one of the crowd that got the Concession: he had lived for years in London, and possibly it will be proved that he had criminal associates. At any rate, he had no difficulty in collecting a houseful of servants, playing as he did on his knowledge of Storn's character. All these men offered to serve Storn for sums at which the average servant would have turned up his nose. It has taken the better part of a year to fill our friend's establishment with these ex-convicts. You remember that the footman who came to us a few months ago said that he had been employed, not by the butler but by Storn himself. They would have taken the first opportunity of getting rid of him, only inadvertently he used an Arabic expression, and Storn, who was suspicious of spies and probably expected the men whom he had betrayed to return, sent him packing.

'On the day Storn was supposed to leave for Egypt, he was seized by the two Italians, locked up in a room and compelled to write such letters and sign such cheques as they dictated. But he remembered, rather late in the day, that the accountant was an old telegraphist, and so he put on the back of the cheque, in pencil marks, a Morse message in the old symbols which were employed when the needle machine was most commonly used.'

He produced the cheque and laid it on the table, running his finger along the pencil mark:

SOSPRSNRPRKLN

'In other words, "Prisoner in Park Lane". The accountant was on his holiday, so he did not read the message.'

Manfred took up the cheque, turned it and examined it.

'What handsome fee will this millionaire send you?' he asked ironically.

The answer did not come till a few days after the Old Bailey trial. It took the form of a cheque – for five guineas.

'Game to the last!' murmured Leon admiringly.

Mr Levingrou's Daughter

Mr Levingrou took his long cigar from his mouth and shook his head sorrowfully. He was a fat man, thick-necked and heavy-cheeked, and he could not afford to spoil a good cigar.

'That is awful . . . that is brutal! Tch! It makes me seek . . . poor José!'

His companion snorted in sympathy.

For José Silva had fallen. An unemotional judge, who spoke rather precociously, had told José that certain crimes were very heinous in the eyes of the law. For example, women were held in special esteem, and to trade on their follies was regarded as being so dreadful that nothing but a very long term of imprisonment could vindicate the law's outraged majesty.

And José had offended beyond forgiveness. He ran the Latin-American Artists Agency to give young and pretty aspirants to the stage a quick and profitable engagement on South American stages. They went away full of joy and they never came back. Letters came from them to their relations, very correctly worded, nicely spelt. They were, they said, happy. They all wrote the same in almost identical language. You might imagine that they wrote to dictation, as indeed they did.

But the vice squad had got on José's tail. A pretty girl applied for a job and went to Buenos Aires, accompanied by her father and brother – they were both Scotland Yard men, and when they learnt all that they had to learn they came back with the girl, a rather shrewd detective herself, and José was arrested. And then they learnt more things about him, and the prison sentence was inevitable.

Nobody arrested Jules Levingrou and haled him from his beautiful little bijou house in Knightsbridge and sent him to a cold bleak prison. And nobody arrested Heinrich Luss, who was his partner. They had financed José and many other Josés, but they were clever.

'José was careless,' sighed Jules as he sucked at his cigar.

Heinrich sighed, too. He was as fat as, but looked fatter than, his companion, because he was a shorter man.

Jules looked round the pretty saloon with its cream and gold decorations, and presently his eyes stopped roving and fixed on a framed photograph that was on the mantelpiece. His big face creased in a smile as he rose with a grunt and, waddling across to the fireplace, took the frame in his hand. The picture was of an extremely pretty girl.

'You see?'

Heinrich took the picture and mumbled ecstatic praise.

'Not goot enough,' he said.

Mr Levingrou agreed. He had never yet seen a picture that quite did justice to the delicate beauty of this only daughter of his. He was a widower; his wife had died when Valerie was a baby. She would never know how many hearts were broken, how many souls destroyed, that she might be brought up in the luxury which surrounded her. This aspect of her upbringing never occurred to Mr Levingrou. He prided himself that he had no sentiment.

He was part proprietor of twenty-three cabarets and dance halls scattered up and down the Argentine and Brazil, and drew large profits from what he regarded as a perfectly legitimate business.

He put down the photograph and came back to the deep armchair.

'It is unfortunate about José; but these men come and go. This new man may or may not be good.'

'What is his name?' asked Heinrich.

Jules searched breathlessly in his pockets, found a letter and opened it, his thick fingers glittering in the light from the crystal chandelier, for he was a lover of rings.

'Leon Gonsalez – *herr Gott!*'

Heinrich was sitting upright in his chair, white as a sheet.

'Name of a pipe! What is the matter with you, Heinrich?'

'Leon Gonsalez!' repeated the other huskily. 'You think he is an applicant for the post . . . you do not know him?'

Jules shook his huge head.

'Why in God's name should I know him – he is a Spaniard, that is good enough for me. This is always the way, Heinrich. No sooner does one of our men make a fool of himself and get caught than another arises. Tomorrow I shall have twenty, thirty, fifty applicants – not to me but through the usual channel.'

Heinrich was looking at him hollow-eyed, and now in his agitation he spoke in German – that brand of German which is heard more frequently in Poland.

'Let me see the letter.' He took it in his hand and read it carefully.

'He asks for an appointment, that is all.'

'Have you ever heard of the Four Just Men?'

Jules frowned.

'They are dead, eh? I read something years ago.'

'They are alive,' said the other grimly, 'pardoned by the English Government. They have a bureau in Curzon Street.'

Rapidly he sketched the history of that strange organization which for years had terrorized the evil-doers who by their natural cunning had evaded the just processes of the law; and, as he spoke, the face of Jules Levingrou lengthened.

'But that – is preposterous!' he spluttered at last. 'How could these men know of me and of you . . . Besides, they dare not.'

Before Heinrich could reply there was a gentle knock at the door and a footman came in. There was a card on the salver he carried in his hand. Jules took it, adjusted his glasses and read, meditated a second, and then: 'Show him up,' he said.

'Leon Gonsalez,' almost whispered Heinrich as the door closed on the servant. 'Do you see a little silver triangle at the corner of the card? That is on the door of their house. It is he!'

'Pshaw!' scoffed his companion. 'He has come – why? To offer his services. You shall see!'

Leon Gonsalez, grey-haired and dapper, swung into the room, his keen, ascetic face tense, his fine eyes alive. A ready smiler was Leon. He was smiling now as he looked from one man to the other.

'You!' he said, and pointed to Jules.

Monsieur Levingrou started. There was almost an accusation in that finger thrust.

'You wish to see me?' He tried to recover some of his lost dignity.

'I did,' said Leon calmly. 'It is my misfortune that I have never seen you before. My friend Manfred, of whom you have heard, knows you very well by sight, and my very dear comrade Poiccart is so well acquainted with you that he could draw you feature by feature – and indeed did upon the table-cloth at dinner last night, much to the annoyance of our thrifty housekeeper!'

Levingrou was on his guard; there was something of the cold devil in those smiling eyes.

'To what am I indebted – ' he began.

'I come in a perfectly friendly spirit,' Leon's smile broadened, his eyes were twinkling, as with suppressed laughter. 'You will forgive that lie, Monsieur Levingrou, for lie it is. I have come to warn you that your wicked little business must be destroyed, or you will be made very unhappy. The police do not know of the Café Espagnol and its peculiar attractions.'

He dived into his overcoat pocket and, with the quick, jerky motion which was characteristic of him, produced a sheet of notepaper and unfolded it.

'I have here a list of thirty-two girls who have gone to one or another of your establishments during the past two years,' he said. 'You may read it' – and thrust the paper into Jules's hand – 'for I have a copy. You will be interested to know that that sheet of paper represents six months' inquiries.'

Jules did not so much as read a name. Instead, he shrugged, pushed the paper back to his visitor and, when Leon did not take it, dropped it on the floor.

'I am entirely in the dark,' he said. 'If you have no business with me you had better go – goodnight.'

'My friend' – Leon's voice was a little lower, and those eyes of his were piercing the very soul of the man who squatted like an ill-shaped toad in the luxurious deeps of silk and down – 'you will send cables to your managers, ordering the release of those girls, the payment of adequate compensation, and first-class return ticket to London.'

Levingrou shrugged.

'I really don't know what you mean, my friend. It seems to me you've come upon a cock and bull story, that you have been deceived.'

M. Jules Levingrou reached out deliberately and pressed an ivory bell-push.

'I think you are mad, therefore I will take a very charitable view of what you say. Now, my friend, we have no more time to give to you.'

But Leon Gonsalez was unperturbed.

'I can only imagine that you have no imagination. Monsieur Levingrou,' he said, a little curtly. 'That you do not realize the torture, the sorrow, the ghastly degradation into which you throw these sisters of ours.'

A gentle tap at the door and the footman entered. Mr Levingrou indicated his visitor with a wave of his hand.

'Show this gentleman to the door.'

If he expected an outburst he was pleasantly disappointed. Leon looked from one man to the other, that mocking smile of his still playing about the corners of his sensitive mouth then, without a word, turned, and the door closed on him.

'You heard – you heard?' Heinrich's voice was quivering with terror, his face the colour of dirty chalk. '*Herr Gott!* you don't understand, Jules! I know of these men. A friend of mine . . . '

He told a story that would have impressed most men; but Levingrou smiled.

'You are scared, my poor friend. You have not my experience of threats. Let him prove what he can and go to the police.'

'You fool!' Heinrich almost howled the words. 'The police! Do I not tell you they want no proof? They punished – '

'Hush!' growled Jules.

He had heard the girl's step in the hall. She was going to the theatre, she said – her explanation stopped short at the sight of Heinrich's white face.

'Daddy,' she said reproachfully, 'you've been quarrelling with Uncle Heinrich.'

She stooped and kissed the forehead of her father and pulled his ear gently. The stout man imprisoned her in both his arms and chuckled.

'No quarrel, my darling. Heinrich is scared of a business deal. You wouldn't imagine he could be such a baby.'

A minute later she stood in front of the fireplace, using a lipstick skilfully. She paused in the operation to tell him an item of news.

'I met such a nice man today, Daddy, at Lady Athery's, a Mr Gordon – do you know him?'

'I know many Mr Gordons,' smiled Jules. And then, in sudden alarm: 'He didn't make love to you, did he?'

She laughed at this.

'My dear, he's almost as old as you. And he's a great artist and very amusing.'

Jules walked with her to the door and saw her go down the steps, cross the little flagged garden, and stood there until her Rolls had passed out of sight. Then he came back to his pretty saloon to argue out this matter of the Four Just Men.

It was a gay party of young people about her own age that Valerie joined. The box was crowded, and was hot and thick, for the theatre was one where smoking was allowed. She was relieved when an attendant tapped her on the shoulder and beckoned her out.

'A gentleman to see you, miss.'

'To see me?' she said in wonder, and came into the vestibule to find a handsome, middle-aged man in evening dress.

'Mr Gordon!' she exclaimed. 'I had no idea you were here!'

He seemed unusually grave.

'I have some rather bad news for you, Miss Levingrou,' he said, and she went pale.

'Not about Father?'

'In a sense it is. I am afraid that he is in rather bad trouble.'

She frowned at this.

'Trouble? What kind of trouble?'

'I can't explain here. Will you come with me to the police station?'

She stared at him incredulously, her mouth open.

'The police station?'

Gordon summoned a waiting attendant.

'Get Miss Levingrou's coat from the box,' he said authoritatively.

A few minutes later they passed out of the theatre together and into a waiting car.

Twelve o'clock was striking when Mr Levingrou rose from his chair stiffly and stretched himself. Heinrich had been gone nearly three hours. He had, indeed, left the house in time to catch the last train for the Continent, whither he fled without even packing so much as a pocket-handkerchief. Unaware of this desertion, Mr Levingrou was on the point of mounting the stairs to bed when a thundering rat-tat shook the house. He turned to the footman.

'See who that is,' he growled, and waited curiously.

When the door was opened he saw the stocky figure of a police inspector.

'Levingrou?' asked the visitor.

Mr Levingrou came forward.

'That is my name,' he said.

The inspector strolled into the hall.

'I want you to come with me to the police station.' His manner was brusque, indeed rude, and Levingrou felt for the first time in his life a qualm of fear.

'The police station? Why?'

'I'll explain that to you when you get there.

'But this is monstrous!' exploded the stout man. I will telephone to my lawyers – '

'Are you going quietly?'

There was such a threat in the tone that Jules became instantly tractable.

'Very good, inspector, I will come. I think you have made a very great mistake and . . . '

He was hustled out of the hall, down the steps and into the waiting car.

It was not an ordinary taxi. The blinds were pulled down. More-over, he discovered as soon as he entered the interior that it was well occupied. Two men sat on seats facing him, the inspector took his place by the prisoner's side.

He could not see where the car was going. Five minutes, ten minutes passed . . . there should be a police station somewhere nearer than that. He put a question.

'I can relieve your mind,' said a calm voice. 'You're not going to a police station.'

'Then where am I being taken?'

'That you will discover,' was the unsatisfactory answer.

Nearly an hour passed before the car drew up before a dark house and the authoritative 'inspector' ordered him curtly to alight. The house had the appearance of being untenanted; the hall was littered with refuse and dust. They led him down a flight of stone stairs to the cellar, unlocked a steel door and pushed him inside.

He had hardly entered before an electric light in the wall glowed dimly, and he saw that he was in what looked to be a concrete chamber, furnished with a bed. At the farther end was a small open doorway, innocent of door, which he was informed led to a washing place. But the revelation which came to Mr Levingrou, and which struck terror to his soul, was the fact that the two men who had brought him were heavily masked – the inspector had disappeared and, try as he did, Jules could not remember what he looked like.

'You will stay here and keep quiet, and you need not be afraid that anybody will be alarmed by your disappearance.'

'But . . . my daughter!' stammered Levingrou in terror.

'Your daughter? Your daughter leaves for the Argentine with a Mr Gordon tomorrow morning – as other men's daughters have left.'

Levingrou stared, took one step forward and fell fainting to the floor.

*　　*　　*

Sixteen days passed; sixteen days of unadulterated hell for the shriek-ing, half-demented man who paced the length of his cell for hours on end till, exhausted, he dropped almost lifeless on his bed. And every morning came a masked man to tell him of plans that had been made, to describe in detail the establishment in Antofagasta which was to be the destination of Valerie Levingrou; of a certain piestro . . . they showed him his photograph . . . who was the master of that hell broth.

'You devils! You devils!' shrieked Levingrou, striking wildly out, but the other caught him and flung him back on the bed.

'You mustn't blame Gordon,' he mocked. 'He has his living to earn . . . he is merely the agent of the man who owns the cabaret.'

Then one morning, the eighteenth, they came and told him, three masked men, that Valerie had arrived and was being initiated into her duties as a dancing girl . . .

Jules Levingrou spent the night shivering in a corner of his cell. They came to him at three in the morning and pricked him with a hypodermic needle. When he woke, he thought he was dreaming, for he was sitting in his own saloon, where these masked men had carried him in the dead of night.

A footman came in, and dropped the tray at the sight of him.

'Good God, sir!' he gasped. 'Where did you come from?'

Levingrou could not speak: he could only shake his head.

'We thought you was in Germany, sir.'

And then, clearing his dry throat, Jules asked harshly: 'Is there any news . . . Miss Valerie . . . ?'

'Miss Valerie, sir?' The footman was astonished. 'Why, yes sir, she's upstairs asleep. She was a bit worried the night she came back and found you weren't here, and then of course she got your letter saying you'd been called abroad.'

The footman was staring at him, an uncomfortable wonder in his gaze. Something peculiar had happened. Jules rose unsteadily to his feet and caught a glance of his face in the mirror. His hair and his beard were white.

He staggered rather than walked to his writing-table, jerked open a drawer and took out an overseas cable form. 'Ring for a messenger.' His voice was hoarse and quavering. 'I want to send fourteen cable-grams to South America.'

The Share Pusher

The man whom Raymond Poiccart ushered into the presence of
Manfred was to all appearances a smart, military looking gentleman approaching the sixties. He was faultlessly dressed and had
the carriage and presence of a soldier. A retired general, thought
Manfred; but he saw something more than the outward personation
of manner revealed. This man was broken. There was a certain
imponderable expression in his face, a tense anguish which this, the
shrewdest of the Three Just Men, instantly interpreted.

'My name is Fole – Major-General Sir Charles Fole,' said the
visitor, as Poiccart placed a chair for him and discreetly withdrew.

'And you have come to see me about Mr Bonsor True,' said
Manfred instantly, and when the other started nervously he laughed.
'No, I am not being very clever,' said Manfred gently. 'So many
people have seen me about Mr Bonsor True. And I think I can
anticipate your story. You have been investing in one of his oil
concerns and you have lost a considerable sum of money. Was it oil?'

'Tin,' said the other. 'Inter-Nigerian Tin. You have heard about
my misfortune?'

Manfred shook his head.

'I have heard about the misfortunes of so many people who have
trusted Mr True. How much have you lost?'

The old man drew a long breath.

'Twenty-five thousand pounds,' he said, 'every penny I possess. I
have consulted the police, but they say there is nothing they can do.
The tin mine actually existed, and no misrepresentation was made by
True in any letter he sent to me.'

Manfred nodded.

Yours is a typical case, General,' he said. 'True never brings himself within the reach of the law. All his misrepresentations are made
over a luncheon table, when there is no other witness, and I presume
that in his letters to you he pointed out the speculative nature of your
investment and warned you that you were not putting your money
into gilt-edged securities.'

'It was at dinner,' said the General. 'I had some doubt on the matter and he asked me to dine with him at the Walkley Hôtel. He told me that immense quantities of tin were in sight, and that while he could not, in justice to his partners, broadcast the exact amount of profit the company would make, he assured me that my money would be doubled in six months. I wouldn't mind so much,' the old man went on, as he raised his trembling hand to his lips, 'but, Mr Manfred, I have a daughter, a brilliant young girl who has, in my opinion, a wonderful future. If she had been a man she would have been a strategist. I hoped to have left her amply provided for, but this means ruin – ruin! Can nothing be done to bring this criminal to justice?'

Manfred did not reply immediately.

'I wonder if you realize. General, that you are the twelfth person who has come to us in the past three months. Mr True is so well protected by the law and by his letters that it is almost impossible to catch him. There was a time' – he smiled faintly – 'when my friends and I would have taken the most dramatic steps to deal with the gentleman, and I think our method would have been effective; but now' – he shrugged his shoulders – 'we are a little restricted. Who introduced you to this gentleman?'

'Mrs Calford Creen. I met the lady at a dinner of a mutual friend, and she asked me to dine with her at her flat in Hanover Mansions.'

Manfred nodded again. He was not at all surprised by this intelligence.

'I am afraid I can promise you very little,' he said. 'The only thing I would ask is that you should keep in touch with me. Where are you living?'

His visitor was at the moment living in a little house near Truro. Manfred noted the address, and a few minutes later was standing by the window watching the weary old man walking slowly down Curzon Street.

Poiccart came in.

'I know nothing of this gentleman's business,' he said, 'but I have a feeling that it concerns our friend True. George, we ought to be able to catch that man. Leon was saying at breakfast this morning that there is a deep pond in the New Forest, where a man suitably anchored by chains and weights might lie without discovery for a hundred years. Personally, I am never in favour of drowning – '

George Manfred laughed.

' 'Ware the law, my good friend,' he said. 'There will be no killing, though a man who has systematically robbed the new poor deserves something with boiling lead in it.'

Nor could Leon Gonsalez offer any solution when he was consulted that afternoon.

'The curious thing is that True has no monies in this country. He runs two bank accounts and is generally overdrawn on both. I should not be surprised if he had a cache somewhere, in which case the matter would be simple – I've been watching him for the greater part of a year, and he never goes abroad, and I have searched his modest Westminster flat so often that I could go blindfolded to the place where he keeps his dress ties.'

* * *

All this had occurred in the previous year and no further complaints came about this fraudulent share pusher. The Three were no nearer to a solution of their problem when came the rather remarkable disappearance of Margaret Lein.

Margaret Lein was not a very important person: she was by all social standards as unimportant a person as one would be likely to meet in a stroll through the West End of London. She occupied the position of maid to the Hon. Mrs Calford Creen, and she had gone out one evening to the chemist to buy a bottle of smelling salts for her mistress, and had never come back.

She was pretty; her age was nineteen; she had no friends in London, being – so she said – an orphan; and, so far as was known, she had no attachments in the accepted sense of the word. But, as the police pointed out, it was extremely unlikely that a rather pretty maid, well spoken and with charming manners, in addition to her physical perfections, could spend a year in London without having acquired something in the shape of a 'follower'.

Mrs Calford Creen, not satisfied with the police inquiries, had called the Three Just Men to her aid. It was a week after the disappearance of Margaret Lein that a well-known lawyer crossed the polished dancing floor of the Leiter Club to greet the man who sat aloof and alone at a very small table near the floor's edge.

'Why, Mr Gonsalez!' he beamed. 'This is the last place in the world I should have expected to find you! In Limehouse, yes, prowling in the haunts of the underworld, yes, but at Leiter's Club . . . Really, I have mistaken your character.'

Leon smiled faintly, poured a little more Rhine wine into his long-stemmed glass and sipped it.

'My dear Mr Thurles,' he drawled, 'this is my underworld. That fat gentleman puffing gallantly with that stout lady is Bill Sikes. It is true he does not break into houses nor carry a life-preserver, but he sells dud shares to thrifty and gullible widows, and has grown fat on the proceeds. Some day I shall take that gentleman and break his heart.'

The red-faced Thurles chuckled as he sat down by the other's side.

'That will be difficult. Mr Bonsor True is too rich a man to pull down, however much a blackguard he may be.'

Leon fixed a cigarette in a long amber tube and seemed wholly absorbed in the operation, which he performed with great care.

'Perhaps I oughtn't to have made that horrific threat,' he said. 'True is a friend of your client's, isn't he?'

'Mrs Creen?' Thurles was genuinely surprised. 'I wasn't aware of the fact.'

'I must have been mistaken,' said Leon, and changed the subject.

He knew right well that he was not mistaken. That stout share plugger had been the *tête-a-tête* guest of Mrs Creen on the night Margaret Lein had disappeared from human ken; and the curious circumstance was that neither to the police nor to the Triangle had Mrs Creen mentioned this interesting fact.

She lived in a modest flat near Hanover Court: a rather pretty, hard-faced young widow, whose source of income was believed to be a legacy left by her late husband. Leon, a very inquisitive man, had made the most careful inquiries without discovering either that she had had a husband or that he had died. All he knew of her was that she took frequent trips abroad, sometimes to out-of-the-way places like Roumania; that she was invariably accompanied by the missing Margaret; that she spent money, not freely but lavishly, gave magnificent entertainments in Paris, Rome, and once in Brussels, and seemed quite content to return from a life which must have cost her at least seven hundred and fifty pounds a week to the modest establishment near Hanover Court where her rent was seven hundred and fifty pounds per annum and her household bills did not exceed twenty pounds a week.

Leon watched the dancing for a little longer, beckoned a waiter and paid his bill. The lawyer had gone back to his party. He saw Mr Bonsor True, the centre of a gay table, and smiled to himself, and wondered whether the share plugger would be as cheerful if he knew that in the right hand inside pocket of Leon Gonsalez' coat was a copy of a marriage certificate that he had dug out that morning.

It had been an inspiration that had led Leon Gonsalez to Somerset House.

He glanced at his watch: late as the hour was, there was still a hope of finding Mrs Creen. His car was waiting in the park in Wellington Place, and ten minutes later he had stopped before the doors of Hanover Mansions. A lift carried him to the third floor. He pressed the bell of No 109. A light showed in the fanlight, and it was Mrs Creen herself who opened the door to him. Evidently she expected somebody else, for she was momentarily taken back.

'Oh, Mr Gonsalez!' And then, quickly: 'Have you had news of Margaret?'

'I am not quite sure whether I have or not,' said Leon. 'May I see you for a few minutes?'

Something in his tone must have warned her.

'It's rather late, isn't it?'

'It will save me a journey in the morning,' he almost pleaded and with some reluctance she admitted him.

It was not the first visit he had paid to her flat, and he had duly noted that, although her method of living was fairly humble, the flat itself was furnished regardless of expense.

She offered him a whisky and soda, which he accepted but did not drink.

'I want to ask you,' he said, when she had settled down, 'how long you have had Margaret in your employ?'

'Over a year,' she replied.

'A nice girl?'

'Very. But I told you about her. It has been a great shock to me.'

'Would you call her accomplished? Did she speak any foreign languages?'

Mrs Creen nodded.

'French and German perfectly – that was why she was such a treasure. She had been brought up with a family in Alsace, and was, I believe, half French.'

'Why did you send her out to the chemist for smelling salts?'

The woman moved impatiently.

'I have already told you, as I told the police, that I had a very bad headache, and Margaret herself suggested she should go to the chemist.'

'For no other reason? Couldn't Mr True have gone?'

She nearly jumped at this.

'Mr True? I don't know what you mean.'

'True was with you that night; you had been dining *tête-a-tête*. In fact, you were dining as one would expect a husband and wife to dine.'

The woman went white, was momentarily bereft of speech.

'I don't know why you're making such a mystery of your marriage, Mrs Creen, but I know that for five years past you have not only been married to True, but you have been his partner, in the sense that you have assisted him in his – er – financial operations. Now, Mrs True, I want you to put your cards on the table. When you went abroad you took this girl with you?'

She nodded dumbly.

'What was your object in going to Paris, Rome and Brussels? Had you any other object than to enjoy yourself? Was there any business reason for your move?'

He saw her lick her dry lips, but she did not reply.

'Let me put it more plainly. Have you in any of those cities a private safe at any of the banking corporations or safe deposits?'

She sprang to her feet, her mouth open in surprise.

'Who told you?' she asked quickly. 'What business is that of yours, anyway?'

As she spoke, came the gentle tinkle of a bell, and she half turned.

'Let me open it for you,' said Leon, and before she could move he was down the passage and had flung open the door.

An astonished financier was standing on the doormat. At the sight of Leon he gaped.

'Come inside, Mr True,' said Leon gently. 'I think I have some interesting news for you.'

'Who – who are you?' stammered the older man, peering at the visitor, and then of a sudden he recognized him. 'My God! One of the Four Just Men, eh? Well, have you found that girl?'

He realized at that moment that the question in itself was a blunder. He was not supposed to be interested in the missing maid.

'I haven't found her, and I think she's going to be rather difficult for any of us to find,' said Leon.

By this time Mrs Creen had recovered her self-possession.

'I'm awfully glad you came, Mr True. This gentleman has been making the most extraordinary statements about us. He is under the impression we are married. Did you ever hear anything so ridiculous?'

Leon did not attempt to refute the absurdity of his suggestion until they were back in the little drawing-room.

'Now, sir,' said Mr Bonsor True, his pompous self, 'whatever do you mean by making – '

Leon cut him short.

'I will tell you briefly what I have already told your wife,' he said; 'and as to your marriage, that is so indisputable a fact that I will not attempt to show you the marriage certificate which is in my pocket. I'm not here to reproach you, True, or this lady. The question of your treatment of the unfortunate people who have invested money with you is a matter for your own conscience. What I do wish to know is, whether it is a fact that in certain continental cities you have safes or deposits where you keep your wealth?'

The significance of the question was not lost upon the stout Mr True.

'There are certain deposits of mine on the Continent,' he said, 'but I don't quite understand – '

'Will you be perfectly frank with me, Mr True?' There was a hint of impatience in Leon's tone. 'Are there in Paris, Rome or Brussels safes of yours, and are you in the habit of carrying the keys of those safes?'

Mr Bonsor True smiled.

'No, sir; I have places of deposit, and they are in fact safes. But they have combinations – '

'Ah ha!' Leon's face lit. 'And do you by any chance carry the combination words in your pocket?'

For a second True hesitated, and then he took from his waistcoat pocket, fastened to a platinum chain, a small golden book about the size of a postage stamp.

'Yes, I carry them here – and why on earth I should be discussing my private business – '

'That's all I wanted to know.'

He stared at the visitor. Leon was laughing softly but heartily, rubbing his hands as at the best joke in the world.

'Now I think I understand,' he said. 'I also know why you sent Miss Margaret Lein to the chemist to get a little smelling salts. It was you they were for!' – his accusing finger pointed at the financier.

True's jaw dropped.

'That's true: I was taken suddenly ill.'

'Mr True fainted,' Mrs Creen broke in. 'I sent Margaret up to my room to get some smelling salts, but they weren't there. It was she who volunteered to buy them from the chemist.'

Leon wiped his eyes.

'That's a great joke,' he said; 'and now I can reconstruct the whole story. What time did you call on Mrs Creen that evening?'

True thought.

'About seven.'

'Are you in the habit of drinking cocktails, and are they usually waiting for you in the dining-room?'

'In the drawing-room,' corrected Mrs Creen.

'You took a cocktail,' Leon went on, 'and then you suddenly went out. In other words, somebody had doctored your drink with a knock-out drop. Mrs Creen was not, of course, in the room. When you fell, Margaret Lein examined your book and got the combination words she wanted. She had been abroad with Mrs Creen, so she knew this playful little method of yours of caching your ill-gotten gains.'

True's face went from livid red to ashy white.

'The combination word?' he said huskily. 'She got the combination word? Oh, my God!'

Without another word he flew from the room and they heard the front door thunder as he slammed it.

Leon went at greater leisure, but he arrived, in Curzon Street in time for supper.

'I'm not going to investigate any further,' he said, 'but it's any odds that those safes in Paris and Rome are empty by now, and that a very clever girl, who is certainly the daughter of one of Mr True's deluded clients, is now in a position to help her parents.'

'How do you know that she has parents?' asked Manfred.

'I don't know,' replied Leon frankly. 'But I am certain she had a father – I wired to General Fole last week to discover if his clever daughter was staying with him, and he wired back that 'Margaret had been abroad finishing her education for the past year'. And I suppose that acting as maid to the partner of a share crook is an education.

The Man Who Sang in Church

To Leon Gonsalez went most of the cases of blackmail which came the way of the Three Just Men.

And yet, from the views he had so consistently expressed, he was the last man in the world to whom such problems should have gone, for in that famous article of his entitled 'Justification', which put up the sales of a quarterly magazine by some thousand per cent, he offered the following opinion:

' . . . as to blackmail, I see no adequate punishment but death in the case of habitual offenders. You cannot parley with the type of criminal who specialises in this loathsome form of livelihood. Obviously there can be no side of him to which appeal can be made: no system of reformation can affect him. He is dehumanised, and may be classified with the secret poisoner, the drug pusher and . . . ' [he mentioned a trade as degrading]

Leon found less drastic means of dealing with these pests; yet we may suppose that the more violent means which distinguished the case of Miss Brown and the man who sang in church had his heartiest approval.

There are so many types of beauty that even Leon Gonsalez, who had a passion for classification, gave up at the eighteenth sub-division of the thirty-third category of brunettes. By which time he had filled two large quarto notebooks.

If he had not wearied of his task before he met Miss Brown, he would assuredly have recognized its hopelessness, for she fell into no category, nor had he her peculiar attractions catalogued in any of his sub-sections. She was dark and slim and elegant. Leon hated the word, but he was compelled to admit this characteristic. The impression she left was one of delicate fragrance. Leon called her the Lavender Girl. She called herself Brown, which was obviously not her name; also, in the matter of simulations, she wore a closely-fitting hat which came down over her eyes and would make subsequent identification extremely difficult.

She timed her visit for the half-light of dusk – the cigarette hour that follows a good dinner, when men are inclined rather to think than to talk, and to doze than either.

Others had come at this hour to the little house in Curzon Street, where the silver triangle on the door marked the habitation of the Three Just Men, and when the bell rang George Manfred looked up at the clock.

'See who it is, Raymond: and before you go, I will tell you. It is a young lady in black, rather graceful of carriage, very nervous and in bad trouble.'

Leon grinned as Poiccart rose heavily from his chair and went out.

'Clairvoyance rather than deduction,' he said, 'and observation rather than either: from where you sit you can see the street. Why mystify our dear friend?'

George Manfred sent a ring of smoke to the ceiling. 'He is not mystified,' he said lazily. 'He has seen her also. If you hadn't been so absorbed in your newspaper you would have seen her, too. She has passed up and down the street three times on the other side. And on each occasion she has glanced toward this door. She is rather typical, and I have been wondering exactly what variety of blackmail has been practised on her.'

Here Raymond Poiccart came back.

'She wishes to see one of you,' he said. 'Her name is Miss Brown – but she doesn't look like a Miss Brown!'

Manfred nodded to Leon. 'It had better be you,' he said.

Gonsalez went to the little front drawing-room, and found the girl standing with her back to the window, her face in shadow. 'I would rather you didn't put on the light, please,' she said, in a calm, steady voice. 'I don't want to be recognized if you meet me again.'

Leon smiled.

'I had no intention of touching the switch,' he said. 'You see, Miss – ' He waited expectantly.

'Brown,' she replied, so definitely that he would have known she desired anonymity even if she had not made her request in regard to the light. 'I told your friend my name.'

'You see, Miss Brown,' he went on, 'we have quite a number of callers who are particularly anxious not to be recognized when we meet them again. Will you sit down? I know that you have not much time, and that you are anxious to catch a train out of town.'

She was puzzled.

'How did you know that?' she asked.

Leon made one of his superb gestures.

'Otherwise you would have waited until it was quite dark before you made your appointment. You have, in point of fact, left it just as late as you could.'

She pulled a chair to the table and sat down slowly, turning her back to the window.

'Of course that is so,' she nodded. 'Yes, I have to leave in time, and I have cut it fine. Are you Mr Manfred?'

'Gonsalez,' he corrected her.

'I want your advice,' she said.

She spoke in an even, unemotional voice, her hands lightly clasped before her on the table. Even in the dark, and unfavourably placed as she was for observation, he could see that she was beautiful. He guessed from the maturity of her voice that she was in the region of twenty-four.

'I am being blackmailed. I suppose you will tell me I should go to the police, but I am afraid the police would be of no assistance, even if I were willing to risk an appearance in Court, which I am not. My father – ' she hesitated – 'is a Government official. It would break his heart if he knew. What a fool I've been!'

'Letters?' asked Leon, sympathetically.

'Letters and other things,' she said. 'About six years ago I was a medical student at St John's Hospital. I didn't take my final exam for reasons which you will understand. My surgical knowledge has not been of very much use to me, except . . . well, I once saved a man's life, though I doubt if it was worth saving. He seems to think it was, but that has nothing to do with the case. When I was at St John's I got to know a fellow-student, a man whose name will not interest you and, as girls of my age sometimes do, I fell desperately in love with him. I didn't know that he was married, although he told me this before our friendship reached a climax.

'For all that followed I was to blame. There were the usual letters – '

'And these are the basis of the blackmail?' asked Leon.

She nodded. 'I was worried ill about the . . . affair. I gave up my work and returned home; but that doesn't interest you, either.'

'Who is blackmailing you?' asked Leon.

She hesitated. 'The man. It's horrible isn't it? But he has gone down and down. I have money of my own – my mother left me two thousand pounds a year – and of course I've paid.'

'When did you see this man last?'

She was thinking of something else, and she did not answer him. As he repeated the question, she looked up quickly.

'Last Christmas Day – only for a moment. He wasn't staying with us – I mean it was at the end of . . . '

She had become suddenly panic-stricken, confused, and was almost breathless as she went on: 'I saw him by accident. Of course he didn't see me, but it was a great shock . . . It was his voice. He always had a wonderful tenor voice.'

'He was singing?' suggested Leon, when she paused, as he guessed, in an effort to recover her self-possession.

'Yes, in church,' she said desperately. 'That is where I saw him.'

She went on speaking with great rapidity, as though she were anxious not only to dismiss from her mind that chance encounter, but to make Leon also forget.

'It was two months after this that he wrote to me – he wrote to our old address in London. He said he was in desperate need of money, and wanted five hundred pounds. I'd already given him more than one thousand pounds, but I was sane enough to write and tell him I intended to do no more. It was then that he horrified me by sending a photograph of the letter – one of the letters – I had sent him. Mr Gonsalez, I have met another man, and . . . well, John had read the news of my engagement.'

'Your fiancé knows nothing about this earlier affair?'

She shook her head.

'No, nothing, and he mustn't know. Otherwise everything would be simple. Do you imagine I would allow myself to be blackmailed any further but for that?'

Leon took a slip of paper from one pocket and a pencil from another.

'Will you tell me the name of this man? John – ?'

'John Letheritt, 27, Lion Row, Whitechurch Street. It's a little room that he has rented, as an office, and a sleeping-place. I've already had inquiries made.'

Leon waited.

'What is the crisis – why have you come now?' he asked.

She took from her bag a letter, and he noted that it was in a clean envelope; evidently she had no intention that her real name and address should be known.

He read it, and found it a typical communication. The letter demanded £3,000 by the third of the month, failing which the writer intended putting 'papers' in 'certain hands'. There was just that little touch of melodrama which for some curious reason the average blackmailer adopts in his communiqués.

'I'll see what I can do – how am I to get in touch with you?' asked Leon. 'I presume that you don't wish that either your real name or your address should be known even to me.'

She did not answer until she had taken from her bag a number of banknotes, which she laid on the table.

Leon smiled. 'I think we'll discuss the question of payment when we have succeeded. What is it you want me to do?'

'I want you to get the letters and, if it is possible, I want you so to frighten this man that he won't trouble me again. As to the money, I shall feel so much happier if you will let me pay you now!'

'It is against the rules of the firm!' said Leon cheerfully.

She gave him a street and a number which he guessed was an accommodation address.

'Please don't see me to the door,' she said, with a half-glance at the watch on her wrist.

He waited till the door closed behind her, and then went upstairs to his companions.

'I know so much about this lady that I could write a monograph on the subject,' he said.

'Tell us a little,' suggested Manfred. But Leon shook his head.

That evening he called at Whitechurch Street. Lion Row was a tiny, miserable thoroughfare, more like an alley than anything, and hardly deserved its grand designation. In one of those ancient houses which must have seen the decline of Alsatia, at the top of three rickety flights of stairs, he found a door, on which had been recently painted: 'J. LETHERITT, EXPORTER'.

His knock produced no response.

He knocked again more heavily, and heard the creaking of a bed, and a harsh voice on the other side asking who was there. It took some time before he could persuade the man to open the door, and then Leon found himself in a very long, narrow room, lighted by a shadeless electric table-lamp. The furniture consisted of a bed, an old washstand and a dingy desk piled high with unopened circulars.

He guessed the man who confronted him, dressed in a soiled shirt and trousers, to be somewhere in the region of thirty-five; he certainly looked older. His face was unshaven and there was in the room an acrid stink of opium.

'What do you want?' growled John Letheritt, glaring suspiciously at the visitor.

With one glance Leon had taken in the man – a weakling, he guessed – one who had found and would always take the easiest way. The little pipe on the table by the bed was a direction post not to be mistaken.

Before he could answer, Letheritt went on: 'If you have come for letters you won't find them here, my friend.' He shook a trembling hand in Leon's face. 'You can go back to dear Gwenda and tell her that you are no more successful than the last gentleman she sent!'

'A blackmailer, eh? You are the dirtiest little blackmailer I ever met,' mused Leon. 'I suppose you know the young lady intends to prosecute you?'

'Let her prosecute. Let her get a warrant and have me pinched! It won't be the first time I've been inside! Maybe she can get a search warrant, then she'll be able to have her letters read in Court. I'm saving you a lot of trouble. I'll save Gwenda trouble, too! Engaged, eh? You're not the prospective bridegroom?' he sneered.

'If I were, I should be wringing your neck,' said Leon calmly. 'If you are a wise man – '

'I'm not wise,' snarled the other. 'Do you think I'd be living in this pigsty if I were? Me . . . a man with a medical degree?'

Then, with a sudden rage, he pushed his visitor towards the door. 'Get out and stay out!'

Leon was so surprised by this onslaught that he was listening to the door being locked and bolted against him before he had realized what had happened.

From the man's manner, he was certain that the letters were in that room – there were a dozen places where they might be hidden: he could have overcome the degenerate with the greatest ease, bound him to the bed and searched the room, but in these days the Three Just Men were very law-abiding people.

Instead he came back to his friends late that night with the story of his partial failure.

'If he left the house occasionally, it would be easy – but he never goes out. I even think that Raymond and I could, without the slightest trouble, make a very thorough search of the place. Letheritt has a bottle of milk left every morning, and it shouldn't be difficult to put him to sleep if we reached the house a little after the milkman.'

Manfred shook his head.

'You'll have to find another way; it's hardly worth while antagonizing the police,' he said.

'Which is putting it mildly,' murmured Poiccart. 'Who's the lady?'

Leon repeated almost word for word the conversation he had had with Miss Brown.

'There are certain remarkable facts in her statement, and I am pretty sure they were facts, and that she was not trying to deceive me,' he said. 'Curious item Number One is that the lady heard this man singing in church last Christmas Day. Is Mr Letheritt the kind of person one would expect to hear exercising his vocal organs on Christmas carols? My brief acquaintance with him leads me to suppose that he isn't. Curious item Number Two was the words: "He wasn't staying with us", or something of that sort; and he was "nearing the end" – of what? Those three items are really remarkable!'

'Not particularly remarkable to me,' growled Poiccart. 'He was obviously a member of a house-party somewhere, and she didn't know he was staying in the neighbourhood, until she saw him in church. It was near the end of his visit.'

Leon shook his head.

'Letheritt has been falling for years. He hasn't reached his present state since Christmas; therefore he must have been as bad – or nearly as bad – nine months ago. I really have taken a violent dislike to him, and I must get those letters.'

Manfred looked at him thoughtfully.

'They would hardly be at his bankers, because he wouldn't have a banker; or at his lawyers, because I should imagine that he is the kind of person whose acquaintance with law begins and ends in the Criminal Courts. I think you are right, Leon; the papers are in his room.'

Leon lost no time. Early the next morning he was in Whitechurch Street, and watched the milkman ascend to the garret where Letheritt had his foul habitation. He waited till the milkman had come out and disappeared but, sharp as he was, he was hardly quick enough. By the time he had reached the top floor, the milk had been taken in, and the little phial of colourless fluid which might have acted as a preservative to the milk was unused.

The next morning he tried again, and again he failed.

On the fourth night, between the hours of one and two, he managed to gain an entry into the house, and crept noiselessly up the stairs. The door was locked from the inside, but he could reach the end of the key with a pair of narrow pliers he carried.

There was no sound from within, when he snapped back the lock and turned the handle softly. He had forgotten the bolts.

The next day he came again, and surveyed the house from the outside. It was possible to reach the window of the room, but he would need a very long ladder, and after a brief consultation with Manfred, he decided against the method.

Manfred made a suggestion.

'Why not send him a wire, asking him to meet your Miss Brown at Liverpool Street Station? You know her Christian name?'

Leon sighed wearily.

'I tried that on the second day, my dear chap, and had little Lew Leveson on hand to "whizz" him the moment he came into the street in case he was carrying the letters on him.'

'By "whizz" you mean to pick his pocket? I can't keep track of modern thief slang,' said Manfred. 'In the days when I was actively interested, we used to call it "dip".'

'You are out of date, George; "whizz" is the word. But of course the beggar didn't come out. If he owed rent I could get the brokers put in; but he does not owe rent. He is breaking no laws, and is living a fairly blameless life – except, of course, one could catch him for being in possession of opium. But that wouldn't be much use, because the police are rather chary of allowing us to work with them.' He shook his head. 'I'm afraid I shall have to give Miss Brown a very bad report.'

It was not until a few days later that he actually wrote to the agreed address, having first discovered that it was, as he suspected, a small stationer's shop where letters could be called for.

A week later Superintendent Meadows, who was friendly with the Three, came down to consult Manfred on a matter of a forged Spanish passport, and since Manfred was an authority on passport forgeries and had a fund of stories about Spanish criminals, it was long after midnight when the conference broke up.

Leon, who needed exercise, walked to Regent Street with Meadows, and the conversation turned to Mr John Letheritt.

'Oh, yes, I know him well. I took him two years ago on a false pretence charge, and got him eighteen months at the London Assizes. A real bad egg, that fellow, and a bit of a squeaker, too. He's the man who put away Joe Benthall, the cleverest cat burglar we've had for a generation. Joe got ten years, and I shouldn't like to be this fellow when he comes out!'

Suddenly Leon asked a question about Letheritt's imprisonment, and when the other had answered, his companion stood stock-still in the middle of the deserted Hanover Square and doubled up with silent laughter.

'I don't see the joke.'

'But I do,' chuckled Leon. 'What a fool I've been! And I thought I understood the case!'

'Do you want Letheritt for anything? I know where he lives,' said Meadows.

Leon shook his head.

'No, I don't want him: but I should very much like to have ten minutes in his room!'

Meadows looked serious.

'He's blackmailing, eh? I wondered where he was getting his money from.'

But Leon did not enlighten him. He went back to Curzon Street and began searching certain works of reference, and followed this by an inspection of a large scale map of the Home Counties. He was the last to go to bed, and the first to waken, for he slept in the front of the house and heard the knocking at the door.

It was raining heavily as he pulled up the window and looked out; and in the dim light of dawn he thought he recognized Superintendent Meadows. A second later he was sure of his visitor's identity.

'Will you come down? I want to see you.'

Gonsalez slipped into his dressing-gown, ran downstairs and opened the door to the Superintendent.

'You remember we were talking about Letheritt last night?' said Meadows as Leon ushered him into the little waiting-room.

The superintendent's voice was distinctly unfriendly, and he was eyeing Leon keenly.

'Yes – I remember.'

'You didn't by any chance go out again last night?'

'No. Why?'

Again that look of suspicion.

'Only Letheritt was murdered at half past one this morning, and his room ransacked.'

Leon stared at him.

'Murdered? Have you got the murderer?' he asked at last.

'No, but we shall get him all right. He was seen coming down the rainpipe by a City policeman. Evidently he had got into Letheritt's room through the window, and it was this discovery by the constable which led to a search of the house. The City Police had to break in the door, and they found Letheritt dead on the bed. He had evidently been hit on the head with a jemmy, and ordinarily that injury would not have killed him, according to the police doctor; but in his state of health it was quite enough to put him out. A policeman went round the house to intercept the burglar, but somehow he must have escaped into one of the little alleys that abound in this part of the city, and he was next seen by a constable in Fleet Street, driving a small car, the number-plate of which had been covered with mud.'

'Was the man recognized?'

'He hasn't been – yet. What he did was to leave three fingerprints on the window, and as he was obviously an old hand at the game, that is as good as a direct identification. The City Detective Force called us in, but we haven't been able to help them except to give them particulars of Letheritt's past life. Incidentally, I supplied them with a copy of your fingerprints. I hope you don't mind.'

Leon grinned.

'Delighted!' he said.

After the officer had left, Leon went upstairs to give the news to his two friends.

But the most startling intelligence was to come when they were sitting at breakfast. Meadows arrived. They saw his car draw up and Poiccart went out to open the door to him. He strode into the little room, his eyes bulging with excitement.

'Here's a mystery which even you fellows will never be able to solve,' he said. 'Do you know that this is a day of great tragedy for Scotland Yard and for the identification system? It means the destruction of a method that has been laboriously built up . . . '

'What are you talking about?' asked Manfred quickly.

'The fingerprint system,' said Meadows, and Poiccart, to whom the fingerprint method was something God-like, gaped at him. 'We've found a duplicate,' said Meadows. 'The prints on the glass were undoubtedly the prints of Joe Benthall – and Joe Benthall is in Wilford County Gaol serving the first part of a ten years' sentence!'

Something made Manfred turn his head toward his friend. Leon's eyes were blazing, his thin face wreathed in one joyous smile.

'The man who sang in church!' he said softly. 'This is the prettiest case that I have ever dealt with. Now sit down, my dear Meadows, and eat! No, no: sit down. I want to hear about Benthall – is it possible for me to see him?'

Meadows stared at him.

'What use would that be? I tell you this is the biggest blow we've ever had. And what is more, when we showed the City policeman a photograph of Benthall, he recognized him as the man he had seen coming down the rainpipe! I thought Benthall had escaped, and phoned the prison. But he's there all right.'

'Can I see Benthall?'

Meadows hesitated.

'Yes – I think it could be managed. The Home Office is rather friendly with you, isn't it?'

Friendly enough, apparently. By noon, Leon Gonsalez was on his way to Wilford Prison and, to his satisfaction, he went alone.

Wilford Gaol is one of the smaller convict establishments, and was brought into use to house long-time convicts of good character who were acquainted with the bookbinding and printing trade. There are several 'trade' prisons in England – Maidstone is the 'printing' prison, Shepton Mallet the 'dyeing' prison – where prisoners may exercise their trades.

The chief warder, whom Leon interviewed, told him that Wilford was to be closed soon, and its inmates transferred to Maidstone. He spoke regretfully of this change.

'We've got a good lot of men here – they give us no trouble, and they have an easy time. We've had no cases of indiscipline for years. We only have one officer on night-duty – that will give you an idea how quiet we are.'

'Who was the officer last night?' asked Leon, and the unexpectedness of the question took the chief warder by surprise.

'Mr Bennett,' he said, 'he's gone sick today by the way – a bilious attack. Curious thing you should ask the question: I've just been to see him. We had an inquiry about the man you've come to visit. Poor old Bennett is in bed with a terrible headache.'

'Can I see the Governor?' asked Leon.

The chief warder shook his head.

'He's gone to Dover with Miss Folian – his daughter. She's gone off to the Continent.'

'Miss Gwenda Folian?' and when the chief warder nodded: 'Is she the lady who was training to be a doctor?'

'She is a doctor,' said the other emphatically. 'Why, when Benthall nearly died from a heart attack, she saved his life – he works in the Governor's house, and I believe he'd cut off his right hand to serve the young lady. There's a lot of good in some of these fellows!'

They were standing in the main prison hall. Leon gazed along the grim vista of steel balconies and little doors.

'This is where the night-warder sits, I suppose?' he asked, as he laid his hand on the high desk near where they were standing: 'and the door leads – ?'

'To the Governor's quarters.'

'And Miss Gwenda often slips through there with a cup of coffee and a sandwich for the night man, I suppose?' he added carelessly.

The chief warder was evasive.

'It would be against regulations if she did,' he said. 'Now you want to see Benthall?'

Leon shook his head.

'I don't think so,' he said quietly.

*   *   *

'Where could a blackguard like Letheritt be singing in church on Christmas Day?' asked Leon when he was giving the intimate history of the case to his companions. 'In only one place – a prison. Obviously our Miss Brown was in that prison: the Governor and his family invariably attend church. Letheritt was "not staying" – it was the end of his sentence, and he had been sent to Wilford for discharge. Poor Meadows! With all his faith in fingerprints gone astray because a released convict was true to his word and went out to get the letters that I missed, whilst the doped Mr Bennett slept at his desk and Miss Gwenda Folian took his place!'

The Lady From Brazil

The journey had begun in a storm of rain and had continued in mist. There was a bumpiness over the land which was rather trying to airsick passengers. The pilot struck the Channel and dropped to less than two hundred feet.

Then came the steward with news that he bawled above the thunder of engines. 'We're landin' at Lympne . . . thick fog in London . . . coaches will take you to London . . . '

Manfred leaned forward to the lady who was sitting on the other side of the narrow gangway.

'Fortunate for you,' he said, tuning his voice so that it reached no other ear.

The Honourable Mrs Peversey raised her glasses and surveyed him cold-bloodedly.

'I beg your pardon?'

They made a perfect landing soon after, and as Manfred descended the steps leading from the Paris plane he offered his hand to assist the charming lady to alight.

'You were saying – ?'

The slim, pretty woman regarded him with cold and open-eyed insolence.

'I was saying that it was rather fortunate for you that we landed here,' said Manfred. 'Your name is Kathleen Zieling, but you are known better as "Claro" May, and there are two detectives waiting for you in London to question you on the matter of a pearl necklace that was lost in London three months ago. I happen to understand French very well and I heard two gentlemen of the Sureté discussing your future just before we left Le Bourget.'

The stare was no longer insolent, but it was not concerned. Apparently her scrutiny of the man who offered such alarming information satisfied her in the matter of his sincerity.

'Thank you,' she said easily, 'but I am not at all worried. Fenniker and Edmonds are the two men. I'll wire them to meet me at my hôtel. You don't look like a "bull" but I suppose you are?'

'Not exactly,' smiled Manfred.

She looked at him oddly. 'You certainly look too honest for a copper. I'm OK, but thank you all the same.'

This was a dismissal, but Manfred stood his ground.

'If you get into any kind of trouble I'd be glad if you'd call me up.' He handed the woman a card, at which she did not even glance. 'And if you wonder why I am interested, I only want to tell you that a year ago a very dear friend of mine would have been killed by the Fouret gang which caught him unprepared on Montmartre, only you very kindly helped him.'

Now, with a start of surprise, she read the card and, reading, changed colour. 'Oh!' she said awkwardly. 'I didn't know that you were one of that bunch – Four Just Men? You folks give me the creeps! Leon something – a dago name . . . '

'Gonsalez,' suggested Manfred, and she nodded.

That's right!'

She was looking at him now with a new interest.

'Honest there's no trouble coming about the pearls. And as to your friend, he saved me. He wouldn't have got into the gang fight, only he came out of the cabaret to help me.'

'Where are you staying in London?'

She told him her address, and at that moment came a Customs officer to break the conversation. Manfred did not see her again – she was not in the closed coach that carried him to London.

In truth he had no great wish to meet her again. Curiosity and a desire to assist one who had given great help to Leon Gonsalez – it was the occasion of Leon's spectacular unravelling of the Lyons forgeries – were behind his action.

Manfred neither sympathized with nor detested criminals. He knew May to be an international swindler on the grand scale, and was fairly well satisfied that she would be well looked after by the English police.

It was on the journey to London that he regretted that he had not asked her for information about Garry, though in all probability they had never met.

George Manfred, by common understanding the leading spirit of the Four Just Men, had in the course of his life removed three-and-twenty social excrescences from all human activities.

The war brought him and his companions a pardon for offences known and offences suspected. But in return the pardoning authorities had exacted from him a promise that he should keep the law in letter and in spirit, and this he had made, not only on his own behalf but on behalf of his companions. Only once did he express regret for having made this covenant, and that was when Garry Lexfield came under his observation.

Garry lived on the outer edge of the law. He was a man of thirty, tall, frank of face, rather good-looking. Women found him fascinating, to their cost, for he was of the ruthless kind; quite nice people invited him to their homes – he even reached the board of a well-known West End Company.

Manfred's first encounter with Garry was over a stupidly insignificant matter. Mr Lexfield was engaged in an argument at the corner of Curzon Street, where he had his flat. Manfred, returning late, saw a man and a woman talking, the man violently, the woman a little timidly. He passed them, thinking that it was one of those quarrels in which wise men are not interested, and then he heard the sound of a blow and a faint scream. He turned to see the woman crouching by the area railings of the house. Quickly he came back.

'Did you hit that woman?' he asked.

'It's none of your dam' business – '

Manfred swung him from his feet and dropped him over the area railings. When he looked round the woman had vanished.

'I might have killed him,' said Manfred penitently, and the spectacle of a penitent Manfred was too much for Leon Gonsalez.

'But you didn't – what happened?'

'When I saw him get up on his feet and knew nothing was broken I bolted,' confessed Manfred. 'I really must guard against these impulses. It must be my advancing years that has spoilt my judgment.'

If Poiccart had a very complete knowledge of the sordid underworld, Manfred was a living encyclopaedia on the swell mob; but for some reason Mr Lexfield was outside his knowledge. Leon made investigations and reported.

'He has been thrown out of India and Australia. He is only "wanted" in New Zealand if he attempts to go back there. His speciality is bigamous marriages into families which are too important to risk a scandal. The swell mob in London only know of him by hearsay. He has a real wife who has followed him to London and was probably the lady who was responsible for his visit to the area.'

Mr Garry Lexfield had 'touched' royally, and luck had been with him, since, unostentatiously and in an assumed name, he had stepped on to the Monrovia at Sydney. He had the charm and the attraction which are three-quarters of the good thief's assets. Certainly he charmed the greater part of three thousand pounds out of the pockets of two wealthy Australian land-owners, and attracted to himself the daughter of one who at any rate had the appearance of being another.

When he landed he was an engaged man: happily and mercifully, his bride-to-be was taken ill on the day of her arrival with a prosaic attack of appendicitis. Before she had left her nursing home, he learned that that bluff squatter, her father, so far from being a millionaire, was in very considerable financial difficulties.

But the luck held: a visit to Monte Carlo produced yet another small fortune – which was not gained at the public tables. Here he met and wooed Elsa Monarty, convent-trained and easily fascinated. A sister, her one relative, had sent her to San Remo – oddly enough, she also was convalescing from an illness – and, straying across the frontier, she met the handsome Mr Lexfield – which was not his name – in the big vestibule of the rooms. She wanted a ticket of admission – the gallant Garry was most obliging. She told him about her sister, who was the manager and part owner of a big dress-making establishment in the Rue de la Paix. Giving confidence for confidence, Garry told her of his rich and titled parents, and described a life which was equally mythical.

He came back to London alone and found himself most inconveniently dogged by the one woman in the world who was entitled to bear his name, which was Jackson – a pertinacious if handsome woman who had no particular affection for him, but was anxious to recover for the benefit of his two neglected children a little of the fortune he had dissipated.

And most pertinacious at a moment when, but for his inherent meanness, he would have gladly paid good money to be rid of her.

It was a week after he had had the shocking experience of finding himself hurled across fairly high railings into a providentially shallow area, and he was still inclined to limp, when Leon Gonsalez, who was investigating his case, came with the full story of the man's misdeeds.

'I would have dropped him a little more heavily if I had known,' said Manfred regretfully. 'The strange thing is that the moment I lifted him – it's a trick you have never quite succeeded in acquiring, Leon – I knew he was something pestilential. We shall have to keep an unfriendly eye on Mr Garry Lexfield. Where does he stay?'

'He has a sumptuous flat in Jermyn Street,' said Leon. 'Before you tell me that there are no sumptuous flats in Jermyn Street, I would like to say that it has the appearance of sumptuousness. I was so interested in this gentleman that I went round to the Yard and had a chat with Meadows. Meadows knows all about him, but he has no evidence to convict. The man's got plenty of money – has an account at the London and Southern, and bought a car this afternoon.'

Manfred nodded thoughtfully.

'A pretty bad man,' he said. 'Is there any chance of finding his wife? I suppose the unfortunate lady who was with him – '

'She lives in Little Titchfield Street – calls herself Mrs Jackson, which is probably our friend's name. Meadows is certain that it is.'

Mr Garry Lexfield was too wise a man not to be aware of the fact that he was under observation; but his was the type of crime which almost defies detection. His pleasant manner and his car, plus a well-organized accident to his punt on one of the upper reaches of the Thames, secured him introductions and honorary membership of a very exclusive river club; and from there was but a step to homes which ordinarily would have been barred to him.

He spent a profitable month initiating two wealthy stockbrokers into the mysteries of bushman poker, at which he was consistently unlucky for five successive nights, losing some £600 to his apologetic hosts. There was no necessity for their apologies as it turned out: on the sixth and seventh days, incredible as it may seem, he cleared the greater part of £5,000 and left his hosts with the impression of his regret that he had been the medium of their loss.

'Very interesting,' said Manfred when this was reported to him.

Then, one night when he was dining at the Ritz-Carlton with a young man to whom he had gained one of his quick introductions, he saw his supreme fortune.

'Do you know her?' he asked in an undertone of his companion.

'That lady? Oh, Lord, yes! I've known her for years. She used to stay with my people in Somerset – Madame Velasquez. She's the widow of a terribly rich chap, a Brazilian.'

Mr Lexfield looked again at the dark, beautiful woman at the next table. She was perhaps a little over-jewelled to please the fastidious. Swathes of diamond bracelets encircled her arm from the wrist up; an immense emerald glittered in a diamond setting on her breast. She was exquisitely dressed and her poise was regal.

'She's terribly rich,' prattled on his informant. 'My colonel, who knows her much better than I, told me her husband had left her six million pounds – it's wicked that people should have so much money.'

It was wicked, thought Garry Lexfield, that anybody should have so much money if he could not 'cut' his share.

'I'd like to meet her,' he said, and a minute later the introduction was made and Garry forgot his arrangement to trim the young guardsman that night in the thrill of confronting a bigger quarry.

He found her a remarkably attractive woman. Her English, though slightly broken, was good. She was obviously pleased to meet him. He danced with her a dozen times and asked to be allowed to call in the morning. But she was leaving for her country place in Seaton Deverel.

'That's rather strange,' he said, with his most dazzling smile. 'I'm driving through Seaton Deverel next Saturday.'

To his joy she bit the bait. At noon on the Saturday his car shot up the long drive to Hanford House.

A week later came Leon with startling news.

'This fellow's got himself engaged to a rich South American widow, George. We can't allow that to go any further. Let us have an orgy of lawlessness – kidnap the brigand and put him on a cattle boat. There's a man in the East India Dock Road who would do it for fifty pounds.'

Manfred shook his head.

'I'll see Meadows,' he said. 'I have an idea that we may catch this fellow.'

Mr Garry Lexfield was not in that seventh heaven of delight to which accepted lovers are supposed to ascend; but he was eminently satisfied with himself as he watched the final touches being made to the dinner table in his flat.

Madame Velasquez had taken a great deal of persuading, had shown an extraordinary suspicion, and asked him to introduce her to those parents of his who were at the moment conveniently attending to their large estates in Canada.

'It is a very serious step I take, Garry dear,' she said, shaking her pretty head dubiously. 'I love you very dearly, of course, but I am so fearful of men who desire only money and not love.'

'Darling, I don't want money,' he said vehemently. 'I have shown you my passbook: I have nine thousand pounds in the bank, apart from my estates.'

She shrugged this off. Madame was a lady of peculiar temperament, never in the same mood for longer than an hour.

She came to dinner and, to his annoyance, brought a chaperon – a girl who spoke no word of English. Mr Lexfield was a very patient man and concealed his anger.

She brought news that made him forget the inconvenience of a chaperon. It was while they were sipping coffee in his over-decorated little drawing-room that she told him:

'Such a nice man I meet today. He came to my house in the country.'

'He was not only nice, but lucky,' smiled Garry, who was really not feeling terribly happy.

'And he spoke about you,' she smiled.

Garry Lexfield became instantly attentive. Nobody in England knew him well enough to make him the subject of conversation. If they did, then the discussion had not been greatly to his advantage.

'Who was this?' he asked.

'He spoke such perfect Spanish, and he has a smile the most delightful! And he said so many funny things that I laughed.'

'A Brazilian?' he asked.

She shook her head.

'In Brazil we speak Portuguese,' she said. 'No, Señor Gonsalez – '

'Gonsalez?' he said quickly. 'Not Leon Gonsalez? One of those swi – men . . . the Three Just Men?'

She raised her eyebrows.

'Do you know them?'

He laughed.

I have heard about them. Blackguards that should have been hanged years ago. They are murderers and thieves. They've got a nerve to come and see you. I suppose he said something pretty bad about me? The truth is, I've been an enemy of theirs for years . . . '

He went on to tell an imaginary story of an earlier encounter he had had with the Three, and she listened intently.

'How interesting!' she said at last. 'No, they simply said of you that you were a bad man, and that you wanted my money; that you had a bad – what is the word? – record. I was very angry really, especially when they told me that you had a wife, which I know is not true, because you would not deceive me. Tomorrow he comes again, this Señor Gonsalez – he really did amuse me when I was not angry. Shall I lunch with you and tell you what he said?'

Garry was annoyed: he was thoroughly alarmed. It had not been difficult to locate and identify the man who had taken such summary action with him; and, once located, he had decided to give a wide berth to the men who lived behind the Silver Triangle. He had sense enough to know they were not to be antagonized, and he had hoped most sincerely that they had been less acute in tracing him than he had been in identifying them.

He changed the conversation and became, in spite of the witness, the most ardent and tender of lovers. All his art and experience was called into play; for here was a prize which had been beyond his dreams.

His immediate objective was some £20,000 which had come to the lady in the shape of dividends. She had displayed a pretty helplessness in the matter of money, though he suspected her of being shrewd enough. Garry Lexfield could talk very glibly and fluently on the subject of the market. It was his pet study; it was likewise his continuous undoing. There never was a thief who did not pride himself on his shrewdness in money matters, and Garry had come in and out of the market from time to time in his short and discreditable life with disastrous results to himself.

He saw her and her silent companion to the car and went back, and in the solitude of his flat turned over the new and alarming threat represented by the interest which the Three Just Men were showing in his activities.

He rose late, as was his practice, and was in his pyjamas when the telephone-bell rang. The voice of the porter informed him that there was a trunk call for him and trunk calls these days meant the lovely Velasquez.

'I have seen Gonsalez,' said her urgent voice. 'He came when I was at breakfast. Tomorrow, he says, they will arrest you because of something you did in Australia. Also today he applies to stop your money coming from the bank.'

'Holding up my account?' said Garry quickly. 'Are you sure?'

'Certain I am sure! They will go to a judge in his rooms and get a paper. Shall I come to lunch?'

'Of course – one o'clock,' he said quickly. He glanced at the little clock on the mantelshelf: it was half-past eleven.

'And about your investments: I think I can fix everything today. Bring your cheque-book.'

He was impatient for her to finish the conversation, and at last rather abruptly he brought it to a termination, dashed down the receiver, and, flying into his bedroom, began to dress.

His bank was in Fleet Street, and the journey seemed interminable. Fleet Street was much too close to the Law Courts for his liking. The judge's order might already be effective.

He pushed his cheque under the brass grille of the tellers' counter and held his breath while the slip of paper was handed to the accountant for verification. And then, to his overwhelming relief, the teller opened his drawer, took out a pad of notes and counted out the amount written on the cheque.

'This leaves only a few pounds to your credit, Mr Lexfield,' he said.

'I know,' said Garry. 'I'm bringing in rather a big cheque after lunch, and I want you to get a special clearance.'

It was then he realized that by that time the judge's order would be in operation. He must find another way of dealing with Madame Velasquez's cheque.

The relief was so great that he could hardly speak calmly. With something short of £9,000 he hurried back to Jermyn Street and arrived simultaneously with Madame Velasquez.

'How funny that *caballero* was, to be sure!' she said in her staccato way. 'I thought I should have laughed in his face. He told me you would not be here tomorrow, which is so absurd!'

'It's blackmail,' said Garry easily. 'Don't you worry about Gonsalez. I have just been to Scotland Yard to report him. Now about these shares – '

They had ten minutes to wait before lunch was ready, and those ten minutes were occupied with many arguments. She had brought her cheque-book, but she was a little fearful. Perhaps, he thought, the visit of Gonsalez had really aroused her suspicions. She was not prepared to invest the whole of her £20,000. He produced the papers and balance sheets that he had intended showing her on the previous night and explained, as he could very readily explain, the sound financial position of the company – one of the most solid on the Rand – in which he wished her to invest.

These shares,' he said impressively, 'will rise in the next twenty-four hours by at least ten per cent. in value. I've got a block held for you, but I must get them this afternoon. My idea is that immediately after lunch you should bring me an open cheque; I'll buy the shares and bring them back to you.'

'But why could not I go?' she asked innocently.

'This is a personal matter,' said Garry with great gravity. 'Sir John is allowing me to buy this stock as a great personal favour.'

To his joy she accepted this assurance – she actually wrote a cheque for £12,500 at the luncheon table, and he could scarcely summon patience to sit through the meal.

The proprietors of the flats in which he had his brief habitation did not cater on a generous scale, but the short time which elapsed before the dessert stage of the lunch arrived was a period of agony. She returned once to the question of her investment, seemed in doubt, referred again to Gonsalez and his warning.

'Perhaps I had better wait for a day – yes?'

'My dear girl, how absurd!' said Garry. 'I really believe you are being frightened by this fellow who called on you this morning! I'll make him sorry!'

He half rose from the table, but she put her hand on his arm.

'Please don't hurry,' she begged, and reluctantly he agreed. The bank did not close until three; there would be time to reach Dover by car and catch the five o'clock boat.

But the bank was situated in the City, and he must not cut his time too fine. He excused himself for a moment, went out in search of the valet he had acquired and gave him a few simple but urgent instructions. When he returned she was reading the balance sheet.

'I am so foolish about these matters,' she said, and suddenly lifted her head. 'What was that?' she asked, as the door slammed.

'My valet – I have sent him out on a little errand.'

She laughed nervously.

'I am what you call on the jump,' she said, as she pushed his coffee towards him. 'Now tell me again, Garry, dear, what does ex-dividend mean?'

He explained at length, and she listened attentively. She was still listening when, with a sudden little choke of alarm, he half rose from his feet, only to fall back on the chair and thence to roll helplessly to the floor. Madame Velasquez took his half-empty cup of coffee, carried it at her leisure into the kitchen and emptied the contents into the sink. When he sent his valet out, Mr Garry Lexfield had saved her a great deal of trouble.

She rolled the unconscious man on to his back, and searched quickly and with a dexterous hand pocket after pocket until she found the fat envelope wherein Garry had placed his banknotes.

There was a knock at the outer door. Without hesitation she went out and opened it to the young guardsman who had so kindly introduced Mr Lexfield to her.

'It's all right, the servant's gone,' she said. 'Here's your two hundred, Tony, and thank you very much.'

Tony grinned.

'The grudge I've got against him is that he took me for a sucker. These Australian crooks – '

'Don't talk – get,' she said tersely.

She went back to the dining-room, removed Garry's collar and tie and, putting a pillow under his head, opened the window. In twenty minutes he would be more or less conscious, by which time his valet would have returned.

She found the cheque she had given to him, burnt it in the empty grate, and with a last look round took her departure.

Outside the airport a tall man was waiting. She saw him signal to the driver of the car to pull up.

'I got your message,' said Manfred sardonically. 'I trust you've had a good killing? I owe you five hundred pounds.'

She shook her head with a laugh. She was still the brown, beautiful Brazilian – it would take weeks before the stain would be removed.

'No, thank you, Mr Manfred. It was a labour of love, and I have been pretty well paid. And the furnished house I took in the country was really not a very expensive proposition – oh, very well, then.'

She took the notes he handed to her and put them in her bag, one eye on the waiting plane. 'You see, Mr Manfred, Garry is an old acquaintance of mine – by hearsay. I sent my sister down to Monte Carlo for her health. She also found Garry.'

Manfred understood. He waited till the plane had passed through the haze out of sight, and then he went back to Curzon Street, well satisfied.

The evening newspapers had no account of the Jermyn Street robbery, which was easily understood. Mr Garry Lexfield had a sense of pride.

The Typist Who Saw Things

About every six months Raymond Poiccart grew restless, and began prodding about in strange corners, opening deed boxes and trunks, and sorting over old documents. It was a few days before the incident of the Curzon Street 'murder' that he appeared in the dining room with an armful of old papers, and placed them on that portion of the table which had not been laid for dinner.

Leon Gonsalez looked and groaned.

George Manfred did not even smile, though he was laughing internally.

'I am indeed sorry to distress you, my dear friends,' said Poiccart apologetically; 'but these papers must be put in order. I have found a bundle of letters that go back five years, to the time when the agency was a child.'

'Burn 'em,' suggested Leon, returning to his book. 'You never do anything with them, anyway!'

Poiccart said nothing. He went religiously from paper to paper, read them in his short-sighted way, and put them aside so that as one pile diminished another pile grew.

'And I suppose when you've finished you'll put them back where you found them?' said Leon.

Poiccart did not answer. He was reading a letter.

'A strange communication, I don't remember reading this before,' he said.

'What is it, Raymond?' asked George Manfred.

Raymond read.

To the Silver Triangle. Private.

Gentlemen,

I have seen your names mentioned in a case as being reliable agents who can be trusted to work of a confidential character. I would be glad if you would make inquiries and find out for me the prospects of the Persian Oil Fields; also if you could negociate the sale of 967 shares held by me. The reason I do not approach an ordinary share-broker is because there are so many sharks in this profeccion. Also could you tell me whether there is a sale for Okama Biscuit shares (American)? Please let me know this.

Yours faithfully,

J. Rock

'I recall that letter,' said Leon promptly. ' "Negotiate" and "profession" were spelt with c's. Don't you remember, George, I suggested this fellow had stolen some shares and was anxious to make us the means by which he disposed of his stolen property?'

Manfred nodded.

'Rock,' said Leon softly. 'No, I have never met Mr Rock. He wrote from Melbourne, didn't he, and gave a box number and a telegraphic address? Did we hear again from him? I think not.'

None of the three could recollect any further communication: the letter passed with the others and might have remained eternally buried, but for Leon's uncanny memory for numbers and spelling errors.

And then one night –

A police whistle squealed in Curzon Street. Gonsalez, who slept in the front of the house, heard the sound in his dreams, and was standing by the open window before he was awake. Again the whistle sounded, and then Gonsalez heard the sound of flying feet. A girl was racing along the sidewalk. She passed the house, stopped, and ran back, and again came to a standstill.

Leon went down the narrow stairs two at a time, unlocked the front door and flung it open. The fugitive stood immediately before him.

'In here – quickly!' said Leon.

She hesitated only a second; stepping backward through the doorway, she waited. Leon gripped her by the arm and pulled her into the passage.

'You needn't be frightened of me or my friends,' he said.

But he felt the arm in his hand strain for release. 'Let me go, please – I don't want to stay here!'

Leon pushed her into the back room and switched on the light.

'You saw a policeman running up toward you, that's why you came back,' he said, in his quiet, conversational way. 'Sit down and rest – you look all in!'

'I'm innocent . . . !' she began, in a trembling voice.

He patted her shoulder.

'Of course you are. I, on the contrary, am guilty, for whether you're innocent or not, I am undoubtedly helping a fugitive from justice.'

She was very young – scarcely more than a child. The pale, drawn face was pretty. She was well, but not expensively, dressed, and it struck Leon as a significant circumstance that on one finger was an emerald ring, which, if the stone were real, must have been worth hundreds of pounds. He glanced at the clock. A few minutes after two. There came to them the sound of heavy, hurrying feet.

'Did anybody see me come in?' she asked, fearfully.

'Nobody was in sight. Now, what is the trouble?'

Danger and fear had held her tense, almost capable. The reaction had come now: she was shaking. Shoulders, hands, body quivered pitiably. She was crying noiselessly, her lips trembled; for the time being she was inarticulate. Leon poured water into a glass and held it to her chattering teeth. If the others had heard him, they had no intention of coming down to investigate. The curiosity of Leon Gonsalez was a household proverb. Any midnight brawl would bring him out of bed and into the street.

After a while, she was calm enough to tell her story, and it was not the story he expected.

'My name is Farrer – Eileen Farrer. I am a typist attached to Miss Lewley's All-Night Typing Agency. Usually there are two girls on duty, one a senior; but Miss Leah went home early. We call ourselves an all-night agency, but really we close down about one o'clock. Most of our work is theatrical. Often, after a first-night performance, certain changes have to be made in a script – and sometimes new contracts are arranged over supper, and we prepare the rough drafts. At other times it is just letter-work. I know all the big managers, and I've often gone to their offices quite late to do work for them. We never, of course, go to strange people and at the offices we have a porter who is also a messenger, to see that we are not annoyed. At twelve o'clock I had a phone message from Mr Grasleigh, of the Orpheum, asking me if I would do two letters for him. He sent his car for me, and I went to his flat in Curzon Street. We're not allowed to go to the private houses of our clients, but I knew Mr Grasleigh was a client, though I had never met him before.'

Leon Gonsalez had often seen Mr Jesse Grasleigh's bright yellow car. That eminent theatrical manager lived in some exclusive flats in Curzon Street, occupying the first floor, and paying – as Leon, who was insatiably curious, discovered – £3,000 a year. He had dawned on London three years before, had acquired the lease of the Orpheum, and had been interested in half a dozen productions, most of which had been failures.

'What time was this?' he asked.

'A quarter to one,' said the girl. 'I reached Curzon Street at about a quarter after. I had several things to do at the office before I left, besides which he told me there was no immediate hurry. I knocked at the door and Mr Grasleigh admitted me. He was in evening dress, and looked as if he had come from a party. He had a big white flower in the buttonhole of his tail coat. I saw no servants, and I know now there were none in the flat. He showed me into his study, which was a large room, and pulled up a chair to a little table by his desk. I don't know exactly what happened. I remember sitting down and taking my notebook out of my attache case and opening it, and I was stooping to find a pencil in the case when I heard a groan, and, looking up, I saw Mr Grasleigh lying back in his chair with a red mark on his white shirt-front – it was horrible!'

'You heard no other sound, no shot?' asked Leon.

She shook her head.

'I was so horrified I couldn't move. And then I heard somebody scream and, looking round, I saw a lady, very beautifully dressed, standing in the doorway. "What have you done to him?" she said. "You horrible woman, you've killed him!" I was so terrified that I couldn't speak, and then I must have got into a panic, for I ran past her and out of the front door – '

'It was open?' suggested Leon.

She frowned.

'Yes, it was open. I think the lady must have left it open. I heard somebody blow a police whistle, but I can't remember how I got down the stairs or into the street. You're not going to give me up, are you?' she asked wildly.

He leaned over and patted her hand.

'My young friend,' he said, gently, 'you have nothing whatever to fear. Stay down here while I dress, and then you and I will go down to Scotland Yard and you will tell them all you know.'

'But I can't. They'll arrest me!'

She was on the verge of hysteria, and it was perhaps a mistake to attempt to argue with her.

'Oh, it's horrible. I hate London . . . I wish I'd never left Australia . . . First the dogs and then the black man and now this . . . '

Leon was startled, but this was not a moment to question her. The thing to do was to bring her to a calm understanding of the situation.

'Don't you realize that they won't blame you, and that your story is such that no police officer in the world would dream of suspecting it?'

'But I ran away – ' she began.

'Of course you ran away,' he said soothingly. 'I should probably have run away too. Just wait here.'

He was half-way through dressing when he heard the front door slam and, running down the stairs, found that the girl had disappeared.

Manfred was awake when he went into his room and told him the story.

'No, I don't think it's a pity that you didn't call me earlier,' he interrupted Leon's apology. 'We couldn't very well have detained her in any circumstances. You know where she is employed. See if you can get Lewley's Agency on the telephone.'

Leon found the number in the book, but had no answer from his call.

When he was dressed he went into the street and made his way to Curzon House. To his surprise he found no policeman on guard at the door, though he saw one at the corner of the street, nor was there any evidence that there had been a tragedy. The front door of the flat was fastened, but inserted in the wall were a number of small bell-pushes, each evidently communicating with one of the flats, and after a while he discovered that which bore the name Grasleigh and was on the point of ringing when the policeman he had seen came silently across from the other side of the road. He evidently knew Leon.

'Good evening, Mr Gonsalez,' he said. It wasn't you blowing that police whistle, was it?'

'No – I heard it, though.'

'So did I and three or four of my mates,' said the policeman. 'We've been flying round these streets for a quarter of an hour, but we haven't found the man who blew it.'

'Probably I'll be able to help you.'

It was at that moment that he heard the door unlocked, and nearly dropped, for the man who opened the door to him he recognized as Grasleigh himself. He was in a dressing-gown; the half of a cigar was in the corner of his mouth.

'Hullo!' he said in surprise. 'What's the trouble?'

'Can I see you for a few minutes?' said Leon when he had recovered from his surprise.

'Certainly,' said the 'dead man', 'though it's hardly the time I like to receive callers. Come up.'

Wonderingly Leon followed him up the stairs to the first floor. He saw no servants, but there was not the slightest evidence to associate this place with the dramatic scene which the girl had described. Once they were in the big study, Leon told his story. When he had finished, Grasleigh shook his head.

'The girl's mad! It's perfectly true that I did telephone for her, and as a matter of fact I thought it was her when you rang the bell. I assure you she hasn't been here tonight . . . Yes, I heard the police whistle blow, but I never mix myself up in these midnight troubles.' He was looking at Leon keenly. 'You're one of the Triangle people, aren't you, Mr Gonsalez? What was this girl like?'

Leon described her, and again the theatrical manager shook his head.

'I've never heard of her,' he said. 'I'm afraid you've been the victim of a hoax, Mr Gonsalez.'

Leon went back to join his two friends, a very bewildered man.

The next morning he called at Lewles Agency, which he knew by repute as a well-conducted establishment of its kind, and interviewed its good-natured spinster-proprietress. He had to exercise a certain amount of caution: he was most anxious not to get the girl into trouble. Fortunately, he knew an important client of Miss Lewley's and he was able to use this unconscious man as a lever to extract the information he required.

'Miss Farrer is doing night duty this week, and she will not be in until this evening,' she explained. 'She has been with us about a month.'

'How long has Mr Grasleigh been a client of yours?'

'Exactly the same time,' she said with a smile. 'I rather think he likes Miss Farrer's work, because previous to that he sent all his work to Danton's Agency, where she was employed, and the moment she came to us he changed his agency.'

'Do you know anything about her?'

The woman hesitated.

'She is an Australian. I believe at one time her family were very wealthy. She's never told me anything about her troubles, but I have an idea that she will be entitled to a lot of money some day. One of the partners of Colgate's, the lawyers, came to see her once.'

Leon managed to get the girl's address, and then went on to the City to find Messrs Colgate. Luck was with him, for Colgate's had employed the Three on several occasions, and at least one of their commissions had been of a most delicate character.

It was one of those old-fashioned firms that had its offices in the region of Bedford Row, and though it was generally known as 'Colgate's', it consisted of seven partners, the names of all of whom were inscribed on the brass plate before the office.

Mr Colgate himself was a man of sixty, and at first rather uncommunicative. It was an inspiration for Leon to tell him of what had happened the night before. To his amazement, he saw the lawyer's face drop.

'That's very bad,' he said, 'very bad indeed. But I'm afraid I can tell you nothing more than you know.'

'Why is it so very bad?' asked Leon.

The lawyer pursed his lips thoughtfully.

'You understand that she is not our client, although we represent a firm of Melbourne solicitors who are acting for this young lady. Her father died in a mental home and left his affairs rather involved. During the past three years, however, some of his property has become very valuable, and there is no reason why this young lady should work at all, except, as I suspect, that she wishes to get away from the scene of this family trouble and has to work to occupy her mind. I happen to know that the taint of madness is a cause of real distress to the girl, and I believe it was on the advice of her only relative that she came to England, in the hope that the change of scene would put out of her mind this misfortune which has overshadowed her.'

'But she has been to see you?'

The lawyer shook his head.

'One of my clients called on her. Some property in Sydney which was overlooked in the settlement of her father's estate came into the market. He had a tenth share, it seems. We tried to get in touch with the executor, Mr Flane, but we were unsuccessful – he's travelling in the East – so we got the girl's signature to the transfer.'

'Flane?'

Mr Colgate was a busy man; he had intimated as much. He was now a little impatient.

'A cousin of the late Joseph Farrer – the only other relative. As a matter of fact, Farrer was staying in Western Australia on his cousin's station just before he went mad.'

Leon was blessed with an imagination, but even this, vivid as it was, could not quite bridge the gaps in what he suspected was an unusual story.

'My own impression,' said the lawyer, 'and I tell you this in the strictest confidence, is that the girl is not quite . . . ' He tapped his forehead. 'She told my clerk, a man who is skilled in gaining the confidence of young people, that she had been followed about for weeks by a black man, on another occasion had been followed about by a black retriever. Apparently, whenever she takes her Saturday stroll, this retriever has appeared and never leaves her. So far as I can discover, nobody else has seen either the black man or the dog. You don't need to be a doctor to know that this delusion of being followed is one of the commonest signs of an unbalanced mind.'

Leon knew something more than the average about police work. He knew that discovery is not a thing of a dramatic moment, but patiently accrued evidence, and he followed the same line of inquiry that a detective from Scotland Yard would follow.

Eileen Farrer lived in Landsbury Road, Clapham, and No 209 proved to be a house in a respectable terrace. The motherly-looking landlady who interviewed him in the hall was palpably relieved to see him when he stated the object of his visit.

'I'm so glad you've come,' she said. 'Are you a relation?'

Leon disclaimed that association.

'She's a very peculiar young lady,' the landlady went on, 'and I don't know what to make of her. She's been up all night walking about her room – she sleeps in the room above me – and this morning she's taken no breakfast. I can't help feeling that there's something wrong – she's so strange.'

'You mean that she's not quite right in her head?' asked Leon brutally.

'Yes, that's what I mean. I thought of sending for my doctor, but she wouldn't hear of it. She told me she'd had a great shock. Do you know her?'

'I've met her,' said Leon. 'May I go upstairs?'

The landlady hesitated.

'I think I'd better tell her you're here. What name?'

'I think it would be better if I saw her without being announced,' said Leon, 'if you will show me the door. Where is she?'

Eileen Farrer was, he learnt, in her sitting-room – she could afford the luxury of an extra apartment Leon tapped at the door and a startled voice asked: 'Who is it?'

He did not answer but, turning the knob, entered the room. The girl was standing by the window, staring out; apparently the taxi that brought Leon had excited her apprehension.

'Oh!' she said in dismay, as she saw her visitor. 'You're the man . . . you haven't come to arrest me?'

Out of the corner of his eye he saw that the floor was strewn with papers. Evidently she had bought every available newspaper to discover tidings of the crime.

'No, I haven't come to arrest you,' said Leon in an even tone. 'I don't exactly know what you could be arrested for – Mr Grasleigh is not dead. He's not even hurt.'

She stared at him, wide-eyed.

'Not even hurt?' she repeated slowly.

'He was quite well when I saw him last night.'

She passed her hand over her eyes.

'I don't understand. I saw him – oh, it's terrible!'

'You saw him, as you thought, very badly hurt. I had the pleasure of meeting him a few minutes afterwards and he was quite uninjured; and, what is more – ' he was watching her as he spoke – 'he said that he had never seen you.'

Wonder, incredulity, terror were in her eyes.

'Now won't you sit down, Miss Farrer, and tell me all about yourself. You see, I know quite a lot. I know, for example, that your father died in an institution.'

She was staring at him as though unable to grasp his words. Leon became instantly practical.

'Now I want you to tell me. Miss Farrer, why your father went mad. Was there any other history of insanity in the family?'

Leon's calmness was of the dominant kind: under its influence she had recovered something of her self-possession.

'No, the cause was a fall from a horse; the full effect of it wasn't known for years afterwards.'

He nodded and smiled.

'I thought not. Where were you when he was taken away?'

'I was at school in Melbourne,' she said, 'or rather, just outside of Melbourne. I never saw my father from the time I was seven. He was a long time in that horrible place, and they wouldn't let me see him.'

'Now tell me this: who is Mr Flane? Do you know him?'

She shook her head.

'He was my father's cousin. The only thing I know about him is that Daddy used to lend him money, and he was staying on the farm when he became ill. I've had several letters from him about money. He paid my fare to England. It was he who suggested I should go home and try to forget all the troubles I'd had.'

'You never saw him?'

'Never,' she said. 'He came once to school, but I was away on a picnic.'

'You don't know what money your father left?'

She shook her head again. 'No, I've no idea.'

'Now tell me, Miss Farrer, about the Negro you have seen following you, and the dog.'

She had very little to tell except the bare fact. The persecution had begun two years before, and her doctor had once called to inquire the cause. Here Leon stopped her quickly.

'Did you send for the doctor?'

'No,' she said in surprise, 'but he must have heard from somebody, though who I can't think, because I told very few people.'

'Can you show me any of the letters that Mr Flane sent you?'

These she had in a drawer, and Leon examined them carefully. Their tone was rather unusual, not the tone one would have expected from a guardian or from one who had control of her destinies. In the main they were protestations of the difficulties the writer found in providing for her schooling, for her clothes, and eventually for the trip to England, and each letter insisted on the fact that her father had left very little money.

'And that was true,' she said. 'Poor Daddy was rather eccentric about money. He never kept his stocks at the bank but always carried them about with him in a big iron box. In fact, he was terribly secretive, and nobody knew exactly what money he had. I thought he was very rich, because he was a little – ' she hesitated – ' "near" is the word. I hate saying anything disparaging about the poor darling, but he was never generous with money, and when I found that he had only left a few hundred pounds and a very few shares, and those not of any particular value, I was astonished. And so, of course, was everybody in Melbourne – everybody who knew us, I mean. In fact, I always regarded myself as poor until a few months ago. We then discovered that father had a large interest in the West Australian Gold Mine, which nobody knew anything about. It came to light by accident. If all they say is true, I shall be very rich. The lawyers have been trying to get into touch with Mr Flane, but they have only had a letter or two, one posted from China addressed to me, and another posted I think in Japan.'

'Have you got the letter addressed to you?'

She produced it. It was written on thick paper. Leon held it up to the light and saw the watermark.

'What shares did your father leave? I mean, what shares was he known to leave?'

She puzzled over this question.

'There were some absolutely valueless, I know. I remember them because of the number – 967. What's the matter?'

Leon was laughing.

'I think I can promise you freedom from any further persecution, Miss Farrer, and my advice to you is that you get immediately in touch with the best firm of lawyers in London. I think I can give you their address. There's one thing I want to tell you – ' there was a very kindly smile in Leon Gonsalez's eyes – 'and it is that you are not mad, that you haven't imagined you were followed by Negroes and by black dogs and that you didn't imagine you saw Mr Grasleigh murdered. There's one more question I want to ask you, and it's about Mr Flane. Do you know what he did for a living?'

'He had a small station – farm, you would call it,' she said. 'I think Daddy bought it for him and his wife. Before that I think he had the lease of a theatre in Adelaide, and he lost a lot of money.'

'Thank you,' said Leon. 'That is all I want to know.'

He drove straight back to the flats in Curzon Street, and met Mr Grasleigh as he was leaving his flat.

'Hullo! You've not come to tell me about another murder?' said that jovial man with a loud laugh.

'Worse than murder,' said Leon, and something in his tone struck the smile from Mr Grasleigh's lips.

Leon followed him into the study and himself closed the door.

'Mr Flane, I understand?' he said, and saw the colour fade from the man's face.

'I don't know what you mean,' blustered Grasleigh. 'My name is – '

'Your name is Flane,' said Leon very gently. 'A few years ago you got an inkling that the man you had robbed – Eileen Farrer's father – was richer than you thought, and you evolved a rather clumsy, and certainly a diabolical scheme to retain possession of Eileen Farrer's property. A shallow-brained man as you are, I have no doubt, would imagine that because the father was mad the daughter could also be driven into a mental asylum. I don't know where you got your Negro from or where you found your trained dog, but I know where you got the money to take the lease of the Orpheum. And, Mr Flane, I want to tell you something more, and you might pass the information on to your wife, who is, I gather, a fellow-conspirator. "Negotiate" is spelt with a "t" and "profession" with an "s". Both words occur in the letters you wrote to Miss Farrer.'

The man was breathing loudly through his nose, and the hand that went up to take out the dead stump of his cigar was shaking.

'You've got to prove all this,' he blustered.

'Unfortunately I have,' said Leon sadly. 'In the old days when the Four Just Men were not quite so legally minded as they are today, you would not have been taken into a court of law: I rather imagine that my friends and I would have opened a manhole in Curzon Street and dropped you through.'

The Mystery of Mr Drake

All events go in threes – that was the considered opinion of Leon Gonsalez. This, for example, was his second meeting with Cornelius Malan. The last time Mr Roos Malan, the bearded brother of Cornelius, had been a third party, but now Roos was dead – though of this fact Leon was at the moment unaware.

This alert and bright-eyed man had never had a driving accident. The fact that he was alive proved this, for he was never quite happy if the needle of the speedometer on his big sports car fell below the seventy mark. By an odd chance it was well below thirty when he skidded on the slush and snow of a lonely Oxford road and slithered a back wheel into a four-foot ditch. That the car did not overturn was a miracle.

Leon climbed out and looked round. The squat farmstead beyond the stone wall which flanked the road had a familiar appearance. He grinned as he leapt the wall and made his way across the rough surface of an uncultivated field towards the building. A dog barked gruffly, but he saw no human creature. And when he knocked at the door there was no answer. Leon was not surprised. Cornelius kept few servants, even in the summer – he was unlikely to have his house well staffed in the unprofitable days of late autumn.

He made a tour of the house, passed through an untidy and weed-grown garden, and still could find no sign of life. And then from the ground, not a dozen yards away, arose a big, broad-shouldered giant of a man. He came veritably from the ground. For a moment the observer was staggered, and then he realized that the man had come out of a well. The back of Cornelius Malan was turned to his uninvited guest. Leon saw him stoop, heard the clang of steel and the click of a lock fastened. Presently the big man dusted his knees and stretched himself and, turning, came straight towards where Leon was standing. At the sight of a stranger, the broad, red face of Cornelius went a shade redder.

'Hi, you!' he began wrathfully, and then recognized his visitor. 'Ah!' he said. 'The detective!'

He spoke with scarcely a trace of accent, unlike his dead brother, who could hardly speak English.

'What do you want, eh? Do more people think that poor Roos has swindled them? Well, he is dead, so you get nothing out of him.'

Leon was looking past him, and the man must have divined what was in his mind, for he said quickly: 'There is a bad well here, full of gas. I must have it filled up – '

'In the meantime you've had it sensibly fastened,' smiled Leon. 'I'm sorry to barge in upon your Arcadian pursuits, Mr Malan, but the fact is my car has ditched itself, and I wanted help to get it up.'

There had been a strange look of apprehension on the man's face, and this cleared away as Leon explained the object of his visit.

'I myself could pick a car out of any ditch,' he boasted. 'You shall see.'

As he walked across the field with Leon he was almost affable.

'I do not like you people from London, and you especially, Mr What's-your-name. You are like the lawyer who swindled me and my poor brother by Potchefstroom, so many years ago that I forget his name. Poor Roos! You and such people as you have hounded him into his grave! Inspectors of taxes and God knows what. And we are both poor men and have nothing to say to them.'

When they got to the car, he found that his strength was hardly sufficient, and they returned to the farm and from some mysterious place gathered two hungry-looking labourers, who, with planks and ropes, succeeded in hauling the Bentley to road level. By this time, Cornelius Malan was his old self.

'That will cost you one pound, my friend,' he said. 'I cannot afford to pay these men for extra work. I am poor, and now that Roos is dead, who knows that I may not have to take that lazy wench of our sister's . . . '

Very solemnly Leon produced a pound note, and handed it to the old miser.

When he got back to Curzon Street he related his experience.

'I'll bet you we're going to meet for the third time,' he said. 'It is odd, but it's a fact. One of these days I am going to write a book on the Law of Coincidence – I've any amount of data.'

'Add this,' said Poiccart briefly, as he tossed a letter across the table.

Leon smoothed it out: the first thing he read was an Oxfordshire address. He turned quickly to the end of the letter, and saw it was signed, 'Leonora Malan'.

Manfred was watching him with a smile in his eyes. 'There's a job after your own heart, Leon,' he said.

Leon read the letter.

Dear Sirs,
Some time ago you came into town to see my uncle, who has now, I am sorry to say, passed over. Will you please grant me an interview on Wednesday morning in regard to my late uncle's money? I don't suppose you can help me, but there is just a chance.

It was signed 'Leonora Malan', and there was a postscript.

Please do not let my Uncle Cornelius know I have written.

Leon scratched his chin.

'Leon and Leonora,' murmured Manfred. 'That alone is sufficient basis for a chapter on coincidences.'

On Wednesday morning, rainy and gusty, Miss Malan called, and with her was the young man who was to be the fourth and the greatest coincidence of all.

A scrawny man of thirty, with irregular features and eyes that were never still, she introduced him as Mr Jones, the late manager of her dead uncle.

Leonora Malan was astonishingly pretty. That was the first impression Leon had of his visitor. He had expected something dumpy and plain – Leonora was a name to shy at. Malan was obviously Cape Dutch. He would have known this even if he had not been aware, from personal experience, of the nationality of her two uncles. He had had an encounter with the notorious Jappy, and the no less objectionable Roos – less objectionable now, since he had been gathered to his fathers. And he was agreeably surprised, for this slim, bright-eyed girl with the peach and rose complexion was a very happy upsetting of preconceived ideas.

She came with him into the bright little drawing-room which was also the office of the Three, and sat down in the chair which Poiccart pushed forward for her before, in his role of butler, he glided out, closing the door respectfully and noiselessly behind him.

She looked up at Leon, her eyes twinkling, and smiled.

'You can do nothing for me, Mr Gonsalez, but Mr Jones thought I ought to see you,' she said, with a trustful glance at her ill-favoured companion which appalled Gonsalez. 'That isn't a very promising beginning, is it? I suppose you'll wonder why I'm wasting your time if I believe that? But just now I'm clutching at straws, and – '

'I am a very substantial straw,' laughed Leon.

Mr Jones spoke. His voice was harsh and coarse.

'It's like this. Leonora is entitled to about eighty thousand pounds. I know it was there before the old boy died. Got the will, Leonora?'

She nodded quickly and sighed, half-opened her little hand-bag, reached mechanically for a battered silver case, but quickly withdrew her hand and snapped the bag tight. Leon reached for the cigarette box and passed it to her.

'You know my uncle?' she said, as she took a cigarette. 'Poor Uncle Roos often spoke about you – '

'Very uncomplimentarily, I am sure,' said Leon.

She nodded.

'Yes, he didn't like you. He was rather afraid of you, and you cost him money.'

Roos Malan had figured in one of Leon's more humdrum cases. Roos and his brother Cornelius had been prosperous farmers in South Africa. And then gold was discovered on their farm, and they became, of a sudden, very rich men; both came to England and settled on two desolate farms in Oxfordshire. It was Roos who had adopted his dead sister's baby with much grumbling and complaining for, like his brother, he was that rarest of misers who grudges every farthing spent even on himself. Yet both brothers were shrewd speculators; too shrewd sometimes. It was a case in which their cupidity had overrun their discretion, that had brought Leon into their orbit.

'Uncle Roos,' said the girl, 'was not so bad as you think. Of course, he was terribly mean about money, and even about the food that was eaten on the farm; and life was a little difficult with him. Sometimes he was kindness itself, and I feel a pig that I am bothering about his wretched money.'

'Don't worry about him,' began Jones impatiently.

'You find that there is no wretched money?' interrupted Leon, glancing again at the letter she had sent him.

She shook her head.

'I can't understand it,' she said.

'Show him the will,' Jones snapped.

She opened her bag again and took out a folded paper.

'Here is a copy.'

Leon took the paper and opened it. It was a short, hand-written document in Dutch. Beneath was the English translation. In a few lines the late Roos Malan had left 'all the property I possess to my niece Leonora Mary Malan'.

'Every penny,' said Jones, with satisfaction that he did not attempt to conceal. 'Leonora and I were going into business in London. Her money, my brains. See what I mean?'

Leon saw very clearly.

'When did he die?' he asked.

'Six months ago.' Leonora frowned as at an unpleasant memory. 'You'll think I am heartless, but really I had no love for him, though at times I was very fond of him.'

'And the property?' said Leon.

She frowned.

'All that is left seems to be the farm and the furniture. The valuers say that it's worth five thousand pounds, and it's mortgaged for four thousand. Uncle Cornelius holds the mortgage. Yet Roos Malan must have been very rich; he drew royalties from his property in South Africa, and I've seen the money in the house; it came every quarter and was always paid in banknotes.'

'I could explain the mortgage,' said Jones. 'Those two mean old skunks exchanged mortgages to protect one another in case the authorities ever tried to play tricks on 'em! The money's gone, mister – I've searched the house from top to bottom. There's a strongroom built in a corner of the cellar – we've had that door opened, but there's not a penny to be found. They're great for strongrooms, the Malans. I know where Cornelius keeps his too. He doesn't know it, but by God, if he doesn't play fair with this kid . . . !'

The girl seemed a little embarrassed by the championship of the man. The friendship was a little one-sided, he thought, and had the impression that Mr Jones's glib plans for 'going into business' were particularly his own.

Jones gave him one piece of news. Neither of the brothers had banking accounts. Though they speculated heavily and wisely in South African stocks, their dividends were paid or their stock was bought with ready money, and invariably cash payments were made in the same medium.

'Both these old blighters objected to paying taxation, and they used all sorts of dirty tricks to avoid payment. They suspected all banks, because they believed that banks tell the Government their clients' business.'

Leonora shook her head again despairingly.

'I don't think you can do anything, Mr Gonsalez, and I almost wish I hadn't written. The money isn't there; there's no record that it ever was there. I really don't mind very much, because I can work.

Happily I took typing lessons and improved my speed at the farm: I did most of Uncle's correspondence.'

'During the last illness was Cornelius at the farm?'

She nodded.

'All the time?'

She nodded again.

And he left – ?'

'Immediately after poor Roos's death. I haven't seen him again, and the only communication I've had from him was a letter in which he told me that I ought to earn my living and that I couldn't depend on him. Now what can I do?'

Leon considered this problem for a long time.

'I'll be perfectly frank with you, Mr Gonsalez,' she went on. 'I am sure Uncle Cornelius collected what money there was in the house before he left. Mr Jones thinks that too.'

'Think it – I know it!' The hatchet-faced man was very emphatic. 'I saw him coming out of the cellar with a big Gladstone bag. Old Roos was in the habit of keeping his key of the strongroom under his pillow; when he died it wasn't there – I found it on the kitchen mantelpiece!'

When the man and the girl were leaving, Leon so manoeuvred the departure that she was the last to go.

'Who is Jones?' he asked, dropping his voice.

She was a little uncomfortable.

'He was Uncle's farm manager – he's been very nice . . . a little too nice.'

Leon nodded, and as he heard Mr Jones returning, asked her immediate plans. She was, she said, staying the week in London, making preparations to earn her own livelihood. After he had taken down her address and seen the party to the door, he walked thoughtfully back to the common room where his two companions were playing chess – an immoral occupation for eleven o'clock in the forenoon.

'She is very pretty,' said Poiccart, not looking up from the piece he was fingering, 'and she has come about her inheritance. And the man with her is no good.'

'You were listening at the door,' accused Leon.

'I have read the local newspapers and I know that Mr Roos Malan died penniless – not sufficient to meet the demands of the Inspector of Taxes,' said Poiccart as he checked Manfred's king. 'Both men were terrible misers, both are enormously rich, and both men have got Somerset House tearing their hair.'

'And naturally,' George Manfred went on, 'she came to you to recover her property. What did the man want?'

He sat back in his chair and sighed.

'We're fearfully respectable, aren't we? It was so easy ten, fifteen years ago. I know so many ways of making Cornelius disgorge.'

'And I know one,' interrupted Leon promptly. 'And if all my theories and views are correct – and I cannot imagine them being anything else – Mr Drake will make the recovery.'

'Mr Who?' Poiccart looked up with a heavy frown.

'Mr Drake,' said Leon glibly; 'an old enemy of mine. We have been at daggers drawn for ten years. He knows one of my most precious secrets, and I have lived in mortal terror of him, so much so that I contemplate removing him from his present sphere of activity.'

George looked at him thoughtfully; then a light dawned in his face.

'Oh, I think I know your mysterious Mr Drake. We used him before, didn't we?'

'We used him before,' agreed Leon gravely. 'But this time he dies the death of a dog!'

'Who is this Jones?' asked Poiccart. 'I've seen him at the Old Bailey – and he has a Dartmoor manner. You remember, George – an unpleasant case, eight-ten years ago. Not a fit companion for the pretty Leonora.'

Leon's car took him the next morning to a famous market town, ten miles from Mr Malan's farm. Here he sought and had an interview with the local inspector of taxes, producing the brief authorization which he had suggested Leonora should sign. The harassed official was both willing and anxious to give Leon all the information he required.

'I have the devil of a job with these people. We know their main income, which arrives from South Africa every quarter, but they've got a score of other South African interests which we're unable to trace. We knew that they are in the habit of receiving their money in cash. Both men have obviously been cheating the Revenue for years, but we could get no evidence against them. If Mr Malan keeps books, he also keeps them well out of sight! A few months ago we put a detective on to watch Cornelius, and we found his hiding place. It lies about twenty feet down a half-filled-in well in his garden.'

Leon nodded.

'And it's a solid rock chamber approached by a steel door. It sounds like a fairy tale, doesn't it? It's one of the many in which Charles II was reputedly hidden, and the existence of the rock chamber has been known for centuries. Cornelius had the steel door fitted, and as the well is right under his window and is fastened by an iron trapdoor and is, moreover, visible from the road, it's much more secure than any safe he could have in his house.'

'Then why not search the strong-room?' asked Leon.

The inspector shook his head.

'We've no authority to do that – the most difficult thing in the world to secure is a search warrant, and our department, unless it institutes criminal proceedings, has never applied for such an authority.'

Leon smiled broadly.

'Mr Drake will have to get it for you,' he said cryptically.

The puzzled official frowned.

'I don't quite get that.'

'You will get more than that,' said the mysterious Leon.

As Leon walked up the muddy cart-track, he became aware of the sound of voices, one deep and bellowing, one high and shrill. Their words, incoherent in themselves, were indistinguishable. He turned the corner of an untidy clump of bushes, and saw the two: Cornelius the giant, and the rat-faced Mr Jones, who was white with passion.

'I'm going to get you, you damned Dutch thief!' he cried shrilly. 'Robbing the orphan – that's what you're doing. You haven't heard the last of me.'

What Cornelius said was impossible to understand, for in his rage he had relapsed into Cape Dutch, which is one of the most expressive mediums of vituperation. He caught sight of Leon, and came striding towards him.

'You're a detective: take that man from here. He's a thief, a gaol-bird. My brother gave him a job because he could get no other.'

The thin lips of Mr Jones curled in a sneer.

'A hell of a job! A stable to sleep in and stuff to eat that Dartmoor would turn up its nose at – not that I know anything about Dartmoor,' he added hastily. 'All that this man says is lies. He's a thief; he took the money from old Roos's safe – '

'And you come and say "Give me ten thousand and I'll tell Leonora not to trouble about the rest," eh?' snarled Cornelius.

Leon knew it was not the moment to tell the story of Mr Drake. That must come later. He made an excuse for his calling and then accompanied the man Jones back to the road.

'Don't you take any notice of what he said, mister, I mean about my trying to doublecross Leonora. She's a good girl; she trusts me, she does, and I'm going to do the right thing by her . . . Old Roos led her the life of a dog.'

Leon wondered what kind of life this ex-convict would lead Leonora Malan and was quite satisfied that, whatever happened, the girl should be saved from such an association.

'And when he says I was a convict – ' began Jones again.

'I can save you a lot of trouble,' said Leon. 'I saw you sentenced.'

He mentioned the offence, and the man went red and then white.

'Now you can go back to London, and I'm warning you not to go near Miss Leonora Malan. If you do, there is going to be trouble.'

Jones opened his mouth as if to say something, changed his mind and lurched up the road. It was later in the evening when Leon returned to tell the story of Mr Drake.

He reached the farm of Mr Cornelius Malan at nine o'clock. It was pitch dark; rain and sleet were falling, and the house offered no promise that his discomfort would be relieved, for not so much as a candle gleam illuminated the dark windows. He knocked for some time, but had no reply. Then he heard the sound of laboured breathing: somebody was walking towards him in the darkness, and he spun round.

'Mr Cornelius Malan?' he asked, and heard the man grunt, and then: 'Who is it?'

'An old friend,' said Leon coolly, and though Cornelius could not see his face, he must have recognized him.

'What do you want?' His voice was shrill with anxiety.

'I want to see you. It's rather an important matter,' said Leon.

The man pushed past him, unlocked the door and led the way into the darkness. Leon waited in the doorway until he saw the yellow flame of a match and heard the tinkle of a lamp chimney being lifted.

The room was big and bare. Only the glow of a wood fire burnt in the hearth, yet this apparently was the farmer's living and sleeping room, for his untidy bed was in one corner of the room. In the centre was a bare deal table, and on this Leon sat uninvited. The man stood at the far end of the table, scowling down at him; his face was pale and haggard.

'What do you want?' he asked again.

'It's about John Drake,' said Leon deliberately. 'He's an old enemy of mine; we have chased one another across three continents before now, and tonight, for the first time in ten years, we met.'

The man was puzzled, bewildered. 'What's this to do with me?'

Leon shrugged. 'Only tonight I killed him.'

He saw the man's jaw drop. 'Killed him?' – incredulously.

Leon nodded.

'I stabbed him with a long knife,' he said, with some relish. 'You've probably heard about the Three Just Men: they do such things. And I've concealed the body on your farm. For the first time in my life I am conscious that I have acted unfairly, and it is my intention to give myself up to the police.'

Cornelius looked down at him.

'On my farm?' he said dully. 'Where did you put the body?'

Not a muscle of Leon's face moved.

'I dropped it down the well.'

'That's a lie!' stormed the other. 'It is impossible that it was you who opened the cover! . . . '

Leon shrugged his shoulders.

'That you must tell the police. They at any rate will learn from me that I dropped him down that well. At the bottom I found a door which I succeeded in opening with a skeleton key, and inside that door is my unhappy victim.'

Malan's lips were quivering.

Suddenly he turned and rushed from the room.

Leon heard the shot and ran through the door into the night . . . the next second he sprawled over the dead body of Cornelius Roos.

Later, when the police came and forced the cover of the well, they found another dead man huddled at the bottom of the well, where Cornelius had thrown him.

* * *

'Jones must have been detected in the act of forcing the well, and been shot,' said Leon. 'Weird, isn't it . . . after my yarn about having buried a man there? I expected no more than that Cornelius would pay up rather than have the well searched.'

'Very weird,' said Manfred drily, 'and the weirdest thing is Jones's real name.'

'What is it?'

'Drake,' said Manfred. 'The police phoned it through half-an-hour before you came in.'

'The Englishman Konnor'

The Three Just Men sat longer over dinner than usual. Poiccart had been unusually talkative – and serious.

'The truth is, my dear George,' he appealed to the silent Manfred, 'we are fiddling with things. There are still offences for which the law does not touch a man; for which death is the only and logical punishment. We do a certain amount of good – yes. We right certain wrongs – yes. But could not any honest detective agency do as much?'

'Poiccart is a lawless man,' murmured Leon Gonsalez; 'he is going *fantee* – there is a murderous light in his eyes!'

Poiccart smiled good-humouredly.

'We know this is true, all of us. There are three men I know, every one of them worthy of destruction. They have wrecked lives, and are within the pale of the law . . . Now, my view is . . . '

They let him talk and talk, and to the eyes of Manfred came a vision of Merrell, the Fourth of the Four Just Men – he who died in Bordeaux and, in dying completed his purpose. Some day the story of Merrell the Fourth may be told. Manfred remembered a warm, still night, when Poiccart had spoken in just this strain. They were younger then: eager for justice, terribly swift to strike . . .

'We are respectable citizens,' said Leon, getting up, 'and you are trying to corrupt us, my friend. I refuse to be corrupted!'

Poiccart looked up at him from under his heavy eyelids.

'Who shall be the first to break back to the old way?' he asked significantly.

Leon did not answer.

This was a month before the appearance of the tablet. It came into the possession of the Four in a peculiar way. Poiccart was in Berlin, looking for a man who called himself Lefèvre. One sunny afternoon, when he was lounging through Charlonenburg, he called in at an antique shop to buy some old Turkish pottery that was exhibited for sale. Two large blue vases were his purchase, and these he had packed and sent to the House with the Silver Triangle, in Curzon Street.

It was Manfred who found the gold badge. He had odd moments of domesticity, and one day decided to wash the pottery. There were all sorts of oddments at the bottom of the vases: one was stuffed with old pieces of Syrian newspaper for half its depth, and it needed a great deal of patience and groping with pieces of wire to bring these to light. Nearing the end of his task, he heard a metallic tinkle and, as he turned the jar upside down, there dropped into the kitchen sink a gold chain bracelet that held an oblong gold tablet, inscribed on both sides with minute Arabic writing.

Now it so happened that Mr Dorian of the *Evening Herald* was in the kitchen when this interesting find was made, and Mr Dorian, as everybody knows, is the greatest gossip-writer that ever went into Fleet Street. He is a youngish man of forty-something who looks twenty-something. You meet him at first nights and very select functions, at the unveiling of war memorials – he was a very good artilleryman during the war. Sometimes he called and stayed to dinner to talk over the old days on the *Megaphone*, but never before had he made professional profit out of his visits. 'Poiccart will be indifferent – but Leon will be delighted,' said Manfred as he examined the bracelet link by link. 'Gold, of course. Leon loves mysteries and usually makes his own. This will go into his little story box.'

The little story box was Leon's especial eccentricity. Disdaining safes and strong rooms, that battered steel deed-box reposed beneath his bed. It is true that it contained nothing of great value intrinsically: a jumble of odds and ends, from the torn tickets of bookmakers to two inches of the rope that should have hanged Manfred, each inconsiderable object had its attachment in the shape of a story.

The imagination of the journalist was fired. He took the bracelet in his hand and examined it.

'What is it?' he asked curiously.

Manfred was examining the inscription.

'Leon understands Arabic better than I – it rather looks like the identification disc of a Turkish officer. He must be, or must have been, rather an exquisite.'

Curious, mused Dorian aloud. Here in smoky London a jar or vase bought in Berlin, and out of it tumbles something of Eastern romance. He asked it he might muse in print to the same purpose, and George Manfred had no objection.

Leon came back that evening: he had been asked by the American Government to secure exact information about a certain general cargo which was being shipped from lighters in the port of London.

'Certain raw materials,' he reported, 'which could have caused a great deal of trouble for our friends in America.'

Manfred told him of his find.

'Dorian was here – I told him he could write about this if he liked.'

'H'm!' said Leon, reading the inscription. 'Did you tell him what this writing stood for? But you're not a whale at Arabic, are you? There's one word in Roman characters, "Konnor" – did you see that? "Konnor"? Now what is "Konnor"?' He looked up at the ceiling. '"The Englishman Konnor" – that was the owner of this interesting exhibit. Konnor? I've got it – "Connor"!'

The next evening, under 'The Man in Town,' Mr Dorian's daily column, Leon read of the find, and was just a little irritated to discover that the thorough Mr Dorian had referred to the story box. If the truth be told, Leon was not proud of this little box of his; it stood for romance and sentiment, two qualities which he was pleased to believe were absent from his spiritual make-up.

'George, you're becoming a vulgar publicity agent,' he complained. 'The next thing that will happen will be that I shall receive fabulous offers from a Sunday newspaper for a series of ten articles on "Stories from my Story Box", and if I do I shall sulk for three days.'

Nevertheless, into the black box went the bracelet. What the writing was all about, and where 'the Englishman Konnor' came into it, Leon refused to say.

Yet it was clear to his two companions that Leon was pursuing some new inquiry in the days that followed. He haunted Fleet Street and Whitehall, and even paid a visit to Dublin. Once Manfred questioned him and Leon smiled amiably.

'The whole thing is rather amusing. Connor isn't even Irish. Probably isn't Connor, though it is certain that he bore that name. I found it on the roll of a very fine Irish regiment. He is most likely a Levantine. Stewarts, the Dublin photographers, have a picture of him in a regimental group. That is what I went to Ireland to see. There's a big bookmaker in Dublin who was an officer in the same regiment, and he says "Connor" spoke with a foreign accent.'

'But who is Connor?' asked Manfred.

Leon showed his even white teeth in a grin of delight.

'He is my story,' was all that he would say.

Three weeks later Leon Gonsalez found adventure.

He had something of the qualities of a cat; he slept noiselessly; the keenest ear must strain to hear him breathing; he woke noiselessly. He could pass from complete oblivion to complete wakefulness in a flash. As a cat opens her eyes and is instantly and cold-bloodedly alert, so was Leon.

He had the rare power of looking back into sleep and rediscovering causes, and he knew without remembering that what had wakened him was not the tap-tap of the blind cords for, the night being windy, this had been a normal accompaniment to sleep, but rather the sound of human movement.

His room was a large one for so small a house, but there could never be enough ventilation for Leon, so that, in addition to windows, the door was wedged open . . . He snuffled picturesquely, like a man in heavy sleep, grumbled drowsily, and turned in the bed; but when he had finished turning, his feet were on the floor and he was standing upright, tightening the cord of his pyjamas.

Manfred and Poiccart were away for the weekend, and he was alone in the house – a satisfactory state of affairs, since Leon preferred to deal with such situations as these single-handed.

Waiting, his head bent, he heard the sound again. It came at the end of a whining gust of wind that should have drowned the noise – a distinct creak. Now the stairs gave seven distinct creakings. This one came from the second tread. He lifted his dressing-gown and drew it on as his bare feet groped for his slippers. Then he slipped out on to the landing, and switched on the light.

There was a man on the landing; his yellow, uncleanly face was upraised to Leon's. Fear, surprise, hateful resentment were there.

'Keep your hand out of your pocket, or I'll shoot you through the stomach,' said Leon calmly. 'It will take you four days to die, and you'll regret every minute of it.'

The second man, half-way up the stairs, stood stock-still, paralysed with fright. He was small and slim. Leon waved the barrel of his Browning in his direction, and the smaller figure shrank against the wall and screamed.

Leon smiled. He had not met a lady burglar for years.

'Turn about, both of you, and walk downstairs,' he ordered; 'don't try to run – that would be fatal.'

They obeyed him, the man sullenly, the girl, he guessed, rather weak in the knees.

Presently they came to the ground floor.

'To the left,' said Leon.

He stepped swiftly up to the man, dropped the Browning against his spine, and put his hand into the jacket pocket. He took out a short-barrelled revolver, and slipped it into the pocket of his dressing-gown.

'Through the doorway – the light switch is on the left, turn it.' Following them into the little dining-room, he closed the door behind him. 'Now sit down – both of you.'

The man he could place: a typical prison man; irregular features, bad-complexioned: a creature of low mentality, who spent his short periods of liberty qualifying for further imprisonment.

His companion had not spoken, and until she spoke Leon could not place her into a category.

'I'm very sorry – I am entirely to blame.'

So she spoke, and Leon was enlightened.

It was an educated voice – the voice you might hear in Bond Street ordering the chauffeur to drive to the Ritz.

She was pretty, but then, most women were pretty to Leon; he had that amount of charity in his soul. Dark eyes, fine arches of eyebrows, rather full, red lips. The nervous fingers that twined in and out of one another were white, shapely, rather over-manicured. There was a small purple spot on the back of one finger, where a big ring had been.

'This man is not responsible,' she said, in a low voice. 'I hired him. A – a friend of mine used to help him, and he came to the house one night last week; and I asked him to do this for me. That's really true.'

'Asked him to burgle my house?'

She nodded. 'I wish you'd let him go – I could talk to you then . . . and feel more comfortable. It really isn't his fault. I'm entirely to blame.'

Leon pulled open the drawer of a small writing-table, and took out a sheet of paper and an inkpad. He put them on the table before the girl's unshaven companion.

'Put your finger and thumb on the pad – press 'em.'

'Whaffor?' The man was husky and suspicious.

'I want your finger-prints in case I have to come after you. Be slippy!'

Reluctantly, the burglar obeyed – first one hand and then the other. Leon examined the prints on the paper, and was satisfied.

'Step this way.'

He pushed his visitor to the street door, opened it, and walked out after him.

'You must not carry a gun,' he said. As he spoke his fist shot up and caught the man under the jaw, and the man went sprawling to the ground.

He got up whimpering.

'She made me carry it,' he whined.

'Then she earned you a punch on the jaw,' said Leon brightly, and closed the door on one who called himself, rather unimaginatively, 'John Smith'.

When he returned to the dining-room, the girl had loosened the heavy coat she wore, and was sitting back in her chair, rather white of face but perfectly calm.

'Has he gone? I'm so glad! You hit him, didn't you? I thought I heard you. What do you think of me?'

'I wouldn't have missed tonight for a thousand pounds!' said Leon, and he was telling the truth.

Only for a fraction of a second did she smile.

'Why do you think I did this mad, stupid thing?' she asked quietly. Leon shook his head.

'That is exactly what I can't think: we've no very important case on hand; the mysterious documents which figure in all sensation stories are entirely missing. I can only suppose that we've been rather unkind to some friend of yours – a lover, a father, a brother – '

He saw the ghost of a smile appear and disappear.

'No; it isn't revenge. You've done me no harm, directly or indirectly. And there are no secret documents.'

'Then it's not revenge and it's not robbery; I confess that I am beaten!' Leon's smile was dazzling, and this time she responded without reservation.

'I suppose I'd better tell you everything,' she said, 'and I'd best start by telling you that my name is Lois Martin, my father is Sir Charles Martin, the surgeon, and I shall be married in three weeks' time to Major John Rutland, of the Cape Police. And that is why I burgled your house.'

Leon was amused.

'You were – er – looking for a wedding-present?' he asked, mildly sarcastic.

To his surprise, she nodded.

'That is just what I came for,' she said. 'I've been very silly. If I'd known you better, I should have come to you and asked for it.'

Her steady eyes were fixed upon Leon.

'Well?' he asked. 'What is this interesting object?'

She spoke very slowly.

'A gold chain bangle, with an identification disc . . . '

Leon was not surprised, except that she was speaking the truth. He jotted down the names she had given him. A gold bracelet,' he repeated, 'the property of – ?'

She hesitated.

'I suppose you've got to know the whole story – I'm rather in your hands.'

He nodded.

'Very much in my hands,' he said pleasantly. 'It seems to me that you will get less discomfort in telling me now than in explaining the matter to a police magistrate.'

He was geniality itself yet she, womanlike, could detect a hardness in his tone that made her shiver a little.

'Major Rutland knows nothing about my coming here – he would be horrified if he knew I had taken this risk,' she began.

She told him, haltingly at first, how her older brother had been killed in Africa during the War.

'That's how I come to know Jack,' she said. 'He was in the desert, too. He wrote to me two years ago from Paris – said he had some papers belonging to poor Frank. He had taken them from his – from his body, after he was killed. Naturally, Daddy asked him to come over, and we became good friends, although Daddy isn't very keen on – our marriage.'

She was silent for a little while, and then went on quickly.

'Father doesn't like the marriage at all, and really the fact that we are getting married is a secret. You see, Mr Gonsalez, I am a comparatively rich woman: my mother left me a large sum of money. And John will be rich, too. During the War, when he was a prisoner, he located a big gold mine in Syria, and that is what the inscription is all about. John saved the life of an Arab, and in his gratitude he revealed to him where the mine was located, and had it all inscribed on a little gold tablet, in Arabic. John lost it at the end of the War, and he'd heard nothing more of it until he read in the *Evening Herald* about your discovery. Poor John was naturally terribly upset at the thought that he might be forestalled by some-body who could decipher the tablet, so I suggested he should call and see you and ask for the bracelet back; but he wouldn't hear of this. Instead, he's been getting more and more worried and upset and nervous, and at last I thought of this mad scheme. Jack has quite a number of acquaintances amongst the criminal classes – being a police officer he very naturally can deal with them; and he's done a lot to help them to keep straight. This man who came tonight was one of them. It was I who saw him, and suggested this idea of getting into the house and taking the bracelet. We knew that you kept it under your bed – '

'Are you sure it was you and not Major John Rutland who thought out this burglary?'

Again she hesitated.

'I think he did in fun suggest that the house should be burgled.'

'And that you should do the burgling?' asked Leon blandly.

She avoided his eyes.

'In fun . . . yes. He said nobody would hurt me, and I could always pretend it was a practical joke. It was very stupid, I know, Mr Gonsalez; if my father knew . . . '

'Exactly,' said Leon brusquely. 'You needn't tell me any more – about the burglary. How much money have you at the bank?'

She looked at him in surprise.

'Nearly forty thousand pounds,' she said. 'I've sold a lot of securities lately – they were not very productive – '

Leon smiled.

'And you've heard of a better investment?'

She was quick to see what he meant.

'You're altogether wrong, Mr Gonsalez,' she said coldly. 'John is only allowing me to put a thousand pounds into his exploration syndicate – he isn't quite sure whether it is a thousand or eight hundred he will require. He won't let me invest a penny more. He's going to Paris tomorrow night, to start these people on their way; and then he is coming back, and we are to be married and follow them.'

Leon looked at her thoughtfully.

'Tomorrow night – do you mean tonight?'

She glanced quickly at the clock, and laughed.

'Of course, tonight.'

Then she leaned across the table and spoke earnestly.

'Mr Gonsalez, I've heard so much about you and your friends, and I'm sure you wouldn't betray our secret. If I'd any sense I should have come to you yesterday and asked you for the tablet – I would even pay a good sum to relieve John's anxiety. Is it too late now?'

Leon nodded.

'Much too late. I am keeping that as a memento. The enterprising gentleman who wrote the paragraph told you that it is part of my story collection – and I never part with stories. By the way, when do you give your cheque?'

Her lips twitched at this.

'You still think John is a wicked swindler? I gave him the cheque yesterday.'

'A thousand or eight hundred?'

'That is for him to decide,' she said.

Leon nodded, and rose.

'I will not trouble you any further. Burglary, Miss Martin, is evidently not your speciality, and I should advise you to avoid that profession in the future.'

'You're not giving me in charge?' she smiled.

'Not yet,' said Leon.

He opened the door for her, and stood in his dressing-gown, watching her. He saw her cross the road to the taxi rank, and take the last vehicle available. Then he bolted the door and went back to bed.

His alarm clock called him at seven, and he arose cheerfully, having before him work which was after his own heart. In the morning he called at a tourist agency and bought a ticket to Paris – it seemed a waste of time to go to the office of the High Commissioner for South Africa and examine the available records of the Cape Police; but he was a conscientious man. The afternoon he spent idling near the Northern and Southern Bank in Threadneedle Street, and at a quarter to three his vigil was rewarded, for he saw Major John Rutland descend from a cab, go into the bank, and emerge a few minutes before the big doors closed. The Major looked very pleased with himself – a handsome fellow, rather slim, with a short-cropped military moustache.

Manfred came back in the afternoon, but Leon told him nothing of the burglary. After dinner he went up to his own room, took from a drawer an automatic, laid a few spots of oil in the sliding jacket, and loaded it carefully. From a small box he took a silencer, which he fixed to the muzzle. He put the apparatus into his overcoat pocket, found his suitcase, and came downstairs. George was standing in the hallway.

'Going out, Leon?'

'I shall be away a couple of days,' said Leon, and Manfred, who never asked questions, opened the door for him.

Leon was hunched up in a corner of a first-class carriage when he saw Major Rutland and the girl pass. Behind them, an unwanted third, was a tall, thin-faced man with grey hair, obviously the surgeon. Leon saw them from the corner of his eye, and as the train pulled out had another glimpse of the girl waving her hand to her departing lover.

It was a dark, gusty night; the weather conditions chalked on a board at the railway station promised an unpleasant crossing, and when he stepped on to the boat at midnight he found it rolling uneasily, even in the comparatively calm waters of the harbour.

He made a quick scrutiny of the purser's list. Major Rutland had taken a cabin and this, after the boat began to move out of harbour, he located. It was the aft cabin de luxe, not a beautiful apartment, for the ship was an old one.

He waited till the assistant purser came along to collect his ticket, and then: 'I'm afraid I've lost my ticket,' he said, and paid.

His ticket from Dover to Calais was in his pocket, but Major Rutland had not taken the Calais but the Ostend boat. He watched the assistant purser go into the cabin de luxe, and peered through the window. The Major was lying on a sofa, his cap pulled down over his eyes.

After the assistant purser had taken his ticket and departed, Leon waited for another half-hour; then he saw the cabin go dark. He wandered round the ship: the last light of England showed glittering-ly on the south-western horizon. There were no passengers on deck: the few that the ship carried had gone below, for she was tossing and rolling diabolically. Another quarter of an hour passed, and then Leon turned the handle of the stateroom door, stepped into the cabin and sent the light of his small torch round the room. Evidently the Major was travelling without a great deal of luggage: there were two small suitcases and nothing more.

These Leon took out on to the deck and, walking to the rail, dropped them into the water. The man's hat went the same way. He put the torch back into his pocket and, returning for the second time to the cabin, gently shook the sleeper.

'I want to speak to you, Konnor,' he said, in a voice little above a whisper.

The man was instantly awake. 'Who are you?'

'Come outside: I want to talk to you.'

'Major Rutland' followed on to the dim deck.

'Where are you going?' he asked.

The aft of the ship was reserved for second-class passengers, and this, too, was deserted. They made their way to the rail above the stern. They were in complete darkness.

'You know who I am?'

'Haven't the slightest idea,' was the cool reply.

'My name is Gonsalez. Yours, of course, is Eugene Konnor – or Bergstoft,' said Leon. 'You were at one time an officer in the – ' He mentioned the regiment. 'In the desert you went over to the enemy by arrangements made through an agency in Cairo. You were reported killed, but in reality you were employed by the enemy as a spy. You were responsible for the disaster at El Masjid – don't try to draw that gun or your life will be shorter.'

'Well,' said the man, a little breathlessly, 'what do you want?'

'I want first of all the money you drew from the bank this afternoon. I've an idea that Miss Martin gave you a blank cheque, and I've a stronger idea that you filled that almost to the limit of her balance, as she will discover tomorrow morning.'

'A hold-up, eh?' Konnor laughed harshly.

'That money, and quick!' said Leon, between his teeth.

Konnor felt the point of the gun against his stomach, and obeyed. Leon took the thick pad of notes from the man, and slipped it into his pocket.

'I suppose you realize, Mr Leon Gonsalez, that you're going to get into very serious trouble?' began Konnor. 'I thought you'd probably decipher the pass – '

'I deciphered the pass without any trouble at all, if you're referring to the gold tablet,' said Leon. 'It said that "the Englishman Konnor is permitted to enter our lines at any moment of the day or night and is to be afforded every assistance," and it was signed by the Commander of the Third Army. Yes, I know all about that.'

'When I get back to England – ' began the man.

'You've no intention of going back to England. You're married. You were married in Dublin – and that was probably not your first bigamy. How much money is there here?'

'Thirty or forty thousand – you needn't think that Miss Martin will prosecute me.'

'Nobody is going to prosecute you,' said Leon, in a low voice.

He took one quick glance around: the decks were empty.

'You're a traitor to your country – if you have a country; a man who has sent thousands of the men who were his comrades to their death. That is all.'

There was a flash of fire from his hand, a guttural '*plop*!' Konnor's knees went under him, but before he reached the ground Leon Gonsalez caught him under the arms, threw the pistol into the water, lifted the man without an effort and heaved him into the dark sea . . .

When Ostend harbour came into sight, and the steward went to collect Major Rutland's luggage, he found it had gone, and with it the owner. Passengers are very often mean, and carry their own luggage on to the deck in order to save porterage. The steward shrugged his shoulders and thought no more of the matter.

As for Leon Gonsalez, he stayed in Brussels one day, posted without comment the £34,000 in notes to Miss Lois Martin, caught the train to Calais and was back in London that night. Manfred glanced up as his friend strode into the dining-room.

'Had a good time, Leon?' he asked.

'Most interesting,' said Leon.

THE END